T5-ACY-354

The
DECAMERON
GIOVANNI BOCCACCIO
100 TALES of LIFE & LOVE
TRANSLATED BY J.M. RIGG

This is a FLAME TREE Book

Publisher & Creative Director: Nick Wells
Editorial Director: Catherine Taylor
Editorial Board: Josie Mitchell, Gillian Whitaker, Taylor Bentley, Jocelyn Pontes

Publisher's Note: Due to the historical nature of classic fiction, we're aware that there may be some language used which has the potential to cause offence to the modern reader. However, wishing overall to preserve the integrity of the text, rather than imposing contemporary sensibilities, we have left it unaltered.

FLAME TREE PUBLISHING
6 Melbray Mews, Fulham,
London SW6 3NS, United Kingdom
www.flametreepublishing.com

First published 2023

Copyright © 2023 Flame Tree Publishing Ltd

23 25 27 26 24
1 3 5 7 9 10 8 6 4 2

ISBN: 978-1-80417-344-2
Special ISBN: 978-1-80417-348-0

All rights reserved. No part of this publication may be reproduced, stored in a retrieval system, or transmitted in any form or by any means, electronic, mechanical, photocopying, recording or otherwise, without the prior written permission of the publisher.

Cover artwork created by Flame Tree Studio. Front cover image based on a painting by J.L.E. Meissonnier (1815–91), etched by Abel Mignon (1861–1936).

A copy of the CIP data for this book is available from the British Library.

Printed and bound in China

The DECAMERON
GIOVANNI BOCCACCIO
100 TALES of LIFE & LOVE

TRANSLATED BY J.M. RIGG

Foreword by Dr. Susanna Barsella

FLAME TREE PUBLISHING

Contents

Foreword by Dr. Susanna Barsella 8
Publisher's Note 9
Proem 13

First Day

Novel I 26
Novel II 33
Novel III 36
Novel IV 38
Novel V 41
Novel VI 43
Novel VII 45
Novel VIII 48
Novel IX 50
Novel X 51

Second Day

Novel I 56
Novel II 59
Novel III 63
Novel IV 68
Novel V 71
Novel VI 78
Novel VII 86
Novel VIII 98
Novel IX 107
Novel X 114

Third Day

Novel I 123
Novel II 127

Novel III 130
Novel IV 135
Novel V 138
Novel VI 142
Novel VII 147
Novel VIII 156
Novel IX 161
Novel X 166

Fourth Day

Novel I 176
Novel II 182
Novel III 188
Novel IV 192
Novel V 195
Novel VI 199
Novel VII 203
Novel VIII 206
Novel IX 210
Novel X 212

Fifth Day

Novel I 221
Novel II 227
Novel III 231
Novel IV 235
Novel V 238
Novel VI 242
Novel VII 246
Novel VIII 250
Novel IX 254
Novel X 258

Sixth Day

Novel I	267
Novel II	268
Novel III	270
Novel IV	272
Novel V	274
Novel VI	276
Novel VII	278
Novel VIII	280
Novel IX	281
Novel X	283

Seventh Day

Novel I	293
Novel II	296
Novel III	299
Novel IV	302
Novel V	305
Novel VI	310
Novel VII	313
Novel VIII	317
Novel IX	322
Novel X	328

Eighth Day

Novel I	334
Novel II	336
Novel III	340
Novel IV	345
Novel V	348
Novel VI	350
Novel VII	354
Novel VIII	367

Novel IX 370
Novel X 379

Ninth Day

Novel I 389
Novel II 393
Novel III 395
Novel IV 398
Novel V 401
Novel VI 406
Novel VII 409
Novel VIII 411
Novel IX 413
Novel X 416

Tenth Day

Novel I 421
Novel II 423
Novel III 426
Novel IV 430
Novel V 434
Novel VI 437
Novel VII 441
Novel VIII 446
Novel IX 456
Novel X 466

The Author's Epilogue 474

Biographies & Sources 478

Foreword: The Decameron

AS ALL GREAT TEXTS, the *Decameron* reflects the great complexity of the times in which it was written and the innovative cultural perspective of its author, Giovanni Boccaccio. Its three-layered narrative structure illustrates the unique character of the *Decameron*: one hundred stories narrated by ten young Florentines during the great plague of 1348 and collected by a principal narrator wishing to comfort young women pining for love. More than a mere collection of stories, the *Decameron* is the first work in the vernacular aspiring to the dignity of a work of moral philosophy intended to teach 'what to avoid and what to pursue' through beautifully written, pleasurable tales. The elaborate structure of the text, the solemn title, literally meaning 'ten days' in Boccaccio's approximate Greek etymology, the authoritative figure of a principal narrator explicitly declaring to write out of compassion for the afflicted, are just some elements pointing at the ethical nature of the *Decameron*. Born and raised in an affluent family of merchant bankers (1313), educated in mercantile practices and law as well as in the liberal arts, exposed to mercantile as well as to aristocratic culture during his years in Naples (1327–40) where his father, Boccaccino di Chellino, directed the local branch of the Florentine Bardi bank, it is not surprising that the *Decameron* reflects not just Boccaccio's individual literary ambition but also the need for a moral reform of society compatible with mercantile culture.

Beauty and ethics are the two pillars that support the ideological architecture of the *Decameron*. As its subtitle 'Galeotto' (Galehaut) suggests, the book mediates between the author and the readers, much as Galehaut mediates between Lancelot and Queen Guinevere, inviting them to reflect on the various cases the one hundred *novellas* present them. The responsibility for extracting good advice from these cases, however, relies on the readers; a perspective making the *Decameron* a text of extraordinary modernity. In reading the stories, we should never forget that its capacity to entertain, which depends on the beauty of the writing, is a means to the end of providing useful advice. This end is explicit in the very beginning of the *Decameron*.

In the Proem, the principal narrator (not to be confused with the real author Boccaccio) tells his readers that he decided to collect one hundred stories out of compassion, moved by gratitude toward a friend whose tales saved him from despair when he was afflicted with lovesickness. He dedicates his stories to those incapable of containing the destructive effects of love because of social limitations, particularly, but not exclusively, the women. The tales he collects are narrated by ten young Florentines, seven women and three men, who during the great plague of 1348 leave the devastated city and spend a fortnight in the countryside to restore their minds and bodies by playing, singing, dancing and telling stories. They organize their little community like a miniature court, electing each day a queen or a king who decide, with the exceptions of the free days 1 and 9, the topics of their respective days. The principal narrator writes the rubrics (brief summaries) of the novellas, intervenes in the introductions and conclusions to each day, in Day 1 authors the horrifying description of the plague in Florence that constitutes the backdrop against which the book is set, defends his work from his critics and narrates his own exemplary one-hundredth-and-one novella in Day 4, and finally addresses his readers in the 'Conclusions of the Author', thus giving an authorial 'closure' to the book.

The sophisticated textual architecture of the *Decameron* allows for a multifocal perspective where the tension between what is and what should be is never completely resolved within the text. Rather, these two dimensions are continually at play across the stories of the days, of the *cornice* (framework) and of the principal narrator. The dialectic between the reality of the tales and the ephemeral ideal court of the ten youths under the ordering figure of the principal narrator is the core essence of the meditation on life in time of death the *Decameron* represents, and maybe one of the reasons it still fascinates the modern reader.

Susanna Barsella
Fordham University

Publisher's Note

Less famous than Dante's *Divine Comedy*, Boccaccio's *Decameron* is nonetheless at once informed by and in direct contrast to its predecessor – and is just as valuable and engaging a work. While the former deals with divine matters, the latter deals with the essentially human; while Dante wrote in epic verse, Boccaccio went further with his innovative structure and use of vernacular prose – this is both a groundbreaking and accessible text that should be enjoyed by more readers.

Various translations of the *Decameron* exist. We have chosen that by J.M. Rigg (1855–1926). Though some of the vocabulary may now be outdated or seem a little esoteric, it retains an elegant style and, compared to other translations, is often more accurate in passages that are of crucial importance to understanding the *Decameron*.

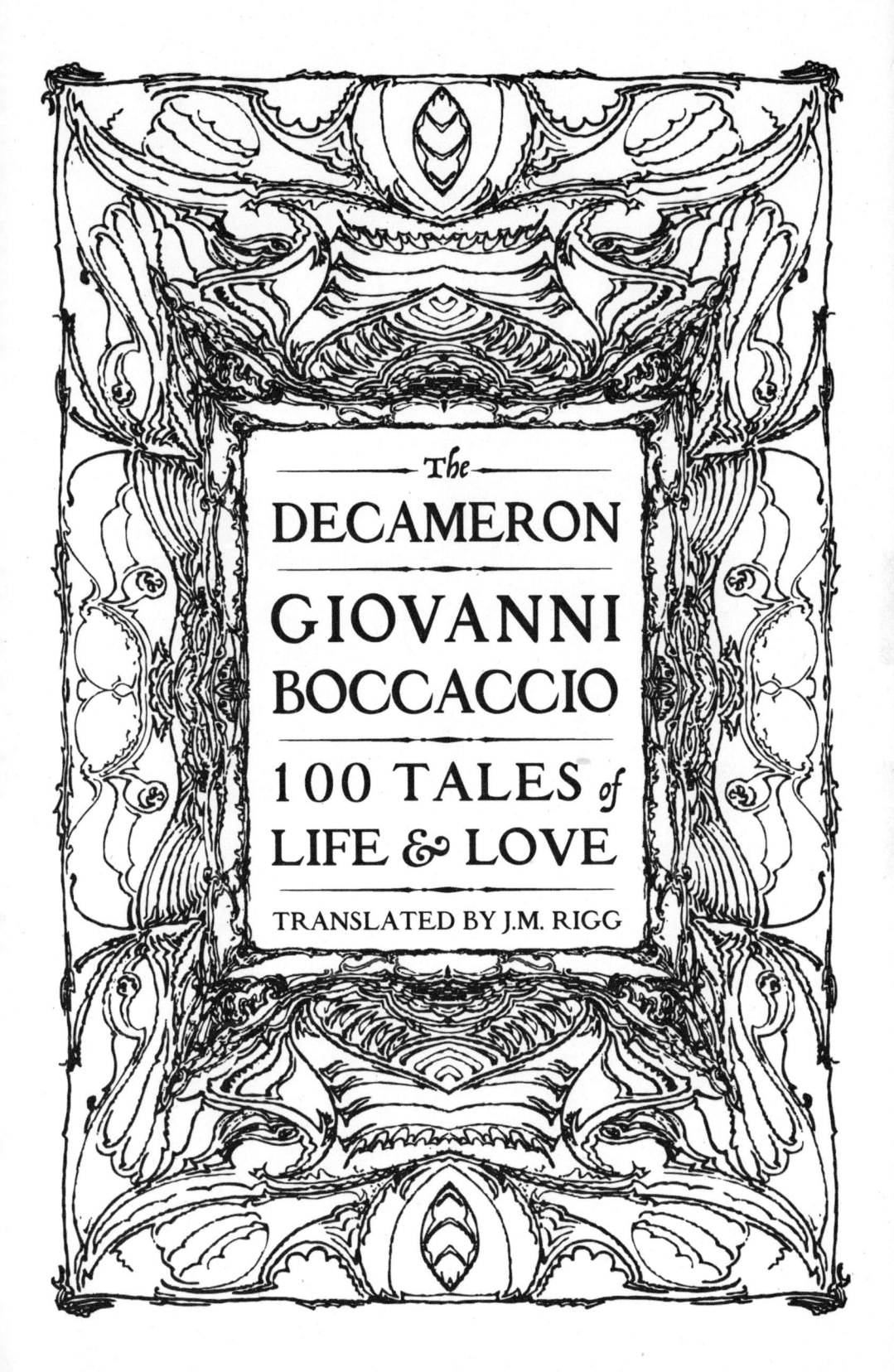

The DECAMERON

GIOVANNI BOCCACCIO

100 TALES of LIFE & LOVE

TRANSLATED BY J.M. RIGG

— Beginneth here the book called Decameron, otherwise Prince Galeotto, wherein are contained one hundred novels told in ten days by seven ladies and three young men. —

Proem

'TIS HUMANE to have compassion on the afflicted and as it shews well in all, so it is especially demanded of those who have had need of comfort and have found it in others: among whom, if any had ever need thereof or found it precious or delectable, I may be numbered; seeing that from my early youth even to the present I was beyond measure aflame with a most aspiring and noble love more perhaps than, were I to enlarge upon it, would seem to accord with my lowly condition. Whereby, among people of discernment to whose knowledge it had come, I had much praise and high esteem, but nevertheless extreme discomfort and suffering not indeed by reason of cruelty on the part of the beloved lady, but through superabundant ardour engendered in the soul by ill-bridled desire; the which, as it allowed me no reasonable period of quiescence, frequently occasioned me an inordinate distress. In which distress so much relief was afforded me by the delectable discourse of a friend and his commendable consolations, that I entertain a very solid conviction that to them I owe it that I am not dead. But, as it pleased Him, who, being infinite, has assigned by immutable law an end to all things mundane, my love, beyond all other fervent, and neither to be broken nor bent by any force of determination, or counsel of prudence, or fear of manifest shame or ensuing danger, did nevertheless in course of time me abate of its own accord, in such wise that it has now left nought of itself in my mind but that pleasure which it is wont to afford to him who does not adventure too far out in navigating its deep seas; so that, whereas it was used to be grievous, now, all discomfort being done away, I find that which remains to be delightful. But the cessation of the pain has not banished the memory of the kind offices done me by those who shared by sympathy the burden of my griefs; nor will it ever, I believe, pass from me except by death. And as among the virtues, gratitude is in my judgment most especially to be commended, and ingratitude in equal measure to be censured, therefore, that I show myself not ungrateful, I have resolved, now that I may call myself to endeavour, in return for what I have received, to afford, so far as in me lies, some solace, if not to those who succoured and who, perchance, by reason of their good sense or good fortune, need it not, at least to such as may be apt to receive it.

And though my support or comfort, so to say, may be of little avail to the needy, nevertheless it seems to me meet to offer it most readily where the need is most apparent, because it will there be most serviceable and also most kindly received. Who will deny, that it should be given, for all that it may be worth, to gentle ladies much rather than to men? Within their soft bosoms, betwixt fear and shame, they harbour secret fires of love, and how much of strength concealment adds to those fires, they know who have proved it. Moreover, restrained by the will, the caprice, the commandment of fathers, mothers, brothers, and husbands, confined most part of their time within the narrow compass of their chambers, they live, so to say, a life of vacant ease, and, yearning and renouncing in the same moment, meditate divers matters which cannot all be cheerful. If thereby a melancholy bred of amorous desire make entrance into their minds, it is like to tarry there to their sore distress, unless it be dispelled by a change of ideas. Besides which they have much less power to support such a weight than men. For, when men are enamoured, their case is very different, as we may readily perceive. They, if they are afflicted by a melancholy and heaviness of mood, have many ways of relief and diversion; they may go where they will, may hear and see many things, may hawk, hunt, fish, ride, play or traffic. By which means all are able to compose their minds, either in whole or in part, and repair the ravage wrought by the dumpish mood, at least for some space of time; and shortly after, by one way or another, either solace ensues, or the dumps become less grievous. Wherefore, in some measure to compensate the injustice of Fortune, which to those whose strength is least, as we see it to be in the delicate frames of ladies, has been most niggard of support, I, for the succour and diversion of such of them as love (for others may find sufficient solace in the needle and the spindle and the reel), do intend to recount one hundred Novels or Fables or Parables or Stories, as we may please to call them, which were recounted in ten days by an honourable company of seven ladies and three young men in the time of the late mortal pestilence, as also some canzonets sung by the said ladies for their delectation. In which pleasant novels will be found some passages of love rudely crossed, with other courses of events of which the issues are felicitous, in times as well modern as ancient: from which stories the said ladies, who shall read them, may derive both pleasure from the entertaining matters set forth therein, and also good counsel, in that they may learn what to shun, and likewise what to pursue. Which cannot, I believe, come to pass unless the dumps be banished by diversion of mind. And if it so happen (as God grant it may) let them give thanks to Love, who, liberating me from his fetters, has given me the power to devote myself to their gratification.

— Beginneth here the first day of the Decameron, in which, when the author has set forth, how it came to pass that the persons, who appear hereafter met together for interchange of discourse, they, under the rule of Pampinea, discourse of such matters as most commend themselves to each in turn. —

As often, most gracious ladies, as I bethink me, how compassionate you are by nature one and all, I do not disguise from myself that the present work must seem to you to have but a heavy and distressful prelude, in that it bears upon its very front what must needs revive the sorrowful memory of the late mortal pestilence, the course whereof was grievous not merely to eye- witnesses but to all who in any other wise had cognisance of it. But I would have you know, that you need not therefore be fearful to read further, as if your reading were ever to be accompanied by sighs and tears. This horrid beginning will be to you even such as to wayfarers is a steep and rugged mountain, beyond which stretches a plain most fair and delectable, which the toil of the ascent and descent does but serve to render more agreeable to them; for, as the last degree of joy brings with it sorrow, so misery has ever its sequel of happiness. To this brief exordium of woe – brief, I say, inasmuch as it can be put within the compass of a few letters – succeed forthwith the sweets and delights which I have promised you, and which, perhaps, had I not done so, were not to have been expected from it. In truth, had it been honestly possible to guide you whither I would bring you by a road less rough than this will be, I would gladly have so done. But, because without this review of the past, it would not be in my power to shew how the matters, of which you will hereafter read, came to pass, I am almost bound of necessity to enter upon it, if I would write of them at all.

I say, then, that the years of the beatific incarnation of the Son of God had reached the tale of one thousand three hundred and forty-eight when in the illustrious city of Florence, the fairest of all the cities of Italy, there made its appearance that deadly pestilence, which, whether disseminated by the influence of the celestial bodies, or sent upon us mortals by God in His just wrath by way of retribution for our iniquities, had had its origin some years before in the East, whence, after destroying an innumerable multitude of living beings, it had propagated itself without respite from place to place, and so, calamitously, had spread into the West.

In Florence, despite all that human wisdom and forethought could devise to avert it, as the cleansing of the city from many impurities by officials appointed for the purpose, the refusal of entrance to all sick folk, and the adoption of many precautions for the preservation of health; despite also humble supplications addressed to God, and often repeated both in public procession and otherwise, by the devout; towards the beginning of the spring of the said year the doleful effects of the pestilence began to be horribly apparent by symptoms that shewed as if miraculous.

Not such were they as in the East, where an issue of blood from the nose was a manifest sign of inevitable death; but in men and women alike it first betrayed itself by the emergence of certain tumours in the groin or the armpits, some of which grew as large as a common apple, others as an egg, some more, some less, which the common folk called gavoccioli. From the two said parts of the body this deadly gavocciolo soon began to propagate and spread itself in all directions indifferently; after which the form of the malady began to change, black spots or livid making their appearance in many cases on the arm or the thigh or elsewhere, now few and large, now minute and numerous. And as the gavocciolo had been and still was an infallible token of approaching death, such also were these spots on whomsoever they shewed themselves. Which maladies seemed to set entirely at naught both the art of the physician and the virtues of physic; indeed, whether it was that the disorder was of a nature to defy such treatment, or that the physicians were at fault – besides the qualified there was now a multitude both of men and of women who practised without having received the slightest tincture of medical science – and, being in ignorance of its source, failed to apply the proper remedies; in either case, not merely were those that recovered few, but almost all within three days from the appearance of the said symptoms, sooner or later, died, and in most cases without any fever or other attendant malady.

Moreover, the virulence of the pest was the greater by reason that intercourse was apt to convey it from the sick to the whole, just as fire devours things dry or greasy when they are brought close to it. Nay, the evil went yet further, for not merely by speech or association with the sick was the malady communicated to the healthy with consequent peril of common death; but any that touched the cloth of the sick or aught else that had been touched or used by them, seemed thereby to contract the disease.

So marvellous sounds that which I have now to relate, that, had not many, and I among them, observed it with their own eyes, I had hardly dared to credit it, much less to set it down in writing, though I had had it from the lips of a credible witness.

I say, then, that such was the energy of the contagion of the said pestilence, that it was not merely propagated from man to man but, what is much more startling, it was frequently observed, that things which had belonged to one sick or dead of the disease, if touched by some other living creature, not of the human species, were the occasion, not merely of sickening, but of an almost instantaneous death. Whereof my own eyes (as I said a little before) had cognisance, one day among others, by the following experience. The rags of a poor man who had died of the disease being strewn about the open street, two hogs came thither, and after, as is their wont, no little trifling with their snouts, took the rags between their teeth and tossed them to and fro about their chaps; whereupon, almost immediately, they gave a few turns, and fell down dead, as if by poison, upon the rags which in an evil hour they had disturbed.

In which circumstances, not to speak of many others of a similar or even graver complexion, divers apprehensions and imaginations were engendered in the minds of such as were left alive, inclining almost all of them to the same harsh resolution, to wit, to shun and abhor all contact with the sick and all that belonged to them, thinking thereby to make each his own health secure. Among whom there were those who thought that to live temperately and avoid all excess would count for much as a preservative against seizures of this kind. Wherefore they banded together, and, dissociating themselves from all others, formed communities in houses where there were no sick, and lived a separate and secluded life, which they regulated with the utmost care, avoiding every kind of luxury, but eating and drinking very moderately of the most delicate viands and the finest wines, holding converse with none but one another, lest tidings of sickness or death should reach them, and diverting their minds with music and such other delights as they could devise. Others, the bias of whose minds was in the opposite direction, maintained, that to drink freely, frequent places of public resort, and take their pleasure with song and revel, sparing to satisfy no appetite, and to laugh and mock at no event, was the sovereign remedy for so great an evil: and that which they affirmed they also put in practice, so far as they were able, resorting day and night, now to this tavern, now to that, drinking with an entire disregard of rule or measure, and by preference making the houses of others, as it were, their inns, if they but saw in them aught that was particularly to their taste or liking; which they were readily able to do, because the owners, seeing death imminent, had become as reckless of their property as of their lives; so that most of the houses were open to all comers, and no distinction was observed between the stranger who presented himself and the rightful lord. Thus, adhering ever to their inhuman determination to shun the sick, as far as possible, they ordered their life. In this extremity of our city's suffering and tribulation the venerable authority of laws, human and divine, was abased and all but totally dissolved, for lack of those who should have administered and enforced them, most of whom, like the rest of the citizens, were either dead or sick, or so hard bested for servants that they were unable to execute any office; whereby every man was free to do what was right in his own eyes.

Not a few there were who belonged to neither of the two said parties, but kept a middle course between them, neither laying the same restraint upon their diet as the former, nor allowing themselves the same license in drinking and other dissipations as the latter, but living with a degree of freedom sufficient to satisfy their appetites, and not as recluses. They therefore walked abroad, carrying in their hands flowers or fragrant herbs or divers sorts of spices, which they frequently raised to their noses, deeming it an excellent thing thus to comfort the brain with such perfumes, because the air seemed to be everywhere laden and reeking with the stench emitted by the dead and the dying and the odours of drugs.

Some again, the most sound, perhaps, in judgment, as they we also the most harsh in temper, of all, affirmed that there was no medicine for the disease superior or equal in efficacy to flight; following which prescription a multitude of men and women, negligent of all but themselves, deserted their city, their houses, their estate, their kinsfolk, their goods, and went into voluntary exile, or migrated to the country parts, as if God in visiting men with this pestilence in requital of their iniquities would not pursue them with His wrath, wherever they might be, but intended the destruction of such alone as remained within the circuit of the walls of the city; or deeming, perchance, that it was now time for all to flee from it, and that its last hour was come.

Of the adherents of these divers opinions not all died, neither did all escape; but rather there were, of each sort and in every place, many that sickened, and by those who retained their health were treated after the example which they themselves, while whole, had set, being everywhere left to languish in almost total neglect. Tedious were it to recount, how citizen avoided citizen, how among neighbours was scarce found any that shewed fellow-feeling for another, how kinsfolk held aloof, and never met, or but rarely; enough that this sore affliction entered so deep into the minds of men and women, that in the horror thereof brother was forsaken by brother, nephew by uncle, brother by sister, and oftentimes husband by wife; nay, what is more, and scarcely to be believed, fathers and mothers were found to abandon their own children, untended, unvisited, to their fate, as if they had been strangers. Wherefore the sick of both sexes, whose number could not be estimated, were left without resource but in the charity of friends (and few such there were), or the interest of servants, who were hardly to be had at high rates and on unseemly terms, and being, moreover, one and all men and women of gross understanding, and for the most part unused to such offices, concerned themselves no farther than to supply the immediate and expressed wants of the sick, and to watch them die; in which service they themselves not seldom perished with their gains. In consequence of which dearth of servants and dereliction of the sick by neighbours, kinsfolk and friends, it came to pass – a thing, perhaps, never before heard of that no woman, however dainty, fair or well-born she might be, shrank, when stricken with the disease, from the ministrations of a man, no matter whether he were young or no, or scrupled to expose to him every part of her body, with no more shame than if he had been a woman, submitting of necessity to that which her malady required; wherefrom, perchance, there resulted in after time some loss of modesty in such as recovered. Besides which many succumbed, who with proper attendance, would, perhaps, have escaped death; so that, what with the virulence of the plague and the lack of due tendance of the sick, the multitude of the deaths, that daily and nightly took place in the city, was such that those who heard the tale – not to say witnessed the fact – were struck dumb with amazement. Whereby, practices contrary to the former habits of the citizens could hardly fail to grow up among the survivors.

It had been, as to-day it still is, the custom for the women that were neighbours and of kin to the deceased to gather in his house with the women that were most closely connected with him, to wail with them in common, while on the other hand his male kinsfolk and neighbours, with not a few of the other citizens, and a due proportion of the clergy according to his quality, assembled without, in front of the house, to receive the corpse; and so the dead man was borne on the shoulders of his peers, with funeral pomp of taper and dirge, to the church selected by him before his death. Which rites, as the pestilence waxed in fury, were either in whole or in great part disused, and gave way to others of a novel order. For not only did no crowd of women surround the bed of the dying, but many passed from this life unregarded, and few indeed were they to whom were accorded the lamentations and bitter tears of sorrowing relations; nay, for the most part, their place was taken by the laugh, the jest, the festal gathering; observances which the women, domestic piety in large measure set aside, had adopted with very great advantage to their health. Few also there were whose bodies were attended to the church by more than ten or twelve of their neighbours, and those not the honourable and respected citizens; but a sort of corpse-carriers drawn from the baser ranks who called themselves becchini and performed such offices for hire, would shoulder the bier, and with hurried steps carry it, not to the church of the dead man's choice, but to that which was nearest at hand, with four or six priests in front and a candle or two, or, perhaps, none; nor did the priests distress themselves with too long and solemn an office, but with the aid of the becchini hastily consigned the corpse to the first tomb which they found untenanted. The condition of lower, and, perhaps, in great measure of the middle ranks, of the people shewed even worse and more deplorable; for, deluded by hope or constrained by poverty, they stayed in their quarters, in their houses, where they sickened by thousands a day, and, being without service or help of any kind, were, so to speak, irredeemably devoted to the death which overtook them. Many died daily or nightly in the public streets; of many others, who died at home, the departure was hardly observed by their neighbours, until the stench of their putrefying bodies carried the tidings; and what with their corpses and the corpses of others who died on every hand the whole place was a sepulchre.

It was the common practice of most of the neighbours, moved no less by fear of contamination by the putrefying bodies than by charity towards the deceased, to drag the corpses out of the houses with their own hands, aided, perhaps, by a porter, if a porter was to be had, and to lay them in front of the doors, where any one who made the round might have seen, especially in the morning, more of them than he could count; afterwards they would have biers brought up, or, in default, planks, whereon they laid them. Nor was it once or twice only that one and the same bier carried two or three corpses at once; but quite a considerable number of such cases occurred, one bier sufficing for husband and wife, two or three brothers, father and son, and so forth. And times without number it happened, that, as two priests, bearing the cross, were on their way to perform the last office for some one, three or four biers were brought up by the porters in rear of them, so that, whereas the priests supposed that they had but one corpse to bury, they discovered that there were six or eight, or sometimes more. Nor, for all their number, were their obsequies honoured by either tears or lights or crowds of mourners; rather, it was come to this, that a dead man was then of no more account than a dead goat would be to-day. From all which it is abundantly manifest, that that lesson of patient resignation, which the sages were never able to learn from the slight and infrequent mishaps which occur in the natural course of events, was now brought home even to the minds of the simple by the magnitude of their disasters, so that they became indifferent to them.

As consecrated ground there was not in extent sufficient to provide tombs for the vast multitude of corpses which day and night, and almost every hour, were brought in eager haste to the churches for interment, least of all, if ancient custom were to be observed and a separate resting-place assigned to each, they dug, for each graveyard, as soon as it was full, a huge trench, in which they laid the corpses as they arrived by hundreds at a time, piling them up as merchandise is stowed in the hold of a ship, tier upon tier, each covered with a little earth, until the trench would hold no more. But I spare to rehearse with minute particularity each of the woes that came upon our city, and say in brief, that, harsh as was the tenor of her fortunes, the surrounding country knew no mitigation, for there – not to speak of the castles, each, as it were, a little city in itself – in sequestered village, or on the open champaign, by the wayside, on the farm, in the homestead, the poor hapless husbandmen and their families, forlorn of physicians' care or servants' tendance, perished day and night alike, not as men, but rather as beasts. Wherefore, they too, like the citizens, abandoned all rule of life, all habit of industry, all counsel of prudence; nay, one and all, as if expecting each day to be their last, not merely ceased to aid Nature to yield her fruit in due season of their beasts and their lands and their past labours, but left no means unused, which ingenuity could devise, to waste their accumulated store; denying shelter to their oxen, asses, sheep, goats, pigs, fowls, nay, even to their dogs, man's most faithful companions, and driving them out into the fields to roam at large amid the unsheaved, nay, unreaped corn. Many of which, as if endowed with reason, took their fill during the day, and returned home at night without any guidance of herdsman. But enough of the country! What need we add, but (reverting to the city) that such and so grievous was the harshness of heaven, and perhaps in some degree of man, that, what with the fury of the pestilence, the panic of those whom it spared, and their consequent neglect or desertion of not a few of the stricken in their need, it is believed without any manner of doubt, that between March and the ensuing July upwards of a hundred thousand human beings lost their lives within the walls of the city of Florence, which before the deadly visitation would not have been supposed to contain so many people! How many grand palaces, how many stately homes, how many splendid residences, once full of retainers, of lords, of ladies, were now left desolate of all, even to the meanest servant! How many families of historic fame, of vast ancestral domains, and wealth proverbial, found now no scion to continue the succession! How many brave men, how many fair ladies, how many gallant youths, whom any physician, were he Galen, Hippocrates, or Aesculapius himself, would have pronounced in the soundest of health, broke fast with their kinsfolk, comrades and friends in the morning, and when evening came, supped with their forefathers in the other world.

Irksome it is to myself to rehearse in detail so sorrowful a history. Wherefore, being minded to pass over so much thereof as I fairly can, I say, that our city, being thus well-nigh depopulated, it so happened, as I afterwards learned from one worthy of credit, that on a Tuesday morning after Divine Service the venerable church of Santa Maria Novella was almost deserted save for the presence of seven young ladies habited sadly in keeping with the season. All were connected either by blood or at least as friends or neighbours and fair and of good understanding were they all, as also of noble birth, gentle manners, and a modest sprightliness. In age none exceeded twenty-eight, or fell short of eighteen years. Their names I would set down in due form, had I not good reason to with hold them, being solicitous lest the matters which here ensue, as told and heard by them, should in after time be occasion of reproach to any of them, in view of the ample indulgence which was then, for the reasons heretofore set forth, accorded to the lighter hours of persons of much riper years than they, but which the manners of to-day have somewhat restricted; nor would I furnish material to detractors, ever ready to bestow their bite where praise is due, to cast by invidious speech the least slur upon the honour of these noble ladies. Wherefore, that what each says may be apprehended without confusion, I intend to give them names more or less appropriate to the character of each. The first, then, being the eldest of the seven, we will call Pampinea, the second Fiammetta, the third Filomena, the fourth Emilia, the fifth we will distinguish as Lauretta, the sixth as Neifile, and the last, not without reason, shall be named Elisa.

'Twas not of set purpose but by mere chance that these ladies met in the same part of the church; but at length grouping themselves into a sort of circle, after heaving a few sighs, they gave up saying paternosters, and began to converse (among other topics) on the times.

So they continued for awhile, and then Pampinea, the rest listening in silent attention, thus began: – "Dear ladies mine, often have I heard it said, and you doubtless as well as I, that wrong is done to none by whoso but honestly uses his reason. And to fortify, preserve, and defend his life to the utmost of his power is the dictate of natural reason in everyone that is born. Which right is accorded in such measure that in defence thereof men have been held blameless in taking life. And if this be allowed by the laws, albeit on their stringency depends the well-being of every mortal, how much more exempt from censure should we, and all other honest folk, be in taking such means as we may for the preservation of our life? As often as I bethink me how we have been occupied this morning, and not this morning only, and what has been the tenor of our conversation, I perceive – and you will readily do the like – that each of us is apprehensive on her own account; nor thereat do I marvel, but at this I do marvel greatly, that, though none of us lacks a woman's wit, yet none of us has recourse to any means to avert that which we all justly fear. Here we tarry, as if, methinks, for no other purpose than to bear witness to the number of the corpses that are brought hither for interment, or to hearken if the brothers there within, whose number is now almost reduced to nought, chant their offices at the canonical hours, or, by our weeds of woe, to obtrude on the attention of every one that enters, the nature and degree of our sufferings.

"And if we quit the church, we see dead or sick folk carried about, or we see those, who for their crimes were of late condemned to exile by the outraged majesty of the public laws, but who now, in contempt of those laws, well knowing that their ministers are a prey to death or disease, have returned, and traverse the city in packs, making it hideous with their riotous antics; or else we see the refuse of the people, fostered on our blood, becchini, as they call themselves, who for our torment go prancing about here and there and everywhere, making mock of our miseries in scurrilous songs. Nor hear we aught but: – Such and such are dead; or, Such and such art dying; and should hear dolorous wailing on every hand, were there but any to wail. Or go we home, what see we there? I know not if you are in like case with me; but there, where once were servants in plenty, I find none left but my maid, and shudder with terror, and feel the very hairs of my head to stand on end; and turn or tarry where I may, I encounter the ghosts of the departed, not with their wonted mien, but with something horrible in their aspect that appals me. For which reasons church and street and home are alike distressful to me, and the more so that none, methinks, having means and place of retirement as we have, abides here save only we; or if any such there be, they are of those, as my senses too often have borne witness, who make no distinction between things honourable and their opposites, so they but answer the cravings of appetite, and, alone or in company, do daily and nightly what things soever give promise of most gratification. Nor are these secular persons alone; but such as live recluse in monasteries break their rule, and give themselves up to carnal pleasures, persuading themselves that they are permissible to them, and only forbidden to others, and, thereby thinking to escape, are become unchaste and dissolute. If such be our circumstances – and such most manifestly they are – what do we here? what wait we for? what dream we of? why are we less prompt to provide for our own safety than the rest of the citizens? Is life less dear to us than to all other women? or think we that the bond, which unites soul and body is stronger in us than in others, so that there is no blow that may light upon it, of which we need be apprehensive? If so, we err, we are deceived. What insensate folly were it in us so to believe! We have but to call to mind the number and condition of those, young as we, and of both sexes, who have succumbed to this cruel pestilence, to find therein conclusive evidence to the contrary. And lest from lethargy or indolence we fall into the vain imagination that by some lucky accident we may in some way or another, when we would, escape – I know not if your opinion accord with mine – I should deem it most wise in us, our case being what it is, if, as many others have done before us, and are still doing, we were to quit this place, and, shunning like death the evil example of others, betake ourselves to the country, and there live as honourable women on one of the estates, of which none of us has any lack, with all cheer of festal gathering and other delights, so long as in no particular we overstep the bounds of reason. There we shall hear the chant of birds, have sight of verdant hills and plains, of cornfields undulating like the sea, of trees of a thousand sorts; there also we shall have a larger view of the heavens, which, however harsh to usward yet deny not their eternal beauty; things fairer far for eye to rest on than the desolate walls of our city. Moreover, we shall there breathe a fresher air, find ampler store of things meet for such as live in these times, have fewer causes of annoy. For, though the husbandmen die there, even as here the citizens, they are dispersed in scattered homesteads, and 'tis thus less painful to witness. Nor, so far as I can see, is there a soul here whom we shall desert; rather we may truly say, that we are ourselves deserted; for, our kinsfolk being either dead or fled in fear of death, no more regardful of us than if we were strangers, we are left alone in our great affliction. No censure, then, can fall on us if we do as I propose; and otherwise grievous suffering, perhaps death, may ensue. Wherefore, if you agree, 'tis my advice, that, attended by our maids with all things needful, we sojourn, now on this, now on the other estate, and in such way of life continue, until we see – if death should not first overtake us – the end which Heaven reserves for these events. And I remind you that it will be at least as seemly in us to leave with honour, as in others, of whom there are not a few, to stay with dishonour."

The other ladies praised Pampinea's plan, and indeed were so prompt to follow it, that they had already begun to discuss the manner in some detail, as if they were forthwith to rise from their seats and take the road, when Filomena, whose judgment was excellent, interposed, saying: – "Ladies, though Pampinea has spoken to most excellent effect, yet it were not well to be so precipitate as you seem disposed to be. Bethink you that we are all women; nor is there any here so young, but she is of years to understand how women are minded towards one another, when they are alone together, and how ill they are able to rule themselves without the guidance of some man. We are sensitive, perverse, suspicious, pusillanimous and timid; wherefore I much misdoubt, that, if we find no other guidance than our own, this company is like to break up sooner, and with less credit to us, than it should. Against which it were well to provide at the outset." Said then Elisa: – "Without doubt man is woman's head, and, without man's governance, it is seldom that aught that we do is brought to a commendable conclusion. But how are we to come by the men? Every one of us here knows that her kinsmen are for the most part dead, and that the survivors are dispersed, one here, one there, we know not where, bent each on escaping the same fate as ourselves; nor were it seemly to seek the aid of strangers; for, as we are in quest of health, we must find some means so to order matters that, wherever we seek diversion or repose, trouble and scandal do not follow us."

While the ladies were thus conversing, there came into the church three young men, young, I say, but not so young that the age of the youngest was less than twenty-five years; in whom neither the sinister course of events, nor the loss of friends or kinsfolk, nor fear for their own safety, had availed to quench, or even temper, the ardour of their love. The first was called Pamfilo, the second Filostrato, and the third Dioneo. Very debonair and chivalrous were they all; and in this troublous time they were seeking if haply, to their exceeding great solace, they might have sight of their fair friends, all three of whom chanced to be among the said seven ladies, besides some that were of kin to the young men. At one and the same moment they recognised the ladies and were recognised by them: wherefore, with a gracious smile, Pampinea thus began: – "Lo, fortune is propitious to our enterprise, having vouchsafed us the good offices of these young men, who are as gallant as they are discreet, and will gladly give us their guidance and escort, so we but take them into our service." Whereupon Neifile, crimson from brow to neck with the blush of modesty, being one of those that had a lover among the young men, said: – "For God's sake, Pampinea, have a care what you say. Well assured am I that nought but good can be said of any of them, and I deem them fit for office far more onerous than this which you propose for them, and their good and honourable company worthy of ladies fairer by far and more tenderly to be cherished than such as we. But 'tis no secret that they love some of us here; wherefore I misdoubt that, if we take them with us, we may thereby give occasion for scandal and censure merited neither by us nor by them." "That," said Filomena, "is of no consequence; so I but live honestly, my conscience gives me no disquietude; if others asperse me, God and the truth will take arms in my defence. Now, should they be disposed to attend us, of a truth we might say with Pampinea, that fortune favours our enterprise." The silence which followed betokened consent on the part of the other ladies, who then with one accord resolved to call the young men, and acquaint them with their purpose, and pray them to be of their company. So without further parley Pampinea, who had a kinsman among the young men, rose and approached them where they stood intently regarding them; and greeting them gaily, she opened to them their plan, and besought them on the part of herself and her friends to join their company on terms of honourable and fraternal comradeship. At first the young men thought she did but trifle with them; but when they saw that she was in earnest, they answered with alacrity that they were ready, and promptly, even before they left the church, set matters in train for their departure. So all things meet being first sent forward in due order to their intended place of sojourn, the ladies with some of their maids, and the three young men, each attended by a man-servant, sallied forth of the city on the morrow, being Wednesday, about daybreak, and took the road; nor had they journeyed more than two short miles when they arrived at their destination. The estate lay upon a little hill some distance from the nearest highway, and, embowered in shrubberies of divers hues, and other greenery, afforded the eye a pleasant prospect. On the summit of the hill was a palace with galleries, halls and chambers, disposed around a fair and spacious court, each very fair in itself, and the goodlier to see for the gladsome pictures with which it was adorned; the whole set amidst meads and gardens laid out with marvellous art, wells of the coolest water, and vaults of the finest wines, things more suited to dainty drinkers than to sober and honourable women. On their arrival the company, to their no small delight, found their beds already made, the rooms well swept and garnished with flowers of every sort that the season could afford, and the floors carpeted with rushes. When they were seated, Dioneo, a gallant who had not his match for courtesy and wit, spoke thus: – "My ladies, 'tis not our forethought so much as your own mother-wit that has guided us hither. How you mean to dispose of your cares I know not; mine I left behind me within the city-gate when I issued thence with you a brief while ago. Wherefore, I pray you, either address yourselves to make merry, to laugh and sing with me (so far, I mean, as may consist with your dignity), or give me leave to hie me back to the stricken city, there to abide with my cares." To whom blithely Pampinea replied, as if she too had cast off all her cares: – "Well sayest thou, Dioneo, excellent well; gaily we mean to live; 'twas a refuge from sorrow that here we sought, nor had we other cause to come hither. But, as no anarchy can long endure, I who initiated the deliberations of which this fair company is the fruit, do now, to the end that our joy may be lasting, deem it expedient, that there be one among us in chief authority, honoured and obeyed by us as our superior, whose exclusive care it shall be to devise how we may pass our time blithely. And that each in turn may prove the weight of the care, as well as enjoy the pleasure, of sovereignty, and, no distinction being made of sex, envy be felt by none by reason of exclusion from the office; I propose, that the weight and honour be borne by each one for a day; and let the first to bear sway be chosen by us all, those that follow to be appointed towards the vesper hour by him or her who shall have had the signory for that day; and let each holder of the signory be, for the time, sole arbiter of the place and manner in which we are to pass our time."

Pampinea's speech was received with the utmost applause, and with one accord she was chosen queen for the first day. Whereupon Filomena hied her lightly to a bay-tree, having often heard of the great honour in which its leaves, and such as were deservedly crowned therewith, were worthy to be holden; and having gathered a few sprays, she made thereof a goodly wreath of honour, and set it on Pampinea's head; which wreath was thenceforth, while their company endured, the visible sign of the wearer's sway and sovereignty.

No sooner was Queen Pampinea crowned than she bade all be silent. She then caused summon to her presence their four maids, and the servants of the three young men, and, all keeping silence, said to them: – "That I may shew you all at once, how, well still giving place to better, our company may flourish and endure, as long as it shall pleasure us, with order meet and assured delight and without reproach, I first of all constitute Dioneo's man, Parmeno, my seneschal, and entrust him with the care and control of all our household, and all that belongs to the service of the hall. Pamfilo's man, Sirisco, I appoint treasurer and chancellor of our exchequer; and be he ever answerable to Parmeno. While Parmeno and Sirisco are too busy about their duties to serve their masters, let Filostrato's man, Tindaro, have charge of the chambers of all three. My maid, Misia, and Filomena's maid, Licisca, will keep in the kitchen, and with all due diligence prepare such dishes as Parmeno shall bid them. Lauretta's maid, Chimera, and Fiammetta's maid, Stratilia we make answerable for the ladies' chambers, and wherever we may take up our quarters, let them see that all is spotless. And now we enjoin you, one and all alike, as you value our favour, that none of you, go where you may, return whence you may, hear or see what you may, bring us any tidings but such as be cheerful." These orders thus succinctly given were received with universal approval. Whereupon Pampinea rose, and said gaily: – "Here are gardens, meads, and other places delightsome enough, where you may wander at will, and take your pleasure; but on the stroke of tierce, let all be here to breakfast in the shade."

Thus dismissed by their new queen the gay company sauntered gently through a garden, the young men saying sweet things to the fair ladies, who wove fair garlands of divers sorts of leaves and sang love-songs.

Having thus spent the time allowed them by the queen, they returned to the house, where they found that Parmeno had entered on his office with zeal; for in a hall on the ground-floor they saw tables covered with the whitest of cloths, and beakers that shone like silver, and sprays of broom scattered everywhere. So, at the bidding of the queen, they washed their hands, and all took their places as marshalled by Parmeno. Dishes, daintily prepared, were served, and the finest wines were at hand; the three serving-men did their office noiselessly; in a word all was fair and ordered in a seemly manner; whereby the spirits of the company rose, and they seasoned their viands with pleasant jests and sprightly sallies. Breakfast done, the tables were removed, and the queen bade fetch instruments of music; for all, ladies and young men alike, knew how to tread a measure, and some of them played and sang with great skill: so, at her command, Dioneo having taken a lute, and Fiammetta a viol, they struck up a dance in sweet concert; and, the servants being dismissed to their repast, the queen, attended by the other ladies and the two young men, led off a stately carol; which ended they fell to singing ditties dainty and gay. Thus they diverted themselves until the queen, deeming it time to retire to rest, dismissed them all for the night. So the three young men and the ladies withdrew to their several quarters, which were in different parts of the palace. There they found the beds well made, and abundance of flowers, as in the hall; and so they undressed, and went to bed.

Shortly after none the queen rose, and roused the rest of the ladies, as also the young men, averring that it was injurious to health to sleep long in the daytime. They therefore hied them to a meadow, where the grass grew green and luxuriant, being nowhere scorched by the sun, and a light breeze gently fanned them. So at the queen's command they all ranged themselves in a circle on the grass, and hearkened while she thus spoke: –

"You mark that the sun is high, the heat intense, and the silence unbroken save by the cicalas among the olive-trees. It were therefore the height of folly to quit this spot at present. Here the air is cool and the prospect fair, and here, observe, are dice and chess. Take, then, your pleasure as you may be severally minded; but, if you take my advice, you will find pastime for the hot hours before us, not in play, in which the loser must needs be vexed, and neither the winner nor the onlooker much the better pleased, but in telling of stories, in which the invention of one may afford solace to all the company of his hearers. You will not each have told a story before the sun will be low, and the heat abated, so that we shall be able to go and severally take our pleasure where it may seem best to each. Wherefore, if my proposal meet with your approval – for in this I am disposed to consult your pleasure – let us adopt it; if not, divert yourselves as best you may, until the vesper hour."

The queen's proposal being approved by all, ladies and men alike, she added: – "So please you, then, I ordain, that, for this first day, we be free to discourse of such matters as most commend themselves, to each in turn." She then addressed Pamfilo, who sat on her right hand, bidding him with a gracious air to lead off with one of his stories. And prompt at the word of command, Pamfilo, while all listened intently, thus began: –

The DECAMERON
GIOVANNI BOCCACCIO
100 TALES of LIFE & LOVE
FIRST DAY

First Day

Novel I

— *Ser Ciappelletto cheats a holy friar by a false confession, and dies; and, having lived as a very bad man, is, on his death, reputed a saint, and called San Ciappelletto.* —

A SEEMLY THING it is, dearest ladies, that whatever we do, it be begun in the holy and awful name of Him who was the maker of all. Wherefore, as it falls to me to lead the way in this your enterprise of story telling, I intend to begin with one of His wondrous works, that, by hearing thereof, our hopes in Him, in whom is no change, may be established, and His name be by us forever lauded. 'Tis manifest that, as things temporal are all doomed to pass and perish, so within and without they abound with trouble and anguish and travail, and are subject to infinite perils; nor, save for the especial grace of God, should we, whose being is bound up with and forms part of theirs, have either the strength to endure or the wisdom to combat their adverse influences. By which grace we are visited and penetrated (so we must believe) not by reason of any merit of our own, but solely out of the fulness of God's own goodness, and in answer to the prayers of those who, being mortal like ourselves, did faithfully observe His ordinances during their lives, and are now become blessed for ever with Him in heaven. To whom, as to advocates taught by experience all that belongs to our frailty, we, not daring, perchance, to present our petitions in the presence of so great a judge, make known our requests for such things as we deem expedient for us. And of His mercy richly abounding to usward we have further proof herein, that, no keenness of mortal vision being able in any degree to penetrate the secret counsels of the Divine mind, it sometimes, perchance, happens, that, in error of judgment, we make one our advocate before His Majesty, who is banished from His presence in eternal exile, and yet He to whom nothing is hidden, having regard rather to the sincerity of our prayers than to our ignorance or the banishment of the intercessor, hears us no less than if the intercessor were in truth one of the blest who enjoy the light of His countenance. Which the story that I am about to relate may serve to make apparent; apparent, I mean, according to the standard or the judgment of man, not of God.

The story goes, then, that Musciatto Franzesi, a great and wealthy merchant, being made a knight in France, and being to attend Charles Sansterre, brother of the King of France, when he came into Tuscany at the instance and with the support of Pope Boniface, found his affairs, as often happens to merchants, to be much involved in divers quarters, and neither easily nor suddenly to be adjusted; wherefore he determined to place them in the hands of commissioners, and found no difficulty except as to certain credits given to some Burgundians, for the recovery of which he doubted whether he could come by a competent agent; for well he knew that the Burgundians were violent men and ill-conditioned and faithless; nor could he call to mind any man so bad that he could with confidence oppose his guile to theirs. After long pondering the matter, he recollected one Ser Ciapperello da Prato, who much frequented his house in Paris. Who being short of stature and very affected, the French who knew not the meaning of Cepparello, but supposed that it meant the same as Cappello, i. e. garland, in their vernacular, called him not Cappello, but Ciappelletto by reason of his diminutive size; and as Ciappelletto he was known everywhere, whereas few people knew him as Ciapperello. Now Ciappelletto's manner of life was thus. He was by profession a notary, and his pride was to make false documents; he would have made them as often as he was asked, and more readily without fee than another at a great price; few indeed he made that were not false, and, great was his shame when they were discovered. False witness he bore, solicited or unsolicited, with boundless delight; and, as oaths were in those days had in very great respect in France, he, scrupling not to forswear himself, corruptly carried the day in every case in which he was summoned faithfully to attest the truth. He took inordinate delight, and bestirred himself with great zeal, in fomenting ill-feeling, enmities, dissensions between friends, kinsfolk and all other folk; and the more calamitous were the consequences the better he was pleased. Set him on murder, or any other foul crime, and he never hesitated, but went about it with alacrity; he had been known on more than one occasion to inflict wounds or death by preference with his own hands. He was a profuse blasphemer of God and His saints, and that on the most trifling occasions, being of all men the most irascible. He was never seen at Church, held all the sacraments vile things, and derided them in language of horrible ribaldry. On the other hand he resorted readily to the tavern and other places of evil repute, and frequented them. He was as fond of women as a dog is of the stick: in the use against nature he had not his match among the most abandoned. He would have pilfered and stolen as a matter of conscience, as a holy man would make an oblation. Most gluttonous he was and inordinately fond of his cups, whereby he sometimes brought upon himself both shame and suffering. He was also a practised gamester and thrower of false dice. But why enlarge so much upon him? Enough that he was, perhaps, the worst man that ever was born.

The rank and power of Musciatto Franzesi had long been this reprobate's mainstay, serving in many instances to secure him considerate treatment on the part of the private persons whom he frequently, and the court which he unremittingly, outraged. So Musciatto, having bethought him of this Ser Cepparello, with whose way of life he was very well acquainted, judged him to be the very sort of person to cope with the guile of the Burgundians. He therefore sent for him, and thus addressed him: – "Ser Ciappelletto, I am, as thou knowest, about to leave this place for good; and among those with whom I have to settle accounts are certain Burgundians, very wily knaves; nor know I the man whom I could more fitly entrust with the recovery of my money than thyself. Wherefore, as thou hast nothing to do at present, if thou wilt undertake this business, I will procure thee the favour of the court, and give thee a reasonable part of what thou shalt recover." Ser Ciappelletto, being out of employment, and by no means in easy circumstances, and about to lose Musciatto, so long his mainstay and support, without the least demur, for in truth he had hardly any choice, made his mind up and answered that he was ready to go. So the bargain was struck. Armed with the power of attorney and the royal letters commendatory, Ser Ciappelletto took leave of Messer Musciatto and hied him to Burgundy, where he was hardly known to a soul. He set about the business which had brought him thither, the recovery of the money, in a manner amicable and considerate, foreign to his nature, as if he were minded to reserve his severity to the last. While thus occupied, he was frequently at the house of two Florentine usurers, who treated him with great distinction out of regard for Messer Musciatto; and there it so happened that he fell sick. The two brothers forthwith placed physicians and servants in attendance upon him, and omitted no means meet and apt for the restoration of his health. But all remedies proved unavailing; for being now old, and having led, as the physicians reported, a disorderly life, he went daily from bad to worse like one stricken with a mortal disease. This greatly disconcerted the two brothers; and one day, hard by the room in which Ser

Ciappelletto lay sick, they began to talk about him; saying one to the other: – "What shall we do with this man? We are hard bested indeed on his account. If we turn him out of the house, sick as he is, we shall not only incur grave censure, but shall evince a signal want of sense; for folk must know the welcome we gave him in the first instance, the solicitude with which we have had him treated and tended since his illness, during which time he could not possibly do aught to displease us, and yet they would see him suddenly turned out of our house sick unto death. On the other hand he has been so bad a man that he is sure not to confess or receive any of the Church's sacraments; and dying thus unconfessed, he will be denied burial in church, but will be cast out into some ditch like a dog; nay, 'twill be all one if he do confess, for such and so horrible have been his crimes that no friar or priest either will or can absolve him; and so, dying without absolution, he will still be cast out into the ditch. In which case the folk of these parts, who reprobate our trade as iniquitous and revile it all day long, and would fain rob us, will seize their opportunity, and raise a tumult, and make a raid upon our houses, crying: – 'Away with these Lombard whom the Church excludes from her pale;' and will certainly strip us of our goods, and perhaps take our lives also; so that in any case we stand to lose if this man die."

Ser Ciappelletto, who, as we said, lay close at hand while they thus spoke, and whose hearing was sharpened, as is often the case, by his malady, overheard all that they said about him. So he called them to him, and said to them: – "I would not have you disquiet yourselves in regard of me, or apprehend loss to befall you by my death. I have heard what you have said of me and have no doubt that 'twould be as you say, if matters took the course you anticipate; but I am minded that it shall be otherwise. I have committed so many offences against God in the course of my life, that one more in the hour of my death will make no difference whatever to the account. So seek out and bring hither the worthiest and most holy friar you can find, and leave me to settle your affairs and mine upon a sound and solid basis, with which you may rest satisfied." The two brothers had not much hope of the result, but yet they went to a friary and asked for a holy and discreet man to hear the confession of a Lombard that was sick in their house, and returned with an aged man of just and holy life, very learned in the Scriptures, and venerable and held in very great and especial reverence by all the citizens. As soon as he had entered the room where Ser Ciappelletto was lying, and had taken his place by his side, he began gently to comfort him: then he asked him how long it was since he was confessed. Whereto Ser Ciappelletto, who had never been confessed, answered: – "Father, it is my constant practice to be confessed at least once a week, and many a week I am confessed more often; but true it is, that, since I have been sick, now eight days, I have made no confession, so sore has been my affliction. "Son," said the friar, "thou hast well done, and well for thee, if so thou continue to do; as thou dost confess so often, I see that my labour of hearkening and questioning will be slight." "Nay but, master friar," said Ser Ciappelletto, "I say not so; I have not confessed so often but that I would fain make a general confession of all my sins that I have committed, so far as I can recall them, from the day of my birth to the present time; and therefore I pray you, my good father, to question me precisely in every particular just as if I had never been confessed. And spare me not by reason of my sickness, for I had far rather do despite to my flesh than, sparing it, risk the perdition of my soul, which my Saviour redeemed with His precious blood."

The holy man was mightily delighted with these words, which seemed to him to betoken a soul in a state of grace. He therefore signified to Ser Ciappelletto his high approval of this practice; and then began by asking him whether he had ever sinned carnally with a woman. Whereto Ser Ciappelletto answered with a sigh: – "My father, I scruple to tell you the truth in this matter, fearing lest I sin in vain-glory." "Nay, but," said the friar, "speak boldly; none ever sinned by telling the truth, either in confession or otherwise." "Then," said Ser Ciappelletto, "as you bid me speak boldly, I will tell you the truth of this matter. I am virgin even as when I issued from my mother's womb." "Now God's blessing on thee," said the friar, "well done; and the greater is thy merit in that, hadst thou so willed, thou mightest have done otherwise far more readily than we who are under constraint of rule." He then proceeded to ask, whether he had offended God by gluttony. Whereto Ser Ciappelletto, heaving a heavy sigh, answered that he had so offended for, being wont to fast not only in Lent like other devout persons, but at least thrice days in every week, taking nothing but bread and water, he had quaffed the water with as good a gusto and as much enjoyment, more particularly when fatigued by devotion or pilgrimage, as great drinkers quaff their wine; and oftentimes he had felt a craving for such dainty dishes of herbs as ladies make when they go into the country, and now and again he had relished his food more than seemed to him meet in one who fasted, as he did, for devotion. "Son," said the friar, "these sins are natural and very trifling; and therefore I would not have thee burden thy conscience too much with them. There is no man, however holy he may be, but must sometimes find it pleasant to eat after a long fast and to drink after exertion." "O, my father," said Ser Ciappelletto, "say not this to comfort me. You know well that I know, that the things which are done in the service of God ought to be done in perfect purity of an unsullied spirit; and whoever does otherwise sins." The friar, well content, replied: – "Glad I am that thou dost think so, and I am mightily pleased with thy pure and good conscience which therein appears; but tell me: hast thou sinned by avarice, coveting more than was reasonable, or withholding more than was right? My father," replied Ser Ciappelletto, "I would not have you disquiet yourself, because I am in the house of these usurers: no part have I in their concerns; nay, I did but come here to admonish and reprehend them, and wean them from this abominable traffic; and so, I believe, I had done, had not God sent me this visitation. But you must know, that my father left me a fortune, of which I dedicated the greater part to God; and since then for my own support and the relief of Christ's poor I have done a little trading, whereof I have desired to make gain; and all that I have gotten I have shared with God's poor, reserving one half for my own needs and giving the other half to them; and so well has my Maker prospered me, that I have ever managed my affairs to better and better account." "Well, done," said the friar, "but how? hast thou often given way to anger?" "Often indeed, I assure you," said Ser Ciappelletto. "And who could refrain therefrom, seeing men doing frowardly all day long, breaking the commandments of God and recking nought of His judgments? Many a time in the course of a single day I had rather be dead than alive, to see the young men going after vanity, swearing and forswearing themselves, haunting taverns, avoiding the churches, and in short walking in the way of the world rather than in God's way." "My son," said the friar, "this is a righteous wrath; nor could I find occasion therein to lay a penance upon thee. But did anger ever by any chance betray thee into taking human life, or affronting or otherwise wronging any?" "Alas," replied Ser Ciappelletto, "alas, sir, man of God though you seem to me, how come you to speak after this manner? If I had had so much as the least thought of doing any of the things of which you speak, should I believe, think you, that I had been thus supported of God? These are the deeds of robbers and such like evil men, to whom I have ever said, when any I saw: – 'Go, God change your heart.'" Said then the friar: – "Now, my son, as thou hopest to be blest of God, tell me, hast thou never borne false witness against any, or spoken evil of another, or taken the goods of another without his leave?" "Yes, master friar," answered Ser Ciappelletto, "most true it is that I have spoken evil of another; for I had once a neighbour who without the least excuse in the world was ever beating his wife, and so great was my pity of the poor creature, whom, when he was in his cups, he would thrash as God alone knows how, that once I spoke evil of him to his wife's kinsfolk." "Well, well," said the friar, "thou tellest me thou hast been a merchant; hast thou ever cheated any, as merchants use to do?" "I'faith, yes, master friar," said Ser Ciappelletto; "but I know not who he was; only that he brought me some money which he owed me for some cloth that I had sold him, and I put it in a box without counting it, where a month afterwards I found four farthings more than there should have been, which I kept for a year to return to him, but not seeing him again, I bestowed them in alms for the love of God." "This," said the friar, "was a small matter; and thou didst well to bestow them as thou didst." The holy friar went on to ask him many other questions, to which he made answer in each case in this sort. Then, as the friar was about to give him absolution, Ser Ciappelletto interposed: – "Sir, I have yet a sin to confess." "What?" asked the friar. "I remember," he said, "that I once caused my servant to sweep my house on a Saturday after none; and that my observance of Sunday was less devout than it should have been." "O, my son," said the friar, "this is a light matter." "No," said Ser Ciappelletto, "say not a light matter; for Sunday is the more to be had in honour because on that day our Lord rose from the dead." Then said the holy friar: – "Now is there aught else that thou hast done?" "Yes, master friar," replied Ser Ciappelletto, "once by inadvertence I spat in the church of God." At this the friar began to smile, and said: – "My son, this is not a matter to trouble about; we, who are religious, spit there all day long." "And great impiety it is when you so do," replied Ser Ciappelletto, "for there is nothing that is so worthy to be kept from all impurity as the holy temple in which sacrifice is offered to God." More he said in the same strain, which I pass over; and then at last he began to sigh, and by and by to weep bitterly, as he was well able to do when he chose. And the friar demanding: – "My son, why weepest thou?" "Alas, master friar" answered Ser Ciappelletto, "a sin yet remains, which I have never confessed, such shame were it to me to tell it; and as often as I call it to mind, I weep as you now see me weep, being well assured that God will never forgive me this sin." Then said the holy friar: – "Come, come, son, what is this that thou sayst? If all the sins of all the men, that ever were or ever shall be, as long as the world shall endure, were concentrated in one man, so great is the goodness of God that He would freely pardon them all, were he but penitent and contrite as I see thou art, and confessed them: wherefore tell me thy sin with a good courage." Then said Ser Ciappelletto, still weeping bitterly: – "Alas, my father, mine is too great a sin, and scarce can I believe, if your prayers do not co-operate, that God will ever grant me His pardon thereof." "Tell it with a good courage," said the friar; "I promise thee to pray God for thee." Ser Ciappelletto, however, continued to weep, and would not speak, for all the friar's encouragement. When he had kept him for a good while in suspense, he heaved a mighty sigh, and said: – "My father, as you promise me to pray God for me, I will tell it you. Know, then, that once, when I was a little child, I cursed my mother;" and having so said he began again to weep bitterly. "O, my son," said the friar, "does this seem to thee so great a sin? Men curse God all day long, and he pardons them freely, if they repent them of having so done; and thinkest thou he will not pardon thee this? Weep not, be comforted, for truly, hadst thou been one of them that set Him on the Cross, with the contrition that I see in thee, thou wouldst not fail of His pardon." "Alas! my father," rejoined Ser Ciappelletto, "what is this you say? To curse my sweet mother that carried me in her womb for nine months day and night, and afterwards on her shoulder more than a hundred times! Heinous indeed was my offence; 'tis too great a sin; nor will it be pardoned, unless you pray God for me."

The friar now perceiving that Ser Ciappelletto had nothing more to say, gave him absolution and his blessing, reputing him for a most holy man, fully believing that all that he had said was true. And who would not have so believed, hearing him so speak at the point of death? Then, when all was done, he said: – "Ser Ciappelletto, if God so will, you will soon be well; but should it so come to pass that God call your blessed soul to Himself in this state of grace, is it well pleasing to you that your body be buried in our convent?" "Yea, verily, master friar," replied Ser

Ciappelletto; "there would I be, and nowhere else, since you have promised to pray God for me; besides which I have ever had a special devotion to your order. Wherefore I pray you, that, on your return to your convent, you cause to be sent me that very Body of Christ, which you consecrate in the morning on the altar; because (unworthy though I be) I purpose with your leave to take it, and afterwards the holy and extreme unction, that, though I have lived as a sinner, I may die at any rate as a Christian." The holy man said that he was greatly delighted, that it was well said of Ser Ciappelletto, and that he would cause the Host to be forthwith brought to him; and so it was.

The two brothers, who much misdoubted Ser Ciappelletto's power to deceive the friar, had taken their stand on the other side of a wooden partition which divided the room in which Ser Ciappelletto lay from another, and hearkening there they readily heard and understood what Ser Ciappelletto said to the friar; and at times could scarce refrain their laughter as they followed his confession; and now and again they said one to another: – "What manner of man is this, whom neither age nor sickness, nor fear of death, on the threshold of which he now stands, nor yet of God, before whose judgment-seat he must soon appear, has been able to turn from his wicked ways, that he die not even as he has lived?" But seeing that his confession had secured the interment of his body in church, they troubled themselves no further. Ser Ciappelletto soon afterwards communicated, and growing immensely worse, received the extreme unction, and died shortly after vespers on the same day on which he had made his good confession. So the two brothers, having from his own moneys provided the wherewith to procure him honourable sepulture, and sent word to the friars to come at even to observe the usual vigil, and in the morning to fetch the corpse, set all things in order accordingly. The holy friar who had confessed him, hearing that he was dead, had audience of the prior of the friary; a chapter was convened and the assembled brothers heard from the confessor's own mouth how Ser Ciappelletto had been a holy man, as had appeared by his confession, and were exhorted to receive the body with the utmost veneration and pious care, as one by which there was good hope that God would work many miracles. To this the prior and the rest of the credulous confraternity assenting, they went in a body in the evening to the place where the corpse of Ser Ciappelletto lay, and kept a great and solemn vigil over it; and in the morning they made a procession habited in their surplices and copes with books in their hands and crosses in front; and chanting as they went, they fetched the corpse and brought it back to their church with the utmost pomp and solemnity, being followed by almost all the folk of the city, men and women alike. So it was laid in the church, and then the holy friar who had heard the confession got up in the pulpit and began to preach marvellous things of Ser Ciapelletto's life, his fasts, his virginity, his simplicity and guilelessness and holiness; narrating among the other matters that of which Ser Ciappelletto had made tearful confession as his greatest sin, and how he had hardly been able to make him conceive that God would pardon him; from which he took occasion to reprove his hearers; saying: – "And you, accursed of God, on the least pretext, blaspheme God and His Mother, and all the celestial court. And much beside he told of his loyalty and purity; and, in short, so wrought upon the people by his words, to which they gave entire credence, that they all conceived a great veneration for Ser Ciappelletto, and at the close of the office came pressing forward with the utmost vehemence to kiss the feet and the hands of the corpse, from which they tore off the cerements, each thinking himself blessed to have but a scrap thereof in his possession; and so it was arranged that it should be kept there all day long, so as to be visible and accessible to all. At nightfall it was honourably interred in a marble tomb in one of the chapels, where on the morrow, one by one, folk came and lit tapers and prayed and paid their vows, setting there the waxen images which they had dedicated. And the fame of

Ciappelletto's holiness and the devotion to him grew in such measure that scarce any there was that in any adversity would vow aught to any saint but he, and they called him and still call him San Ciappelletto affirming that many miracles have been and daily are wrought by God through him for such as devoutly crave his intercession.

So lived, so died Ser Cepperello da Prato, and came to be reputed a saint, as you have heard. Nor would I deny that it is possible that he is of the number of the blessed in the presence of God, seeing that, though his life was evil and depraved, yet he might in his last moments have made so complete an act of contrition that perchance God had mercy on him and received him into His kingdom. But, as this is hidden from us, I speak according to that which appears, and I say that he ought rather to be in the hands of the devil in hell than in Paradise. Which, if so it be, is a manifest token of the superabundance of the goodness of God to usward, inasmuch as he regards not our error but the sincerity of our faith, and hearkens unto us when, mistaking one who is at enmity with Him for a friend, we have recourse to him, as to one holy indeed, as our intercessor for His grace. Wherefore, that we of this gay company may by His grace be preserved safe and sound throughout this time of adversity, commend we ourselves in our need to Him, whose name we began by invoking, with lauds and reverent devotion and good confidence that we shall be heard.

And so he was silent.

First Day
Novel II

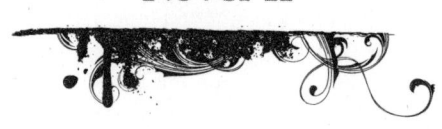

— *Abraham, a Jew, at the instance of Jehannot de Chevigny, goes to the court of Rome, and having marked the evil life of the clergy, returns to Paris, and becomes a Christian.* —

PAMFILO'S STORY elicited the mirth of some of the ladies and the hearty commendation of all, who listened to it with close attention until the end. Whereupon the queen bade Neifile, who sat next her, to tell a story, that the commencement thus made of their diversions might have its sequel. Neifile, whose graces of mind matched the beauty of her person, consented with a gladsome goodwill, and thus began: –

Pamfilo has shewn by his story that the goodness of God spares to regard our errors when they result from unavoidable ignorance, and in mine I mean to shew you how the same goodness, bearing patiently with the shortcomings of those who should be its faithful witness in deed and word, draws from them contrariwise evidence of His infallible truth; to the end that what we believe we may with more assured conviction follow.

In Paris, gracious ladies, as I have heard tell, there was once a great merchant, a large dealer in drapery, a good man, most loyal and righteous, his name Jehannot de Chevigny, between whom and a Jew, Abraham by name, also a merchant, and a man of great wealth, as also most loyal and righteous, there subsisted a very close friendship. Now Jehannot, observing Abraham's loyalty and rectitude, began to be sorely vexed in spirit that the soul of one so worthy and wise and good should perish for want of faith. Wherefore he began in a friendly manner to plead with him, that he should leave the errors of the Jewish faith and turn to the Christian verity, which, being sound and holy, he might see daily prospering and gaining ground, whereas, on the contrary, his own religion was dwindling and was almost come to nothing. The Jew replied that he believed that there was no faith sound and holy except the Jewish faith, in which he was born, and in which he meant to live and die; nor would anything ever turn him therefrom. Nothing daunted, however, Jehannot some days afterwards began again to ply Abraham with similar arguments, explaining to him in such crude fashion as merchants use the reasons why our faith is better than the Jewish. And though the Jew was a great master in the Jewish law, yet, whether it was by reason of his friendship for Jehannot, or that the Holy Spirit dictated the words that the simple merchant used, at any rate the Jew began to be much interested in Jehannot's arguments, though still too staunch in his faith to suffer himself to be converted. But Jehannot was no less assiduous in plying him with argument than he was obstinate in adhering to his law, insomuch that at length the Jew, overcome by such incessant appeals, said: – "Well, well, Jehannot, thou wouldst have me become a Christian, and I am disposed to do so, provided I first go to Rome and there see him whom thou callest God's vicar on earth, and observe what manner of life he leads and his brother cardinals with him; and if such it be that thereby, in conjunction with thy words, I may understand that thy faith is better than mine, as thou hast sought to shew me, I will do as I have said: otherwise, I will remain as I am a Jew." When

Jehannot heard this, he was greatly distressed, saying to himself: – "I thought to have converted him; but now I see that the pains which I took for so excellent a purpose are all in vain; for, if he goes to the court of Rome and sees the iniquitous and foul life which the clergy lead there, so far from turning Christian, had he been converted already, he would without doubt relapse into Judaism." Then turning to Abraham he said: – "Nay, but, my friend, why wouldst thou be at all this labour and great expense of travelling from here to Rome? to say nothing of the risks both by sea and by land which a rich man like thee must needs run. Thinkest thou not, to find here one that can give thee baptism? And as for any doubts that thou mayst have touching the faith to which I point thee, where wilt thou find greater masters and sages therein than here, to resolve thee of any question thou mayst put to them? Wherefore in my opinion this journey of thine is superfluous. Think that the prelates there are such as thou mayst have seen here, nay, as much better as they are nearer to the Chief Pastor. And so, by my advice thou wilt spare thy pains until some time of indulgence, when I, perhaps, may be able to bear thee company." The Jew replied: – "Jehannot, I doubt not that so it is as thou sayst; but once and for all I tell thee that I am minded to go there, and will never otherwise do that which thou wouldst have me and hast so earnestly besought me to do." "Go then," said Jehannot, seeing that his mind was made up, "and good luck go with thee;" and so he gave up the contest because nothing would be lost, though he felt sure that he would never become a Christian after seeing the court of Rome. The Jew took horse, and posted with all possible speed to Rome; where on his arrival he was honourably received by his fellow Jews. He said nothing to any one of the purpose for which he had come; but began circumspectly to acquaint himself with the ways of the Pope and the cardinals and the other prelates and all the courtiers; and from what he saw for himself, being a man of great intelligence, or learned from others, he discovered that without distinction of rank they were all sunk in the most disgraceful lewdness, sinning not only in the way of nature but after the manner of the men of Sodom, without any restraint of remorse or shame, in such sort that, when any great favour was to be procured, the influence of the courtesans and boys was of no small moment. Moreover he found them one and all gluttonous, wine-bibbers, drunkards, and next after lewdness, most addicted to the shameless service of the belly, like brute beasts. And, as he probed the matter still further, he perceived that they were all so greedy and avaricious that human, nay Christian blood, and things sacred of what kind soever, spiritualities no less than temporalities, they bought and sold for money; which traffic was greater and employed more brokers than the drapery trade and all the other trades of Paris put together; open simony and gluttonous excess being glosed under such specious terms as "arrangement" and "moderate use of creature comforts," as if God could not penetrate the thoughts of even the most corrupt hearts, to say nothing of the signification of words, and would suffer Himself to be misled after the manner of men by the names of things. Which matters, with many others which are not to be mentioned, our modest and sober-minded Jew found by no means to his liking, so that, his curiosity being fully satisfied, he was minded to return to Paris; which accordingly he did. There, on his arrival, he was met by Jehannot; and the two made great cheer together. Jehannot expected Abraham's conversion least of all things, and allowed him some days of rest before he asked what he thought of the Holy Father and the cardinals and the other courtiers. To which the Jew forthwith replied: – "I think God owes them all an evil recompense: I tell thee, so far as I was able to carry my investigations, holiness, devotion, good works or exemplary living in any kind was nowhere to be found in any clerk; but only lewdness, avarice, gluttony, and the like, and worse, if worse may be, appeared to be held in such honour of all, that (to my thinking) the place is a centre of diabolical rather than of divine activities. To the best of my judgment, your Pastor, and by consequence all that are about him devote all their zeal and ingenuity and subtlety to devise how best and most speedily they may bring the Christian religion to nought and banish it from the world. And because I see that what they so zealously endeavour does not come to pass, but that on the contrary your religion continually grows, and shines more and more clear, therein I seem to discern a very evident token that it, rather than any other, as being more true and holy than any other, has the Holy Spirit for its foundation and support. For which cause, whereas I met your exhortations in a harsh and obdurate temper, and would not become a Christian, now I frankly tell you that I would on no account omit to become such. Go we then to the church, and there according to the traditional rite of your holy faith let me receive baptism." Jehannot, who had anticipated a diametrically opposite conclusion, as soon as he heard him so speak, was the best pleased man that ever was in the world. So taking Abraham with him to Notre Dame he prayed the clergy there to baptise him. When they heard that it was his own wish, they forthwith did so, and Jehannot raised him from the sacred font, and named him Jean; and afterwards he caused teachers of great eminence thoroughly to instruct him in our faith, which he readily learned, and afterwards practised in a good, a virtuous, nay, a holy life.

First Day

Novel III

— Melchisedech, a Jew, by a story of three rings averts a great danger with which he was menaced by Saladin. —

WHEN NEIFILE had brought her story to a close amid the commendations of all the company, Filomena, at the queen's behest, thus began: –

The story told by Neifile brings to my mind another in which also Jew appears, but this time as the hero of a perilous adventure; and as enough has been said of God and of the truth our faith, it will not now be inopportune if we descend to mundane events and the actions of men. Wherefore I propose to tell you a story, which will perhaps dispose you to be more circumspect than you have been wont to be in answering questions addressed to you. Well ye know, or should know, loving gossips, that, as it often happens that folk by their own folly forfeit a happy estate and are plunged in most grievous misery, so good sense will extricate the wise from extremity of peril, and establish them in complete and assured peace. Of the change from good to evil fortune, which folly may effect, instances abound; indeed, occurring as they do by the thousand day by day, they are so conspicuous that their recital would be beside our present purpose. But that good sense may be our succour in misfortune, I will now, as I promised, make plain to you within the narrow compass of a little story.

Saladin, who by his great valour had from small beginnings made himself Soldan of Egypt, and gained many victories over kings both Christian and Saracen, having in divers wars and by divers lavish displays of magnificence spent all his treasure, and in order to meet a certain emergency being in need of a large sum of money, and being at a loss to raise it with a celerity adequate to his necessity, bethought him of a wealthy Jew, Melchisedech by name, who lent at usance in Alexandria, and who, were he but willing, was, as he believed, able to accommodate him, but was so miserly that he would never do so of his own accord, nor was Saladin disposed to constrain him thereto. So great, however, was his necessity that, after pondering every method whereby the Jew might be induced to be compliant, at last he determined to devise a colourably reasonable pretext for extorting the money from him. So he sent for him, received him affably, seated him by his side, and presently said to him: – "My good man, I have heard from many people that thou art very wise, and of great discernment in divine things; wherefore I would gladly know of thee, which of the three laws thou reputest the true law, the law of the Jews, the law of the Saracens, or the law of the Christians?" The Jew, who was indeed a wise man, saw plainly enough that Saladin meant to entangle him in his speech, that he might have occasion to harass him, and bethought him that he could not praise any of the three laws above another without furnishing Saladin with the pretext which he sought. So, concentrating all the force of his mind to shape such an answer as might avoid the snare, he presently lit on what he sought, saying: – "My lord, a pretty question indeed is this which you propound, and fain would I answer it; to which end it is apposite that I tell you a story, which, if you will hearken, is as follows: – If I mistake not, I remember to have often heard tell of a great and rich man of old time, who among other most precious jewels had in his treasury a ring of extraordinary beauty and value, which by reason of its value and beauty he was minded to leave to his heirs for ever; for which cause he ordained, that, whichever of his sons was found in possession of the ring as by his bequest, should thereby be designate his heir, and be entitled to receive from the rest the honour and homage due to a superior. The son, to whom he bequeathed the ring, left it in like manner to his descendants, making the like ordinance as his predecessor. In short the ring passed from hand to hand for many generations; and in the end came to the hands of one who had three sons, goodly and virtuous all, and very obedient to their father, so that he loved them all indifferently. The rule touching the descent of the ring was known to the young men, and each aspiring to hold the place of honour among them did all he could to persuade his father, who was now old, to leave the ring to him at his death. The worthy man, who loved them all equally, and knew not how to choose from among them a sole legatee, promised the ring to each in turn, and in order to satisfy all three, caused a cunning artificer secretly to make two other rings, so like the first, that the maker himself could hardly tell which was the true ring. So, before he died, he disposed of the rings, giving one privily to each of his sons; whereby it came to pass, that after his decease each of the sons claimed the inheritance and the place of honour, and, his claim being disputed by his brothers, produced his ring in witness of right. And the rings being found so like one to another that it was impossible to distinguish the true one, the suit to determine the true heir remained pendent, and still so remains. And so, my lord, to your question, touching the three laws given to the three peoples by God the Father, I answer: – Each of these peoples deems itself to have the true inheritance, the true law, the true commandments of God; but which of them is justified in so believing, is a question which, like that of the rings, remains pendent." The excellent adroitness with which the Jew had contrived to evade the snare which he had laid for his feet was not lost upon Saladin. He therefore determined to let the Jew know his need, and did so, telling him at the same time what he had intended to do, in the event of his answering less circumspectly than he had done.

Thereupon the Jew gave the Soldan all the accommodation that he required, which the Soldan afterwards repaid him in full. He also gave him most munificent gifts with his lifelong amity and a great and honourable position near his person.

First Day

Novel IV

— *A monk lapses into a sin meriting the most severe punishment, justly censures the same fault in his abbot, and thus evades the penalty.* —

THE SILENCE which followed the conclusion of Filomena's tale was broken by Dioneo, who sate next her, and without waiting for the queen's word, for he knew that by the rule laid down at the commencement it was now his turn to speak, began on this wise: –

Loving ladies, if I have well understood the intention of you all, we are here to afford entertainment to one another by story-telling; wherefore, provided only nought is done that is repugnant to this end, I deem it lawful for each (and so said our queen a little while ago) to tell whatever story seems to him most likely to be amusing. Seeing, then, that we have heard how Abraham saved his soul by the good counsel of Jehannot de Chevigny, and Melchisedech by his own good sense safe-guarded his wealth against the stratagems of Saladin, I hope to escape your censure in narrating a brief story of a monk, who by his address delivered his body from imminent peril of most severe chastisement.

In the not very remote district of Lunigiana there flourished formerly a community of monks more numerous and holy than is there to be found to-day, among whom was a young brother, whose vigour and lustihood neither the fasts nor the vigils availed to subdue. One afternoon, while the rest of the confraternity slept, our young monk took a stroll around the church, which lay in a very sequestered spot, and chanced to espy a young and very beautiful girl, a daughter, perhaps, of one of the husbandmen of those parts, going through the fields and gathering herbs as she went. No sooner had he seen her than he was sharply assailed by carnal concupiscence, insomuch that he made up to and accosted her; and (she hearkening) little by little they came to an understanding, and unobserved by any entered his cell together. Now it so chanced that, while they fooled it within somewhat recklessly, he being overwrought with passion, the abbot awoke and passing slowly by the young monk's cell, heard the noise which they made within, and the better to distinguish the voices, came softly up to the door of the cell, and listening discovered that beyond all doubt there was a woman within. His first thought was to force the door open; but, changing his mind, he returned to his chamber and waited until the monk should come out.

Delightsome beyond measure though the monk found his intercourse with the girl, yet was he not altogether without anxiety. He had heard, as he thought, the sound of footsteps in the dormitory, and having applied his eye to a convenient aperture had had a good view of the abbot as he stood by the door listening. He was thus fully aware that the abbot might have detected the presence of a woman in the cell. Whereat he was exceedingly distressed, knowing that he had a severe punishment to expect; but he concealed his vexation from the girl while he busily cast about in his mind for some way of escape from his embarrassment. He thus hit on a novel stratagem which was exactly suited to his purpose. With the air of one who had had enough of the girl's company he said to her: – "I shall now leave you in order that I may arrange for your departure hence unobserved. Stay here quietly until I return." So out he went, locking the door of the cell, and withdrawing the key, which he carried straight to the abbot's chamber and handed to him, as was the custom when a monk was going out, saying with a composed air: – "Sir, I was not able this morning to bring in all the faggots which I had made ready, so with your leave I will go to the wood and bring them in." The abbot, desiring to have better cognisance of the monk's offence, and not dreaming that the monk knew that he had been detected, was pleased with the turn matters had taken, and received the key gladly, at the same time giving the monk the desired leave. So the monk withdrew, and the abbot began to consider what course it were best for him to take, whether to assemble the brotherhood and open the door in their presence, that, being witnesses of the delinquency, they might have no cause to murmur against him when he proceeded to punish the delinquent, or whether it were not better first to learn from the girl's own lips how it had come about. And reflecting that she might be the wife or daughter of some man who would take it ill that she should be shamed by being exposed to the gaze of all the monks, he determined first of all to find out who she was, and then to make up his mind. So he went softly to the cell, opened the door, and, having entered, closed it behind him. The girl, seeing that her visitor was none other than the abbot, quite lost her presence of mind, and quaking with shame began to weep. Master abbot surveyed her from head to foot, and seeing that she was fresh and comely, fell a prey, old though he was, to fleshly cravings no less poignant and sudden than those which the young monk had experienced, and began thus to commune with himself: – "Alas! why take I not my pleasure when I may, seeing that I never need lack for occasions of trouble and vexation of spirit? Here is a fair wench, and no one in the world to know. If I can bring her to pleasure me, I know not why I should not do so. Who will know? No one will ever know; and sin that is hidden is half forgiven; this chance may never come again; so, methinks, it were the part of wisdom to take the boon which God bestows." So musing, with an altogether different purpose from that with which he had come, he drew near the girl, and softly bade her to be comforted, and besought her not to weep; and so little by little he came at last to show her what he would be at. The girl, being made neither of iron nor of adamant, was readily induced to gratify the abbot, who after bestowing upon her many an embrace and kiss, got upon the monk's bed, where, being sensible, perhaps, of the disparity between his reverend portliness and her tender youth, and fearing to injure her by his excessive weight, he refrained from lying upon her, but laid her upon him, and in that manner disported himself with her for a long time. The monk, who had only pretended to go to the wood, and had concealed himself in the dormitory, no sooner saw the abbot enter his cell than he was overjoyed to think that his plan would succeed; and when he saw that he had locked the door, he was well assured thereof. So he stole out of his hiding-place, and set his eye to an aperture through which he saw and heard all that the abbot did and said. At length the abbot, having had enough of dalliance with the girl, locked her in the cell and returned to his chamber. Catching sight of the monk soon afterwards, and supposing him to have returned from the wood, he determined to give him a sharp reprimand and have him imprisoned, that he might thus secure the prey for himself alone. He therefore caused him to be summoned, chid him very severely and with a stern countenance, and ordered him to be put in prison. The monk replied trippingly: – "I Sir, I have not been so long in the order of St. Benedict as to have every particular of the rule by heart; nor did you teach me before to-day in what posture it behoves the monk to have intercourse with women, but limited your instruction to such matters as fasts and vigils. As, however, you have now given me my lesson, I promise you, if you also pardon my offence, that I will never repeat it, but will always follow the example which you have set me."

The abbot, who was a shrewd man, saw at once that the monk was not only more knowing than he, but had actually seen what he had done; nor, conscience-stricken himself, could he for shame mete out to the monk a measure which he himself merited. So pardon given, with an injunction to bury what had been seen in silence, they decently conveyed the young girl out of the monastery, whither, it is to be believed, they now and again caused her to return.

First Day
Novel V

— *The Marchioness of Monferrato by a banquet of hens seasoned with wit checks the mad passion of the King of France.* —

THE STORY TOLD by Dioneo evoked at first some qualms of shame in the minds of the ladies, as was apparent by the modest blush that tinged their faces: then exchanging glances, and scarce able to refrain their mirth, they listened to it with half-suppressed smiles. On its conclusion they bestowed upon Dioneo a few words of gentle reprehension with intent to admonish him that such stories were not to be told among ladies. The queen then turned to Fiammetta, who was seated on the grass at her side, and bade her follow suit and Fiammetta with a gay and gracious mien thus began: –

The line upon which our story-telling proceeds, to wit, to shew the virtue that resides in apt and ready repartees, pleases me well; and as in affairs of love men and women are in diverse case, for to aspire to the love of a woman of higher lineage than his own is wisdom in man, whereas a woman's good sense is then most conspicuous when she knows how to preserve herself from becoming enamoured of a man, her superior in rank, I am minded, fair my ladies, to shew you by the story which I am now to tell, how by deed and word a gentlewoman both defended herself against attack, and weaned her suitor from his love.

The Marquis of Monferrato, a paladin of distinguished prowess, was gone overseas as gonfalonier of the Church in a general array of the Christian forces. Whose merits being canvassed at the court of Philippe le Borgne, on the eve of his departure from France on the same service, a knight observed, that there was not under the stars a couple comparable to the Marquis and his lady; in that, while the Marquis was a paragon of the knightly virtues, his lady for beauty, and honour was without a peer among all the other ladies of the world. These words made so deep an impression on the mind of the King of France that, though he had never seen the lady, he fell ardently in love with her, and, being to join the armada, resolved that his port of embarcation should be no other than Genoa, in order that, travelling thither by land, he might find a decent pretext for visiting the Marchioness, with whom in the absence of the Marquis he trusted to have the success which he desired; nor did he fail to put his design in execution. Having sent his main army on before, he took the road himself with a small company of gentlemen, and, as they approached the territory of the Marquis, he despatched a courier to the Marchioness, a day in advance, to let her know that he expected to breakfast with her the next morning. The lady, who knew her part and played it well, replied graciously, that he would be indeed welcome, and that his presence would be the greatest of all favours. She then began to commune with herself, what this might import, that so great a king should come to visit her in her husband's absence, nor was she so deluded as not to surmise that it was the fame of her beauty that drew him thither. Nevertheless she made ready to do him honour in a manner befitting her high degree, summoning to her presence such of the retainers as remained in the castle, and giving all needful directions with their advice, except that the order of the banquet and the choice of the dishes she reserved entirely to herself. Then, having caused all the hens that could be found in the country-side to be brought with all speed into the castle, she bade her cooks furnish forth the royal table with divers dishes made exclusively of such fare. The King arrived on the appointed day, and was received by the lady with great and ceremonious cheer. Fair and noble and gracious seemed she in the eyes of the King beyond all that he had conceived from the knight's words, so that he was lost in admiration and inly extolled her to the skies, his passion being the more inflamed in proportion as he found the lady surpass the idea which he had formed of her. A suite of rooms furnished with all the appointments befitting the reception of so great a king, was placed at his disposal, and after a little rest, breakfast-time being come, he and the Marchioness took their places at the same table, while his suite were honourably entertained at other boards according to their several qualities. Many courses were served with no lack of excellent and rare wines, whereby the King was mightily pleased, as also by the extraordinary beauty of the Marchioness, on whom his eye from time to time rested. However, as course followed course, the King observed with some surprise, that, though the dishes were diverse, yet they were all but variations of one and the same fare, to wit, the pullet. Besides which he knew that the domain was one which could not but afford plenty of divers sorts of game, and by forewarning the lady of his approach, he had allowed time for hunting; yet, for all his surprise, he would not broach the question more directly with her than by a reference to her hens; so, turning to her with a smile, he said: – "Madam, do hens grow in this country without so much as a single cock?" The Marchioness, who perfectly apprehended the drift of the question, saw in it an opportunity, sent her by God, of evincing her virtuous resolution; so casting a haughty glance upon the King she answered thus: – "Sire, no; but the women, though they may differ somewhat from others in dress and rank, are yet of the same nature here as elsewhere." The significance of the banquet of pullets was made manifest to the King by these words, as also the virtue which they veiled. He perceived that on a lady of such a temper words would be wasted, and that force was out of the question. Wherefore, yielding to the dictates of prudence and honour, he was now as prompt to quench, as he had been inconsiderate in conceiving, his unfortunate passion for the lady; and fearing her answers, he refrained from further jesting with her, and dismissing his hopes devoted himself to his breakfast, which done, he disarmed suspicion of the dishonourable purpose of his visit by an early departure, and thanking her for the honour she had conferred upon him, and commending her to God, took the road to Genoa.

First Day
Novel VI

— A worthy man by an apt saying puts to shame the wicked hypocrisy of the religious. —

WHEN ALL HAD commended the virtue of the Marchioness and the spirited reproof which she administered to the King of France, Emilia, who sate next to Fiammetta, obeyed the queen's behest, and with a good courage thus began: –

My story is also of a reproof, but of one administered by a worthy man, who lived the secular life, to a greedy religious, by a jibe as merry as admirable. Know then, dear ladies, that there was in our city, not long ago, a friar minor, an inquisitor in matters of heresy, who, albeit he strove might and main to pass himself off as a holy man and tenderly solicitous for the integrity of the Christian Faith, as they all do, yet he had as keen a scent for a full purse as for a deficiency of faith. Now it so chanced that his zeal was rewarded by the discovery of a good man far better furnished with money than with sense, who in an unguarded moment, not from defect of faith, but rather, perhaps from excess of hilarity, being heated with wine, had happened to say to his boon companions, that he had a wine good enough for Christ Himself to drink. Which being reported to the inquisitor, he, knowing the man to be possessed of large estates and a well-lined purse, set to work in hot haste, "cum gladiis et fustibus," to bring all the rigour of the law to bear upon him, designing thereby not to lighten the load of his victim's misbelief, but to increase the weight of his own purse by the florins, which he might, as he did, receive from him. So he cited him to his presence, and asked him whether what was alleged against him were true. The good man answered in the affirmative, and told him how it had happened. "Then," said our most holy and devout inquisitor of St. John Goldenbeard, "then hast thou made Christ a wine-bibber, and a lover of rare vintages, as if he were a sot, a toper and a tavern-haunter even as one of you. And thinkest thou now by a few words of apology to pass this off as a light matter? It is no such thing as thou supposest. Thou hast deserved the fire; and we should but do our duty, did we inflict it upon thee." With these and the like words in plenty he upbraided him, bending on him meanwhile a countenance as stern as if Epicurus had stood before him denying the immortality of the soul. In short he so terrified him that the good man was fain to employ certain intermediaries to anoint his palms with a liberal allowance of St. John Goldenmouth's grease, an excellent remedy for the disease of avarice which spreads like a pestilence among the clergy, and notably among the friars minors, who dare not touch a coin, that he might deal gently with him. And great being the virtue of this ointment, albeit no mention is made thereof by Galen in any part of his Medicines, it had so gracious an effect that the threatened fire gave place to a cross, which he was to wear as if he were bound for the emprise over seas; and to make the ensign more handsome the inquisitor ordered that it should be yellow upon a black ground. Besides which, after pocketing the coin, he kept him dangling about him for some days, bidding him by way of penance hear mass every morning at Santa Croce, and afterwards wait upon him at the breakfast-hour, after which he was free to do as he pleased for the rest of the day. All which he most carefully observed; and so it fell out that one of these mornings there were chanted at the mass at which he assisted the following words of the Gospel: – You shall receive an hundredfold and shall possess eternal life. With these words deeply graven in his memory, he presented himself, as he was bidden, before the inquisitor, where he sate taking his breakfast, and being asked whether he had heard mass that morning, he promptly answered: – "Yes, sir." And being further asked: – "Heardest thou aught therein, as to which thou art in doubt, or hast thou any question to propound?" the good man responded: – "Nay indeed, doubt have I none of aught that I heard; but rather assured faith in the verity of all. One thing, however, I heard, which caused me to commiserate you and the rest of you friars very heartily, in regard of the evil plight in which you must find yourselves in the other world." "And what," said the inquisitor, "was the passage that so moved thee to commiserate us?" "Sir," rejoined the good man, "it was that passage in the Gospel which says: – "You shall receive an hundredfold." "You heard aright," said the inquisitor; "but why did the passage so affect you?" "Sir," replied the good man, "I will tell you. Since I have been in attendance here, I have seen a crowd of poor folk receive a daily dole, now of one, now of two, huge tureens of swill, being the refuse from your table, and that of the brothers of this convent; whereof if you are to receive an hundredfold in the other world, you will have so much that it will go hard but you are all drowned therein." This raised a general laugh among those who sat at the inquisitor's table, whereat the inquisitor, feeling that their gluttony and hypocrisy had received a home-thrust, was very wroth, and, but that what he had already done had not escaped censure, would have instituted fresh proceedings against him in revenge for the pleasantry with which he had rebuked the baseness of himself and his brother friars; so in impotent wrath he bade him go about his business and shew himself there no more.

First Day
Novel VII

— *Bergamino, with a story of Primasso and the Abbot of Cluny, finely censures a sudden access of avarice in Messer Cane della Scala.* —

EMILIA'S CHARMING manner and her story drew laughter and commendation from the queen and all the company, who were much tickled by her new type of crusader. When the laughter had subsided, and all were again silent, Filostrato, on whom the narration now fell, began on this wise: –

A fine thing it is, noble ladies, to hit a fixed mark; but if, on the sudden appearance of some strange object, it be forthwith hit by the bowman, 'tis little short of a miracle. The corrupt and filthy life of the clergy offers on many sides a fixed mark of iniquity at which, whoever is so minded, may let fly, with little doubt that they will reach it, the winged words of reproof and reprehension. Wherefore, though the worthy man did well to censure in the person of the inquisitor the pretended charity of the friars who give to the poor what they ought rather to give to the pigs or throw away, higher indeed is the praise which I accord to him, of whom, taking my cue from the last story, I mean to speak; seeing that by a clever apologue he rebuked a sudden and unwonted access of avarice in Messer Cane della Scala, conveying in a figure what he had at heart to say touching Messer Cane and himself; which apologue is to follow.

Far and wide, almost to the ends of the earth, is borne the most illustrious renown of Messer Cane della Scala, in many ways the favoured child of fortune, a lord almost without a peer among the notables and magnificoes of Italy since the time of the Emperor Frederic II. Now Messer Cane, being minded to hold high festival at Verona, whereof fame should speak marvellous things, and many folk from divers parts, of whom the greater number were jesters of every order, being already arrived, Messer Cane did suddenly (for some cause or another) abandon his design, and dismissed them with a partial recompense. One only, Bergamino by name, a speaker ready and polished in a degree credible only to such as heard him, remained, having received no recompense or conge, still cherishing the hope that this omission might yet turn out to his advantage. But Messer Cane was possessed with the idea that whatever he might give Bergamino would be far more completely thrown away than if he had tossed it into the fire; so never a word of the sort said he or sent he to him. A few days thus passed, and then Bergamino, seeing that he was in no demand or request for aught that belonged to his office, and being also at heavy charges at his inn for the keep of his horses and servants, fell into a sort of melancholy; but still he waited a while, not deeming it expedient to leave. He had brought with him three rich and goodly robes, given him by other lords, that he might make a brave show at the festival, and when his host began to press for payment he gave him one of the robes; afterwards, there being still much outstanding against him, he must needs, if he would tarry longer at the inn, give the host the second robe; after which he began to live on the third, being minded remain there, as long as it would hold out, in expectation of better luck, and then to take his departure. Now, while he was thus living on the third robe, it chanced that Messer Cane encountered him one day as he sate at breakfast with a very melancholy visage. Which Messer Cane observing, said, rather to tease him than expecting to elicit from him any pleasant retort: – "What ails thee, Bergamino, that thou art still so melancholy? Let me know the reason why." Whereupon Bergamino, without a moment's reflection, told the following story, which could not have fitted his own case more exactly if it had been long premeditated.

My lord, you must know that Primasso was a grammarian of great eminence, and excellent and quick beyond all others in versifying; whereby he waxed so notable and famous that, albeit he was not everywhere known by sight, yet there were scarce any that did not at least by name and report know who Primasso was. Now it so happened that, being once at Paris in straitened circumstances, as it was his lot to be most of his time by reason that virtue is little appreciated by the powerful, he heard speak of the Abbot of Cluny, who, except the Pope, is supposed to be the richest prelate, in regard of his vast revenues, that the Church of God can shew; and marvellous and magnificent things were told him of the perpetual court which the abbot kept, and how, wherever he was, he denied not to any that came there either meat or drink, so only that he preferred his request while the abbot was at table. Which when Primasso heard, he determined to go and see for himself what magnificent state this abbot kept, for he was one that took great delight in observing the ways of powerful and lordly men; wherefore he asked how far from Paris was the abbot then sojourning. He was informed that the abbot was then at one of his places distant perhaps six miles; which Primasso concluded he could reach in time for breakfast, if he started early in the morning. When he had learned the way, he found that no one else was travelling by it, and fearing lest by mischance he should lose it, and so find himself where it would not be easy for him to get food, he determined to obviate so disagreeable a contingency by taking with him three loaves of bread – as for drink, water, though not much to his taste, was, he supposed, to be found everywhere. So, having disposed the loaves in the fold of his tunic, he took the road and made such progress that he reached the abbot's place of sojourn before the breakfast-hour. Having entered, he made the circuit of the entire place, observing everything, the vast array of tables, and the vast kitchen well-appointed with all things needful for the preparation and service of the breakfast, and saying to himself: – "In very truth this man is even such a magnifico as he is reported to be." While his attention was thus occupied, the abbot's seneschal, it being now breakfast-time, gave order to serve water for the hands, which being washen, they sat them all down to breakfast. Now it so happened that Primasso was placed immediately in front of the door by which the abbot must pass from his chamber, into the hall, in which, according to rule of his court, neither wine, nor bread, nor aught else drinkable or eatable was ever set on the tables before he made his appearance and was seated. The seneschal, therefore, having set the tables, sent word to the abbot, that all was now ready, and they waited only his pleasure. So the abbot gave the word, the door of his chamber was thrown open, and he took a step or two forward towards the hall, gazing straight in front of him as he went. Thus it fell out that the first man on whom he set eyes was Primasso, who was in very sorry trim. The abbot, who knew him not by sight, no sooner saw him, than, surprised by a churlish mood to which he had hitherto been an entire stranger, he said to himself: – "So it is to such as this man that I give my hospitality;" and going back into the chamber he bade lock the door, and asked of his attendants whether the vile fellow that sate at table directly opposite the door was known to any of them, who, one and all, answered in the negative. Primasso waited a little, but he was not used to fast, and his journey had whetted his appetite. So, as the abbot did not return, he drew out one of the loaves which he had brought with him, and began to eat. The abbot, after a while, bade one of his servants go see whether Primasso were gone. The servant returned with the answer: – "No, sir, and (what is more) he is eating a loaf of bread, which he seems to have brought with him." "Be it so then," said the abbot, who was vexed that he was not gone of his own accord, but was not disposed to turn him out; "let him eat his own bread, if he have any, for he shall have none of ours today." By and by Primasso, having finished his first loaf, began, as the abbot did not make his appearance, to eat the second; which was likewise reported to the abbot, who had again sent to see if he were gone. Finally, as the abbot still delayed his coming, Primasso, having finished the second loaf, began upon the third; whereof, once more, word was carried to the abbot, who now began to commune with himself and say: – "Alas! my soul, what unwonted mood harbourest thou to-day? What avarice? what scorn? and of whom? I have given my hospitality, now for many a year, to whoso craved it, without looking to see whether he were gentle or churl, poor or rich, merchant or cheat, and mine eyes have seen it squandered on vile fellows without number; and nought of that which I feel towards this man ever entered my mind. Assuredly it cannot be that he is a man of no consequence, who is the occasion of this access of avarice in me. Though he seem to me a vile fellow, he must be some great man, that my mind is thus obstinately averse to do him honour." Of which musings the upshot was that he sent to inquire who the vile fellow was, and learning that he was Primasso, come to see if what he had heard of his magnificent state were true, he was stricken with shame, having heard of old Primasso's fame, and knowing him to be a great man. Wherefore, being zealous to make him the amend, he studied to do him honour in many ways; and after breakfast, that his garb might accord with his native dignity, he caused him to be nobly arrayed, and setting him upon a palfrey and filling his purse, left it to his own choice, whether to go or to stay. So Primasso, with a full heart, thanked him for his courtesy in terms the amplest that he could command, and, having left Paris afoot, returned thither on horseback."

Messer Cane was shrewd enough to apprehend Bergamino's meaning perfectly well without a gloss, and said with a smile: – "Bergamino, thy parable is apt, and declares to me very plainly thy losses, my avarice, and what thou desirest of me. And in good sooth this access of avarice, of which thou art the occasion, is the first that I have experienced. But I will expel the intruder with the baton which thou thyself hast furnished." So he paid Bergamino's reckoning, habited him nobly in one of his own robes, gave him money and a palfrey, and left it for the time at his discretion, whether to go or to stay.

First Day
Novel VIII

— Guglielmo Borsiere by a neat retort sharply censures avarice in Messer Ermino de' Grimaldi. —

NEXT FILOSTRATO was seated Lauretta, who, when the praises bestowed on Bergamino's address had ceased, knowing that it was now her turn to speak, waited not for the word of command, but with a charming graciousness thus began: –

The last novel, dear gossips, prompts me to relate how a worthy man, likewise a jester, reprehended not without success the greed of a very wealthy merchant; and, though the burden of my story is not unlike the last, yet, perchance, it may not on that account be the less appreciated by you, because it has a happy termination.

Know then that in Genoa there dwelt long ago a gentleman, who was known as Messer Ermino de' Grimaldi, and whose wealth, both in lands and money, was generally supposed to be far in excess of that of any other burgher then in Italy, and as in wealth he was without a rival in Italy, so in meanness and avarice there was not any in the entire world, however richly endowed with those qualities, whom he did not immeasurably surpass, insomuch that, not only did he keep a tight grip upon his purse when honour was to be done to another, but in his personal expenditure, even upon things meet and proper, contrary to the general custom of the Genoese, whose wont is to array themselves nobly, he was extremely penurious, as also in his outlay upon his table. Wherefore, not without just cause, folk had dropped his surname de' Grimaldi, and called him instead Messer Ermino Avarizia. While thus by thrift his wealth waxed greater and greater, it so chanced that there came to Genoa a jester of good parts, a man debonair and ready of speech, his name Guglielmo Borsiere, whose like is not to be found to-day when jesters (to the great reproach be it spoken of those that claim the name and reputation of gentlemen) are rather to be called asses, being without courtly breeding, and formed after the coarse pattern of the basest of churls. And whereas in the days of which I speak they made it their business, they spared no pains, to compose quarrels, to allay heart-burnings, between gentlemen, or arrange marriages, or leagues of amity, ministering meanwhile relief to jaded minds and solace to courts by the sprightly sallies of their wit, and with keen sarcasm, like fathers, censuring churlish manners, being also satisfied with very trifling guerdons; nowadays all their care is to spend their time in scandal-mongering, in sowing discord, in saying, and (what is worse) in doing in the presence of company things churlish and flagitious, in bringing accusations, true or false, of wicked, shameful or flagitious conduct against one another; and in drawing gentlemen into base and nefarious practices by sinister and insidious arts. And by these wretched and depraved lords he is held most dear and best rewarded whose words and deeds are the most atrocious, to the great reproach and scandal of the world of to-day; whereby it is abundantly manifest that virtue has departed from the earth, leaving a degenerate generation to wallow in the lowest depths of vice.

But reverting to the point at which I started, wherefrom under stress of just indignation I have deviated somewhat further than I intended, I say that the said Guglielmo was had in honour, and was well received by all the gentlemen of Genoa; and tarrying some days in the city, heard much of the meanness and avarice of Messer Ermino, and was curious to see him. Now Messer Ermino had heard that this Guglielmo Borsiere was a man of good parts, and, notwithstanding his avarice, having in him some sparks of good breeding, received him with words of hearty greeting and a gladsome mien, and conversed freely with him and of divers matters, and so conversing, took him with other Genoese that were of his company to a new and very beautiful house which he had built, and after shewing him over the whole of it, said to him: – "Now, Messer Guglielmo, you have seen and heard many things; could you suggest to me something, the like of which has not hitherto been seen, which I might have painted here in the saloon of this house?" To which ill-judged question Guglielmo replied: – "Sir, it would not, I think, be in my power to suggest anything the like of which has never been seen, unless it were a sneeze or something similar; but if it so please you, I have something to suggest, which, I think, you have never seen." "Prithee, what may that be?" said Messer Ermino, not expecting to get the answer which he got. For Guglielmo replied forthwith: – "Paint Courtesy here;" which Messer Ermino had no sooner heard, than he was so stricken with shame that his disposition underwent a complete change, and he said: – "Messer, Guglielmo, I will see to it that Courtesy is here painted in such wise that neither you nor any one else shall ever again have reason to tell me that I have not seen or known that virtue." And henceforward (so enduring was the change wrought by Guglielmo's words) there was not in Genoa, while he lived, any gentleman so liberal and so gracious and so lavish of honour both to strangers and to his fellow-citizens as Messer Ermino de' Grimaldi.

First Day
Novel IX

— The censure of a Gascon lady converts the King of Cyprus from a churlish to an honourable temper. —

EXCEPT ELISA none now remained to answer the call of the queen, and she without waiting for it, with gladsome alacrity thus began: –

Bethink you, damsels, how often it has happened that men who have been obdurate to censures and chastisements have been reclaimed by some unpremeditated casual word. This is plainly manifest by the story told by Lauretta; and by mine, which will be of the briefest, I mean further to illustrate it; seeing that, good stories, being always pleasurable, are worth listening to with attention, no matter by whom they may be told.

'Twas, then, in the time of the first king of Cyprus, after the conquest made of the Holy Land by Godfrey de Bouillon, that a lady of Gascony made a pilgrimage to the Holy Sepulchre, and on her way home, having landed at Cyprus, met with brutal outrage at the hands of certain ruffians. Broken-hearted and disconsolate she determined to make her complaint to the king; but she was told that it would be all in vain, because so spiritless and faineant was he that he not only neglected to avenge affronts put upon others, but endured with a reprehensible tameness those which were offered to himself, insomuch that whoso had any ill-humour to vent, took occasion to vex or mortify him. The lady, hearing this report, despaired of redress, and by way of alleviation of her grief determined to make the king sensible of his baseness. So in tears she presented herself before him and said: – "Sire, it is not to seek redress of the wrong done me that I come here before you: but only that, so please you, I may learn of you how it is that you suffer patiently the wrongs which, as I understand, are done you; that thus schooled by you in patience I may endure my own, which, God knows, I would gladly, were it possible, transfer to you, seeing that you are so well fitted to bear them." These words aroused the hitherto sluggish and apathetic king as it were from sleep. He redressed the lady's wrong, and having thus made a beginning, thenceforth meted out the most rigorous justice to all that in any wise offended against the majesty of his crown.

First Day
Novel X

— Master Alberto da Bologna honourably puts to shame a lady who sought occasion to put him to shame in that he was in love with her. —

AFTER ELISA had done, it only remained for the queen to conclude the day's story-telling, and thus with manner debonair did she begin: –

As stars in the serene expanse of heaven, as in spring-time flowers in the green pastures, so, honourable damsels, in the hour of rare and excellent converse is wit with its bright sallies. Which, being brief, are much more proper for ladies than for men, seeing that prolixity of speech, when brevity is possible, is much less allowable to them; albeit (shame be to us all and all our generation) few ladies or none are left to-day who understand aught that is wittily said, or understanding are able to answer it. For the place of those graces of the spirit which distinguished the ladies of the past has now been usurped by adornments of the person; and she whose dress is most richly and variously and curiously dight, accounts herself more worthy to be had in honour, forgetting, that, were one but so to array him, an ass would carry a far greater load of finery than any of them, and for all that be not a whit the more deserving of honour. I blush to say this, for in censuring others I condemn myself. Tricked out, bedecked, bedizened thus, we are either silent and impassive as statues, or, if we answer aught that is said to us, much better were it we had held our peace. And we make believe, forsooth, that our failure to acquit ourselves in converse with our equals of either sex does but proceed from guilelessness; dignifying stupidity by the name of modesty, as if no lady could be modest and converse with other folk than her maid or laundress or bake-house woman; which if Nature had intended, as we feign she did, she would have set other limits to our garrulousness. True it is that in this, as in other matters, time and place and person are to be regarded; because it sometimes happens that a lady or gentleman thinking by some sally of wit to put another to shame, has rather been put to shame by that other, having failed duly to estimate their relative powers. Wherefore, that you may be on your guard against such error, and, further, that in you be not exemplified the common proverb, to wit, that women do ever and on all occasions choose the worst, I trust that this last of to-day's stories, which falls to me to tell, may serve you as a lesson; that, as you are distinguished from others by nobility of nature, so you may also shew yourselves separate from them by excellence of manners.

There lived not many years ago, perhaps yet lives, in Bologna, a very great physician, so great that the fame of his skill was noised abroad throughout almost the entire world.

Now Master Alberto (such was his name) was of so noble a temper that, being now nigh upon seventy years of age, and all but devoid of natural heat of body, he was yet receptive of the flames of love; and having at an assembly seen a very beautiful widow lady, Madonna Malgherida de' Ghisolieri, as some say, and being charmed with her beyond measure, was, notwithstanding his age, no less ardently enamoured than a young man, insomuch that he was not well able to sleep at night, unless during the day he had seen the fair lady's lovely and delicate features. Wherefore he began to frequent the vicinity of her house, passing to and fro in front of it, now on foot now on horseback, as occasion best served. Which she and many other ladies perceiving, made merry together more than once, to see a man of his years and discretion in love, as if they deemed that this most delightful passion of love were only fit for empty-headed youths, and could not in men be either harboured or engendered. Master Alberto thus continuing to haunt the front of the house, it so happened that one feast-day the lady with other ladies was seated before her door, and Master Alberto's approach being thus observed by them for some time before he arrived, they complotted to receive him and shew him honour, and then to rally him on his love; and so they did, rising with one accord to receive him, bidding him welcome, and ushering him into a cool courtyard, where they regaled him with the finest wines and comfits; which done, in a tone of refined and sprightly banter they asked him how it came about that he was enamoured of this fair lady, seeing that she was beloved of many a fine gentleman of youth and spirit. Master Alberto, being thus courteously assailed, put a blithe face on it, and answered: – "Madam, my love for you need surprise none that is conversant with such matters, and least of all you that are worthy of it. And though old men, of course, have lost the strength which love demands for its full fruition, yet are they not therefore without the good intent and just appreciation of what beseems the accepted lover, but indeed understand it far better than young men, by reason that they have more experience. My hope in thus old aspiring to love you, who are loved by so many young men, is founded on what I have frequently observed of ladies' ways at lunch, when they trifle with the lupin and the leek. In the leek no part is good, but the head is at any rate not so bad as the rest, and indeed not unpalatable; you, however, for the most part, following a depraved taste, hold it in your hand and munch the leaves, which are not only of no account but actually distasteful. How am I to know, madam, that in your selection of lovers, you are not equally eccentric? In which case I should be the man of your choice, and the rest would be cast aside." Whereto the gentle lady, somewhat shame-stricken, as were also her fair friends, thus made answer: – "Master Alberto, our presumption has received from you a most just and no less courteous reproof; but your love is dear to me, as should ever be that of a wise and worthy man. And therefore, saving my honour, I am yours, entirely and devotedly at your pleasure and command." This speech brought Master Alberto to his feet, and the others also rising, he thanked the lady for her courtesy, bade her a gay and smiling adieu, and so left the house. Thus the lady, not considering on whom she exercised her wit, thinking to conquer was conquered herself – against which mishap you, if you are discreet, will ever be most strictly on your guard.

 As the young ladies and the three young men finished their storytelling the sun was westering and the heat of the day in great measure abated. Which their queen observing, debonairly thus she spoke: – "Now, dear gossips, my day of sovereignty draws to a close, and nought remains for me to do but to give you a new queen, by whom on the morrow our common life may be ordered as she may deem best in a course of seemly pleasure; and though there seems to be still some interval between day and night, yet, as whoso does not in some degree anticipate the course of time, cannot well provide for the future; and in order that what the new queen shall decide to be meet for the morrow may be made ready beforehand, I decree that from this time forth the days begin at this hour. And so in reverent submission to Him in whom is the life of all beings, for our comfort and solace we commit the governance of our realm for the morrow into the hands of Queen Filomena, most discreet of damsels." So saying she arose, took the laurel wreath from her brow, and with a gesture of reverence set it on the brow of Filomena, whom she then, and after her all the other ladies and the young men, saluted as queen, doing her due and graceful homage.

 Queen Filomena modestly blushed a little to find herself thus invested with the sovereignty; but, being put on her mettle by Pampinea's recent admonitions, she was minded not to seem awkward, and soon recovered her composure. She then began by confirming all the appointments made by Pampinea, and making all needful arrangements for the following morning and evening, which they were to pass where they then were. Whereupon she thus spoke: – "Dearest gossips, though, thanks rather to Pampinea's courtesy than to merit of mine, I am made queen of you all, yet I am not on that account minded to have respect merely to my own judgment in the governance of our life, but to unite your wisdom with mine; and that you may understand what I think of doing, and by consequence may be able to amplify or curtail it at your pleasure, I will in few words make known to you my purpose. The course observed by Pampinea to-day, if I have judged aright, seems to be alike commendable and delectable; wherefore, until by lapse of time, or for some other cause, it grow tedious, I purpose not to alter it. So when we have arranged for what we have already taken in hand, we will go hence and enjoy a short walk; at sundown we will sup in the cool; and we will then sing a few songs and otherwise divert ourselves, until it is time to go to sleep. To-morrow we will rise in the cool of the morning, and after enjoying another walk, each at his or her sweet will, we will return, as to-day, and in due time break our fast, dance, sleep, and having risen, will here resume our story-telling, wherein, methinks, pleasure and profit unite in superabundant measure. True it is that Pampinea, by reason of her late election to the sovereignty, neglected one matter, which I mean to introduce, to wit, the circumscription of the topic of our story-telling, and its preassignment, that each may be able to premeditate some apt story bearing upon the theme; and seeing that from the beginning of the world Fortune has made men the sport of divers accidents, and so it will continue until the end, the theme, so please you, shall in each case be the same; to wit, the fortune of such as after divers adventures have at last attained a goal of unexpected felicity.

 The ladies and the young men alike commended the rule thus laid down, and agreed to follow it. Dioneo, however, when the rest had done speaking, said: – "Madam, as all the rest have said, so say I, briefly, that the rule prescribed by you is commendable and delectable; but of your especial grace I crave a favour, which, I trust, may be granted and continued to me, so long as our company shall endure; which favour is this: that I be not bound by the assigned theme if I am not so minded, but that I have leave to choose such topic as best shall please me. And lest any suppose that I crave this grace as one that has not stories ready to hand, I am henceforth content that mine be always the last." The queen, knowing him to be a merry and facetious fellow, and feeling sure that he only craved this favour in order that, if the company were jaded, he might have an opportunity to recreate them by some amusing story, gladly, with the consent of the rest, granted his petition. She then rose, and attended by the rest sauntered towards a stream, which, issuing clear as crystal from a neighbouring hill, precipitated itself into a valley shaded by trees close set amid living rock and fresh green herbage. Bare of foot and arm they entered the stream, and roving hither and thither amused themselves in divers ways till in due time they returned to the palace, and gaily supped. Supper ended, the queen sent for instruments of music, and bade Lauretta lead a dance, while Emilia was to sing a song accompanied by Dioneo on the lute.

 Accordingly Lauretta led a dance, while Emilia with passion sang the following song:

> *So fain I am of my own loveliness,*
> *I hope, nor think not e'er*
> *The weight to feel of other amorousness.*
> *When in the mirror I my face behold,*
> *That see I there which doth my mind content,*
> *Nor any present hap or memory old*

> May me deprive of such sweet ravishment.
> Where else, then, should I find such blandishment
>   Of sight and sense that e'er
> My heart should know another amorousness?
>
> Nor need I fear lest the fair thing retreat,
>   When fain I am my solace to renew;
> Rather, I know, 'twill me advance to meet,
> To pleasure me, and shew so sweet a view
> That speech or thought of none its semblance true
>   Paint or conceive may e'er,
> Unless he burn with ev'n such amorousness.
>
> Thereon as more intent I gaze, the fire
>   Waxeth within me hourly, more and more,
> Myself I yield thereto, myself entire,
> And foretaste have of what it hath in store,
> And hope of greater joyance than before,
>   Nay, such as ne'er
> None knew; for ne'er was felt such amorousness.

This ballade, to which all heartily responded, albeit its words furnished much matter of thought to some, was followed by some other dances, and part of the brief night being thus spent, the queen proclaimed the first day ended, and bade light the torches that all might go to rest until the following morning; and so, seeking their several chambers, to rest they went.

— Endeth here the first day of the Decameron; beginneth the second, in which, under the rule of Filomena, they discourse of the fortunes of such as after divers misadventures have at last attained a goal of unexpected felicity. —

THE SUN was already trailing the new day in his wake of light, and the birds, blithely chanting their lays among the green boughs, carried the tidings to the ear, when with one accord all the ladies and the three young men arose, and entered the gardens, where for no little time they found their delight in sauntering about the dewy meads, straying hither and thither, culling flowers, and weaving them into fair garlands. The day passed like its predecessor; they breakfasted in the shade, and danced and slept until noon, when they rose, and, at their queen's behest, assembled in the cool meadow, and sat them down in a circle about her. Fair and very debonair she shewed, crowned with her laurel wreath, as for a brief space she scanned the company, and then bade Neifile shew others the way with a story. Neifile made no excuse, and gaily thus began.

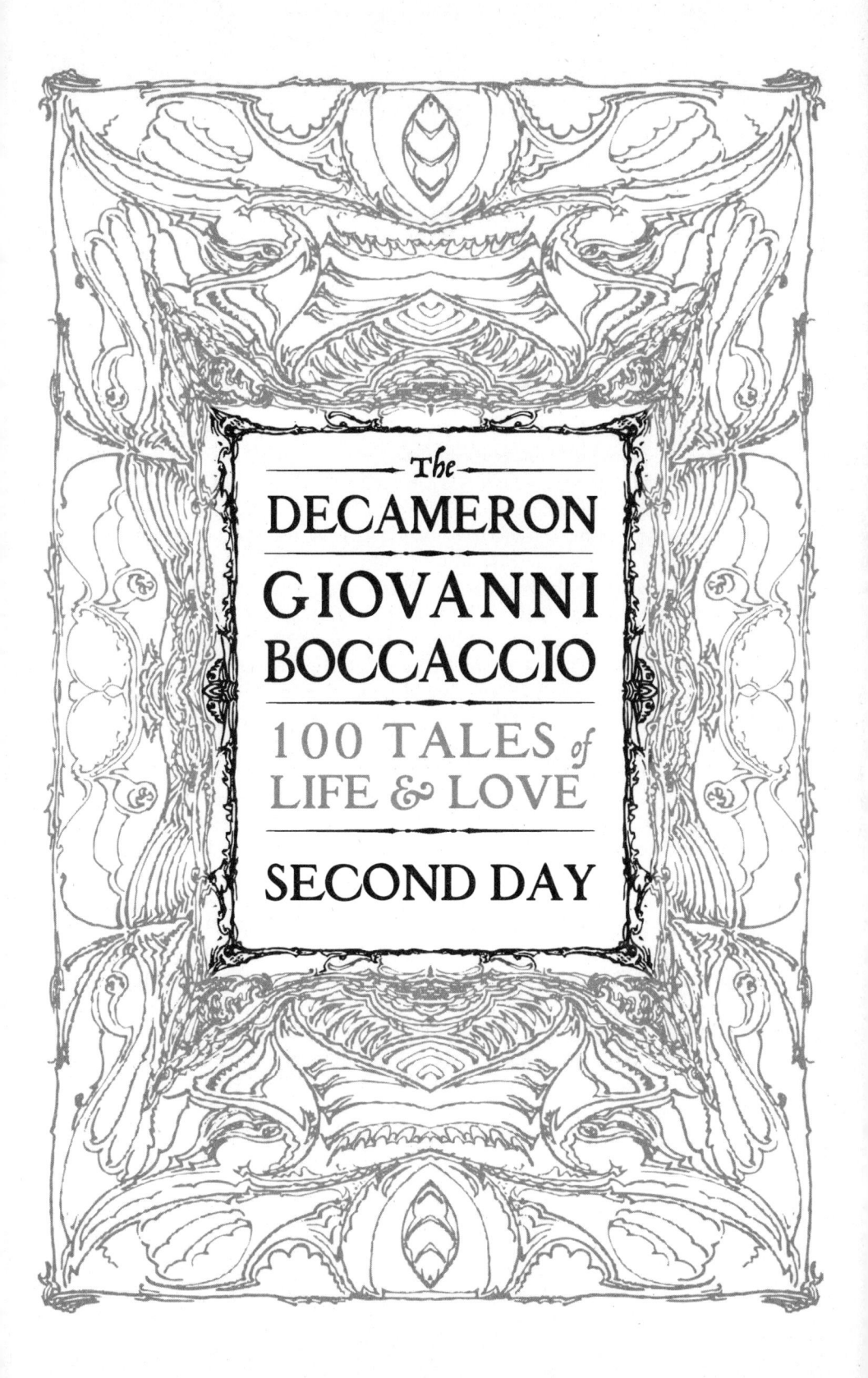

The DECAMERON
GIOVANNI BOCCACCIO
100 TALES of LIFE & LOVE
SECOND DAY

Second Day

Novel I

— *Martellino pretends to be a paralytic, and makes it appear as if he were cured by being placed upon the body of St. Arrigo. His trick is detected; he is beaten and arrested, and is in peril of hanging, but finally escapes.* —

OFTEN HAS IT happened, dearest ladies, that one who has studied to raise a laugh at others' expense, especially in regard of things worthy to be had in reverence, has found the laugh turn against himself, and sometimes to his loss: as, in obedience to the queen's command, and by way of introducing our theme, I am about to shew you, by the narrative of an adventure which befell one of our own citizens, and after a course of evil fortune had an entirely unexpected and very felicitous issue.

Not long ago there was at Treviso a German, named Arrigo, a poor man who got his living as a common hired porter, but though of so humble a condition, was respected by all, being accounted not only an honest but a most holy man; insomuch that, whether truly or falsely I know not, the Trevisans affirm, that on his decease all the bells of the cathedral of Treviso began to toll of their own accord. Which being accounted a miracle, this Arrigo was generally reputed a saint; and all the people of the city gathered before the house where his body lay, and bore it, with a saint's honours, into the cathedral, and brought thither the halt and paralytic and blind, and others afflicted with disease or bodily defects, as hoping that by contact with this holy body they would all be healed. The people thus tumultuously thronging the church, it so chanced that there arrived in Treviso three of our own citizens, of whom one was named Stecchi, another Martellino, and the third Marchese; all three being men whose habit it was to frequent the courts of the nobles and afford spectators amusement by assuming disguises and personating other men. Being entire strangers to the place, and seeing everybody running to and fro, they were much astonished, and having learned the why and wherefore, were curious to go see what was to be seen. So at the inn, where they put up, Marchese began: – "We would fain go see this saint; but for my part I know not how we are to reach the spot, for I hear the piazza is full of Germans and other armed men, posted there by the Lord who rules here to prevent an uproar, and moreover the church, so far as one may learn, is so full of folk that scarce another soul may enter it." Whereupon Martellino, who was bent on seeing what was to be seen, said: – "Let not this deter us; I will assuredly find a way of getting to the saint's body." "How?" rejoined Marchese. "I will tell you," replied Martellino; "I will counterfeit a paralytic, and thou wilt support me on one side and Stecchi on the other, as if I were not able to go alone, and so you will enter the church, making it appear as if you were leading me up to the body of the saint that he may heal me, and all that see will make way and give us free passage." Marchese and Stecchi approved the plan; so all three forthwith left the inn and repaired to a lonely place, where Martellino distorted his hands, his fingers, his arms, his legs, and also his mouth and eyes and his entire face in a manner horrible to contemplate; so that no stranger that saw him could have doubted that he was impotent and paralysed in every part of his body. In this guise

Marchese and Stecchi laid hold of him, and led him towards the church, assuming a most piteous air, and humbly beseeching everybody for God's sake to make way for them. Their request was readily granted; and, in short, observed by all, and crying out at almost every step, "make way, make way," they reached the place where St. Arrigo's body was laid. Whereupon some gentlemen who stood by, hoisted Martellino on to the saint's body, that thereby he might receive the boon of health. There he lay still for a while, the eyes of all in the church being riveted upon him in expectation of the result; then, being a very practised performer, he stretched, first, one of his fingers, next a hand, afterwards an arm, and so forth, making as if he gradually recovered the use of all his natural powers. Which the people observing raised such a clamour in honour of St. Arrigo that even thunder would have been inaudible. Now it chanced that hard by stood a Florentine, who knew Martellino well, though he had failed to recognise him, when, in such strange guise, he was led into the church; but now, seeing him resume his natural shape, the Florentine recognised him, and at once said with a laugh, "God's curse upon him. Who that saw him come but would have believed that he was really paralysed?" These words were overheard by some of the Trevisans, who began forthwith to question the Florentine. "How?" said they; "was he then not paralysed? No, by God returned the Florentine he has always been as straight as any of us; he has merely shewn you that he knows better than any man alive how to play this trick of putting on any counterfeit semblance that he chooses." Thereupon the Trevisans, without further parley, made a rush, clearing the way and crying out as they went: – "Seize this traitor who mocks at God and His saints; who, being no paralytic, has come hither in the guise of a paralytic to deride our patron saint and us." So saying, they laid hands on him, dragged him down from where he stood, seized him by the hair, tore the clothes from his back, and fell to beating and kicking him, so that it seemed to him as if all the world were upon him. He cried out: – "Pity, for God's sake," and defended himself as best he could: all in vain, however; the press became thicker and thicker moment by moment. Which Stecchi and Marchese observing began to say one to the other that 'twas a bad business; yet, being apprehensive on their own account, they did not venture to come to his assistance, but cried out with the rest that he ought to die, at the same time, however, casting about how they might find the means to rescue him from the hands of the people, who would certainly have killed him, but for a diversion which Marchese hastily effected. The entire posse of the signory being just outside, he ran off at full speed to the Podesta's lieutenant, and said to him: – "Help, for God's sake; there is a villain here that has cut my purse with full a hundred florins of gold in it; prithee have him arrested that I may have my own again." Whereupon, twelve sergeants or more ran forthwith to the place where hapless Martellino was being carded without a comb, and, forcing their way with the utmost difficulty through the throng, rescued him all bruised and battered from their hands, and led him to the palace; whither he was followed by many who, resenting what he had done, and hearing that he was arrested as a cutpurse, and lacking better pretext for harassing him, began one and all to charge him with having cut their purses. All which the deputy of the Podesta had no sooner heard, than, being a harsh man, he straightway took Martellino aside and began to examine him. Martellino answered his questions in a bantering tone, making light of the arrest; whereat the deputy, losing patience, had him bound to the strappado, and caused him to receive a few hints of the cord with intent to extort from him a confession of his guilt, by way of preliminary to hanging him. Taken down from the strappado, and questioned by the deputy if what his accusers said were true, Martellino, as nothing was to be gained by denial, answered: – "My lord, I am ready to confess the truth; let but my accusers say, each of them, when and where I cut his purse, and I will tell you what I have and what I have not done." "So be it," said the deputy, and caused a few of them to be summoned. Whereupon Martellino, being charged with having cut this, that or the other man's purse eight, six or four days ago, while others averred that he had cut their purses that very day, answered thus: – "My lord, these men lie in the throat, and for token that I speak true, I tell you that, so far from having been here as long as they make out, it is but very lately that I came into these parts, where I never was before; and no sooner was I come, than, as my ill-luck would have it, I went to see the body of this saint, and so have been carded as you see; and that what I say is true, his Lordship's intendant of arrivals, and his book, and also my host may certify. Wherefore, if you find that even so it is as I say, hearken not to these wicked men, and spare me the torture and death which they would have you inflict." In this posture of affairs Marchese and Stecchi, learning that the Podesta's deputy was dealing rigorously with Martellino, and had already put him to the strappado, grew mightily alarmed. "We have made a mess of it," they said to themselves; "we have only taken him out of the frying-pan to toss him into the fire." So, hurrying hither and thither with the utmost zeal, they made diligent search until they found their host, and told him how matters stood. The host had his laugh over the affair, and then brought them to one Sandro Agolanti, who dwelt in Treviso and had great interest with the Lord of the place. The host laid the whole matter before Sandro, and, backed by Marchese and Stecchi, besought him to undertake Martellino's cause. Sandro, after many a hearty laugh, hied him to the Lord, who at his instance sent for Martellino. The messengers found Martellino still in his shirt before the deputy, at his wits' end, and all but beside himself with fear, because the deputy would hear nothing that he said in his defence. Indeed, the deputy, having a spite against Florentines, had quite made up his mind to have him hanged; he was therefore in the last degree reluctant to surrender him to the Lord, and only did so upon compulsion. Brought at length before the Lord, Martellino detailed to him the whole affair, and prayed him as the greatest of favours to let him depart in peace. The Lord had a hearty laugh over the adventure, and bestowed a tunic on each of the three. So, congratulating themselves on their unexpected deliverance from so great a peril, they returned home safe and sound.

Second Day
Novel II

— *Rinaldo d'Asti is robbed, arrives at Castel Guglielmo, and is entertained by a widow lady; his property is restored to him, and he returns home safe and sound.* —

THE LADIES and the young men, especially Filostrato, laughed inordinately at Neifile's narrative of Martellino's misadventures. Then Filostrato, who sate next Neifile, received the queen's command to follow her, and promptly thus began: –

Fair ladies, 'tis on my mind to tell you a story in which are mingled things sacred and passages of adverse fortune and love, which to hear will perchance be not unprofitable, more especially to travellers in love's treacherous lands; of whom if any fail to say St. Julian's paternoster, it often happens that, though he may have a good bed, he is ill lodged.

Know, then, that in the time of the Marquis Azzo da Ferrara, a merchant, Rinaldo d'Asti by name, having disposed of certain affairs which had brought him to Bologna, set his face homeward, and having left Ferrara behind him was on his way to Verona, when he fell in with some men that looked like merchants, but were in truth robbers and men of evil life and condition, whose company he imprudently joined, riding and conversing with them. They, perceiving that he was a merchant, and judging that he must have money about him, complotted to rob him on the first opportunity; and to obviate suspicion they played the part of worthy and reputable men, their discourse of nought but what was seemly and honourable and leal, their demeanour at once as respectful and as cordial as they could make it; so that he deemed himself very lucky to have met with them, being otherwise alone save for a single mounted servant. Journeying thus, they conversed after the desultory manner of travellers, of divers matters, until at last they fell a talking of the prayers which men address to God, and one of the robbers – there were three of them – said to Rinaldo: – "And you, gentle sir, what is your wonted orison when you are on your travels?" Rinaldo answered: – "Why, to tell the truth, I am a man unskilled, unlearned in such matters, and few prayers have I at my command, being one that lives in the good old way and lets two soldi count for twenty-four deniers; nevertheless it has always been my custom in journeying to say of a morning, as I leave the inn, a paternoster and an avemaria for the souls of the father and mother of St. Julian, after which I pray God and St. Julian to provide me with a good inn for the night. And many a time in the course of my life have I met with great perils by the way, and evading them all have found comfortable quarters for the night: whereby my faith is assured, that St. Julian, in whose honour I say my paternoster, has gotten me this favour of God; nor should I look for a prosperous journey and a safe arrival at night, if I had not said it in the morning." Then said his interrogator: – "And did you say it this morning?" Whereto Rinaldo answered, "Troth, did I," which caused the other, who by this time knew what course matters would take, to say to himself: – "'Twill prove to have been said in the nick of time; for if we do not miscarry, I take it thou wilt have but a sorry lodging." Then turning to Rinaldo he said: – "I also have travelled much, and never a prayer have I said though I have heard them much, commended by many, nor has it ever been my lot to find other than good quarters for the night; it may be that this very evening you will be able to determine which of us has the better lodging, you that have said the paternoster, or I that have not said it. True, however, it is that in its stead I am accustomed to say the 'Dirupisti,' or the 'Intemerata,' or the 'De profundis,' which, if what my grandmother used to say is to be believed, are of the greatest efficacy." So, talking of divers matters, and ever on the look-out for time and place suited to their evil purpose, they continued their journey, until towards evening, some distance from Castel Guglielmo, as they were about to ford a stream, these three ruffians, profiting by the lateness of the hour, and the loneliness and straitness of the place, set upon Rinaldo and robbed him, and leaving him afoot and in his shirt, said by way of adieu: – "Go now, and see if thy St. Julian will provide thee with good lodging to-night; our saint, we doubt not, will do as much by us;" and so crossing the stream, they went their way. Rinaldo's servant, coward that he was, did nothing to help his master when he saw him attacked, but turned his horse's head, and was off at a smart pace; nor did he draw rein until he was come to Castel Guglielmo; where, it being now evening, he put up at an inn and gave himself no further trouble. Rinaldo, left barefoot, and stripped to his shirt, while the night closed in very cold and snowy, was at his wits' end, and shivering so that his teeth chattered in his head, began to peer about, if haply he might find some shelter for the night, that so he might not perish with the cold; but, seeing none (for during a recent war the whole country had been wasted by fire), he set off for Castel Guglielmo, quickening his pace by reason of the cold. Whether his servant had taken refuge in Castel Guglielmo or elsewhere, he knew not, but he thought that, could he but enter the town, God would surely send him some succour. However, dark night overtook him while he was still about a mile from the castle; so that on his arrival he found the gates already locked and the bridges raised, and he could not pass in. Sick at heart, disconsolate and bewailing his evil fortune, he looked about for some place where he might ensconce himself, and at any rate find shelter from the snow. And by good luck he espied a house, built with a balcony a little above the castle-wall, under which balcony he purposed to shelter himself until daybreak. Arrived at the spot, he found beneath the balcony a postern, which, however, was locked; and having gathered some bits of straw that lay about, he placed them in front of the postern, and there in sad and sorrowful plight took up his quarters, with many a piteous appeal to St. Julian, whom he reproached for not better rewarding the faith which he reposed in him. St. Julian, however, had not abandoned him, and in due time provided him with a good lodging.

There was in the castle a widow lady of extraordinary beauty (none fairer) whom Marquis Azzo loved as his own life, and kept there for his pleasure. She lived in the very same house beneath the balcony of which Rinaldo had posted himself. Now it chanced that that very day the Marquis had come to Castel Guglielmo to pass the night with her, and had privily caused a bath to be made ready, and a supper suited to his rank, in the lady's own house. The arrangements were complete; and only the Marquis was stayed for, when a servant happened to present himself at the castle-gate, bringing tidings for the Marquis which obliged him suddenly to take horse. He therefore sent word to the lady that she must not wait for him, and forthwith took his departure. The lady, somewhat disconsolate, found nothing better to do than to get into the bath which had been intended for the Marquis, sup and go to bed: so into the bath she went. The bath was close to the postern on the other side of which hapless Rinaldo had ensconced himself, and, thus the mournful and quavering music which Rinaldo made as he shuddered in the cold, and which seemed rather to proceed from a stork's beak than from the mouth of a human being, was audible to the lady in the bath. She therefore called her maid, and said to her: – "Go up and look out over the wall and down at the postern, and mark who is there, and what he is, and what he does there." The maid obeyed, and, the night being fine, had no difficulty in making out Rinaldo as he sate there, barefoot, as I have, said, and in his shirt, and trembling in every limb. So she called out to him, to know who he was. Rinaldo, who could scarcely articulate for shivering, told as briefly as he could, who he was, and how and why he came to be there; which done, he began piteously to, beseech her not, if she could avoid it, to leave him there all night to perish of cold. The maid went back to her mistress full of pity for Rinaldo, and told her all she had seen and heard. The lady felt no less pity for Rinaldo; and bethinking her that she had the key of the postern by which the Marquis sometimes entered when he paid her a secret visit, she said to the maid: – "Go, and let him in softly; here is this supper, and there will be none to eat it; and we can very well put him up for the night." Cordially commending her mistress's humanity, the maid went and let Rinaldo in, and brought him to the lady, who, seeing that he was all but dead with cold, said to him: – "Quick, good man, get into that bath, which is still warm." Gladly he did so, awaiting no second invitation, and was so much comforted by its warmth that he seemed to have passed from death to life. The lady provided him with a suit of clothes, which had been worn by her husband shortly before his death, and which, when he had them on, looked as if they had been made for him. So he recovered heart, and, while he awaited the lady's commands, gave thanks to God and St. Julian for delivering him from a woful night and conducting him, as it seemed, to comfortable quarters.

The lady meanwhile took a little rest, after which she had a roaring fire put in one of her large rooms, whither presently she came, and asked her maid how the good man did. The maid replied: – "Madam, he has put on the clothes, in which he shews to advantage, having a handsome person, and seeming to be a worthy man, and well-bred." "Go, call him then," said the lady, "tell him to come hither to the fire, and we will sup; for I know that he has not supped." Rinaldo, on entering the room and seeing the lady, took her to be of no small consequence. He therefore made her a low bow, and did his utmost to thank her worthily for the service she had rendered him. His words pleased her no less than his person, which accorded with what the maid had said: so she made him heartily welcome, installed him at his ease by her side before the fire, and questioned him of the adventure which had brought him thither. Rinaldo detailed all the circumstances, of which the lady had heard somewhat when Rinaldo's servant made his appearance at the castle. She therefore gave entire credence to what he said, and told him what she knew about his servant, and how he might easily find him on the morrow. She then bade set the table, which done, Rinaldo and she washed their hands and sate down together to sup. Tall he was and comely of form and feature, debonair and gracious of mien and manner, and in his lusty prime. The lady had eyed him again and again to her no small satisfaction, and, her wantonness being already kindled for the Marquis, who was to have come to lie with her, she had let Rinaldo take the vacant place in her mind. So when supper was done, and they were risen from the table, she conferred with her maid, whether, after the cruel trick played upon her by the Marquis, it were not well to take the good gift which Fortune had sent her. The maid knowing the bent of her mistress's desire, left no word unsaid that might encourage her to follow it. Wherefore the lady, turning towards Rinaldo, who was standing where she had left him by the fire, began thus: – "So! Rinaldo, why still so pensive? Will nothing console you for the loss of a horse and a few clothes? Take heart, put a blithe face on it, you are at home; nay more, let me tell you that, seeing you in those clothes which my late husband used to wear, and taking you for him, I have felt, not once or twice, but perhaps a hundred times this evening, a longing to throw my arms round you and kiss you; and, in faith, I had so done, but that I feared it might displease you." Rinaldo, hearing these words, and marking the flame which shot from the lady's eyes, and being no laggard, came forward with open arms, and confronted her and said: – "Madam, I am not unmindful that I must ever acknowledge that to you I owe my life, in regard of the peril whence you rescued me. If then there be any way in which I may pleasure you, churlish indeed were I not to devise it. So you may even embrace and kiss me to your heart's content, and I will embrace and kiss you with the best of good wills." There needed no further parley. The lady, all aflame with amorous desire, forthwith threw herself into his arms, and straining him to her bosom with a thousand passionate embraces, gave and received a thousand kisses before they sought her chamber. There with all speed they went to bed, nor did day surprise them until again and again and in full measure they had satisfied their desire. With the first streaks of dawn they rose, for the lady was minded that none should surmise aught of the affair. So, having meanly habited Rinaldo, and replenished his purse, she enjoined him to keep the secret, shewed him the way to the castle, where he was to find his servant, and let him out by the same postern by which he had entered. When it was broad day the gates were opened, and Rinaldo, passing himself off as a traveller from distant parts, entered the castle, and found his servant. Having put on the spare suit which was in his valise, he was about to mount the servant's horse, when, as if by miracle, there were brought into the castle the three gentlemen of the road who had robbed him the evening before, having been taken a little while after for another offence. Upon their confession Rinaldo's horse was restored to him, as were also his clothes and money; so that he lost nothing except a pair of garters, of which the robbers knew not where they had bestowed them. Wherefore Rinaldo, giving thanks to God and St. Julian, mounted his horse, and returned home safe and sound, and on the morrow the three robbers kicked heels in the wind.

Second Day
Novel III

— *Three young men squander their substance and are reduced to poverty. Their nephew, returning home a desperate man, falls in with an abbot, in whom he discovers the daughter of the King of England. She marries him, and he retrieves the losses and reestablishes the fortune of his uncles.* —

THE LADIES MARVELLED to hear the adventures of Rinaldo d'Asti, praised his devotion, and gave thanks to God and St. Julian for the succour lent him in his extreme need. Nor, though the verdict was hardly outspoken, was the lady deemed unwise to take the boon which God had sent her. So they tittered and talked of her night of delight, while Pampinea, being seated by Filostrato, and surmising that her turn would, as it did, come next, was lost in meditation on what she was to say. Roused from her reverie by the word of the queen, she put on a cheerful courage, and thus began: –

Noble ladies, discourse as we may of Fortune's handiwork, much still remains to be said if we but scan events aright, nor need we marvel thereat, if we but duly consider that all matters, which we foolishly call our own, are in her hands and therefore subject, at her inscrutable will, to every variety of chance and change without any order therein by us discernible. Which is indeed signally manifest everywhere and all day long; yet, as 'tis our queen's will that we speak thereof, perhaps 'twill not be unprofitable to you, if, notwithstanding it has been the theme of some of the foregoing stories, I add to them another, which, I believe, should give you pleasure.

There was formerly in our city a knight, by name Messer Tedaldo, of the Lamberti, according to some, or, as others say, of the Agolanti family, perhaps for no better reason than that the occupation of his sons was similar to that which always was and is the occupation of the Agolanti. However, without professing to determine which of the two houses he belonged to, I say, that he was in his day a very wealthy knight, and had three sons, the eldest being by name Lamberto, the second Tedaldo, and the third Agolante. Fine, spirited young men were they all, though the eldest was not yet eighteen years old when their father, Messer Tedaldo, died very rich, leaving to them as his lawful heirs the whole of his property both movable and immovable. Finding themselves thus possessed of great wealth, both in money and in lands and chattels, they fell to spending without stint or restraint, indulging their every desire, maintaining a great establishment, and a large and well-filled stable, besides dogs and hawks, keeping ever open house, scattering largesses, jousting, and, not content with these and the like pastimes proper to their condition, indulging every appetite natural to their youth. They had not long followed this course of life before the cash left them by their father was exhausted; and, their rents not sufficing to defray their expenditure, they began to sell and pledge their property, and disposing of it by degrees, one item to-day and another to-morrow, they hardly perceived that they were approaching the verge of ruin, until poverty opened the eyes which wealth had fast sealed. So one day Lamberto called his brothers to him, reminded them of the position of wealth and dignity which had been theirs and their father's before them, and shewed them the poverty to which their extravagance had reduced them, and adjured them most earnestly that, before their destitution was yet further manifest, they should all three sell what little remained to them and depart thence; which accordingly they did. Without leave-taking, or any ceremony, they quitted Florence; nor did they rest until they had arrived in England and established themselves in a small house in London, where, by living with extreme parsimony and lending at exorbitant usances, they prospered so well that in the course of a few years they amassed a fortune; and so, one by one, they returned to Florence, purchased not a few of their former estates besides many others, and married. The management of their affairs in England, where they continued their business of usurers, they left to a young nephew, Alessandro by name, while, heedless alike of the teaching of experience and of marital and parental duty, they all three launched out at Florence into more extravagant expenditure than before, and contracted debts on all hands and to large amounts. This expenditure they were enabled for some years to support by the remittances made by Alessandro, who, to his great profit, had lent money to the barons on the security of their castles and rents.

While the three brothers thus continued to spend freely, and, when short of money, to borrow it, never doubting of help from England, it so happened that, to the surprise of everybody, there broke out in England a war between the King and his son, by which the whole island was divided into two camps; whereby Alessandro lost all his mortgages, of the baronial castles and every other source of income whatsoever. However, in the daily expectation that peace would be concluded between the King and his son, Alessandro, hoping that in that event all would be restored to him, principal and interest, tarried in the island; and the three brothers at Florence in no degree retrenched their extravagant expenditure, but went on borrowing from day to day. Several years thus passed; and, their hopes being frustrated, the three brothers not only lost credit, but, being pressed for payment by their creditors, were suddenly arrested, and, their property proving deficient, were kept in prison for the balance, while their wives and little children went into the country parts, or elsewhere, wretchedly equipped, and with no other prospect than to pass the rest of their days in destitution. Alessandro, meanwhile, seeing that the peace, which he had for several years awaited in England, did not come, and deeming that he would hazard his life to no purpose by tarrying longer in the country, made up his mind to return to Italy. He travelled at first altogether alone; but it so chanced that he left Bruges at the same time with an abbot, habited in white, attended by a numerous retinue, and preceded by a goodly baggage-train. Behind the abbot rode two greybeard knights, kinsmen of the King, in whom Alessandro recognised acquaintances, and, making himself known to them, was readily received into their company. As thus they journeyed together, Alessandro softly asked them who the monks were that rode in front with so great a train, and whither they were bound. "The foremost rider," replied one of the knights, "is a young kinsman of ours, the newly-elected abbot of one of the greatest abbeys of England,; and as he is not of legal age for such a dignity, we are going with him to Rome to obtain the Holy Father's dispensation and his confirmation in the office; but this is not a matter for common talk." Now the new abbot, as lords are wont to do when they travel, was sometimes in front, sometimes in rear of his train; and thus it happened that, as he passed, he set eyes on Alessandro, who was still quite young, and very shapely and well-favoured, and as courteous, gracious and debonair as e'er another. The abbot was marvellously taken with him at first sight, having never seen aught that pleased him so much, called him to his side, addressed him graciously, and asked him who he was, whence he came, and whither he was bound. Alessandro frankly told all about himself, and having thus answered the abbot's questions, placed himself at his service as far as his small ability might extend. The abbot was struck by his easy flow of apt speech, and observing his bearing more closely, he made up his mind that, albeit his occupation was base, he was nevertheless of gentle blood, which added no little to his interest in him; and being moved to compassion by his misfortunes, he gave him friendly consolation, bidding him be of good hope, that if he lived a worthy life, God would yet set him in a place no less or even more exalted than that whence Fortune had cast him down, and prayed him to be of his company as far as Tuscany, as both were going the same way. Alessandro thanked him for his words of comfort, and professed himself ready to obey his every command.

So fared on the abbot, his mind full of new ideas begotten by the sight of Alessandro, until some days later they came to a town which was none too well provided with inns; and, as the abbot must needs put up there, Alessandro, who was well acquainted with one of the innkeepers, arranged that the abbot should alight at his house, and procured him the least discomfortable quarters which it could afford. He thus became for the nonce the abbot's seneschal, and being very expert for such office, managed excellently, quartering the retinue in divers parts of the town. So the abbot supped, and, the night being far spent, all went to bed except Alessandro, who then asked the host where he might find quarters for the night. "In good sooth, I know not," replied the host; "thou seest that every place is occupied, and that I and my household must lie on the benches. However, in the abbot's chamber there are some corn-sacks. I can shew thee the way thither, and lay a bit of a bed upon them, and there, an it like thee, thou mayst pass the night very well." "How sayst thou?" said Alessandro; "in the abbot's chamber, which thou knowest is small, so that there was not room for any of the monks to sleep there? Had I understood this when the curtains were drawn, I would have quartered his monks on the corn-sacks, and slept myself where the monks sleep." "'Tis even so, however," replied the host, "and thou canst, if thou wilt, find excellent quarters there: the abbot sleeps, the curtains are close drawn; I will go in softly and lay a small bed there, on which thou canst sleep." Alessandro, satisfied that it might be managed without disturbing the abbot, accepted the offer, and made his arrangements for passing the night as quietly as he could.

The abbot was not asleep; his mind being far too overwrought by certain newly-awakened desires. He had heard what had passed between Alessandro and the host, he had marked the place where Alessandro had lain down, and in the great gladness of his heart had begun thus to commune with himself: – "God has sent me the opportunity of gratifying my desire; if I let it pass, perchance it will be long before another such opportunity occurs." So, being minded by no means to let it slip, when all was quiet in the inn, he softly called Alessandro, and bade him lie down by his side. Alessandro made many excuses, but ended by undressing and obeying whereupon the abbot laid a hand on Alessandro's breast, and began to caress him just as amorous girls do their lovers; whereat Alessandro marvelled greatly, doubting the abbot was prompted to such caresses by a shameful love. Which the abbot speedily divined, or else surmised from some movement on Alessandro's part, and, laughing, threw off a chemise which she had upon her, and taking Alessandro's hand, laid it on her bosom, saying: – "Alessandro, dismiss thy foolish thought, feel here, and learn what I conceal." Alessandro obeyed, laying a hand upon the abbot's bosom, where he encountered two little teats, round, firm and delicate, as they had been of ivory; whereby he at once knew that 'twas a woman, and without awaiting further encouragement forthwith embraced her, and would have kissed her, when she said: – "Before thou art more familiar with me hearken to what I have to say to thee. As thou mayst perceive, I am no man, but a woman. Virgin I left my home, and was going to the Pope to obtain his sanction for my marriage, when, as Fortune willed, whether for thy gain or my loss, no sooner had I seen thee the other day, than I burned for thee with such a flame of love as never yet had lady for any man. Wherefore I am minded to have thee for my husband rather than any other; so, if thou wilt not have me to wife, depart at once, and return to thine own place." Albeit he knew not who she was, Alessandro by the retinue which attended her conjectured that she must be noble and wealthy, and he saw that she was very fair; so it was not long before he answered that, if such were her pleasure, it was very much to his liking. Whereupon she sate up, set a ring on his finger, and espoused him before a tiny picture of our Lord; after which they embraced, and to their no small mutual satisfaction solaced themselves for the rest of the night. At daybreak Alessandro rose, and by preconcert with the lady, left the chamber as he had entered it, so that none knew where he had passed the night: then, blithe at heart beyond measure, he rejoined the abbot and his train, and so, resuming their journey, they after many days arrived at Rome. They had not been there more than a few days, when the abbot, attended by the two knights and Alessandro, waited on the Pope, whom, after making the due obeisance, he thus addressed: – "Holy Father, as you must know better than any other, whoso intends to lead a true and honourable life ought, as far as may be, to shun all occasion of error; for which cause I, having a mind to live honourably, did, the better to accomplish my purpose, assume the habit in which you see me, and depart by stealth from the court of my father, the King of England, who was minded to marry me, young as you see me to be, to the aged King of Scotland; and, carrying with me not a little of his treasure, set my face hitherward that your Holiness might bestow me in marriage. Nor was it the age of the King of Scotland that moved me to flee so much as fear lest the frailty of my youth should, were I married to him, betray me to commit some breach of divine law, and sully the honour of my father's royal blood. And as in this frame of mind I journeyed, God, who knows best what is meet for every one, did, as I believe, of His mercy shew me him whom He is pleased to appoint me for my husband, even this young man" (pointing to Alessandro) "whom you see by my side, who for nobility of nature and bearing is a match for any great lady, though the strain of his blood, perhaps, be not of royal purity. Him, therefore, have I chosen. Him will I have, and no other, no matter what my father or any one else may think. And albeit the main purpose with which I started is fulfilled, yet I have thought good to continue my journey, that I may visit the holy and venerable places which abound in this city, and your Holiness, and that so in your presence, and by consequence in the presence of others, I may renew my marriage-vow with Alessandro, whereof God alone was witness. Wherefore I humbly pray you that God's will and mine may be also yours, and that you pronounce your benison thereon, that therewith, having the more firm assurance of the favour of Him, whose vicar you are, we may both live together, and, when the time comes, die to God's glory and yours."

Alessandro was filled with wonder and secret delight, when he heard that his wife was the daughter of the King of England; but greater still was the wonder of the two knights, and such their wrath that, had they been anywhere else than in the Pope's presence, they would not have spared to affront Alessandro, and perhaps the lady too. The Pope, on his part, found matter enough for wonder as well in the lady's habit as in her choice; but, knowing that he could not refuse, he consented to grant her request.

He therefore began by smoothing the ruffled tempers of the knights, and having reconciled them with the lady and Alessandro, proceeded to put matters in train for the marriage. When the day appointed was come, he gave a great reception, at which were assembled all the cardinals and many other great lords; to whom he presented the lady royally robed, and looking so fair and so gracious that she won, as she deserved, the praise of all, and likewise Alessandro, splendidly arrayed, and bearing himself not a whit like the young usurer but rather as one of royal blood, for which cause he received due honour from the knights. There, before the Pope himself, the marriage-vows were solemnly renewed; and afterwards the marriage, which was accompanied by every circumstance that could add grace and splendour to the ceremony, received the sanction of his benediction. Alessandro and the lady on leaving Rome saw fit to visit Florence, whither fame had already wafted the news, so that they were received by the citizens with every token of honour. The lady set the three brothers at liberty, paying all their creditors, and reinstated them and their wives in their several properties. So, leaving gracious memories behind them, Alessandro and his lady, accompanied by Agolante, quitted Florence, and arriving at Paris were honourably received by the King. The two knights went before them to England, and by their influence induced the King to restore the lady to his favour, and receive her and his son-in-law with every circumstance of joy and honour. Alessandro he soon afterwards knighted with unwonted ceremony, and bestowed on him the earldom of Cornwall. And such was the Earl's consequence and influence at court that he restored peace between father and son, thereby conferring a great boon on the island and gaining the love and esteem of all the people. Agolante, whom he knighted, recovered all the outstanding debts in full, and returned to Florence immensely rich. The Earl passed the rest of his days with his lady in great renown. Indeed there are those who say, that with the help of his father-in-law he effected by his policy and valour the conquest of Scotland, and was crowned king of that country.

Second Day
Novel IV

— Landolfo Ruffolo is reduced to poverty, turns corsair, is captured by Genoese, is shipwrecked, escapes on a chest full of jewels, and, being cast ashore at Corfu, is hospitably entertained by a woman, and returns home wealthy. —

WHEN PAMPINEA had brought her story to this glorious conclusion, Lauretta, who sate next her, delayed not, but thus began: –

Most gracious ladies, the potency of Fortune is never, methinks, more conspicuous than when she raises one, as in Pampinea's story we have seen her raise Alessandro, from abject misery to regal state. And such being the limits which our theme henceforth imposes on our invention, I shall feel no shame to tell a story wherein reverses yet greater are compensated by a sequel somewhat less dazzling. Well I know that my story, being compared with its predecessor, will therefore be followed with the less interest; but, failing of necessity, I shall be excused.

Scarce any part of Italy is reputed so delectable as the sea-coast between Reggio and Gaeta; and in particular the slope which overlooks the sea by Salerno, and which the dwellers there call the Slope of Amalfi, is studded with little towns, gardens and fountains, and peopled by men as wealthy and enterprising in mercantile affairs as are anywhere to be found; in one of which towns, to wit, Ravello, rich as its inhabitants are to-day, there was formerly a merchant, who surpassed them all in wealth, Landolfo Ruffolo by name, who yet, not content with his wealth, but desiring to double it, came nigh to lose it all and his own life to boot. Know, then, that this man, having made his calculations, as merchants are wont, bought a great ship, which, entirely at his own expense, he loaded with divers sorts of merchandise, and sailed to Cyprus. There he found several other ships, each laden with just such a cargo as his own, and was therefore fain to dispose of his goods at a very cheap rate, insomuch that he might almost as well have thrown them away, and was brought to the verge of ruin. Mortified beyond measure to find himself thus reduced in a short space of time from opulence to something like poverty, he was at his wits' end, and rather than go home poor, having left home rich, he was minded to retrieve his losses by piracy or die in the attempt. So he sold his great ship, and with the price and the proceeds of the sale of his merchandise bought a light bark such as corsairs use, and having excellently well equipped her with the armament and all things else meet for such service, took to scouring the seas as a rover, preying upon all folk alike, but more particularly upon the Turk.

In this enterprise he was more favoured by Fortune than in his trading adventures. A year had scarce gone by before he had taken so many ships from the Turk that not only had he recovered the fortune which he had lost in trade, but was well on the way to doubling it. The bitter memory of his late losses taught him sobriety; he estimated his gains and found them ample; and lest he should have a second fall, he schooled himself to rest content with them, and made up his mind to return home without attempting to add to them. Shy of adventuring once more in trade, he refrained from investing them in any way, but shaped his course for home, carrying them with him in the very same bark in which he had gotten them. He had already entered the Archipelago when one evening a contrary wind sprang up from the southeast, bringing with it a very heavy sea, in which his bark could not well have lived. He therefore steered her into a bay under the lee of one of the islets, and there determined to await better weather. As he lay there two great carracks of Genoa, homeward-bound from Constantinople, found, not without difficulty, shelter from the tempest in the same bay. The masters of the carracks espied the bark, and found out to whom she belonged: the fame of Landolfo and his vast wealth had already reached them, and had excited their natural cupidity and rapacity. They therefore determined to capture the bark, which lay without means of escape. Part of their men, well armed with cross-bows and other weapons, they accordingly sent ashore, so posting them that no one could leave the bark without being exposed to the bolts; the rest took to their boats, and rowed up to the side of Landolfo's little craft, which in a little time, with little trouble and no loss or risk, they captured with all aboard her. They then cleared the bark of all she contained, allowing Landolfo, whom they set aboard one of the carracks, only a pitiful doublet, and sunk her. Next day the wind shifted, and the carracks set sail on a westerly course, which they kept prosperously enough throughout the day; but towards evening a tempest arose, and the sea became very boisterous, so that the two ships were parted one from the other. And such was the fury of the gale that the ship, aboard which was poor, hapless Landolfo, was driven with prodigious force upon a shoal off the island of Cephalonia, and broke up and went to pieces like so much glass dashed against a wall. Wherefore the unfortunate wretches that were aboard her, launched amid the floating merchandise and chests and planks with which the sea was strewn, did as men commonly do in such a case; and, though the night was of the murkiest and the sea rose and fell in mountainous surges, such as could swim sought to catch hold of whatever chance brought in their way. Among whom hapless Landolfo, who only the day before had again and again prayed for death, rather than he should return home in such poverty, now, seeing death imminent, was afraid; and, like the rest, laid hold of the first plank that came to hand, in the hope that, if he could but avoid immediate drowning, God would in some way aid his escape. Gripping the beam with his legs as best he might, while wind and wave tossed him hither and thither, he contrived to keep himself afloat until broad day: when, looking around him, he discerned nothing but clouds and sea and a chest, which, borne by the wave, from time to time drew nigh him to his extreme terror, for he apprehended it might strike against the plank, and do him a mischief; and ever, as it came near him, he pushed it off with all the little force he had in his hand. But, as it happened, a sudden gust of wind swept down upon the sea, and struck the chest with such force that it was driven against the plank on which Landolfo was, and upset it, and Landolfo went under the waves. Swimming with an energy begotten rather of fear than of strength, he rose to the surface only to see the plank so far from him that, doubting he could not reach it, he made for the chest, which was close at hand; and resting his breast upon the lid, he did what he could to keep it straight with his arms. In this manner, tossed to and fro by the sea, without tasting food, for not a morsel had he with him, and drinking more than he cared for, knowing not where he was, and seeing nothing but the sea, he remained all that day, and the following night. The next day, as the will of God, or the force of the wind so ordered, more like a sponge than aught else, but still with both hands holding fast by the edges of the chest, as we see those do that clutch aught to save themselves from drowning, he was at length borne to the coast of the island of Corfu, where by chance a poor woman was just then scrubbing her kitchen-ware with sand and salt-water to make it shine. The woman caught sight of him as he drifted shorewards, but making out only a shapeless mass, was at first startled, and shrieked and drew back. Landolfo was scarce able to see, and uttered no sound, for his power of speech was gone. However, when the sea brought him close to the shore, she distinguished the shape of the chest, and gazing more intently, she first made out the arms strained over the chest, and then discerned the face and divined the truth. So, prompted by pity, she went out a little way into the sea, which was then calm, took him by the hair of the head, and drew him to land, chest and all. Then, not without difficulty she disengaged his hands from the chest, which she set on the head of a little girl, her daughter, that was with her, carried him home like a little child, and set him in a bath, where she chafed and laved him with warm water, until, the vital heat and some part of the strength which he had lost being restored, she saw fit to take him out and regale him with some good wine and comfits. Thus for some days she tended him as best she could, until he recovered his strength, and knew where he was. Then, in due time, the good woman, who had kept his chest safe, gave it back to him, and bade him try his fortune.

Landolfo could not recall the chest, but took it when she brought it to him, thinking that, however slight its value, it must suffice for a few days' charges. He found it very light, and quite lost hope; but when the good woman was out of doors, he opened it to see what was inside, and found there a great number of precious stones, some set, others unset. Having some knowledge of such matters, he saw at a glance that the stones were of great value; wherefore, feeling that he was still not forsaken by God, he praised His name, and quite recovered heart. But, having in a brief space of time been twice shrewdly hit by the bolts of Fortune, he was apprehensive of a third blow, and deemed it meet to use much circumspection in conveying his treasure home; so he wrapped it up in rags as best he could, telling the good woman that he had no more use for the chest, but she might keep it if she wished, and give him a sack in exchange. This the good woman readily did; and he, thanking her as heartily as he could for the service she had rendered him, threw his sack over his shoulders, and, taking ship, crossed to Brindisi. Thence he made his way by the coast as far as Trani, where he found some of his townsfolk that were drapers, to whom he narrated all his adventures except that of the chest. They in charity gave him a suit of clothes, and lent him a horse and their escort as far as Ravello, whither, he said, he was minded to return. There, thanking God for bringing him safe home, he opened his sack, and examining its contents with more care than before, found the number, and fashion of the stones to be such that the sale of them at a moderate price, or even less, would leave him twice as rich as when he left Ravello. So, having disposed of his stones, he sent a large sum of money to Corfu in recompense of the service done him by the good woman who had rescued him from the sea, and also to his friends at Trani who had furnished him with the clothes; the residue he retained, and, making no more ventures in trade, lived and died in honourable estate.

Second Day
Novel V

— *Andreuccio da Perugia comes to Naples to buy horses, meets with three serious adventures in one night, comes safe out of them all, and returns home with a ruby.* —

LANDOLFO'S FIND of stones, began Fiammetta, on whom the narration now fell, has brought to my mind a story in which there are scarce fewer perilous scapes than in Lauretta's story, but with this difference: that, instead of a course of perhaps several years, a single night, as you shall hear, sufficed for their occurrence.

In Perugia, by what I once gathered, there lived a young man, Andreuccio di Pietro by name, a horse-dealer, who, having learnt that horses were to be had cheap at Naples, put five hundred florins of gold in his purse, and in company with some other merchants went thither, never having been away from home before. On his arrival at Naples, which was on a Sunday evening, about vespers, he learnt from his host that the fair would be held on the following morning. Thither accordingly he then repaired, and looked at many horses which pleased him much, and cheapening them more and more, and failing to strike a bargain with any one, he from time to time, being raw and unwary, drew out his purse of florins in view of all that came and went, to shew that he meant business.

While he was thus chaffering, and after he had shewn his purse, there chanced to come by a Sicilian girl, fair as fair could be, but ready to pleasure any man for a small consideration. He did not see her, but she saw him and his purse, and forthwith said to herself: – "Who would be in better luck than I if all those florins were mine?" and so she passed on. With the girl was an old woman, also a Sicilian, who, when she saw Andreuccio, dropped behind the girl, and ran towards him, making as if she would tenderly embrace him. The girl observing this said nothing, but stopped and waited a little way off for the old woman to rejoin her. Andreuccio turned as the old woman came up, recognised her, and greeted her very cordially; but time and place not permitting much converse, she left him, promising to visit him at his inn; and he resumed his chaffering, but bought nothing that morning.

Her old woman's intimate acquaintance with Andreuccio had no more escaped the girl's notice than the contents of Andreuccio's purse; and with the view of devising, if possible, some way to make the money, either in whole or in part, her own, she began cautiously to ask the old woman, who and whence he was, what he did there, and how she came to know him. The old woman gave her almost as much and as circumstantial information touching Andreuccio and his affairs as he might have done himself, for she had lived a great while with his father, first in Sicily, and afterwards at Perugia. She likewise told the girl the name of his inn, and the purpose with which he had come to Naples. Thus fully armed with the names and all else that it was needful for her to know touching Andreuccio's kith and kin, the girl founded thereon her hopes of gratifying her cupidity, and forthwith devised a cunning stratagem to effect her purpose. Home she went, and gave the old woman work enough to occupy her all day, that she might not be able to visit Andreuccio; then, summoning to her aid a little girl whom she had well trained for such services, she sent her about vespers to the inn where Andreuccio lodged. Arrived there, the little girl asked for Andreuccio of Andreuccio himself, who chanced to be just outside the gate. On his answering that he was the man, she took him aside, and said: – "Sir, a lady of this country, so please you, would fain speak with you." Whereto he listened with all his ears, and having a great conceit of his person, made up his mind that the lady was in love with him, as if there were ne'er another handsome fellow in Naples but himself; so forthwith he replied, that he would wait on the lady, and asked where and when it would be her pleasure to speak with him. "Sir," replied the little girl, "she expects you in her own house, if you be pleased to come." "Lead on then, I follow thee," said Andreuccio promptly, vouchsafing never a word to any in the inn. So the little girl guided him to her mistress's house, which was situated in a quarter the character of which may be inferred from its name, Evil Hole. Of this, however, he neither knew nor suspected aught, but, supposing that the quarter was perfectly reputable and that he was going to see a sweet lady, strode carelessly behind the little girl into the house of her mistress, whom she summoned by calling out, "Andreuccio is here;" and Andreuccio then saw her advance to the head of the stairs to await his ascent. She was tall, still in the freshness of her youth, very fair of face, and very richly and nobly clad. As Andreuccio approached, she descended three steps to meet him with open arms, and clasped him round the neck, but for a while stood silent as if from excess of tenderness; then, bursting into a flood of tears, she kissed his brow, and in slightly broken accents said: – "O Andreuccio, welcome, welcome, my Andreuccio." Quite lost in wonder to be the recipient of such caresses, Andreuccio could only answer: – "Madam, well met." Whereupon she took him by the hand, led him up into her saloon, and thence without another word into her chamber, which exhaled throughout the blended fragrance of roses, orange-blossoms and other perfumes. He observed a handsome curtained bed, dresses in plenty hanging, as is customary in that country, on pegs, and other appointments very fair and sumptuous; which sights, being strange to him, confirmed his belief that he was in the house of no other than a great lady. They sate down side by side on a chest at the foot of the bed, and thus she began to speak: – "Andreuccio, I cannot doubt that thou dost marvel both at the caresses which I bestow upon thee, and at my tears, seeing that thou knowest me not, and, maybe, hast never so much as heard my name; wait but a moment and thou shalt learn what perhaps will cause thee to marvel still, more to wit, that I am thy sister; and I tell thee, that, since of God's especial grace it is granted me to see one, albeit I would fain see all, of my brothers before I die, I shall not meet death, when the hour comes, without consolation; but thou, perchance, hast never heard aught of this; wherefore listen to what I shall say to thee. Pietro, my father and thine, as I suppose thou mayst have heard, dwelt a long while at Palermo, where his good heart and gracious bearing caused him to be (as he still is) much beloved by all that knew him; but by none was he loved so much as by a gentlewoman, afterwards my mother, then a widow, who, casting aside all respect for her father and brothers, ay, and her honour, grew so intimate with him that a child was born, which child am I thy sister, whom thou seest before thee. Shortly after my birth it so befell that Pietro must needs leave Palermo and return to Perugia, and I, his little daughter, was left behind with my mother at Palermo; nor, so far as I have been able to learn, did he ever again bestow a thought upon either of us. Wherefore – to say nothing of the love which he should have borne me, his daughter by no servant or woman of low degree – I should, were he not my father, gravely censure the ingratitude which he shewed towards my mother, who, prompted by a most loyal love, committed her fortune and herself to his keeping, without so much as knowing who he was. But to what end? The wrongs of long-ago are much more easily censured than redressed;

enough that so it was. He left me a little girl at Palermo, where, when I was grown to be almost as thou seest me, my mother, who was a rich lady, gave me in marriage to an honest gentleman of the Girgenti family, who for love of my mother and myself settled in Palermo, and there, being a staunch Guelf, entered into correspondence with our King Charles; which being discovered by King Frederic before the time was ripe for action, we had perforce to flee from Sicily just when I was expecting to become the greatest lady that ever was in the island. So, taking with us such few things as we could, few, I say, in comparison of the abundance which we possessed, we bade adieu to our estates and palaces, and found a refuge in this country, and such favour with King Charles that, in partial compensation for the losses which we had sustained on his account, he has granted us estates and houses and an ample pension, which he regularly pays to my husband and thy brother-in-law, as thou mayst yet see. In this manner I live here but that I am blest with the sight of thee, I ascribe entirely to the mercy of God; and no thanks to thee, my sweet brother." So saying she embraced him again, and melting anew into tears kissed his brow.

This story, so congruous, so consistent in every detail, came trippingly and without the least hesitancy from her tongue. Andreuccio remembered that his father had indeed lived at Palermo; he knew by his own experience the ways of young folk, how prone they are to love; he saw her melt into tears, he felt her embraces and sisterly kisses; and he took all she said for gospel. So, when she had done, he answered: – "Madam, it should not surprise you that I marvel, seeing that, in sooth, my father, for whatever cause, said never a word of you and your mother, or, if he did so, it came not to my knowledge, so that I knew no more of you than if you had not been; wherefore, the lonelier I am here, and the less hope I had of such good luck, the better pleased I am to have found here my sister. And indeed, I know not any man, however exalted his station, who ought not to be well pleased to have such a sister; much more, then, I, who am but a petty merchant; but, I pray you, resolve me of one thing: how came you to know that I was here?" Then answered she: – "'Twas told me this morning by a poor woman who is much about the house, because, as she tells me, she was long in the service of our father both at Palermo and at Perugia, and, but that it seemed more fitting that thou shouldst come to see me at home than that I should visit thee at an inn, I had long ago sought thee out." She then began to inquire particularly after all his kinsfolk by name, and Andreuccio, becoming ever more firmly persuaded of that which it was least for his good to believe, answered all her questions. Their conversation being thus prolonged and the heat great, she had Greek wine and sweetmeats brought in, and gave Andreuccio to drink; and when towards supper-time he made as if he would leave, she would in no wise suffer it; but, feigning to be very much vexed, she embraced him, saying: – "Alas! now 'tis plain how little thou carest for me: to think that thou art with thy sister, whom thou seest for the first time, and in her own house, where thou shouldst have alighted on thine arrival, and thou wouldst fain depart hence to go sup at an inn! Nay but, for certain, thou shalt sup with me; and albeit, to my great regret, my husband is not here, thou shalt see that I can do a lady's part in shewing thee honour." Andreuccio, not knowing what else to say, replied: – "Sister, I care for you with all a brother's affection; but if I go not, supper will await me all the evening at the inn, and I shall justly be taxed with discourtesy." Then said she: – "Blessed be God, there is even now in the house one by whom I can send word that they are not to expect thee at the inn, albeit thou wouldst far better discharge the debt of courtesy by sending word to thy friends, that they come here to sup; and then, if go thou must, you might all go in a body." Andreuccio replied, that he would have none of his friends that evening, but since she would have him stay, he would even do her the pleasure. She then made a shew of sending word to the inn that they should not expect him at dinner. Much more talk followed; and then they sate down to a supper of many courses splendidly served, which she cunningly protracted until nightfall; nor, when they were risen from table, and Andreuccio was about to take his departure, would she by any means suffer it, saying that Naples was no place to walk about in after dark, least of all for a stranger, and that, as she had sent word to the inn that they were not to expect him at supper, so she had done the like in regard of his bed. Believing what she said, and being (in his false confidence) overjoyed to be with her, he stayed. After supper there was matter enough for talk both various and prolonged; and, when the night was in a measure spent, she gave up her own chamber to Andreuccio, leaving him with a small boy to shew him aught that he might have need of, while she retired with her women to another chamber.

It was a very hot night, so, no sooner was Andreuccio alone than he stripped himself to his doublet, and drew off his stockings and laid them on the bed's head; and nature demanding a discharge of the surplus weight which he carried within him, he asked the lad where this might be done, and was shewn a door in a corner of the room, and told to go in there. Andreuccio, nothing doubting, did so, but, by ill luck, set his foot on a plank which was detached from the joist at the further end, whereby down it went, and he with it. By God's grace he took no hurt by the fall, though it was from some height, beyond sousing himself from head to foot in the ordure which filled the whole place, which, that you may the better understand what has been said, and that which is to follow, I will describe to you. A narrow and blind alley, such as we commonly see between two houses, was spanned by planks supported by joists on either side, and on the planks was the stool; of which planks that which fell with Andreuccio was one. Now Andreuccio, finding himself down there in the alley, fell to calling on the lad, who, as soon as he heard him fall, had run off, and promptly let the lady know what had happened. She hied forthwith to her chamber, and after a hasty search found Andreuccio's clothes and the money in them, for he foolishly thought to secure himself against risk by carrying it always on his person, and thus being possessed of the prize for which she had played her ruse, passing herself off as the sister of a man of Perugia, whereas she was really of Palermo, she concerned herself no further with Andreuccio except to close with all speed the door by which he had gone out when he fell. As the lad did not answer, Andreuccio began to shout more loudly; but all to no purpose. Whereby his suspicions were aroused, and he began at last to perceive the trick that had been played upon him; so he climbed over a low wall that divided the alley from the street, and hied him to the door of the house, which he knew very well. There for a long while he stood shouting and battering the door till it shook on its hinges; but all again to no purpose. No doubt of his misadventure now lurking in his mind, he fell to bewailing himself, saying: – "Alas! in how brief a time have I lost five hundred florins and a sister!" with much more of the like sort. Then he recommenced battering the door and shouting, to such a tune that not a few of the neighbours were roused, and finding the nuisance intolerable, got up; and one of the lady's servant-girls presented herself at the window with a very sleepy air, and said angrily: – "Who knocks below there?" "Oh!" said Andreuccio, "dost not know me? I am Andreuccio, Madam Fiordaliso's brother." "Good man," she rejoined, "if thou hast had too much to drink, go, sleep it off, and come back to-morrow. I know not Andreuccio, nor aught of the fantastic stuff thou pratest; prithee begone and be so good as to let us sleep in peace." "How?" said Andreuccio, "dost not understand what I say? For sure thou dost understand; but if Sicilian kinships are of such a sort that folk forget them so soon, at least return me my clothes, which I left within, and right glad shall I be to be off." Half laughing, she rejoined: – "Good man, methinks thou dost dream;" and, so saying, she withdrew and closed the window. Andreuccio by this time needed no further evidence of his wrongs; his wrath knew no bounds, and mortification well-nigh converted it into frenzy; he was minded to exact by force what he had failed to obtain by entreaties; and so, arming himself with a large stone, he renewed his attack upon the door with fury, dealing much heavier blows than at first. Wherefore, not a few of the neighbours, whom he had already roused from their beds, set him down as an ill-conditioned rogue, and his story as a mere fiction intended to annoy the good woman, and resenting the din which he now made, came to their windows, just as, when a stranger dog makes his appearance, all the dogs of the quarter will run to bark at him, and called out in chorus: – "'Tis a gross affront to come at this time of night to the house of the good woman with this silly story. Prithee, good man, let us sleep in peace; begone in God's name; and if thou hast a score to settle with her, come to-morrow, but a truce to thy pestering to-night."

Emboldened, perhaps, by these words, a man who lurked within the house, the good woman's bully, whom Andreuccio had as yet neither seen nor heard, shewed himself at the window, and said in a gruff voice and savage, menacing tone: – "Who is below there?" Andreuccio looked up in the direction of the voice, and saw standing at the window, yawning and rubbing his eyes as if he had just been roused from his bed, or at any rate from deep sleep, a fellow with a black and matted beard, who, as far as Andreuccio's means of judging went, bade fair to prove a most redoubtable champion. It was not without fear, therefore, that he replied: – "I am a brother of the lady who is within." The bully did not wait for him to finish his sentence, but, addressing him in a much sterner tone than before, called out: – "I know not why I come not down and give thee play with my cudgel, whilst thou givest me sign of life, ass, tedious driveller that thou must needs be, and drunken sot, thus to disturb our night's rest." Which said, he withdrew, and closed the window. Some of the neighbours who best knew the bully's quality gave Andreuccio fair words. "For God's sake," said they, "good man, take thyself off, stay not here to be murdered. 'Twere best for thee to go." These counsels, which seemed to be dictated by charity, reinforced the fear which the voice and aspect of the bully had inspired in Andreuccio, who, thus despairing of recovering his money and in the deepest of dumps, set his face towards the quarter whence in the daytime he had blindly followed the little girl, and began to make his way back to the inn. But so noisome was the stench which he emitted that he resolved to turn aside and take a bath in the sea. So he bore leftward up a street called Ruga Catalana, and was on his way towards the steep of the city, when by chance he saw two men coming towards him, bearing a lantern, and fearing that they might be patrols or other men who might do him a mischief, he stole away and hid himself in a dismantled house to avoid them. The house, however, was presently entered by the two men, just as if they had been guided thither; and one of them having disburdened himself of some iron tools which he carried on his shoulder, they both began to examine them, passing meanwhile divers comments upon them. While they were thus occupied, "What," said one, means this? Such a stench as never before did I smell the like. "So saying, he raised the lantern a little; whereby they had a view of hapless Andreuccio, and asked in amazement: – "Who is there?" Whereupon Andreuccio was at first silent, but when they flashed the light close upon him, and asked him what he did there in such a filthy state, he told them all that had befallen him. Casting about to fix the place where it occurred, they said one to another: – "Of a surety 'twas in the house of Scarabone Buttafuoco." Then said one, turning to Andreuccio: – "Good man, albeit thou hast lost thy money, thou hast cause enough to praise God that thou hadst the luck to fall; for hadst thou not fallen, be sure that, no sooner wert thou asleep, than thou hadst been knocked on the head, and lost not only thy money but thy life. But what boots it now to bewail thee? Thou mightest as soon pluck a star from the firmament as recover a single denier; nay, 'tis as much as thy life is worth if he do but hear that thou breathest a word of the affair."

The two men then held a short consultation, at the close of which they said: – "Lo now; we are sorry for thee, and so we make thee a fair offer. If thou wilt join with us in a little matter which we have in hand, we doubt not but thy share of the gain will greatly exceed what thou hast lost." Andreuccio, being now desperate, answered that he was ready to join them. Now Messer Filippo Minutolo, Archbishop of Naples, had that day been buried with a ruby on his finger, worth over five hundred florins of gold, besides other ornaments of extreme value. The two men were minded to despoil the Archbishop of his fine trappings, and imparted their design to Andreuccio, who, cupidity getting the better of caution, approved it; and so they all three set forth. But as they were on their way to the cathedral, Andreuccio gave out so rank an odour that one said to the other: – "Can we not contrive that he somehow wash himself a little, that he stink not so shrewdly?" "Why yes," said the other, "we are now close to a well, which is never without the pulley and a large bucket; 'tis but a step thither, and we will wash him out of hand." Arrived at the well, they found that the rope was still there, but the bucket had been removed; so they determined to attach him to the rope, and lower him into the well, there to wash himself, which done, he was to jerk the rope, and they would draw him up. Lowered accordingly he was; but just as, now washen, he jerked the rope, it so happened that a company of patrols, being thirsty because 'twas a hot night and some rogue had led them a pretty dance, came to the well to drink. The two men fled, unobserved, as soon as they caught sight of the newcomers, who, parched with thirst, laid aside their bucklers, arms and surcoats, and fell to hauling on the rope, that it bore the bucket, full of water. When, therefore, they saw Andreuccio, as he neared the brink of the well, loose the rope and clutch the brink with his hands, they were stricken with a sudden terror, and without uttering a word let go the rope, and took to flight with all the speed they could make. Whereat Andreuccio marvelled mightily, and had he not kept a tight grip on the brink of the well, he would certainly have gone back to the bottom and hardly have escaped grievous hurt, or death. Still greater was his astonishment, when, fairly landed on terra firma, he found the patrols' arms lying there, which he knew had not been carried by his comrades. He felt a vague dread, he knew not why; he bewailed once more his evil fortune; and without venturing to touch the arms, he left the well and wandered he knew not whither. As he went, however, he fell in with his two comrades, now returning to draw him out of the well; who no sooner saw him than in utter amazement they demanded who had hauled him up. Andreuccio answered that he knew not, and then told them in detail how it had come about, and what he had found beside the well. They laughed as they apprehended the circumstances, and told him why they had fled, and who they were that had hauled him up. Then without further parley, for it was now midnight, they hied them to the cathedral. They had no difficulty in entering and finding the tomb, which was a magnificent structure of marble, and with their iron implements they raised the lid, albeit it was very heavy, to a height sufficient to allow a man to enter, and propped it up. This done, a dialogue ensued. "Who shall go in?" said one. "Not I," said the other. "Nor I," rejoined his companion; "let Andreuccio go in." "That will not I," said Andreuccio. Whereupon both turned upon him and said: – "How? thou wilt not go in? By God, if thou goest not in, we will give thee that over the pate with one of these iron crowbars that thou shalt drop down dead." Terror-stricken, into the tomb Andreuccio went, saying to himself as he did so: – "These men will have me go in, that they may play a trick upon me: when I have handed everything up to them, and am sweating myself to get out of the tomb, they will be off about their business, and I shall be left, with nothing for my pains." So he determined to make sure of his own part first; and bethinking him of the precious ring of which he had heard them speak, as soon as he had completed the descent, he drew the ring off the Archbishop's finger, and put it on his own: he then handed up one by one the crosier, mitre and gloves, and other of the Archbishop's trappings, stripping him to his shirt; which done, he told his comrades that there was nothing more. They insisted that the ring must be there, and bade him search everywhere. This he feigned to do, ejaculating from time to time that he found it not; and thus he kept them a little while in suspense. But they, who, were in their way as cunning as he, kept on exhorting him to make a careful search, and, seizing their opportunity, withdrew the prop that supported the lid of the tomb, and took to their heels, leaving him there a close prisoner. You will readily conceive how Andreuccio behaved when he understood his situation. More than once he applied his head and shoulders to the lid and sought with might and main to heave it up; but all his efforts were fruitless; so that at last, overwhelmed with anguish he fell in a swoon on the corpse of the Archbishop, and whether of the twain were the more lifeless, Andreuccio or the Archbishop, 'twould have puzzled an observer to determine.

When he came to himself he burst into a torrent of tears, seeing now nothing in store for him but either to perish there of hunger and fetid odours beside the corpse and among the worms, or, should the tomb be earlier opened, to be taken and hanged as a thief. These most lugubrious meditations were interrupted by a sound of persons walking and talking in the church. They were evidently a numerous company, and their purpose, as Andreuccio surmised, was the very same with which he and his comrades had come thither: whereby his terror was mightily increased. Presently the folk opened the tomb, and propped up the lid, and then fell to disputing as to who should go in. None was willing, and the contention was protracted; but at length one – 'twas a priest – said: – "Of what are ye afeared? Think ye to be eaten by him? Nay, the dead eat not the living. I will go in myself." So saying he propped his breast upon the edge of the lid, threw his head back, and thrust his legs within, that he might go down feet foremost. On sight whereof Andreuccio started to his feet, and seizing hold of one of the priest's legs, made as if he would drag him down; which caused the priest to utter a prodigious yell, and bundle himself out of the tomb with no small celerity. The rest took to flight in a panic, as if a hundred thousand devils were at their heels. The tomb being thus left open, Andreuccio, the ring still on his finger, spring out. The way by which he had entered the church served him for egress, and roaming at random, he arrived towards daybreak at the coast. Diverging thence he came by chance upon his inn, where he found that his host and his comrades had been anxious about him all night. When he told them all that had befallen him, they joined with the host in advising him to leave Naples at once. He accordingly did so, and returned to Perugia, having invested in a ring the money with which he had intended to buy horses.

Second Day
Novel VI

— *Madam Beritola loses two sons, is found with two kids on an island, goes thence to Lunigiana, where one of her sons takes service with her master, and lies with his daughter, for which he is put in prison. Sicily rebels against King Charles, the son is recognised by the mother, marries the master's daughter, and, his brother being discovered, is reinstated in great honour.* —

THE LADIES and the young men alike had many a hearty laugh over Fiammetta's narrative of Andreuccio's adventures, which ended, Emilia, at the queen's command, thus began: –

Grave and grievous are the vicissitudes with which Fortune makes us acquainted, and as discourse of such matter serves to awaken our minds, which are so readily lulled to sleep by her flatteries, I deem it worthy of attentive hearing by all, whether they enjoy her favour or endure her frown, in that it ministers counsel to the one sort and consolation to the other. Wherefore, albeit great matters have preceded it, I mean to tell you a story, not less true than touching, of adventures whereof the issue was indeed felicitous, but the antecedent bitterness so long drawn out that scarce can I believe that it was ever sweetened by ensuing happiness.

Dearest ladies, you must know that after the death of the Emperor Frederic II. the crown of Sicily passed to Manfred; whose favour was enjoyed in the highest degree by a gentleman of Naples, Arrighetto Capece by name, who had to wife Madonna Beritola Caracciola, a fair and gracious lady, likewise a Neapolitan. Now when Manfred was conquered and slain by King Charles I. at Benevento, and the whole realm transferred its allegiance to the conqueror, Arrighetto, who was then governor of Sicily, no sooner received the tidings than he prepared for instant flight, knowing that little reliance was to be placed on the fleeting faith of the Sicilians, and not being minded to become a subject of his master's enemy. But the Sicilians having intelligence of his plans, he and many other friends and servants of King Manfred were surprised, taken prisoners and delivered over to King Charles, to whom the whole island was soon afterwards surrendered. In this signal reversal of the wonted course of things Madam Beritola, knowing not what was become of Arrighetto, and from the past ever auguring future evil, lest she should suffer foul dishonour, abandoned all that she possessed, and with a son of, perhaps, eight years, Giusfredi by name, being also pregnant, fled in a boat to Lipari, where she gave birth to another male child, whom she named Outcast. Then with her sons and a hired nurse she took ship for Naples, intending there to rejoin her family. Events, however, fell out otherwise than she expected; for by stress of weather the ship was carried out of her course to the desert island of Ponza, where they put in to a little bay until such time as they might safely continue their voyage. Madam Beritola landed with the rest on the island, and, leaving them all, sought out a lonely and secluded spot, and there abandoned herself to melancholy brooding on the loss of her dear Arrighetto. While thus she spent her days in solitary preoccupation with her grief it chanced that a galley of corsairs swooped down upon the island, and, before either the mariners or any other folk were aware of their peril, made an easy capture of them all and sailed away; so that, when Madam Beritola, her wailing for that day ended, returned, as was her wont, to the shore to solace herself with the sight of her sons, she found none there. At first she was lost in wonder, then with a sudden suspicion of the truth she bent her eyes seaward, and there saw the galley still at no great distance, towing the ship in her wake. Thus apprehending beyond all manner of doubt that she had lost her sons as well as her husband, and that, alone, desolate and destitute, she might not hope, that any of her lost ones would ever be restored to her, she fell down on the shore in a swoon with the names of her husband and sons upon her lips. None was there to administer cold water or aught else that might recall her truant powers; her animal spirits might even wander whithersoever they would at their sweet will: strength, however, did at last return to her poor exhausted frame, and therewith tears and lamentations, as, plaintively repeating her sons' names, she roamed in quest of them from cavern to cavern. Long time she sought them thus; but when she saw that her labour was in vain, and that night was closing in, hope, she knew not why, began to return, and with it some degree of anxiety on her own account. Wherefore she left the shore and returned to the cavern where she had been wont to indulge her plaintive mood. She passed the night in no small fear and indescribable anguish; the new day came, and, as she had not supped, she was fain after tierce to appease her hunger, as best she could, by a breakfast of herbs: this done, she wept and began to ruminate on her future way of life. While thus engaged, she observed a she-goat come by and go into an adjacent cavern, and after a while come forth again and go into the wood: thus roused from her reverie she got up, went into the cavern from which the she-goat had issued, and there saw two kids, which might have been born that very day, and seemed to her the sweetest and the most delicious things in the world: and, having, by reason of her recent delivery, milk still within her, she took them up tenderly, and set them to her breast. They, nothing loath, sucked at her teats as if she had been their own dam; and thenceforth made no distinction between her and the dam. Which caused the lady to feel that she had found company in the desert; and so, living on herbs and water, weeping as often as she bethought her of her husband and sons and her past life, she disposed herself to live and die there, and became no less familiar with the she-goat than with her young.

 The gentle lady thus leading the life of a wild creature, it chanced that after some months stress of weather brought a Pisan ship to the very same bay in which she had landed. The ship lay there for several days, having on board a gentleman, Currado de' Malespini by name (of the same family as the Marquis), who with his noble and most devout lady was returning home from a pilgrimage, having visited all the holy places in the realm of Apulia. To beguile the tedium of the sojourn Currado with his lady, some servants and his dogs, set forth one day upon a tour through the island. As they neared the place where Madam Beritola dwelt, Currado's dogs on view of the two kids, which, now of a fair size, were grazing, gave chase. The kids, pursued by the dogs, made straight for Madam Beritola's cavern. She, seeing what was toward, started to her feet, caught up a stick, and drove the dogs back. Currado and his lady coming up after the dogs, gazed on Madam Beritola, now tanned and lean and hairy, with wonder, which she more than reciprocated. At her request Currado called off the dogs; and then he and his lady besought her again and again to say who she was and what she did there. So she told them all about herself, her rank, her misfortunes, and the savage life which she was minded to lead. Currado, who had known Arrighetto Capece very well, was moved to tears by compassion, and exhausted all his eloquence to induce her to change her mind, offering to escort her home, or to take her to live with him in honourable estate as his sister until God should vouchsafe her kindlier fortune. The lady, declining all his offers, Currado left her with his wife, whom he bade see that food was brought thither, and let Madam Beritola, who was all in rags, have one of her own dresses to wear, and do all that she could to persuade her to go with them. So the gentle lady stayed with Madam Beritola, and after condoling with her at large on her misfortunes had food and clothing brought to her, and with the greatest difficulty in the world prevailed upon her to eat and dress herself. At last, after much beseeching, she induced her to depart from her oft-declared intention never to go where she might meet any that knew her, and accompany them to Lunigiana, taking with her the two kids and the dam, which latter had in the meantime returned, and to the gentle lady's great surprise had greeted Madam Beritola with the utmost affection. So with the return of fair weather Madam Beritola, taking with her the dam and the two kids, embarked with Currado and his lady on their ship, being called by them – for her true name was not to be known of all – Cavriuola; and the wind holding fair, they speedily reached the mouth of the Magra, and landing hied them to Currado's castle where Madam Beritola abode with Currado's lady in the quality of her maid, serving her well and faithfully, wearing widow's weeds, and feeding and tending her kids with assiduous and loving care.

The corsairs, who, not espying Madam Beritola, had left her at Ponza when they took the ship on which she had come thither, had made a course to Genoa, taking with them all the other folk. On their arrival the owners of the galley shared the booty, and so it happened that as part thereof Madam Beritola's nurse and her two boys fell to the lot of one Messer Guasparrino d'Oria, who sent all three to his house, being minded to keep them there as domestic slaves. The nurse, beside herself with grief at the loss of her mistress and the woful plight in which she found herself and her two charges, shed many a bitter tear. But, seeing that they were unavailing, and that she and the boys were slaves together, she, having, for all her low estate, her share of wit and good sense, made it her first care to comfort them; then, regardful of the condition to which they were reduced, she bethought her, that, if the lads were recognised, 'twould very likely be injurious to them. So, still hoping that some time or another Fortune would change her mood, and they be able, if living, to regain their lost estate, she resolved to let none know who they were, until she saw a fitting occasion; and accordingly, whenever she was questioned thereof by any, she gave them out as her own children. The name of the elder she changed from Giusfredi to Giannotto di Procida; the name of the younger she did not think it worth while to change. She spared no pains to make Giusfredi understand the reason why she had changed his name, and, the risk which he might run if he were recognised. This she impressed upon him not once only but many times; and the boy, who was apt to learn, followed the instructions of the wise nurse with perfect exactitude.

So the two boys, ill clad and worse shod, continued with the nurse in Messer Guasparrino's house for two years, patiently performing all kinds of menial offices. But Giannotto, being now sixteen years old, and of a spirit that consorted ill with servitude, brooked not the baseness of his lot, and dismissed himself from Messer Guasparrino's service by getting aboard a galley bound for Alexandria, and travelled far and wide, and fared never the better. In the course of his wanderings he learned that his father, whom he had supposed to be dead, was still living, but kept in prison under watch and ward by King Charles. He was grown a tall handsome young man, when, perhaps three or four years after he had given Messer Guasparrino the slip, weary of roaming and all but despairing of his fortune, he came to Lunigiana, and by chance took service with Currado Malespini, who found him handy, and was well-pleased with him. His mother, who was in attendance on Currado's lady, he seldom saw, and never recognised her, nor she him; so much had time changed both from their former aspect since they last met. While Giannotto was thus in the service of Currado, it fell out by the death of Niccolo da Grignano that his widow, Spina, Currado's daughter, returned to her father's house. Very fair she was and loveable, her age not more than sixteen years, and so it was that she saw Giannotto with favour, and he her, and both fell ardently in love with one another. Their passion was early gratified; but several months elapsed before any detected its existence. Wherefore, growing overbold, they began to dispense with the precautions which such an affair demanded. So one day, as they walked with others through a wood, where the trees grew fair and close, the girl and Giannotto left the rest of the company some distance behind, and, thinking that they were well in advance, found a fair pleasaunce girt in with trees and carpeted with abundance of grass and flowers, and fell to solacing themselves after the manner of lovers. Long time they thus dallied, though such was their delight that all too brief it seemed to them, and so it befell that they were surprised first by the girl's mother and then by Currado. Pained beyond measure by what he had seen, Currado, without assigning any cause, had them both arrested by three of his servants and taken in chains to one of his castles; where in a frenzy of passionate wrath he left them, resolved to put them to an ignominious death. The girl's mother was also very angry, and deemed her daughter's fall deserving of the most rigorous chastisement, but, when by one of Currado's chance words she divined the doom which he destined for the guilty pair, she could not reconcile herself to it, and hasted to intercede with her angry husband, beseeching him to refrain the impetuous wrath which would hurry him in his old age to murder his daughter and imbrue his hands in the blood of his servant, and vent it in some other way, as by close confinement and duress, whereby the culprits should be brought to repent them of their fault in tears. Thus, and with much more to the like effect, the devout lady urged her suit, and at length prevailed upon her husband to abandon his murderous design. Wherefore, he commanded that the pair should be confined in separate prisons, and closely guarded, and kept short of food and in sore discomfort, until further order; which was accordingly done; and the life which the captives led, their endless tears, their fasts of inordinate duration, may be readily imagined.

Giannotto and Spina had languished in this sorry plight for full a year, entirely ignored by Currado, when in concert with Messer Gian di Procida, King Peter of Arragon raised a rebellion in the island of Sicily, and wrested it from King Charles, whereat Currado, being a Ghibelline, was overjoyed. Hearing the tidings from one of his warders, Giannotto heaved a great sigh, and said: – "Alas, fourteen years have I been a wanderer upon the face of the earth, looking for no other than this very event; and now, that my hopes of happiness may be for ever frustrate, it has come to pass only to find me in prison, whence I may never think to issue alive." "How?" said the warder; "what signify to thee these doings of these mighty monarchs? What part hadst thou in Sicily?" Giannotto answered: – "'Tis as if my heart were breaking when I bethink me of my father and what part he had in Sicily. I was but a little lad when I fled the island, but yet I remember him as its governor in the time of King Manfred." "And who then was thy father?" demanded the warder. "His name," rejoined Giannotto, "I need no longer scruple to disclose, seeing that I find myself in the very strait which I hoped to avoid by concealing it. He was and still is, if he live, Arrighetto Capece; and my name is not Giannotto but Giusfredi; and I doubt not but, were I once free, and back in Sicily, I might yet hold a very honourable position in the island."

The worthy man asked no more questions, but, as soon as he found opportunity, told what he had learned to Currado, who, albeit he made light of it in the warder's presence, repaired to Madam Beritola, and asked her in a pleasant manner, whether she had had by Arrighetto a son named Giusfredi. The lady answered, in tears, that, if the elder of her two sons were living, such would be his name, and his age twenty-two years. This inclined Currado to think that Giannotto and Giusfredi were indeed one and the same; and it occurred to him, that, if so it were, he might at once shew himself most merciful and blot out his daughter's shame and his own by giving her to him in marriage; wherefore he sent for Giannotto privily, and questioned him in detail touching his past life. And finding by indubitable evidence that he was indeed Giusfredi, son of Arrighetto Capece, he said to him: – "Giannotto, thou knowest the wrong which thou hast done me in the person of my daughter, what and how great it is, seeing that I used thee well and kindly, and thou shouldst therefore, like a good servant, have shewn thyself jealous of my honour, and zealous in my interest; and many there are who, hadst thou treated them as thou hast treated me, would have caused thee to die an ignominious death; which my clemency would not brook. But now, as it is even so as thou sayst, and thou art of gentle blood by both thy parents, I am minded to put an end to thy sufferings as soon as thou wilt, releasing thee from the captivity in which thou languishest, and setting thee in a happy place, and reinstating at once thy honour and my own. Thy intimacy with Spina – albeit, shameful to both – was yet prompted by love. Spina, as thou knowest, is a widow, and her dower is ample and secure. What her breeding is, and her father's and her mother's, thou knowest: of thy present condition I say nought. Wherefore, when thou wilt, I am consenting, that, having been with dishonour thy friend, she become with honour thy wife, and that, so long as it seem good to thee, thou tarry here with her and me as my son."

Captivity had wasted Giannotto's flesh, but had in no degree impaired the generosity of spirit which he derived from his ancestry, or the whole-hearted love which he bore his lady. So, albeit he ardently desired that which Currado offered, and knew that he was in Currado's power, yet, even as his magnanimity prompted, so, unswervingly, he made answer: – "Currado, neither ambition nor cupidity nor aught else did ever beguile me to any treacherous machination against either thy person or thy property. Thy daughter I loved, and love and shall ever love, because I deem her worthy of my love, and, if I dealt with her after a fashion which to the mechanic mind seems hardly honourable, I did but commit that fault which is ever congenial to youth, which can never be eradicated so long as youth continues, and which, if the aged would but remember that they were once young and would measure the delinquencies of others by their own and their own by those of others, would not be deemed so grave as thou and many others depict it; and what I did, I did as a friend, not as an enemy. That which thou offerest I have ever desired and should long ago have sought, had I supposed that thou wouldst grant it, and 'twill be the more grateful to me in proportion to the depth of my despair. But if thy intent be not such, as thy words import, feed me not with vain hopes, but send me back to prison there to suffer whatever thou mayst be pleased to inflict; nor doubt that even as I love Spina, so for love of her shall I ever love thee, though thou do thy worst, and still hold thee in reverent regard."

Currado marvelled to hear him thus speak, and being assured of his magnanimity and the fervour of his love, held him the more dear; wherefore he rose, embraced and kissed him, and without further delay bade privily bring thither Spina, who left her prison wasted and wan and weak, and so changed that she seemed almost another woman than of yore, even as Giannotto was scarce his former self. Then and there in Currado's presence they plighted their troth according to our custom of espousals; and some days afterwards Currado, having in the meantime provided all things meet for their convenience and solace, yet so as that none should surmise what had happened, deemed it now time to gladden their mothers with the news. So he sent for his lady and Cavriuola, and thus, addressing Cavriuola, he spoke: – "What would you say, madam, were I to restore you your elder son as the husband of one of my daughters?" Cavriuola answered: – "I should say, that, were it possible for you to strengthen the bond which attaches me to you, then assuredly you had so done, in that you restored to me that which I cherish more tenderly than myself, and in such a guise as in some measure to renew within me the hope which I had lost: more I could not say." And so, weeping, she was silent. Then, turning to his lady, Currado said: – "And thou, madam, what wouldst thou think if I were to present thee with such a son-in-law?" "A son-in-law," she answered, "that was not of gentle blood, but a mere churl, so he pleased you, would well content me." "So!" returned Currado; "I hope within a few days to gladden the hearts of both of you."

He waited only until the two young folk had recovered their wonted mien, and were clad in a manner befitting their rank. Then, addressing Giusfredi, he said: – "Would it not add to thy joy to see thy mother here?" "I dare not hope," returned Giusfredi, "that she has survived calamities and sufferings such as hers; but were it so, great indeed would be my joy, and none the less that by her counsel I might be aided to the recovery (in great measure) of my lost heritage in Sicily." Whereupon Currado caused both the ladies to come thither, and presented to them the bride. The gladness with which they both greeted her was a wonder to behold, and no less great was their wonder at the benign inspiration that had prompted Currado to unite her in wedlock with Giannotto, whom Currado's words caused Madam Beritola to survey with some attention. A hidden spring of memory was thus touched; she recognised in the man the lineaments of her boy, and awaiting no further evidence she ran with open arms and threw herself upon his neck. No word did she utter, for very excess of maternal tenderness and joy; but, every avenue of sense closed, she fell as if bereft of life within her son's embrace. Giannotto, who had often seen her in the castle and never recognised her, marvelled not a little, but nevertheless it at once flashed upon him that 'twas his mother, and blaming himself for his past inadvertence he took her in his arms and wept and tenderly kissed her. With gentle solicitude Currado's lady and Spina came to her aid, and restored her suspended animation with cold water and other remedies. She then with many tender and endearing words kissed him a thousand times or more, which tokens of her love he received with a look of reverential acknowledgment. Thrice, nay a fourth time were these glad and gracious greetings exchanged, and joyful indeed were they that witnessed them, and hearkened while mother and son compared their past adventures. Then Currado, who had already announced his new alliance to his friends, and received their felicitations proceeded to give order for the celebration of the event with all becoming gaiety and splendour. As he did so, Giusfredi said to him: – "Currado, you have long given my mother honourable entertainment, and on me you have conferred many boons; wherefore, that you may fill up the measure of your kindness, 'tis now my prayer that you be pleased to gladden my mother and my marriage feast and me with the presence of my brother, now in servitude in the house of Messer Guasparrino d'Oria, who, as I have already told you, made prize of both him and me; and that then you send some one to Sicily, who shall make himself thoroughly acquainted with the circumstances and condition of the country, and find out how it has fared with my father Arrighetto, whether he be alive or dead, and if alive, in what circumstances, and being thus fully informed, return to us with the tidings." Currado assented, and forthwith sent most trusty agents both to Genoa and to Sicily. So in due time an envoy arrived at Genoa, and made instant suit to Guasparrino on Currado's part for the surrender of Outcast and the nurse, setting forth in detail all that had passed between Currado and Giusfredi and his mother. Whereat Messer Guasparrino was mightily astonished, and said: – "Of a surety there is nought that, being able, I would not do to pleasure Currado; and, true it is that I have had in my house for these fourteen years the boy whom thou dost now demand of me, and his mother, and gladly will I surrender them; but tell Currado from me to beware of excessive credulity, and to put no faith in the idle tales of Giannotto, or Giusfredi, as thou sayst he calls himself, who is by no means so guileless as he supposes."

Then, having provided for the honourable entertainment of the worthy envoy, he sent privily for the nurse, and cautiously sounded her as to the affair. The nurse had heard of the revolt of Sicily, and had learned that Arrighetto was still alive. She therefore banished fear, and told Messer Guasparrino the whole story, and explained to him the reasons why she had acted as she had done. Finding that what she said accorded very well with what he had learned from Currado's envoy, he inclined to credit the story, and most astutely probing the matter in divers ways, and always finding fresh grounds for confidence, he reproached himself for the sorry manner in which he had treated the boy, and by way of amends gave him one of his own daughters, a beautiful girl of eleven years, to wife with a dowry suited to Arrighetto's rank, and celebrated their nuptials with great festivity, He then brought the boy and girl, Currado's envoy, and the nurse in a well-armed galliot to Lerici, being there met by Currado, who had a castle not far off, where great preparations had been made for their entertainment: and thither accordingly he went with his whole company. What cheer the mother had of her son, the brothers of one another, and all the three of the faithful nurse; what cheer Messer Guasparrino and his daughter had of all, and all of them, and what cheer all had of Currado and his lady and their sons and their friends, words may not describe; wherefore, my ladies, I leave it to your imagination. And that their joy might be full, God, who, when He gives, gives most abundantly, added the glad tidings that Arrighetto Capece was alive and prosperous. For, when in the best of spirits the ladies and gentlemen had sat them down to feast, and they were yet at the first course, the envoy from Sicily arrived, and among other matters reported, that, no sooner had the insurrection broken out in the island than the people hied them in hot haste to the prison where Arrighetto was kept in confinement by King Charles, and despatching the guards, brought him forth, and knowing him to be a capital enemy to King Charles made him their captain, and under his command fell upon and massacred the French. Whereby he had won the highest place in the favour of King Peter, who had granted him restitution of all his estates and honours, so that he was now both prosperous and mighty. The envoy added that Arrighetto had received him with every token of honour, had manifested the utmost delight on hearing of his lady and son, of whom no tidings had reached him since his arrest, and had sent, to bring them home, a brigantine with some gentlemen aboard, whose arrival might hourly be expected.

The envoy, and the good news which he brought, were heartily welcome; and presently Currado, with some of his friends, encountered the gentlemen who came for Madam Beritola and Giusfredi, and saluting them cordially invited them to his feast, which was not yet half done. Joy unheard of was depicted on the faces of the lady, of Giusfredi, and of all the rest as they greeted them; nor did they on their part take their places at the table before, as best they might, they had conveyed to Currado and his lady Arrighetto's greetings and grateful acknowledgments of the honour which they had conferred upon his lady and his son, and had placed Arrighetto, to the uttermost of his power, entirely at their service. Then, turning to Messer Guasparrino, of whose kindness Arrighetto surmised nothing, they said that they were very sure that, when he learned the boon which Outcast had received at his hands, he would pay him the like and an even greater tribute of gratitude. This speech ended, they feasted most joyously with the brides and bridegrooms. So passed the day, the first of many which Currado devoted to honouring his son-in-law and his other intimates, both kinsfolk and friends. The time of festivity ended, Madam Beritola and Giusfredi and the rest felt that they must leave: so, taking Spina with them, they parted, not without many tears, from Currado and his lady and Guasparrino, and went aboard the brigantine, which, wafted by a prosperous wind, soon brought them to Sicily. At Palermo they were met by Arrighetto, who received them all, ladies and sons alike, with such cheer as it were vain to attempt to describe. There it is believed that they all lived long and happily and in amity with God, being not unmindful of the blessings which He had conferred upon them.

Second Day
Novel VII

— The Soldan of Babylon sends one of his daughters overseas, designing to marry her to the King of Algarve. By divers adventures she comes in the space of four years into the hands of nine men in divers places. At last she is restored to her father, whom she quits again in the guise of a virgin, and, as was at first intended, is married to the King of Algarve. —

HAD EMILIA'S STORY but lasted a little longer, the young ladies would perhaps have been moved to tears, so great was the sympathy which they felt for Madam Beritola in her various fortunes. But now that it was ended, the Queen bade Pamfilo follow suit; and he, than whom none was more obedient, thus began: –

Hardly, gracious ladies, is it given to us to know that which makes for our good; insomuch that, as has been observable in a multitude of instances, many, deeming that the acquisition of great riches would ensure them an easy and tranquil existence, have not only besought them of God in prayer, but have sought them with such ardour that they have spared no pains and shrunk from no danger in the quest, and have attained their end only to lose, at the hands of some one covetous of their vast inheritance, a life with which before the days of their prosperity they were well content. Others, whose course, perilous with a thousand battles, stained with the blood of their brothers and their friends, has raised them from base to regal estate, have found in place of the felicity they expected an infinity of cares and fears, and have proved by experience that a chalice may be poisoned, though it be of gold, and set on the table of a king. Many have most ardently desired beauty and strength and other advantages of person, and have only been taught their error by the death or dolorous life which these very advantages entailed upon them. And so, not to instance each particular human desire, I say, in sum, that there is none of, them that men may indulge in full confidence as exempt from the chances and changes of fortune; wherefore, if we would act rightly, we ought to school ourselves to take and be content with that which He gives us, who alone knows and can afford us that of which we have need. But, divers as are the aberrations of desire to which men are prone, so, gracious ladies, there is one to which you are especially liable, in that you are unduly solicitous of beauty, insomuch, that, not content with the charms which nature has allotted you, you endeavour to enhance them with wondrous ingenuity of art; wherefore I am minded to make you acquainted with the coil of misadventures in which her beauty involved a fair Saracen, who in the course of, perhaps, four years was wedded nine several times.

There was of yore a Soldan of Babylon, by name of Beminedab, who in his day had cause enough to be well content with his luck. Many children male and female had he, and among them a daughter, Alatiel by name, who by common consent of all that saw her was the most beautiful woman then to be found in the world. Now the Soldan, having been signally aided by the King of Algarve in inflicting a great defeat upon a host of Arabs that had attacked him, had at his instance and by way of special favour given Alatiel to the King to wife; wherefore, with an honourable escort of gentlemen and ladies most nobly and richly equipped, he placed her aboard a well-armed, well-furnished ship, and, commending her to God, sped her on her journey. The mariners, as soon as the weather was favourable, hoisted sail, and for some days after their departure from Alexandria had a prosperous voyage; but when they had passed Sardinia, and were beginning to think that they were nearing their journey's end, they were caught one day between divers cross winds, each blowing with extreme fury, whereby the ship laboured so sorely that not only the lady but the seamen from time to time gave themselves up for lost. But still, most manfully and skilfully they struggled might and main with the tempest, which, ever waxing rather than waning, buffeted them for two days with immense unintermittent surges; and being not far from the island of Majorca, as the third night began to close in, wrapt in clouds and mist and thick darkness, so that they saw neither the sky nor aught else, nor by any nautical skill might conjecture where they were, they felt the ship's timbers part. Wherefore, seeing no way to save the ship, each thought only how best to save himself, and, a boat being thrown out, the masters first, and then the men, one by one, though the first-comers sought with knives in their hands to bar the passage of the rest, all, rather than remain in the leaky ship, crowded into it, and there found the death which they hoped to escape. For the boat, being in such stress of weather, and with such a burden quite unmanageable, went under, and all aboard her perished; whereas the ship, leaky though she was, and all but full of water, yet, driven by the fury of the tempest, was hurled with prodigious velocity upon the shore of the island of Majorca, and struck it with such force as to embed herself in the sand, perhaps a stone's throw from terra firma, where she remained all night beaten and washed by the sea, but no more to be moved by the utmost violence of the gale. None had remained aboard her but the lady and her women, whom the malice of the elements and their fears had brought to the verge of death. When it was broad day and the storm was somewhat abated, the lady, half dead, raised her head, and in faltering accents began to call first one and then another of her servants. She called in vain, however; for those whom she called were too far off to hear. Great indeed was her wonder and fear to find herself thus without sight of human face or sound of other voice than her own; but, struggling to her feet as best she might, she looked about her, and saw the ladies that were of her escort, and the other women, all prostrate on the deck; so, after calling them one by one, she began at length to touch them, and finding few that shewed sign of life, for indeed, between grievous sea-sickness and fear, they had little life left, she grew more terrified than before. However, being in sore need of counsel, all alone as she was, and without knowledge or means of learning where she was, she at last induced such as had life in them to get upon their feet, with whom, as none knew where the men were gone, and the ship was now full of water and visibly breaking up, she abandoned herself to piteous lamentations.

 It was already none before they descried any one on the shore or elsewhere to whom they could make appeal for help; but shortly after none it so chanced that a gentleman, Pericone da Visalgo by name, being on his return from one of his estates, passed that way with some mounted servants. Catching sight of the ship, he apprehended the circumstances at a glance, and bade one of his servants try to get aboard her, and let him know the result. The servant with some difficulty succeeded in boarding the vessel, and found the gentle lady with her few companions ensconced under shelter of the prow, and shrinking timidly from observation. At the first sight of him they wept, and again and again implored him to have pity on them; but finding that he did not understand them, nor they him, they sought by gestures to make him apprehend their forlorn condition.

 With these tidings the servant, after making such survey of the ship as he could, returned to Pericone, who forthwith caused the ladies, and all articles of value which were in the ship and could be removed, to be brought off her, and took them with him to one of his castles. The ladies' powers were soon in a measure restored by food and rest, and by the honour which was paid to Alatiel, and Alatiel alone by all the rest, as well as by the richness of her dress, Pericone perceived that she must be some great lady. Nor, though she was still pale, and her person bore evident marks of the sea's rough usage, did he fail to note that it was cast in a mould of extraordinary beauty. Wherefore his mind was soon made up that, if she lacked a husband, he would take her to wife and that, if he could not have her to wife, then he would make her his mistress. So this ardent lover, who was a man of powerful frame and haughty mien, devoted himself for several days to the service of the lady with excellent effect, for the lady completely recovered her strength and spirits, so that her beauty far exceeded Pericone's most sanguine conjectures. Great therefore beyond measure was his sorrow that he understood not her speech, nor she his, so that neither could know who the other was; but being inordinately enamoured of her beauty, he sought by such mute blandishments as he could devise to declare his love, and bring her of her own accord to gratify his desire. All in vain, however; she repulsed his advances point blank; whereby his passion only grew the stronger. So some days passed; and the lady perceiving Pericone's constancy, and bethinking her that sooner or later she must yield either to force or to love, and gratify his passion, and judging by what she observed of the customs of the people that she was amongst Christians, and in a part where, were she able to speak their language, she would gain little by making herself known, determined with a lofty courage to stand firm and immovable in this extremity of her misfortunes. Wherefore she bade the three women, who were all that were left to her, on no account to let any know who they were, unless they were so circumstanced that they might safely count on assistance in effecting their escape: she also exhorted them most earnestly to preserve their chastity, averring that she was firmly resolved that none but her husband should enjoy her. The women heartily assented, and promised that her injunctions should be obeyed to the utmost of their power.

Day by day Pericone's passion waxed more ardent, being fomented by the proximity and contrariety of its object. Wherefore seeing that blandishment availed nothing, he was minded to have recourse to wiles and stratagems, and in the last resort to force. The lady, debarred by her law from the use of wine, found it, perhaps, on that account all the more palatable, which Pericone observing determined to enlist Bacchus in the service of Venus. So, ignoring her coyness, he provided one evening a supper, which was ordered with all possible pomp and beauty, and graced by the presence of the lady. No lack was there of incentives to hilarity; and Pericone directed the servant who waited on Alatiel to ply her with divers sorts of blended wines; which command the man faithfully executed. She, suspecting nothing, and seduced by the delicious flavour of the liquor, drank somewhat more freely than was seemly, and forgetting her past woes, became frolicsome, and incited by some women who trod some measures in the Majorcan style, she shewed the company how they footed it in Alexandria. This novel demeanour was by no means lost on Pericone, who saw in it a good omen of his speedy success; so, with profuse relays of food and wine he prolonged the supper far into the night.

When the guests were at length gone, he attended the lady alone to her chamber, where, the heat of the wine overpowering the cold counsels of modesty, she made no more account of Pericone's presence than if he had been one of her women, and forthwith undressed and went to bed. Pericone was not slow to follow her, and as soon as the light was out lay down by her side, and taking her in his arms, without the least demur on her part, began, to solace himself with her after the manner of lovers; which experience – she knew not till then with what horn men butt – caused her to repent that she had not yielded to his blandishments; nor did she thereafter wait to be invited to such nights of delight, but many a time declared her readiness, not by words, for she had none to convey her meaning, but by gestures.

But this great felicity which she now shared with Pericone was not to last: for not content with making her, instead of the consort of a king, the mistress of a castellan, Fortune had now in store for her a harsher experience, though of an amorous character. Pericone had a brother, twenty-five years of age, fair and fresh as a rose, his name Marato. On sight of Alatiel Marato had been mightily taken with her; he inferred from her bearing that he stood high in her good graces; he believed that nothing stood between him and the gratification of his passion but the jealous vigilance with which Pericone guarded her. So musing, he hit upon a ruthless expedient, which had effect in action as hasty as heinous.

It so chanced that there then lay in the port of the city a ship, commanded by two Genoese, bound with a cargo of merchandise for Klarenza in the Morea: her sails were already hoist; and she tarried only for a favourable breeze. Marato approached the masters and arranged with them to take himself and the lady aboard on the following night. This done he concerted further action with some of his most trusty friends, who readily lent him their aid to carry his design into execution. So on the following evening towards nightfall, the conspirators stole unobserved into Pericone's house, which was entirely unguarded, and there hid themselves, as pre-arranged. Then, as the night wore on, Marato shewed them where Pericone and the lady slept, and they entered the room, and slew Pericone. The lady thus rudely roused wept; but silencing her by menaces of death they carried her off with the best part of Pericone's treasure, and hied them unobserved to the coast, where Marato parted from his companions, and forthwith took the lady aboard the ship. The wind was now fair and fresh, the mariners spread the canvas, and the vessel sped on her course.

This new misadventure, following so hard upon the former, caused the lady no small chagrin; but Marato, with the aid, of the good St. Crescent-in-hand that God has given us, found means to afford her such consolation that she was already grown so familiar with him as entirely to forget Pericone, when Fortune, not content with her former caprices, added a new dispensation of woe; for what with. the beauty of her person, which, as we have often said, was extra ordinary, and the exquisite charm of her manners the two young men, who commanded the ship, fell so desperately in love with her that they thought of nothing but how they might best serve and please her, so only that Marato should not discover the reason of their assiduous attentions. And neither being ignorant of the other's love, they held secret counsel together, and resolved to make conquest of the lady on joint account: as if love admitted of being held in partnership like merchandise or money. Which design being thwarted by the jealousy with which Alatiel was guarded by Marato, they chose a day and hour, when the ship was speeding amain under canvas, and Marato was on the poop looking out over the sea and quite off his guard; and going stealthily up behind him, they suddenly laid hands on him, and threw him into the sea, and were already more than a mile on their course before any perceived that Marato was overboard. Which when the lady learned, and knew that he was irretrievably lost, she relapsed into her former plaintive mood. But the twain were forthwith by her side with soft speeches and profuse promises, which, however ill she understood them, were not altogether inapt to allay a grief which had in it more of concern for her own hapless self than of sorrow for her lost lover. So, in course of time, the lady beginning visibly to recover heart, they began privily to debate which of them should first take her to bed with him; and neither being willing to give way to the other, and no compromise being discoverable, high words passed between them, and the dispute grew so hot, that they both waxed very wroth, drew their knives, and rushed madly at one another, and before they could be parted by their men, several stabs had been given and received on either side, whereby the one fell dead on the spot, and the other was severely wounded in divers parts of the body. The lady was much disconcerted to find herself thus alone with none to afford her either succour or counsel, and was mightily afraid lest the wrath of the kinsfolk and friends of the twain should vent itself upon her. From this mortal peril she was, however, delivered by the intercessions of the wounded man and their speedy arrival at Klarenza.

As there she tarried at the same inn with her wounded lover, the fame of her great beauty was speedily bruited abroad, and reached the ears of the Prince of the Morea, who was then staying there. The Prince was curious to see her, and having so done, pronounced her even more beautiful than rumour had reported her; nay, he fell in love with her in such a degree that he could think of nought else; and having heard in what guise she had come thither, he deemed that he might have her. While he was casting about how to compass his end, the kinsfolk of the wounded man, being apprised of the fact, forthwith sent her to him to the boundless delight, as well of the lady, who saw therein her deliverance from a great peril, as of the Prince. The royal bearing, which enhanced the lady's charms, did not escape the Prince, who, being unable to discover her true rank, set her down as at any rate of noble lineage; wherefore he loved her as much again as before, and shewed her no small honour, treating her not as his mistress but as his wife. So the lady, contrasting her present happy estate with her past woes, was comforted; and, as her gaiety revived, her beauty waxed in such a degree that all the Morea talked of it and of little else: insomuch that the Prince's friend and kinsman, the young, handsome and gallant Duke of Athens, was smitten with a desire to see her, and taking occasion to pay the Prince a visit, as he was now and again wont to do, came to Klarenza with a goodly company of honourable gentlemen. The Prince received him with all distinction and made him heartily welcome, but did not at first shew him the lady. By and by, however, their conversation began to turn upon her and her charms, and the Duke asked if she were really so marvellous a creature as folk said. The Prince replied: – "Nay, but even more so; and thereof thou shalt have better assurance than my words, to wit, the witness of thine own eyes." So, without delay, for the Duke was now all impatience, they waited on the lady, who was prepared for their visit, and received them very courteously and graciously. They seated her between them, and being debarred from the pleasure of conversing with her, for of their speech she understood little or nothing, they both, and especially the Duke, who was scarce able to believe that she was of mortal mould, gazed upon her in mute admiration; whereby the Duke, cheating himself with the idea that he was but gratifying his curiosity, drank with his eyes, unawares, deep draughts of the poisoned chalice of love, and, to his own lamentable hurt, fell a prey to a most ardent passion. His first thought, when they had left her, and he had time for reflection, was that the Prince was the luckiest man in the world to have a creature so fair to solace him; and swayed by his passion, his mind soon inclined to divers other and less honourable meditations, whereof the issue was that, come what might, he would despoil the Prince of his felicity, and, if possible, make it his own. This resolution was no sooner taken than, being of a hasty temperament, he cast to the winds all considerations of honour and justice, and studied only how to compass his end by craft. So, one day, as the first step towards the accomplishment of his evil purpose, he arranged with the Prince's most trusted chamberlain, one Ciuriaci, that his horses and all other his personal effects should, with the utmost secrecy, be got ready against a possible sudden departure: and then at nightfall, attended by a single comrade (both carrying arms), he was privily admitted by Ciuriaci into the Prince's chamber. It was a hot night, and the Prince had risen without disturbing the lady, and was standing bare to the skin at an open window fronting the sea, to enjoy a light breeze that blew thence. So, by preconcert with his comrade, the Duke stole up to the window, and in a trice ran the Prince through the body, and caught him up, and threw him out of the window. The palace was close by the sea, but at a considerable altitude above it, and the window, through which the Prince's body was thrown, looked over some houses, which, being sapped by the sea, had become ruinous, and were rarely or never visited by a soul; whereby, as the Duke had foreseen, the fall of the Prince's body passed, as indeed it could not but pass, unobserved. Thereupon the Duke's accomplice whipped out a halter, which he had brought with him for the purpose, and, making as if he were but in play, threw it round Ciuriaci's neck, drew it so tight that he could not utter a sound, and then, with the Duke's aid, strangled him, and sent him after his master. All this was accomplished, as the Duke knew full well, without awakening any in the palace, not even the lady, whom he now approached with a light, and holding it over the bed gently uncovered her person, as she lay fast asleep, and surveyed her from head to foot to his no small satisfaction; for fair as she had seemed to him dressed, he found her unadorned charms incomparably greater. As he gazed, his passion waxed beyond measure, and, reckless of his recent crime, and of the blood which still stained his hands, he got forthwith into the bed; and she, being too sound asleep to distinguish between him and the Prince, suffered him to lie with her.

But, boundless as was his delight, it brooked no long continuance, so, rising, he called to him some of his comrades, by whom he had the lady secured in such manner that she could utter no sound, and borne out of the palace by the same secret door by which he had gained entrance; he then set her on horseback and in dead silence put his troop in motion, taking the road to Athens. He did not, however, venture to take the lady to Athens, where she would have encountered his Duchess – for he was married – but lodged her in a very beautiful villa which he had hard by the city overlooking the sea, where, most forlorn of ladies, she lived secluded, but with no lack of meet and respectful service.

On the following morning the Prince's courtiers awaited his rising until none, but perceiving no sign of it, opened the doors, which had not been secured, and entered his bedroom. Finding it vacant, they supposed that the Prince was gone off privily somewhere to have a few days of unbroken delight with his fair lady; and so they gave themselves no further trouble. But the next day it so chanced that an idiot, roaming about the ruins where lay the corpses of the Prince and Ciuriaci, drew the latter out by the halter and went off dragging it after him. The corpse was soon recognised by not a few, who, at first struck dumb with amazement, soon recovered sense enough to cajole the idiot into retracing his steps and shewing them the spot where he had found it; and having thus, to the immeasurable grief of all the citizens, discovered the Prince's body, they buried it with all honour. Needless to say that no pains were spared to trace the perpetrators of so heinous a crime, and that the absence and evidently furtive departure of the Duke of Athens caused him to be suspected both of the murder and of the abduction of the lady. So the citizens were instant with one accord that the Prince's brother, whom they chose as his successor, should exact the debt of vengeance; and he, having satisfied himself by further investigation that their suspicion was well founded, summoned to his aid his kinsfolk, friends and divers vassals, and speedily gathered a large, powerful and well-equipped army, with intent to make war upon the Duke of Athens. The Duke, being informed of his movements, made ready likewise to defend himself with all his power; nor had he any lack of allies, among whom the Emperor of Constantinople sent his son, Constantine, and his nephew, Manuel, with a great and goodly force. The two young men were honourably received by the Duke, and still more so by the Duchess, who was Constantine's sister.

Day by day war grew more imminent, and at last the Duchess took occasion to call Constantine and Manuel into her private chamber, and with many tears told them the whole story at large, explaining the casus belli, dilating on the indignity which she suffered at the hands of the Duke if as was believed, he really kept a mistress in secret, and beseeching them in most piteous accents to do the best they could to devise some expedient whereby the Duke's honour might be cleared, and her own peace of mind assured. The young men knew exactly how matters stood; and so, without wearying the Duchess with many questions, they did their best to console her, and succeeded in raising her hopes. Before taking their leave they learned from her where the lady was, whose marvellous beauty they had heard lauded so often; and being eager to see her, they besought the Duke to afford them an opportunity. Forgetful of what a like complaisance had cost the Prince, he consented, and next morning brought them to the villa where the lady lived, and with her and a few of his boon companions regaled them with a lordly breakfast, which was served in a most lovely garden. Constantine had no sooner seated himself and surveyed the lady, than he was lost in admiration, inly affirming that he had never seen so beautiful a creature, and that for such a prize the Duke, or any other man, might well be pardoned treachery or any other crime: he scanned her again and again, and ever with more and more admiration; where-by it fared with him even as it had fared with the Duke. He went away hotly in love with her, and dismissing all thought of the war, cast about for some method by which, without betraying his passion to any, he might devise some means of wresting the lady from the Duke.

As he thus burned and brooded, the Prince drew dangerously near the Duke's dominions; wherefore order was given for an advance, and the Duke, with Constantine and the rest, marshalled his forces and led them forth from Athens to bar the Prince's passage of the frontier at certain points. Some days thus passed, during which Constantine, whose mind and soul were entirely absorbed by his passion for the lady, bethought him, that, as the Duke was no longer in her neighbourhood, he might readily compass his end. He therefore feigned to be seriously unwell, and, having by this pretext obtained the Duke's leave, he ceded his command to Manuel, and returned to his sister at Athens. He had not been there many days before the Duchess recurred to the dishonour which the Duke did her by keeping the lady; whereupon he said that of that, if she approved, he would certainly relieve her by seeing that the lady was removed from the villa to some distant place. The Duchess, supposing that Constantine was prompted not by jealousy of the Duke but by jealousy for her honour, gave her hearty consent to his plan, provided he so contrived that the Duke should never know that she had been privy to it; on which point Constantine gave her ample assurance. So, being authorised by the Duchess to act as he might deem best, he secretly equipped a light bark and manned her with some of his men, to whom he confided his plan, bidding them lie to off the garden of the lady's villa; and so, having sent the bark forward, he hied him with other of his men to the villa. He gained ready admission of the servants, and was made heartily welcome by the lady, who, at his desire, attended by some of her servants, walked with him and some of his comrades in the garden. By and by, feigning that he had a message for her from the Duke, he drew her aside towards a gate that led down to the sea, and which one of his confederates had already opened. A concerted signal brought the bark alongside, and to seize the lady and set her aboard the bark was but the work of an instant. Her retinue hung back as they heard Constantine menace with death whoso but stirred or spoke, and suffered him, protesting that what he did was done not to wrong the Duke, but solely to vindicate his sister's honour, to embark with his men. The lady wept, of course, but Constantine was at her side, the rowers gave way, and the bark, speeding like a thing of life over the waves, made Egina shortly after dawn. There Constantine and the lady landed, she still lamenting her fatal beauty, and took a little rest and pleasure. Then, re-embarking, they continued their voyage, and in the course of a few days reached Chios, which Constantine, fearing paternal censure, and that he might be deprived of his fair booty, deemed a safe place of sojourn. So, after some days of repose the lady ceased to bewail her harsh destiny, and suffering Constantine to console her as his predecessors had done, began once more to enjoy the good gifts which Fortune sent her.

Now while they thus dallied, Osbech, King of the Turks, who was perennially at war with the Emperor, came by chance to Smyrna; and there learning, that Constantine was wantoning in careless ease at Chios with a lady of whom he had made prize, he made a descent by night upon the island with an armed flotilla. Landing his men in dead silence, he made captives of not a few of the Chians whom he surprised in their beds; others, who took the alarm and rushed to arms, he slew; and having wasted the whole island with fire, he shipped the booty and the prisoners, and sailed back to Smyrna. As there he overhauled the booty, he lit upon the fair lady, and knew her for the same that had been taken in bed and fast asleep with Constantine: whereat, being a young man, he was delighted beyond measure, and made her his wife out of hand with all due form and ceremony. And so for several months he enjoyed her.

Now there had been for some time and still was a treaty pending between the Emperor and Basano, King of Cappadocia, whereby Basano with his forces was to fall on Osbech on one side while the Emperor attacked him on the other. Some demands made by Basano, which the Emperor deemed unreasonable, had so far retarded the conclusion of the treaty; but no sooner had the Emperor learned the fate of his son than, distraught with grief, he forthwith conceded the King of Cappadocia's demands, and was instant with him to fall at once upon Osbech while he made ready to attack him on the other side. Getting wind of the Emperor's design, Osbech collected his forces, and, lest he should be caught and crushed between the convergent armies of two most mighty potentates, advanced against the King of Cappadocia. The fair lady he left at Smyrna in the care of a faithful dependant and friend, and after a while joined battle with the King of Cappadocia, in which battle he was slain, and his army defeated and dispersed. Wherefore Basano with his victorious host advanced, carrying everything before him, upon Smyrna, and receiving everywhere the submission due to a conqueror.

Meanwhile Osbech's dependant, by name Antioco, who had charge of the fair lady, was so smitten with her charms that, albeit he was somewhat advanced in years, he broke faith with his friend and lord, and allowed himself to become enamoured of her. He had the advantage of knowing her language, which counted for much with one who for some years had been, as it were, compelled to live the life of a deaf mute, finding none whom she could understand or by whom she might be understood; and goaded by passion, he in the course of a few days established such a degree of intimacy with her that in no long time it passed from friendship into love, so that their lord, far away amid the clash of arms and the tumult of the battle, was forgotten, and marvellous pleasure had they of one another between the sheets.

However, news came at last of Osbech's defeat and death, and the victorious and unchecked advance of Basano, whose advent they were by no means minded to await. Wherefore, taking with them the best part of the treasure that Osbech had left there, they hied them with all possible secrecy to Rhodes. There they had not along abode before Antioco fell ill of a mortal disease. He had then with him a Cypriote merchant, an intimate and very dear friend, to whom, as he felt his end approach, he resolved to leave all that he possessed, including his dear lady. So, when he felt death imminent, he called them to him and said: – "'Tis now quite evident to me that my life is fast ebbing away; and sorely do I regret it, for never had I so much pleasure of life as now. Well content indeed I am in one respect, in that, as die I must, I at least die in the arms of the two persons whom I love more than any other in the world, to wit, in thine arms, dearest friend, and those of this lady, whom, since I have known her, I have loved more than myself. But yet 'tis grievous to me to know that I must leave her here in a strange land with none to afford her either protection or counsel; and but that I leave her with thee, who, I doubt not, wilt have for my sake no less care of her than thou wouldst have had of me, 'twould grieve me still more; wherefore with all my heart and soul I pray thee, that, if I die, thou take her with all else that belongs to me into thy charge, and so acquit thyself of thy trust as thou mayst deem conducive to the peace of my soul. And of thee, dearest lady, I entreat one favour, that I be not forgotten of, thee, after my death, so that there whither I go it may still be my boast to be beloved here of the most beautiful lady that nature ever formed. Let me but die with these two hopes assured, and without doubt I shall depart in peace."

Both the merchant and the lady wept to hear him thus speak, and, when he had done, comforted him, and promised faithfully, in the event of his death, to do even as he besought them. He died almost immediately afterwards, and was honourably buried by them. A few days sufficed the merchant to wind up all his affairs in Rhodes and being minded to return to Cyprus aboard a Catalan boat that was there, he asked the fair lady what she purposed to do if he went back to Cyprus. The lady answered, that, if it were agreeable to him, she would gladly accompany him, hoping that for love of Antioco, he would treat and regard her as his sister. The merchant replied, that it would afford him all the pleasure in the world; and, to protect her from insult until their arrival in Cyprus, he gave her out as his wife, and, suiting action to word, slept with her on the boat in an alcove in a little cabin in the poop. Whereby that happened which on neither side was intended when they left Rhodes, to wit, that the darkness and the comfort and the warmth of the bed, forces of no mean efficacy, did so prevail with them that dead Antioco was forgotten alike as lover and as friend, and by a common impulse they began to wanton together, insomuch that before they were arrived at Baffa, where the Cypriote resided, they were indeed man and wife. At Baffa the lady tarried with the merchant a good while, during which it so befell that a gentleman, Antigono by name, a man of ripe age and riper wisdom but no great wealth, being one that had had vast and various experience of affairs in the service of the King of Cyprus but had found fortune adverse to him, came to Baffa on business; and passing one day by the house where the fair lady was then living by herself, for the Cypriote merchant was gone to Armenia with some of his wares, he chanced to catch sight of the lady at one of the windows, and, being struck by her extraordinary beauty, regarded her attentively, and began to have some vague recollection of having seen her before, but could by no means remember where. The fair lady, however, so long the sport of Fortune, but now nearing the term of her woes, no sooner saw Antigono than she remembered to have seen him in her father's service, and in no mean capacity, at Alexandria. Wherefore she forthwith sent for him, hoping that by his counsel she might elude her merchant and be reinstated in her true character and dignity of princess. When he presented himself, she asked him with some embarrassment whether he were, as she took him to be, Antigono of Famagosta. He answered in the affirmative, adding: – "And of you, madam, I have a sort of recollection, though I cannot say where I have seen you; wherefore so it irk you not, bring, I pray you, yourself to my remembrance." Satisfied that it was Antigono himself, the lady in a flood of tears threw herself upon him to his no small amazement, and embraced his neck: then, after a little while, she asked him whether he had never see her in Alexandria. The question awakened Antigono's memory; he at once recognised Alatiel, the Soldan's daughter, whom he had though to have been drowned at sea, and would have paid her due homage; but she would not suffer it, and bade him be seated with her for a while. Being seated, he respectfully asked her, how, and when and whence she had come thither, seeing that all Egypt believed for certain that she had been drowned at sea some years before. "And would that so it had been," said the lady, "rather than I should have led the life that

I have led; and so doubtless will my father say, if he shall ever come to know of it." And so saying, she burst into such a flood of tears that 'twas a wonder to see. Wherefore Antigono said to her: – "Nay but, madam, be not distressed before the occasion arises. I pray you, tell me the story of your adventures, and what has been the tenor of your life; perchance 'twill prove to be no such matter but, God helping us, we may set it all straight." "Antigono," said the fair lady, "when I saw thee, 'twas as if I saw my father, and 'twas the tender love by which I am holden to him that prompted me to make myself known to thee, though I might have kept my secret; and few indeed there are, whom to have met would have afforded me such pleasure as this which I have in meeting and recognising thee before all others; wherefore I will now make known to thee as to my father that which in my evil fortune I have ever kept close. If, when thou hast heard my story, thou seest any means whereby I may be reinstated in my former honour, I pray thee use it. If not, disclose to none that thou hast seen me or heard aught of me."

Then, weeping between every word, she told him her whole story from the day of the shipwreck at Majorca to that hour. Antigono wept in sympathy, and then said: – "Madam, as throughout this train of misfortunes you have happily escaped recognition, I undertake to restore you to your father in such sort that you shall be dearer to him than ever before, and be afterwards married to the King of Algarve. "How?" she asked. Whereupon he explained to her in detail how he meant to proceed; and, lest delay should give occasion to another to interfere, he went back at once to Famagosta, and having obtained audience of the King, thus he spoke: – "Sire, so please you, you have it in your power at little cost to yourself to do a thing, which will at once redound most signally to your honour and confer a great boon on me, who have grown poor in your service." "How?" asked the King. Then said Antigono: – "At Baffa is of late arrived a fair damsel, daughter of the Soldan, long thought to be drowned, who to preserve her chastity has suffered long and severe hardship. She is now reduced to poverty, and is desirous of returning to her father. If you should be pleased to send her back to him under my escort, your honour and my interest would be served in high and equal measure; nor do I think that such a service would ever be forgotten by the Soldan."

With true royal generosity the King forthwith signified his approval, and had Alatiel brought under honourable escort to Famagosta, where, attended by his Queen, he received her with every circumstance of festal pomp and courtly magnificence. Schooled by Antigono, she gave the King and Queen such a version of her adventures as satisfied their inquiries in every particular. So, after a few days, the King sent her back to the Soldan under escort of Antigono, attended by a goodly company of honourable men and women; and of the cheer which the Soldan made her, and not her only but Antigono and all his company, it boots not to ask. When she was somewhat rested, the Soldan inquired how it was that she was yet alive, and where she had been so long without letting him know how it fared with her. Whereupon the lady, who had got Antigono's lesson by heart, answered thus: – "My father, 'twas perhaps the twentieth night after my departure from you when our ship parted her timbers in a terrible storm and went ashore nigh a place called Aguamorta, away there in the West: what was the fate of the men that were aboard our ship I know not, nor knew I ever; I remember only, that, when day came, and I returned, as it were, from death to life, the wreck, having been sighted, was boarded by folk from all the country-side, intent on plunder; and I and two of my women were taken ashore, where the women were forthwith parted from me by the young men, nor did I ever learn their fate. Now hear my own. Struggling might and main, I was seized by two young men, who dragged me, weeping bitterly, by the hair of the head, towards a great forest; but, on sight of four men who were then passing that way on horseback, they forthwith loosed me and took to flight. Whereupon the four men, who struck me as persons of great authority, ran up to me; and much they questioned me, and much I said to them; but neither did they understand me, nor I them. So, after long time conferring together, they set me on one of their horses and brought me to a house, where dwelt a community of ladies, religious according to their law; and what the men may have said I know not, but there I was kindly received and ever honourably entreated by all; and with them I did afterwards most reverentially pay my devotions to St. Crescent-in-Hollow, who is held in great honour by the women of that country. When I had been some time with them, and had learned something of their language, they asked me who and whence I was: whereto I, knowing that I was in a convent, and fearing to be cast out as a foe to their law if I told the truth, answered that I was the daughter of a great gentleman of Cyprus, who had intended to marry me to a gentleman of Crete; but that on the voyage we had been driven out of our course and wrecked at Aguamorta. And so I continued, as occasion required, observing their usages with much assiduity, lest worse should befall me; but being one day asked by their superior, whom they call abbess, whether I was minded to go back to Cyprus, I answered that, there was nought that I desired so much. However, so solicitous for my honour was the abbess, that there was none going to Cyprus to whom she would entrust me, until, two months or so ago, there arrived some worthy men from France, of whom one was a kinsman of the abbess, with their wives. They were on their way to visit the sepulchre where He whom they hold to be God was buried after He had suffered death at the hands of the Jews; and the abbess, learning their destination, prayed them to take charge of me, and restore me to my father in Cyprus. With what cheer, with what honour, these gentlemen and their wives entertained me, 'twere long to tell. But, in brief, we embarked, and in the course of a few days arrived at Baffa, where it was so ordered by the providence of God, who perchance took pity on me, that in the very hour of our disembarkation I, not knowing a soul and being at a loss how to answer the gentlemen, who would fain have discharged the trust laid upon them by the reverend abbess and restored me to my father, fell in, on the shore, with Antigono, whom I forthwith called, and in our language, that I might be understood neither of the gentlemen nor of their wives, bade him acknowledge me as his daughter. He understood my case at once, made much of me, and to the utmost of his slender power honourably requited the gentlemen. He then brought me to the King of Cyprus, who accorded me welcome there and conduct hither so honourable as words of mine can never describe. If aught remains to tell, you had best learn it from the lips of Antigono, who has often heard my story."

Then Antigono, addressing the Soldan, said: – "Sire, what she has told you accords with what she has often told me, and, with what I have learned from the gentlemen and ladies who accompanied her. One thing, however, she has omitted, because, I suppose, it hardly becomes her to tell it; to wit, all that the gentlemen and ladies, who accompanied her, said of the virtuous and gracious and noble life which she led with the devout ladies, and of the tears and wailings of both the ladies and the gentlemen, when they parted with her to me. But were I to essay to repeat all that they said to me, the day that now is, and the night that is to follow, were all too short: suffice it to say so much as this, that, by what I gathered from their words and have been able to see for myself, you may make it your boast, that among all the daughters of all your peers that wear the crown none can be matched with yours for virtue and true worth."

By all which the Soldan was so overjoyed that 'twas a wonder to see. Again and again he made supplication to God, that of His grace power might be vouchsafed him adequately to recompense all who had done honour to his daughter, and most especially the King of Cyprus, for the honourable escort under which he had sent her thither; for Antigono he provided a magnificent guerdon, and some days later gave him his conge to return to Cyprus, at the same time by a special ambassage conveying to the King his grateful acknowledgments of the manner in which he had treated his daughter. Then, being minded that his first intent, to wit, that his daughter should be the bride of the King of Algarve, should not be frustrate, he wrote to the King, telling him all, and adding that, if he were still minded to have her, he might send for her. The King was overjoyed by these tidings, and having sent for her with great pomp, gave her on her arrival a hearty welcome. So she, who had lain with eight men, in all, perhaps, ten thousand times, was bedded with him as a virgin, and made him believe that a virgin she was, and lived long and happily with him as his queen: wherefore 'twas said: – "Mouth, for kisses, was never the worse: like as the moon reneweth her course."

Second Day
Novel VIII

— *The Count of Antwerp, labouring under a false accusation goes into exile. He leaves his two children in different places in England, and takes service in Ireland. Returning to England an unknown man, he finds his sons prosperous. He serves as a groom in the army of the King of France; his innocence is established and he is restored to his former honours.* —

THE LADIES HEAVED many sighs over the various fortunes of the fair lady: but what prompted those sighs who shall say? With some, perchance, 'twas as much envy as pity of one to whose lot fell so many nights of delight. But, however this may be, when Pamfilo's story was ended, and the laughter which greeted his last words had subsided, the queen turned to Elisa, and bade her follow suit with one of her stories. So Elisa with a cheerful courage thus began: –

Vast indeed is the field that lies before us, wherein to roam at large; 'twould readily afford each of us not one course but ten, so richly has Fortune diversified it with episodes both strange and sombre; wherefore selecting one such from this infinite store, I say: – That, after the transference of the Roman Empire from the Franks to the Germans, the greatest enmity prevailed between the two nations, with warfare perpetual and relentless: wherefore, deeming that the offensive would be their best defence, the King of France and his son mustered all the forces they could raise from their own dominions and those of their kinsmen and allies, and arrayed a grand army for the subjugation of their enemies. Before they took the field, as they could not leave the realm without a governor, they chose for that office Gautier, Count of Antwerp, a true knight and sage counsellor, and their very loyal ally and vassal, choosing him the rather, because, albeit he was a thorough master of the art of war, yet they deemed him less apt to support its hardships than for the conduct of affairs of a delicate nature. Him, therefore, they set in their place as their vicar-general and regent of the whole realm of France, and having so done, they took the field.

Count Gautier ordered his administration wisely and in a regular course, discussing all matters with the queen and her daughter-in-law; whom, albeit they were left under his charge and jurisdiction, he nevertheless treated as his ladies paramount. The Count was about forty years of age, and the very mould of manly beauty; in bearing as courteous and chivalrous as ever a gentleman might be, and withal so debonair and dainty, so feat and trim of person that he had not his peer, among the gallants of that day. His wife was dead, leaving him two children and no more, to wit, a boy and a girl, still quite young. Now the King and his son being thus away at the war, and the Count frequenting the court of the two said ladies, and consulting with them upon affairs of state, it so befell, that the Prince's lady regarded him with no small favour, being very sensible alike of the advantages of his person and the nobility of his bearing; whereby she conceived for him a passion which was all the more ardent because it was secret. And, as he was without a wife, and she was still in the freshness of her youth, she saw not why she should not readily be gratified; but supposing that nothing stood in the way but her own shamefastness, she resolved to be rid of that, and disclose her mind to him without any reserve. So one day, when she was alone, she seized her opportunity, and sent for him, as if she were desirous to converse with him on indifferent topics. The Count, his mind entirely aloof from the lady's purpose, presented himself forthwith, and at her invitation sate down by her side on a settee. They were quite alone in the room; but the Count had twice asked her the reason why she had so honoured him, before, overcome by passion, she broke silence, and crimson from neck with shame, half sobbing, trembling in every limb, and at every word, she thus spoke: – "Dearest friend and sweet my lord, sagacity such as yours cannot but be apt to perceive how great is the frailty of men and women, and how, for divers reasons, it varies in different persons in such a degree that no just judge would mete out the same measure to each indifferently, though the fault were apparently the same. Who would not acknowledge that a poor man or woman, fain to earn daily bread by the sweat of the brow, is far more reprehensible in yielding to the solicitations of love, than a rich lady, whose life is lapped in ease and unrestricted luxury? Not a soul, I am persuaded, but would so acknowledge! Wherefore I deem that the possession of these boons of fortune should go far indeed to acquit the possessor, if she, perchance, indulge an errant love; and, for the rest, that, if she have chosen a wise and worthy lover, she should be entirely exonerated. And as I think I may fairly claim the benefit of both these pleas, and of others beside, to wit, my youth and my husband's absence, which naturally incline me to love, 'tis meet that I now urge them in your presence in defence of my passion; and if they have the weight with you which they should have with the wise, I pray you to afford me your help and counsel in the matter wherein I shall demand it. I avow that in the absence of my husband I have been unable to withstand the promptings of the flesh and the power of love, forces of such potency that even the strongest men – not to speak of delicate women – have not seldom been, nay daily are, overcome by them; and so, living thus, as you see me, in ease and luxury, I have allowed the allurements of love to draw me on until at last I find myself a prey to passion. Wherein were I discovered, I were, I confess, dishonoured; but discovery being avoided, I count the dishonour all but nought. Moreover, love has been so gracious to me that not only has he spared to blind me in the choice of my lover, but he has even lent me his most effective aid, pointing me to one well worthy of the love of a lady such as I, even to yourself; whom, if I misread not my mind, I deem the most handsome and courteous and debonair, and therewithal the sagest cavalier that the realm of France may shew. And as you are without a wife, so may I say that I find myself without a husband. Wherefore in return for this great love I bear you, deny me not, I pray you, yours; but have pity on my youth, which wastes away for you like ice before the fire."

These words were followed by such a flood of tears, that, albeit she had intended yet further to press her suit, speech failed her; her eyes drooped, and, almost swooning with emotion, she let her head fall upon the Count's breast. The Count, who was the most loyal of knights, began with all severity to chide her mad passion and to thrust her from him – for she was now making as if she would throw her arms around his neck – and to asseverate with oaths that he would rather be hewn in pieces than either commit, or abet another in committing such an offence against the honour of his lord; when the lady, catching his drift, and forgetting all her love in a sudden frenzy of rage, cried out: – "So! unknightly knight, is it thus you flout my love? Now Heaven forbid, but, as you would be the death of me, I either do you to death or drive you from the world!" So saying, she dishevelled and tore her hair and rent her garments to shreds about her bosom. Which done, she began shrieking at the top of her voice: – "Help! help! The Count of Antwerp threatens to violate me!" Whereupon the Count, who knew that a clear conscience was no protection against the envy of courtiers, and doubted that his innocence would prove scarce a match for the cunning of the lady, started to his feet, and hied him with all speed out of the room, out of the palace, and back to his own house. Counsel of none he sought; but forthwith set his children on horseback, and taking horse himself, departed post haste for Calais. The lady's cries brought not a few to her aid, who, observing her plight, not only gave entire credence to her story, but improved upon it, alleging that the debonair and accomplished Count had long employed all the arts of seduction to compass his end. So they rushed in hot haste to the Count's house, with intent to arrest him, and not finding him, sacked it and razed it to the ground. The news, as glosed and garbled, being carried to the King and Prince in the field, they were mightily incensed, and offered a great reward for the Count, dead or alive, and condemned him and his posterity to perpetual banishment.

Meanwhile the Count, sorely troubled that by his flight his innocence shewed as guilt, pursued his journey, and concealing his identity, and being recognised by none, arrived with his two children at Calais. Thence he forthwith crossed to England, and, meanly clad, fared on for London, taking care as he went to school his children in all that belonged to their new way of life, and especially in two main articles: to wit, that they should bear with resignation the poverty to which, by no fault of theirs, but solely by one of Fortune's caprices, they and he were reduced, and that they should be most sedulously on their guard to betray to none, as they valued their lives, whence they were, or who their father was. The son, Louis by name, was perhaps nine, and the daughter, Violante, perhaps seven years of age. For years so tender they proved apt pupils, and afterwards shewed by their conduct that they had well learned their father's lesson. He deemed it expedient to change their names, and accordingly called the boy Perrot and the girl Jeannette. So, meanly clad, the Count and his two children arrived at London, and there made shift to get a living by going about soliciting alms in the guise of French mendicants.

Now, as for this purpose they waited one morning outside a church, it so befell that a great lady, the wife of one of the marshals of the King of England, observed them, as she left the church, asking alms, and demanded of the Count whence he was, and whether the children were his. He answered that he was from Picardy, that the children were his, and that he had been fain to leave Picardy by reason of the misconduct of their reprobate elder brother. The lady looked at the girl, who being fair, and of gentle and winning mien and manners, found much favour in her eyes. So the kind-hearted lady said to the Count: – "My good man, if thou art willing to leave thy little daughter with me, I like her looks so well that I will gladly take her; and if she grow up a good woman, I will see that she is suitably married when the right time comes." The Count was much gratified by the proposal, which he forthwith accepted, and parted with the girl, charging the lady with tears to take every care of her.

Having thus placed the girl with one in whom he felt sure that he might trust, he determined to tarry no longer in London; wherefore, taking Perrot with him and begging as he went, he made his way to Wales, not without great suffering, being unused to go afoot. Now in Wales another of the King's marshals had his court, maintaining great state and a large number of retainers; to which court, the Count and his son frequently repaired, there to get food; and there Perrot, finding the marshal's son and other gentlemen's sons vying with one another in boyish exercises, as running and leaping, little by little joined their company, and shewed himself a match or more for them all in all their contests. The marshal's attention being thus drawn to him, he was well pleased with the boy's mien and bearing, and asked who he was. He was told that he was the son of a poor man who sometimes came there to solicit alms. Whereupon he asked the Count to let him have the boy, and the Count, to whom God could have granted no greater boon, readily consented, albeit he was very loath to part with Perrot.

Having thus provided for his son and daughter, the Count resolved to quit the island; and did so, making his way as best he could to Stamford, in Ireland, where he obtained a menial's place in the service of a knight, retainer to one of the earls of that Country, and so abode there a long while, doing all the irksome and wearisome drudgery of a lackey or groom.

Meanwhile under the care of the gentle lady at London Violante or Jeannette increased, as in years and stature so also in beauty, and in such favour with the lady and her husband and every other member of the household and all who knew her that 'twas a wonder to see; nor was there any that, observing her bearing and manners, would not have said that estate or dignity there was none so high or honourable but she was worthy of it. So the lady, who, since she had received her from her father, had been unable to learn aught else about him than what he had himself told, was minded to marry her honourably according to what she deemed to be her rank. But God, who justly apportions reward according to merit, having regard to her noble birth, her innocence, and the load of suffering which the sin of another had laid upon her, ordered otherwise; and in His good providence, lest the young gentlewoman should be mated with a churl, permitted, we must believe, events to take the course they did.

The gentle lady with whom Jeannette lived had an only son, whom she and her husband loved most dearly, as well because he was a son as for his rare and noble qualities, for in truth there were few that could compare with him in courtesy and courage and personal beauty. Now the young man marked the extraordinary beauty and grace of Jeannette, who was about six years his junior, and fell so desperately in love with her that he had no eyes for any other maiden; but, deeming her to be of low degree, he not only hesitated to ask her of his parents in marriage, but, fearing to incur reproof for indulging a passion for an inferior, he did his utmost to conceal his love. Whereby it gave him far more disquietude than if he had avowed it; insomuch that – so extreme waxed his suffering – he fell ill, and that seriously. Divers physicians were called in, but, for all their scrutiny of his symptoms, they could not determine the nature of his malady, and one and all gave him up for lost. Nothing could exceed the sorrow and dejection of his father and mother, who again and again piteously implored him to discover to them the cause of his malady, and received no other answer than sighs or complaints that he seemed to be wasting away. Now it so happened that one day, Jeannette, who from regard for his mother was sedulous in waiting upon him, for some reason or another came into the room where he lay, while a very young but very skilful physician sate by him and held his pulse. The young man gave her not a word or other sign of recognition; but his passion waxed, his heart smote him, and the acceleration of his pulse at once betrayed his inward commotion to the physician, who, albeit surprised, remained quietly attentive to see how long it would last, and observing that it ceased when Jeannette left the room, conjectured that he was on the way to explain the young man's malady. So, after a while, still holding the young man's pulse, he sent for Jeannette, as if he had something to ask of her. She returned forthwith; the young man's pulse mounted as soon as she entered the room, and fell again as soon as she left it. Wherefore the physician no longer hesitated, but rose, and taking the young man's father and mother aside, said to them: – "The restoration of your son's health rests not with medical skill, but solely with Jeannette, whom, as by unmistakable signs I have discovered, he ardently loves, though, so far I can see, she is not aware of it. So you know what you have to do, if you value his life." The prospect thus afforded of their son's deliverance from death reassured the gentleman and his lady, albeit they were troubled, misdoubting it must be by his marriage with Jeannette. So, when the physician was gone, they went to the sick lad, and the lady thus spoke: – "My son, never would I have believed that thou wouldst have concealed from me any desire of thine, least of all if such it were that privation should cause thee to languish; for well assured thou shouldst have been and shouldst be, that I hold thee dear as my very self, and that whatever may be for thy contentment, even though it were scarce seemly, I would do it for thee; but, for all thou hast so done, God has shewn Himself more merciful to theeward than thyself, and, lest thou die of this malady, has given me to know its cause, which is nothing else than the excessive love which thou bearest to a young woman, be she who she may. Which love in good sooth thou needest not have been ashamed to declare; for it is but natural at thy age; and hadst thou not loved, I should have deemed thee of very little worth. So, my son, be not shy of me, but frankly discover to me thy whole heart; and away with this gloom and melancholy whereof thy sickness is engendered, and be comforted, and assure thyself that there is nought that thou mayst require of me which I will not do to give thee ease, so far as my powers may reach, seeing that thou art dearer to me than my own life. Away with thy shamefastness and fears, and tell me if there is aught wherein I may be helpful to thee in the matter of thy love; and if I bestir not myself and bring it to pass, account me the most harsh mother that ever bore son."

The young man was at first somewhat shamefast to hear his mother thus speak, but, reflecting that none could do more for his happiness than she, he took courage, and thus spoke: – "Madam, my sole reason for concealing my love from you was that I have observed that old people for the most part forget that they once were young; but, as I see that no such unreasonableness is to be apprehended in you, I not only acknowledge the truth of what you say that you have discerned, but I will also disclose to you the object of my passion, on the understanding that your promise shall to the best of your power be performed, as it must be, if I am to be restored to you in sound health." Whereupon the lady, making too sure of that which was destined to fall out otherwise than she expected, gave him every encouragement to discover all his heart, and promised to lose no time and spare no pains in endeavouring to compass his gratification. "Madam," said then the young man, "the rare beauty and exquisite manners of our Jeannette, my powerlessness to make her understand – I do not say commiserate – my love, and my reluctance to disclose it to any, have brought me to the condition in which you see me; and if your promise be not in one way or another performed, be sure that my life will be brief." The lady, deeming that the occasion called rather for comfort than for admonition, replied with a smile: – "Ah! my son, was this then of all things the secret of thy suffering? Be of good cheer, and leave me to arrange the affair, when you are recovered." So, animated by a cheerful hope, the young man speedily gave sign of a most marked improvement, which the lady observed with great satisfaction, and then began to cast about how she might keep her promise. So one day she sent for Jeannette, and in a tone of gentle raillery asked her if she had a lover. Jeannette turned very red as she answered: – "Madam, 'twould scarce, nay, 'twould ill become a damsel such as I, poor, outcast from home, and in the service of another, to occupy herself with thoughts of love." Whereto the lady answered: – "So you have none, we will give you one, who will brighten all your life and give you more joy of your beauty; for it is not right that so fair a damsel as you remain without a lover." "Madam," rejoined Jeannette, "you found me living in poverty with my father, you adopted me, you have brought me up as your daughter; wherefore I should, if possible, comply with your every wish; but in this matter I will render you no compliance, nor do I doubt that I do well. So you will give me a husband, I will love him, but no other will I love; for, as patrimony I now have none save my honour, that I am minded to guard and preserve while my life shall last." Serious though the obstacle was which these words opposed to the plan by which the lady had intended to keep her promise to her son, her sound judgment could not but secretly acknowledge that the spirit which they evinced was much to be commended in the damsel. Wherefore she said: – "Nay but, Jeannétte; suppose that our Lord the King, who is a young knight as thou art a most fair damsel, craved some indulgence of thy love, wouldst thou deny him?" "The King," returned Jeannette without the least hesitation, "might constrain me, but with my consent he should never have aught of me that was not honourable." Whereto the lady made no answer, for she now understood the girl's temper; but, being minded to put her to the proof, she told her son that, as soon as he was recovered, she would arrange that he should be closeted with her in the same room, and be thus able to use all his arts to bring her to his will, saying that it ill became her to play the part of procuress and urge her son's suit upon her own maid. But as the young man, by no means approving this idea, suddenly grew worse, the lady at length opened her mind to Jeannette, whom she found in the same frame as before, and indeed even more resolute. Wherefore she told her husband all that she had done; and as both preferred that their son should marry beneath him, and live, than that he should remain single and die, they resolved, albeit much disconcerted, to give Jeannette to him to wife; and so after long debate they did. Whereat Jeannette was overjoyed, and with devout heart gave thanks to God that He had not forgotten her; nevertheless she still gave no other account of herself than that she was the daughter of a Picard. So the young man recovered, and blithe at heart as ne'er another, was married, and began to speed the time gaily with his bride.

Meanwhile Perrot, left in Wales with the marshal of the King of England, had likewise with increase of years increase of favour with his master, and grew up most shapely and well-favoured, and of such prowess that in all the island at tourney or joust or any other passage of arms he had not his peer; being everywhere known and renowned as Perrot the Picard. And as God had not forgotten Jeannette, so likewise He made manifest by what follows that He had not forgotten Perrot. Well-nigh half the population of those parts being swept off by a sudden visitation of deadly pestilence, most of the survivors fled therefrom in a panic, so that the country was, to all appearance, entirely deserted. Among those that died of the pest were the marshal, his lady, and his son, besides brothers and nephews and kinsfolk in great number; whereby of his entire household there were left only one of his daughters, now marriageable, and a few servants, among them Perrot. Now Perrot being a man of such notable prowess, the damsel, soon after the pestilence had spent itself, took him, with the approval and by the advice of the few folk that survived, to be her husband, and made him lord of all that fell to her by inheritance. Nor was it long before the King of England, learning that the marshal was dead, made Perrot the Picard, to whose merit he was no stranger, marshal in the dead man's room. Such, in brief, was the history of the two innocent children, with whom the Count of Antwerp had parted, never expecting to see them again.

'Twas now the eighteenth year since the Count of Antwerp had taken flight from Paris, when, being still in Ireland, where he had led a very sorry and suffering sort of life, and feeling that age was now come upon him, he felt a longing to learn, if possible, what was become of his children. The fashion of his outward man was now completely changed; for long hardship had (as he well knew) given to his age a vigour which his youth, lapped in ease, had lacked. So he hesitated not to take his leave of the knight with whom he had so long resided, and poor and in sorry trim he crossed to England, and made his way to the place where he had left Perrot – to find him a great lord and marshal of the King, and in good health, and withal a hardy man and very handsome. All which was very grateful to the old man; but yet he would not make himself known to his son, until he had learned the fate of Jeannette. So forth he fared again, nor did he halt until he was come to London, where, cautiously questing about for news of the lady with whom he had left his daughter, and how it fared with her, he learned that Jeannette was married to the lady's son. Whereat, in the great gladness of his heart, he counted all his past adversity but a light matter, since he had found his children alive and prosperous. But sore he yearned to see Jeannette. Wherefore he took to loitering, as poor folk are wont, in the neighbourhood of the house. And so one day Jacques Lamiens – such was the name of Jeannette's husband – saw him and had pity on him, observing that he was poor and aged, and bade one of his servants take him indoors, and for God's sake give him something to eat; and nothing loath the servant did so. Now Jeannette had borne Jacques several children, the finest and the most winsome children in the world, the eldest no more than eight years old; who gathered about the Count as he ate, and, as if by instinct divining that he was their grandfather, began to make friends with him. He, knowing them for his grandchildren, could not conceal his love, and repaid them with caresses; insomuch that they would not hearken to their governor when he called them, but remained with the Count. Which being reported to Jeannette, she came out of her room, crossed to where the Count was sitting with the children, and bade them do as their master told them, or she would certainly have them whipped. The children began to cry, and to say that they would rather stay with the worthy man, whom they liked much better than their master; whereat both the lady and the Count laughed in sympathy. The Count had risen, with no other intention – for he was not minded to disclose his paternity – than to pay his daughter the respect due from his poverty to her rank, and the sight of her had thrilled his soul with a wondrous delight. By her he was and remained unrecognised; utterly changed as he was from his former self; aged, grey-haired, bearded, lean and tanned – in short to all appearance another man than the Count.

However, seeing that the children were unwilling to leave him, but wept when she made as if she would constrain them, she bade the master let them be for a time. So the children remained with the worthy man, until by chance Jacques' father came home, and learned from the master what had happened. Whereupon, having a grudge against Jeannette, he said: – "Let them be; and God give them the ill luck which He owes them: whence they sprang, thither they must needs return; they descend from a vagabond on the mother's side, and so 'tis no wonder that they consort readily with vagabonds." The Count caught these words and was sorely pained, but, shrugging his shoulders, bore the affront silently as he had borne many another. Jacques, who had noted his children's fondness for the worthy man, to wit, the Count, was displeased; but nevertheless, such was the love he bore them, that, rather than see them weep, he gave order that, if the worthy man cared to stay there in his service, he should be received. The Count answered that he would gladly do so, but that he was fit for nothing except to look after horses, to which he had been used all his life. So a horse was assigned him, and when he had groomed him, he occupied himself in playing with the children.

While Fortune thus shaped the destinies of the Count of Antwerp and his children, it so befell that after a long series of truces made with the Germans the King of France died, and his crown passed to his son, whose wife had been the occasion of the Count's banishment. The new king, as soon as the last truce with the Germans was run out, renewed hostilities with extraordinary vigour, being aided by his brother of England with a large army under the command of his marshal, Perrot, and his other marshal's son, Jacques Lamiens. With them went the worthy man, that is to say, the Count, who, unrecognised by any, served for a long while in the army in the capacity of groom, and acquitted himself both in counsel and in arms with a wisdom and valour unwonted in one of his supposed rank. The war was still raging when the Queen of France fell seriously ill, and, as she felt her end approach, made a humble and contrite confession of all her sins to the Archbishop of Rouen, who was universally reputed a good and most holy man. Among her other sins she confessed the great wrong that she had done to the Count of Antwerp; nor was she satisfied to confide it to the Archbishop, but recounted the whole affair, as it had passed, to not a few other worthy men, whom she besought to use their influence with the King to procure the restitution of the Count, if he were still alive, and if not, of his children, to honour and estate. And so, dying shortly afterwards, she was honourably buried.

The Queen's confession wrung from the King a sigh or two of compunction for a brave man cruelly wronged; after which he caused proclamation to be made throughout the army and in many other parts, that whoso should bring him tidings of the Count of Antwerp, or his children, should receive from him such a guerdon for each of them as should justly be matter of marvel; seeing that he held him acquitted, by confession of the Queen, of the crime for which he had been banished, and was therefore now minded to grant him not only restitution but increase of honour and estate.

Now the Count, being still with the army in his character of groom, heard the proclamation, which he did not doubt was made in good faith. Wherefore he hied him forthwith to Jacques, and begged a private interview with him and Perrot, that he might discover to them that whereof the King was in quest. So the meeting was had; and Perrot was on the point of declaring himself, when the Count anticipated him: – "Perrot," he said, "Jacques here has thy sister to wife, but never a dowry had he with her. Wherefore that thy sister be not dowerless, 'tis my will that he, and no other, have this great reward which the King offers for thee, son, as he shall certify, of the Count of Antwerp, and for his wife and thy sister, Violante, and for me, Count of Antwerp, thy father." So hearing, Perrot scanned the Count closely, and forthwith recognising him, burst into tears, and throwing himself at his feet embraced him, saying: – "My father, welcome, welcome indeed art thou." Whereupon, between what he had heard from the Count and what he had witnessed on the part of Perrot, Jacques was so overcome with wonder and delight, that at first he was at a loss to know how to act. However, giving entire credence to what he had heard, and recalling insulting language which he had used towards the quondam groom, the Count, he was sore stricken with shame, and wept, and fell at the Count's feet, and humbly craved his pardon for all past offences; which the Count, raising him to his feet, most graciously granted him. So with many a tear and many a hearty laugh the three men compared their several fortunes; which done, Perrot and Jacques would have arrayed the Count in manner befitting his rank, but he would by no means suffer it, being minded that Jacques, so soon as he was well assured that the guerdon was forthcoming, should present him to the King in his garb of groom, that thereby the King might be the more shamed. So Jacques, with the Count and Perrot, went presently to the King and offered to present to him the Count and his children, provided the guerdon were forthcoming according to the proclamation. Jacques wondered not a little as forthwith at a word from the King a guerdon was produced ample for all three, and he was bidden take it away with him, so only that he should in very truth produce, as he had promised, the Count and his children in the royal presence. Then, withdrawing a little and causing his quondam groom, now Count, to come forward with Perrot, he said: – "Sire, father and son are before you; the daughter, my wife, is not here, but, God willing, you shall soon see her." So hearing, the King surveyed the Count, whom, notwithstanding his greatly changed appearance, he at length recognised, and well-nigh moved to tears, he raised him from his knees to his feet, and kissed and embraced him. He also gave a kindly welcome to Perrot, and bade forthwith furnish the Count with apparel, servants and horses, suited to his rank; all which was no sooner said than done. Moreover the King shewed Jacques no little honour, and particularly questioned him of all his past adventures.

As Jacques was about to take the noble guerdons assigned him for the discovery of the Count and his children, the Count said to him: – "Take these tokens of the magnificence of our Lord the King, and forget not to tell thy father that 'tis from no vagabond that thy children, his and my grandchildren, descend on the mother's side." So Jacques took the guerdons, and sent for his wife and mother to join him at Paris. Thither also came Perrot's wife: and there with all magnificence they were entertained by the Count, to whom the King had not only restored all his former estates and honours, but added thereto others, whereby he was now become a greater man than he had ever been before. Then with the Count's leave they all returned to their several houses. The Count himself spent the rest of his days at Paris in greater glory than ever.

Second Day
Novel IX

— *Bernabo of Genoa, deceived by Ambrogiuolo, loses his money and commands his innocent wife to be put to death. She escapes, habits herself as a man, and serves the Soldan. She discovers the deceiver, and brings Bernabo to Alexandria, where the deceiver is punished. She then resumes the garb of a woman, and with her husband returns wealthy to Genoa.* —

WHEN ELISA had performed her part, and brought her touching story to a close, Queen Philomena, a damsel no less stately than fair of person, and of a surpassingly sweet and smiling mien, having composed herself to speak, thus began: –

Our engagements with Dioneo shall be faithfully observed; wherefore, as he and I alone remain to complete the day's narration, I will tell my story first, and he shall have the grace he craved, and be the last to speak. After which prelude she thus began her story: – 'Tis a proverb current among the vulgar that the deceived has the better of the deceiver; a proverb which, were it not exemplified by events, might hardly in any manner be justified. Wherefore, while adhering to our theme, I am minded at the same time dearest ladies to shew you that there is truth in this proverb; the proof whereof should be none the less welcome to you that it may put you on your guard against deceivers.

Know then that certain very great merchants of Italy, being met, as merchants use, for divers reasons proper to each, at a hostelry in Paris, and having one evening jovially supped together, fell a talking of divers matters, and so, passing from one topic to another, they came at last to discuss the ladies whom they had left at home, and one jocosely said: – "I cannot answer for my wife; but for myself I own, that, whenever a girl that is to my mind comes in my way, I give the go-by to the love that I bear my wife, and take my pleasure of the new-comer to the best of my power." "And so do I," said another, "because I know that, whether I suspect her or no, my wife tries her fortune, and so 'tis do as you are done by; the ass and the wall are quits." A third added his testimony to the same effect; and in short all seemed to concur in the opinion that the ladies they had left behind them were not likely to neglect their opportunities, when one, a Genoese, Bernabo Lomellin by name, dissociated himself from the rest, affirming that by especial grace of God he was blessed with a wife who was, perhaps, the most perfect paragon to be found in Italy of all the virtues proper to a lady, ay, and in great measure, to a knight or squire; inasmuch as she was fair, still quite young, handy, hardy, and clever beyond all other women in embroidery work and all other forms of lady's handicraft. Moreover so well-mannered, discreet and sensible was she that she was as fit to wait at a lord's table as any squire or manservant or such like, the best and most adroit that could be found. To which encomium he added that she knew how to manage a horse, fly a hawk, read, write and cast up accounts better than as if she were a merchant; and after much more in the same strain of commendation he came at length to the topic of their conversation, asseverating with an oath that 'twas not possible to find a woman more honest, more chaste than she: nay, he verily believed that, if he remained from home for ten years, or indeed for the rest of his days, she would never think of any of these casual amours with any other man.

Among the merchants who thus gossiped was a young man, Ambrogiuolo da Piacenza, by name, who, when Bernabo thus concluded his eulogy of his wife, broke out into a mighty laugh, and asked him with a leer, whether he of all men had this privilege by special patent of the Emperor. Bernabo replied, somewhat angrily, that 'twas a boon conferred upon him by God, who was rather more powerful than the Emperor. To which Ambrogiuolo rejoined: – "I make no doubt, Bernabo, that thou believest that what thou sayst is true; but, methinks, thou hast been but a careless observer of the nature of things; otherwise, I do not take thee to be of so gross understanding but that thou must have discerned therein reasons for speaking more judiciously of this matter. And that thou mayst not think that we, who have spoken with much freedom about our wives, deem them to be of another nature and mould than thine, but mayst know that we have but uttered what common sense dictates, I am minded to go a little further into this matter with thee. I have always understood, that of all mortal beings created by God man is the most noble, and next after him woman: man, then, being, as is universally believed, and is indeed apparent by his works, more perfect than woman, must without doubt be endowed with more firmness and constancy, women being one and all more mobile, for reasons not a few and founded in nature, which I might adduce, but mean for the present to pass over. And yet, for all his greater firmness, man cannot withstand – I do not say a woman's supplications, but – the mere lust of the eye which she unwittingly excites, and that in such sort that he will do all that is in his power to induce her to pleasure him, not once, perhaps, in the course of a month, but a thousand times a day. How, then, shouldst thou expect a woman, mobile by nature, to resist the supplications, the flatteries, the gifts, and all the other modes of attack that an accomplished seducer will employ? Thou thinkest that she may hold out! Nay verily, affirm it as thou mayst, I doubt thou dost not really so think. Thou dost not deny that thy wife is a woman, a creature of flesh and blood like the rest; and if so, she must have the same cravings, the same natural propensities as they, and no more force to withstand them; wherefore 'tis at least possible, that, however honest she be, she will do as others do; and nought that is possible admits such peremptory denial or affirmation of its contrary as this of thine."

Whereto Bernabo returned – "I am a merchant and no philosopher, and I will give thee a merchant's answer. I acknowledge that what thou sayst is true of vain and foolish women who have no modesty, but such as are discreet are so sensitive in regard of their honour that they become better able to preserve it than men, who have no such solicitude; and my wife is one of this sort." "Doubtless," observed Ambrogiuolo, "few would be found to indulge in these casual amours, if every time they did so a horn grew out on the brow to attest the fact; but not only does no horn make its appearance but not so much as a trace or vestige of a horn, so only they be but prudent; and the shame and dishonour consist only in the discovery: wherefore, if they can do it secretly, they do it, or are fools to refrain. Hold it for certain that she alone is chaste who either had never suit made to her, or, suing herself, was repulsed. And albeit I know that for reasons true and founded in nature this must needs be, yet I should not speak so positively thereof as I do, had I not many a time with many a woman verified it by experience. And I assure thee that, had I but access to this most saintly wife of thine, I should confidently expect very soon to have the same success with her as with others." Then Bernabo angrily: – "'Twere long and tedious to continue this discussion. I should have my say, and thou thine, and in the end 'twould come to nothing. But, as thou sayst that they are all so compliant, and that thou art so accomplished a seducer, I give thee this pledge of the honour of my wife: I consent to forfeit my head, if thou shouldst succeed in bringing her to pleasure thee in such a sort; and shouldst thou fail, thou shalt forfeit to me no more than one thousand florins of gold."

Elated by this unexpected offer, Ambrogiuolo replied: – "I know not what I should do with thy blood, Bernabo, if I won the wager; but, if thou wouldst have proof of what I have told thee, lay five thousand florins of gold, which must be worth less to thee than thy head, against a thousand of mine, and, whereas thou makest no stipulation as to time, I will bind myself to go to Genoa, and within three months from my departure hence to have had my pleasure of thy wife, and in witness thereof to bring back with me, of the things which she prizes most dearly, evidence of her compliance so weighty and conclusive that thou thyself shalt admit the fact; nor do I require ought of thee but that thou pledge thy faith neither to come to Genoa nor to write word to her of this matter during the said three months." Bernabo professed himself well content; and though the rest of the company, seeing that the compact might well have very evil consequences, did all that they could to frustrate it, yet the two men were now so heated that, against the will of the others, they set it down fairly in writing, and signed it each with his own hand. This done, Ambrogiuolo, leaving Bernabo at Paris, posted with all speed for Genoa. Arrived there, he set to work with great caution; and having found out the quarter in which the lady resided, he learned in the course of a few days enough about her habits of life and her character to know that what Bernabo had told him was rather less than the truth. So, recognising that his enterprise was hopeless, he cast about for some device whereby he might cover his defeat; and having got speech of a poor woman, who was much in the lady's house, as also in her favour, he bribed her (other means failing) to convey him in a chest, which he had had made for the purpose, not only into the house but into the bedroom of the lady, whom the good woman, following Bernabo's instructions, induced to take charge of it for some days, during which, she said, she would be away.

So the lady suffered the chest to remain in the room; and when the night was so far spent that Bernabo thought she must be asleep, he opened it with some tools with which he had provided himself, and stole softly out. There was a light in the room, so that he was able to form an idea of its situation, to take note of the pictures and everything else of consequence that it contained, and to commit the whole to memory. This done, he approached the bed; and observing that the lady, and a little girl that was with her, were fast asleep, he gently uncovered her, and saw that nude she was not a whit less lovely than when dressed: he looked about for some mark that might serve him as evidence that he had seen her in this state, but found nothing except a mole, which she had under the left breast, and which was fringed with a few fair hairs that shone like gold. So beautiful was she that he was tempted at the hazard of his life to take his place by her side in the bed; but, remembering what he had heard of her inflexible obduracy in such affairs, he did not venture; but quietly replaced the bedclothes; and having passed the best part of the night very much at his ease in her room, he took from one of the lady's boxes a purse, a gown, a ring and a girdle, and with these tokens returned to the chest, and locked himself in as before. In this manner he passed two nights, nor did the lady in the least suspect his presence. On the third day the good woman came by preconcert to fetch her chest, and took it back to the place whence she had brought it. So Ambrogiuolo got out, paid her the stipulated sum, and hied him back with all speed to Paris, where he arrived within the appointed time. Then, in presence of the merchants who were witnesses of his altercation with Bernabo, and the wager to which it had given occasion, he told Bernabo that he had won the bet, having done what he had boasted that he would do; and in proof thereof he first of all described the appearance of the room and the pictures, and then displayed the articles belonging to the lady which he had brought away with him, averring that she had given them to him. Bernabo acknowledged the accuracy of his description of the room, and that the articles did really belong to his wife, but objected that Ambrogiuolo might have learned characteristic features of the room from one of the servants, and have come by the things in a similar way, and therefore, unless he had something more to say, he could not justly claim to have won the bet. "Verily," rejoined Ambrogiuolo, "this should suffice; but, as thou requirest that I say somewhat further, I will satisfy thee. I say, then, that Madam Zinevra, thy wife, has under her left breast a mole of some size, around which are, perhaps, six hairs of a golden hue." As Bernabo heard this, it was as if a knife pierced his heart, so poignant was his suffering; and, though no word escaped him, the complete alteration of his mien bore unmistakable witness to the truth of Ambrogiuolo's words. After a while he said: – "Gentlemen, 'tis even as Ambrogiuolo says; he has won the bet; he has but to come when he will, and he shall be paid." And so the very next day Ambrogiuolo was paid in full, and Bernabo, intent on wreaking vengeance on his wife, left Paris and set his face towards Genoa. He had no mind, however, to go home, and accordingly halted at an estate which he had some twenty miles from the city, whither he sent forward a servant, in whom he reposed much trust, with two horses and a letter advising the lady of his return, and bidding her come out to meet him. At the same time he gave the servant secret instructions to choose some convenient place, and ruthlessly put the lady to death, and so return to him. On his arrival at Genoa the servant delivered his message and the letter to the lady, who received him with great cheer, and next morning got on horseback and set forth with him for her husband's estate. So they rode on, talking of divers matters, until they came to a deep gorge, very lonely, and shut in by high rocks and trees. The servant, deeming this just the place in which he might without risk of discovery fulfil his lord's behest, whipped out a knife, and seizing the lady by the arm, said: – "Madam, commend your soul to God, for here must end at once your journey and your life." Terror-stricken by what she saw and heard, the lady cried out: – "Mercy for God's sake; before thou slay me, tell me at least wherein I have wronged thee, that thou art thus minded to put me to death." "Madam," said the servant, "me you have in no wise wronged; but your husband – how you may have wronged him I know not – charged me shew you no mercy, but to slay you on this journey, and threatened to have me hanged by the neck, should I not do so. You know well how bound I am to him, and that I may not disobey any of his commands: God knows I pity you, but yet I can no otherwise." Whereat the lady burst into tears, saying: – "Mercy for God's sake; make not thyself the murderer of one that has done thee no wrong, at the behest of another. The all-seeing God knows that I never did aught to merit such requital at my husband's hands. But enough of this for the present: there is a way in which thou canst serve at once God and thy master and myself, if thou wilt do as I bid thee: take, then, these clothes of mine and give me in exchange just thy doublet and a hood; and carry the clothes with thee to my lord and thine, and tell him that thou hast slain me; and I swear to thee by the life which I shall have received at thy hands, that I will get me gone, and there abide whence news of me shall never reach either him or thee or these parts." The servant, being loath to put her to death, soon yielded to pity; and so he took her clothes, allowing her to retain a little money that she had, and gave her one of his worser doublets and a hood; then, praying her to depart the country, he left her afoot in the gorge, and returned to his master, whom he gave to understand that he had not only carried out his orders but had left the lady's body a prey to wolves. Bernabo after a while returned to Genoa, where, the supposed murder being bruited abroad, he was severely censured.

Alone and disconsolate, the lady, as night fell, disguised herself as best she could, and hied her to a neighbouring village, where, having procured what was needful from an old woman, she shortened the doublet and fitted it to her figure, converted her chemise into a pair of breeches, cut her hair close, and, in short, completely disguised herself as a sailor. She then made her way to the coast, where by chance she encountered a Catalan gentleman, by name Segner Encararch, who had landed from one of his ships, which lay in the offing, to recreate himself at Alba, where there was a fountain. So she made overture to him of her services, was engaged and taken aboard the ship, assuming the name Sicurano da Finale. The gentleman put her in better trim as to clothes, and found her so apt and handy at service that he was exceeding well pleased with her.

Not long afterwards the Catalan sailed one of his carracks to Alexandria. He took with him some peregrine falcons, which he presented to the Soldan, who feasted him once or twice; and noting with approbation the behaviour of Sicurano, who always attended his master, he craved him of the Catalan, which request the Catalan reluctantly granted. Sicurano proved so apt for his new service that he was soon as high in grace and favour with the Soldan as he had been with the Catalan. Wherefore, when the time of year came at which there was wont to be held at Acre, then under the Soldan's sway, a great fair, much frequented by merchants, Christian and Saracen alike, and to which, for the security of the merchants and their goods, the Soldan always sent one of his great officers of state with other officers and a guard to attend upon them, he determined to send Sicurano, who by this time knew the language very well. So Sicurano was sent to Acre as governor and captain of the guard for the protection of the merchants and merchandise. Arrived there, he bestirred himself with great zeal in all matters appertaining to his office; and as he went his rounds of inspection, he espied among the merchants not a few from Italy, Sicilians, Pisans, Genoese, Venetians, and so forth, with whom he consorted the more readily because they reminded him of his native land. And so it befell that, alighting once at a shop belonging to some Venetian merchants, he saw there among other trinkets a purse and a girdle, which he forthwith recognised as having once been his own. Concealing his surprise, he blandly asked whose they were, and if they were for sale. He was answered by Ambrogiuolo da Piacenza, who had come thither with much merchandise aboard a Venetian ship, and hearing that the captain of the guard was asking about the ownership of the purse and girdle, came forward, and said with a smile: – "The things are mine, Sir, and I am not disposed to sell them, but, if they take your fancy, I will gladly give them to you." Observing the smile, Sicurano misdoubted that something had escaped him by which Ambrogiuolo had recognised him; but he answered with a composed air: – "Thou dost smile, perchance, to see me, a soldier, come asking about this woman's gear?" "Not so, Sir," returned Ambrogiuolo; "I smile to think of the manner in which I came by it." "And pray," said Sicurano, "if thou hast no reason to conceal it, tell me, in God's name, how thou didst come by the things." " Why, Sir," said Ambrogiuolo, "they were given me by a Genoese lady, with whom I once spent a night, Madam Zinevra by name, wife of Bernabo Lomellin, who prayed me to keep them as a token of her love. I smiled just now to think of the folly of Bernabo, who was so mad as to stake five thousand florins of gold, against my thousand that I could not bring his wife to surrender to me; which I did. I won the bet; and he, who should rather have been punished for his insensate folly, than she for doing what all women do, had her put to death, as I afterwards gathered, on his way back from Paris to Genoa."

Ambrogiuolo had not done speaking before Sicurano had discerned in him the evident cause of her husband's animosity against her, and all her woe, and had made up her mind that he should not escape with impunity. She therefore feigned to be much interested by this story, consorted frequently and very familiarly with Ambrogiuolo, and insidiously captured his confidence, insomuch that at her suggestion, when the fair was done, he, taking with him all his wares, accompanied her to Alexandria, where she provided him with a shop, and put no little of her own money in his hands; so that he, finding it very profitable, was glad enough to stay. Anxious to make her innocence manifest to Bernabo, Sicurano did not rest until, with the help of some great Genoese merchants that were in Alexandria, she had devised an expedient to draw him thither. Her plan succeeded; Bernabo arrived; and, as he was now very poor, she privily arranged that he should be entertained by one of her friends until occasion should serve to carry out her design. She had already induced Ambrogiuolo to tell his story to the Soldan, and the Soldan to interest himself in the matter. So Bernabo being come, and further delay inexpedient, she seized her opportunity, and persuaded the Soldan to cite Ambrogiuolo and Bernabo before him, that in Bernabo's presence Ambrogiuolo might be examined of his boast touching Bernabo's wife, and the truth hereof, if not to be had from him by gentle means, be elicited by torture. So the Soldan, having Ambrogiuolo and Bernabo before him, amid a great concourse of his people questioned Ambrogiuolo of the five thousand florins of gold that he had won from Bernabo, and sternly bade him tell the truth. Still more harsh was the aspect of Sicurano, in whom Ambrogiuolo had placed his chief reliance, but who now threatened him with the direst torments if the truth were not forthcoming. Thus hard bested on this side and on that, and in a manner coerced, Ambrogiuolo, thinking he had but to refund, in presence of Bernabo and many others accurately recounted the affair as it had happened. When he had done, Sicurano, as minister of the Soldan for the time being, turned to Bernabo and said: – "And thy wife, thus falsely accused, what treatment did she meet with at thy hands?" "Mortified," said Bernabo, "by the loss of my money, and the dishonour which I deemed to have been done me by my wife, I was so overcome by wrath that I had her put to death by one of my servants, who brought me word that her corpse had been instantly devoured by a pack of wolves."

Albeit the Soldan had heard and understood all that had passed, yet he did not as yet apprehend the object for which Sicurano had pursued the investigation. Wherefore Sicurano thus addressed him: – "My lord, what cause this good lady has to boast of her lover and her husband you have now abundant means of judging; seeing that the lover at one and the same time despoils her of her honour, blasting her fair fame with slanderous accusations, and ruins her husband; who, more prompt to trust the falsehood of another than the verity of which his own long experience should have assured him, devotes her to death and the devouring wolves; and, moreover, such is the regard, such the love which both bear her that, though both tarry a long time with her, neither recognises her. However, that you may know full well what chastisements they have severally deserved, I will now cause her to appear in your presence and theirs, provided you, of your especial grace, be pleased to punish the deceiver and pardon the deceived." The Soldan, being minded in this matter to defer entirely to Sicurano, answered that he was well content, and bade produce the lady. Bernabo, who had firmly believed that she was dead, was lost in wonder; likewise Ambrogiuolo, who now divined his evil plight, and dreading something worse than the disbursement of money, knew not whether to expect the lady's advent with fear or with hope. His suspense was not of long duration; for, as soon as the Soldan signified his assent, Sicurano, weeping, threw herself on her knees at his feet, and discarding the tones, as she would fain have divested herself of the outward semblance, of a man, said: – "My lord, that forlorn, hapless Zinevra am I, falsely and foully slandered by this traitor Ambrogiuolo, and by my cruel and unjust husband delivered over to his servant to slaughter and cast out as a prey to the wolves; for which cause I have now for six years been a wanderer on the face of the earth in the guise of a man." Then rending her robes in front and baring her breast, she made it manifest to the Soldan and all others who were present, that she was indeed a woman; then turning to Ambrogiuolo she haughtily challenged him to say when she had ever lain with him, as he had boasted. Ambrogiuolo said never a word, for he now recognised her, and it was as if shame had reft from him the power of speech. The Soldan, who had never doubted that

Sicurano was a man, was so wonder-struck by what he saw and heard that at times he thought it must be all a dream. But, as wonder gave place to conviction of the truth, he extolled in the amplest terms the constancy and virtue and seemliness with which Zinevra, erstwhile Sicurano, had ordered her life. He then directed that she should be most nobly arrayed in the garb of her sex and surrounded by a bevy of ladies. Mindful of her intercession, he granted to Bernabo the life which he had forfeited; and she, when Bernabo threw himself at her feet and wept and craved her pardon, raised him, unworthy though he was, to his feet and generously forgave him, and tenderly embraced him as her husband. Ambrogiuolo the Soldan commanded to be bound to a stake, that his bare flesh, anointed with honey, might be exposed to the sun on one of the heights of the city, there to remain until it should fall to pieces of its own accord: and so 'twas done. He then decreed that the lady should have the traitor's estate, which was worth not less but rather more than ten thousand doubloons; whereto he added, in jewels and vessels of gold and silver and in money, the equivalent of upwards of other ten thousand doubloons, having first entertained her and her husband with most magnificent and ceremonious cheer, accordant with the lady's worth. Which done, he placed a ship at their disposal, and gave them leave to return to Genoa at their pleasure. So to Genoa they returned very rich and happy, and were received with all honour, especially Madam Zinevra, whom all the citizens had believed to be dead, and whom thenceforth, so long as she lived, they held of great consequence and excellency. As for Ambrogiuolo, the very same day that he was bound to the stake, the honey with which his body was anointed attracted such swarms of flies, wasps and gadflies, wherewith that country abounds, that not only was his life sucked from him but his very bones were completely denuded of flesh; in which state, hanging by the sinews, they remained a long time undisturbed, for a sign and a testimony of his baseness to all that passed by. And so the deceived had the better of the deceiver.

Second Day
Novel X

— *Paganino da Monaco carries off the wife of Messer Ricciardo di Chinzica, who, having learned where she is, goes to Paganino and in a friendly manner asks him to restore her. He consents, provided she be willing. She refuses to go back with her husband. Messer Ricciardo dies, and she marries Paganino.* —

THEIR QUEEN'S STORY, by its beauty, elicited hearty commendation from all the honourable company, and most especially from Dioneo, with whom it now rested to conclude the day's narration. Again and again he renewed his eulogy of the queen's story; and then began on this wise: –

Fair ladies, there is that in the queen's story which has caused me to change my purpose, and substitute another story for that which I had meant to tell: I refer to the insensate folly of Bernabo (well though it was with him in the end) and of all others who delude themselves, as he seemed to do, with the vain imagination that, while they go about the world, taking their pleasure now of this, now of the other woman, their wives, left at home, suffer not their hands to stray from their girdles; as if we who are born of them and bred among them, could be ignorant of the bent of their desires. Wherefore, by my story I purpose at one and the same time to shew you how great is the folly of all such, and how much greater is the folly of those who, deeming themselves mightier than nature, think by sophistical arguments to bring that to pass which is beyond their power, and strive might and main to conform others to their own pattern, however little the nature of the latter may brook such treatment. Know then that there was in Pisa a judge, better endowed with mental than with physical vigour, by name Messer Ricciardo di Chinzica, who, being minded to take a wife, and thinking, perhaps, to satisfy her by the same resources which served him for his studies, was to be suited with none that had not both youth and beauty, qualities which he would rather have eschewed, if he had known how to give himself as good counsel as he gave to others. However, being very rich, he had his desire. Messer Lotto Gualandi gave him in marriage one of his daughters, Bartolomea by name, a maid as fair and fit for amorous dalliance as any in Pisa, though few maids be there that do not shew as spotted lizards. The judge brought her home with all pomp and ceremony, and had a brave and lordly wedding; but in the essay which he made the very first night to serve her so as to consummate the marriage he made a false move, and drew the game much to his own disadvantage; for next morning his lean, withered and scarce animate frame was only to be re-quickened by draughts of vernaccia, artificial restoratives and the like remedies. So, taking a more sober estimate of his powers than he had been wont, the worthy judge began to give his wife lessons from a calendar, which might have served as a horn-book, and perhaps had been put together at Ravenna inasmuch as, according to his shewing, there was not a day in the year but was sacred, not to one saint only, but to many; in honour of whom for divers reasons it behoved men and women to abstain from carnal intercourse; whereto he added fast-days, Ember-days, vigils of Apostles and other saints, Friday, Saturday, Sunday, the whole of Lent, certain lunar mansions, and many other exceptions, arguing perchance, that the practice of men with women abed should have its times of vacation no less than the administration of the law. In this method, which caused the lady grievous dumps, he long persisted, hardly touching her once a month, and observing her closely, lest another should give her to know working-days, as he had taught her holidays.

Now it so befell that, one hot season, Messer Ricciardo thought he would like to visit a very beautiful estate which he had near Monte Nero, there to take the air and recreate himself for some days, and thither accordingly he went with his fair lady. While there, to amuse her, he arranged for a day's fishing; and so, he in one boat with the fishermen, and she in another with other ladies, they put out to watch the sport, which they found so delightsome, that almost before they knew where they were they were some miles out to sea. And while they were thus engrossed with the sport, a galliot of Paganino da Mare, a very famous corsair of those days, hove in sight and bore down upon the boats, and, for all the speed they made, came up with that in which were the ladies; and on sight of the fair lady Paganino, regardless of all else, bore her off to his galliot before the very eyes of Messer Ricciardo, who was by this time ashore, and forthwith was gone. The chagrin of the judge, who was jealous of the very air, may readily be imagined. But 'twas to no purpose that, both at Pisa and elsewhere, he moaned and groaned over the wickedness of the corsairs, for he knew neither by whom his wife had been abducted, nor whither she had been taken. Paganino, meanwhile, deemed himself lucky to have gotten so beautiful a prize; and being unmarried, he was minded never to part with her, and addressed himself by soft words to soothe the sorrow which kept her in a flood of tears. Finding words of little avail, he at night passed – the more readily that the calendar had slipped from his girdle, and all feasts and holidays from his mind – to acts of love, and on this wise administered consolation so effective that before they were come to Monaco she had completely forgotten the judge and his canons, and had begun to live with Paganino as merrily as might be. So he brought her to Monaco, where, besides the daily and nightly solace which he gave her, he honourably entreated her as his wife.

Not long afterwards Messer Ricciardo coming to know where his wife was, and being most ardently desirous to have her back, and thinking none but he would understand exactly what to do in the circumstances, determined to go and fetch her himself, being prepared to spend any sum of money that might be demanded by way of ransom. So he took ship, and being come to Monaco, he both saw her and was seen by her; which news she communicated to Paganino in the evening, and told him how she was minded to behave. Next morning Messer Ricciardo, encountering Paganino, made up to him; and soon assumed a very familiar and friendly air, while Paganino pretended not to know him, being on his guard to see what he would be at. So Messer Ricciardo, as soon as he deemed the time ripe, as best and most delicately he was able, disclosed to Paganino the business on which he had come, praying him to take whatever in the way of ransom he chose and restore him the lady. Paganino replied cheerily: – "Right glad I am to see you here, Sir; and briefly thus I answer you: – True it is that I have here a young woman; whether she be your wife or another man's, I know not, for you are none of my acquaintance, nor is she, except for the short time that she has been with me. If, as you say, you are her husband, why, as you seem to me to be a pleasant gentleman, I will even take you to her, and I doubt not she will know you well; if she says that it is even as you say, and is minded to go with you, you shall give me just what you like by way of ransom, so pleasant have I found you; otherwise 'twill be churlish in you to think of taking her from me, who am a young man, and as fit to keep a woman as another, and moreover never knew any woman so agreeable." "My wife," said Ricciardo, "she is beyond all manner of doubt, as thou shalt see; for so soon as thou bringest me to her, she will throw her arms about my neck; wherefore as thou art minded, even so be it; I ask no more." "Go we then," said Paganino; and forthwith they went into the house, and Paganino sent for the lady while they waited in one of the halls. By and by she entered from one of the adjoining rooms all trim and tricked out, and advanced to the place where Paganino and Messer Ricciardo were standing, but never a word did she vouchsafe to her husband, any more than if he had been some stranger whom Paganino had brought into the house. Whereat the judge was mightily amazed, having expected to be greeted by her with the heartiest of cheer, and began to ruminate thus: – Perhaps I am so changed by the melancholy and prolonged heartache, to which I have been a prey since I lost her, that she does not recognise me. Wherefore he said: – "Madam, cause enough have I to rue it that I took thee a fishing, for never yet was known such grief as has been mine since I lost thee; and now it seems as if thou dost not recognise me, so scant of courtesy is thy greeting. Seest thou not that I am thy Messer Ricciardo, come hither prepared to pay whatever this gentleman, in whose house we are, may demand, that I may have thee back and take thee away with me: and he is so good as to surrender thee on my own terms?" The lady turned to him with a slight smile, and said: – "Is it to me you speak, Sir? Bethink you that you may have mistaken me for another, for I, for my part, do not remember ever to have seen you." "Nay," said Messer Ricciardo, "but bethink thee what thou sayst; scan me closely; and if thou wilt but search thy memory, thou wilt find that I am thy Ricciardo di Chinzica." "Your pardon, Sir," answered the lady, "'tis not, perhaps, as seemly for me, as you imagine, to gaze long upon you; but I have gazed long enough to know that I never saw you before." Messer Ricciardo supposed that she so spoke for fear of Paganino, in whose presence she durst not acknowledge that she knew him: so, after a while, he craved as a favour of Paganino that he might speak with her in a room alone. Which request Paganino granted, so only that he did not kiss her against her will. He then bade the lady go with Messer Ricciardo into a room apart, and hear what he had to say, and give him such answer as she deemed meet. So the lady and Messer Ricciardo went together into a room alone, and sate down, and Messer Ricciardo began on this wise: – "Ah! dear heart of me, sweet soul of me, hope of me, dost not recognise thy Ricciardo that loves thee better than himself? how comes it thus to pass? am I then so changed? Ah! goodly eye of me, do but look on me a little." Whereat the lady burst into a laugh, and interrupting him, said: – "Rest assured that my memory is not so short but that I know you for what you are, my husband, Messer Ricciardo di Chinzica; but far enough you shewed yourself to be, while I was with you, from knowing me for what I was, young, lusty, lively; which, had you been the wise man you would fain be reputed, you would not have ignored, nor by consequence that which, besides food and clothing, it behoves men to give young ladies, albeit for shame they demand it not; which in what sort you gave, you know. You should not have taken a wife if she was to be less to you than the study of the law, albeit 'twas never as a judge that I regarded you, but rather as a bellman of encaenia and saints' days, so well you knew them all, and fasts and vigils. And I tell you that, had you imposed the observance of as many saints' days on the labourers that till your lands as on yourself who had but my little plot to till, you would never have harvested a single grain of corn. God in His mercy, having regard unto my youth, has caused me to fall in with this gentleman, with whom I am much closeted in this room, where nought is known of feasts, such feasts, I mean, as you, more devoted to the service of God than to the service of ladies, were wont to observe in such profusion; nor was this threshold ever crossed by Saturday or Friday or vigil or Ember-days or Lent, that is so long; rather here we are at work day and night, threshing the wool, and well I know how featly it went when the matin bell last sounded. Wherefore with him I mean to stay, and to work while I am young, and postpone the observance of feasts and times of indulgence and fasts until I am old: so get you hence, and good luck go with you, but depart with what speed you may, and observe as many feasts as you like, so I be not with you."

The pain with which Messer Ricciardo followed this outburst was more than he could bear, and when she had done, he exclaimed: – "Ah! sweet soul of me, what words are these that thou utterest? Hast thou no care for thy parents' honour and thine own? Wilt thou remain here to be this man's harlot, and to live in mortal sin, rather than live with me at Pisa as my wife? Why, when he is tired of thee, he will cast thee out to thy most grievous dishonour. I will ever cherish thee, and ever, will I nill I, thou wilt be the mistress of my house. Wouldst thou, to gratify this unbridled and unseemly passion, part at once with thy honour and with me, who love thee more dearly than my very life? Ah! cherished hope of me, say not so again: make up thy mind to come with me. As I now know thy bent, I will henceforth constrain myself to pleasure thee: wherefore, sweet my treasure, think better of it, and come with me, who have never known a happy hour since thou wert reft from me." The lady answered: – "I expect not, nor is it possible, that another should be more tender of my honour than I am myself. Were my parents so, when they gave me to you? I trow not; nor mean I to be more tender of their honour now than they were then of mine. And if now I live in mortar sin, I will ever abide there until it be pestle sin: concern yourself no further on my account. Moreover, let me tell you, that, whereas at Pisa 'twas as if I were your harlot, seeing that the planets in conjunction according to lunar mansion and geometric square intervened between you and me, here with Paganino I deem myself a wife, for he holds me in his arms all night long and hugs and bites me, and how he serves me, God be my witness. Ah! but you say you will constrain yourself to serve me: to what end? to do it on the third essay, and raise it by stroke of baton? I doubt not you are become a perfect knight since last I saw you. Begone, and constrain yourself to live; for here, methinks, your tenure is but precarious, so hectic and wasted is your appearance. Nay more; I tell you this, that, should Paganino desert me (which he does not seem disposed to do so long as I am willing to stay with him), never will I return to your house, where for one while I staid to my most grievous loss and prejudice, but will seek my commodity elsewhere, than with one from whose whole body I could not wring a single cupful of sap. So, again, I tell you that here is neither feast nor vigil; wherefore here I mean to abide; and you, get you gone, in God's name with what speed you may, lest I raise the cry that you threaten to violate me."

Messer Ricciardo felt himself hard bested, but he could not but recognise that, worn out as he was, he had been foolish to take a young wife; so sad and woebegone he quitted the room, and, after expending on Paganino a wealth of words which signified nothing, he at last gave up his bootless enterprise, and leaving the lady to her own devices, returned to Pisa; where for very grief he lapsed into such utter imbecility that, when he was met by any with greeting or question in the street, he made no other answer than "the evil hole brooks no holiday," and soon afterwards died. Which when Paganino learned, being well assured of the love the lady bore him, he made her his lawful wife; and so, keeping neither feast nor vigil nor Lent, they worked as hard as their legs permitted, and had a good time. Wherefore, dear my ladies, I am of opinion that Messer Bernabo in his altercation with Ambrogiuolo rode the goat downhill.

This story provoked so much laughter that the jaws of every one in the company ached; and all the ladies by common consent acknowledged that Dioneo was right, and pronounced Bernabo a blockhead. But when the story was ended and the laughter had subsided, the queen, observing that the hour was now late, and that with the completion of the day's story-telling the end of her sovereignty was come, followed the example of her predecessor, and took off her wreath and set it on Neifile's brow, saying with gladsome mien, "Now, dear gossip, thine be the sovereignty of this little people;" and so she resumed her seat. Neifile coloured somewhat to receive such honour, shewing of aspect even as the fresh-blown rose of April or May in the radiance of the dawn, her eyes rather downcast, and glowing with love's fire like the morning-star. But when the respectful murmur, by which the rest of the company gave blithe token of the favour in which they held their queen, was hushed, and her courage revived, she raised herself somewhat more in her seat than she was wont, and thus spoke: – "As so it is that I am your queen, I purpose not to depart from the usage observed by my predecessors, whose rule has commanded not only your obedience but your approbation. I will therefore in few words explain to you the course which, if it commend itself to your wisdom, we will follow. To-morrow, you know, is Friday, and the next day Saturday, days which most folk find somewhat wearisome by reason of the viands which are then customary, to say nothing of the reverence in which Friday is meet to be held, seeing that 'twas on that day that He who died for us bore His passion; wherefore 'twould be in my judgment both right and very seemly, if, in honour of God, we then bade story-telling give place to prayer. On Saturday ladies are wont to wash the head, and rid their persons of whatever of dust or other soilure they may have gathered by the labours of the past week; not a few, likewise, are wont to practise abstinence for devotion to the Virgin Mother of the Son of God, and to honour the approaching Sunday by an entire surcease from work. Wherefore, as we cannot then completely carry out our plan of life, we shall, I think, do well to intermit our story-telling on that day also. We shall then have been here four days; and lest we should be surprised by new-comers, I deem it expedient that we shift our quarters, and I have already taken thought for our next place of sojourn. Where, being arrived on Sunday, we will assemble after our sleep; and, whereas to-day our discourse has had an ample field to range in, I propose, both because you will thereby have more time for thought, and it will be best to set some limits to the license of our story-telling, that of the many diversities of Fortune's handiwork we make one our theme, whereof I have also made choice, to wit, the luck of such as have painfully acquired some much-coveted thing, or having lost, have recovered it. Whereon let each meditate some matter, which to tell may be profitable or at least delectable to the company, saving always Dioneo's privilege." All applauded the queen's speech and plan, to which, therefore, it was decided to give effect. Thereupon the queen called her seneschal, told him where to place the tables that evening, and then explained to him all that he had to do during the time of her sovereignty. This done, she rose with her train, and gave leave to all to take their pleasure as to each might seem best. So the ladies and the men hied them away to a little garden, where they diverted themselves a while; then supper-time being come, they supped with all gay and festal cheer. When they were risen from the table, Emilia, at the queen's command, led the dance, while Pampinea, the other ladies responding, sang the ensuing song.

> *Shall any lady sing, if I not sing,*
> *I to whom Love did full contentment bring?*
>
> *Come hither, Love, thou cause of all my joy,*
> *Of all my hope, and all its sequel blest,*
>   *And with me tune the lay,*
> *No more to sighs and bitter past annoy,*
> *That now but serve to lend thy bliss more zest;*
>   *But to that fire's clear ray,*
> *Wherewith enwrapt I blithely live and gay,*
> *Thee as my God for ever worshipping.*

> 'Twas thou, O Love, didst set before mine eyes,
> When first thy fire my soul did penetrate,
>   A youth to be my fere,
> So fair, so fit for deeds of high emprise,
> That ne'er another shall be found more great,
>   Nay, nor, I ween, his peer:
> Such flame he kindled that my heart's full cheer
> I now pour out in chant with thee, my King.
>
> And that wherein I most delight is this,
> That as I love him, so he loveth me:
>   So thank thee, Love, I must.
> For whatsoe'er this world can yield of bliss
> Is mine, and in the next at peace to be
>   I hope through that full trust
> I place in him. And thou, O God, that dost
> It see, wilt grant of joy thy plenishing.

Some other songs and dances followed, to the accompaniment of divers sorts of music; after which, the queen deeming it time to go to rest, all, following in the wake of the torches, sought their several chambers. The next two days they devoted to the duties to which the queen had adverted, looking forward to the Sunday with eager expectancy.

> — Endeth here the second day of the Decameron, beginneth the third, in which, under the rule of Neifile, discourse is had of the fortune of such as have painfully acquired some much-coveted thing, or, having lost, have recovered it. —

THE DAWN OF SUNDAY was already changing from vermilion to orange, as the sun hasted to the horizon, when the queen rose and roused all the company. The seneschal had early sent forward to their next place of sojourn ample store of things meet with folk to make all things ready, and now seeing the queen on the road, and the decampment, as it were, begun, he hastily completed the equipment of the baggage-train, and set off therewith, attended by the rest of the servants, in rear of the ladies and gentlemen. So, to the chant of, perhaps, a score of nightingales and other birds, the queen, her ladies and the three young men trooping beside or after her, paced leisurely westward by a path little frequented and overgrown with herbage and flowers, which, as they caught the sunlight, began one and all to unfold their petals. So fared she on with her train, while the quirk and the jest and the laugh passed from mouth to mouth; nor had they completed more than two thousand paces when, well before half tierce, they arrived at a palace most fair and sumptuous, which stood out somewhat from the plain, being situate upon a low eminence. On entering, they first traversed its great halls and dainty chambers furnished throughout with all brave and meet appointments; and finding all most commendable, they reputed its lord a magnifico. Then descending, they surveyed its spacious and cheerful court, its vaults of excellent wines and copious springs of most cool water, and found it still more commendable. After which, being fain of rest, they sat them down in a gallery which commanded the court, and was close imbosked with leafage and such flowers as the season afforded, and thither the discreet seneschal brought comfits and wines most choice and excellent, wherewith they were refreshed. Whereupon they hied them to a walled garden adjoining the palace; which, the gate being opened, they entered, and wonder-struck by the beauty of the whole passed on to examine more attentively the several parts. It was bordered and traversed in many parts by alleys, each very wide and straight as an arrow and roofed in with trellis of vines, which gave good promise of bearing clusters that year, and, being all in flower, dispersed such fragrance throughout the garden as blended with that exhaled by many another plant that grew therein made the garden seem redolent of all the spices that ever grew in the East. The sides of the alleys were all, as it were, walled in with roses white and red and jasmine; insomuch that there was no part of the garden but one might walk there not merely in the morning but at high noon in grateful shade and fragrance, completely screened from the sun. As for the plants that were in the garden, 'twere long to enumerate them, to specify their sorts, to describe the order of their arrangement; enough, in brief, that there was abundance of every rarer species that our climate allows. In the middle of the garden, a thing not less but much more to be commended than aught else, was a lawn of the finest turf, and so green that it seemed almost black, pranked with flowers of, perhaps, a thousand sorts, and girt about with the richest living verdure of orange-trees and cedars, which shewed not only flowers but fruits both new and old, and were no less grateful to the smell by their fragrance than to the eye by their shade. In the middle of the lawn was a basin of whitest marble, graven with marvellous art; in the centre whereof – whether the spring were natural or artificial I know not – rose a column supporting a figure which sent forth a jet of water of such volume and to such an altitude that it fell, not without a delicious plash, into the basin in quantity amply sufficient to turn a mill-wheel. The overflow was carried away from the lawn by a hidden conduit, and then, reemerging, was distributed through tiny channels, very fair and cunningly contrived, in such sort as to flow round the entire lawn, and by similar derivative channels to penetrate almost every part of the fair garden, until, re-uniting at a certain point, it issued thence, and, clear as crystal, slid down towards the plain, turning by the way two mill-wheels with extreme velocity to the no small profit of the lord. The aspect of this garden, its fair order, the plants and the fountain and the rivulets that flowed from it, so charmed the ladies and the three young men that with one accord they affirmed that they knew not how it could receive any accession of beauty, or what other form could be given to Paradise, if it were to be planted on earth. So, excellently well pleased, they roved about it, plucking sprays from the trees, and weaving them into the fairest of garlands, while songsters of, perhaps, a score of different sorts warbled as if in mutual emulation, when suddenly a sight as fair and delightsome as novel, which, engrossed by the other beauties of the place, they had hitherto overlooked, met their eyes. For the garden, they now saw, was peopled with a host of living creatures, fair and of, perhaps, a hundred sorts; and they pointed out to one another how here emerged a cony, or there scampered a hare, or couched a goat, or grazed a fawn, or many another harmless, all but domesticated, creature roved carelessly seeking his pleasure at his own sweet will. All which served immensely to reinforce their already abundant delight. At length, however, they had enough of wandering about the garden and observing this thing and that: wherefore they repaired to the beautiful fountain, around which were ranged the tables, and there, after they had sung half-a-dozen songs and trod some measures, they sat them down, at the queen's command, to breakfast, which was served with all celerity and in fair and orderly manner, the viands being both good and delicate; whereby their spirits rose, and up they got, and betook themselves again to music and song and dance, and so sped the hours, until, as the heat increased, the queen deemed it time that whoso was so minded should go to sleep. Some there were that did so; others were too charmed by the beauty of the place to think of leaving it; but tarried there, and, while the rest slept, amused themselves with reading romances or playing at chess or dice. However, after none, there was a general levee; and, with faces laved and refreshed with cold water, they gathered by the queen's command upon the lawn, and, having sat them down in their wonted order by the fountain, waited for the story-telling to begin upon the theme assigned by the queen. With this duty the queen first charged Filostrato, who began on this wise.

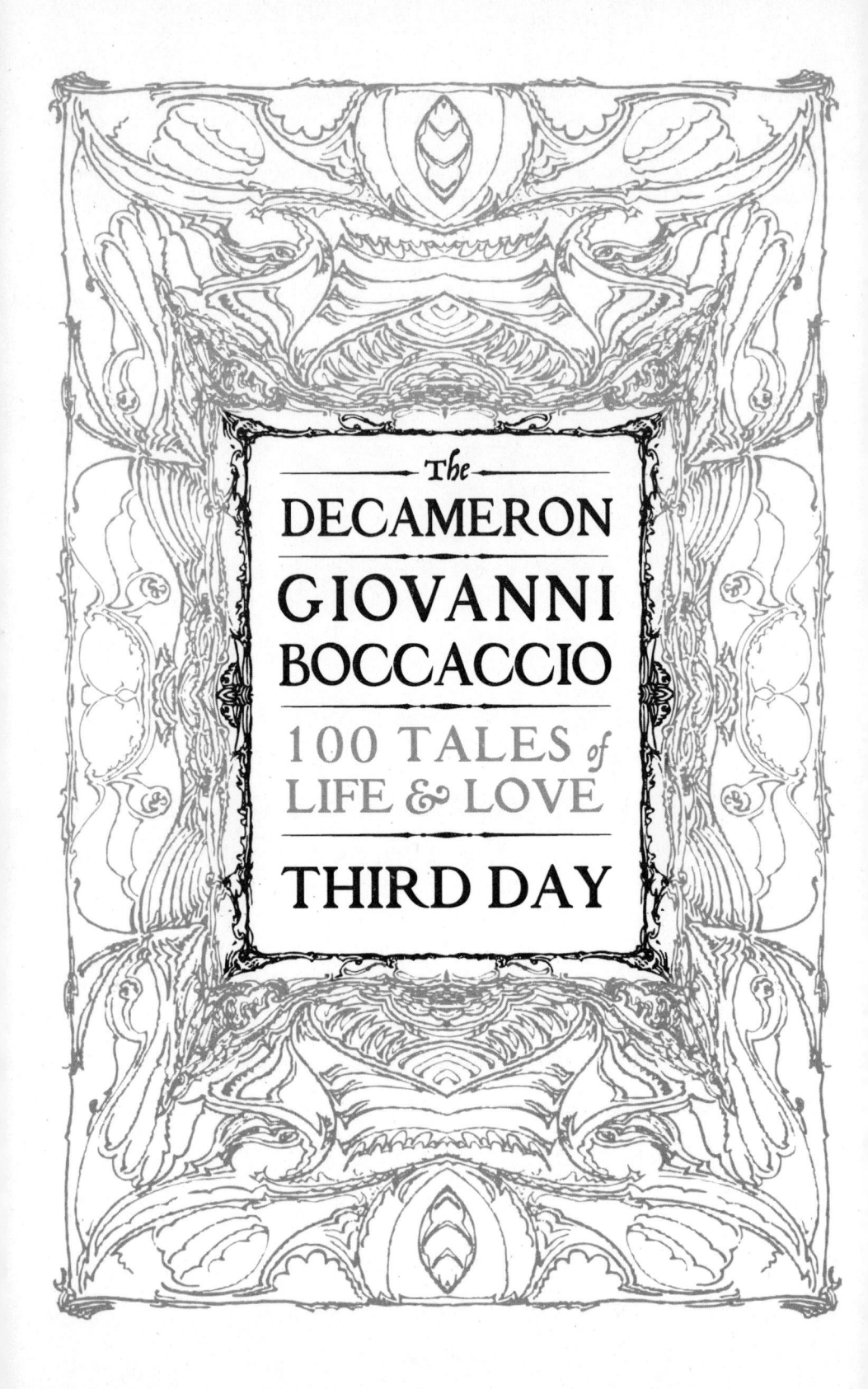

The DECAMERON
GIOVANNI BOCCACCIO
100 TALES of LIFE & LOVE
THIRD DAY

Third Day

Novel I

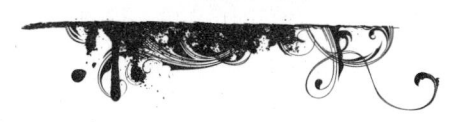

— *Masetto da Lamporecchio feigns to be dumb, and obtains a gardener's place at a convent of women, who with one accord make haste to lie with him.* —

FAIREST LADIES, not a few there are both of men and of women, who are so foolish as blindly to believe that, so soon as a young woman has been veiled in white and cowled in black, she ceases to be a woman, and is no more subject to the cravings proper to her sex, than if, in assuming the garb and profession of a nun, she had put on the nature of a stone: and if, perchance, they hear of aught that is counter to this their faith, they are no less vehement in their censure than if some most heinous and unnatural crime had been committed; neither bethinking them of themselves, whom unrestricted liberty avails not to satisfy, nor making due allowance for the prepotent forces of idleness and solitude. And likewise not a few there are that blindly believe that, what with the hoe and the spade and coarse fare and hardship, the carnal propensities are utterly eradicated from the tillers of the soil, and therewith all nimbleness of wit and understanding. But how gross is the error of such as so suppose, I, on whom the queen has laid her commands, am minded, without deviating from the theme prescribed by her, to make manifest to you by a little story.

In this very country-side of ours there was and yet is a convent of women of great repute for sanctity – name it I will not, lest I should in some measure diminish its repute – the nuns being at the time of which I speak but nine in number, including the abbess, and all young women. Their very beautiful garden was in charge of a foolish fellow, who, not being content with his wage, squared accounts with their steward and hied him back to Lamporecchio, whence he came. Among others who welcomed him home was a young husbandman, Masetto by name, a stout and hardy fellow, and handsome for a contadino, who asked him where he had been so long. Nuto, as our good friend was called, told him. Masetto then asked how he had been employed at the convent, and Nuto answered: – "I kept their large and beautiful garden in good trim, and, besides, I sometimes went to the wood to fetch the faggots, I drew water, and did some other trifling services; but the ladies gave so little wage that it scarce kept me in shoes. And moreover they are all young, and, I think, they are one and all possessed of the devil, for 'tis impossible to do anything to their mind; indeed, when I would be at work in the kitchen-garden, 'put this here,' would say one, 'put that here,' would say another, and a third would snatch the hoe from my hand, and say, 'that is not as it should be'; and so they would worry me until I would give up working and go out of the garden; so that, what with this thing and that, I was minded to stay there no more, and so I am come hither. The steward asked me before I left to send him any one whom on my return I might find fit for the work, and I promised; but God bless his loins, I shall be at no pains to find out and send him any one."

As Nuto thus ran on, Masetto was seized by such a desire to be with these nuns that he quite pined, as he gathered from what Nuto said that his desire might be gratified. And as that could not be, if he said nothing to Nuto, he remarked: – "Ah! 'twas well done of thee to come hither.

A man to live with women! he might as well live with so many devils: six times out of seven they know not themselves what they want." There the conversation ended; but Masetto began to cast about how he should proceed to get permission to live with them. He knew that he was quite competent for the services of which Nuto spoke, and had therefore no fear of failing on that score; but he doubted he should not be received, because he was too young and well-favoured. So, after much pondering, he fell into the following train of thought: – The place is a long way off, and no one there knows me; if I make believe that I am dumb, doubtless I shall be admitted. Whereupon he made his mind up, laid a hatchet across his shoulder, and saying not a word to any of his destination, set forth, intending to present himself at the convent in the character of a destitute man. Arrived there, he had no sooner entered than he chanced to encounter the steward in the courtyard, and making signs to him as dumb folk do, he let him know that of his charity he craved something to eat, and that, if need were, he would split firewood. The steward promptly gave him to eat, and then set before him some logs which Nuto had not been able to split, all which Masetto, who was very strong, split in a very short time. The steward, having occasion to go to the wood, took him with him, and there set him at work on the lopping; which done he placed the ass in front of him, and by signs made him understand that he was to take the loppings back to the convent. This he did so well that the steward kept him for some days to do one or two odd jobs. Whereby it so befell that one day the abbess saw him, and asked the steward who he was. "Madam," replied the steward, "'tis a poor deaf mute that came here a day or two ago craving alms, so I have treated him kindly, and have let him make himself useful in many ways. If he knew how to do the work of the kitchen-garden and would stay with us, I doubt not we should be well served; for we have need of him, and he is strong, and would be able for whatever he might turn his hand to; besides which you would have no cause to be apprehensive lest he should be cracking his jokes with your young women." "As I trust in God," said the abbess, "thou sayst sooth; find out if he can do the garden work, and if he can, do all thou canst to keep him with us; give him a pair of shoes, an old hood, and speak him well, make much of him, and let him be well fed." All which the steward promised to do.

Masetto, meanwhile, was close at hand, making as if he were sweeping the courtyard, and heard all that passed between the abbess and the steward, whereat he gleefully communed with himself on this wise: – Put me once within there, and you will see that I will do the work of the kitchen-garden as it never was done before. So the steward set him to work in the kitchen-garden, and finding that he knew his business excellently well, made signs to him to know whether he would stay, and he made answer by signs that he was ready to do whatever the steward wished. The steward then signified that he was engaged, told him to take charge of the kitchen-garden, and shewed him what he had to do there. Then, having other matters to attend to, he went away, and left him there. Now, as Masetto worked there day by day, the nuns began to tease him, and make him their butt (as it commonly happens that folk serve the dumb) and used bad language to him, the worst they could think of, supposing that he could not understand them, all which passed scarce heeded by the abbess, who perhaps deemed him as destitute of virility as of speech. Now it so befell that after a hard day's work he was taking a little rest, when two young nuns, who were walking in the garden, approached the spot where he lay, and stopped to look at him, while he pretended to be asleep. And so the bolder of the two said to the other: – "If I thought thou wouldst keep the secret, I would tell thee what I have sometimes meditated, and which thou perhaps mightest also find agreeable." The other replied: – "Speak thy mind freely and be sure that I will never tell a soul." Whereupon the bold one began: – "I know not if thou hast ever considered how close we are kept here, and that within these precincts dare never enter any man, unless it be the old steward or this mute: and I have often heard from ladies that have come hither, that all the other sweets that the world has to offer signify not a jot in comparison of the pleasure that a woman has in connexion with a man. Whereof I have more than once been minded to make experiment with this mute, no other man being available. Nor, indeed, could one find any man in the whole world so meet therefor; seeing that he could not blab if he would; thou seest that he is but a dull clownish lad, whose size has increased out of all proportion to his sense; wherefore I would fain hear what thou hast to say to it." "Alas!" said the other, "what is't thou sayst? Knowest thou not that we have vowed our virginity to God?" "Oh," rejoined the first, "think but how many vows are made to Him all day long, and never a one performed: and so, for our vow, let Him find another or others to perform it." "But," said her companion, "suppose that we conceived, how then?" "Nay but," protested the first, "thou goest about to imagine evil before it befalls, thee: time enough to think of that when it comes to pass; there will be a thousand ways to prevent its ever being known, so only we do not publish it ourselves." Thus reassured, the other was now the more eager of the two to test the quality of the male human animal. "Well then," she said, "how shall we go about it?" and was answered: – "Thou seest 'tis past none; I make no doubt but all the sisters are asleep, except ourselves; search we through the kitchen-garden, to see if there be any there, and if there be none, we have but to take him by the hand and lead him hither to the hut where he takes shelter from the rain; and then one shall mount guard while the other has him with her inside. He is such a simpleton that he will do just whatever we bid him." No word of this conversation escaped Masetto, who, being disposed to obey, hoped for nothing so much as that one of them should take him by the hand. They, meanwhile, looked carefully all about them, and satisfied themselves that they were secure from observation: then she that had broached the subject came close up to Masetto, and shook him; whereupon he started to his feet. So she took him by the hand with a blandishing air, to which he replied with some clownish grins. And then she led him into the hut, where he needed no pressing to do what she desired of him. Which done, she changed places with the other, as loyal comradeship required; and Masetto, still keeping up the pretence of simplicity, did their pleasure. Wherefore before they left, each must needs make another assay of the mute's powers of riding; and afterwards, talking the matter over many times, they agreed that it was in truth not less but even more delightful than they had been given to understand; and so, as they found convenient opportunity, they continued to go and disport themselves with the mute.

Now it so chanced that one of their gossips, looking out of the window of her cell, saw what they did, and imparted it to two others. The three held counsel together whether they should not denounce the offenders to the abbess, but soon changed their mind, and came to an understanding with them, whereby they became partners in Masetto. And in course of time by divers chances the remaining three nuns also entered the partnership. Last of all the abbess, still witting nought of these doings, happened one very hot day, as she walked by herself through the garden, to find Masetto, who now rode so much by night that he could stand very little fatigue by day, stretched at full length asleep under the shade of an almond-tree, his person quite exposed in front by reason that the wind had disarranged his clothes. Which the lady observing, and knowing that she was alone, fell a prey to the same appetite to which her nuns had yielded: she aroused Masetto, and took him with her to her chamber, where, for some days, though the nuns loudly complained that the gardener no longer came to work in the kitchen-garden, she kept him, tasting and re-tasting the sweetness of that indulgence which she was wont to be the first to censure in others. And when at last she had sent him back from her chamber to his room, she must needs send for him again and again, and made such exorbitant demands upon him, that Masetto, not being able to satisfy so many women, bethought him that his part of mute, should he persist in it, might entail disastrous consequences. So one night, when he was with the abbess, he cut the tongue-string, and thus broke silence: – "Madam, I have understood that a cock may very well serve ten hens, but that ten men are sorely tasked to satisfy a single woman; and here am I expected to serve nine, a burden quite beyond my power to bear; nay, by what I have already undergone I am now so reduced that my strength is quite spent; wherefore either bid me Godspeed, or find some means to make matters tolerable." Wonder-struck to hear the supposed mute thus speak, the lady exclaimed: – "What means this? I took thee to be dumb." "And in sooth, Madam, so was I," said Masetto, "not indeed from my birth, but through an illness which took from me the power of speech, which only this very night have I recovered; and so I praise God with all my heart." The lady believed him; and asked him what he meant by saying that he had nine to serve. Masetto told her how things stood; whereby she perceived that of all her nuns there was not any but was much wiser than she; and lest, if Masetto were sent away, he should give the convent a bad name, she discreetly determined to arrange matters with the nuns in such sort that he might remain there. So, the steward having died within the last few days, she assembled all the nuns; and their and her own past errors being fully avowed, they by common consent, and with Masetto's concurrence, resolved that the neighbours should be given to understand that by their prayers and the merits of their patron saint, Masetto, long mute, had recovered the power of speech; after which they made him steward, and so ordered matters among themselves that he was able to endure the burden of their service. In the course of which, though he procreated not a few little monastics, yet 'twas all managed so discreetly that no breath of scandal stirred, until after the abbess's death, by which time Masetto was advanced in years and minded to return home with the wealth that he had gotten; which he was suffered to do, as soon as he made his desire known. And so Masetto, who had left Lamporecchio with a hatchet on his shoulder, returned thither in his old age rich and a father, having by the wisdom with which he employed his youth, spared himself the pains and expense of rearing children, and averring that such was the measure that Christ meted out to the man that set horns on his cap.

Third Day
Novel II

— *A groom lies with the wife of King Agilulf, who learns the fact, keeps his own counsel, finds out the groom and shears him. The shorn shears all his fellows, and so comes safe out of the scrape.* —

FILOSTRATO'S STORY, which the ladies had received now with blushes now with laughter, being ended, the queen bade Pampinea follow suit. Which behest Pampinea smilingly obeyed, and thus began: –

Some there are whose indiscretion is such that they must needs evince that they are fully cognizant of that which it were best they should not know, and censuring the covert misdeeds of others, augment beyond measure the disgrace which they would fain diminish. The truth whereof, fair ladies, I mean to shew you in the contrary case, wherein appears the astuteness of one that held, perhaps, an even lower place than would have been Masetto's in the esteem of a doughty king.

Agilulf, King of the Lombards, who like his predecessors made the city of Pavia in Lombardy the seat of his government, took to wife Theodelinde, the widow of Authari, likewise King of the Lombards, a lady very fair, wise and virtuous, but who was unfortunate in her lover. For while the Lombards prospered in peace under the wise and firm rule of King Agilulf, it so befell that one of the Queen's grooms, a man born to very low estate, but in native worth far above his mean office, and moreover not a whit less tall and goodly of person than the King, became inordinately enamoured of her. And as, for all his base condition he had sense enough to recognize that his love was in the last degree presumptuous, he disclosed it to none, nay, he did not even venture to tell her the tale by the mute eloquence of his eyes. And albeit he lived without hope that he should ever be able to win her favour, yet he inwardly gloried that he had fixed his affections in so high a place; and being all aflame with passion, he shewed himself zealous beyond any of his comrades to do whatever he thought was likely to please the Queen. Whereby it came about, that, when the Queen had to take horse, she would mount the palfrey that he groomed rather than any other; and when she did so, he deemed himself most highly favoured, and never quitted her stirrup, esteeming himself happy if he might but touch her clothes. But as 'tis frequently observed that love waxes as hope wanes, so was it with this poor groom, insomuch that the burden of this great hidden passion, alleviated by no hope, was most grievous to bear, and from time to time, not being able to shake it off, he purposed to die. And meditating on the mode, he was minded that it should be of a kind to make it manifest that he died for the love which he had borne and bore to the Queen, and also to afford him an opportunity of trying his fortune whether his desire might in whole or in part be gratified. He had no thought of speaking to the Queen, nor yet of declaring his love to her by letter, for he knew that 'twould be vain either to speak or to write; but he resolved to try to devise some means whereby he might lie with the Queen; which end might in no other way be compassed than by contriving to get access to her in her bedroom; which could only be by passing himself off as the King, who, as he knew, did not always lie with her. Wherefore, that he might observe the carriage and dress of the King as he passed to her room, he contrived to conceal himself for several nights in a great hall of the King's palace which separated the King's room from that of the Queen: and on one of these nights he saw the King issue from his room, wrapped in a great mantle, with a lighted torch in one hand and a wand in the other, and cross the hall, and, saying nothing, tap the door of the Queen's room with the wand once or twice; whereupon the door was at once opened and the torch taken from his hand. Having observed the King thus go and return, and being bent on doing likewise, he found means to come by a mantle like that which he had seen the King wear, and also a torch and a wand: he then took a warm bath, and having thoroughly cleansed himself, that the smell of the foul straw might not offend the lady, or discover to her the deceit, he in this guise concealed himself as he was wont in the great hall. He waited only until all were asleep, and then, deeming the time come to accomplish his purpose, or by his presumption clear a way to the death which he coveted, he struck a light with the flint and steel which he had brought with him; and having kindled his torch and wrapped himself close in his mantle, he went to the door of the Queen's room, and tapped on it twice with his wand. The door was opened by a very drowsy chambermaid, who took the torch and put it out of sight; whereupon without a word he passed within the curtain, laid aside the mantle, and got into the bed where the Queen lay asleep. Then, taking her in his arms and straining her to him with ardour, making as if he were moody, because he knew that, when the King was in such a frame, he would never hear aught, in such wise, without word said either on his part or on hers, he had more than once carnal cognizance of the Queen. Loath indeed was he to leave her, but, fearing lest by too long tarrying his achieved delight might be converted into woe, he rose, resumed the mantle and the light, and leaving the room without a word, returned with all speed to his bed. He was hardly there when the King got up and entered the Queen's room; whereat she wondered not a little; but, reassured by the gladsome greeting which he gave her as he got into bed, she said: – "My lord, what a surprise is this to-night! 'Twas but now you left me after an unwonted measure of enjoyment, and do you now return so soon? consider what you do." From these words the King at once inferred that the Queen had been deceived by some one that had counterfeited his person and carriage; but, at the same time, bethinking himself that, as neither the Queen nor any other had detected the cheat, 'twas best to leave her in ignorance, he wisely kept silence. Which many a fool would not have done, but would have said: – "Nay, 'twas not I that was here. Who was it that was here? How came it to pass? Who came hither?" Whereby in the sequel he might have caused the lady needless chagrin, and given her occasion to desire another such experience as she had had, and so have brought disgrace upon himself by uttering that, from which, unuttered, no shame could have resulted. Wherefore, betraying little, either by his mien or by his words, of the disquietude which he felt, the King replied: – "Madam, seem I such to you that you cannot suppose that I should have been with you once, and returned to you immediately afterwards?" "Nay, not so, my lord," returned the lady, "but none the less I pray you to look to your health." Then said the King: – "And I am minded to take your advice; wherefore, without giving you further trouble I will leave you." So, angered and incensed beyond measure by the trick which, he saw, had been played upon him, he resumed his mantle and quitted the room with the intention of privily detecting the offender, deeming that he must belong to the palace, and that, whoever he might be, he could not have quitted it. So, taking with him a small lantern which shewed only a glimmer of light, he went into the dormitory which was over the palace-stables and was of great length, insomuch that well-nigh all the men-servants slept there in divers beds, and arguing that, by whomsoever that of which the Queen spoke was done, his heart and pulse could not after such a strain as yet have ceased to throb, he began cautiously with one of the head-grooms, and so went from bed to bed feeling at the heart of each man to see if it was thumping. All were asleep, save only he that had been with the Queen, who, seeing the King come, and guessing what he sought to discover, began to be mightily afraid, insomuch that to the agitation which his late exertion had communicated to his heart, terror now added one yet more violent; nor did he doubt that, should the King perceive it, he would kill him. Divers alternatives of action thronged his mind; but at last, observing that the King was unarmed, he resolved to make as if he were asleep, and wait to see what the King would do. So, having tried many and found none that he deemed the culprit, the King came at last to the culprit himself, and marking the thumping of his heart, said to himself: – This is he. But being minded to afford no clue to his ulterior purpose, he did no more than with a pair of scissors which he had brought with him shear away on one side of the man's head a portion of his locks, which, as was then the fashion, he wore very long, that by this token he might recognize him on the morrow; and having so done, he departed and returned to his room. The groom, who was fully sensible of what the King had done, and being a shrewd fellow understood very well to what end he was so marked, got up without a moment's delay; and, having found a pair of scissors – for, as it chanced, there were several pairs there belonging to the stables for use in grooming the horse – he went quietly through the dormitory and in like manner sheared the locks of each of the sleepers just above the ear; which done without disturbing any, he went back to bed.

On the morrow, as soon as the King was risen, and before the gates of the palace were opened, he summoned all his men-servants to his presence, and, as they stood bareheaded before him, scanned them closely to see whether the one whom he had sheared was there; and observing with surprise that the more part of them were all sheared in the same manner, said to himself: – Of a surety this fellow, whom I go about to detect, evinces, for all his base condition, a high degree of sense. Then, recognising that he could not compass his end without causing a bruit, and not being minded to brave so great a dishonour in order to be avenged upon so petty an offender, he was content by a single word of admonition to shew him that his offence had not escaped notice. Wherefore turning to them all, he said: – "He that did it, let him do it no more, and get you hence in God's peace." Another would have put them to the strappado, the question, the torture, and thereby have brought to light that which one should rather be sedulous to cloak; and having so brought it to light, would, however complete the retribution which he exacted, have not lessened but vastly augmented his disgrace, and sullied the fair fame of his lady. Those who heard the King's parting admonition wondered, and made much question with one another, what the King might have meant to convey by it; but 'twas understood by none but him to whom it referred: who was discreet enough never to reveal the secret as long as the King lived, or again to stake his life on such a venture.

Third Day

Novel III

— *Under cloak of confession and a most spotless conscience, a lady, enamoured of a young man, induces a booby friar unwittingly to provide a means to the entire gratification of her passion.* —

WHEN PAMPINEA had done, and several of the company had commended the hardihood and wariness of the groom, as also the wisdom of the King, the queen, turning to Filomena, bade her follow suit: wherefore with manner debonair Filomena thus began: –

The story which I shall tell you is of a trick which was actually played by a fair lady upon a booby religious, and which every layman should find the more diverting that these religious, being, for the most part, great blockheads and men of odd manners and habits, do nevertheless credit themselves with more ability and knowledge in all kinds than fall to the lot of the rest of the world; whereas, in truth, they are far inferior, and so, not being able, like others, to provide their own sustenance, are prompted by sheer baseness to fly thither for refuge where they may find provender, like pigs. Which story, sweet my ladies, I shall tell you, not merely that thereby I may continue the sequence in obedience to the queen's behest, but also to the end that I may let you see that even the religious, in whom we in our boundless credulity repose exorbitant faith, may be, and sometimes are, made – not to say by men – even by some of us women the sport of their sly wit.

In our city, where wiles do more abound than either love or faith, there dwelt, not many years ago, a gentlewoman richly endowed (none more so) by nature with physical charms, as also with gracious manners, high spirit and fine discernment. Her name I know, but will not disclose it, nor yet that of any other who figures in this story, because there yet live those who might take offence thereat, though after all it might well be passed off with a laugh. High-born and married to an artificer of woollen fabrics, she could not rid her mind of the disdain with which, by reason of his occupation, she regarded her husband; for no man, however wealthy, so he were of low condition, seemed to her worthy to have a gentlewoman to wife; and seeing that for all his wealth he was fit for nothing better than to devise a blend, set up a warp, or higgle about yarn with a spinster, she determined to dispense with his embraces, save so far as she might find it impossible to refuse them; and to find her satisfaction elsewhere with one that seemed to her more meet to afford it than her artificer of woollens. In this frame of mind she became enamoured of a man well worthy of her love and not yet past middle age, insomuch that, if she saw him not in the day, she must needs pass an unquiet night. The gallant, meanwhile, remained fancy-free, for he knew nought of the lady's case; and she, being apprehensive of possible perils to ensue, was far too circumspect to make it known to him either by writing or by word of mouth of any of her female friends. Then she learned that he had much to do with a religious, a simple, clownish fellow, but nevertheless, as being a man of most holy life, reputed by almost everybody a most worthy friar, and decided that she could not find a better intermediary between herself and her lover than this same friar. So, having matured her plan, she hied her at a convenient time to the convent where the friar abode and sent for him, saying, that, if he so pleased, she would be confessed by him. The friar, who saw at a glance that she was a gentlewoman, gladly heard her confession; which done, she said: – "My father, I have yet a matter to confide to you, in which I must crave your aid and counsel. Who my kinsfolk and husband are, I wot you know, for I have myself told you. My husband loves me more dearly than his life, and being very wealthy, he can well and does forthwith afford me whatever I desire. Wherefore, as he loves me, even so I love him more dearly than myself; nor was there ever yet wicked woman that deserved the fire so richly as should I, were I guilty – I speak not of acts, but of so much as a single thought of crossing his will or tarnishing his honour. Now a man there is – his name, indeed, I know not, but he seems to me to be a gentleman, and, if I mistake not, he is much with you – a fine man and tall, his garb dun and very decent, who, the bent of my mind being, belike, quite unknown to him, would seem to have laid siege to me, insomuch that I cannot shew myself at door or casement, or quit the house, but forthwith he presents himself before me; indeed I find it passing strange that he is not here now; whereat I am sorely troubled, because, when men so act, unmerited reproach will often thereby be cast upon honest women. At times I have been minded to inform my brothers of the matter; but then I have bethought me that men sometimes frame messages in such a way as to evoke untoward answers, whence follow high words; and so they proceed to rash acts: wherefore, to obviate trouble and scandal, I have kept silence, and by preference have made you my confidant, both because you are the gentleman's friend, and because it befits your office to censure such behaviour not only in friends but in strangers. And so I beseech you for the love of our only Lord God to make him sensible of his fault, and pray him to offend no more in such sort. Other ladies there are in plenty, who may, perchance, be disposed to welcome such advances, and be flattered to attract his fond and assiduous regard, which to me, who am in no wise inclined to encourage it, is but a most grievous molestation."

Having thus spoken, the lady bowed her head as if she were ready to weep. The holy friar was at no loss to apprehend who it was of whom she spoke; he commended her virtuous frame, firmly believing that what she said was true, and promised to take such action that she should not again suffer the like annoyance; nor, knowing that she was very wealthy, did he omit to extol works of charity and almsgiving, at the same time opening to her his own needs. "I make my suit to you," said she, "for the love of God; and if your friend should deny what I have told you, tell him roundly that 'twas from me you had it, and that I made complaint to you thereof." So, her confession ended and penance imposed, bethinking her of the hints which the friar had dropped touching almsgiving, she slipped into his hand as many coins as it would hold, praying him to say masses for the souls of her dead. She then rose and went home.

Not long afterwards the gallant paid one of his wonted visits to the holy friar. They conversed for a while of divers topics, and then the friar took him aside, and very courteously reproved him for so haunting and pursuing the lady with his gaze, as from what she had given him to understand, he supposed was his wont. The gallant, who had never regarded her with any attention, and very rarely passed her house, was amazed, and was about to clear himself, when the friar closed his mouth, saying: – "Now away with this pretence of amazement, and waste not words in denial, for 'twill not avail thee. I have it not from the neighbours; she herself, bitterly complaining of thy conduct, told it me. I say not how ill this levity beseems thee; but of her I tell thee so much as this, that, if I ever knew woman averse to such idle philandering, she is so; and therefore for thy honour's sake, and that she be no more vexed, I pray thee refrain therefrom, and let her be in peace." The gallant, having rather more insight than the holy friar, was not slow to penetrate the lady's finesse; he therefore made as if he were rather shame-stricken, promised to go no further with the matter, and hied him straight from the friar to the lady's house, where she was always posted at a little casement to see if he were passing by. As she saw him come, she shewed him so gay and gracious a mien that he could no longer harbour any doubt that he had put the true construction upon what he had heard from the friar; and thenceforth, to his own satisfaction and the immense delight and solace of the lady, he omitted not daily to pass that way, being careful to make it appear as if he came upon other business. 'Twas thus not long before the lady understood that she met with no less favour in his eyes than he in hers; and being desirous to add fuel to his flame, and to assure him of the love she bore him, as soon as time and occasion served, she returned to the holy friar, and having sat herself down at his feet in the church, fell a weeping. The friar asked her in a soothing tone what her new trouble might be. Whereto the lady answered: – "My father, 'tis still that accursed friend of thine, of whom I made complaint to you some days ago, and who would now seem to have been born for my most grievous torment, and to cause me to do that by reason whereof I shall never be glad again, nor venture to place myself at your feet." "How?" said the friar; "has he not forborne to annoy thee?" "Not he, indeed," said the lady; "on the contrary, 'tis my belief that, since I complained to you of him, he has, as if in despite, being offended, belike, that I did so, passed my house seven times for once that he did so before. Nay, would to God he were content to pass and fix me with his eyes; but he is waxed so bold and unabashed that only yesterday he sent a woman to me at home with his compliments and cajoleries, and, as if I had not purses and girdles enough, he sent me a purse and a girdle; whereat I was, as I still am, so wroth, that, had not conscience first, and then regard for you, weighed with me, I had flown into a frenzy of rage. However, I restrained myself, and resolved neither to do nor to say aught without first letting you know it. Nor only so; but, lest the woman who brought the purse and girdle, and to whom I at first returned them, shortly bidding her begone and take them back to the sender, should keep them and tell him that I had accepted them, as I believe they sometimes do, I recalled her and had them back, albeit 'twas in no friendly spirit that I received them from her hand; and I have brought them to you, that you may return them to him and tell him that I stand in no need of such gifts from him, because, thanks be to God and my husband, I have purses and girdles enough to smother him in. And if after this he leave me not alone, I pray you as my father to hold me excused if, come what may, I tell it to my husband and brothers; for much liefer had I that he suffer indignity, if so it must be, than that my fair fame should be sullied on his account: that holds good, friar." Weeping bitterly as she thus ended, she drew from under her robe a purse of very fine and ornate workmanship and a dainty and costly little girdle, and threw them into the lap of the friar, who, fully believing what she said, manifested the utmost indignation as he took them, and said: – "Daughter, that by these advances thou shouldst be moved to anger, I deem neither strange nor censurable; but I am instant with thee to follow my advice in the matter. I chid him some days ago, and ill has he kept the promise that he made me; for which cause and this last feat of his I will surely make his ears so tingle that he will give thee no more trouble; wherefore, for God's sake, let not thyself be so overcome by wrath as to tell it to any of thy kinsfolk; which might bring upon him a retribution greater than he deserves. Nor fear lest thereby thy fair fame should suffer; for I shall ever be thy most sure witness before God and men that thou art innocent." The lady made a shew of being somewhat comforted: then, after a pause – for well she knew the greed of him and his likes – she said: – "Of late, Sir, by night, the spirits of divers of my kinsfolk have appeared to me in my sleep, and methinks they are in most grievous torment; alms, alms, they crave, nought else, especially my mother, who seems to be in so woful and abject a plight that 'tis pitiful to see. Methinks 'tis a most grievous torment to her to see the tribulation which this enemy of God has brought upon me. I would therefore have you say for their souls the forty masses of St. Gregory and some of your prayers, that God may deliver them from this purging fire." So saying she slipped a florin into the hand of the holy friar, who took it gleefully, and having with edifying words and many examples fortified her in her devotion, gave her his benediction, and suffered her to depart.

The lady gone, the friar, who had still no idea of the trick that had been played upon him, sent for his friend; who was no sooner come than he gathered from the friar's troubled air that he had news of the lady, and waited to hear what he would say. The friar repeated what he had said before, and then broke out into violent and heated objurgation on the score of the lady's latest imputation. The gallant, who did not as yet apprehend the friar's drift, gave but a very faint denial to the charge of sending the purse and girdle, in order that he might not discredit the lady with the friar, if, perchance, she had given him the purse and girdle. Whereupon the friar exclaimed with great heat: – "How canst thou deny it, thou wicked man? Why, here they are; she brought them to me in tears with her own hand. Look at them, and say if thou knowest them not." The gallant now feigned to be much ashamed, and said: – "Why, yes, indeed, I do know them; I confess that I did wrong; and I swear to you that, now I know her character, you shall never hear word more of this matter." Many words followed; and then the blockheadly friar gave the purse and girdle to his friend, after which he read him a long lecture, besought him to meddle no more with such matters, and on his promising obedience dismissed him.

Elated beyond measure by the assurance which he now had of the lady's love, and the beautiful present, the gallant, on leaving the friar, hied him straight to a spot whence he stealthily gave the lady to see that he had both her gifts: whereat the lady was well content, the more so as her intrigue seemed ever to prosper more and more. She waited now only for her husband's departure from home to crown her enterprise with success. Nor was it long before occasion required that her husband should go to Genoa. The very morning that he took horse and rode away she hied her to the holy friar, and after many a lamentation she said to him betwixt her sobs: – "My father, now at last I tell you out and out that I can bear my suffering no longer. I promised you some days ago to do nought in this matter without first letting you know it; I am now come to crave release from that promise; and that you may believe that my lamentations and complaints are not groundless, I will tell you how this friend of yours, who should rather be called a devil let loose from hell, treated me only this very morning, a little before matins. As ill-luck would have it, he learned, I know not how, that yesterday morning my husband went to Genoa, and so this morning at the said hour he came into my garden, and got up by a tree to the window of my bedroom, which looks out over the garden, and had already opened the casement, and was about to enter the room, when I suddenly awoke, and got up and uttered a cry, and should have continued to cry out, had not he, who was still outside, implored my mercy for God's sake and yours, telling me who he was. So, for love of you I was silent, and naked as I was born, ran and shut the window in his face, and he – bad luck to him – made off, I suppose, for I saw him no more. Consider now if such behaviour be seemly and tolerable: I for my part am minded to put up with no more of it; indeed I have endured too much already for love of you."

Wroth beyond measure was the friar, as he heard her thus speak, nor knew he what to say, except that he several times asked her if she were quite certain that it was no other than he. "Holy name of God!" replied the lady, "as if I did not yet know him from another! He it was, I tell you; and do you give no credence to his denial." "Daughter," said then the friar, "there is here nought else to say but that this is a monstrous presumption and a most heinous offence; and thou didst well to send him away as thou didst. But seeing that God has preserved thee from shame, I would implore thee that as thou hast twice followed my advice, thou do so likewise on this occasion, and making no complaint to any of thy kinsfolk, leave it to me to try if I can control this devil that has slipt his chain, whom I supposed to be a saint; and if I succeed in weaning him from this insensate folly, well and good; and if I fail, thenceforth I give thee leave, with my blessing, to do whatsoever may commend itself to thy own judgment." "Lo now," answered the lady, "once again I will not vex or disobey you; but be sure that you so order matters that he refrain from further annoyance, as I give you my word that never will I have recourse to you again touching this matter." Then, without another word, and with a troubled air, she took leave of him. Scarcely was she out of the church when the gallant came up. The friar called him, took him aside, and gave him the affront in such sort as 'twas never before given to any man reviling him as a disloyal and perjured traitor. The gallant, who by his two previous lessons had been taught how to value the friar's censures, listened attentively, and sought to draw him out by ambiguous answers. "Wherefore this wrath, Sir?" he began. "Have I crucified Christ?" "Ay, mark the fellow's effrontery!" retorted the friar: "list to what he says! He talks, forsooth, as if 'twere a year or so since, and his villanies and lewdnesses were clean gone from his memory for lapse of time. Between matins and now hast thou forgotten this morning's outrage? Where wast thou this morning shortly before daybreak?" "Where was I?" rejoined the gallant; "that know not I. 'Tis indeed betimes that the news has reached you." "True indeed it is," said the friar, "that the news has reached me: I suppose that, because the husband was not there, thou never doubtedst that thou wouldst forthwith be received by the lady with open arms. Ah! the gay gallant! the honourable gentleman! he is now turned prowler by night, and breaks into gardens, and climbs trees! Dost thou think by sheer importunity to vanquish the virtue of this lady, that thou escaladest her windows at night by the trees? She dislikes thee of all things in the world, and yet thou must still persist. Well indeed hast thou laid my admonitions to heart, to say nothing of the many proofs which she has given thee of her disdain! But I have yet a word for thee: hitherto, not that she bears thee any love, but that she has yielded to my urgent prayers, she has kept silence as to thy misdeeds: she will do so no more: I have given her leave to act as she may think fit, if thou givest her any further annoyance. And what wilt thou do if she informs her brothers?" The gallant, now fully apprised of what it imported him to know, was profuse in promises, whereby as best he might he reassured the friar, and so left him. The very next night, as soon as the matin hour was come, he entered the garden, climbed up the tree, found the window open, entered the chamber, and in a trice was in the embrace of his fair lady. Anxiously had she expected him, and blithely did she now greet him, saying: – "All thanks to master friar that he so well taught thee the way hither." Then, with many a jest and laugh at the simplicity of the asinine friar, and many a flout at distaff-fuls and combs and cards, they solaced themselves with one another to their no small delight. Nor did they omit so to arrange matters that they were well able to dispense with master friar, and yet pass many another night together with no less satisfaction: to which goal I pray that I, and all other Christian souls that are so minded, may be speedily guided of God in His holy mercy.

Third Day
Novel IV

— *Dom Felice instructs Fra Puccio how to attain blessedness by doing a penance. Fra Puccio does the penance, and meanwhile Dom Felice has a good time with Fra Puccio's wife.* —

WHEN FILOMENA, having concluded her story, was silent, and Dioneo had added a few honeyed phrases in praise of the lady's wit and Filomena's closing prayer, the queen glanced with a smile to Pamfilo, and said: –

"Now, Pamfilo, give us some pleasant trifle to speed our delight." "That gladly will I," returned forthwith Pamfilo, and then: – "Madam," he began, "not a few there are that, while they use their best endeavours to get themselves places in Paradise, do, by inadvertence, send others thither: as did, not long ago, betide a fair neighbour of ours, as you shall hear.

Hard by San Pancrazio there used to live, as I have heard tell, a worthy man and wealthy, Puccio di Rinieri by name, who in later life, under an overpowering sense of religion, became a tertiary of the order of St. Francis, and was thus known as Fra Puccio. In which spiritual life he was the better able to persevere that his household consisted but of a wife and a maid, and having no need to occupy himself with any craft, he spent no small part of his time at church; where, being a simple soul and slow of wit, he said his paternosters, heard sermons, assisted at the mass, never missed lauds (i. e. when chanted by the seculars), fasted and mortified his flesh; nay – so 'twas whispered – he was of the Flagellants. His wife, Monna Isabetta by name, a woman of from twenty-eight to thirty summers, still young for her age, lusty, comely and plump as a casolan apple, had not unfrequently, by reason of her husband's devoutness, if not also of his age, more than she cared for, of abstinence; and when she was sleepy, or, maybe, riggish, he would repeat to her the life of Christ, and the sermons of Fra Nastagio, or the lament of the Magdalen, or the like. Now, while such was the tenor of her life, there returned from Paris a young monk, by name Dom Felice, of the convent of San Pancrazio, a well-favoured man and keen-witted, and profoundly learned, with whom Fra Puccio became very intimate; and as there was no question which he could put to him but Dom Felice could answer it, and moreover he made great shew of holiness, for well he knew Fra Puccio's bent, Fra Puccio took to bringing him home and entertaining him at breakfast and supper, as occasion served; and for love of her husband the lady also grew familiar with Dom Felice, and was zealous to do him honour. So the monk, being a constant visitor at Fra Puccio's house, and seeing the lady so lusty and plump, surmised that of which she must have most lack, and made up his mind to afford, if he could, at once relief to Fra Puccio and contentment to the lady. So cautiously, now and again, he cast an admiring glance in her direction with such effect that he kindled in her the same desire with which he burned, and marking his success, took the first opportunity to declare his passion to her. He found her fully disposed to gratify it; but how this might be, he was at a loss to discover, for she would not trust herself with him in any place whatever except her own house, and there it could not be, because Fra Puccio never travelled; whereby the monk was greatly dejected. Long he pondered the matter, and at length thought of an expedient, whereby he might be with the lady in her own house without incurring suspicion, notwithstanding that Fra Puccio was there. So, being with Fra Puccio one day, he said to him: – "Reasons many have I to know, Fra Puccio, that all thy desire is to become a saint; but it seems to me that thou farest by a circuitous route, whereas there is one very direct, which the Pope and the greater prelates that are about him know and use, but will have it remain a secret, because otherwise the clergy, who for the most part live by alms, and could not then expect alms or aught else from the laity, would be speedily ruined. However, as thou art my friend, and hast shewn me much honour, I would teach thee that way, if I were assured that thou wouldst follow it without letting another soul in the world hear of it." Fra Puccio was now all agog to hear more of the matter, and began most earnestly entreating Dom Felice to teach him the way, swearing that without Dom Felice's leave none should ever hear of it from him, and averring that, if he found it practicable, he would certainly follow it. "I am satisfied with thy promises," said the monk, "and I will shew thee the way. Know then that the holy doctors hold that whoso would achieve blessedness must do the penance of which I shall tell thee; but see thou take me judiciously. I do not say that after the penance thou wilt not be a sinner, as thou art; but the effect will be that the sins which thou hast committed up to the very hour of the penance will all be purged away and thereby remitted to thee, and the sins which thou shalt commit thereafter will not be written against thee to thy damnation, but will be quit by holy water, like venial sins. First of all then the penitent must with great exactitude confess his sins when he comes to begin the penance. Then follows a period of fasting and very strict abstinence which must last for forty days, during which time he is to touch no woman whomsoever, not even his wife. Moreover, thou must have in thy house some place whence thou mayst see the sky by night, whither thou must resort at compline; and there thou must have a beam, very broad, and placed in such a way, that, standing, thou canst rest thy nether part upon it, and so, not raising thy feet from the ground, thou must extend thy arms, so as to make a sort of crucifix, and if thou wouldst have pegs to rest them on thou mayst; and on this manner, thy gaze fixed on the sky, and never moving a jot, thou must stand until matins. And wert thou lettered, it were proper for thee to say meanwhile certain prayers that I would give thee; but as thou art not so, thou must say three hundred paternosters and as many avemarias in honour of the Trinity; and thus contemplating the sky, be ever mindful that God was the creator of the heaven and the earth, and being set even as Christ was upon the cross, meditate on His passion. Then, when the matin-bell sounds, thou mayst, if thou please, go to bed – but see that thou undress not – and sleep; but in the morning thou must go to church, and hear at least three masses, and say fifty paternosters and as many avemarias; after which thou mayst with a pure heart do aught that thou hast to do, and breakfast; but at vespers thou must be again at church, and say there certain prayers, which I shall give thee in writing and which are indispensable, and after compline thou must repeat thy former exercise. Do this, and I, who have done it before thee, have good hope that even before thou shalt have reached the end of the penance, thou wilt, if thou shalt do it in a devout spirit, have already a marvellous foretaste of the eternal blessedness." "This," said Fra Puccio, "is neither a very severe nor a very long penance, and can be very easily managed: wherefore in God's name I will begin on Sunday." And so he took his leave of Dom Felice, and went home, and, by Dom Felice's permission, informed his wife of every particular of his intended penance.

 The lady understood very well what the monk meant by enjoining him not to stir from his post until matins; and deeming it an excellent device, she said that she was well content that he should do this or aught else that he thought good for his soul; and to the end that his penance might be blest of, she would herself fast with him, though she would go no further. So they did as they had agreed: when Sunday came Fra Puccio began his penance, and master monk, by understanding with the lady, came most evenings, at the hour when he was secure from discovery, to sup with her, always bringing with him abundance both of meat and of drink, and after slept with her till the matin hour, when he got up and left her, and Fra Puccio went to bed. The place which Fra Puccio had chosen for his penance was close to the room in which the lady slept, and only separated from it by the thinnest of partitions; so that, the monk and the lady disporting themselves with one another without stint or restraint, Fra Puccio thought he felt the floor of the house shake a little, and pausing at his hundredth paternoster, but without leaving his post, called out to the lady to know what she was about. The lady, who dearly loved a jest, and was just then riding the horse of St. Benedict or St. John Gualbert, answered: – "I'faith, husband, I am as restless as may be." "Restless," said Fra Puccio, "how so? What means this restlessness?" Whereto with a hearty laugh, for which she doubtless had good occasion, the bonny lady replied: – "What means it? How should you ask such a question? Why, I have heard you say a thousand times: – 'Who fasting goes to bed, uneasy lies his head.'" Fra Puccio, supposing that her wakefulness and restlessness abed was due to want of food, said in good faith: – "Wife, I told thee I would have thee not fast; but as thou hast chosen to fast, think not of it, but think how thou mayst compose thyself to sleep; thou tossest about the bed in such sort that the shaking is felt here." "That need cause thee no alarm," rejoined the lady. "I know what I am about; I will manage as well as I can, and do thou likewise." So Fra Puccio said no more to her, but resumed his paternosters; and thenceforth every night, while Fra Puccio's penance lasted, the lady and master monk, having had a bed made up for them in another part of the house, did there wanton it most gamesomely, the monk departing and the lady going back to her bed at one and the same time, being shortly before Fra Puccio's return from his nightly vigil. The friar thus persisting in his penance while the lady took her fill of pleasure with the monk, she would from time to time say jestingly to him: – "Thou layest a penance upon Fra Puccio whereby we are rewarded with Paradise." So well indeed did she relish the dainties with which the monk regaled her, the more so by contrast with the abstemious life to which her husband had long accustomed her, that, when Fra Puccio's penance was done, she found means to enjoy them elsewhere, and ordered her indulgence with such discretion as to ensure its long continuance. Whereby (that my story may end as it began) it came to pass that Fra Puccio, hoping by his penance to win a place for himself in Paradise, did in fact translate thither the monk who had shewn him the way, and the wife who lived with him in great dearth of that of which the monk in his charity gave her superabundant largess.

Third Day

Novel V

— *Zima gives a palfrey to Messer Francesco Vergellesi, who in return suffers him to speak with his wife. She keeping silence, he answers in her stead, and the sequel is in accordance with his answer.* —

WHEN PAMFILO had brought the story of Fra Puccio to a close amid the laughter of the ladies, the queen debonairly bade Elisa follow suit; and she, whose manner had in it a slight touch of severity, which betokened not despite, but was habitual to her, thus began: –

Many there are that, being very knowing, think that others are quite the reverse; and so, many a time, thinking to beguile others, are themselves beguiled; wherefore I deem it the height of folly for any one wantonly to challenge another to a contest of wit. But, as, perchance, all may not be of the same opinion, I am minded, without deviating from the prescribed order, to acquaint you with that which thereby befell a certain knight of Pistoia. Know then that at Pistoia there lived a knight, Messer Francesco, by name, of the Vergellesi family, a man of much wealth and good parts, being both wise and clever, but withal niggardly beyond measure. Which Messer Francesco, having to go to Milan in the capacity of podesta, had provided himself with all that was meet for the honourable support of such a dignity, save only a palfrey handsome enough for him; and not being able to come by any such, he felt himself at a loss. Now there was then in Pistoia a young man, Ricciardo by name, of low origin but great wealth, who went always so trim and fine and foppish of person, that folk had bestowed upon him the name of Zima, by which he was generally known. Zima had long and to no purpose burned and yearned for love of Messer Francesco's very fair and no less virtuous wife. His passion was matter of common notoriety; and so it befell that some one told Messer Francesco that he had but to ask Zima, who was the possessor of one of the handsomest palfreys in Tuscany, which on that account he greatly prized, and he would not hesitate to give him the horse for the love which he bore his wife. So our niggardly knight sent for Zima, and offered to buy the horse of him, hoping thereby to get him from Zima as a gift. Zima heard the knight gladly, and thus made answer: – "Sell you my horse, Sir, I would not, though you gave me all that you have in the world; but I shall be happy to give him to you, when you will, on this condition, that, before he pass into your hands, I may by your leave and in your presence say a few words to your wife so privately that I may be heard by her alone." Thinking at once to gratify his cupidity and to outwit Zima, the knight answered that he was content that it should be even as Zima wished. Then, leaving him in the hall of the palace, he went to his lady's chamber, and told her the easy terms on which he might acquire the palfrey, bidding her give Zima his audience, but on no account to vouchsafe him a word of reply. This the lady found by no means to her mind, but, as she must needs obey her husband's commands, she promised compliance, and followed him into the hall to hear what Zima might have to say. Zima then renewed his contract with the knight in due form; whereupon, the lady being seated in a part of the hall where she was quite by herself, he sate down by her side, and thus began: – "Noble lady, I have too much respect for your understanding to doubt that you have long been well aware of the extremity of passion whereto I have been brought by your beauty, which certainly exceeds that of any other lady that I have ever seen, to say nothing of your exquisite manners and incomparable virtues, which might well serve to captivate every soaring spirit that is in the world; wherefore there need no words of mine to assure you that I love you with a love greater and more ardent than any that man yet bore to woman, and so without doubt I shall do, as long as my woful life shall hold this frame together; nay, longer yet, for, if love there be in the next world as in this, I shall love you evermore. And so you may make your mind secure that there is nothing that is yours, be it precious or be it common, which you may count as in such and so sure a sort your own as me, for all that I am and have. And that thereof you may not lack evidence of infallible cogency, I tell you, that I should deem myself more highly favoured, if I might at your command do somewhat to pleasure you, than if at my command the whole world were forthwith to yield me obedience. And as 'tis even in such sort that I am yours, 'tis not unworthily that I make bold to offer my petitions to Your Highness, as being to me the sole, exclusive source of all peace, of all bliss, of all health. Wherefore, as your most lowly vassal, I pray you, dear my bliss, my soul's one hope, wherein she nourishes herself in love's devouring flame, that in your great benignity you deign so far to mitigate the harshness which in the past you have shewn towards me, yours though I am, that, consoled by your compassion, I may say, that, as 'twas by your beauty that I was smitten with love, so 'tis to your pity that I owe my life, which, if in your haughtiness you lend not ear unto my prayers, will assuredly fail, so that I shall die, and, it may be, 'twill be said that you slew me. 'Twould not redound to your honour that I died for love of you; but let that pass; I cannot but think, however, that you would sometimes feel a touch of remorse, and would grieve that 'twas your doing, and that now and again, relenting, you would say to yourself: – 'Ah! how wrong it was of me that I had not pity on my Zima;' by which too late repentance you would but enhance your grief. Wherefore, that this come not to pass, repent you while it is in your power to give me ease, and shew pity on me before I die, seeing that with you it rests to make me either the gladdest or the saddest man that lives. My trust is in your generosity, that 'twill not brook that a love so great and of such a sort as mine should receive death for guerdon, and that by a gladsome and gracious answer you will repair my shattered spirits, which are all a-tremble in your presence for very fear." When he had done, he heaved several very deep sighs, and a few tears started from his eyes, while he awaited the lady's answer.

Long time he had wooed her with his eyes, had tilted in her honour, had greeted her rising with music; and against these and all like modes of attack she had been proof; but the heartfelt words of her most ardent lover were not without their effect, and she now began to understand what she had never till then understood, to wit, what love really means. So, albeit she obeyed her lord's behest, and kept silence, yet she could not but betray by a slight sigh that which, if she might have given Zima his answer, she would readily have avowed. After waiting a while, Zima found it strange that no answer was forthcoming; and he then began to perceive the trick which the knight had played him. However, he kept his eyes fixed on the lady, and observing that her eyes glowed now and again, as they met his, and noting the partially suppressed sighs which escaped her, he gathered a little hope, which gave him courage to try a novel plan of attack. So, while the lady listened, he began to make answer for her to himself on this wise: – "Zima mine, true indeed it is that long since I discerned that thou didst love me with a love exceeding great and whole-hearted, whereof I have now yet ampler assurance by thine own words, and well content I am therewith, as indeed I ought to be. And however harsh and cruel I may have seemed to thee, I would by no means have thee believe, that I have been such at heart as I have seemed in aspect; rather, be assured that I have ever loved thee and held thee dear above all other men; the mien which I have worn was but prescribed by fear of another and solicitude for my fair fame. But a time will soon come when I shall be able to give thee plain proof of my love, and to accord the love which thou hast borne and dost bear me its due guerdon. Wherefore be comforted and of good hope; for, Messer Francesco is to go in a few days' time to Milan as podesta, as thou well knowest, seeing that for love of me thou hast given him thy fine palfrey; and I vow to thee upon my faith, upon the true love which I bear thee, that without fail, within a few days thereafter thou shalt be with me, and we will give our love complete and gladsome consummation. And that I may have no more occasion to speak to thee of this matter, be it understood between us that henceforth when thou shalt observe two towels disposed at the window of my room which overlooks the garden, thou shalt come to me after nightfall of that same day by the garden door (and look well to it that thou be not seen), and thou shalt find me waiting for thee, and we will have our fill of mutual cheer and solace all night long."

Having thus answered for the lady, Zima resumed his own person and thus replied to the lady: – "Dearest madam, your boon response so overpowers my every faculty that scarce can I frame words to render you due thanks; and, were I able to utter all I feel, time, however long, would fail me fully to thank you as I would fain and as I ought: wherefore I must even leave it to your sage judgment to divine that which I yearn in vain to put in words. Let this one word suffice, that as you bid me, so I shall not fail to do; and then, having, perchance, firmer assurance of the great boon which you have granted me, I will do my best endeavour to thank you in terms the amplest that I may command. For the present there is no more to say; and so, dearest my lady, I commend you to God; and may He grant you your heart's content of joy and bliss." To all which the lady returned never a word: wherefore Zima rose and turned to rejoin the knight, who, seeing him on his feet, came towards him, and said with a laugh: – "How sayst thou? Have I faithfully kept my promise to thee?" "Not so, Sir," replied Zima; "for by thy word I was to have spoken with thy wife, and by thy deed I have spoken to a statue of marble." Which remark was much relished by the knight, who, well as he had thought of his wife, thought now even better of her, and said: – "So thy palfrey, that was, is now mine out and out." "'Tis even so, Sir," replied Zima; "but had I thought to have gotten such fruit as I have from this favour of yours, I would not have craved it, but would have let you have the palfrey as a free gift: and would to God I had done so, for, as it is, you have bought the palfrey and I have not sold him." This drew a laugh from the knight, who within a few days thereafter mounted the palfrey which he had gotten, and took the road for Milan, there to enter on his podestate. The lady, now mistress of herself, bethought her of Zima's words, and the love which he bore her, and for which he had parted with his palfrey; and observing that he frequently passed her house, said to herself: – "What am I about? Why throw I my youth away? My husband is gone to Milan, and will not return for six months, and when can he ever restore them to me? When I am old! And besides, shall I ever find another such lover as Zima? I am quite by myself. There is none to fear, I know not why I take not my good time while I may: I shall not always have the like opportunity as at present: no one will ever know; and if it should get known, 'tis better to do and repent than to forbear and repent." Of which meditations the issue was that one day she set two towels in the window overlooking the garden, according to Zima's word, and Zima having marked them with much exultation, stole at nightfall alone to the door of the lady's garden, and finding it open, crossed to another door that led into the house, where he found the lady awaiting him. On sight of him she rose to meet him, and gave him the heartiest of welcomes. A hundred thousand times he embraced and kissed her, as he followed her upstairs: then without delay they hied them to bed, and knew love's furthest bourne. And so far was the first time from being in this case the last, that, while the knight was at Milan, and indeed after his return, there were seasons not a few at which Zima resorted thither to the immense delight of both parties.

Third Day
Novel VI

— *Ricciardo Minutolo loves the wife of Filippello Fighinolfi, and knowing her to be jealous, makes her believe that his own wife is to meet Filippello at a bagnio on the ensuing day; whereby she is induced to go thither, where, thinking to have been with her husband, she discovers that she has tarried with Ricciardo.* —

WHEN ELISA had quite done, the queen, after some commendation of Zima's sagacity, bade Fiammetta follow with a story. Whereto Fiammetta, all smiles, responded: – "Madam, with all my heart;" and thus began: –

Richly though our city abounds, as in all things else, so also in instances to suit every topic, yet I am minded to journey some distance thence, and, like Elisa, to tell you something of what goes on in other parts of the world: wherefore pass we to Naples, where you shall hear how one of these sanctified that shew themselves so shy of love, was by the subtlety of her lover brought to taste of the fruit before she had known the flowers of love; whereby at one and the same time you may derive from the past counsel of prudence for the future, and present delectation.

In the very ancient city of Naples, which for loveliness has not its superior or perhaps its equal in Italy, there once lived a young man, renowned alike for noble blood and the splendour of his vast wealth, his name Ricciardo Minutolo. He was mated with a very fair and loving wife; but nevertheless he became enamoured of a lady who in the general opinion vastly surpassed in beauty every other lady in Naples. Catella – such was the lady's name – was married to a young man, likewise of gentle blood, Filippello Fighinolfi by name, whom she, most virtuous of ladies, loved and held dear above all else in the world. Being thus enamoured of Catella, Ricciardo Minutolo left none of those means untried whereby a lady's favour and love are wont to be gained, but for all that he made no way towards the attainment of his heart's desire: whereby he fell into a sort of despair, and witless and powerless to loose himself from his love, found life scarce tolerable, and yet knew not how to die. While in this frame he languished, it befell one day that some ladies that were of kin to him counselled him earnestly to be quit of such a love, whereby he could but fret himself to no purpose, seeing that Catella cared for nought in the world save Filippello, and lived in such a state of jealousy on his account that never a bird flew but she feared lest it should snatch him from her. So soon as Ricciardo heard of Catella's jealousy, he forthwith began to ponder how he might make it subserve his end. He feigned to have given up his love for Catella as hopeless, and to have transferred it to another lady, in whose honour he accordingly began to tilt and joust and do all that he had been wont to do in honour of Catella. Nor was it long before well-nigh all the Neapolitans, including Catella herself, began to think that he had forgotten Catella, and was to the last degree enamoured of the other lady. In this course he persisted, until the opinion was so firmly rooted in the minds of all that even Catella laid aside a certain reserve which she had used towards him while she deemed him her lover, and, coming and going, greeted him in friendly, neighbourly fashion, like the rest. Now it so befell that during the hot season, when, according to the custom of the

Neapolitans, many companies of ladies and gentlemen went down to the sea-coast to recreate themselves and breakfast and sup, Ricciardo, knowing that Catella was gone thither with her company, went likewise with his, but, making as if he were not minded to stay there, he received several invitations from the ladies of Catella's company before he accepted any. When the ladies received him, they all with one accord, including Catella, began to rally him on his new love, and he furnished them with more matter for talk by feigning a most ardent passion. At length most of the ladies being gone off, one hither, another thither, as they do in such places, leaving Catella and a few others with Ricciardo, he tossed at Catella a light allusion to a certain love of her husband Filippello, which threw her at once into such a fit of jealousy, that she inly burned with a vehement desire to know what Ricciardo meant. For a while she kept her own counsel; then, brooking no more suspense, she adjured Ricciardo, by the love he bore the lady whom most he loved, to expound to her what he had said touching Filippello. He answered thus: – "You have adjured me by her to whom I dare not deny aught that you may ask of me; my riddle therefore I will presently read you, provided you promise me that neither to him nor to any one else will you impart aught of what I shall relate to you, until you shall have ocular evidence of its truth; which, so you desire it, I will teach you how you may obtain." The lady accepted his terms, which rather confirmed her belief in his veracity, and swore that she would not tell a soul. They then drew a little apart, that they might not be overheard by the rest, and Ricciardo thus began: – "Madam, did I love you, as I once did, I should not dare to tell you aught that I thought might cause you pain; but, now that that love is past, I shall have the less hesitation in telling you the truth. Whether Filippello ever resented the love which I bore you, or deemed that it was returned by you, I know not: whether it were so or no, he certainly never shewed any such feeling to me; but so it is that now, having waited, perhaps, until, as he supposes, I am less likely to be on my guard, he shews a disposition to serve me as I doubt he suspects that I served him; that is to say, he would fain have his pleasure of my wife, whom for some time past he has, as I discover, plied with messages through most secret channels. She has told me all, and has answered him according to my instructions: but only this morning, just before I came hither, I found a woman in close parley with her in the house, whose true character and purpose I forthwith divined; so I called my wife, and asked what the woman wanted. Whereto she answered: – 'Tis this persecution by Filippello which thou hast brought upon me by the encouraging answers that thou wouldst have me give him: he now tells me that he is most earnestly desirous to know my intentions, and that, should I be so minded, he would contrive that I should have secret access to a bagnio in this city, and he is most urgent and instant that I should consent. And hadst thou not, wherefore I know not, bidden me keep the affair afoot, I would have dismissed him in such a sort that my movements would have been exempt from his prying observation for ever.' Upon this I saw that the affair was going too far; I determined to have no more of it, and to let you know it, that you may understand how he requites your wholehearted faith, which brought me of late to the verge of death. And that you may not suppose that these are but empty words and idle tales, but may be able, should you so desire, to verify them by sight and touch, I caused my wife to tell the woman who still waited her answer, that she would be at the bagnio to-morrow about none, during the siesta: with which answer the woman went away well content. Now you do not, I suppose, imagine that I would send her thither; but if I were in your place, he should find me there instead of her whom he thinks to find there; and when I had been some little time with him, I would give him to understand with whom he had been, and he should have of me such honour as he deserved. Whereby, I doubt not, he would be put to such shame as would at one and the same time avenge both the wrong which he has done to you and that which he plots against me."

Catella, as is the wont of the jealous, hearkened to Ricciardo's words without so much as giving a thought to the speaker or his wiles, inclined at once to credit his story, and began to twist certain antecedent matters into accord with it; then, suddenly kindling with wrath, she answered that to the bagnio she would certainly go; 'twould cause her no great inconvenience, and if he should come, she would so shame him that he should never again set eyes on woman but his ears would tingle. Satisfied by what he heard, that his stratagem was well conceived, and success sure, Ricciardo added much in corroboration of his story, and having thus confirmed her belief in it, besought her to keep it always close, whereto she pledged her faith.

Next morning Ricciardo hied him to the good woman that kept the bagnio to which he had directed Catella, told her the enterprise which he had in hand, and prayed her to aid him therein so far as she might be able. The good woman, who was much beholden to him, assured him that she would gladly do so, and concerted with him all that was to be said and done. She had in the bagnio a room which was very dark, being without any window to admit the light. This room, by Ricciardo's direction, she set in order, and made up a bed there as well as she could, into which bed Ricciardo got, as soon as he had breakfasted, and there awaited Catella's coming.

Now Catella, still giving more credence to Ricciardo's story than it merited, had gone home in the evening in a most resentful mood, and Filippello, returning home the same evening with a mind greatly preoccupied, was scarce as familiar with her as he was wont to be. Which she marking, grew yet more suspicious than before, and said to herself: – "Doubtless he is thinking of the lady of whom he expects to take his pleasure to-morrow, as most assuredly he shall not;" and so, musing and meditating what she should say to him after their rencounter at the bagnio, she spent the best part of the night. But – to shorten my story – upon the stroke of none Catella, taking with her a single attendant, but otherwise adhering to her original intention, hied her to the bagnio which Ricciardo had indicated; and finding the good woman there, asked her whether Filippello had been there that day. Primed by Ricciardo, the good woman asked her, whether she were the lady that was to come to speak with him; to which she answered in the affirmative. "Go to him, then," said the good woman. And so Catella, in quest of that which she would gladly not have found, was shewn to the chamber where Ricciardo was, and having entered without uncovering her head, closed the door behind her. Overjoyed to see her, Ricciardo sprang out of bed, took her in his arms, and said caressingly: – "Welcome, my soul." Catella, dissembling, for she was minded at first to counterfeit another woman, returned his embrace, kissed him, and lavished endearments upon him; saying, the while, not a word, lest her speech should betray her. The darkness of the room, which was profound, was equally welcome to both; nor were they there long enough for their eyes to recover power. Ricciardo helped Catella on to the bed, where, with no word said on either side in a voice that might be recognized, they lay a long while, much more to the solace and satisfaction of the one than of the other party. Then, Catella, deeming it high time to vent her harboured resentment, burst forth in a blaze of wrath on this wise: – "Alas! how wretched is the lot of women, how misplaced of not a few the love they bear their husbands! Ah, woe is me! for eight years have I loved thee more dearly than my life; and now I find that thou, base miscreant that thou art, dost nought but burn and languish for love of another woman! Here thou hast been – with whom, thinkest thou? Even with her whom thou hast too long deluded with thy false blandishments, making pretence to love her while thou art enamoured of another. 'Tis I, Catella, not the wife of Ricciardo, false traitor that thou art; list if thou knowest my voice; 'tis I indeed! Ah! would we were but in the light! – it seems to me a thousand years till then – that I might shame thee as thou deservest, vile, pestilent dog that thou art! Alas! woe is me! such love as I have borne so many years – to whom? To this faithless dog, that, thinking to have a strange woman in his embrace, has in the brief while that I have been with him here lavished upon me more caresses and endearments than during all the forepast time that I have been his! A lively spark indeed art thou to-day, renegade dog, that shewest thyself so limp and enervate and impotent at home! But, God be praised, thou hast tilled thine own plot, and not another's, as thou didst believe. No wonder that last night thou heldest aloof from me; thou wast thinking of scattering thy seed elsewhere, and wast minded to shew thyself a lusty knight when thou shouldst join battle. But praise be to God and my sagacity, the water has nevertheless taken its proper course. Where is thy answer, culprit? Hast thou nought to say? Have my words struck thee dumb? God's faith I know not why I forbear to pluck thine eyes out with my fingers. Thou thoughtest to perpetrate this treason with no small secrecy; but, by God, one is as knowing as another; thy plot has failed; I had better hounds on thy trail than thou didst think for." Ricciardo, inly delighted by her words, made no answer, but embraced and kissed her more than ever, and overwhelmed her with his endearments. So she continued her reproaches, saying: – "Ay, thou thinkest to cajole me with thy feigned caresses, wearisome dog that thou art, and so to pacify and mollify me; but thou art mistaken. I shall never be mollified, until I have covered thee with infamy in the presence of all our kinsfolk and friends and neighbours. Am I not, miscreant, as fair as the wife of Ricciardo Minutolo? Am I not as good a lady as she? Why dost not answer, vile dog? Wherein has she the advantage of me? Away with thee! touch me not; thou hast done feats of arms more than enough for to-day. Well I know that, now that thou knowest who I am, thou wilt wreak thy will on me by force: but by God's grace I will yet disappoint thee. I know not why I forbear to send for Ricciardo, who loved me more than himself and yet was never able to boast that he had a single glance from me; nor know I why 'twere wrong to do so. Thou thoughtest to have his wife here, and 'tis no fault of thine that thou hadst her not: so, if I had him, thou couldst not justly blame me."

Enough had now been said: the lady's mortification was extreme; and, as she ended, Ricciardo bethought him that, if he suffered her, thus deluded, to depart, much evil might ensue. He therefore resolved to make himself known, and disabuse her of her error. So, taking her in his arms, and clipping her so close that she could not get loose, he said: – "Sweet my soul, be not wroth: that which, while artlessly I loved, I might not have, Love has taught me to compass by guile: know that I am thy Ricciardo."

At these words and the voice, which she recognized, Catella started, and would have sprung out of the bed; which being impossible, she essayed a cry; but Ricciardo laid a hand upon her mouth, and closed it, saying: – "Madam, that which is done can never be undone, though you should cry out for the rest of your days, and should you in such or any other wise publish this matter to any, two consequences will ensue. In the first place (and this is a point which touches you very nearly) your honour and fair fame will be blasted; for, however you may say that I lured you hither by guile, I shall deny it, and affirm, on the contrary, that I induced you to come hither by promises of money and gifts, and that 'tis but because you are vexed that what I gave you did not altogether come up to your expectations, that you make such a cry and clamour; and you know that folk are more prone to believe evil than good, and therefore I am no less likely to be believed than you. The further consequence will be mortal enmity between your husband and me, and the event were as like to be that I killed him as that he killed me: which if I did, you would never more know joy or peace. Wherefore, heart of my body, do not at one and the same time bring dishonour upon yourself and set your husband and me at strife and in jeopardy of our lives. You are not the first, nor will you be the last to be beguiled; nor have I beguiled you to rob you of aught, but for excess of love that I bear, and shall ever bear, you, being your most lowly vassal. And though it is now a great while that I, and what I have and can and am worth, are yours, yet I am minded that so it shall be henceforth more than ever before. Your discretion in other matters is not unknown to me, and I doubt not 'twill be equally manifest in this."

Ricciardo's admonitions were received by Catella with many a bitter tear; but though she was very wroth and very sad at heart, yet Ricciardo's true words so far commanded the assent of her reason, that she acknowledged that 'twas possible they might be verified by the event. Wherefore she made answer: "Ricciardo, I know not how God will grant me patience to bear the villainy and knavery which thou hast practised upon me; and though in this place, to which simplicity and excess of jealousy guided my steps, I raise no cry, rest assured that I shall never be happy, until in one way or another I know myself avenged of that which thou hast done to me. Wherefore unhand me, let me go: thou hast had thy desire of me, and hast tormented me to thy heart's content: 'tis time to release me; let me go, I pray thee." But Ricciardo, seeing that she was still much ruffled in spirit, was resolved not to let her go, until he had made his peace with her. So he addressed himself to soothe her; and by dint of most dulcet phrases and entreaties and adjurations he did at last prevail with her to give him her pardon; nay, by joint consent, they tarried there a great while to the exceeding great delight of both. Indeed the lady, finding her lover's kisses smack much better than those of her husband, converted her asperity into sweetness, and from that day forth cherished a most tender love for Ricciardo; whereof, using all circumspection, they many a time had solace. God grant us solace of ours.

Third Day
Novel VII

— Tedaldo, being in disfavour with his lady, departs from Florence. He returns thither after a while in the guise of a pilgrim, has speech of his lady, and makes her sensible of her fault. Her husband, convicted of slaying him, he delivers from peril of death, reconciles him with his brothers, and thereafter discreetly enjoys his lady. —

SO CEASED FIAMMETTA; and, when all had bestowed on her their meed of praise, the queen – to lose no time – forthwith bade Emilia resume the narration. So thus Emilia began: –

I am minded to return to our city, whence my two last predecessors saw fit to depart, and to shew you how one of our citizens recovered the lady he had lost. Know then that there was in Florence a young noble, his name Tedaldo Elisei, who being beyond measure enamoured of a lady hight Monna Ermellina, wife of one Aldobrandino Palermini, and by reason of his admirable qualities richly deserving to have his desire, found Fortune nevertheless adverse, as she is wont to be to the prosperous. Inasmuch as, for some reason or another, the lady, having shewn herself gracious towards Tedaldo for a while, completely altered her mien, and not only shewed him no further favour, but would not so much as receive a message from him or suffer him to see her face; whereby he fell a prey to a grievous and distressful melancholy; but so well had he concealed his love that the cause of his melancholy was surmised by none. He tried hard in divers ways to recover the love which he deemed himself to have lost for no fault of his, and finding all his efforts unavailing, he resolved to bid the world adieu, that he might not afford her who was the cause of his distress the satisfaction of seeing him languish. So he got together as much money as he might, and secretly, no word said to friend or kinsman except only a familiar gossip, who knew all, he took his departure for Ancona. Arrived there, he assumed the name of Filippo Santodeccio, and having forgathered with a rich merchant, entered his service. The merchant took him with him to Cyprus aboard one of his ships, and was so well pleased with his bearing and behaviour that he not only gave him a handsome salary but made him in a sort his companion, and entrusted him with the management of no small part of his affairs: wherein he proved himself so apt and assiduous, that in the course of a few years he was himself established in credit and wealth and great repute as a merchant. Seven years thus passed, during which, albeit his thoughts frequently reverted to his cruel mistress, and sorely love smote him, and much he yearned to see her again, yet such was his firmness that he came off conqueror, until one day in Cyprus it so befell that there was sung in his hearing a song that he had himself composed, and of which the theme was the mutual love that was between his lady and him, and the delight that he had of her; which as he heard, he found it incredible that she should have forgotten him, and burned with such a desire to see her once more, that, being able to hold out no longer, he made up his mind to return to Florence. So, having set all his affairs in order, he betook him, attended only by a single servant, to Ancona; whence he sent all his effects, as they arrived, forward to Florence, consigning them to a friend of his Ancontan partner, and followed with his servant in the disguise of a pilgrim returned from the Holy Sepulchre. Arrived at

Florence, he put up at a little hostelry kept by two brothers hard by his lady's house, whither he forthwith hied him, hoping that, perchance, he might have sight of her from the street; but, finding all barred and bolted, doors, windows and all else, he doubted much, she must be dead, or have removed thence. So, with a very heavy heart, he returned to the house of the two brothers, and to his great surprise found his own four brothers standing in front of it, all in black. He knew that he was so changed from his former semblance, both in dress and in person, that he might not readily be recognized, and he had therefore no hesitation in going up to a shoemaker and asking him why these men were all dressed in black. The shoemaker answered: – "'Tis because 'tis not fifteen days since a brother of theirs, Tedaldo by name, that had been long abroad, was slain; and I understand that they have proved in court that one Aldobrandino Palermini, who is under arrest, did the deed, because Tedaldo, who loved his wife, was come back to Florence incognito to forgather with her." Tedaldo found it passing strange that there should be any one so like him as to be mistaken for him, and deplored Aldobrandino's evil plight. He had learned, however, that the lady was alive and well. So, as 'twas now night, he hied him, much perplexed in mind, into the inn, and supped with his servant. The bedroom assigned him was almost at the top of the house, and the bed was none of the best. Thoughts many and disquieting haunted his mind, and his supper had been but light. Whereby it befell that midnight came and went, and Tedaldo was still awake. As thus he watched, he heard shortly after midnight, a noise as of persons descending from the roof into the house, and then through the chinks of the door of his room he caught the flicker of an ascending light. Wherefore he stole softly to the door, and peeping through a chink to make out what was afoot, he saw a very fine young woman bearing a light, and three men making towards her, being evidently those that had descended from the roof. The men exchanged friendly greetings with the young woman, and then one said to her: – "Now, God be praised, we may make our minds easy, for we are well assured that judgment for the death of Tedaldo Elisei is gotten by his brothers against Aldobrandino Palermini, and he has confessed, and the sentence is already drawn up; but still it behoves us to hold our peace; for, should it ever get abroad that we were guilty, we shall stand in the like jeopardy as Aldobrandino." So saying, they took leave of the woman, who seemed much cheered, and went to bed. What he had heard set Tedaldo musing on the number and variety of the errors to which men are liable: as, first, how his brothers had mourned and interred a stranger in his stead, and then charged an innocent man upon false suspicion, and by false witness brought him into imminent peril of death: from which he passed to ponder the blind severity of laws and magistrates, who from misguided zeal to elicit the truth not unfrequently become ruthless, and, adjudging that which is false, forfeit the title which they claim of ministers of God and justice, and do but execute the mandates of iniquity and the Evil One. And so he came at last to consider the possibility of saving Aldobrandino, and formed a plan for the purpose. Accordingly, on the morrow, when he was risen, he left his servant at the inn, and hied him alone, at what he deemed a convenient time, to his lady's house, where, finding, by chance, the door open, he entered, and saw his lady sitting, all tears and lamentations, in a little parlour on the ground-floor. Whereat he all but wept for sympathy; and drawing near her, he said: – "Madam, be not troubled in spirit: your peace is nigh you." Whereupon the lady raised her head, and said between her sobs: – "Good man, what dost thou, a pilgrim, if I mistake not, from distant parts, know either of my peace or of my affliction?" "Madam," returned the pilgrim, "I am of Constantinople, and am but now come hither, at God's behest, that I may give you laughter for tears, and deliver your husband from death." "But," said the lady, "if thou art of Constantinople, and but now arrived, how is't that thou knowest either who my husband is, or who I am?" Whereupon the pilgrim gave her the whole narrative, from the very beginning, of Aldobrandino's sufferings; he also told her, who she was, how long she had been married, and much besides that was known to him of her affairs: whereat the lady was lost in wonder, and, taking him to be a prophet, threw herself on her knees at his feet, and besought him for God's sake, if he were come to save Aldobrandino, to lose no time, for the matter brooked no delay. Thus adjured, the pilgrim assumed an air of great sanctity, as he said: – "Arise, Madam, weep not, but hearken diligently to what I shall say to you, and look to it that you impart it to none. I have it by revelation of God that the tribulation wherein you stand is come upon you in requital of a sin which you did once commit, of which God is minded that this suffering be a partial purgation, and that you make reparation in full, if you would not find yourself in a far more grievous plight." "Sir," replied the lady, "many sins have I committed, nor know I how among them all to single out that whereof, more than another, God requires reparation at my hands – wherefore, if you know it, tell it me, and what by way of reparation I may do, that will I do." "Madam," returned the pilgrim, "well wot I what it is, nor shall I question you thereof for my better instruction, but that the rehearsal may give you increase of remorse therefor. But pass we now to fact. Tell me, mind you ever to have had a lover?" Whereat the lady heaved a deep sigh; then, marvelling not a little, for she had thought 'twas known to none, albeit on the day when the man was slain, who was afterwards buried as Tedaldo, there had been some buzz about it, occasioned by some indiscreet words dropped by Tedaldo's gossip and confidant, she made answer: – "I see that there is nought that men keep secret but God reveals it to you; wherefore I shall not endeavour to hide my secrets from you. True it is that in my youth I was beyond measure enamoured of the unfortunate young man whose death is imputed to my husband; whom I mourned with grief unfeigned, for, albeit I shewed myself harsh and cruel towards him before his departure, yet neither thereby, nor by his long absence, nor yet by his calamitous death was my heart estranged from him." Then said the pilgrim: – "'Twas not the unfortunate young man now dead that you did love, but Tedaldo Elisei. But let that pass; now tell me: wherefore lost he your good graces? Did he ever offend you?" "Nay verily," answered the lady, "he never offended me at all. My harshness was prompted by an accursed friar, to whom I once confessed, and who, when I told him of the love I bore Tedaldo, and my intimacy with him, made my ears so tingle and sing that I still shudder to think of it, warning me that, if I gave it not up, I should fall into the jaws of the Devil in the abyss of hell, and be cast into the avenging fire. Whereby I was so terrified that I quite made my mind up to discontinue my intimacy with him, and, to trench the matter, I would thenceforth have none of his letters or messages; and so, I suppose, he went away in despair, though I doubt not, had he persevered a while longer, I should not have seen him wasting away like snow in sunshine without relenting of my harsh resolve; for in sooth there was nothing in the world I would so gladly have done." Then said the pilgrim: – "Madam, 'tis this sin, and this only, that has brought upon you your present tribulation. I know positively that Tedaldo did never put force upon you: 'twas of your own free will, and for that he pleased you, that you became enamoured of him, your constant visitor, your intimate friend he became, because you yourself would have it so; and in the course of your intimacy you shewed him such favour by word and deed that, if he loved you first, you multiplied his love full a thousandfold. And if so it was, and well I know it was so, what justification had you for thus harshly severing yourself from him? You should have considered the whole matter before the die was cast, and not have entered upon it, if you deemed you might have cause to repent you of it as a sin. As soon as he became yours, you became his. Had he not been yours, you might have acted as you had thought fit, at your own unfettered discretion, but, as you were his, 'twas robbery, 'twas conduct most disgraceful, to sever yourself from him against his will. Now you must know that I am a friar; and therefore all the ways of friars are familiar to me; nor does it misbecome me, as it might another, to speak for your behoof somewhat freely of them; as I am minded to do that you may have better understanding of them in the future than you would seem to have had in the past. Time was when the friars were most holy and worthy men, but those who to-day take the name and claim the reputation of friars have nought of the friar save only the habit: nay, they have not even that: for, whereas their founders ordained that their habits should be strait, of a sorry sort, and of coarse stuff, apt symbols of a soul that in arraying the body in so mean a garb did despite to all things temporal, our modern friars will have them full, and double, and resplendent, and of the finest stuff, and of a fashion goodly and pontifical, wherein without shame they flaunt it like peacocks in the church, in the piazza, even as do the laity in their robes. And as the fisherman casts his net into the stream with intent to take many fish at one throw: so 'tis the main solicitude and study, art and craft of these friars to embrace and entangle within the ample folds of their vast swelling skirts beguines, widows and other foolish women, ay, and men likewise in great number. Wherefore, to speak with more exactitude, the friars of to-day have nought of the habit of the friar save only the colour thereof. And, whereas the friars of old time sought to win men to their salvation, those of to-day seek to win their women and their wealth; wherefore they have made it and make it their sole concern by declamation and imagery to strike terror into the souls of fools, and to make believe that sins are purged by alms and masses; to the end that they, base wretches that have fled to friarage not to ensue holiness but to escape hardship, may receive from this man bread, from that man wine, and from the other man a donation for masses for the souls of his dead. True indeed it is that sins are purged by almsgiving and prayer; but, did they who give the alms know, did they but understand to whom they give them, they would be more apt to keep them to themselves, or throw them to so many pigs. And, knowing that the fewer be they that share great riches, the greater their ease, 'tis the study of each how best by declamation and intimidation to oust others from that whereof he would fain be the sole owner. They censure lust in men, that, they turning therefrom, the sole use of their women may remain to the censors: they condemn usury and unlawful gains, that, being entrusted with the restitution thereof, they may be able to enlarge their habits, and to purchase bishoprics and other great preferments with the very money which they have made believe must bring its possessor to perdition. And when they are taxed with these and many other discreditable practices, they deem that there is no censure, however grave, of which they may not be quit by their glib formula: – 'Follow our precepts, not our practice:' as if 'twere possible that the sheep should be of a more austere and rigid virtue than the shepherds. And how many of these, whom they put off with this formula, understand it not in the way in which they enunciate it, not a few of them know. The friars of to-day would have you follow their precepts, that is to say, they would have you fill their purses with coin, confide to them your secrets, practise continence, be longsuffering, forgive those that trespass against you, keep yourselves from evil speaking; all which things are good, seemly, holy. But to what end? To the end that they may be able to do that which, if the laity do it, they will not be able to do. Who knows not that idleness cannot subsist without money? Spend thy money on thy pleasures, and the friar will not be able to live in sloth in his order. Go after women, and there will be no place for the friar. Be not longsuffering, pardon not the wrong-doer, and the friar will not dare to cross thy threshold to corrupt thy family. But wherefore pursue I the topic through every detail? They accuse themselves as often as they so excuse themselves in the hearing of all that have understanding. Why seclude they not themselves, if they misdoubt their power to lead continent and holy lives? Or if they must needs not live as recluses, why follow they not that other holy text of the Gospel: – Christ began to do and to teach? Let them practise first, and school us with their precepts afterwards. A thousand such have I seen in my day, admirers, lovers, philanderers, not of ladies of the world alone, but of nuns; ay, and they too such as made the most noise in the pulpits. Is it such as they that we are to follow? He that does so, pleases himself; but God knows if he do wisely. But assume that herein we must allow that your censor, the friar, spoke truth, to wit, that none may break the marriage-vow without very grave sin. What then? to rob a man, to slay him, to make of him an exile and a wanderer on the face of the earth, are not these yet greater sins? None will deny that so they are. A woman that indulges herself in the intimate use with a man commits but a sin of nature; but if she rob him, or slay him, or drive him out into exile, her sin proceeds from depravity of spirit. That you did rob Tedaldo, I have already shewn you, in that, having of your own free will become his, you reft you from him. I now go further and say that, so far as in you lay, you slew him, seeing that, shewing yourself ever more and more cruel, you did your utmost to drive him to take his own life; and in the law's intent he that is the cause that wrong is done is as culpable as he that does it. Nor is it deniable that you were the cause that for seven years he has been an exile and a wanderer upon the face of the earth. Wherefore upon each of the said three articles you are found guilty of a greater crime than you committed by your intimacy with him. But consider we the matter more closely: perchance Tedaldo merited such treatment: nay, but assuredly 'twas not so. You have yourself so confessed: besides which I know that he loves you more dearly than himself. He would laud, he would extol, he would magnify you above all other ladies so as never was heard the like, wheresoever 'twas seemly for him to speak of you, and it might be done without exciting suspicion. All his bliss, all his honour, all his liberty he avowed was entirely in your disposal. Was he not of noble birth? And for beauty might he not compare with the rest of his townsfolk? Did he not excel in all the exercises and accomplishments proper to youth? Was he not beloved, held dear, well seen of all men? You will not deny it. How then could you at the behest of a paltry friar, silly, brutish and envious, bring yourself to deal with him in any harsh sort? I cannot estimate the error of those ladies who look askance on men and hold them cheap; whereas, bethinking them of what they are themselves, and what and how great is the nobility with which God has endowed man above all the other animals, they ought rather to glory in the love which men give them, and hold them most dear, and with all zeal study to please them, that so their love may never fail. In what sort you did so, instigated by the chatter of a friar, some broth-guzzling, pastry-gorging knave without a doubt, you know; and peradventure his purpose was but to instal himself in the place whence he sought to oust another. This then is the sin which the Divine justice, which, ever operative, suffers no perturbation of its even balance, or arrest of judgment, has decreed not to leave unpunished: wherefore, as without due cause you devised how you might despoil Tedaldo of yourself, so without due cause your husband has been placed and is in jeopardy of his life on Tedaldo's account, and to your sore affliction. Wherefrom if you would be delivered, there is that which you must promise, ay, and (much more) which you must perform: to wit, that, should it ever betide that Tedaldo return hither from his long exile, you will restore to him your favour, your love, your tender regard, your intimacy, and reinstate him in the position which he held before you foolishly hearkened to the halfwitted friar."

Thus ended the pilgrim; and the lady, who had followed him with the closest attention, deeming all that he advanced very sound, and doubting not that her tribulation was, as he said, in requital of her sin, spoke thus: – "Friend of God, well I wot that the matters which you discourse are true, and, thanks to your delineation, I now in great measure know what manner of men are the friars, whom I have hitherto regarded as all alike holy; nor doubt I that great was my fault in the course which I pursued towards Tedaldo; and gladly, were it in my power, would I make reparation in the manner which you have indicated. But how is this feasible? Tedaldo can never return to us. He is dead. Wherefore I know not why I must needs give you a promise which cannot be performed." "Madam," returned the pilgrim, "'tis revealed to me by God that Tedaldo is by no means dead, but alive and well and happy, so only he enjoyed your favour." "Nay, but," said the lady, "speak advisedly; I saw his body done to death by more than one knife-wound; I folded it in these arms, and drenched the dead face with many a tear; whereby, perchance, I gave occasion for the bruit that has been made to my disadvantage." "Say what you may, Madam," rejoined the pilgrim," I assure you that Tedaldo lives, and if you will but give the promise, then, for its fulfilment, I have good hope that you will soon see him." Whereupon: "I give the promise," said the lady, "and right gladly will I make it good; nor is there aught that might happen that would yield me such delight as to see my husband free and scatheless, and Tedaldo alive." Tedaldo now deemed it wise to make himself known, and establish the lady in a more sure hope of her husband's safety. Wherefore he said: – "Madam, to set your mind at ease in regard of your husband, I must first impart to you a secret, which be mindful to disclose to none so long as you live." Then – for such was the confidence which the lady reposed in the pilgrim's apparent sanctity that they were by themselves in a place remote from observation – Tedaldo drew forth a ring which he had guarded with the most jealous care, since it had been given him by the lady on the last night when they were together, and said, as he shewed it to her: – "Madam, know you this?" The lady recognized it forthwith, and answered: – "I do, Sir; I gave it long ago to Tedaldo." Then the pilgrim, rising and throwing off his sclavine and hat, said with the Florentine accent: – "And know you me?" The lady recognizing forthwith the form and semblance of Tedaldo, was struck dumb with wonder and fear as of a corpse that is seen to go about as if alive, and was much rather disposed to turn and flee from Tedaldo returned from the tomb than to come forward and welcome Tedaldo arrived from Cyprus. But when Tedaldo said to her: – "Fear not, Madam, your Tedaldo am I, alive and well, nor was I ever dead, whatever you and my brothers may think," the lady, partly awed, partly reassured by his voice, regarded him with rather more attention, and inly affirming that 'twas in very truth Tedaldo, threw herself upon his neck, and wept, and kissed him, saying: – "Sweet my Tedaldo, welcome home." "Madam," replied Tedaldo after he had kissed and embraced her, "time serves not now for greetings more intimate. 'Tis for me to be up and doing, that Aldobrandino may be restored to you safe and sound; touching which matter you will, I trust, before to-morrow at even hear tidings that will gladden your heart; indeed I expect to have good news to-night, and, if so, will come and tell it you, when I shall be less straitened than I am at present." He then resumed his sclavine and hat, and having kissed the lady again, and bade her be of good cheer, took his leave, and hied him to the prison, where Aldobrandino lay more occupied with apprehension of imminent death than hope of deliverance to come. As ministrant of consolation, he gained ready admittance of the warders, and, seating himself by Aldobrandino's side, he said: – "Aldobrandino, in me thou seest a friend sent thee by God, who is touched with pity of thee by reason of thy innocence; wherefore, if in reverent submission to Him thou wilt grant me a slight favour that I shall ask of thee, without fail, before to-morrow at even, thou shalt, in lieu of the doom of death that thou awaitest, hear thy acquittal pronounced." "Worthy man," replied Aldobrandino, "I know thee not, nor mind I ever to have seen thee; wherefore, as thou shewest thyself solicitous for my safety, my friend indeed thou must needs be, even as thou sayst. And in sooth the crime, for which they say I ought to be doomed to death, I never committed, though others enough I have committed, which perchance have brought me to this extremity. However, if so be that God has now pity on me, this I tell thee in reverent submission to Him, that, whereas 'tis but a little thing that thou cravest of me, there is nought, however great, but I would not only promise but gladly do it; wherefore, even ask what thou wilt, and, if so be that I escape, I will without fail keep my word to the letter." "Nay," returned the pilgrim, "I ask but this of thee, that thou pardon Tedaldo's four brothers, that in the belief that thou wast guilty of their brother's death they brought thee to this strait, and, so they ask thy forgiveness, account them as thy brothers and friends." "How sweet," replied Aldobrandino, "is the savour, how ardent the desire, of vengeance, none knows but he that is wronged; but yet, so God may take thought for my deliverance, I will gladly pardon, nay, I do now pardon them, and if I go hence alive and free, I will thenceforth have them in such regard as shall content thee." Satisfied with this answer, the pilgrim, without further parley, heartily exhorted Aldobrandino to be of good cheer; assuring him that, before the next day was done, he should be certified beyond all manner of doubt of his deliverance; and so he left him.

On quitting the prison the pilgrim hied him forthwith to the signory, and being closeted with a knight that was in charge, thus spoke: – "My lord, 'tis the duty of all, and most especially of those who hold your place, zealously to bestir themselves that the truth be brought to light, in order as well that those bear not the penalty who have not committed the crime, as that the guilty be punished. And that this may come to pass to your honour and the undoing of the delinquent, I am come hither to you. You wot that you have dealt rigorously with Aldobrandino Palermini, and have found, as you think, that 'twas he that slew Tedaldo Elisei, and you are about to condemn him; wherein you are most certainly in error, as I doubt not before midnight to prove to you, delivering the murderers into your hands." The worthy knight, who was not without pity for Aldobrandino, readily gave ear to the pilgrim's words. He conversed at large with him, and availing himself of his guidance, made an easy capture of the two brothers that kept the inn and their servant in their first sleep. He was about to put them the torture, to elicit the true state of the case, when, their courage failing, they confessed without the least reserve, severally at first, and then jointly, that 'twas they that had slain Tedaldo Elisei, not knowing who he was. Asked for why, they answered that 'twas because he had sorely harassed the wife of one of them, and would have constrained her to do his pleasure, while they were out of doors. Whereof the pilgrim was no sooner apprised, than by leave of the knight he withdrew, and hied him privily to the house of Madonna Ermellina, whom (the rest of the household being gone to bed) he found awaiting him alone, and equally anxious for good news of her husband and a complete reconciliation with her Tedaldo. On entering, he blithely exclaimed: – "Rejoice, dearest my lady, for thou mayst rest assured that to-morrow thou shalt have thy Aldobrandino back here safe and sound;" and to confirm her faith in his words, he told her all that he had done. Greater joy was never woman's than hers of two such glad surprises; to wit, to have Tedaldo with her alive again, whom she had wailed for verily dead, and to know Aldobrandino, whom she had thought in no long time to wail for dead, now out of jeopardy. Wherefore, when she had affectionately embraced and kissed her Tedaldo, they hied them to bed together, and with hearty goodwill made gracious and gladsome consummation of their peace by interchange of sweet solace.

With the approach of day Tedaldo rose, and having first apprised the lady of his purpose and enjoined her, as before, to keep it most secret, resumed his pilgrim's habit, and sallied forth of her house, to be ready, as occasion should serve, to act in Aldobrandino's interest. As soon as 'twas day, the signory, deeming themselves amply conversant with the affair, set Aldobrandino at large; and a few days later they caused the malefactors to be beheaded in the place where they had done the murder.

Great was Aldobrandino's joy to find himself free, not less great was that of his lady and all his friends and kinsfolk; and as 'twas through the pilgrim that it had come about, they brought him to their house, there to reside as long as he cared to tarry in the city; nor could they do him honour and cheer enough, and most of all the lady, who knew her man. But after awhile, seeing that his brothers were not only become a common laughing-stock by reason of Aldobrandino's acquittal, but had armed themselves for very fear, he felt that their reconciliation with him brooked no delay, and accordingly craved of him performance of his promise. Aldobrandino replied handsomely that it should be had at once. The pilgrim then bade him arrange for the following day a grand banquet, at which he and his kinsfolk and their ladies were to entertain the four brothers and their ladies, adding that he would himself go forthwith as Aldobrandino's envoy, and bid them welcome to his peace and banquet. All which being approved by Aldobrandino, the pilgrim hied him with all speed to the four brothers, whom by ample, apt and unanswerable argument he readily induced to reinstate themselves in Aldobrandino's friendship by suing for his forgiveness: which done, he bade them and their ladies to breakfast with Aldobrandino on the morrow, and they, being assured of his good faith, were consenting to come. So, on the morrow, at the breakfast hour, Tedaldo's four brothers, still wearing their black, came with certain of their friends to Aldobrandino's house, where he awaited them; and, in presence of the company that had been bidden to meet them, laid down their arms, and made surrender to Aldobrandino, asking his pardon of that which they had done against him. Aldobrandino received them compassionately, wept, kissed each on the mouth, and let few words suffice to remit each offence. After them came their sisters and their wives, all habited sadly, and were graciously received by Madonna Ermellina and the other ladies. The guests, men and women alike, found all things ordered at the banquet with magnificence, nor aught unmeet for commendation save the restraint which the yet recent grief, betokened by the sombre garb of Tedaldo's kinsfolk, laid upon speech (wherein some had found matter to except against the banquet and the pilgrim for devising it, as he well knew), but, as he had premeditated, in due time, he stood up, the others being occupied with their dessert, and spoke thus: – "Nothing is wanting to complete the gaiety of this banquet except the presence of Tedaldo; whom, as you have been long time with him and have not known him, I will point out to you." So, having divested himself of his sclavine and whatever else in his garb denoted the pilgrim, he remained habited in a tunic of green taffeta, in which guise, so great was the wonder with which all regarded him that, though they recognized him, 'twas long before any dared to believe that 'twas actually Tedaldo. Marking their surprise, Tedaldo told them not a little about themselves, their family connexions, their recent history, and his own adventures. Whereat his brothers and the rest of the men, all weeping for joy, hasted to embrace him, followed by the women, as well those that were not, as those that were, of kin to him, save only Madonna Ermellina. Which Aldobrandino observing, said: – "What is this, Ermellina? How comes it that, unlike the other ladies, thou alone dost Tedaldo no cheer?" "Cheer," replied the lady in the hearing of all, "would I gladly do him such as no other woman has done or could do, seeing that I am more beholden to him than any other woman, in that to him I owe it that I have thee with me again; 'tis but the words spoken to my disadvantage, while we mourned him that we deemed Tedaldo, that give me pause." "Now out upon thee," said Aldobrandino, "thinkest thou that I heed the yelping of these curs? His zeal for my deliverance has abundantly disproved it, besides which I never believed it. Quick, get thee up, and go and embrace him." The lady, who desired nothing better, was in this not slow to obey her husband; she rose forthwith, and embraced Tedaldo as the other ladies had done, and did him gladsome cheer. Tedaldo's brothers and all the company, men and women alike, heartily approved Aldobrandino's handsomeness; and so whatever of despite the rumour had engendered in the minds of any was done away. And, now that all had done him cheer, Tedaldo with his own hands rent his brothers' suits of black upon their backs, as also the sad-hued garments which his sisters and sisters-in-law wore, and bade bring other apparel. Which when they had donned, there was no lack of singing, dancing and other sorts of merry-making; whereby the banquet, for all its subdued beginning, had a sonorous close. Then, just as they were, in the blithest of spirits, they hied them all to Tedaldo's house, where in the evening they supped; and in this manner they held festival for several days.

'Twas some time before the Florentines ceased to look on Tedaldo as a portent, as if he were risen from the dead; and a shadow of doubt whether he were really Tedaldo or no continued to lurk in the minds of not a few, including even his brothers: they had no assured belief; and in that frame had perchance long continued, but for a casual occurrence that shewed them who the murdered man was. It so befell that one day some men-at-arms from Lunigiana passed by their house, and seeing Tedaldo accosted him, saying: – "Good-morrow to thee, Faziuolo." To whom Tedaldo, in the presence of his brothers, answered: – "You take me for another." Whereat they were abashed, and asked his pardon, saying: – "Sooth to tell, you are liker than we ever knew any man like to another to a comrade of ours, Faziuolo da Pontremoli by name, who came hither a fortnight ago, or perhaps a little more, since when we have not been able to learn what became of him. Most true it is that your dress surprised us, because he, like ourselves, was a soldier." Whereupon Tedaldo's eldest brother came forward, and asked how their comrade had been accoutred. They told him, and 'twas found to have been exactly as they said: by which and other evidence 'twas established that 'twas Faziuolo that had been murdered, and not Tedaldo; of whom thenceforth no suspicion lurked in the minds of his brothers or any one else.

So, then, Tedaldo returned home very rich, and remained constant in his love; nor did the lady again treat him harshly; but, using discretion, they long had mutual solace of their love. God grant us solace of ours.

Third Day
Novel VIII

— *Ferondo, having taken a certain powder, is interred for dead; is disinterred by the abbot, who enjoys his wife; is put in prison and taught to believe that he is in purgatory; is then resuscitated, and rears as his own a boy begotten by the abbot upon his wife.* —

ENDED EMILIA'S long story, which to none was the less pleasing for its length, but was deemed of all the ladies brief in regard of the number and variety of the events therein recounted, a gesture of the queen sufficed to convey her behest to Lauretta, and cause her thus to begin: –

"Dearest ladies, I have it in mind to tell you a true story, which wears far more of the aspect of a lie than of that which it really was: 'tis brought to my recollection by that which we have heard of one being bewailed and buried in lieu of another. My story then is of one that, living, was buried for dead, and after believed with many others that he came out of the tomb not as one that had not died but as one risen from the dead; whereby he was venerated as a saint who ought rather to have been condemned as a criminal."

Know then that there was and still is in Tuscany an abbey, situate, as we see not a few, in a somewhat solitary spot, wherein the office of abbot was held by a monk, who in all other matters ordered his life with great sanctity, save only in the commerce with women, and therein knew so well how to cloak his indulgence, that scarce any there were that so much as suspected – not to say detected it – so holy and just was he reputed in all matters. Now the abbot consorted much with a very wealthy contadino, Ferondo by name, a man coarse and gross beyond measure, whose friendship the abbot only cared for because of the opportunities which it afforded of deriving amusement from his simplicity; and during their intercourse the abbot discovered that Ferondo had a most beautiful wife of whom he became so hotly enamoured that he could think of nought else either by day or by night. But learning that, however simple and inept in all other matters, Ferondo shewed excellent good sense in cherishing and watching over this wife of his, he almost despaired. However, being very astute, he prevailed so far with Ferondo, that he would sometimes bring his wife with him to take a little recreation in the abbey-garden, where he discoursed to them with all lowliness of the blessedness of life eternal, and the most pious works of many men and women of times past, insomuch that the lady conceived a desire to confess to him, and craved and had Ferondo's leave therefor. So, to the abbot's boundless delight, the lady came and seated herself at his feet to make her confession, whereto she prefixed the following exordium: – "If God, Sir, had given me a husband, or had not permitted me to have one, perchance 'twould be easy for me, under your guidance, to enter the way, of which you have spoken, that leads to life eternal. But, considering what manner of man Ferondo is, and his stupidity, I may call myself a widow, while yet I am married in that, so long as he lives, I may have no other husband; and he, fool that he is, is without the least cause so inordinately jealous of me that 'tis not possible but that my life with him be one of perpetual tribulation and woe. Wherefore before I address myself to make further confession, I in all humility beseech you to be pleased to give me some counsel of this matter, for here or nowhere is to be found the source of the amelioration of my life, and if it be not found, neither confession nor any other good work will be of any avail." The abbot was overjoyed to hear her thus speak, deeming that Fortune had opened a way to the fulfilment of his hearts desire. Wherefore he said: – "My daughter, I doubt not that 'tis a great affliction to a lady, fair and delicate as you are, to have a fool for a husband, and still more so he should be jealous: and as your husband is both the one and the other, I readily credit what you say of your tribulation. But, to come to the point, I see no resource or remedy in this case, save this only, that Ferondo be cured of his jealousy. The medicine that shall cure him I know very well how to devise, but it behoves you to keep secret what I am about to tell you." "Doubt not of it, my father," said the lady; "for I had rather suffer death than tell any aught that you forbade me to tell. But the medicine, how is it to be devised?" "If we would have him cured," replied the abbot, "it can only be by his going to purgatory." "And how may that be?" returned the lady; "can he go thither while he yet lives?" "He must die," answered the abbot; "and so he will go thither; and when he has suffered pain enough to be cured of his jealousy, we have certain prayers with which we will supplicate God to restore him to life, and He will do so." "Then," said the lady; "am I to remain a widow?" "Yes," replied the abbot, "for a certain time, during which you must be very careful not to let yourself be married to another, because 'twould offend God, and when Ferondo was restored to life, you would have to go back to him, and he would be more jealous than ever." "Be it so then," said the lady; "if he be but cured of his jealousy, and so I be not doomed to pass the rest of my days in prison, I shall be content: do as you think best." "And so will I," said the abbot; "but what reward shall I have for such a service?" "My father," said the lady, "what you please; so only it be in my power. But what may the like of me do that may be acceptable to a man such as you?" "Madam," replied the abbot, "'tis in your power to do no less for me than I am about to do for you: as that which I am minded to do will ensure your comfort and consolation, so there is that which you may do which will be the deliverance and salvation of my life." "If so it be," said the lady, "I shall not be found wanting." "In that case," said the abbot, "you will give me your love, and gratify my passion for you, with which I am all afire and wasting away." Whereto the lady, all consternation, replied: – "Alas! my father, what is this you crave? I took you for a holy man; now does it beseem holy men to make such overtures to ladies that come to them for counsel?" "Marvel not, fair my soul," returned the abbot; "hereby is my holiness in no wise diminished, for holiness resides in the soul, and this which I ask of you is but a sin of the flesh. But, however it may be, such is the might of your bewitching beauty, that love constrains me thus to act. And, let me tell you, good cause have you to vaunt you of your beauty more than other women, in that it delights the saints, who are used to contemplate celestial beauties; whereto I may add that, albeit I am an abbot, yet I am a man even as others, and, as you see, not yet old. Nor need this matter seem formidable to you, but rather to be anticipated with pleasure, for, while Ferondo is in purgatory, I shall be your nightly companion, and will give you such solace as he should have given you; nor will it ever be discovered by any, for all think of me even as you did a while ago, or even more so. Reject not the grace that God accords you; for 'tis in your power to have, and, if you are wise and follow my advice, you shall have that which women not a few desire in vain to have. And moreover I have jewels fair and rare, which I am minded shall be yours and none other's. Wherefore, sweet my hope, deny me not due guerdon of the service which I gladly render you."

    The lady, her eyes still downcast, knew not how to deny him, and yet scrupled to gratify him: wherefore the abbot, seeing that she had hearkened and hesitated to answer, deemed that she was already half won, and following up what he had said with much more to the like effect, did not rest until he had persuaded her that she would do well to comply: and so with some confusion she told him that she was ready to obey his every behest; but it might not be until

Ferondo was in purgatory. The abbot, well content, replied: – "And we will send him thither forthwith: do but arrange that he come hither to stay with me to-morrow or the day after." Which said, he slipped a most beautiful ring on her finger, and dismissed her. Pleased with the gift, and expecting more to come, the lady rejoined her attendants, with whom she forthwith fell a talking marvellous things of the abbot's sanctity, and so went home with them.

Some few days after, Ferondo being come to the abbey, the abbot no sooner saw him than he resolved to send him to purgatory. So he selected from among his drugs a powder of marvellous virtue, which he had gotten in the Levant from a great prince, who averred that 'twas wont to be used by the Old Man of the Mountain, when he would send any one to or bring him from his paradise, and that, without doing the recipient any harm, 'twould induce in him, according to the quantity of the dose, a sleep of such duration and quality that, while the efficacy of the powder lasted, none would deem him to be alive. Whereof he took enough to cause a three days' sleep, and gave it to Ferondo in his cell in a beaker that had still some wine in it, so that he drank it unwittingly: after which he took Ferondo to the cloister, and there with some of his monks fell to making merry with him and his ineptitudes. In no long time, however, the powder so wrought, that Ferondo was seized in the head with a fit of somnolence so sudden and violent that he slept as he stood, and sleeping fell to the ground. The abbot put on an agitated air, caused him to be untrussed, sent for cold water, and had it sprinkled on his face, and applied such other remedies as if he would fain call back life and sense banished by vapours of the stomach, or some other intrusive force; but, as, for all that he and his monks did, Ferondo did not revive, they, after feeling his pulse and finding there no sign of life, one and all pronounced him certainly dead. Wherefore they sent word to his wife and kinsfolk, who came forthwith, and mourned a while; after which Ferondo in his clothes was by the abbot's order laid in a tomb. The lady went home, saying that nothing should ever part her from a little son that she had borne Ferondo; and so she occupied herself with the care of her son and Ferondo's estate. At night the abbot rose noiselessly, and with the help of a Bolognese monk, in whom he reposed much trust, and who was that very day arrived from Bologna, got Ferondo out of the tomb, and bore him to a vault, which admitted no light, having been made to serve as a prison for delinquent monks; and having stripped him of his clothes, and habited him as a monk, they laid him on a truss of straw, and left him there until he should revive. Expecting which event, and instructed by the abbot how he was then to act, the Bolognese monk (none else knowing aught of what was afoot) kept watch by the tomb.

The day after, the abbot with some of his monks paid a pastoral visit to the lady's house, where he found her in mourning weeds and sad at heart; and, after administering a little consolation, he gently asked her to redeem her promise. Free as she now felt herself, and hampered neither by Ferondo nor by any other, the lady, who had noticed another beautiful ring on the abbot's finger, promised immediate compliance, and arranged with the abbot that he should visit her the very next night. So, at nightfall, the abbot donned Ferondo's clothes, and, attended by his monk, paid his visit, and lay with her until matins to his immense delight and solace, and so returned to the abbey; and many visits he paid her on the same errand; whereby some that met him, coming or going that way, supposed that 'twas Ferondo perambulating those parts by way of penance; and fables not a few passed from mouth to mouth of the foolish rustics, and sometimes reached the ears of the lady, who was at no loss to account for them.

As for Ferondo, when he revived, 'twas only to find himself he knew not where, while the Bolognese monk entered the tomb, gibbering horribly, and armed with a rod, wherewith, having laid hold of Ferondo, he gave him a severe thrashing. Blubbering and bellowing for pain, Ferondo could only ejaculate: – "Where am I?" "In purgatory," replied the monk. "How?"

returned Ferondo, "am I dead then?" and the monk assuring him that 'twas even so, he fell a bewailing his own and his lady's and his son's fate, after the most ridiculous fashion in the world. The monk brought him somewhat to eat and drink. Of which when Ferondo caught sight, "Oh!" said he, "dead folk eat then, do they?" "They do," replied the monk, "And this, which I bring thee, is what the lady that was thy wife sent this morning to the church by way of alms for masses for thy soul; and God is minded that it be assigned to thee." "Now God grant her a happy year," said Ferondo; "dearly I loved her while I yet lived, and would hold her all night long in my arms, and cease not to kiss her, ay, and would do yet more to her, when I was so minded." Whereupon he fell to eating and drinking with great avidity, and finding the wine not much to his taste, he said: – "Now God do her a mischief! Why gave she not the priest of the wine that is in the cask by the wall?" When he had done eating, the monk laid hold of him again, and gave him another sound thrashing with the rod. Ferondo bellowed mightily, and then cried out: – "Alas! why servest thou me so?" "God," answered the monk, "has decreed that thou be so served twice a day." "For why?" said Ferondo. "Because," returned the monk, "thou wast jealous, notwithstanding thou hadst to wife a woman that has not her peer in thy countryside." "Alas," said Ferondo, "she was indeed all that thou sayst, ay, and the sweetest creature too, – no comfit so honeyed – but I knew not that God took it amiss that a man should be jealous, or I had not been so." "Of that," replied the monk, "thou shouldst have bethought thee while thou wast there, and have amended thy ways; and should it fall to thy lot ever to return thither, be sure that thou so lay to heart the lesson that I now give thee, that thou be no more jealous." "Oh!" said Ferondo; "dead folk sometimes return to earth, do they?" "They do," replied the monk; "if God so will." "Oh!" said Ferondo; "if I ever return, I will be the best husband in the world; never will I beat her or scold her, save for the wine that she has sent me this morning, and also for sending me never a candle, so that I have had perforce to eat in the dark." "Nay," said the monk, "she sent them, but they were burned at the masses." "Oh!" said Ferondo, "I doubt not you say true; and, of a surety, if I ever return, I will let her do just as she likes. But tell me, who art thou that entreatest me thus?" "Late of Sardinia I," answered the monk, "dead too; and, for that I gave my lord much countenance in his jealousy, doomed by God for my proper penance to entreat thee thus with food and drink and thrashings, until such time as He may ordain otherwise touching thee and me." "And are we two the only folk here?" inquired Ferondo. "Nay, there are thousands beside," answered the monk; "but thou canst neither see nor hear them, nor they thee." "And how far," said Ferondo, "may we be from our country?" "Oh! ho!" returned the monk, "why, 'tis some miles clean out of shitrange." "I'faith," said Ferondo, "that is far indeed: methinks we must be out of the world."

In such a course, alternately beaten, fed and amused with idle tales, was Ferondo kept for ten months, while the abbot, to his great felicity, paid many a visit to the fair lady, and had the jolliest time in the world with her. But, as misfortunes will happen, the lady conceived, which fact, as soon as she was aware of it, she imparted to the abbot; whereupon both agreed that Ferondo must without delay be brought back from purgatory to earth and her, and be given to understand that she was with child of him. So the very next night the abbot went to the prison, and in a disguised voice pronounced Ferondo's name, and said to him: – "Ferondo, be of good cheer, for God is minded that thou return to earth; and on thy return thou shalt have a son by thy lady, and thou shalt call him Benedetto; because 'tis in answer to the prayers of thy holy abbot and thy lady, and for love of St. Benedict, that God accords thee this grace." Whereat Ferondo was overjoyed, and said: – "It likes me well. God give a good year to Master Lord God, and the abbot, and St. Benedict, and my cheese-powdered, honey-sweet wife." Then, in the wine that he sent him, the abbot administered enough of the powder to cause him to sleep for four hours; and so, with the aid of the monk, having first habited him in his proper clothes, he privily conveyed him back to the tomb in which he had been buried. On the morrow at daybreak Ferondo revived, and perceiving through a chink in the tomb a glimmer of light, to which he had been a stranger for full ten months, he knew that he was alive, and began to bellow: – "Let me out, let me out:" then, setting his head to the lid of the tomb, he heaved amain; whereby the lid, being insecure, started; and he was already thrusting it aside, when the monks, matins being now ended, ran to the spot and recognized Ferondo's voice, and saw him issue from the tomb; by which unwonted event they were all so affrighted that they took to flight, and hied them to the abbot: who, rising as if from prayer, said: – "Sons, be not afraid; take the cross and the holy water, and follow me, and let us see what sign of His might God will vouchsafe us." And so he led the way to the tomb; beside which they found Ferondo, standing, deathly pale by reason of his long estrangement from the light. On sight of the abbot he ran and threw himself at his feet, saying: – "My father, it has been revealed to me that 'tis to your prayers and those of St. Benedict and my lady that I owe my release from purgatorial pain, and restoration to life; wherefore 'tis my prayer that God give you a good year and good calends, to-day and all days." "Laud we the power of God!" said the abbot. "Go then, son, as God has restored thee to earth, comfort thy wife, who, since thou didst depart this life, has been ever in tears, and mayst thou live henceforth in the love and service of God." "Sir," answered Ferondo, "'tis well said; and, for the doing, trust me that, as soon as I find her, I shall kiss her, such is the love I bear her." So saying, he went his way; and the abbot, left alone with his monks, made as if he marvelled greatly at the affair, and caused devoutly chant the Miserere. So Ferondo returned to his hamlet, where all that saw him fleeing, as folk are wont to flee from spectacles of horror, he called them back, asseverating that he was risen from the tomb. His wife at first was no less timorous: but, as folk began to take heart of grace, perceiving that he was alive, they plied him with many questions, all which he answered as one that had returned with ripe experience, and gave them tidings of the souls of their kinsfolk, and told of his own invention the prettiest fables of the purgatorial state, and in full folkmoot recounted the revelation vouchsafed him by the mouth of Ragnolo Braghiello before his resuscitation.

Thus was Ferondo reinstated in his property and reunited to his wife, who, being pregnant, as he thought, by himself, chanced by the time of her delivery to countenance the vulgar error that the woman must bear the infant in the womb for exactly nine months, and gave birth to a male child, who was named Benedetto Ferondi. Ferondo's return from purgatory, and the report he brought thence, immeasurably enhanced the fame of the abbot's holiness. So Ferondo, cured of his jealousy by the thrashings which he had gotten for it, verified the abbot's prediction, and never offended the lady again in that sort. Wherefore she lived with him, as before, in all outward seemliness; albeit she failed not, as occasion served, to forgather with the holy abbot, who had so well and sedulously served her in her especial need.

Third Day
Novel IX

— Gillette of Narbonne cures the King of France of a fistula, craves for spouse Bertrand de Roussillon, who marries her against his will, and hies him in despite to Florence, where, as he courts a young woman, Gillette lies with him in her stead, and has two sons by him; for which cause he afterwards takes her into favour and entreats her as his wife. —

LAURETTA'S STORY being ended, and the queen being minded not to break her engagement with Dioneo, 'twas now her turn to speak. Wherefore without awaiting the call of her subjects, thus with mien most gracious she began: – Now that we have heard Lauretta's story, who shall tell any to compare with it for beauty? Lucky indeed was it that she was not the first; for few that followed would have pleased; and so, I misdoubt me, 'twill fare ill with those that remain to complete the day's narration. However, for what it may be worth, I will tell you a story which seems to me germane to our theme.

Know, then, that in the realm of France there was a gentleman, Isnard, Comte de Roussillon, by name, who, being in ill-health, kept ever in attendance on him a physician, one Master Gerard of Narbonne. The said Count had an only son named Bertrand, a very fine and winsome little lad; with whom were brought up other children of his own age, among them the said physician's little daughter Gillette; who with a love boundless and ardent out of all keeping with her tender years became enamoured of this Bertrand. And so, when the Count died, and his son, being left a ward of the King, must needs go to Paris, the girl remained beside herself with grief, and, her father dying soon after, would gladly have gone to Paris to see Bertrand, might she but have found a fair excuse; but no decent pretext could she come by, being left a great and sole heiress and very closely guarded. So being come of marriageable age, still cherishing Bertrand's memory, she rejected not a few suitors, to whom her kinsfolk would fain have married her, without assigning any reason.

Now her passion waxing ever more ardent for Bertrand, as she learned that he was grown a most goodly gallant, tidings reached her that the King of France, in consequence of a tumour which he had had in the breast, and which had been ill tended, was now troubled with a fistula, which occasioned him extreme distress and suffering; nor had he as yet come by a physician that was able, though many had essayed, to cure him, but had rather grown worse under their hands; wherefore in despair he was minded no more to have recourse to any for counsel or aid. Whereat the damsel was overjoyed, deeming not only that she might find therein lawful occasion to go to Paris, but, that, if the disease was what she took it to be, it might well betide that she should be wedded to Bertrand. So – for not a little knowledge had she gotten from her father – she prepared a powder from certain herbs serviceable in the treatment of the supposed disease, and straightway took horse, and hied her to Paris. Arrived there she made it her first concern to have sight of Bertrand; and then, having obtained access to the King, she besought him of his grace to shew her his disease. The King knew not how to refuse so young, fair and winsome a damsel, and let her see the place. Whereupon, no longer doubting that she should cure him, she said: – "Sire, so please you, I hope in God to cure you of this malady within eight days without causing you the least distress or discomfort." The King inly scoffed at her words, saying to himself: – "How should a damsel have come by a knowledge and skill that the greatest physicians in the world do not possess?" He therefore graciously acknowledged her good intention, and answered that he had resolved no more to follow advice of physician. "Sire," said the damsel, "you disdain my art, because I am young and a woman; but I bid you bear in mind that I rely not on my own skill, but on the help of God, and the skill of Master Gerard of Narbonne, my father, and a famous physician in his day." Whereupon the King said to himself: – "Perchance she is sent me by God; why put I not her skill to the proof, seeing that she says that she can cure me in a short time, and cause me no distress?" And being minded to make the experiment, he said: – "Damsel, and if, having caused me to cancel my resolve, you should fail to cure me, what are you content should ensue?" "Sire," answered the damsel, "set a guard upon me; and if within eight days I cure you not, have me burned; but if I cure you, what shall be my guerdon?" "You seem," said the King, "to be yet unmarried; if you shall effect the cure, we will marry you well and in high place." "Sire," returned the damsel, "well content indeed am I that you should marry me, so it be to such a husband as I shall ask of you, save that I may not ask any of your sons or any other member of the royal house." Whereto the King forthwith consented, and the damsel, thereupon applying her treatment, restored him to health before the period assigned. Wherefore, as soon as the King knew that he was cured: – "Damsel," said he, "well have you won your husband." She, answered: – "In that case, Sire, I have won Bertrand de Roussillon, of whom, while yet a child, I was enamoured, and whom I have ever since most ardently loved." To give her Bertrand seemed to the King no small matter; but, having pledged his word, he would not break it: so he sent for Bertrand, and said to him: – "Bertrand, you are now come to man's estate, and fully equipped to enter on it; 'tis therefore our will that you go back and assume the governance of your county, and that you take with you a damsel, whom we have given you to wife." "And who is the damsel, Sire?" said Bertrand. "She it is," answered the King, "that has restored us to health by her physic." Now Bertrand, knowing Gillette, and that her lineage was not such as matched his nobility, albeit, seeing her, he had found her very fair, was overcome with disdain, and answered: – "So, Sire, you would fain give me a she-doctor to wife. Now God forbid that I should ever marry any such woman." "Then," said the King, "you would have us fail of the faith which we pledged to the damsel, who asked you in marriage by way of guerdon for our restoration to health." "Sire," said Bertrand, "you may take from me all that I possess, and give me as your man to whomsoever you may be minded; but rest assured that I shall never be satisfied with such a match." "Nay, but you will," replied the King; "for the damsel is fair and discreet, and loves you well; wherefore we anticipate that you will live far more happily with her than with a dame of much higher lineage." Bertrand was silent; and the King made great preparations for the celebration of the nuptials. The appointed day came, and Bertrand, albeit reluctantly, nevertheless complied, and in the presence of the King was wedded to the damsel, who loved him more dearly than herself. Which done, Bertrand, who had already taken his resolution, said that he was minded to go down to his county, there to consummate the marriage; and so, having craved and had leave of absence of the King, he took horse, but instead of returning to his county he hied him to Tuscany; where, finding the Florentines at war with the Sienese, he determined to take service with the Florentines, and being made heartily and honourably welcome, was appointed to the command of part of their forces, at a liberal stipend, and so remained in their service for a long while. Distressed by this turn of fortune, and hoping by her wise management to bring

Bertrand back to his county, the bride hied her to Roussillon, where she was received by all the tenants as their liege lady. She found that, during the long absence of the lord, everything had fallen into decay and disorder; which, being a capable woman, she rectified with great and sedulous care, to the great joy of the tenants, who held her in great esteem and love, and severely censured the Count, that he was not satisfied with her. When the lady had duly ordered all things in the county, she despatched two knights to the Count with the intelligence, praying him, that, if 'twas on her account that he came not home, he would so inform her; in which case she would gratify him by departing. To whom with all harshness he replied: – "She may even please herself in the matter. For my part I will go home and live with her, when she has this ring on her finger and a son gotten of me upon her arm." The ring was one which he greatly prized, and never removed from his finger, by reason of a virtue which he had been given to understand that it possessed. The knights appreciated the harshness of a condition which contained two articles, both of which were all but impossible; and, seeing that by no words of theirs could they alter his resolve, they returned to the lady, and delivered his message. Sorely distressed, the lady after long pondering determined to try how and where the two conditions might be satisfied, that so her husband might be hers again. Having formed her plan, she assembled certain of the more considerable and notable men of the county, to whom she gave a consecutive and most touching narrative of all that she had done for love of the Count, with the result; concluding by saying that she was not minded to tarry there to the Count's perpetual exile, but to pass the rest of her days in pilgrimages and pious works for the good of her soul: wherefore she prayed them to undertake the defence and governance of the county, and to inform the Count that she had made entire and absolute cession of it to him, and was gone away with the intention of never more returning to Roussillon. As she spoke, tears not a few coursed down the cheeks of the honest men, and again and again they besought her to change her mind, and stay. All in vain, however; she commended them to God, and, accompanied only by one of her male cousins and a chambermaid (all three habited as pilgrims and amply provided with money and precious jewels), she took the road, nor tarried until she was arrived at Florence. There she lodged in a little inn kept by a good woman that was a widow, bearing herself lowly as a poor pilgrim, and eagerly expectant of news of her lord.

Now it so befell that the very next day she saw Bertrand pass in front of the inn on horseback at the head of his company; and though she knew him very well, nevertheless she asked the good woman of the inn who he was. The hostess replied: – "'Tis a foreign gentleman – Count Bertrand they call him – a very pleasant gentleman, and courteous, and much beloved in this city; and he is in the last degree enamoured of one of our neighbours here, who is a gentlewoman, but in poor circumstances. A very virtuous damsel she is too, and, being as yet unmarried by reason of her poverty, she lives with her mother, who is an excellent and most discreet lady, but for whom, perchance, she would before now have yielded and gratified the Count's desire." No word of this was lost on the lady; she pondered and meditated every detail with the closest attention, and having laid it all to heart, took her resolution: she ascertained the names and abode of the lady and her daughter that the Count loved, and hied her one day privily, wearing her pilgrim's weeds, to their house, where she found the lady and her daughter in very evident poverty, and after greeting them, told the lady that, if it were agreeable to her, she would speak with her. The gentlewoman rose and signified her willingness to listen to what she had to say; so they went into a room by themselves and sate down, and then the Countess began thus: – "Madam, methinks you are, as I am, under Fortune's frown; but perchance you have it in your power, if you are so minded, to afford solace to both of us." The lady answered that, so she might honourably find it, solace indeed was what she craved most of all things in the world. Whereupon the Countess continued: – "I must first be assured of your faith, wherein if I confide and am deceived, the interests of both of us will suffer." "Have no fear," said the gentlewoman, "speak your whole mind without reserve, for you will find that there is no deceit in me." So the Countess told who she was, and the whole course of her love affair, from its commencement to that hour, on such wise that the gentlewoman, believing her story the more readily that she had already heard it in part from others, was touched with compassion for her. The narrative of her woes complete, the Countess added: – "Now that you have heard my misfortunes, you know the two conditions that I must fulfil, if I would come by my husband; nor know I any other person than you, that may enable me to fulfil them; but so you may, if this which I hear is true, to wit, that my husband is in the last degree enamoured of your daughter." "Madam," replied the gentlewoman, "I know not if the Count loves my daughter, but true it is that he makes great shew of loving her; but how may this enable me to do aught for you in the matter that you have at heart?" "The how, madam," returned the Countess, "I will shortly explain to you; but you shall first hear what I intend shall ensue, if you serve me. Your daughter, I see, is fair and of marriageable age, and, by what I have learned and may well understand, 'tis because you have not the wherewith to marry her that you keep her at home. Now, in recompense of the service that you shall do me, I mean to provide her forthwith from my own moneys with such a dowry as you yourself shall deem adequate for her marriage." The lady was too needy not to be gratified by the proposal; but, nevertheless, with the true spirit of the gentlewoman, she answered: – "Nay but, madam, tell me that which I may do for you, and if it shall be such as I may honourably do, gladly will I do it, and then you shall do as you may be minded." Said then the Countess: – "I require of you, that through some one in whom you trust you send word to the Count, my husband, that your daughter is ready to yield herself entirely to his will, so she may be sure that he loves her even as he professes; whereof she will never be convinced, until he send her the ring which he wears on his finger, and which, she understands, he prizes so much: which, being sent, you shall give to me, and shall then send him word that your daughter is ready to do his pleasure, and, having brought him hither secretly, you shall contrive that I lie by his side instead of your daughter. Perchance, by God's grace I shall conceive, and so, having his ring on my finger, and a son gotten of him on my arm, shall have him for my own again, and live with him even as a wife should live with her husband, and owe it all to you."

The lady felt that 'twas not a little that the Countess craved of her, for she feared lest it should bring reproach upon her daughter: but she reflected that to aid the good lady to recover her husband was an honourable enterprise, and that in undertaking it she would be subserving a like end; and so, trusting in the good and virtuous disposition of the Countess, she not only promised to do as she was required, but in no long time, proceeding with caution and secrecy, as she had been bidden, she both had the ring from the Count, loath though he was to part with it, and cunningly contrived that the Countess should lie with him in place of her daughter. In which first commingling, so ardently sought by the Count, it so pleased God that the lady was gotten, as in due time her delivery made manifest, with two sons. Nor once only, but many times did the lady gratify the Countess with the embraces of her husband, using such secrecy that no word thereof ever got wind, the Count all the while supposing that he lay, not with his wife, but with her that he loved, and being wont to give her, as he left her in the morning, some fair and rare jewel, which she jealously guarded.

When she perceived that she was with child, the Countess, being minded no more to burden the lady with such service, said to her: – "Madam, thanks be to God and to you, I now have that which I desired, and therefore 'tis time that I make you grateful requital, and take my leave of you." The lady answered that she was glad if the Countess had gotten aught that gave her joy; but that 'twas not as hoping to have guerdon thereof that she had done her part, but simply because she deemed it meet and her duty so to do. "Well said, madam," returned the Countess, "and in like manner that which you shall ask of me I shall not give you by way of guerdon, but because I deem it meet and my duty to give it." Whereupon the lady, yielding to necessity, and abashed beyond measure, asked of her a hundred pounds wherewith to marry her daughter. The Countess, marking her embarrassment, and the modesty of her request, gave her five hundred pounds besides jewels fair and rare, worth, perhaps, no less; and having thus much more than contented her, and received her superabundant thanks, she took leave of her and returned to the inn. The lady, to render purposeless further visits or messages on Bertrand's part, withdrew with her daughter to the house of her kinsfolk in the country; nor was it long before Bertrand, on the urgent entreaty of his vassals and intelligence of the departure of his wife, quitted Florence and returned home. Greatly elated by this intelligence, the Countess tarried awhile in Florence, and was there delivered of two sons as like as possible to their father, whom she nurtured with sedulous care. But by and by she saw fit to take the road, and being come, unrecognized by any, to Montpellier, rested there a few days; and being on the alert for news of the Count and where he was, she learned that on All Saints' day he was to hold a great reception of ladies and gentlemen at Roussillon. Whither, retaining her now wonted pilgrim's weeds, she hied her, and finding that the ladies and gentlemen were all gathered in the Count's palace and on the point of going to table, she tarried not to change her dress, but went up into the hall, bearing her little ones in her arms, and threading her way through the throng to the place where she saw the Count stand, she threw herself at his feet, and sobbing, said to him: – "My lord, thy hapless bride am I, who to ensure thy homecoming and abidance in peace have long time been a wanderer, and now demand of thee observance of the condition whereof word was brought me by the two knights whom I sent to thee. Lo in my arms not one son only but twain, gotten of thee, and on my finger thy ring. 'Tis time, then, that I be received of thee as thy wife according to thy word." Whereat the Count was all dumfounded, recognizing the ring and his own lineaments in the children, so like were they to him; but saying to himself nevertheless: – "How can it have come about?" So the Countess, while the Count and all that were present marvelled exceedingly, told what had happened, and the manner of it, in precise detail. Wherefore the Count, perceiving that she spoke truth, and having regard to her perseverance and address and her two fine boys, and the wishes of all his vassals and the ladies, who with one accord besought him to own and honour her thenceforth as his lawful bride, laid aside his harsh obduracy, and raised the Countess to her feet, and embraced and kissed her, and acknowledged her for his lawful wife, and the children for his own. Then, having caused her to be rearrayed in garments befitting her rank, he, to the boundless delight of as many as were there, and of all other his vassals, gave up that day and some that followed to feasting and merrymaking; and did ever thenceforth honour, love and most tenderly cherish her as his bride and wife.

Third Day
Novel X

— *Alibech turns hermit, and is taught by Rustico, a monk, how the Devil is put in hell. She is afterwards conveyed thence, and becomes the wife of Neerbale.* —

DIONEO, OBSERVING that the queen's story, which he had followed with the closest attention, was now ended, and that it only remained for him to speak, waited not to be bidden, but smilingly thus began: –

Gracious ladies, perchance you have not yet heard how the Devil is put in hell; wherefore, without deviating far from the topic of which you have discoursed throughout the day, I will tell you how 'tis done; it may be the lesson will prove inspiring; besides which, you may learn therefrom that, albeit Love prefers the gay palace and the dainty chamber to the rude cabin, yet, for all that, he may at times manifest his might in wilds matted with forests, rugged with alps, and desolate with caverns: whereby it may be understood that all things are subject to his sway. But – to come to my story – I say that in the city of Capsa in Barbary there was once a very rich man, who with other children had a fair and dainty little daughter, Alibech by name. Now Alibech, not being a Christian, and hearing many Christians, that were in the city, speak much in praise of the Christian Faith and the service of God, did one day inquire of one of them after what fashion it were possible to serve God with as few impediments as might be, and was informed that they served God best who most completely renounced the world and its affairs; like those who had fixed their abode in the wilds of the Thebaid desert. Whereupon, actuated by no sober predilection, but by childish impulse, the girl, who was very simple and about fourteen years of age, said never a word more of the matter, but stole away on the morrow, and quite alone set out to walk to the Thebaid desert; and, by force of resolution, albeit with no small suffering, she after some days reached those wilds; where, espying a cabin a great way off, she hied her thither, and found a holy man by the door, who, marvelling to see her there, asked her what she came there to seek. She answered that, guided by the spirit of God, she was come thither, seeking, if haply she might serve Him, and also find some one that might teach her how He ought to be served. Marking her youth and great beauty, the worthy man, fearing lest, if he suffered her to remain with him, he should be ensnared by the Devil, commended her good intention, set before her a frugal repast of roots of herbs, crab-apples and dates, with a little water to wash them down, and said to her: – "My daughter, there is a holy man not far from here, who is much better able to teach thee that of which thou art in quest than I am; go to him, therefore;" and he shewed her the way. But when she was come whither she was directed, she met with the same answer as before, and so, setting forth again, she came at length to the cell of a young hermit, a worthy man and very devout – his name Rustico – whom she interrogated as she had the others. Rustico, being minded to make severe trial of his constancy, did not send her away, as the others had done, but kept her with him in his cell, and when night came, made her a little bed of palm-leaves; whereon he bade her compose herself to sleep. Hardly had she done so before the solicitations of the flesh joined battle with the powers of Rustico's spirit, and he, finding himself left in the lurch by the latter, endured not many assaults before he beat a retreat, and surrendered at discretion: wherefore he bade adieu to holy meditation and prayer and discipline, and fell a musing on the youth and beauty of his companion, and also how he might so order his conversation with her, that without seeming to her to be a libertine he might yet compass that which he craved of her. So, probing her by certain questions, he discovered that she was as yet entirely without cognizance of man, and as simple as she seemed: wherefore he excogitated a plan for bringing her to pleasure him under colour of serving God. He began by giving her a long lecture on the great enmity that subsists between God and the Devil; after which he gave her to understand that, God having condemned the Devil to hell, to put him there was of all services the most acceptable to God. The girl asking him how it might be done, Rustico answered: – "Thou shalt know it in a trice; thou hast but to do that which thou seest me do." Then, having divested himself of his scanty clothing, he threw himself stark naked on his knees, as if he would pray; whereby he caused the girl, who followed his example, to confront him in the same posture. Whereupon Rustico, seeing her so fair, felt an accession of desire, and therewith came an insurgence of the flesh, which Alibech marking with surprise, said: – "Rustico, what is this, which I see thee have, that so protrudes, and which I have not?" "Oh! my daughter," said Rustico, "'tis the Devil of whom I have told thee: and, seest thou? he is now tormenting me most grievously, insomuch that I am scarce able to hold out." Then: – "Praise be to God," said the girl, "I see that I am in better case than thou, for no such Devil have I." "Sooth sayst thou," returned Rustico; "but instead of him thou hast somewhat else that I have not." "Oh!" said Alibech, "what may that be?" "Hell," answered Rustico: "and I tell thee, that 'tis my belief that God has sent thee hither for the salvation of my soul; seeing that, if this Devil shall continue to plague me thus, then, so thou wilt have compassion on me and permit me to put him in hell, thou wilt both afford me great and exceeding great solace, and render to God an exceeding most acceptable service, if, as thou sayst, thou art come into these parts for such a purpose." In good faith the girl made answer: – "As I have hell to match your Devil, be it, my father, as and when you will." Whereupon: – "Bless thee, my daughter," said Rustico, "go we then, and put him there, that he leave me henceforth in peace." Which said, he took the girl to one of the beds and taught her the posture in which she must lie in order to incarcerate this spirit accursed of God. The girl, having never before put any devil in hell, felt on this first occasion a twinge of pain: wherefore she said to Rustico: – "Of a surety, my father, he must be a wicked fellow, this devil, and in very truth a foe to God; for there is sorrow even in hell – not to speak of other places – when he is put there." "Daughter," said Rustico, "'twill not be always so." And for better assurance thereof they put him there six times before they quitted the bed; whereby they so thoroughly abased his pride that he was fain to be quiet. However, the proud fit returning upon him from time to time, and the girl addressing herself always obediently to its reduction, it so befell that she began to find the game agreeable, and would say to Rustico: – "Now see I plainly that 'twas true, what the worthy men said at Capsa, of the service of God being so delightful: indeed I cannot remember that in aught that ever I did I had so much pleasure, so much solace, as in putting the Devil in hell; for which cause I deem it insensate folly on the part of any one to have a care to aught else than the service of God." Wherefore many a time she would come to Rustico, and say to him: – "My father, 'twas to serve God that I came hither, and not to pass my days in idleness: go we then, and put the Devil in hell." And while they did so, she would now and again say: – "I know not, Rustico, why the Devil should escape from hell; were he but as ready to stay there as hell is to receive and retain him, he would never come out of it." So, the girl thus frequently inviting and exhorting Rustico to the service of God, there came at length a time when she had so thoroughly lightened his doublet that he shivered when another would have sweated; wherefore he began to instruct her that the Devil was not to be corrected and put in hell, save when his head was exalted with pride; adding, "and we by God's grace have brought him to so sober a mind that he prays God he may be left in peace;" by which means he for a time kept the girl quiet. But when she saw that Rustico had no more occasion for her to put the Devil in hell, she said to him one day: – "Rustico, if thy Devil is chastened and gives thee no more trouble, my hell, on the other hand, gives me no peace; wherefore, I with my hell have holpen thee to abase the pride of thy Devil, so thou wouldst do well to lend me the aid of thy Devil to allay the fervent heat of my hell." Rustico, whose diet was roots of herbs and water, was scarce able to respond to her demands: he told her that 'twould require not a few devils to allay the heat of hell; but that he would do what might be in his power; and so now and again he satisfied her; but so seldom that 'twas as if he had tossed a bean into the jaws of a lion. Whereat the girl, being fain of more of the service of God than she had, did somewhat repine. However, the case standing thus (deficiency of power against superfluity of desire) between Rustico's Devil and Alibech's hell, it chanced that a fire broke out in Capsa, whereby the house of Alibech's father was burned, and he and all his sons and the rest of his household perished; so that Alibech was left sole heiress of all his estate. And a young gallant, Neerbale by name, who by reckless munificence had wasted all his substance, having discovered that she was alive, addressed himself to the pursuit of her, and, having found her in time to prevent the confiscation of her father's estate as an escheat for failure of heirs, took her, much to Rustico's relief and against her own will, back to Capsa, and made her his wife, and shared with her her vast patrimony. But before he had lain with her, she was questioned by the ladies of the manner in which she had served God in the desert; whereto she answered, that she had been wont to serve Him by putting the Devil in hell, and that Neerbale had committed a great sin, when he took her out of such service. The ladies being curious to know how the Devil was put in hell, the girl satisfied them, partly by words, partly by signs. Whereat they laughed exorbitantly (and still laugh) and said to her: – "Be not down-hearted, daughter; 'tis done here too; Neerbale will know well how to serve God with you in that way." And so the story passing from mouth to mouth throughout the city, it came at last to be a common proverb, that the most acceptable service that can be rendered to God is to put the Devil in hell; which proverb, having travelled hither across the sea, is still current. Wherefore, young ladies, you that have need of the grace of God, see to it that you learn how to put the Devil in hell, because 'tis mightily pleasing to God, and of great solace to both the parties, and much good may thereby be engendered and ensue.

A thousand times or more had Dioneo's story brought the laugh to the lips of the honourable ladies, so quaint and curiously entertaining found they the fashion of it. And now at its close the queen, seeing the term of her sovereignty come, took the laurel wreath from her head, and with mien most debonair, set it on the brow of Filostrato, saying: – "We shall soon see whether the wolf will know better how to guide the sheep than the sheep have yet succeeded in guiding the wolves." Whereat Filostrato said with a laugh: – "Had I been hearkened to, the wolves would have taught the sheep to put the Devil in hell even as Rustico taught Alibech. Wherefore call us not wolves, seeing that you have not shewn yourselves sheep: however, as best I may be able, I will govern the kingdom committed to my charge." Whereupon Neifile took him up: "Hark ye, Filostrato," she said, "while you thought to teach us, you might have learnt a lesson from us, as did Masetto da Lamporecchio from the nuns, and have recovered your speech when the bones had learned to whistle without a master." Filostrato, perceiving that there was a scythe for each of his arrows, gave up jesting, and addressed himself to the governance of his kingdom. He called the seneschal, and held him strictly to account in every particular; he then judiciously ordered all matters as he deemed would be best and most to the satisfaction of the company, while his sovereignty should last; and having so done, he turned to the ladies, and said: – "Loving ladies, as my ill luck would have it, since I have had wit to tell good from evil, the charms of one or other of you have kept me ever a slave to Love: and for all I shewed myself humble and obedient and conformable, so far as I knew how, to all his ways, my fate has been still the same, to be discarded for another, and go ever from bad to worse; and so, I suppose, 'twill be with me to the hour of my death. Wherefore I am minded that to-morrow our discourse be of no other topic than that which is most germane to my condition, to wit, of those whose loves had a disastrous close: because mine, I expect, will in the long run be most disastrous; nor for other cause was the name, by which you address me, given me by one that well knew its signification." Which said, he arose, and dismissed them all until supper-time.

So fair and delightsome was the garden that none saw fit to quit it, and seek diversion elsewhere. Rather – for the sun now shone with a tempered radiance that caused no discomfort – some of the ladies gave chase to the kids and conies and other creatures that haunted it, and, scampering to and fro among them as they sate, had caused them a hundred times, or so, some slight embarrassment. Dioneo and Fiammetta fell a singing of Messer Guglielmo and the lady of Vergiu. Filomena and Pamfilo sat them down to a game of chess; and, as thus they pursued each their several diversions, time sped so swiftly that the supper-hour stole upon them almost unawares: whereupon they ranged the tables round the beautiful fountain, and supped with all glad and festal cheer.

When the tables were removed, Filostrato, being minded to follow in the footsteps of his fair predecessors in sway, bade Lauretta lead a dance and sing a song. She answered: – "My lord, songs of others know I none, nor does my memory furnish me with any of mine own that seems meet for so gay a company; but, if you will be content with what I have, gladly will I give you thereof." "Nought of thine," returned the king, "could be other than goodly and delectable. Wherefore give us even what thou hast." So encouraged, Lauretta, with dulcet voice, but manner somewhat languishing, raised the ensuing strain, to which the other ladies responded: –

> *What dame disconsolate*
> *May so lament as I,*
> *That vainly sigh, to Love still dedicate?*
>
> *He that the heaven and every orb doth move*
> *Formed me for His delight*
> *Fair, debonair and gracious, apt for love;*
> *That here on earth each soaring spirit might*
> *Have foretaste how, above,*
> *That beauty shews that standeth in His sight.*
> *Ah! but dull wit and slight,*
> *For that it judgeth ill,*
> *Liketh me not, nay, doth me vilely rate.*
>
> *There was who loved me, and my maiden grace*
> *Did fondly clip and strain,*
> *As in his arms, so in his soul's embrace,*
> *And from mine eyes Love's fire did drink amain,*
> *And time that glides apace*
> *In nought but courting me to spend was fain*
> *Whom courteous I did deign*
> *Ev'n as my peer to entreat;*
> *But am of him bereft! Ah! dolorous fate!*

> *Came to me next a gallant swol'n with pride,*
>   *Brave, in his own conceit,*
>   *And no less noble eke. Whom woe betide*
>   *That he me took, and holds in all unmeet*
>   *Suspicion, jealous-eyed!*
>   *And I, who wot that me the world should greet*
>   *As the predestined sweet*
>   *Of many men, well-nigh*
>   *Despair, to be to one thus subjugate.*
>
> *Ah! woe is me! cursed be the luckless day,*
>   *When, a new gown to wear,*
>   *I said the fatal ay; for blithe and gay*
>   *In that plain gown I lived, no whit less fair;*
>   *While in this rich array*
>   *A sad and far less honoured life I bear!*
>   *Would I had died, or e'er*
>   *Sounded those notes of joy*
>   *(Ah! dolorous cheer!) my woe to celebrate!*
>
> *So list my supplication, lover dear,*
>   *Of whom such joyance I,*
>   *As ne'er another, had. Thou that in clear*
>   *Light of the Maker's presence art, deny*
>   *Not pity to thy fere,*
>   *Who thee may ne'er forget; but let one sigh*
>   *Breathe tidings that on high*
>   *Thou burnest still for me;*
>   *And sue of God that He me there translate.*

So ended Lauretta her song, to which all hearkened attentively, though not all interpreted it alike. Some were inclined to give it a moral after the Milanese fashion, to wit, that a good porker was better than a pretty quean. Others construed it in a higher, better and truer sense, which 'tis not to the present purpose to unfold. Some more songs followed by command of the king, who caused torches not a few to be lighted and ranged about the flowery mead; and so the night was prolonged until the last star that had risen had begun to set. Then, bethinking him that 'twas time for slumber, the king bade all good-night, and dismissed them to their several chambers.

— *Endeth here the third day of the Decameron, beginneth the fourth, in which, under the rule of Filostrato, discourse is had of those whose loves had a disastrous close.* —

DEAREST LADIES, as well from what I heard in converse with the wise, as from matters that not seldom fell within my own observation and reading, I formed the opinion that the vehement and scorching blast of envy was apt to vent itself only upon lofty towers or the highest tree-tops: but therein I find that I misjudged; for, whereas I ever sought and studied how best to elude the buffetings of that furious hurricane, and to that end kept a course not merely on the plain, but, by preference, in the depth of the valley; as should be abundantly clear to whoso looks at these little stories, written as they are not only in the vulgar Florentine, and in prose, and without dedicatory flourish, but also in as homely and simple a style as may be; nevertheless all this has not stood me in such stead but that I have been shrewdly shaken, nay, all but uprooted by the blast, and altogether lacerated by the bite of this same envy. Whereby I may very well understand that 'tis true, what the sages aver, that only misery is exempt from envy in the present life. Know then, discreet my ladies, that some there are, who, reading these little stories, have alleged that I am too fond of you, and that 'tis not a seemly thing that I should take so much pleasure in ministering to your gratification and solace; and some have found more fault with me for praising you as I do. Others, affecting to deliver a more considered judgment, have said that it ill befits my time of life to ensue such matters, to wit, the discoursing of women, or endeavouring to pleasure them. And not a few, feigning a mighty tender regard to my fame, aver that I should do more wisely to keep ever with the Muses on Parnassus, than to forgather with you in such vain dalliance. Those again there are, who, evincing less wisdom than despite, have told me that I should shew sounder sense if I bethought me how to get my daily bread, than, going after these idle toys, to nourish myself upon the wind; while certain others, in disparagement of my work, strive might and main to make it appear that the matters which I relate fell out otherwise than as I set them forth. Such then, noble ladies, are the blasts, such the sharp and cruel fangs, by which, while I champion your cause, I am assailed, harassed and well-nigh pierced through and through. Which censures I hear and mark, God knows, with equal mind: and, though to you belongs all my defence, yet I mean not to be niggard of my own powers, but rather, without dealing out to them the castigation they deserve, to give them such slight answer as may secure my ears some respite of their clamour; and that without delay; seeing that, if already, though I have not completed the third part of my work, they are not a few and very presumptuous, I deem it possible, that before I have reached the end, should they receive no check, they may have grown so numerous, that 'twould scarce tax their powers to sink me; and that your forces, great though they be, would not suffice to withstand them. However I am minded to answer none of them, until I have related in my behoof, not indeed an entire story, for I would not seem to foist my stories in among those of so honourable a company as that with which I have made you acquainted, but a part of one, that its very incompleteness may shew that it is not one of them: wherefore, addressing my assailants, I say: – That in our city there was in old time a citizen named Filippo Balducci, a man of quite low origin, but of good substance and well versed and expert in matters belonging to his condition, who had a wife that he most dearly loved, as did she him, so that their life passed in peace and concord, nor there was aught they studied so much as how to please each other perfectly. Now it came to pass, as it does to every one, that the good lady departed this life, leaving Filippo nought of hers but an only son, that she had had by him, and who was then about two years old. His wife's death left Filippo as disconsolate as ever was any man for the loss of a loved one: and sorely missing the companionship that was most dear to him, he resolved to have done with the world, and devote himself and his little son to the service of God. Wherefore, having dedicated all his goods to charitable uses, he forthwith betook him to the summit of Monte Asinaio, where he installed himself with his son in a little cell, and living on alms, passed his days in fasting and prayer, being careful above all things to say nothing to the boy of any temporal matters, nor to let him see aught of the kind, lest they should distract his mind from his religious exercises, but discoursing with him continually of the glory of the life eternal and of God and the saints, and teaching him nought else but holy orisons: in which way of life he kept him not a few years, never suffering him to quit the cell or see aught but himself. From time to time the worthy man would go Florence, where divers of the faithful would afford him relief according to his needs, and so he would return to his cell. And thus it fell out that one day Filippo, now an aged man, being asked by the boy, who was about eighteen years old, whither he went, told him. Whereupon: – "Father," said the boy, "you are now old, and scarce able to support fatigue; why take you me not with you for once to Florence, and give me to know devout friends of God and you, so that I, who am young and fitter for such exertion than you, may thereafter go to Florence for our supplies at your pleasure, and you remain here?"

The worthy man, bethinking him that his son was now grown up, and so habituated to the service of God as hardly to be seduced by the things of the world, said to himself: – "He says well." And so, as he must needs go to Florence, he took the boy with him. Where, seeing the palaces, the houses, the churches, and all matters else with which the city abounds, and of which he had no more recollection than if he had never seen them, the boy found all passing strange, and questioned his father of not a few of them, what they were and how they were named; his curiosity being no sooner satisfied in one particular than he plied his father with a further question. And so it befell that, while son and father were thus occupied in asking and answering questions, they encountered a bevy of damsels, fair and richly arrayed, being on their return from a wedding; whom the young man no sooner saw, than he asked his father what they might be. "My son," answered the father, "fix thy gaze on the ground, regard them not at all, for naughty things are they." "Oh!" said the son, "and what is their name?" The father, fearing to awaken some mischievous craving of concupiscence in the young man, would not denote them truly, to wit, as women, but said: – "They are called goslings." Whereupon, wonderful to tell! the lad who had never before set eyes on any woman, thought no more of the palaces, the oxen, the horses, the asses, the money, or aught else that he had seen, but exclaimed: – "Prithee, father, let me have one of those goslings." "Alas, my son," replied the father, "speak not of them; they are naughty things." "Oh!" questioned the son; "but are naughty things made like that?" "Ay," returned the father. Whereupon the son: – "I know not," he said, "what you say, nor why they should be naughty things: for my part I have as yet seen nought that seemed to me so fair and delectable. They are fairer than the painted angels that you have so often shewn me. Oh! if you love me, do but let us take one of these goslings up there, and I will see that she have whereon to bill." "Nay," said the father, "that will not I. Thou knowest not whereon they bill;" and straightway, being ware that nature was more potent than his art, he repented him that he had brought the boy to Florence.

But enough of this story: 'tis time for me to cut it short, and return to those, for whose instruction 'tis told. They say then, some of these my censors, that I am too fond of you, young ladies, and am at too great pains to pleasure you. Now that I am fond of you, and am at pains to pleasure you, I do most frankly and fully confess; and I ask them whether, considering only all that it means to have had, and to have continually, before one's eyes your debonair demeanour, your bewitching beauty and exquisite grace, and therewithal your modest womanliness, not to speak of having known the amorous kisses, the caressing embraces, the voluptuous comminglings, whereof our intercourse with you, ladies most sweet, not seldom is productive, they do verily marvel that I am fond of you, seeing that one who was nurtured, reared, and brought up on a savage and solitary mountain, within the narrow circuit of a cell, without other companion than his father, had no sooner seen you than 'twas you alone that he desired, that he demanded, that he sought with ardour? Will they tear, will they lacerate me with their censures, if I, whose body Heaven fashioned all apt for love, whose soul from very boyhood was dedicate to you, am not insensible to the power of the light of your eyes, to the sweetness of your honeyed words, to the flame that is kindled by your gentle sighs, but am fond of you and sedulous to pleasure you; you, again I bid them remember, in whom a hermit, a rude, witless lad, liker to an animal than to a human being, found more to delight him than in aught else that he saw? Of a truth whoso taxes me thus must be one that, feeling, knowing nought of the pleasure and power of natural affection, loves you not, nor craves your love; and such an one I hold in light esteem. And as for those that go about to find ground of exception in my age, they do but shew that they ill understand that the leek, albeit its head is white, has a green tail. But jesting apart, thus I answer them, that never to the end of my life shall I deem it shameful to me to pleasure those to whom Guido Cavalcanti and Dante Alighieri in their old age, and Messer Cino da Pistoia in extreme old age, accounted it an honour and found it a delight to minister gratification. And but that 'twere a deviation from the use and wont of discourse, I would call history to my aid, and shew it to abound with stories of noble men of old time, who in their ripest age studied above all things else to pleasure the ladies; whereof if they be ignorant, go they and get them to school. To keep with the Muses on Parnassus is counsel I approve; but tarry with them always we cannot, nor they with us, nor is a man blameworthy, if, when he happen to part from them, he find his delight in those that resemble them. The Muses are ladies, and albeit ladies are not the peers of the Muses, yet they have their outward semblance; for which cause, if for no other, 'tis reasonable that I should be fond of them. Besides which, ladies have been to me the occasion of composing some thousand verses, but of never a verse that I made were the Muses the occasion. Howbeit 'twas with their aid, 'twas under their influence that I composed those thousand verses, and perchance they have sometimes visited me to encourage me in my present task, humble indeed though it be, doing honour and paying, as it were, tribute, to the likeness which the ladies have to them; wherefore, while I weave these stories, I stray not so far from Mount Parnassus and the Muses as not a few perchance suppose. But what shall we say to those, in whom my hunger excites such commiseration that they bid me get me bread? Verily I know not, save this: – Suppose that in my need I were to beg bread of them, what would be their answer? I doubt not they would say: – "Go seek it among the fables." And in sooth the poets have found more bread among their fables than many rich men among their treasures. And many that have gone after fables have crowned their days with splendour, while, on the other hand, not a few, in the endeavour to get them more bread than they needed, have perished miserably. But why waste more words on them? Let them send me packing, when I ask bread of them; not that, thank God, I have yet need of it, and should I ever come to be in need of it, I know, like the Apostle, how to abound and to be in want, and so am minded to be beholden to none but myself. As for those who say that these matters fell out otherwise than as I relate them, I should account it no small favour, if they would produce the originals, and should what I write not accord with them, I would acknowledge the justice of their censure, and study to amend my ways; but, until better evidence is forthcoming than their words, I shall adhere to my own opinion without seeking to deprive them of theirs, and give them tit for tat. And being minded that for this while this answer suffice, I say that with God and you, in whom I trust, most gentle ladies, to aid and protect me, and patience for my stay, I shall go forward with my work, turning my back on this tempest, however it may rage; for I see not that I can fare worse than the fine dust, which the blast of the whirlwind either leaves where it lies, or bears aloft, not seldom over the heads of men, over the crowns of kings, of emperors, and sometimes suffers to settle on the roofs of lofty palaces, and the summits of the tallest towers, whence if it fall, it cannot sink lower than the level from which it was raised. And if I ever devoted myself and all my powers to minister in any wise to your gratification, I am now minded more than ever so to do, because I know that there is nought that any can justly say in regard thereof, but that I, and others who love you, follow the promptings of nature, whose laws whoso would withstand, has need of powers pre-eminent, and, even so, will oft-times labour not merely in vain but to his own most grievous disadvantage. Such powers I own that I neither have, nor, to such end, desire to have; and had I them, I would rather leave them to another than use them myself. Wherefore let my detractors hold their peace, and if they cannot get heat, why, let them shiver their life away; and, while they remain addicted to their delights, or rather corrupt tastes, let them leave me to follow my own bent during the brief life that is accorded us. But this has been a long digression, fair ladies, and 'tis time to retrace our steps to the point where we deviated, and continue in the course on which we started.

The sun had chased every star from the sky, and lifted the dank murk of night from the earth, when, Filostrato being risen, and having roused all his company, they hied them to the fair garden, and there fell to disporting themselves: the time for breakfast being come, they took it where they had supped on the preceding evening, and after they had slept they rose, when the sun was in his zenith, and seated themselves in their wonted manner by the beautiful fountain; where Fiammetta, being bidden by Filostrato to lead off the story-telling, awaited no second command, but debonairly thus began.

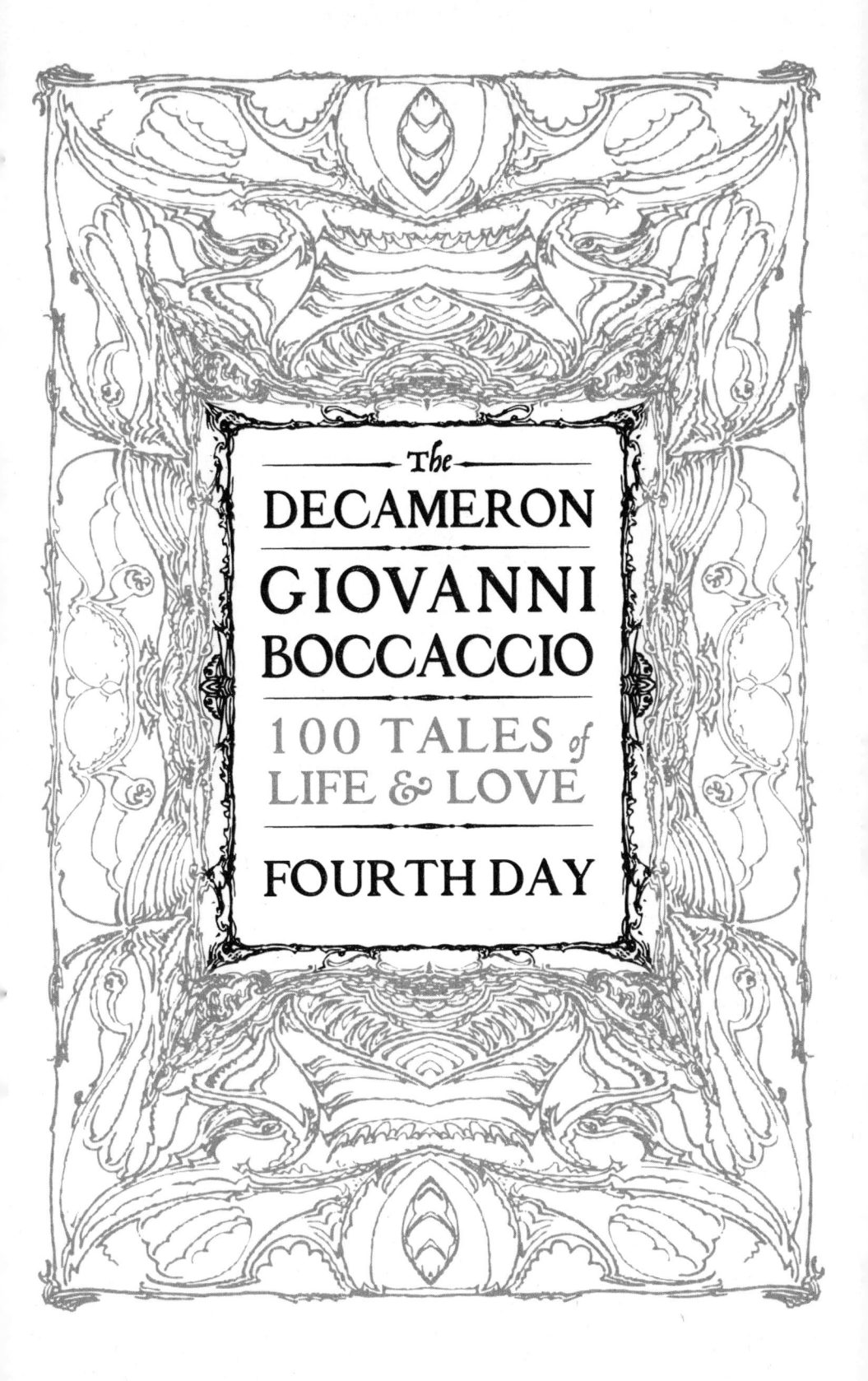

The DECAMERON
GIOVANNI BOCCACCIO
100 TALES of LIFE & LOVE
FOURTH DAY

Fourth Day

Novel I

— Tancred, Prince of Salerno, slays his daughter's lover, and sends her his heart in a golden cup: she pours upon it a poisonous distillation, which she drinks and dies. —

A DIREFUL THEME has our king allotted us for to-day's discourse seeing that, whereas we are here met for our common delectation, needs must we now tell of others' tears, whereby, whether telling or hearing, we cannot but be moved to pity. Perchance 'twas to temper in some degree the gaiety of the past days that he so ordained, but, whatever may have been his intent, his will must be to me immutable law; wherefore I will narrate to you a matter that befell piteously, nay woefully, and so as you may well weep thereat.

Tancred, Prince of Salerno, a lord most humane and kind of heart, but that in his old age he imbrued his hands in the blood of a lover, had in the whole course of his life but one daughter; and had he not had her, he had been more fortunate.

Never was daughter more tenderly beloved of father than she of the Prince, who, for that cause not knowing how to part with her, kept her unmarried for many a year after she had come of marriageable age: then at last he gave her to a son of the Duke of Capua, with whom she had lived but a short while, when he died and she returned to her father. Most lovely was she of form and feature (never woman more so), and young and light of heart, and more knowing, perchance, than beseemed a woman. Dwelling thus with her loving father, as a great lady, in no small luxury, nor failing to see that the Prince, for the great love he bore her, was at no pains to provide her with another husband, and deeming it unseemly on her part to ask one of him, she cast about how she might come by a gallant to be her secret lover. And seeing at her father's court not a few men, both gentle and simple, that resorted thither, as we know men use to frequent courts, and closely scanning their mien and manners, she preferred before all others the Prince's page, Guiscardo by name, a man of very humble origin, but preeminent for native worth and noble bearing; of whom, seeing him frequently, she became hotly enamoured, hourly extolling his qualities more and more highly. The young man, who for all his youth by no means lacked shrewdness, read her heart, and gave her his own on such wise that his love for her engrossed his mind to the exclusion of almost everything else. While thus they burned in secret for one another, the lady, desiring of all things a meeting with Guiscardo, but being shy of making any her confidant, hit upon a novel expedient to concert the affair with him. She wrote him a letter containing her commands for the ensuing day, and thrust it into a cane in the space between two of the knots, which cane she gave to Guiscardo, saying: – "Thou canst let thy servant have it for a bellows to blow thy fire up to night." Guiscardo took it, and feeling sure that 'twas not unadvisedly that she made him such a present, accompanied with such words, hied him straight home, where, carefully examining the cane, he observed that it was cleft, and, opening it, found the letter; which he had no sooner read, and learned what he was to do, than, pleased as ne'er another, he fell to devising how to set all in order that he might not fail to meet the lady on the following day, after the manner she had prescribed.

Now hard by the Prince's palace was a grotto, hewn in days of old in the solid rock, and now long disused, so that an artificial orifice, by which it received a little light, was all but choked with brambles and plants that grew about and overspread it. From one of the ground-floor rooms of the palace, which room was part of the lady's suite, a secret stair led to the grotto, though the entrance was barred by a very strong door. This stair, having been from time immemorial disused, had passed out of mind so completely that there was scarce any that remembered that it was there: but Love, whose eyes nothing, however secret, may escape, had brought it to the mind of the enamoured lady. For many a day, using all secrecy, that none should discover her, she had wrought with her tools, until she had succeeded in opening the door; which done, she had gone down into the grotto alone, and having observed the orifice, had by her letter apprised Guiscardo of its apparent height above the floor of the grotto, and bidden him contrive some means of descending thereby. Eager to carry the affair through, Guiscardo lost no time in rigging up a ladder of ropes, whereby he might ascend and descend; and having put on a suit of leather to protect him from the brambles, he hied him the following night (keeping the affair close from all) to the orifice, made the ladder fast by one of its ends to a massive trunk that was rooted in the mouth of the orifice, climbed down the ladder, and awaited the lady. On the morrow, making as if she would fain sleep, the lady dismissed her damsels, and locked herself into her room: she then opened the door of the grotto, hied her down, and met Guiscardo, to their marvellous mutual satisfaction. The lovers then repaired to her room, where in exceeding great joyance they spent no small part of the day. Nor were they neglectful of the precautions needful to prevent discovery of their amour; but in due time Guiscardo returned to the grotto; whereupon the lady locked the door and rejoined her damsels. At nightfall Guiscardo reascended his ladder, and, issuing forth of the orifice, hied him home; nor, knowing now the way, did he fail to revisit the grotto many a time thereafter.

But Fortune, noting with envious eye a happiness of such degree and duration, gave to events a dolorous turn, whereby the joy of the two lovers was converted into bitter lamentation. 'Twas Tancred's custom to come from time to time quite alone to his daughter's room, and tarry talking with her a while. Whereby it so befell that he came down there one day after breakfast, while Ghismonda – such was the lady's name – was in her garden with her damsels; so that none saw or heard him enter; nor would he call his daughter, for he was minded that she should not forgo her pleasure. But, finding the windows closed and the bed-curtains drawn down, he seated himself on a divan that stood at one of the corners of the bed, rested his head on the bed, drew the curtain over him, and thus, hidden as if of set purpose, fell asleep. As he slept Ghismonda, who, as it happened, had caused Guiscardo to come that day, left her damsels in the garden, softly entered the room, and having locked herself in, unwitting that there was another in the room, opened the door to Guiscardo, who was in waiting. Straightway they got them to bed, as was their wont; and, while they there solaced and disported them together, it so befell that Tancred awoke, and heard and saw what they did: whereat he was troubled beyond measure, and at first was minded to upbraid them; but on second thoughts he deemed it best to hold his peace, and avoid discovery, if so he might with greater stealth and less dishonour carry out the design which was already in his mind. The two lovers continued long together, as they were wont, all unwitting of Tancred; but at length they saw fit to get out of bed, when Guiscardo went back to the grotto, and the lady hied her forth of the room. Whereupon Tancred, old though he was, got out at one of the windows, clambered down into the garden, and, seen by none, returned sorely troubled to his room. By his command two men took Guiscardo early that same night, as he issued forth of the orifice accoutred in his suit of leather, and brought him privily to Tancred; who, as he saw him, all but wept, and said: – "Guiscardo, my kindness to thee is ill requited by the outrage and dishonour which thou hast done me in the person of my daughter, as to-day I have seen with my own eyes." To whom Guiscardo could answer nought but: – "Love is more potent than either, you or I." Tancred then gave order to keep him privily under watch and ward in a room within the palace; and so 'twas done. Next day, while Ghismonda wotted nought of these matters, Tancred, after pondering divers novel expedients, hied him after breakfast, according to his wont, to his daughter's room, where, having called her to him and locked himself in with her, he began, not without tears, to speak on this wise: – "Ghismonda, conceiving that I knew thy virtue and honour, never, though it had been reported to me, would I have credited, had I not seen with my own eyes, that thou wouldst so much as in idea, not to say fact, have ever yielded thyself to any man but thy husband: wherefore, for the brief residue of life that my age has in store for me, the memory of thy fall will ever be grievous to me. And would to God, as thou must needs demean thyself to such dishonour, thou hadst taken a man that matched thy nobility; but of all the men that frequent my court, thou must needs choose Guiscardo, a young man of the lowest condition, a fellow whom we brought up in charity from his tender years; for whose sake thou hast plunged me into the abyss of mental tribulation, insomuch that I know not what course to take in regard of thee. As to Guiscardo, whom I caused to be arrested last night as he issued from the orifice, and keep in durance, my course is already taken, but how I am to deal with thee, God knows, I know not. I am distraught between the love which I have ever borne thee, love such as no father ever bare to daughter, and the most just indignation evoked in me by thy signal folly; my love prompts me to pardon thee, my indignation bids me harden my heart against thee, though I do violence to my nature. But before I decide upon my course, I would fain hear what thou hast to say to this." So saying, he bent his head, and wept as bitterly as any child that had been soundly thrashed.

Her father's words, and the tidings they conveyed that not only was her secret passion discovered, but Guiscardo taken, caused Ghismonda immeasurable grief, which she was again and again on the point of evincing, as most women do, by cries and tears; but her high spirit triumphed over this weakness; by a prodigious effort she composed her countenance, and taking it for granted that her Guiscardo was no more, she inly devoted herself to death rather than a single prayer for herself should escape her lips. Wherefore, not as a woman stricken with grief or chidden for a fault, but unconcerned and unabashed, with tearless eyes, and frank and utterly dauntless mien, thus answered she her father: – "Tancred, your accusation I shall not deny, neither will I cry you mercy, for nought should I gain by denial, nor aught would I gain by supplication: nay more; there is nought I will do to conciliate thy humanity and love; my only care is to confess the truth, to defend my honour by words of sound reason, and then by deeds most resolute to give effect to the promptings of my high soul. True it is that I have loved and love Guiscardo, and during the brief while I have yet to live shall love him, nor after death, so there be then love, shall I cease to love him; but that I love him, is not imputable to my womanly frailty so much as to the little zeal thou shewedst for my bestowal in marriage, and to Guiscardo's own worth. It should not have escaped thee, Tancred, creature of flesh and blood as thou art, that thy daughter was also a creature of flesh and blood, and not of stone or iron; it was, and is, thy duty to bear in mind (old though thou art) the nature and the might of the laws to which youth is subject; and, though thou hast spent part of thy best years in martial exercises, thou shouldst nevertheless have not been ignorant how potent is the influence even upon the aged – to say nothing of the young – of ease and luxury. And not only am I, as being thy daughter, a creature of flesh and blood, but my life is not so far spent but that I am still young, and thus doubly fraught with fleshly appetite, the vehemence whereof is marvellously enhanced by reason that, having been married, I have known the pleasure that ensues upon the satisfaction of such desire. Which forces being powerless to withstand, I did but act as was natural in a young woman, when I gave way to them, and yielded myself to love. Nor in sooth did I fail to the utmost of my power so to order the indulgence of my natural propensity that my sin should bring shame neither upon thee nor upon me. To which end Love in his pity, and Fortune in a friendly mood, found and discovered to me a secret way, whereby, none witting, I attained my desire: this, from whomsoever thou hast learned it, howsoever thou comest to know it, I deny not. 'Twas not at random, as many women do, that I loved Guiscardo; but by deliberate choice I preferred him before all other men, and of determinate forethought I lured him to my love, whereof, through his and my discretion and constancy, I have long had joyance. Wherein 'twould seem that thou, following rather the opinion of the vulgar than the dictates of truth, find cause to chide me more severely than in my sinful love, for, as if thou wouldst not have been vexed, had my choice fallen on a nobleman, thou complainest that I have forgathered with a man of low condition; and dost not see that therein thou censurest not my fault but that of Fortune, which not seldom raises the unworthy to high place and leaves the worthiest in low estate. But leave we this: consider a little the principles of things, thou seest that in regard of our flesh we are all moulded of the same substance, and that all souls are endowed by one and the same Creator with equal faculties, equal powers, equal virtues. 'Twas merit that made the first distinction between us, born as we were, nay, as we are, all equal, and those whose merits were and were approved in act the greatest were called noble, and the rest were not so denoted. Which law, albeit overlaid by the contrary usage of after times, is not yet abrogated, nor so impaired but that it is still traceable in nature and good manners; for which cause whoso with merit acts, does plainly shew himself a gentleman; and if any denote him otherwise, the default is his own and not his whom he so denotes. Pass in review all thy nobles, weigh their merits, their manners and bearing, and then compare Guiscardo's qualities with theirs: if thou wilt judge without prejudice, thou wilt pronounce him noble in the highest degree, and thy nobles one and all churls. As to Guiscardo's merits and worth I did but trust the verdict which thou thyself didst utter in words, and which mine own eyes confirmed. Of whom had he such commendation as of thee for all those excellences whereby a good man and true merits commendation? And in sooth thou didst him but justice; for, unless mine eyes have played me false, there was nought for which thou didst commend him but I had seen him practise it, and that more admirably than words of thine might express; and had I been at all deceived in this matter, 'twould have been by thee. Wilt thou say then that I have forgathered with a man of low condition? If so, thou wilt not say true. Didst thou say with a poor man, the impeachment might be allowed, to thy shame, that thou so ill hast known how to requite a good man and true that is thy servant; but poverty, though it take away all else, deprives no man of gentilesse. Many kings, many great princes, were once poor, and many a ditcher or herdsman has been and is very wealthy. As for thy last perpended doubt, to wit, how thou shouldst deal with me, banish it utterly from thy thoughts. If in thy extreme old age thou art minded to manifest a harshness unwonted in thy youth, wreak thy harshness on me, resolved as I am to cry thee no mercy, prime cause as I am that this sin, if sin it be, has been committed; for of this I warrant thee, that as thou mayst have done or shalt do to Guiscardo, if to me thou do not the like, I with my own hands will do it. Now get thee gone to shed thy tears with the women, and when thy melting mood is over, ruthlessly destroy Guiscardo and me, if such thou deem our merited doom, by one and the same blow."

The loftiness of his daughter's spirit was not unknown to the Prince; but still he did not credit her with a resolve quite as firmly fixed as her words implied, to carry their purport into effect.

So, parting from her without the least intention of using harshness towards her in her own person, he determined to quench the heat of her love by wreaking his vengeance on her lover, and bade the two men that had charge of Guiscardo to strangle him noiselessly that same night, take the heart out of the body, and send it to him. The men did his bidding: and on the morrow the Prince had a large and beautiful cup of gold brought to him, and having put Guiscardo's heart therein, sent it by the hand of one of his most trusted servants to his daughter, charging the servant to say, as he gave it to her: – "Thy father sends thee this to give thee joy of that which thou lovest best, even as thou hast given him joy of that which he loved best."

Now when her father had left her, Ghismonda, wavering not a jot in her stern resolve, had sent for poisonous herbs and roots, and therefrom had distilled a water, to have it ready for use, if that which she apprehended should come to pass. And when the servant appeared with the Prince's present and message, she took the cup unblenchingly, and having lifted the lid, and seen the heart, and apprehended the meaning of the words, and that the heart was beyond a doubt Guiscardo's, she raised her head, and looking straight at the servant, said: – "Sepulture less honourable than of gold had ill befitted heart such as this: herein has my father done wisely." Which said, she raised it to her lips, and kissed it, saying: – "In all things and at all times, even to this last hour of my life, have I found my father most tender in his love, but now more so than ever before; wherefore I now render him the last thanks which will ever be due from me to him for this goodly present." So she spoke, and straining the cup to her, bowed her head over it, and gazing at the heart, said: – "Ah! sojourn most sweet of all my joys, accursed be he by whose ruthless act I see thee with the bodily eye: 'twas enough that to the mind's eye thou wert hourly present. Thou hast run thy course; thou hast closed the span that Fortune allotted thee; thou hast reached the goal of all; thou hast left behind thee the woes and weariness of the world; and thy enemy has himself granted thee sepulture accordant with thy deserts. No circumstance was wanting to duly celebrate thy obsequies, save the tears of her whom, while thou livedst, thou didst so dearly love; which that thou shouldst not lack, my remorseless father was prompted of God to send thee to me, and, albeit my resolve was fixed to die with eyes unmoistened and front all unperturbed by fear, yet will I accord thee my tears; which done, my care shall be forthwith by thy means to join my soul to that most precious soul which thou didst once enshrine. And is there other company than hers, in which with more of joy and peace I might fare to the abodes unknown? She is yet here within, I doubt not, contemplating the abodes of her and my delights, and – for sure I am that she loves me – awaiting my soul that loves her before all else."

Having thus spoken, she bowed herself low over the cup; and, while no womanish cry escaped her, 'twas as if a fountain of water were unloosed within her head, so wondrous a flood of tears gushed from her eyes, while times without number she kissed the dead heart. Her damsels that stood around her knew not whose the heart might be or what her words might mean, but melting in sympathy, they all wept, and compassionately, as vainly, enquired the cause of her lamentation, and in many other ways sought to comfort her to the best of their understanding and power. When she had wept her fill, she raised her head, and dried her eyes. Then: – "O heart," said she, "much cherished heart, discharged is my every duty towards thee; nought now remains for me to do but to come and unite my soul with thine." So saying, she sent for the vase that held the water which the day before she had distilled, and emptied it into the cup where lay the heart bathed in her tears; then, nowise afraid, she set her mouth to the cup, and drained it dry, and so with the cup in her hand she got her upon her bed, and having there disposed her person in guise as seemly as she might, laid her dead lover's heart upon her own, and silently awaited death. Meanwhile the damsels, seeing and hearing what passed, but knowing not what the water was that she had drunk, had sent word of each particular to Tancred; who, apprehensive of that which came to pass, came down with all haste to his daughter's room, where he arrived just as she got her upon her bed, and, now too late, addressed himself to comfort her with soft words, and seeing in what plight she was, burst into a flood of bitter tears. To whom the lady: – "Reserve thy tears, Tancred, till Fortune send thee hap less longed for than this: waste them not on me who care not for them. Whoever yet saw any but thee bewail the consummation of his desire? But, if of the love thou once didst bear me any spark still lives in thee, be it thy parting grace to me, that, as thou brookedst not that I should live with Guiscardo in privity and seclusion, so wherever thou mayst have caused Guiscardo's body to be cast, mine may be united with it in the common view of all." The Prince replied not for excess of grief; and the lady, feeling that her end was come, strained the dead heart to her bosom, saying: – "Fare ye well; I take my leave of you;" and with eyelids drooped and every sense evanished departed this life of woe. Such was the lamentable end of the loves of Guiscardo and Ghismonda; whom Tancred, tardily repentant of his harshness, mourned not a little, as did also all the folk of Salerno, and had honourably interred side by side in the same tomb.

Fourth Day
Novel II

— Fra Alberto gives a lady to understand that she is beloved of the Angel Gabriel, in whose shape he lies with her sundry times; afterward, for fear of her kinsmen, he flings himself forth of her house, and finds shelter in the house of a poor man, who on the morrow leads him in the guise of a wild man into the piazza, where, being recognized, he is apprehended by his brethren and imprisoned. —

MORE THAN ONCE had Fiammetta's story brought tears to the eyes of her fair companions; but now that it was ended the king said with an austere air: – "I should esteem my life but a paltry price to pay for half the delight that Ghismonda had with Guiscardo: whereat no lady of you all should marvel, seeing that each hour that I live I die a thousand deaths; nor is there so much as a particle of compensating joy allotted me. But a truce to my own concerns: I ordain that Pampinea do next ensue our direful argument, wherewith the tenor of my life in part accords, and if she follow in Fiammetta's footsteps, I doubt not I shall presently feel some drops of dew distill upon my fire." Pampinea received the king's command in a spirit more accordant with what from her own bent she divined to be the wishes of her fair gossips than with the king's words; wherefore, being minded rather to afford them some diversion, than, save as in duty bound, to satisfy the king, she made choice of a story which, without deviating from the prescribed theme, should move a laugh, and thus began: –

'Tis a proverb current among the vulgar, that: – "Whoso, being wicked, is righteous reputed, May sin as he will, and 'twill ne'er be imputed." Which proverb furnishes me with abundant matter of discourse, germane to our theme, besides occasion to exhibit the quality and degree of the hypocrisy of the religious, who flaunt it in ample flowing robes, and, with faces made pallid by art, with voices low and gentle to beg alms, most loud and haughty to reprove in others their own sins, would make believe that their way of salvation lies in taking from us and ours in giving to them; nay, more, as if they had not like us Paradise to win, but were already its lords and masters, assign therein to each that dies a place more or less exalted according to the amount of the money that he has bequeathed to them; which if they believe, 'tis by dint of self-delusion, and to the effect of deluding all that put faith in their words. Of whose guile were it lawful for me to make as full exposure as were fitting, not a few simple folk should soon be enlightened as to what they cloak within the folds of their voluminous habits. But would to God all might have the like reward of their lies as a certain friar minor, no novice, but one that was reputed among their greatest at Venice; whose story, rather than aught else, I am minded to tell you, if so I may, perchance, by laughter and jollity relieve in some degree your souls that are heavy laden with pity for the death of Ghismonda.

Know then, noble ladies, that there was in Imola a man of evil and corrupt life, Berto della Massa by name, whose pestilent practices came at length to be so well known to the good folk of Imola that 'twas all one whether he lied or spoke the truth, for there was not a soul in Imola that believed a word he said: wherefore, seeing that his tricks would pass no longer there, he removed, as in despair, to Venice, that common sink of all abominations, thinking there to find other means than he had found elsewhere to the prosecution of his nefarious designs. And, as if conscience-stricken for his past misdeeds, he assumed an air of the deepest humility, turned the best Catholic of them all, and went and made himself a friar minor, taking the name of Fra Alberto da Imola. With his habit he put on a shew of austerity, highly commending penitence and abstinence, and eating or drinking no sort of meat or wine but such as was to his taste. And scarce a soul was there that wist that the thief, the pimp, the cheat, the assassin, had not been suddenly converted into a great preacher without continuing in the practice of the said iniquities, whensoever the same was privily possible. And withal, having got himself made priest, as often as he celebrated at the altar, he would weep over the passion of our Lord, so there were folk in plenty to see, for tears cost him little enough, when he had a mind to shed them. In short, what with his sermons and his tears, he duped the folk of Venice to such a tune that scarce a will was there made but he was its executor and depositary; nay, not a few made him trustee of their moneys, and most, or well-nigh most, men and women alike, their confessor and counsellor: in short, he had put off the wolf and put on the shepherd, and the fame of his holiness was such in those parts that St. Francis himself had never the like at Assisi.

Now it so befell that among the ladies that came to confess to this holy friar was one Monna Lisetta of Ca' Quirino, the young, silly, empty-headed wife of a great merchant, who was gone with the galleys to Flanders. Like a Venetian – for unstable are they all – though she placed herself at his feet, she told him but a part of her sins, and when Fra Alberto asked her whether she had a lover, she replied with black looks: – "How now, master friar? have you not eyes in your head? See you no difference between my charms and those of other women? Lovers in plenty might I have, so I would: but charms such as mine must not be cheapened: 'tis not every man that might presume to love me. How many ladies have you seen whose beauty is comparable to mine? I should adorn Paradise itself." Whereto she added so much more in praise of her beauty that the friar could scarce hear her with patience. Howbeit, discerning at a glance that she was none too well furnished with sense, he deemed the soil meet for his plough, and fell forthwith inordinately in love with her, though he deferred his blandishments to a more convenient season, and by way of supporting his character for holiness began instead to chide her, telling her (among other novelties) that this was vainglory: whereto the lady retorted that he was a blockhead, and could not distinguish one degree of beauty from another. Wherefore Fra Alberto, lest he should occasion her too much chagrin, cut short the confession, and suffered her to depart with the other ladies. Some days after, accompanied by a single trusty friend, he hied him to Monna Lisetta's house, and having withdrawn with her alone into a saloon, where they were safe from observation, he fell on his knees at her feet, and said: – "Madam, for the love of God I crave your pardon of that which I said to you on Sunday, when you spoke to me of your beauty, for so grievously was I chastised therefor that very night, that 'tis but to-day that I have been able to quit my bed." "And by whom," quoth my Lady Battledore, "were you so chastised?" "I will tell you," returned Fra Alberto. "That night I was, as is ever my wont, at my orisons, when suddenly a great light shone in my cell, and before I could turn me to see what it was, I saw standing over me a right goodly youth with a stout cudgel in his hand, who seized me by the habit and threw me at his feet and belaboured me till I was bruised from head to foot. And when I asked him why he used me thus, he answered: – "Tis because thou didst to-day presume to speak slightingly of the celestial charms of Monna Lisetta, whom I love next to God Himself.' Whereupon I asked: – 'And who are you?' And he made answer that he was the Angel Gabriel. Then said I: – 'O my lord, I pray you pardon me.' Whereto he answered: – 'I pardon thee on condition that thou go to her, with what speed thou mayst, and obtain her pardon, which if she accord thee not, I shall come back hither and give thee belabourings enough with my cudgel to make thee a sad man for the rest of thy days.' What more he said, I dare not tell you, unless you first pardon me." Whereat our flimsy pumpion-pated Lady Lackbrain was overjoyed, taking all the friar's words for gospel. So after a while she said: – "And did I not tell you, Fra Alberto, that my charms were celestial? But, so help me God, I am moved to pity of you, and forthwith I pardon you, lest worse should befall you, so only you tell me what more the Angel said." "So will I gladly, Madam," returned Fra Alberto, "now that I have your pardon; this only I bid you bear in mind, that you have a care that never a soul in the world hear from you a single word of what I shall say to you, if you would not spoil your good fortune, wherein there is not to-day in the whole world a lady that may compare with you. Know then that the Angel Gabriel bade me tell you that you stand so high in his favour that again and again he would have come to pass the night with you, but that he doubted he should affright you. So now he sends you word through me that he would fain come one night, and stay a while with you; and seeing that, being an angel, if he should visit you in his angelic shape, he might not be touched by you, he would, to pleasure you, present himself in human shape; and so he bids you send him word, when you would have him come, and in whose shape, and he will come; for which cause you may deem yourself more blessed than any other lady that lives." My Lady Vanity then said that she was highly flattered to be beloved of the Angel Gabriel; whom she herself loved so well that she had never grudged four soldi to burn a candle before his picture, wherever she saw it, and that he was welcome to visit her as often as he liked, and would always find her alone in her room; on the understanding, however, that he should not desert her for the Virgin Mary, whom she had heard he did mightily affect, and indeed 'twould so appear, for, wherever she saw him, he was always on his knees at her feet: for the rest he might even come in what shape he pleased, so that it was not such as to terrify her. Then said Fra Alberto: – "Madam, 'tis wisely spoken; and I will arrange it all with him just as you say. But 'tis in your power to do me a great favour, which will cost you nothing; and this favour is that you be consenting that he visit you in my shape. Now hear wherein you will confer this favour: thus will it be: he will disembody my soul, and set it in Paradise, entering himself into my body; and, as long as he shall be with you, my soul will be in Paradise." Whereto my Lady Slenderwit: – "So be it," she said; "I am well pleased that you have this solace to salve the bruises that he gives you on my account." "Good," said Fra Alberto; "then you will see to it that to-night he find, when he comes, your outer door unlatched, that he may have ingress; for, coming, as he will, in human shape, he will not be able to enter save by the door." "It shall be done," replied the lady. Whereupon Fra Alberto took his leave, and the lady remained in such a state of exaltation that her nether end knew not her chemise, and it seemed to her a thousand years until the Angel Gabriel should come to visit her. Fra Alberto, bethinking him that 'twas not as an angel, but as a cavalier that he must acquit himself that night, fell to fortifying himself with comfits and other dainties, that he might not lose his saddle for slight cause. Then, leave of absence gotten, he betook him at nightfall, with a single companion, to the house of a woman that was his friend, which house had served on former occasions as his base when he went a chasing the fillies; and having there disguised himself, he hied him, when he deemed 'twas time, to the house of the lady, where, donning the gewgaws he had brought with him, he transformed himself into an angel, and going up, entered the lady's chamber. No sooner saw she this dazzling apparition than she fell on her knees before the Angel, who gave her his blessing, raised her to her feet, and motioned her to go to bed. She, nothing loath, obeyed forthwith, and the Angel lay down beside his devotee. Now, Fra Alberto was a stout, handsome fellow, whose legs bore themselves right bravely; and being bedded with Monna Lisetta, who was lusty and delicate, he covered her after another fashion than her husband had been wont, and took many a flight that night without wings, so that she heartily cried him content; and not a little therewithal did he tell her of the glory celestial. Then towards daybreak, all being ready for his return, he hied him forth, and repaired, caparisoned as he was, to his friend, whom, lest he should be affrighted, sleeping alone, the good woman of the house had solaced with her company. The lady, so soon as she had breakfasted, betook her to Fra Alberto, and reported the Angel Gabriel's visit, and what he had told her of the glory of the life eternal, describing his appearance, not without some added marvels of her own invention. Whereto Fra Alberto replied: – "Madam, I know not how you fared with him; but this I know, that last night he came to me, and for that I had done his errand with you, he suddenly transported my soul among such a multitude of flowers and roses as was never seen here below, and my soul – what became of my body I know not – tarried in one of the most delightful places that ever was from that hour until matins." "As for your body," said the lady, "do I not tell you whose it was? It lay all night long with the Angel Gabriel in my arms; and if you believe me not, you have but to took under your left pap, where I gave the Angel a mighty kiss, of which the mark will last for some days." "Why then," said Fra Alberto, "I will even do to-day what 'tis long since I did, to wit, undress, that I may see if you say sooth." So they fooled it a long while, and then the lady went home, where Fra Alberto afterwards paid her many a visit without any let. However, one day it so befell that while Monna Lisetta was with one of her gossips canvassing beauties, she, being minded to exalt her own charms above all others, and having, as we know, none too much wit in her pumpion-pate, observed: – "Did you but know by whom my charms are prized, then, for sure, you would have nought to say of the rest." Her gossip, all agog to hear, for well she knew her foible, answered: – "Madam, it may be as you say, but still, while one knows not who he may be, one cannot alter one's mind so rapidly." Whereupon my Lady Featherbrain: – "Gossip," said she, "'tis not for common talk, but he that I wot of is the Angel Gabriel, who loves me more dearly than himself, for that I am, so he tells me, the fairest lady in all the world, ay, and in the Maremma to boot." Whereat her gossip would fain have laughed, but held herself in, being minded to hear more from her. Wherefore she said: – "God's faith, Madam, if 'tis the Angel Gabriel, and he tells you so, why, so of course it must needs be; but I wist not the angels meddled with such matters." "There you erred, gossip," said the lady: "zounds, he does it better than my husband, and he tells me they do it above there too, but, as he rates my charms above any that are in heaven, he is enamoured of me, and not seldom visits me: so now dost see?" So away went the gossip so agog to tell the story, that it seemed to her a thousand years till she was where it might be done; and being met for recreation with a great company of ladies, she narrated it all in detail: whereby it passed to the ladies' husbands, and to other ladies, and from them to yet other ladies, so that in less than two days all Venice was full of it. But among others, whose ears it reached, were Monna Lisetta's brothers-in-law, who, keeping their own counsel, resolved to find this angel and make out whether he knew how to fly; to which end they kept watch for some nights. Whereof no hint, as it happened, reached Fra Alberto's ears; and so, one night when he was come to enjoy the lady once more, he was scarce undressed when her brothers-in-law, who had seen him come, were at the door of the room and already opening it, when Fra Alberto, hearing the noise and apprehending the danger, started up, and having no other resource, threw open a window that looked on to the Grand Canal, and plunged into the water. The depth was great, and he was an expert swimmer; so that he took no hurt, but, having reached the other bank, found a house open, and forthwith entered it, praying the good man that was within, for God's sake to save his life, and trumping up a story to account for his being there at so late an hour, and stripped to the skin. The good man took pity on him, and having occasion to go out, he put him in his own bed, bidding him stay there until his return; and so, having locked him in, he went about his business.

Now when the lady's brothers-in-law entered the room, and found that the Angel Gabriel had taken flight, leaving his wings behind him, being baulked of their prey, they roundly rated the lady, and then, leaving her disconsolate, betook themselves home with the Angel's spoils. Whereby it befell, that, when 'twas broad day, the good man, being on the Rialto, heard tell how the Angel Gabriel had come to pass the night with Monna Lisetta, and, being surprised by her brothers-in-law, had taken fright, and thrown himself into the Canal, and none knew what was become of him. The good man guessed in a trice that the said Angel was no other than the man he had at home, whom on his return he recognized, and, after much chaffering, brought him to promise him fifty ducats that he might not be given up to the lady's brothers-in-law. The bargain struck, Fra Alberto signified a desire to be going. Whereupon: – "There is no way," said the good man, "but one, if you are minded to take it. To-day we hold a revel, wherein folk lead others about in various disguises; as, one man will present a bear, another a wild man, and so forth; and then in the piazza of San Marco there is a hunt, which done, the revel is ended; and then away they hie them, whither they will, each with the man he has led about. If you are willing to be led by me in one or another of these disguises, before it can get wind that you are here, I can bring you whither you would go; otherwise I see not how you are to quit this place without being known; and the lady's brothers-in-law, reckoning that you must be lurking somewhere in this quarter, have set guards all about to take you." Loath indeed was Fra Alberto to go in such a guise, but such was his fear of the lady's relations that he consented, and told the good man whither he desired to be taken, and that he was content to leave the choice of the disguise to him. The good man then smeared him all over with honey, and covered him with down, set a chain on his neck and a vizard on his face, gave him a stout cudgel to carry in one hand, and two huge dogs, which he had brought from the shambles, to lead with the other, and sent a man to the Rialto to announce that whoso would see the Angel Gabriel should hie him to the piazza of San Marco; in all which he acted as a leal Venetian. And so, after a while, he led him forth, and then, making him go before, held him by the chain behind, and through a great throng that clamoured: – "What manner of thing is this? what manner of thing is this?" he brought him to the piazza, where, what with those that followed them, and those that had come from the Rialto on hearing the announcement, there were folk without end. Arrived at the piazza, he fastened his wild man to a column in a high and exposed place, making as if he were minded to wait till the hunt should begin; whereby the flies and gadflies, attracted by the honey with which he was smeared, caused him most grievous distress. However, the good man waited only until the piazza was thronged, and then, making as if he would unchain his wild man, he tore the vizard from Fra Alberto's face, saying: – "Gentlemen, as the boar comes not to the hunt, and the hunt does not take place, that it be not for nothing that you are come hither, I am minded to give you a view of the Angel Gabriel, who comes down from heaven to earth by night to solace the ladies of Venice." The vizard was no sooner withdrawn than all recognized Fra Alberto, and greeted him with hootings, rating him in language as offensive and opprobrious as ever rogue was abused withal, and pelting him in the face with every sort of filth that came to hand: in which plight they kept him an exceeding great while, until by chance the bruit thereof reached his brethren, of whom some six thereupon put themselves in motion, and, arrived at the piazza, clapped a habit on his back, and unchained him, and amid an immense uproar led him off to their convent, where, after languishing a while in prison, 'tis believed that he died.

So this man, by reason that, being reputed righteous, he did evil, and 'twas not imputed to him, presumed to counterfeit the Angel Gabriel, and, being transformed into a wild man, was in the end put to shame, as he deserved, and vainly bewailed his misdeeds. God grant that so it may betide all his likes.

Fourth Day

Novel III

— *Three young men love three sisters, and flee with them to Crete. The eldest of the sisters slays her lover for jealousy. The second saves the life of the first by yielding herself to the Duke of Crete. Her lover slays her, and makes off with the first: the third sister and her lover are charged with the murder, are arrested and confess the crime. They escape death by bribing the guards, flee destitute to Rhodes, and there in destitution die.* —

PAMPINEA'S STORY ended, Filostrato mused a while, and then said to her: – "A little good matter there was that pleased me at the close of your story, but, before 'twas reached, there was far too much to laugh at, which I could have wished had not been there." Then, turning to Lauretta, he said: – "Madam, give us something better to follow, if so it may be." Lauretta replied with a laugh: – "Harsh beyond measure are you to the lovers, to desire that their end be always evil; but, as in duty bound, I will tell a story of three, who all alike came to a bad end, having had little joyance of their loves;" and so saying, she began.

Well may ye wot, young ladies, for 'tis abundantly manifest, that there is no vice but most grievous disaster may ensue thereon to him that practises it, and not seldom to others; and of all the vices that which hurries us into peril with loosest rein is, methinks, anger; which is nought but a rash and hasty impulse, prompted by a feeling of pain, which banishes reason, shrouds the eyes of the mind in thick darkness, and sets the soul ablaze with a fierce frenzy. Which, though it not seldom befall men, and one rather than another, has nevertheless been observed to be fraught in women with more disastrous consequences, inasmuch as in them the flame is both more readily kindled, and burns more brightly, and with less impediment to its vehemence. Wherein is no cause to marvel, for, if we consider it, we shall see that 'tis of the nature of fire to lay hold more readily of things light and delicate than of matters of firmer and more solid substance; and sure it is that we (without offence to the men be it spoken) are more delicate than they, and much more mobile. Wherefore, seeing how prone we are thereto by nature, and considering also our gentleness and tenderness, how soothing and consolatory they are to the men with whom we consort, and that thus this madness of wrath is fraught with grievous annoy and peril; therefore, that with stouter heart we may defend ourselves against it, I purpose by my story to shew you, how the loves of three young men, and as many ladies, as I said before, were by the anger of one of the ladies changed from a happy to a most woeful complexion.

Marseilles, as you know, is situate on the coast of Provence, a city ancient and most famous, and in old time the seat of many more rich men and great merchants than are to be seen there to-day, among whom was one Narnald Cluada by name, a man of the lowest origin, but a merchant of unsullied probity and integrity, and boundless wealth in lands and goods and money, who had by his lady several children, three of them being daughters, older, each of them, than the other children, who were sons. Two of the daughters, who were twins, were, when my story begins, fifteen years old, and the third was but a year younger, so that in order to their marriage their kinsfolk awaited nothing but the return of Narnald from Spain, whither he was gone with his merchandise. One of the twins was called Ninette, the other Madeleine; the third daughter's name was Bertelle. A young man, Restagnon by name, who, though poor, was of gentle blood, was in the last degree enamoured of Ninette, and she of him; and so discreetly had they managed the affair, that, never another soul in the world witting aught of it, they had had joyance of their love, and that for a good while, when it so befell that two young friends of theirs, the one Foulques, the other Hugues by name, whom their fathers, recently dead, had left very wealthy, fell in love, the one with Madeleine, the other with Bertelle. Whereof Restagnon being apprised by Ninette bethought him that in their love he might find a means to the relief of his necessities. He accordingly consorted freely and familiarly with them, accompanying, now one, now the other, and sometimes both of them, when they went to visit their ladies and his; and when he judged that he had made his footing as friendly and familiar as need was, he bade them one day to his house, and said: – "Comrades most dear, our friendship, perchance, may not have left you without assurance of the great love I bear you, and that for you I would do even as much as for myself: wherefore, loving you thus much, I purpose to impart to you that which is in my mind, that in regard thereof, you and I together may then resolve in such sort as to you shall seem the best. You, if I may trust your words, as also what I seem to have gathered from your demeanour by day and by night, burn with an exceeding great love for the two ladies whom you affect, as I for their sister. For the assuagement whereof, I have good hope that, if you will unite with me, I shall find means most sweet and delightsome; to wit, on this wise. You possess, as I do not, great wealth: now if you are willing to make of your wealth a common stock with me as third partner therein, and to choose some part of the world where we may live in careless ease upon our substance, without any manner of doubt I trust so to prevail that the three sisters with great part of their father's substance shall come to live with us, wherever we shall see fit to go; whereby, each with his own lady, we shall live as three brethren, the happiest men in the world. 'Tis now for you to determine whether you will embrace this proffered solace, or let it slip from you." The two young men, whose love was beyond all measure fervent, spared themselves the trouble of deliberation: 'twas enough that they heard that they were to have their ladies: wherefore they answered, that, so this should ensue, they were ready to do as he proposed. Having thus their answer, Restagnon a few days later was closeted with Ninette, to whom 'twas a matter of no small difficulty for him to get access. Nor had he been long with her before he adverted to what had passed between him and the young men, and sought to commend the project to her for reasons not a few. Little need, however, had he to urge her: for to live their life openly together was the very thing she desired, far more than he: wherefore she frankly answered that she would have it so, that her sisters would do, more especially in this matter, just as she wished, and that he should lose no time in making all the needful arrangements. So Restagnon returned to the two young men, who were most urgent that it should be done even as he said, and told them that on the part of the ladies the matter was concluded. And so, having fixed upon Crete for their destination, and sold some estates that they had, giving out that they were minded to go a trading with the proceeds, they converted all else that they possessed into money, and bought a brigantine, which with all secrecy they handsomely equipped, anxiously expecting the time of their departure, while Ninette on her part, knowing well how her sisters were affected, did so by sweet converse foment their desire that, till it should be accomplished, they accounted their life as nought. The night of their embarcation being come, the three sisters opened a great chest that belonged to their father, and took out therefrom a vast quantity of money and jewels, with which they all three issued forth of the house in dead silence, as they had been charged, and found their three lovers awaiting them; who, having forthwith brought them aboard the brigantine, bade the rowers give way, and, tarrying nowhere, arrived the next evening at Genoa, where the new lovers had for the first time joyance and solace of their love.

Having taken what they needed of refreshment, they resumed their course, touching at this port and that, and in less than eight days, speeding without impediment, were come to Crete. There they bought them domains both beautiful and broad, whereon, hard by Candia they built them mansions most goodly and delightsome, wherein they lived as barons, keeping a crowd of retainers, with dogs, hawks and horses, and speeding the time with their ladies in feasting and revelling and merrymaking, none so light-hearted as they. Such being the tenor of their life, it so befell that (as 'tis matter of daily experience that, however delightsome a thing may be, superabundance thereof will breed disgust) Restagnon, much as he had loved Ninette, being now able to have his joyance of her without stint or restraint, began to weary of her, and by consequence to abate somewhat of his love for her. And being mightily pleased with a fair gentlewoman of the country, whom he met at a merrymaking, he set his whole heart upon her, and began to shew himself marvellously courteous and gallant towards her; which Ninette perceiving grew so jealous that he might not go a step but she knew of it, and resented it to his torment and her own with high words. But as, while superfluity engenders disgust, appetite is but whetted when fruit is forbidden, so Ninette's wrath added fuel to the flame of Restagnon's new love. And whichever was the event, whether in course of time Restagnon had the lady's favour or had it not, Ninette, whoever may have brought her the tidings, firmly believed that he had it; whereby from the depths of distress she passed into a towering passion, and thus was transported into such a frenzy of rage that all the love she bore to Restagnon was converted into bitter hatred, and, blinded by her wrath, she made up her mind to avenge by Restagnon's death the dishonour which she deemed that he had done her. So she had recourse to an old Greek woman, that was very skilful in compounding poisons, whom by promises and gifts she induced to distill a deadly water, which, keeping her own counsel, she herself gave Restagnon to drink one evening, when he was somewhat heated and quite off his guard: whereby – such was the efficacy of the water – she despatched Restagnon before matins. On learning his death Foulques and Hugues and their ladies, who knew not that he had been poisoned, united their bitter with Ninette's feigned lamentations, and gave him honourable sepulture. But so it befell that, not many days after, the old woman, that had compounded the poison for Ninette, was taken for another crime; and, being put to the torture, confessed the compounding of the poison among other of her misdeeds, and fully declared what had thereby come to pass. Wherefore the Duke of Crete, breathing no word of his intent, came privily by night, and set a guard around Foulques' palace, where Ninette then was, and quietly, and quite unopposed, took and carried her off; and without putting her to the torture, learned from her in a trice all that he sought to know touching the death of Restagnon. Foulques and Hugues had learned privily of the Duke, and their ladies of them, for what cause Ninette was taken; and, being mightily distressed thereby, bestirred themselves with all zeal to save Ninette from the fire, to which they apprehended she would be condemned, as having indeed richly deserved it; but all their endeavours seemed to avail nothing, for the Duke was unwaveringly resolved that justice should be done. Madeleine, Foulques' fair wife, who had long been courted by the Duke, but had never deigned to shew him the least favour, thinking that by yielding herself to his will she might redeem her sister from the fire, despatched a trusty envoy to him with the intimation that she was entirely at his disposal upon the twofold condition, that in the first place her sister should be restored to her free and scatheless, and, in the second place, the affair should be kept secret. Albeit gratified by this overture, the Duke was long in doubt whether he should accept it; in the end, however, he made up his mind to do so, and signified his approval to the envoy. Then with the lady's consent he put Foulques and Hugues under arrest for a night, as if he were minded to examine them of the affair, and meanwhile quartered himself privily with Madeleine. Ninette, who, he had made believe, had been set in a sack, and was to be sunk in the sea that same night, he took with him, and presented her to her sister in requital of the night's joyance, which, as he parted from her on the morrow, he prayed her might not be the last, as it was the first, fruit of their love, at the same time enjoining her to send the guilty lady away that she might not bring reproach upon him, nor he be compelled to deal rigorously with her again. Released the same morning, and told that Ninette had been cast into the sea, Foulques and Hugues, fully believing that so it was, came home, thinking how they should console their ladies for the death of their sister; but, though Madeleine was at great pains to conceal Ninette, Foulques nevertheless, to his no small amazement, discovered that she was there; which at once excited his suspicion, for he knew that the Duke had been enamoured of Madeleine; and he asked how it was that Ninette was there. Madeleine made up a long story by way of explanation, to which his sagacity gave little credit, and in the end after long parley he constrained her to tell the truth. Whereupon, overcome with grief, and transported with rage, he drew his sword, and, deaf to her appeals for mercy, slew her. Then, fearing the vengeful justice of the Duke, he left the dead body in the room, and hied him to Ninette, and with a counterfeit gladsome mien said to her: – "Go we without delay whither thy sister has appointed that I escort thee, that thou fall not again into the hands of the Duke." Ninette believed him, and being fain to go for very fear, she forewent further leave-taking of her sister, more particularly as it was now night, and set out with Foulques, who took with him such little money as he could lay his hands upon; and so they made their way to the coast, where they got aboard a bark, but none ever knew where their voyage ended.

Madeleine's dead body being discovered next day, certain evil-disposed folk, that bore a grudge to Hugues, forthwith apprised the Duke of the fact; which brought the Duke – for much he loved Madeleine – in hot haste to the house, where he arrested Hugues and his lady, who as yet knew nothing of the departure of Foulques and Ninette, and extorted from them a confession that they and Foulques were jointly answerable for Madeleine's death. For which cause being justly apprehensive of death, they with great address corrupted the guards that had charge of them, giving them a sum of money which they kept concealed in their house against occasions of need; and together with the guards fled with all speed, leaving all that they possessed behind them, and took ship by night for Rhodes, where, being arrived, they lived in great poverty and misery no long time. Such then was the issue, to which Restagnon, by his foolish love, and Ninette by her wrath brought themselves and others.

Fourth Day
Novel IV

— *Gerbino, in breach of the plighted faith of his grandfather, King Guglielmo, attacks a ship of the King of Tunis to rescue thence his daughter. She being slain by those aboard the ship, he slays them, and afterwards he is beheaded.* —

LAURETTA, HER STORY ended, kept silence; and the king brooded as in deep thought, while one or another of the company deplored the sad fate of this or the other of the lovers, or censured Ninette's wrath, or made some other comment. At length, however, the king roused himself, and raising his head, made sign to Elisa that 'twas now for her to speak. So, modestly, Elisa thus began: –

Gracious ladies, not a few there are that believe that Love looses no shafts save when he is kindled by the eyes, contemning their opinion that hold that passion may be engendered by words; whose error will be abundantly manifest in a story which I purpose to tell you; wherein you may see how mere rumour not only wrought mutual love in those that had never seen one another, but also brought both to a miserable death.

Guglielmo, the Second, as the Sicilians compute, King of Sicily, had two children, a son named Ruggieri, and a daughter named Gostanza. Ruggieri died before his father, and left a son named Gerbino; who, being carefully trained by his grandfather, grew up a most goodly gallant, and of great renown in court and camp, and that not only within the borders of Sicily, but in divers other parts of the world, among them Barbary, then tributary to the King of Sicily. And among others, to whose ears was wafted the bruit of Gerbino's magnificent prowess and courtesy, was a daughter of the King of Tunis, who, by averment of all that had seen her, was a creature as fair and debonair, and of as great and noble a spirit as Nature ever formed. To hear tell of brave men was her delight, and what she heard, now from one, now from another, of the brave deeds of Gerbino she treasured in her mind so sedulously, and pondered them with such pleasure, rehearsing them to herself in imagination, that she became hotly enamoured of him, and there was none of whom she talked, or heard others talk, so gladly. Nor, on the other hand, had the fame of her incomparable beauty and other excellences failed to travel, as to other lands, so also to Sicily, where, falling on Gerbino's ears, it gave him no small delight, to such effect that he burned for the lady no less vehemently than she for him. Wherefore, until such time as he might, upon some worthy occasion, have his grandfather's leave to go to Tunis, yearning beyond measure to see her, he charged every friend of his, that went thither, to give her to know, as best he might, his great and secret love for her, and to bring him tidings of her. Which office one of the said friends discharged with no small address; for, having obtained access to her, after the manner of merchants, by bringing jewels for her to look at, he fully apprised her of Gerbino's passion, and placed him, and all that he possessed, entirely at her disposal. The lady received both messenger and message with gladsome mien, made answer that she loved with equal ardour, and in token thereof sent Gerbino one of her most precious jewels. Gerbino received the jewel with extreme delight, and sent her many a letter and many a most precious gift by the hand of the same messenger; and 'twas well understood between them that, should Fortune accord him opportunity, he should see and know her.

On this footing the affair remained somewhat longer than was expedient; and so, while Gerbino and the lady burned with mutual love, it befell that the King of Tunis gave her in marriage to the King of Granada; whereat she was wroth beyond measure, for that she was not only going into a country remote from her lover, but, as she deemed, was severed from him altogether; and so this might not come to pass, gladly, could she but have seen how, would she have left her father and fled to Gerbino. In like manner, Gerbino, on learning of the marriage, was vexed beyond measure, and was oft times minded, could he but find means to win to her husband by sea, to wrest her from him by force. Some rumour of Gerbino's love and of his intent, reached the King of Tunis, who, knowing his prowess and power, took alarm, and as the time drew nigh for conveying the lady to Granada, sent word of his purpose to King Guglielmo, and craved his assurance that it might be carried into effect without let or hindrance on the part of Gerbino, or any one else. The old King had heard nothing of Gerbino's love affair, and never dreaming that 'twas on such account that the assurance was craved, granted it without demur, and in pledge thereof sent the King of Tunis his glove. Which received, the King made ready a great and goodly ship in the port of Carthage, and equipped her with all things meet for those that were to man her, and with all appointments apt and seemly for the reception of his daughter, and awaited only fair weather to send her therein to Granada. All which the young lady seeing and marking, sent one of her servants privily to Palermo, bidding him greet the illustrious Gerbino on her part, and tell him that a few days would see her on her way to Granada; wherefore 'twould now appear whether, or no, he were really as doughty a man as he was reputed, and loved her as much as he had so often protested. The servant did not fail to deliver her message exactly, and returned to Tunis, leaving Gerbino, who knew that his grandfather, King Guglielmo, had given the King of Tunis the desired assurance, at a loss how to act. But prompted by love, and goaded by the lady's words and loath to seem a craven, he hied him to Messina; and having there armed two light galleys, and manned them with good men and true, he put to sea, and stood for Sardinia, deeming that the lady's ship must pass that way. Nor was he far out in his reckoning; for he had not been there many days, when the ship, sped by a light breeze, hove in sight not far from the place where he lay in wait for her. Whereupon Gerbino said to his comrades: – "Gentlemen, if you be as good men and true as I deem you, there is none of you but must have felt, if he feel not now, the might of love; for without love I deem no mortal capable of true worth or aught that is good; and if you are or have been in love, 'twill be easy for you to understand that which I desire. I love, and 'tis because I love that I have laid this travail upon you; and that which I love is in the ship that you see before you, which is fraught not only with my beloved, but with immense treasures, which, if you are good men and true, we, so we but play the man in fight, may with little trouble make our own; nor for my share of the spoils of the victory demand I aught but a lady, whose love it is that prompts me to take arms: all else I freely cede to you from this very hour. Forward, then; attack we this ship; success should be ours, for God favours our enterprise, nor lends her wind to evade us." Fewer words might have sufficed the illustrious Gerbino; for the rapacious Messinese that were with him were already bent heart and soul upon that to which by his harangue he sought to animate them. So, when he had done, they raised a mighty shout, so that 'twas as if trumpets did blare, and caught up their arms, and smiting the water with their oars, overhauled the ship. The advancing galleys were observed while they were yet a great way off by the ship's crew, who, not being able to avoid the combat, put themselves in a posture of defence. Arrived at close quarters, the illustrious Gerbino bade send the ship's masters aboard the galleys, unless they were minded to do battle. Certified of the challenge, and who they were that made it, the Saracens answered that 'twas in breach of the faith plighted to them by their assailants' king that they were thus attacked, and in token thereof displayed King Guglielmo's glove, averring in set terms that there should be no surrender either of themselves or of aught that was aboard the ship without battle. Gerbino, who had observed the lady standing on the ship's poop, and seen that she was far more beautiful than he had imagined, burned with a yet fiercer flame than before, and to the display of the glove made answer, that, as he had no falcons there just then, the glove booted him not; wherefore, so they were not minded to surrender the lady, let them prepare to receive battle. Whereupon, without further delay, the battle began on both sides with a furious discharge of arrows and stones; on which wise it was long protracted to their common loss; until at last Gerbino, seeing that he gained little advantage, took a light bark which they had brought from Sardinia, and having fired her, bore down with her, and both the galleys, upon the ship. Whereupon the Saracens, seeing that they must perforce surrender the ship or die, caused the King's daughter, who lay beneath the deck weeping, to come up on deck, and led her to the prow, and shouting to Gerbino, while the lady shrieked alternately "mercy" and "succour," opened her veins before his eyes, and cast her into the sea, saying: – "Take her; we give her to thee on such wise as we can, and as thy faith has merited." Maddened to witness this deed of barbarism, Gerbino, as if courting death, recked no more of the arrows and the stones, but drew alongside the ship, and, despite the resistance of her crew, boarded her; and as a famished lion ravens amongst a herd of oxen, and tearing and rending, now one, now another, gluts his wrath before he appeases his hunger, so Gerbino, sword in hand, hacking and hewing on all sides among the Saracens, did ruthlessly slaughter not a few of them; till, as the burning ship began to blaze more fiercely, he bade the seamen take thereout all that they might by way of guerdon, which done, he quitted her, having gained but a rueful victory over his adversaries. His next care was to recover from the sea the body of the fair lady, whom long and with many a tear he mourned: and so he returned to Sicily, and gave the body honourable sepulture in Ustica, an islet that faces, as it were, Trapani, and went home the saddest man alive.

When these tidings reached the King of Tunis, he sent to King Guglielmo ambassadors, habited in black, who made complaint of the breach of faith and recited the manner of its occurrence. Which caused King Guglielmo no small chagrin; and seeing not how he might refuse the justice they demanded, he had Gerbino arrested, and he himself, none of his barons being able by any entreaty to turn him from his purpose, sentenced him to forfeit his head, and had it severed from his body in his presence, preferring to suffer the loss of his only grandson than to gain the reputation of a faithless king. And so, miserably, within the compass of a few brief days, died the two lovers by woeful deaths, as I have told you, and without having known any joyance of their love.

Fourth Day
Novel V

— Lisabetta's brothers slay her lover: he appears to her in a dream, and shews her where he is buried: she privily disinters the head, and sets it in a pot of basil, whereon she daily weeps a great while. The pot being taken from her by her brothers, she dies, not long after. —

ELISA'S STORY ended, the king bestowed a few words of praise upon it, and then laid the burden of discourse upon Filomena, who, full of compassion for the woes of Gerbino and his lady, heaved a piteous sigh, and thus began: –

My story, gracious ladies, will not be of folk of so high a rank as those of whom Elisa has told us, but perchance 'twill not be less touching. 'Tis brought to my mind by the recent mention of Messina, where the matter befell.

Know then that there were at Messina three young men, that were brothers and merchants, who were left very rich on the death of their father, who was of San Gimignano; and they had a sister, Lisabetta by name, a girl fair enough, and no less debonair, but whom, for some reason or another, they had not as yet bestowed in marriage. The three brothers had also in their shop a young Pisan, Lorenzo by name, who managed all their affairs, and who was so goodly of person and gallant, that Lisabetta bestowed many a glance upon him, and began to regard him with extraordinary favour; which Lorenzo marking from time to time, gave up all his other amours, and in like manner began to affect her, and so, their loves being equal, 'twas not long before they took heart of grace, and did that which each most desired. Wherein continuing to their no small mutual solace and delight, they neglected to order it with due secrecy, whereby one night as Lisabetta was going to Lorenzo's room, she, all unwitting, was observed by the eldest of the brothers, who, albeit much distressed by what he had learnt, yet, being a young man of discretion, was swayed by considerations more seemly, and, allowing no word to escape him, spent the night in turning the affair over in his mind in divers ways. On the morrow he told his brothers that which, touching Lisabetta and Lorenzo, he had observed in the night, which, that no shame might thence ensue either to them or to their sister, they after long consultation determined to pass over in silence, making as if they had seen or heard nought thereof, until such time as they in a safe and convenient manner might banish this disgrace from their sight before it could go further. Adhering to which purpose, they jested and laughed with Lorenzo as they had been wont; and after a while pretending that they were all three going forth of the city on pleasure, they took Lorenzo with them; and being come to a remote and very lonely spot, seeing that 'twas apt for their design, they took Lorenzo, who was completely off his guard, and slew him, and buried him on such wise that none was ware of it. On their return to Messina they gave out that they had sent him away on business; which was readily believed, because 'twas what they had been frequently used to do. But as Lorenzo did not return, and Lisabetta questioned the brothers about him with great frequency and urgency, being sorely grieved by his long absence, it so befell that one day, when she was very pressing in her enquiries, one of the brothers said: – "What means this? What hast thou to do with Lorenzo, that thou shouldst ask about him so often? Ask us no more, or we will give thee such answer as thou deservest." So the girl, sick at heart and sorrowful, fearing she knew not what, asked no questions; but many a time at night she called piteously to him, and besought him to come to her, and bewailed his long tarrying with many a tear, and ever yearning for his return, languished in total dejection.

But so it was that one night, when, after long weeping that her Lorenzo came not back, she had at last fallen asleep, Lorenzo appeared to her in a dream, wan and in utter disarray, his clothes torn to shreds and sodden; and thus, as she thought, he spoke: – "Lisabetta, thou dost nought but call me, and vex thyself for my long tarrying, and bitterly upbraid me with thy tears; wherefore be it known to thee that return to thee I may not, because the last day that thou didst see me thy brothers slew me." After which, he described the place where they had buried him, told her to call and expect him no more, and vanished. The girl then awoke, and doubting not that the vision was true, wept bitterly. And when morning came, and she was risen, not daring to say aught to her brothers, she resolved to go to the place indicated in the vision, and see if what she had dreamed were even as it had appeared to her. So, having leave to go a little way out of the city for recreation in company with a maid that had at one time lived with them and knew all that she did, she hied her thither with all speed; and having removed the dry leaves that were strewn about the place, she began to dig where the earth seemed least hard. Nor had she dug long, before she found the body of her hapless lover, whereon as yet there was no trace of corruption or decay; and thus she saw without any manner of doubt that her vision was true. And so, saddest of women, knowing that she might not bewail him there, she would gladly, if she could, have carried away the body and given it more honourable sepulture elsewhere; but as she might not so do, she took a knife, and, as best she could, severed the head from the trunk, and wrapped it in a napkin and laid it in the lap of her maid; and having covered the rest of the corpse with earth, she left the spot, having been seen by none, and went home. There she shut herself up in her room with the head, and kissed it a thousand times in every part, and wept long and bitterly over it, till she had bathed it in her tears. She then wrapped it in a piece of fine cloth, and set it in a large and beautiful pot of the sort in which marjoram or basil is planted, and covered it with earth, and therein planted some roots of the goodliest basil of Salerno, and drenched them only with her tears, or water perfumed with roses or orange-blossoms. And 'twas her wont ever to sit beside this pot, and, all her soul one yearning, to pore upon it, as that which enshrined her Lorenzo, and when long time she had so done, she would bend over it, and weep a great while, until the basil was quite bathed in her tears.

Fostered with such constant, unremitting care, and nourished by the richness given to the soil by the decaying head that lay therein, the basil burgeoned out in exceeding great beauty and fragrance. And, the girl persevering ever in this way of life, the neighbours from time to time took note of it, and when her brothers marvelled to see her beauty ruined, and her eyes as it were evanished from her head, they told them of it, saying: – "We have observed that such is her daily wont." Whereupon the brothers, marking her behaviour, chid her therefore once or twice, and as she heeded them not, caused the pot to be taken privily from her. Which, so soon as she missed it, she demanded with the utmost instance and insistence, and, as they gave it not back to her, ceased not to wail and weep, insomuch that she fell sick; nor in her sickness craved she aught but the pot of basil. Whereat the young men, marvelling mightily, resolved to see what the pot might contain; and having removed the earth they espied the cloth, and therein the head, which was not yet so decayed, but that by the curled locks they knew it for Lorenzo's head. Passing strange they found it, and fearing lest it should be bruited abroad, they buried the head, and, with as little said as might be, took order for their privy departure from Messina, and hied them thence to Naples. The girl ceased not to weep and crave her pot, and, so weeping, died. Such was the end of her disastrous love; but not a few in course of time coming to know the truth of the affair, there was one that made the song that is still sung: to wit: –

> *A thief he was, I swear,*
>   *A sorry Christian he,*
>   *That took my basil of Salerno fair,* etc.[1]

Footnote 1: This Sicilian folk-song, of which Boccaccio quotes only the first two lines, is given in extenso from MS. Laurent. 38, plut. 42, by Fanfani in his edition of the *Decameron* (Florence, 1857). The following is a free rendering:

> *A thief he was, I swear,*
>   *A sorry Christian he,*
>   *That took my basil of Salerno fair,*
>   *That flourished mightily.*
> *Planted by mine own hands with loving care*
> *What time they revelled free:*
>   *To spoil another's goods is churlish spite.*

> *To spoil another's goods is churlish spite,*
>   *Ay, and most heinous sin.*
> *A basil had I (alas! luckless wight!),*
>   *The fairest plant: within*
> *Its shade I slept: 'twas grown to such a height.*
> *But some folk for chagrin*
>   *'Reft me thereof, ay, and before my door.*

> *'Reft me thereof, ay, and before my door.*
>   *Ah! dolorous day and drear!*
> *Ah! woe is me! Would God I were no more!*
>   *My purchase was so dear!*
> *Ah! why that day did I to watch give o'er?*
>   *For him my cherished fere*
>   *With marjoram I bordered it about.*

> *With marjoram I bordered it about*
>   *In May-time fresh and fair,*
> *And watered it thrice ere each week was out,*
>   *And marked it grow full yare:*
> *But now 'tis stolen. Ah! too well 'tis known!*
> *But now 'tis stolen. Ah! too well 'tis known!*
>   *That no more may I hide:*
> *But had to me a while before been shewn*
>   *What then should me betide,*
> *At night before my door I had laid me down*

To watch my plant beside.
Yet God Almighty sure me succour might.

Ay, God Almighty sure me succour might,
  So were it but His will,
  'Gainst him that me hath done so foul despite,
  That in dire torment still
  I languish, since the thief reft from my sight
  My plant that did me thrill,
  And to my inmost Soul such comfort lent!

And to my inmost soul such comfort lent!
  So fresh its fragrance blew,
  That when, what time the sun uprose, I went
  My watering to do,
  I'd hear the people all in wonderment
  Say, whence this perfume new?
  And I for love of it of grief shall die.

And I for love of it of grief shall die,
  Of my fair plant for dole.
  Would one but shew me how I might it buy!
  Ah! how 'twould me console!
  Ounces an hundred of fine gold have I:
  Him would I give the whole,
  Ay, and a kiss to boot, so he were fain.

Fourth Day
Novel VI

— *Andreuola loves Gabriotto: she tells him a dream that she has had; he tells her a dream of his own, and dies suddenly in her arms. While she and her maid are carrying his corpse to his house, they are taken by the Signory. She tells how the matter stands, is threatened with violence by the Podestà, but will not brook it. Her father hears how she is bested; and, her innocence being established, causes her to be set at large; but she, being minded to tarry no longer in the world, becomes a nun.* —

GLAD INDEED were the ladies to have heard Filomena's story, for that, often though they had heard the song sung, they had never yet, for all their enquiries, been able to learn the occasion upon which it was made. When 'twas ended, Pamfilo received the king's command to follow suit, and thus spoke: –

By the dream told in the foregoing story I am prompted to relate one in which two dreams are told, dreams of that which was to come, as Lisabetta's was of that which had been, and which were both fulfilled almost as soon as they were told by those that had dreamed them. Wherefore, loving ladies, you must know that 'tis the common experience of mankind to have divers visions during sleep; and albeit the sleeper, while he sleeps, deems all alike most true, but, being awake, judges some of them to be true, others to be probable, and others again to be quite devoid of truth, yet not a few are found to have come to pass. For which cause many are as sure of every dream as of aught that they see in their waking hours, and so, as their dreams engender in them fear or hope, are sorrowful or joyous. And on the other hand there are those that credit no dream, until they see themselves fallen into the very peril whereof they were forewarned. Of whom I approve neither sort, for in sooth neither are all dreams true, nor all alike false. That they are not all true, there is none of us but may many a time have proved; and that they are not all alike false has already been shewn in Filomena's story, and shall also, as I said before, be shewn in mine. Wherefore I deem that in a virtuous course of life and conduct there is no need to fear aught by reason of any dream that is contrary thereto, or on that account to give up any just design; and as for crooked and sinister enterprises, however dreams may seem to favour them, and flatter the hopes of the dreamer with auspicious omens, none should trust them: rather should all give full credence to such as run counter thereto. But come we to the story.

In the city of Brescia there lived of yore a gentleman named Messer Negro da Ponte Carraro, who with other children had a very fair daughter, Andreuola by name, who, being unmarried, chanced to fall in love with a neighbour, one Gabriotto, a man of low degree, but goodly of person and debonair, and endowed with all admirable qualities; and aided and abetted by the housemaid, the girl not only brought it to pass that Gabriotto knew that he was beloved of her, but that many a time to their mutual delight he came to see her in a fair garden belonging to her father. And that nought but death might avail to sever them from this their gladsome love, they became privily man and wife; and, while thus they continued their clandestine intercourse, it happened that one night, while the girl slept, she saw herself in a dream in her garden with Gabriotto, who to the exceeding great delight of both held her in his arms; and while thus they lay, she saw issue from his body somewhat dark and frightful, the shape whereof she might not discern; which, as she thought, laid hold of Gabriotto, and in her despite with prodigious force reft him from her embrace, and bore him with it underground, so that both were lost to her sight for evermore: whereby stricken with sore and inexpressible grief, she awoke; and albeit she was overjoyed to find that 'twas not as she had dreamed, yet a haunting dread of what she had seen in her vision entered her soul. Wherefore, Gabriotto being minded to visit her on the ensuing night, she did her best endeavour to dissuade him from coming; but seeing that he was bent upon it, lest he should suspect somewhat, she received him in her garden, where, having culled roses many, white and red – for 'twas summer – she sat herself down with him at the base of a most fair and lucent fountain. There long and joyously they dallied, and then Gabriotto asked her wherefore she had that day forbade his coming. Whereupon the lady told him her dream of the night before, and the doubt and fear which it had engendered in her mind. Whereat Gabriotto laughed, and said that 'twas the height of folly to put any faith in dreams, for that they were occasioned by too much or too little food, and were daily seen to be, one and all, things of nought, adding: – "Were I minded to give heed to dreams, I should not be here now, for I, too, had a dream last night, which was on this wise: – Methought I was in a fair and pleasant wood, and there, a hunting, caught a she-goat as beautiful and loveable as any that ever was seen, and, as it seemed to me, whiter than snow, which in a little while grew so tame and friendly that she never stirred from my side. All the same so jealous was I lest she should leave me, that, meseemed, I had set a collar of gold around her neck, and held her by a golden chain. And presently meseemed that, while the she-goat lay at rest with her head in my lap, there came forth, I knew not whence, a greyhound bitch, black as coal, famished, and most fearsome to look upon; which made straight for me, and for, meseemed, I offered no resistance, set her muzzle to my breast on the left side and gnawed through to the heart, which, meseemed, she tore out to carry away with her. Whereupon ensued so sore a pain that it brake my sleep, and as I awoke I laid my hand to my side to feel if aught were amiss there; but finding nothing I laughed at myself that I had searched. But what signifies it all? Visions of the like sort, ay, and far more appalling, have I had in plenty, and nought whatever, great or small, has come of any of them. So let it pass, and think we how we may speed the time merrily."

What she heard immensely enhanced the already great dread which her own dream had inspired in the girl; but, not to vex Gabriotto, she dissembled her terror as best she might. But, though she made great cheer, embracing and kissing him, and receiving his embraces and kisses, yet she felt a doubt, she knew not why, and many a time, more than her wont, she would gaze upon his face, and ever and anon her glance would stray through the garden to see if any black creature were coming from any quarter. While thus they passed the time, of a sudden Gabriotto heaved a great sigh, and embracing her, said: – "Alas! my soul, thy succour! for I die." And so saying, he fell down upon the grassy mead. Whereupon the girl drew him to her, and laid him on her lap, and all but wept, and said: – "O sweet my lord, what is't that ails thee?" But Gabriotto was silent, and gasping sore for breath, and bathed in sweat, in no long time departed this life.

How grievous was the distress of the girl, who loved him more than herself, you, my ladies, may well imagine. With many a tear she mourned him, and many times she vainly called him by his name; but when, having felt his body all over, and found it cold in every part, she could no longer doubt that he was dead, knowing not what to say or do, she went, tearful and woebegone, to call the maid, to whom she had confided her love, and shewed her the woeful calamity that had befallen her. Piteously a while they wept together over the dead face of Gabriotto, and then the girl said to the maid: – "Now that God has reft him from me, I have no mind to linger in this life; but before I slay myself, I would we might find apt means to preserve my honour, and the secret of our love, and to bury the body from which the sweet soul has fled." "My daughter," said the maid, "speak not of slaying thyself, for so wouldst thou lose in the other world, also, him that thou hast lost here; seeing that thou wouldst go to hell, whither, sure I am, his soul is not gone, for a good youth he was; far better were it to put on a cheerful courage, and bethink thee to succour his soul with thy prayers or pious works, if perchance he have need thereof by reason of any sin that he may have committed. We can bury him readily enough in this garden, nor will any one ever know; for none knows that he ever came hither; and if thou wilt not have it so, we can bear him forth of the garden, and leave him there; and on the morrow he will be found, and carried home, and buried by his kinsfolk." The girl, heavy-laden though she was with anguish, and still weeping, yet gave ear to the counsels of her maid, and rejecting the former alternative, made answer to the latter on this wise: – "Now God forbid that a youth so dear, whom I have so loved and made my husband, should with my consent be buried like a dog, or left out there in the street. He has had my tears, and so far as I may avail, he shall have the tears of his kinsfolk, and already wot I what we must do." And forthwith she sent the maid for a piece of silken cloth, which she had in one of her boxes; and when the maid returned with it, they spread it on the ground, and laid Gabriotto's body thereon, resting the head upon a pillow. She then closed the eyes and mouth, shedding the while many a tear, wove for him a wreath of roses, and strewed upon him all the roses that he and she had gathered; which done, she said to the maid: – "'Tis but a short way hence to the door of his house; so thither we will bear him, thou and I, thus as we have dight him, and will lay him at the door. Day will soon dawn, and they will take him up; and, though 'twill be no consolation to them, I, in whose arms he died, shall be glad of it." So saying, she burst once more into a torrent of tears, and fell with her face upon the face of the dead, and so long time she wept. Then, yielding at last to the urgency of her maid, for day was drawing nigh, she arose, drew from her finger the ring with which she had been wedded to Gabriotto, and set it on his finger, saying with tears: – "Dear my lord, if thy soul be witness of my tears, or if, when the spirit is fled, aught of intelligence or sense still lurk in the body, graciously receive the last gift of her whom in life thou didst so dearly love." Which said, she swooned, and fell upon the corpse; but, coming after a while to herself, she arose; and then she and her maid took the cloth whereon the body lay, and so bearing it, quitted the garden, and bent their steps towards the dead man's house. As thus they went, it chanced that certain of the Podesta's guard, that for some reason or another were abroad at that hour, met them, and arrested them with the corpse. Andreuola, to whom death was more welcome than life, no sooner knew them for the officers of the Signory than she frankly said: – "I know you, who you are, and that flight would avail me nothing: I am ready to come with you before the Signory, and to tell all there is to tell; but let none of you presume to touch me, so long as I obey you, or to take away aught that is on this body, if he would not that I accuse him." And so, none venturing to lay hand upon either her person or the corpse, she entered the palace.

So soon as the Podesta was apprised of the affair, he arose, had her brought into his room, and there made himself conversant with the circumstances: and certain physicians being charged to inquire whether the good man had met his death by poison or otherwise, all with one accord averred that 'twas not by poison, but that he was choked by the bursting of an imposthume near the heart. Which when the Podesta heard, perceiving that the girl's guilt could but be slight, he sought to make a pretence of giving what it was not lawful for him to sell her, and told her that he would set her at liberty, so she were consenting to pleasure him; but finding that he did but waste his words he cast aside all decency, and would have used force. Whereupon Andreuola, kindling with scorn, waxed exceeding brave, and defended herself with a virile energy, and with high and contumelious words drove him from her.

When 'twas broad day, the affair reached the ears of Messer Negro, who, half dead with grief, hied him with not a few of his friends to the palace; where, having heard all that the Podesta had to say, he required him peremptorily to give him back his daughter. The Podesta, being minded rather to be his own accuser, than that he should be accused by the girl of the violence that he had meditated towards her, began by praising her and her constancy, and in proof thereof went on to tell what he had done; he ended by saying, that, marking her admirable firmness, he had fallen mightily in love with her, and so, notwithstanding she had been wedded to a man of low degree, he would, if 'twere agreeable to her and to her father, Messer Negro, gladly make her his wife. While they thus spoke, Andreuola made her appearance, and, weeping, threw herself at her father's feet, saying: – "My father, I wot I need not tell you the story of my presumption, and the calamity that has befallen me, for sure I am that you have heard it and know it; wherefore, with all possible humility I crave your pardon of my fault, to wit, that without your knowledge I took for my husband him that pleased me best. And this I crave, not that my life may be spared, but that I may die as your daughter and not as your enemy;" and so, weeping, she fell at his feet. Messer Negro, now an old man, and naturally kindly and affectionate, heard her not without tears, and weeping raised her tenderly to her feet, saying: – "Daughter mine, I had much liefer had it that thou hadst had a husband that I deemed a match for thee; and in that thou hadst taken one that pleased thee I too had been pleased; but thy concealing thy choice from me is grievous to me by reason of thy distrust of me, and yet more so, seeing that thou hast lost him before I have known him. But as 'tis even so, to his remains be paid the honour which, while he lived for thy contentment, I had gladly done him as my son-in-law." Then, turning to his sons and kinsmen, he bade them order Gabriotto's obsequies with all pomp and honourable circumstance.

Meanwhile the young man's kinsmen and kinswomen, having heard the news, had flocked thither, bringing with them almost all the rest of the folk, men and women alike, that were in the city. And so his body, resting on Andreuola's cloth, and covered with her roses, was laid out in the middle of the courtyard, and there was mourned not by her and his kinsfolk alone, but publicly by well-nigh all the women of the city, and not a few men; and shouldered by some of the noblest of the citizens, as it had been the remains of no plebeian but of a noble, was borne from the public courtyard to the tomb with exceeding great pomp.

Some days afterwards, as the Podesta continued to urge his suit, Messer Negro would have discussed the matter with his daughter; but, as she would hear none of it, and he was minded in this matter to defer to her wishes, she and her maid entered a religious house of great repute for sanctity, where in just esteem they lived long time thereafter.

Fourth Day
Novel VII

— Simona loves Pasquino; they are together in a garden; Pasquino rubs a leaf of sage against his teeth, and dies; Simona is arrested, and, with intent to shew the judge how Pasquino died, rubs one of the leaves of the same plant against her teeth, and likewise dies. —

WHEN PAMFILO had done with his story, the king, betraying no compassion for Andreuola, glancing at Emilia, signified to her his desire that she should now continue the sequence of narration. Emilia made no demur, and thus began: –

Dear gossips, Pamfilo's story puts me upon telling you another in no wise like thereto, save in this, that as Andreuola lost her lover in a garden, so also did she of whom I am to speak, and, being arrested like Andreuola, did also deliver herself from the court, albeit 'twas not by any vigour or firmness of mind, but by a sudden death. And, as 'twas said among us a while ago, albeit Love affects the mansions of the noble, he does not, therefore, disdain the dominion of the dwellings of the poor, nay, does there at times give proof of his might no less signal than when he makes him feared of the wealthiest as a most potent lord. Which, though not fully, will in some degree appear in my story, wherewith I am minded to return to our city, from which to-day's discourse, roving from matter to matter, and one part of the world to another, has carried us so far.

Know then that no great while ago there dwelt in Florence a maid most fair, and, for her rank, debonair – she was but a poor man's daughter – whose name was Simona; and though she must needs win with her own hands the bread she ate, and maintain herself by spinning wool; yet was she not, therefore, of so poor a spirit, but that she dared to give harbourage in her mind to Love, who for some time had sought to gain entrance there by means of the gracious deeds and words of a young man of her own order that went about distributing wool to spin for his master, a wool-monger. Love being thus, with the pleasant image of her beloved Pasquino, admitted into her soul, mightily did she yearn, albeit she hazarded no advance, and heaved a thousand sighs fiercer than fire with every skein of yarn that she wound upon her spindle, while she called to mind who he was that had given her that wool to spin. Pasquino on his part became, meanwhile, very anxious that his master's wool should be well spun, and most particularly about that which Simona span, as if, indeed, it and it alone was to furnish forth the whole of the cloth. And so, what with the anxiety which the one evinced, and the gratification that it afforded to the other, it befell that, the one waxing unusually bold, and the other casting off not a little of her wonted shyness and reserve, they came to an understanding for their mutual solace; which proved so delightful to both, that neither waited to be bidden by the other, but 'twas rather which should be the first to make the overture.

While thus they sped their days in an even tenor of delight, and ever grew more ardently enamoured of one another, Pasquino chanced to say to Simona that he wished of all things she would contrive how she might betake her to a garden, whither he would bring her, that there they might be more at their ease, and in greater security. Simona said that she was agreeable; and, having given her father to understand that she was minded to go to San Gallo for the pardoning, she hied her with one of her gossips, Lagina by name, to the garden of which Pasquino had told her. Here she found Pasquino awaiting her with a friend, one Puccino, otherwise Stramba; and Stramba and Lagina falling at once to love-making, Pasquino and Simona left a part of the garden to them, and withdrew to another part for their own solace.

Now there was in their part of the garden a very fine and lovely sage-bush, at foot of which they sat them down and made merry together a great while, and talked much of a junketing they meant to have in the garden quite at their ease. By and by Pasquino, turning to the great sage-bush, plucked therefrom a leaf, and fell to rubbing his teeth and gums therewith, saying that sage was an excellent detergent of aught that remained upon them after a meal. Having done so, he returned to the topic of the junketing of which he had spoken before. But he had not pursued it far before his countenance entirely changed, and forthwith he lost sight and speech, and shortly after died. Whereupon Simona fell a weeping and shrieking and calling Stramba and Lagina; who, notwithstanding they came up with all speed, found Pasquino not only dead but already swollen from head to foot, and covered with black spots both on the face and on the body; whereupon Stramba broke forth with: – "Ah! wicked woman! thou hast poisoned him;" and made such a din that 'twas heard by not a few that dwelt hard by the garden; who also hasted to the spot, and seeing Pasquino dead and swollen, and hearing Stramba bewail himself and accuse Simona of having maliciously poisoned him, while she, all but beside herself for grief to be thus suddenly bereft of her lover, knew not how to defend herself, did all with one accord surmise that 'twas even as Stramba said. Wherefore they laid hands on her, and brought her, still weeping bitterly, to the palace of the Podesta: where at the instant suit of Stramba, backed by Atticciato and Malagevole, two other newly-arrived friends of Pasquino, a judge forthwith addressed himself to question her of the matter; and being unable to discover that she had used any wicked practice, or was guilty, he resolved to take her with him and go see the corpse, and the place, and the manner of the death, as she had recounted it to him; for by her words he could not well understand it. So, taking care that there should be no disturbance, he had her brought to the place where Pasquino's corpse lay swollen like a tun, whither he himself presently came, and marvelling as he examined the corpse, asked her how the death had come about. Whereupon, standing by the sagebush, she told him all that had happened, and that he might perfectly apprehend the occasion of the death, she did as Pasquino had done, plucked one of the leaves from the bush, and rubbed her teeth with it. Whereupon Stramba and Atticciato, and the rest of the friends and comrades of Pasquino, making in the presence of the judge open mock of what she did, as an idle and vain thing, and being more than ever instant to affirm her guilt, and to demand the fire as the sole condign penalty, the poor creature, that, between grief for her lost lover and dread of the doom demanded by Stramba, stood mute and helpless, was stricken no less suddenly, and in the same manner, and for the same cause (to wit, that she had rubbed her teeth with the sage leaf) as Pasquino, to the no small amazement of all that were present.

Oh! happy souls for whom one and the same day was the term of ardent love and earthly life! Happier still, if to the same bourn ye fared! Ay, and even yet more happy, if love there be in the other world, and there, even as here, ye love! But happiest above all Simona, so far as we, whom she has left behind, may judge, in that Fortune brooked not that the witness of Stramba, Atticciato and Malagevole, carders, perchance, or yet viler fellows, should bear down her innocence, but found a more seemly issue, and, appointing her a like lot with her lover, gave her at once to clear herself from their foul accusation, and to follow whither the soul, that she so loved, of her Pasquino had preceded her!

The judge, and all else that witnessed the event, remained long time in a sort of stupefaction, knowing not what to say of it; but at length recovering his wits, the judge said: – "'Twould seem that this sage is poisonous, which the sage is not used to be. Let it be cut down to the roots and burned, lest another suffer by it in like sort." Which the gardener proceeding to do in the judge's presence, no sooner had he brought the great bush down, than the cause of the deaths of the two lovers plainly appeared: for underneath it was a toad of prodigious dimensions, from whose venomous breath, as they conjectured, the whole of the bush had contracted a poisonous quality. Around which toad, none venturing to approach it, they set a stout ring-fence of faggots, and burned it together with the sage. So ended Master judge's inquest on the death of hapless Pasquino, who with his Simona, swollen as they were, were buried by Stramba, Atticciato, Guccio Imbratta, and Malagevole in the church of San Paolo, of which, as it so happened, they were parishioners.

Fourth Day
Novel VIII

— *Girolamo loves Salvestra: yielding to his mother's prayers he goes to Paris; he returns to find Salvestra married; he enters her house by stealth, lays himself by her side, and dies; he is borne to the church, where Salvestra lays herself by his side, and dies.* —

WHEN EMILIA'S STORY was done, Neifile at a word from the king thus began: –
Some there are, noble ladies, who, methinks, deem themselves to be wiser than the rest of the world, and are in fact less so; and by consequence presume to measure their wit against not only the counsels of men but the nature of things; which presumption has from time to time been the occasion of most grievous mishaps; but nought of good was ever seen to betide thereof. And as there is nought in nature that brooks to be schooled or thwarted so ill as love, the quality of which is such that it is more likely to die out of its own accord than to be done away of set purpose, I am minded to tell you a story of a lady, who, while she sought to be more wise than became her, and than she was, and indeed than the nature of the matter, wherein she studied to shew her wisdom, allowed, thinking to unseat Love from the heart that he had occupied, and wherein perchance the stars had established him, did in the end banish at one and the same time Love and life from the frame of her son.

Know, then, that, as 'tis related by them of old time, there was once in our city a very great and wealthy merchant, Leonardo Sighieri by name, who had by his lady a son named Girolamo, after whose birth he departed this life, leaving his affairs in meet and due order; and well and faithfully were they afterwards administered in the interest of the boy by his mother and guardians. As he grew up, consorting more frequently with the neighbours' children than any others of the quarter, he made friends with a girl of his own age that was the daughter of a tailor; and in course of time this friendship ripened into a love so great and vehement, that Girolamo was ever ill at ease when he saw her not; nor was her love for him a whit less strong than his for her. Which his mother perceiving would not seldom chide him therefor and chastise him. And as Girolamo could not give it up, she confided her distress to his guardians, speaking – for by reason of her boy's great wealth she thought to make, as it were, an orange-tree out of a bramble – on this wise: – "This boy of ours, who is now scarce fourteen years old, is so in love with a daughter of one of our neighbours, a tailor – Salvestra is the girl's name – that, if we part them not, he will, peradventure, none else witting, take her to wife some day, and I shall never be happy again; or, if he see her married to another, he will pine away; to prevent which, methinks, you would do well to send him away to distant parts on the affairs of the shop; for so, being out of sight she will come at length to be out of mind, and then we can give him some well-born girl to wife." Whereto the guardians answered, that 'twas well said, and that it should be so done to the best of their power: so they called the boy into the shop, and one of them began talking to him very affectionately on this wise: – "My son, thou art now almost grown up; 'twere well thou shouldst now begin to learn something for thyself of thy own affairs: wherefore we should be very well pleased if thou wert to go stay at Paris a while, where thou wilt see how we trade with not a little of thy wealth, besides which thou wilt there become a much better, finer, and more complete gentleman than thou couldst here, and when thou hast seen the lords and barons and seigneurs that are there in plenty, and hast acquired their manners, thou canst return hither." The boy listened attentively, and then answered shortly that he would have none of it, for he supposed he might remain at Florence as well as another. Whereupon the worthy men plied him with fresh argument, but were unable to elicit other answer from him, and told his mother so. Whereat she was mightily incensed, and gave him a great scolding, not for his refusing to go to Paris, but for his love; which done, she plied him with soft, wheedling words, and endearing expressions and gentle entreaties that he would be pleased to do as his guardians would have him; whereby at length she prevailed so far, that he consented to go to Paris for a year and no more; and so 'twas arranged. To Paris accordingly our ardent lover went, and there under one pretext or another was kept for two years. He returned more in love than ever, to find his Salvestra married to a good youth that was a tent-maker; whereat his mortification knew no bounds. But, seeing that what must be must be, he sought to compose his mind; and, having got to know where she lived, he took to crossing her path, according to the wont of young men in love, thinking that she could no more have forgotten him than he her. 'Twas otherwise, however; she remembered him no more than if she had never seen him; or, if she had any recollection of him, she dissembled it: whereof the young man was very soon ware, to his extreme sorrow. Nevertheless he did all that he could to recall himself to her mind; but, as thereby he seemed to be nothing advantaged, he made up his mind, though he should die for it, to speak to her himself. So, being instructed as to her house by a neighbour, he entered it privily one evening when she and her husband were gone to spend the earlier hours with some neighbours, and hid himself in her room behind some tent-cloths that were stretched there, and waited till they were come back, and gone to bed, and he knew the husband to be asleep. Whereupon he got him to the place where he had seen Salvestra lie down, and said as he gently laid his hand upon her bosom: – "O my soul, art thou yet asleep?" The girl was awake, and was on the point of uttering a cry, when he forestalled her, saying: – "Hush! for God's sake. I am thy Girolamo." Whereupon she, trembling in every limb: – "Nay, but for God's sake, Girolamo, begone: 'tis past, the time of our childhood, when our love was excusable. Thou seest I am married; wherefore 'tis no longer seemly that I should care for any other man than my husband, and so by the one God, I pray thee, begone; for, if my husband were to know that thou art here, the least evil that could ensue would be that I should never more be able to live with him in peace or comfort, whereas, having his love, I now pass my days with him in tranquil happiness." Which speech caused the young man grievous distress; but 'twas in vain that he reminded her of the past, and of his love that distance had not impaired, and therewith mingled many a prayer and the mightiest protestations. Wherefore, yearning for death, he besought her at last that she would suffer him to lie a while beside her till he got some heat, for he was chilled through and through, waiting for her, and promised her that he would say never a word to her, nor touch her, and that as soon as he was a little warmed he would go away. On which terms Salvestra, being not without pity for him, granted his request. So the young man lay down beside her, and touched her not; but, gathering up into one thought the love he had so long borne her, the harshness with which she now requited it, and his ruined hopes, resolved to live no longer, and in a convulsion, without a word, and with fists clenched, expired by her side.

After a while the girl, marvelling at his continence, and fearing lest her husband should awake, broke silence, saying: – "Nay, but, Girolamo, why goest thou not?" But, receiving no answer, she supposed that he slept. Wherefore, reaching forth her hand to arouse him, she touched him and found him to her great surprise cold as ice; and touching him again and again somewhat rudely, and still finding that he did not stir, she knew that he was dead. Her grief was boundless, and 'twas long before she could bethink her how to act. But at last she resolved to sound her husband's mind as to what should be done in such a case without disclosing that 'twas his own. So she awakened him, and told him how he was then bested, as if it were the affair of another, and then asked him, if such a thing happened to her, what course he would take. The good man answered that he should deem it best to take the dead man privily home, and there leave him, bearing no grudge against the lady, who seemed to have done no wrong. "And even so," said his wife, "it is for us to do;" and taking his hand, she laid it on the corpse. Whereat he started up in consternation, and struck a light, and with out further parley with his wife, clapped the dead man's clothes upon him, and forthwith (confident in his own innocence) raised him on his shoulders, and bore him to the door of his house, where he set him down and left him.

Day came, and the dead man being found before his own door, there was a great stir made, particularly by his mother; the body was examined with all care from head to foot, and, no wound or trace of violence being found on it, the physicians were on the whole of opinion that, as the fact was, the man had died of grief. So the corpse was borne to a church, and thither came the sorrowing mother and other ladies, her kinswomen and neighbours, and began to wail and mourn over it without restraint after our Florentine fashion. And when the wailing had reached its height, the good man, in whose house the death had occurred, said to Salvestra: – "Go wrap a mantle about thy head, and hie thee to the church, whither Girolamo has been taken, and go about among the women and list what they say of this matter, and I will do the like among the men, that we may hear if aught be said to our disadvantage." The girl assented, for with tardy tenderness she now yearned to look on him dead, whom living she would not solace with a single kiss, and so to the church she went. Ah! how marvellous to whoso ponders it, is the might of Love, and how unsearchable his ways! That heart, which, while Fortune smiled on Girolamo, had remained sealed to him, opened to him now that he was fordone, and, kindling anew with all its old flame, melted with such compassion that no sooner saw she his dead face, as there she stood wrapped in her mantle, than, edging her way forward through the crowd of women, she stayed not till she was beside the corpse; and there, uttering a piercing shriek, she threw herself upon the dead youth, and as her face met his, and before she might drench it with her tears, grief that had reft life from him had even so reft it from her.

The women strove to comfort her, and bade her raise herself a little, for as yet they knew her not; then, as she did not arise, they would have helped her, but found her stiff and stark, and so, raising her up, they in one and the same moment saw her to be Salvestra and dead. Whereat all the women that were there, overborne by a redoubled pity, broke forth in wailing new and louder far than before. From the church the bruit spread itself among the men, and reached the ears of Salvestra's husband, who, deaf to all that offered comfort or consolation, wept a long while; after which he told to not a few that were there what had passed in the night between the youth and his wife; and so 'twas known of all how they came to die, to the common sorrow of all. So they took the dead girl, and arrayed her as they are wont to array the dead, and laid her on the same bed beside the youth, and long time they mourned her: then were they both buried in the same tomb, and thus those, whom love had not been able to wed in life, were wedded by death in indissoluble union.

Fourth Day

Novel IX

— *Sieur Guillaume de Roussillon slays his wife's paramour, Sieur Guillaume de Cabestaing, and gives her his heart to eat. She, coming to wit thereof, throws herself from a high window to the ground, and dies, and is buried with her lover.* —

NEIFILE'S STORY, which had not failed to move her gossips to no little pity, being ended, none now remained to speak but the king and Dioneo, whose privilege the king was minded not to infringe: wherefore he thus began: –

I propose, compassionate my ladies, to tell you a story, which, seeing that you so commiserate ill-starred loves, may claim no less a share of your pity than the last, inasmuch as they were greater folk of whom I shall speak, and that which befell them was more direful.

You are to know, then, that, as the Provencals relate, there were once in Provence two noble knights, each having castles and vassals under him, the one yclept Sieur Guillaume de Roussillon, and the other Sieur Guillaume de Cabestaing; and being both most doughty warriors, they were as brothers, and went ever together, and bearing the same device, to tournament or joust, or other passage of arms. And, albeit each dwelt in his own castle, and the castles were ten good miles apart, it nevertheless came to pass that, Sieur Guillaume de Roussillon having a most lovely lady, and amorous withal, to wife, Sieur Guillaume de Cabestaing, for all they were such friends and comrades, became inordinately enamoured of the lady, who, by this, that, and the other sign that he gave, discovered his passion, and knowing him for a most complete knight, was flattered, and returned it, insomuch that she yearned and burned for him above all else in the world, and waited only till he should make his suit to her, as before long he did; and so they met from time to time, and great was their love. Which intercourse they ordered with so little discretion that 'twas discovered by the husband, who was very wroth, insomuch that the great love which he bore to Cabestaing was changed into mortal enmity; and, dissembling it better than the lovers their love, he made his mind up to kill Cabestaing. Now it came to pass that, while Roussillon was in this frame, a great tourney was proclaimed in France, whereof Roussillon forthwith sent word to Cabestaing, and bade him to his castle, so he were minded to come, that there they might discuss whether (or no) to go to the tourney, and how. Cabestaing was overjoyed, and made answer that he would come to sup with him next day without fail. Which message being delivered, Roussillon wist that the time was come to slay Cabestaing. So next day he armed himself, and, attended by a few servants, took horse, and about a mile from his castle lay in ambush in a wood through which Cabestaing must needs pass. He waited some time, and then he saw Cabestaing approach unarmed with two servants behind, also unarmed, for he was without thought of peril on Roussillon's part. So Cabestaing came on to the place of Roussillon's choice, and then, fell and vengeful, Roussillon leapt forth lance in hand, and fell upon him, exclaiming: – "Thou art a dead man!" and the words were no sooner spoken than the lance was through Cabestaing's breast. Powerless either to defend himself or even utter a cry, Cabestaing fell to the ground, and soon expired. His servants waited not to see who had done the deed, but turned their horses' heads and fled with all speed to their lord's castle. Roussillon dismounted, opened Cabestaing's breast with a knife, and took out the heart with his own hands, wrapped it up in a banderole, and gave it to one of his servants to carry: he then bade none make bold to breathe a word of the affair, mounted his horse and rode back – 'twas now night – to his castle. The lady, who had been told that Cabestaing was to come to supper that evening, and was all impatience till he should come, was greatly surprised to see her husband arrive without him. Wherefore: – "How is this, my lord?" said she. "Why tarries Cabestaing?" "Madam," answered her husband, "I have tidings from him that he cannot be here until tomorrow:" whereat the lady was somewhat disconcerted.

Having dismounted, Roussillon called the cook, and said to him: – "Here is a boar's heart; take it, and make thereof the daintiest and most delicious dish thou canst, and when I am set at table serve it in a silver porringer." So the cook took the heart, and expended all his skill and pains upon it, mincing it and mixing with it plenty of good seasoning, and made thereof an excellent ragout; and in due time Sieur Guillaume and his lady sat them down to table. The meat was served, but Sieur Guillaume, his mind engrossed with his crime, ate but little. The cook set the ragout before him, but he, feigning that he cared to eat no more that evening, had it passed on to the lady, and highly commended it. The lady, nothing loath, took some of it, and found it so good that she ended by eating the whole. Whereupon: – "Madam," quoth the knight, "how liked you this dish?" "In good faith, my lord," replied the lady, "not a little." "So help me, God," returned the knight, "I dare be sworn you did; 'tis no wonder that you should enjoy that dead, which living you enjoyed more than aught else in the world." For a while the lady was silent; then: – "How say you?" said she; "what is this you have caused me to eat?" "That which you have eaten," replied the knight, "was in good sooth the heart of Sieur Guillaume de Cabestaing, whom you, disloyal woman that you are, did so much love: for assurance whereof I tell you that but a short while before I came back, I plucked it from his breast with my own hands." It boots not to ask if the lady was sorrow-stricken to receive such tidings of her best beloved. But after a while she said: – "'Twas the deed of a disloyal and recreant knight; for if I, unconstrained by him, made him lord of my love, and thereby did you wrong, 'twas I, not he, should have borne the penalty. But God forbid that fare of such high excellence as the heart of a knight so true and courteous as Sieur Guillaume de Cabestaing be followed by aught else." So saying she started to her feet, and stepping back to a window that was behind her, without a moment's hesitation let herself drop backwards therefrom. The window was at a great height from the ground, so that the lady was not only killed by the fall, but almost reduced to atoms. Stunned and conscience-stricken by the spectacle, and fearing the vengeance of the country folk, and the Count of Provence, Sieur Guillaume had his horses saddled and rode away. On the morrow the whole countryside knew how the affair had come about; wherefore folk from both of the castles took the two bodies, and bore them with grief and lamentation exceeding great to the church in the lady's castle, and laid them in the same tomb, and caused verses to be inscribed thereon signifying who they were that were there interred, and the manner and occasion of their death.

Fourth Day
Novel X

— *The wife of a leech, deeming her lover, who has taken an opiate, to be dead, puts him in a chest, which, with him therein, two usurers carry off to their house. He comes to himself, and is taken for a thief; but, the lady's maid giving the Signory to understand that she had put him in the chest which the usurers stole, he escapes the gallows, and the usurers are mulcted in moneys for the theft of the chest.* —

NOW THAT the king had told his tale, it only remained for Dioneo to do his part, which he witting, and being thereto bidden by the king, thus began: –

Sore have I – to say nought of you, my ladies – been of eyne and heart to hear the woeful histories of ill-starred love, insomuch that I have desired of all things that they might have an end. Wherefore, now that, thank God, ended they are, unless indeed I were minded, which God forbid, to add to such pernicious stuff a supplement of the like evil quality, no such dolorous theme do I purpose to ensue, but to make a fresh start with somewhat of a better and more cheerful sort, which perchance may serve to suggest to-morrow's argument.

You are to know, then, fairest my damsels, that 'tis not long since there dwelt at Salerno a leech most eminent in surgery, his name, Master Mazzeo della Montagna, who in his extreme old age took to wife a fair damsel of the same city, whom he kept in nobler and richer array of dresses and jewels, and all other finery that the sex affects, than any other lady in Salerno. Howbeit, she was none too warm most of her time, being ill covered abed by the doctor; who gave her to understand – even as Messer Ricciardo di Chinzica, of whom we spoke a while since, taught his lady the feasts – that for once that a man lay with a woman he needed I know not how many days to recover, and the like nonsense: whereby she lived as ill content as might be; and, lacking neither sense nor spirit, she determined to economize at home, and taking to the street, to live at others' expense. So, having passed in review divers young men, she at last found one that was to her mind, on whom she set all her heart and hopes of happiness. Which the gallant perceiving was mightily flattered, and in like manner gave her all his love. Ruggieri da Jeroli – such was the gallant's name – was of noble birth, but of life, and conversation so evil and reprehensible that kinsman or friend he had none left that wished him well, or cared to see him; and all Salerno knew him for a common thief and rogue of the vilest character. Whereof the lady took little heed, having a mind to him for another reason; and so with the help of her maid she arranged a meeting with him. But after they had solaced themselves a while, the lady began to censure his past life, and to implore him for love of her to depart from such evil ways; and to afford him the means thereto, she from time to time furnished him with money. While thus with all discretion they continued their intercourse, it chanced that a man halt of one of his legs was placed under the leech's care. The leech saw what was amiss with him, and told his kinsfolk, that, unless a gangrened bone that he had in his leg were taken out, he must die, or have the whole leg amputated; that if the bone were removed he might recover; but that otherwise he would not answer for his life: whereupon the relatives assented that the bone should be removed, and left the patient in the hands of the leech; who, deeming that by reason of the pain 'twas not possible for him to endure the treatment without an opiate, caused to be distilled in the morning a certain water of his own concoction, whereby the patient, drinking it, might be ensured sleep during such time as he deemed the operation, which he meant to perform about vespers, would occupy. In the meantime he had the water brought into his house, and set it in the window of his room, telling no one what it was. But when the vesper hour was come, and the leech was about to visit his patient, a messenger arrived from some very great friends of his at Amalfi, bearing tidings of a great riot there had been there, in which not a few had been wounded, and bidding him on no account omit to hie him thither forthwith. Wherefore the leech put off the treatment of the leg to the morrow, and took boat to Amalfi; and the lady, knowing that he would not return home that night, did as she was wont in such a case, to wit, brought Ruggieri in privily, and locked him in her chamber until certain other folk that were in the house were gone to sleep. Ruggieri, then, being thus in the chamber, awaiting the lady, and having – whether it were that he had had a fatiguing day, or eaten something salt, or, perchance, that 'twas his habit of body – a mighty thirst, glancing at the window, caught sight of the bottle containing the water which the leech had prepared for the patient, and taking it to be drinking water, set it to his lips and drank it all, and in no long time fell into a deep sleep.

So soon as she was able the lady hied her to the room, and there finding Ruggieri asleep, touched him and softly told him to get up: to no purpose, however; he neither answered nor stirred a limb. Wherefore the lady, rather losing patience, applied somewhat more force, and gave him a push, saying: – "Get up, sleepy-head; if thou hadst a mind to sleep, thou shouldst have gone home, and not have come hither." Thus pushed Ruggieri fell down from a box on which he lay, and, falling, shewed no more sign of animation than if he had been a corpse. The lady, now somewhat alarmed, essayed to lift him, and shook him roughly, and took him by the nose, and pulled him by the beard; again to no purpose: he had tethered his ass to a stout pin. So the lady began to fear he must be dead: however, she went on to pinch him shrewdly, and singe him with the flame of a candle; but when these methods also failed she, being, for all she was a leech's wife, no leech herself, believed for sure that he was dead; and as there was nought in the world that she loved so much, it boots not to ask if she was sore distressed; wherefore silently, for she dared not lament aloud, she began to weep over him and bewail such a misadventure. But, after a while, fearing lest her loss should not be without a sequel of shame, she bethought her that she must contrive without delay to get the body out of the house; and standing in need of another's advice, she quietly summoned her maid, shewed her the mishap that had befallen her, and craved her counsel. Whereat the maid marvelled not a little; and she too fell to pulling Ruggieri this way and that, and pinching him, and, as she found no sign of life in him, concurred with her mistress that he was verily dead, and advised her to remove him from the house. "And where," said the lady, "shall we put him, that to-morrow, when he is discovered, it be not suspected that 'twas hence he was carried?" "Madam," answered the maid, "late last evening I marked in front of our neighbour the carpenter's shop a chest, not too large, which, if he have not put it back in the house, will come in very handy for our purpose, for we will put him inside, and give him two or three cuts with a knife, and so leave him. When he is found, I know not why it should be thought that 'twas from this house rather than from any other that he was put there; nay, as he was an evil-liver, 'twill more likely be supposed, that, as he hied him on some evil errand, some enemy slew him, and then put him in the chest." The lady said there was nought in the world she might so ill brook as that Ruggieri should receive any wound; but with that exception she approved her maid's proposal, and sent her to see if the chest were still where she had seen it. The maid, returning, reported that there it was, and, being young and strong, got Ruggieri, with the lady's help, upon her shoulders; and so the lady, going before to espy if any folk came that way, and the maid following, they came to the chest, and having laid Ruggieri therein, closed it and left him there.

Now a few days before, two young men, that were usurers, had taken up their quarters in a house a little further on: they had seen the chest during the day, and being short of furniture, and having a mind to make great gain with little expenditure, they had resolved that, if it were still there at night, they would take it home with them. So at midnight forth they hied them, and finding the chest, were at no pains to examine it closely, but forthwith, though it seemed somewhat heavy, bore it off to their house, and set it down beside a room in which their women slept; and without being at pains to adjust it too securely they left it there for the time, and went to bed.

Towards matins Ruggieri, having had a long sleep and digested the draught and exhausted its efficacy, awoke, but albeit his slumber was broken, and his senses had recovered their powers, yet his brain remained in a sort of torpor which kept him bemused for some days; and when he opened his eyes and saw nothing, and stretched his hands hither and thither and found himself in the chest, it was with difficulty that he collected his thoughts. "How is this?" he said to himself. "Where am I? Do I sleep or wake? I remember coming this evening to my lady's chamber; and now it seems I am in a chest. What means it? Can the leech have returned, or somewhat else have happened that caused the lady, while I slept, to hide me here? That was it, I suppose. Without a doubt it must have been so." And having come to this conclusion, he composed himself to listen, if haply he might hear something, and being somewhat ill at ease in the chest, which was none too large, and the side on which he lay paining him, he must needs turn over to the other, and did so with such adroitness that, bringing his loins smartly against one of the sides of the chest, which was set on an uneven floor, he caused it to tilt and then fall; and such was the noise that it made as it fell that the women that slept there awoke, albeit for fear they kept silence. Ruggieri was not a little disconcerted by the fall, but, finding that thereby the chest was come open, he judged that, happen what might, he would be better out of it than in it; and not knowing where he was, and being otherwise at his wits' end, he began to grope about the house, if haply he might find a stair or door whereby he might take himself off. Hearing him thus groping his way, the alarmed women gave tongue with: – "Who is there?" Ruggieri, not knowing the voice, made no answer: wherefore the women fell to calling the two young men, who, having had a long day, were fast asleep, and heard nought of what went on. Which served to increase the fright of the women, who rose and got them to divers windows, and raised the cry: – "Take thief, take thief!" At which summons there came running from divers quarters not a few of the neighbours, who got into the house by the roof or otherwise as each best might: likewise the young men, aroused by the din, got up; and, Ruggieri being now all but beside himself for sheer amazement, and knowing not whither to turn him to escape them, they took him and delivered him to the officers of the Governor of the city, who, hearing the uproar, had hasted to the spot. And so he was brought before the Governor, who, knowing him to be held of all a most arrant evil-doer, put him forthwith to the torture, and, upon his confessing that he had entered the house of the usurers with intent to rob, was minded to make short work of it, and have him hanged by the neck.

In the morning 'twas bruited throughout all Salerno that Ruggieri had been taken a thieving in the house of the usurers. Whereat the lady and her maid were all amazement and bewilderment, insomuch that they were within an ace of persuading themselves that what they had done the night before they had not done, but had only dreamed it; besides which, the peril in which Ruggieri stood caused the lady such anxiety as brought her to the verge of madness.

Shortly after half tierce the leech, being returned from Amalfi, and minded now to treat his patient, called for his water, and finding the bottle empty made a great commotion, protesting that nought in his house could be let alone. The lady, having other cause of annoy, lost temper, and said: – "What would you say, Master, of an important matter, when you raise such a din because a bottle of water has been upset? Is there never another to be found in the world?" "Madam," replied the leech, "thou takest this to have been mere water. 'Twas no such thing, but an artificial water of a soporiferous virtue;" and he told her for what purpose he had made it. Which the lady no sooner heard, than, guessing that Ruggieri had drunk it, and so had seemed to them to be dead, she said: – "Master, we knew it not; wherefore make you another." And so the leech, seeing that there was no help for it, had another made. Not long after, the maid, who by the lady's command had gone to find out what folk said of Ruggieri, returned, saying: – "Madam, of Ruggieri they say nought but evil, nor, by what I have been able to discover, has he friend or kinsman that has or will come to his aid; and 'tis held for certain that to-morrow the Stadic will have him hanged. Besides which, I have that to tell you which will surprise you; for, methinks, I have found out how he came into the usurers' house. List, then, how it was: you know the carpenter in front of whose shop stood the chest we put Ruggieri into: he had to-day the most violent altercation in the world with one to whom it would seem the chest belongs, by whom he was required to make good the value of the chest, to which he made answer that he had not sold it, but that it had been stolen from him in the night. 'Not so,' said the other; 'thou soldst it to the two young usurers, as they themselves told me last night, when I saw it in their house at the time Ruggieri was taken.' 'They lie,' replied the carpenter. 'I never sold it them, but they must have stolen it from me last night; go we to them.' So with one accord off they went to the usurers' house, and I came back here. And so, you see, I make out that 'twas on such wise that Ruggieri was brought where he was found; but how he came to life again, I am at a loss to conjecture." The lady now understood exactly how things were, and accordingly told the maid what she had learned from the leech, and besought her to aid her to get Ruggieri off, for so she might, if she would, and at the same time preserve her honour. "Madam," said the maid, "do but shew me how; and glad shall I be to do just as you wish." Whereupon the lady, to whom necessity taught invention, formed her plan on the spur of the moment, and expounded it in detail to the maid; who (as the first step) hied her to the leech, and, weeping, thus addressed him: – "Sir, it behoves me to ask your pardon of a great wrong that I have done you." "And what may that be?" inquired the leech. "Sir," said the maid, who ceased not to weep, "you know what manner of man is Ruggieri da Jeroli. Now he took a fancy to me, and partly for fear, partly for love, I this year agreed to be his mistress; and knowing yestereve that you were from home, he coaxed me into bringing him into your house to sleep with me in my room. Now he was athirst, and I, having no mind to be seen by your lady, who was in the hall, and knowing not whither I might sooner betake me for wine or water, bethought me that I had seen a bottle of water in your room, and ran and fetched it, and gave it him to drink, and then put the bottle back in the place whence I had taken it; touching which I find that you have made a great stir in the house. Verily I confess that I did wrong; but who is there that does not wrong sometimes? Sorry indeed am I to have so done, but 'tis not for such a cause and that which ensued thereon that Ruggieri should lose his life. Wherefore, I do most earnestly beseech you, pardon me, and suffer me to go help him as best I may be able." Wroth though he was at what he heard, the leech replied in a bantering tone: – "Thy pardon thou hast by thine own deed; for, whereas thou didst last night think to have with thee a gallant that would thoroughly dust thy pelisse for thee, he was but a sleepy head; wherefore get thee gone, and do what thou mayst for the deliverance of thy lover, and for the future look thou bring him not into the house; else I will pay thee for that turn and this to boot." The maid, deeming that she had come off well in the first brush, hied her with all speed to the prison where Ruggieri lay, and by her cajoleries prevailed upon the warders to let her speak with him; and having told him how he must answer the Stadic if he would get off, she succeeded in obtaining preaudience of the Stadic; who, seeing that the baggage was lusty and mettlesome, was minded before he heard her to grapple her with the hook, to which she was by no means averse, knowing that such a preliminary would secure her a better hearing. When she had undergone the operation and was risen: – "Sir," said she, "you have here Ruggieri da Jeroli, apprehended on a charge of theft; which charge is false." Whereupon she told him the whole story from beginning to end, how she, being Ruggieri's mistress, had brought him into the leech's house and had given him the opiate, not knowing it for such, and taking him to be dead, had put him in the chest; and then recounting what she had heard pass between the carpenter and the owner of the chest, she shewed him how Ruggieri came into the house of the usurers. Seeing that 'twas easy enough to find out whether the story were true, the Stadic began by questioning the leech as to the water, and found that 'twas as she had said: he then summoned the carpenter, the owner of the chest and the usurers, and after much further parley ascertained that the usurers had stolen the chest during the night, and brought it into their house: finally he sent for Ruggieri, and asked him where he had lodged that night, to which Ruggieri answered that where he had lodged he knew not, but he well remembered going to pass the night with Master Mazzeo's maid, in whose room he had drunk some water by reason of a great thirst that he had; but what happened to him afterwards, except that, when he awoke, he found himself in a chest in the house of the usurers, he knew not. All which matters the Stadic heard with great interest, and caused the maid and Ruggieri and the carpenter and the usurers to rehearse them several times. In the end, seeing that Ruggieri was innocent, he released him, and mulcted the usurers in fifteen ounces for the theft of the chest. How glad Ruggieri was thus to escape, it boots not to ask; and glad beyond measure was his lady. And so, many a time did they laugh and make merry together over the affair, she and he and the dear maid that had proposed to give him a taste of the knife; and remaining constant in their love, they had ever better and better solace thereof. The like whereof befall me, sans the being put in the chest.

 Heartsore as the gentle ladies had been made by the preceding stories, this last of Dioneo provoked them to such merriment, more especially the passage about the Stadic and the hook, that they lacked not relief of the piteous mood engendered by the others. But the king observing that the sun was now taking a yellowish tinge, and that the end of his sovereignty was come, in terms most courtly made his excuse to the fair ladies, that he had made so direful a theme as lovers' infelicity the topic of their discourse; after which, he rose, took the laurel wreath from his head, and, while the ladies watched to see to whom he would give it, set it graciously upon the blond head of Fiammetta, saying: – "Herewith I crown thee, as deeming that thou, better than any other, wilt know how to make to-morrow console our fair companions for the rude trials of to-day." Fiammetta, whose wavy tresses fell in a flood of gold over her white and delicate shoulders, whose softly rounded face was all radiant with the very tints of the white lily blended with the red of the rose, who carried two eyes in her head that matched those of a peregrine falcon, while her tiny sweet mouth shewed a pair of lips that shone as rubies, replied with a smile: – "And gladly take I the wreath, Filostrato, and that thou mayst more truly understand what thou hast done, 'tis my present will and pleasure that each make ready to discourse to-morrow of good fortune befalling lovers after divers direful or disastrous adventures." The theme propounded was approved by all; whereupon the queen called the seneschal, and having made with him all meet arrangements, rose and gaily dismissed all the company until the supper hour; wherefore, some straying about the garden, the beauties of which were not such as soon to pall, others bending their steps towards the mills that were grinding without, each, as and where it seemed best, they took meanwhile their several pleasures. The supper hour come, they all gathered, in their wonted order, by the fair fountain, and in the gayest of spirits and well served they supped. Then rising they addressed them, as was their wont, to dance and song, and while Filomena led the dance: – "Filostrato," said the queen, "being minded to follow in the footsteps of our predecessors, and that, as by their, so by our command a song be sung; and well witting that thy songs are even as thy stories, to the end that no day but this be vexed with thy misfortunes, we ordain that thou give us one of them, whichever thou mayst prefer." Filostrato answered that he would gladly do so; and without delay began to sing on this wise: –

>   *Full well my tears attest,*
>   *O traitor Love, with what just cause the heart,*
>   *With which thou once hast broken faith, doth smart.*
>
>   *Love, when thou first didst in my heart enshrine*
>   *Her for whom still I sigh, alas! in vain,*
>   *Nor any hope do know,*
>   *A damsel so complete thou didst me shew,*
>   *That light as air I counted every pain,*
>   *Wherewith behest of thine*
>   *Condemned my soul to pine.*
>   *Ah! but I gravely erred; the which to know*
>   *Too late, alas! doth but enhance my woe.*
>
>   *The cheat I knew not ere she did me leave,*
>   *She, she, in whom alone my hopes were placed:*
>   *For 'twas when I did most*
>   *Flatter myself with hope, and proudly boast*
>   *Myself her vassal lowliest and most graced,*
>   *Nor thought Love might bereave,*
>   *Nor dreamed he e'er might grieve,*
>   *'Twas then I found that she another's worth*
>   *Into her heart had ta'en and me cast forth.*
>
>   *A plant of pain, alas! my heart did bear,*
>   *What time my hapless self cast forth I knew;*
>   *And there it doth remain;*
>   *And day and hour I curse and curse again,*
>   *When first that front of love shone on my view*
>   *That front so queenly fair,*
>   *And bright beyond compare!*
>   *Wherefore at once my faith, my hope, my fire*
>   *My soul doth imprecate, ere she expire.*
>   *My lord, thou knowest how comfortless my woe,*
>   *Thou, Love, my lord, whom thus I supplicate*
>   *With many a piteous moan,*
>   *Telling thee how in anguish sore I groan,*

Yearning for death my pain to mitigate.
Come death, and with one blow
Cut short my span, and so
With my curst life me of my frenzy ease;
For wheresoe'er I go, 'twill sure decrease.

Save death no way of comfort doth remain:
No anodyne beside for this sore smart.
The boon, then, Love bestow;
And presently by death annul my woe,
And from this abject life release my heart.
Since from me joy is ta'en,
And every solace, deign
My prayer to grant, and let my death the cheer
Complete, that she now hath of her new fere.

Song, it may be that no one shall thee learn:
Nor do I care; for none I wot, so well
As I may chant thee; so,
This one behest I lay upon thee, go
Hie thee to Love, and him in secret tell,
How I my life do spurn,
My bitter life, and yearn,
That to a better harbourage he bring
Me, of all might and grace that own him king.

Full well my tears attest, etc.

Filostrato's mood and its cause were made abundantly manifest by the words of this song; and perchance they had been made still more so by the looks of a lady that was among the dancers, had not the shades of night, which had now overtaken them, concealed the blush that suffused her face. Other songs followed until the hour for slumber arrived: whereupon at the behest of the queen all the ladies sought their several chambers.

— Endeth here the fourth day of the Decameron, beginneth the fifth, in which under the rule of Fiammetta discourse is had of good fortune befalling lovers after divers direful or disastrous adventures. —

ALL THE EAST WAS WHITE, nor any part of our hemisphere unillumined by the rising beams, when the carolling of the birds that in gay chorus saluted the dawn among the boughs induced Fiammetta to rise and rouse the other ladies and the three gallants; with whom adown the hill and about the dewy meads of the broad champaign she sauntered, talking gaily of divers matters, until the sun had attained some height. Then, feeling his rays grow somewhat scorching, they retraced their steps, and returned to the villa; where, having repaired their slight fatigue with excellent wines and comfits, they took their pastime in the pleasant garden until the breakfast hour; when, all things being made ready by the discreet seneschal, they, after singing a stampita, and a balladette or two, gaily, at the queen's behest, sat them down to eat. Meetly ordered and gladsome was the meal, which done, heedful of their rule of dancing, they trod a few short measures with accompaniment of music and song. Thereupon, being all dismissed by the queen until after the siesta, some hied them to rest, while others tarried taking their pleasure in the fair garden. But shortly after none, all, at the queen's behest, reassembled, according to their wont, by the fountain; and the queen, having seated herself on her throne, glanced towards Pamfilo, and bade him with a smile lead off with the stories of good fortune. Whereto Pamfilo gladly addressed himself, and thus began.

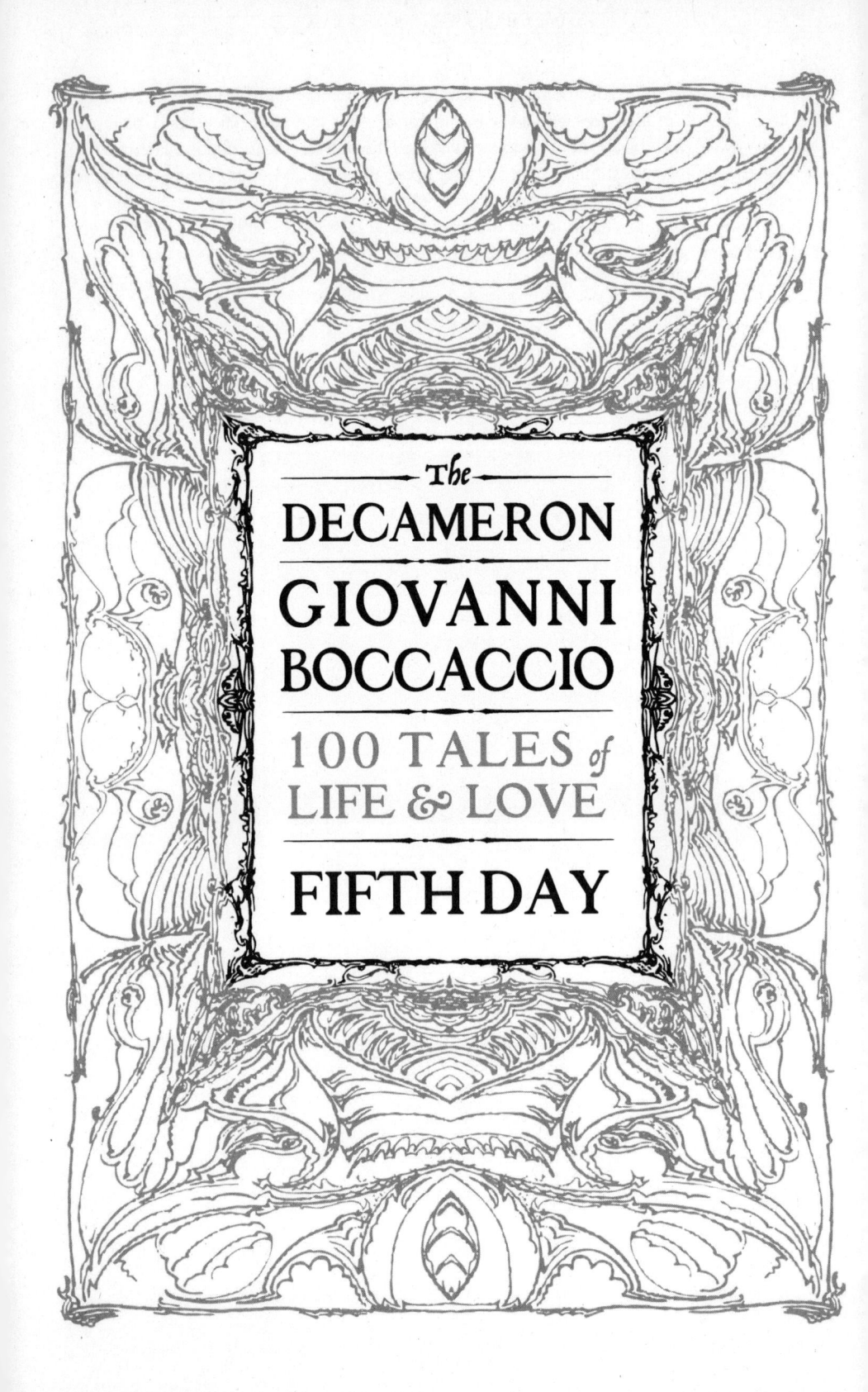

The DECAMERON
GIOVANNI BOCCACCIO
100 TALES of LIFE & LOVE
FIFTH DAY

Fifth Day
Novel I

— *Cimon, by loving, waxes wise, wins his wife Iphigenia by capture on the high seas, and is imprisoned at Rhodes. He is delivered by Lysimachus; and the twain capture Cassandra and recapture Iphigenia in the hour of their marriage. They flee with their ladies to Crete, and having there married them, are brought back to their homes.* —

MANY STORIES, sweet my ladies, occur to me as meet for me to tell by way of ushering in a day so joyous as this will be: of which one does most commend itself to my mind, because not only has it, one of those happy endings of which to-day we are in quest, but 'twill enable you to understand how holy, how mighty and how salutary are the forces of Love, which not a few, witting not what they say, do most unjustly reprobate and revile: which, if I err not, should to you, for that I take you to be enamoured, be indeed welcome.

Once upon a time, then, as we have read in the ancient histories of the Cypriotes, there was in the island of Cyprus a very great noble named Aristippus, a man rich in all worldly goods beyond all other of his countrymen, and who might have deemed himself incomparably blessed, but for a single sore affliction that Fortune had allotted him. Which was that among his sons he had one, the best grown and handsomest of them all, that was well-nigh a hopeless imbecile. His true name was Galesus; but, as neither his tutor's pains, nor his father's coaxing or chastisement, nor any other method had availed to imbue him with any tincture of letters o manners, but he still remained gruff and savage of voice, and in his bearing liker to a beast than to a man, all, as in derision, were wont to call him Cimon, which in their language signifies the same as "bestione" (brute) in ours. The father, grieved beyond measure to see his son's life thus blighted, and having abandoned all hope of his recovery, nor caring to have the cause of his mortification ever before his eyes, bade him betake him to the farm, and there keep with his husbandmen. To Cimon the change was very welcome, because the manners and habits of the uncouth hinds were more to his taste than those of the citizens. So to the farm Cimon hied him, and addressed himself to the work thereof; and being thus employed, he chanced one afternoon as he passed, staff on shoulder, from one domain to another, to enter a plantation, the like of which for beauty there was not in those parts, and which was then – for 'twas the month of May – a mass of greenery; and, as he traversed it, he came, as Fortune was pleased to guide him, to a meadow girt in with trees exceeding tall, and having in one of its corners a fountain most fair and cool, beside which he espied a most beautiful girl lying asleep on the green grass, clad only in a vest of such fine stuff that it scarce in any measure veiled the whiteness of her flesh, and below the waist nought but an apron most white and fine of texture; and likewise at her feet there slept two women and a man, her slaves. No sooner did Cimon catch sight of her, than, as if he had never before seen form of woman, he stopped short, and leaning on his cudgel, regarded her intently, saying never a word, and lost in admiration. And in his rude soul, which, despite a thousand lessons, had hitherto remained impervious to every delight that belongs to urbane life, he felt the awakening of an idea, that bade his gross and coarse mind acknowledge, that this girl was the fairest creature that had ever been seen by mortal eye. And thereupon he began to distinguish her several parts, praising her hair, which shewed to him as gold, her brow, her nose and mouth, her throat and arms, and above all her bosom, which was as yet but in bud, and as he gazed, he changed of a sudden from a husbandman into a judge of beauty, and desired of all things to see her eyes, which the weight of her deep slumber kept close shut, and many a time he would fain have awakened her, that he might see them. But so much fairer seemed she to him than any other woman that he had seen, that he doubted she must be a goddess; and as he was not so devoid of sense but that he deemed things divine more worthy of reverence than things mundane, he forbore, and waited until she should awake of her own accord; and though he found the delay overlong, yet, enthralled by so unwonted a delight, he knew not how to be going. However, after he had tarried a long while, it so befell that Iphigenia – such was the girl's name – her slaves still sleeping, awoke, and raised her head, and opened her eyes, and seeing Cimon standing before her, leaning on his staff, was not a little surprised, and said: – "Cimon, what seekest thou in this wood at this hour?" For Cimon she knew well, as indeed did almost all the country-side, by reason alike of his uncouth appearance as of the rank and wealth of his father. To Iphigenia's question he answered never a word; but as soon as her eyes were open, nought could he do but intently regard them, for it seemed to him that a soft influence emanated from them, which filled his soul with a delight that he had never before known. Which the girl marking began to misdoubt that by so fixed a scrutiny his boorish temper might be prompted to some act that should cause her dishonour: wherefore she roused her women, and got up, saying: – "Keep thy distance, Cimon, in God's name." Whereto Cimon made answer: – "I will come with thee." And, albeit the girl refused his escort, being still in fear of him, she could not get quit of him; but he attended her home; after which he hied him straight to his father's house, and announced that he was minded on no account to go back to the farm: which intelligence was far from welcome to his father and kinsmen; but nevertheless they suffered him to stay, and waited to see what might be the reason of his change of mind. So Cimon, whose heart, closed to all teaching, love's shaft, sped by the beauty of Iphigenia, had penetrated, did now graduate in wisdom with such celerity as to astonish his father and kinsmen, and all that knew him. He began by requesting his father to let him go clad in the like apparel, and with, in all respects, the like personal equipment as his brothers: which his father very gladly did. Mixing thus with the gallants, and becoming familiar with the manners proper to gentlemen, and especially to lovers, he very soon, to the exceeding great wonder of all, not only acquired the rudiments of letters, but waxed most eminent among the philosophic wits. After which (for no other cause than the love he bore to Iphigenia) he not only modulated his gruff and boorish voice to a degree of smoothness suitable to urbane life, but made himself accomplished in singing and music; in riding also and in all matters belonging to war, as well by sea as by land, he waxed most expert and hardy. And in sum (that I go not about to enumerate each of his virtues in detail) he had not completed the fourth year from the day of his first becoming enamoured before he was grown the most gallant, and courteous, ay, and the most perfect in particular accomplishments, of the young cavaliers that were in the island of Cyprus. What then, gracious ladies, are we to say of Cimon? Verily nought else but that the high faculties, with which Heaven had endowed his noble soul, invidious Fortune had bound with the strongest of cords, and circumscribed within a very narrow region of his heart; all which cords Love, more potent than Fortune, burst and brake in pieces; and then with the might, wherewith he awakens dormant powers, he brought them forth of the cruel obfuscation, in which they lay, into clear light, plainly shewing thereby, whence he may draw, and whither he may guide, by his beams the souls that are subject to his sway.

Now, albeit by his love for Iphigenia Cimon was betrayed, as young lovers very frequently are, into some peccadillos, yet Aristippus, reflecting that it had turned him from a booby into a man, not only bore patiently with him, but exhorted him with all his heart to continue steadfast in his love.

And Cimon, who still refused to be called Galesus, because 'twas as Cimon that Iphigenia had first addressed him, being desirous to accomplish his desire by honourable means, did many a time urge his suit upon her father, Cipseus, that he would give her him to wife: whereto Cipseus always made the same answer, to wit, that he had promised her to Pasimondas, a young Rhodian noble, and was not minded to break faith with him. However, the time appointed for Iphigenia's wedding being come, and the bridegroom having sent for her, Cimon said to himself: – 'Tis now for me to shew thee, O Iphigenia, how great is my love for thee: 'tis by thee that I am grown a man, nor doubt I, if I shall have thee, that I shall wax more glorious than a god, and verily thee will I have, or die. Having so said, he privily enlisted in his cause certain young nobles that were his friends, and secretly fitted out a ship with all equipment meet for combat, and put to sea on the look-out for the ship that was to bear Iphigenia to Rhodes and her husband. And at length, when her father had done lavishing honours upon her husband's friends, Iphigenia embarked, and, the mariners shaping their course for Rhodes, put to sea. Cimon was on the alert, and overhauled them the very next day, and standing on his ship's prow shouted amain to those that were aboard Iphigenia's ship: – "Bring to; strike sails, or look to be conquered and sunk in the sea." Then, seeing that the enemy had gotten their arms above deck, and were making ready to make a fight of it, he followed up his words by casting a grapnel upon the poop of the Rhodians, who were making great way; and having thus made their poop fast to his prow, he sprang, fierce as a lion, reckless whether he were followed or no, on to the Rhodians' ship, making, as it were, no account of them, and animated by love, hurled himself, sword in hand, with prodigious force among the enemy, and cutting and thrusting right and left, slaughtered them like sheep; insomuch that the Rhodians, marking the fury of his onset, threw down their arms, and as with one voice did all acknowledge themselves his prisoners. To whom Cimon: – "Gallants," quoth he, "'twas neither lust of booty nor enmity to you that caused me to put out from Cyprus to attack you here with force of arms on the high seas. Moved was I thereto by that which to gain is to me a matter great indeed, which peaceably to yield me is to you but a slight matter; for 'tis even Iphigenia, whom more than aught else I love; whom, as I might not have her of her father in peaceable and friendly sort, Love has constrained me to take from you in this high-handed fashion and by force of arms; to whom I mean to be even such as would have been your Pasimondas: wherefore give her to me, and go your way, and God's grace go with you."

Yielding rather to force than prompted by generosity, the Rhodians surrendered Iphigenia, all tears, to Cimon; who, marking her tears, said to her: – "Grieve not, noble lady; thy Cimon am I, who, by my long love, have established a far better right to thee than Pasimondas by the faith that was plighted to him." So saying, he sent her aboard his ship, whither he followed her, touching nought that belonged to the Rhodians, and suffering them to go their way. To have gotten so dear a prize made him the happiest man in the world, but for a time 'twas all he could do to assuage her grief: then, after taking counsel with his comrades, he deemed it best not to return to Cyprus for the present: and so, by common consent they shaped their course for Crete, where most of them, and especially Cimon, had alliances of old or recent date, and friends not a few, whereby they deemed that there they might tarry with Iphigenia in security. But Fortune, that had accorded Cimon so gladsome a capture of the lady, suddenly proved fickle, and converted the boundless joy of the enamoured gallant into woeful and bitter lamentation. 'Twas not yet full four hours since Cimon had parted from the Rhodians, when with the approach of night, that night from which Cimon hoped such joyance as he had never known, came weather most turbulent and tempestuous, which wrapped the heavens in cloud, and swept the sea with scathing blasts; whereby 'twas not possible for any to see how the ship was to be worked or steered, or to steady himself so as to do any duty upon her deck. Whereat what grief was Cimon's, it boots not to ask. Indeed it seemed to him that the gods had granted his heart's desire only that it might be harder for him to die, which had else been to him but a light matter. Not less downcast were his comrades; but most of all Iphigenia, who, weeping bitterly and shuddering at every wave that struck the ship, did cruelly curse Cimon's love and censure his rashness, averring that this tempest was come upon them for no other cause than that the gods had decreed, that, as 'twas in despite of their will that he purposed to espouse her, he should be frustrate of his presumptuous intent, and having lived to see her expire, should then himself meet a woeful death.

While thus and yet more bitterly they bewailed them, and the mariners were at their wits' end, as the gale grew hourly more violent, nor knew they, nor might conjecture, whither they went, they drew nigh the island of Rhodes, albeit that Rhodes it was they wist not, and set themselves, as best and most skilfully they might, to run the ship aground. In which enterprise Fortune favoured them, bringing them into a little bay, where, shortly before them, was arrived the Rhodian ship that Cimon had let go. Nor were they sooner ware that 'twas Rhodes they had made, than day broke, and, the sky thus brightening a little, they saw that they were about a bow-shot from the ship that they had released on the preceding day. Whereupon Cimon, vexed beyond measure, being apprehensive of that which in fact befell them, bade make every effort to win out of the bay, and let Fortune carry them whither she would, for nowhere might they be in worse plight than there. So might and main they strove to bring the ship out, but all in vain: the violence of the gale thwarted them to such purpose as not only to preclude their passage out of the bay but to drive them, willing nilling, ashore. Whither no sooner were they come, than they were recognized by the Rhodian mariners, who were already landed. Of whom one ran with all speed to a farm hard by, whither the Rhodian gallants were gone, and told them that Fortune had brought Cimon and Iphigenia aboard their ship into the same bay to which she had guided them. Whereat the gallants were overjoyed, and taking with them not a few of the farm-servants, hied them in hot haste to the shore, where, Cimon and his men being already landed with intent to take refuge in a neighbouring wood, they took them all (with Iphigenia) and brought them to the farm. Whence, pursuant to an order of the Senate of Rhodes, to which, so soon as he received the news, Pasimondas made his complaint, Cimon and his men were all marched off to prison by Lysimachus, chief magistrate of the Rhodians for that year, who came down from the city for the purpose with an exceeding great company of men at arms. On such wise did our hapless and enamoured Cimon lose his so lately won Iphigenia before he had had of her more than a kiss or two. Iphigenia was entertained and comforted of the annoy, occasioned as well by her recent capture as by the fury of the sea, by not a few noble ladies of Rhodes, with whom she tarried until the day appointed for her marriage. In recompense of the release of the Rhodian gallants on the preceding day the lives of Cimon and his men were spared, notwithstanding that Pasimondas pressed might and main for their execution; and instead they were condemned to perpetual imprisonment: wherein, as may be supposed, they abode in dolorous plight, and despaired of ever again knowing happiness.

However, it so befell that, Pasimondas accelerating his nuptials to the best of his power, Fortune, as if repenting her that in her haste she had done Cimon so evil a turn, did now by a fresh disposition of events compass his deliverance. Pasimondas had a brother, by name Hormisdas, his equal in all respects save in years, who had long been contract to marry Cassandra, a fair and noble damsel of Rhodes, of whom Lysimachus was in the last degree enamoured; but owing to divers accidents the marriage had been from time to time put off. Now Pasimondas, being about to celebrate his nuptials with exceeding great pomp, bethought him that he could not do better than, to avoid a repetition of the pomp and expense, arrange, if so he might, that his brother should be wedded on the same day with himself. So, having consulted anew with Cassandra's kinsfolk, and come to an understanding with them, he and his brother and they conferred together, and agreed that on the same day that Pasimondas married Iphigenia, Hormisdas should marry Cassandra. Lysimachus, getting wind of this arrangement, was mortified beyond measure, seeing himself thereby deprived of the hope which he cherished of marrying Cassandra himself, if Hormisdas should not forestall him. But like a wise man he concealed his chagrin, and cast about how he might frustrate the arrangement: to which end he saw no other possible means but to carry Cassandra off. It did not escape him that the office which he held would render this easily feasible, but he deemed it all the more dishonourable than if he had not held the office; but, in short, after much pondering, honour yielded place to love, and he made up his mind that, come what might, he would carry Cassandra off. Then, as he took thought what company he should take with him, and how he should go about the affair, he remembered Cimon, whom he had in prison with his men, and it occurred to him that he could not possibly have a better or more trusty associate in such an enterprise than Cimon. Wherefore the same night he caused Cimon to be brought privily to him in his own room, and thus addressed him: – "Cimon, as the gods are most generous and liberal to bestow their gifts on men, so are they also most sagacious to try their virtue; and those whom they find to be firm and steadfast in all circumstances they honour, as the most worthy, with the highest rewards. They have been minded to be certified of thy worth by better proofs than thou couldst afford them, as long as thy life was bounded by thy father's house amid the superabundant wealth which I know him to possess: wherefore in the first place they so wrought upon thee with the shrewd incitements of Love that from an insensate brute, as I have heard, thou grewest to be a man; since when, it has been and is their intent to try whether evil fortune and harsh imprisonment may avail to change thee from the temper that was thine when for a short while thou hadst joyance of the prize thou hadst won. And so thou prove the same that thou wast then, they have in store for thee a boon incomparably greater than aught that they vouchsafed thee before: what that boon is, to the end thou mayst recover heart and thy wonted energies, I will now explain to thee. Pasimondas, exultant in thy misfortune and eager to compass thy death, hastens to the best of his power his nuptials with thy Iphigenia; that so he may enjoy the prize that Fortune, erstwhile smiling, gave thee, and forthwith, frowning, reft from thee. Whereat how sore must be thy grief, if rightly I gauge thy love, I know by my own case, seeing that his brother Hormisdas addresses himself to do me on the same day a like wrong in regard of Cassandra, whom I love more than aught else in the world. Nor see I that Fortune has left us any way of escape from this her unjust and cruel spite, save what we may make for ourselves by a resolved spirit and the might of our right hands: take we then the sword, and therewith make we, each, prize of his lady, thou for the second, I for the first time: for so thou value the recovery, I say not of thy liberty, for without thy lady I doubt thou wouldst hold it cheap, but of thy lady, the gods have placed it in thine own hands, if thou art but minded to join me in my enterprise."

These words restored to Cimon all that he had lost of heart and hope, nor pondered he long, before he replied: – "Lysimachus, comrade stouter or more staunch than I thou mightst not have in such an enterprise, if such indeed it be as thou sayst: wherefore lay upon me such behest as thou shalt deem meet, and thou shalt marvel to witness the vigour of my performance." Whereupon Lysimachus: – "On the third day from now," quoth he, "their husbands' houses will be newly entered by the brides, and on the same day at even we too will enter them in arms, thou with thy men, and I with some of mine, in whom I place great trust, and forcing our way among the guests and slaughtering all that dare to oppose us, will bear the ladies off to a ship which I have had privily got ready." Cimon approved the plan, and kept quiet in prison until the appointed time; which being come, the nuptials were celebrated with great pomp and magnificence, that filled the houses of the two brothers with festal cheer. Then Lysimachus having made ready all things meet, and fired Cimon and his men and his own friends for the enterprise by a long harangue, disposed them in due time, all bearing arms under their cloaks, in three companies; and having privily despatched one company to the port, that, when the time should come to embark, he might meet with no let, he marched with the other two companies to the house of Pasimondas, posted the one company at the gate, that, being entered, they might not be shut in or debarred their egress, and, with the other company and Cimon, ascended the stairs, and gained the saloon, where the brides and not a few other ladies were set at several tables to sup in meet order: whereupon in they rushed, and overthrew the tables and seized each his own lady, and placed them in charge of their men, whom they bade bear them off forthwith to the ship that lay ready to receive them. Whereupon the brides and the other ladies and the servants with one accord fell a sobbing and shrieking, insomuch that a confused din and lamentation filled the whole place. Cimon, Lysimachus and their band, none withstanding, but all giving way before them, gained the stairs, which they were already descending when they encountered Pasimondas, who, carrying a great staff in his hand, was making in the direction of the noise; but one doughty stroke of Cimon's sword sufficed to cleave his skull in twain, and lay him dead at Cimon's feet, and another stroke disposed of hapless Hormisdas, as he came running to his brother's aid. Some others who ventured to approach them were wounded and beaten off by the retinue. So forth of the house, that reeked with blood and resounded with tumult and lamentation and woe, sped Simon and Lysimachus with all their company, and without any let, in close order, with their fair booty in their midst, made good their retreat to the ship; whereon with the ladies they one and all embarked, for the shore was now full of armed men come to rescue the ladies, and, the oarsmen giving way, put to sea elate. Arrived at Crete, they met with a hearty welcome on the part of their many friends and kinsfolk; and, having married their ladies, they made greatly merry, and had gladsome joyance of their fair booty. Their doings occasioned, both in Cyprus and in Rhodes, no small stir and commotion, which lasted for a long while: but in the end, by the good offices of their friends and kinsfolk in both islands, 'twas so ordered as that after a certain term of exile Cimon returned with Iphigenia to Cyprus, and in like manner Lysimachus returned with Cassandra to Rhodes; and long and blithely thereafter lived they, each well contented with his own wife in his own land.

Fifth Day

Novel II

— Gostanza loves Martuccio Gomito, and hearing that he is dead, gives way to despair, and hies her alone aboard a boat, which is wafted by the wind to Susa. She finds him alive in Tunis, and makes herself known to him, who, having by his counsel gained high place in the king's favour, marries her, and returns with her wealthy to Lipari. —

PAMFILO'S STORY being ended, the queen, after commending it not a little, called for one to follow from Emilia; who thus began: –

Meet and right it is that one should rejoice when events so fall out that passion meets with its due reward: and as love merits in the long run rather joy than suffering, far gladlier obey I the queen's than I did the king's behest, and address myself to our present theme. You are to know then, dainty ladies, that not far from Sicily there is an islet called Lipari, in which, no great while ago, there dwelt a damsel, Gostanza by name, fair as fair could be, and of one of the most honourable families in the island. And one Martuccio Gomito, who was also of the island, a young man most gallant and courteous, and worthy for his condition, became enamoured of Gostanza; who in like manner grew so afire for him that she was ever ill at ease, except she saw him. Martuccio, craving her to wife, asked her of her father, who made answer that, Martuccio being poor, he was not minded to give her to him. Mortified to be thus rejected by reason of poverty, Martuccio took an oath in presence of some of his friends and kinsfolk that Lipari should know him no more, until he was wealthy. So away he sailed, and took to scouring the seas as a rover on the coast of Barbary, preying upon all whose force matched not his own. In which way of life he found Fortune favourable enough, had he but known how to rest and be thankful: but 'twas not enough that he and his comrades in no long time waxed very wealthy; their covetousness was inordinate, and, while they sought to gratify it, they chanced in an encounter with certain Saracen ships to be taken after a long defence, and despoiled, and, most part of them, thrown into the sea by their captors, who, after sinking his ship, took Martuccio with them to Tunis, and clapped him in prison, and there kept him a long time in a very sad plight.

Meanwhile, not by one or two, but by divers and not a few persons, tidings reached Lipari that all that were with Martuccio aboard his bark had perished in the sea. The damsel, whose grief on Martuccio's departure had known no bounds, now hearing that he was dead with the rest, wept a great while, and made up her mind to have done with life; but, lacking the resolution to lay violent hands upon herself, she bethought her how she might devote herself to death by some novel expedient. So one night she stole out of her father's house, and hied her to the port, and there by chance she found, lying a little apart from the other craft, a fishing boat, which, as the owners had but just quitted her, was still equipped with mast and sails and oars. Aboard which boat she forthwith got, and being, like most of the women of the island, not altogether without nautical skill, she rowed some distance out to sea, and then hoisted sail, and cast away oars and tiller, and let the boat drift, deeming that a boat without lading or steersman would certainly be either capsized by the wind or dashed against some rock and broken in pieces, so that escape she could not, even if she would, but must perforce drown. And so, her head wrapped in a mantle, she stretched herself weeping on the floor of the boat. But it fell out quite otherwise than she had conjectured: for, the wind being from the north, and very equable, with next to no sea, the boat kept an even keel, and next day about vespers bore her to land hard by a city called Susa, full a hundred miles beyond Tunis. To the damsel 'twas all one whether she were at sea or ashore, for, since she had been aboard, she had never once raised, nor, come what might, meant she ever to raise, her head.

Now it so chanced, that, when the boat grounded, there was on the shore a poor woman that was in the employ of some fishermen, whose nets she was just taking out of the sunlight. Seeing the boat under full sail, she marvelled how it should be suffered to drive ashore, and conjectured that the fishermen on board were asleep. So to the boat she hied her, and finding therein only the damsel fast asleep, she called her many times, and at length awakened her; and perceiving by her dress that she was a Christian, she asked her in Latin how it was that she was come thither all alone in the boat. Hearing the Latin speech, the damsel wondered whether the wind had not shifted, and carried her back to Lipari: so up she started, gazed about her, and finding herself ashore and the aspect of the country strange, asked the good woman where she was. To which the good woman made answer: – "My daughter, thou art hard by Susa in Barbary." Whereupon the damsel, sorrowful that God had not seen fit to accord her the boon of death, apprehensive of dishonour, and at her wits' end, sat herself down at the foot of her boat, and burst into tears. Which the good woman saw not without pity, and persuaded her to come with her into her hut, and there by coaxing drew from her how she was come thither; and knowing that she could not but be fasting, she set before her her own coarse bread and some fish and water, and prevailed upon her to eat a little. Gostanza thereupon asked her, who she was that thus spoke Latin; whereto she answered that her name was Carapresa, and that she was from Trapani, where she had served some Christian fishermen. To the damsel, sad indeed though she was, this name Carapresa, wherefore she knew not, seemed to be of happy augury, so that she began to take hope, she knew not why, and to grow somewhat less fain of death: wherefore without disclosing who or whence she was, she earnestly besought the good woman for the love of God to have pity on her youth, and advise her how best to avoid insult. Whereupon Carapresa, good woman that she was, left her in her hut, while with all speed she picked up her nets; and on her return she wrapped her in her own mantle, and led her to Susa. Arrived there, she said to her: – "Gostanza, I shall bring thee to the house of an excellent Saracen lady, for whom I frequently do bits of work, as she has occasion: she is an old lady and compassionate: I will commend thee to her care as best I may, and I doubt not she will right gladly receive thee, and entreat thee as her daughter: and thou wilt serve her, and, while thou art with her, do all thou canst to gain her favour, until such time as God may send thee better fortune;" and as she said, so she did.

The old lady listened, and then, gazing steadfastly in the damsel's face, shed tears, and taking her hand, kissed her forehead, and led her into the house, where she and some other women dwelt quite by themselves, doing divers kinds of handiwork in silk and palm leaves and leather. Wherein the damsel in a few days acquired some skill, and thenceforth wrought together with them; and rose wondrous high in the favour and good graces of all the ladies, who soon taught her their language.

Now while the damsel, mourned at home as lost and dead, dwelt thus at Susa, it so befell that, Mariabdela being then King of Tunis, a young chieftain in Granada, of great power, and backed by mighty allies, gave out that the realm of Tunis belonged to him, and having gathered a vast army, made a descent upon Tunis with intent to expel the King from the realm. Martuccio

Gomito, who knew the language of Barbary well, heard the tidings in prison, and learning that the King of Tunis was mustering a mighty host for the defence of his kingdom, said to one of the warders that were in charge of him and his comrades: – "If I might have speech of the King, I am confident that the advice that I should give him would secure him the victory." The warder repeated these words to his chief, who forthwith carried them to the King. Wherefore by the King's command Martuccio was brought before him, and being asked by him what the advice, of which he had spoken, might be, answered on this wise: – "Sire, if in old days, when I was wont to visit this country of yours, I duly observed the manner in which you order your battle, methinks you place your main reliance upon archers; and therefore, if you could contrive that your enemy's supply of arrows should give out and your own continue plentiful, I apprehend that you would win the battle." "Ay indeed," replied the King, "I make no doubt that, could I but accomplish that, I should conquer." "Nay but, Sire," returned Martuccio, "you may do it, if you will. Listen, and I will tell you how. You must fit the bows of your archers with strings much finer than those that are in common use, and match them with arrows, the notches of which will not admit any but these fine strings; and this you must do so secretly that your enemy may not know it, else he will find means to be even with you. Which counsel I give you for the following reason: – When your and your enemy's archers have expended all their arrows, you wot that the enemy will fall to picking up the arrows that your men have shot during the battle, and your men will do the like by the enemy's arrows; but the enemy will not be able to make use of your men's arrows, by reason that their fine notches will not suffice to admit the stout strings, whereas your men will be in the contrary case in regard of the enemy's arrows, for the fine string will very well receive the large-notched arrow, and so your men will have an abundant supply of arrows, while the enemy will be at a loss for them."

The King, who lacked not sagacity, appreciated Martuccio's advice, and gave full effect to it; whereby he came out of the war a conqueror, and Martuccio, being raised to the chief place in his favour, waxed rich and powerful. Which matters being bruited throughout the country, it came to the ears of Gostanza that Martuccio Gomito, whom she had long supposed to be dead, was alive; whereby her love for him, some embers of which still lurked in her heart, burst forth again in sudden flame, and gathered strength, and revived her dead hope. Wherefore she frankly told all her case to the good lady with whom she dwelt, saying that she would fain go to Tunis, that her eyes might have assurance of that which the report received by her ears had made them yearn to see. The lady fell heartily in with the girl's desire, and, as if she had been her mother, embarked with her for Tunis, where on their arrival they were honourably received in the house of one of her kinswomen. Carapresa, who had attended her, being sent to discover what she might touching Martuccio, brought back word that he was alive, and high in honour and place. The gentlewoman was minded that none but herself should apprise Martuccio of the arrival of his Gostanza: wherefore she hied her one day to Martuccio, and said: – "Martuccio, there is come to my house a servant of thine from Lipari, who would fain speak with thee here privily, and for that he would not have me trust another, I am come hither myself to deliver his message." Martuccio thanked her, and forthwith hied him with her to her house: where no sooner did the girl see him than she all but died for joy, and carried away by her feelings, fell upon his neck with open arms and embraced him, and, what with sorrow of his past woes and her present happiness, said never a word, but softly wept. Martuccio regarded her for a while in silent wonder; then, heaving a sigh, he said: – "Thou livest then, my Gostanza? Long since I heard that thou wast lost; nor was aught known of thee at home." Which said, he tenderly and with tears embraced her. Gostanza told him all her adventures, and how honourably she had been entreated by the gentlewoman with whom she had dwelt. And so long time they conversed, and then Martuccio parted from her, and hied him back to his lord the King, and told him all, to wit, his own adventures and those of the girl, adding that with his leave he was minded to marry her according to our law. Which matters the King found passing strange; and having called the girl to him, and learned from her that 'twas even as Martuccio had said: – "Well indeed," quoth he, "hast thou won thy husband." Then caused he gifts most ample and excellent to be brought forth, part of which he gave to Gostanza, and part to Martuccio, leaving them entirely to their own devices in regard of one another. Then Martuccio, in terms most honourable, bade farewell to the old lady with whom Gostanza had dwelt, thanking her for the service she had rendered to Gostanza, and giving her presents suited to her condition, and commending her to God, while Gostanza shed many a tear: after which, by leave of the King, they went aboard a light bark, taking with them Carapresa, and, sped by a prosperous breeze, arrived at Lipari, where they were received with such cheer as 'twere vain to attempt to describe. There were Martuccio and Gostanza wedded with all pomp and splendour; and there long time in easeful peace they had joyance of their love.

Fifth Day
Novel III

— *Pietro Boccamazza runs away with Agnolella, and encounters a gang of robbers: the girl takes refuge in a wood, and is guided to a castle. Pietro is taken, but escapes out of the hands of the robbers, and after some adventures arrives at the castle where Agnolella is, marries her, and returns with her to Rome.* —

ENDED EMILIA'S story, which none of the company spared to commend, the queen, turning to Elisa, bade her follow suit; and she, with glad obedience, thus began: –

'Tis a story, sweet ladies, of a woeful night passed by two indiscreet young lovers that I have in mind; but, as thereon ensued not a few days of joy, 'tis not inapposite to our argument, and shall be narrated.

'Tis no long time since at Rome, which, albeit now the tail, was of yore the head, of the world, there dwelt a young man, Pietro Boccamazza by name, a scion of one of the most illustrious of the Roman houses, who became enamoured of a damsel exceeding fair, and amorous withal – her name Agnolella – the daughter of one Gigliuozzo Saullo, a plebeian, but in high repute among the Romans. Nor, loving thus, did Pietro lack the address to inspire in Agnolella a love as ardent as his own. Wherefore, overmastered by his passion, and minded no longer to endure the sore suffering that it caused him, he asked her in marriage. Whereof his kinsfolk were no sooner apprised, than with one accord they came to him and strongly urged him to desist from his purpose: they also gave Gigliuozzo Saullo to understand that he were best to pay no sort of heed to Pietro's words, for that, if he so did, they would never acknowledge him as friend or relative. Thus to see himself debarred of the one way by which he deemed he might attain to his desire, Pietro was ready to die for grief, and, all his kinsfolk notwithstanding, he would have married Gigliuozzo's daughter, had but the father consented. Wherefore at length he made up his mind that, if the girl were willing, nought should stand in the way; and having through a common friend sounded the damsel and found her apt, he brought her to consent to elope with him from Rome. The affair being arranged, Pietro and she took horse betimes one morning, and sallied forth for Anagni, where Pietro had certain friends, in whom he placed much trust; and as they rode, time not serving for full joyance of their love, for they feared pursuit, they held converse thereof, and from time to time exchanged a kiss. Now it so befell, that, the way being none too well known to Pietro, when, perhaps eight miles from Rome, they should have turned to the right, they took instead a leftward road. Whereon when they had ridden but little more than two miles, they found themselves close to a petty castle, whence, so soon as they were observed, there issued some dozen men at arms; and, as they drew near, the damsel, espying them, gave a cry, and said: – "We are attacked, Pietro, let us flee;" and guiding her nag as best she knew towards a great forest, she planted the spurs in his sides, and so, holding on by the saddle-bow, was borne by the goaded creature into the forest at a gallop. Pietro, who had been too engrossed with her face to give due heed to the way, and thus had not been ware, as soon as she, of the approach of the men at arms, was still looking about to see whence they were coming, when they came up with him, and took him prisoner, and forced him to dismount. Then they asked who he was, and, when he told them, they conferred among themselves, saying: – "This is one of the friends of our enemies: what else can we do but relieve him of his nag and of his clothes, and hang him on one of these oaks in scorn of the Orsini?" To which proposal all agreeing, they bade Pietro strip himself: but while, already divining his fate, he was so doing, an ambuscade of full five-and-twenty men at arms fell suddenly upon them, crying: – "Death, death!" Thus surprised, they let Pietro go, and stood on the defensive; but, seeing that the enemy greatly outnumbered them, they took to their heels, the others giving chase. Whereupon Pietro hastily resumed his clothes, mounted his nag, and fled with all speed in the direction which he had seen the damsel take. But finding no road or path through the forest, nor discerning any trace of a horse's hooves, he was – for that he found not the damsel – albeit he deemed himself safe out of the clutches of his captors and their assailants, the most wretched man alive, and fell a weeping and wandering hither and thither about the forest, uttering Agnolella's name. None answered; but turn back he dared not: so on he went, not knowing whither he went; besides which, he was in mortal dread of the wild beasts that infest the forest, as well on account of himself as of the damsel, whom momently he seemed to see throttled by some bear or wolf. Thus did our unfortunate Pietro spend the whole day, wandering about the forest, making it to resound with his cries of Agnolella's name, and harking at times back, when he thought to go forward; until at last, what with his cries and his tears and his fears and his long fasting, he was so spent that he could go no further. 'Twas then nightfall, and, as he knew not what else to do, he dismounted at the foot of an immense oak, and having tethered his nag to the trunk, climbed up into the branches, lest he should be devoured by the wild beasts during the night. Shortly afterwards the moon rose with a very clear sky, and Pietro, who dared not sleep, lest he should fall, and indeed, had he been secure from that risk, his misery and his anxiety on account of the damsel would not have suffered him to sleep, kept watch, sighing and weeping and cursing his evil luck.

Now the damsel, who, as we said before, had fled she knew not whither, allowing her nag to carry her whithersoever he would, strayed so far into the forest that she lost sight of the place where she had entered it, and spent the whole day just as Pietro had done, wandering about the wilderness, pausing from time to time, and weeping, and uttering his name, and bewailing her evil fortune. At last, seeing that 'twas now the vesper hour and Pietro came not, she struck into a path, which the nag followed, until, after riding some two miles, she espied at some distance a cottage, for which she made with all speed, and found there a good man, well stricken in years, with his wife, who was likewise aged. Seeing her ride up alone, they said: – "Daughter, wherefore ridest thou thus alone at this hour in these parts?" Weeping, the damsel made answer that she had lost her companion in the forest, and asked how far might Anagni be from there? "My daughter," returned the good man, "this is not the road to Anagni; 'tis more than twelve miles away." "And how far off," inquired the damsel, "are the nearest houses in which one might find lodging for the night?" "There are none so near," replied the good man, "that thou canst reach them to-day." "Then, so please you," said the damsel, "since go elsewhither I cannot, for God's sake let me pass the night here with you." Whereto the good man made answer: – "Damsel, welcome art thou to tarry the night with us; but still thou art to know that these parts are infested both by day and by night by bands, which, be they friends or be they foes, are alike ill to meet with, and not seldom do much despite and mischief, and if by misadventure one of these bands should visit us while thou wert here, and marking thy youth and beauty should do thee despite and dishonour, we should be unable to afford thee any succour. This we would have thee know, that if it should so come to pass, thou mayst not have cause to reproach us." The damsel heard not the old man's words without dismay; but, seeing that the hour was now late, she answered: – "God, if He be so pleased, will save both you and me from such molestation, and if not, 'tis a much lesser evil to be maltreated by men than to be torn in pieces by the wild beasts in the forest." So saying, she dismounted, and entered the cottage, where, having supped with the poor man and his wife on such humble fare as they had, she laid herself in her clothes beside them in their bed. She slept not, however; for her own evil plight and that of Pietro, for whom she knew not how to augur aught but evil, kept her sighing and weeping all night long. And towards matins she heard a great noise as of men that marched; so up she got and hied her into a large courtyard that was in rear of the cottage, and part of which was covered with a great heap of hay, which she espying, hid herself therein, that, if the men came there, they might not so readily find her. Scarce had she done so than the men, who proved to be a strong company of marauders, were at the door of the cottage, which they forced open; and having entered, and found the damsel's nag, still saddled, they asked who was there. The damsel being out of sight, the good man answered: – "There is none here but my wife and I; but this nag, which has given some one the slip, found his way hither last night, and we housed him, lest he should be devoured by the wolves." "So!" said the chief of the band, "as he has no owner, he will come in very handy for us."

Whereupon, in several parties, they ransacked the cottage from top to bottom; and one party went out into the courtyard, where, as they threw aside their lances and targets, it so befell that one of them, not knowing where else to bestow his lance, tossed it into the hay, and was within an ace of killing the damsel that lay hid there, as likewise she of betraying her whereabouts, for the lance all but grazing her left breast, insomuch that the head tore her apparel, she doubted she was wounded, and had given a great shriek, but that, remembering where she was, she refrained for fear. By and by the company cooked them a breakfast of kid's and other meat, and having eaten and drunken, dispersed in divers directions, as their affairs required, taking the girl's nag with them. And when they were gotten some little way off, the good man asked his wife: – "What became of the damsel, our guest of last night, that I have not seen her since we rose?" The good woman answered that she knew not where the damsel was, and went to look for her. The damsel, discovering that the men were gone, came forth of the hay, and the good man, seeing her, was overjoyed that she had not fallen into the hands of the ruffians, and, as day was breaking, said to her: – "Now that day is at hand, we will, so it like thee, escort thee to a castle, some five miles hence, where thou wilt be in safety; but thou must needs go afoot, because these villains, that are but just gone, have taken thy nag with them." The damsel, resigning herself to her loss, besought them for God's sake to take her to the castle: whereupon they set forth, and arrived there about half tierce. Now the castle belonged to one of the Orsini, Liello di Campo di Fiore by name, whose wife, as it chanced, was there. A most kindly and good woman she was, and, recognizing the damsel as soon as she saw her, gave her a hearty welcome and would fain have from her a particular account of how she came there. So the damsel told her the whole story. The lady, to whom Pietro was also known, as being a friend of her husband, was distressed to hear of his misadventure, and being told where he was taken, gave him up for dead. So she said to the damsel: – "Since so it is that thou knowest not how Pietro has fared, thou shalt stay here with me until such time as I may have opportunity to send thee safely back to Rome."

Meanwhile Pietro, perched on his oak in as woeful a plight as might be, had espied, when he should have been in his first sleep, a full score of wolves, that, as they prowled, caught sight of the nag, and straightway were upon him on all sides. The horse, as soon as he was ware of their approach, strained on the reins till they snapped, and tried to make good his escape; but, being hemmed in, was brought to bay, and made a long fight of it with his teeth and hooves; but in the end they bore him down and throttled him and forthwith eviscerated him, and, the whole pack falling upon him, devoured him to the bone before they had done with him. Whereat Pietro, who felt that in the nag he had lost a companion and a comfort in his travail, was sorely dismayed, and began to think that he should never get out of the forest. But towards dawn, he, perched there in the oak, almost dead with cold, looking around him as he frequently did, espied about a mile off a huge fire. Wherefore, as soon as 'twas broad day, he got down, not without trepidation, from the oak, and bent his steps towards the fire; and being come to it, he found, gathered about it, a company of shepherds, eating and making merry, who took pity on him and made him welcome. And when he had broken his fast and warmed himself, he told them the mishap that had befallen him, and how it was that he was come there alone, and asked them if there was a farm or castle in those parts, whither he might betake him. The shepherds said that about three miles away there was a castle belonging to Liello di Campo di Fiore, where his lady was then tarrying. Pietro, much comforted, requested to be guided thither by some of their company; whereupon two of them right gladly escorted him. So Pietro arrived at the castle, where he found some that knew him; and while he was endeavouring to set on foot a search for the damsel in the forest, the lady summoned him to her presence, and he, forthwith obeying, and seeing Agnolella with her, was the happiest man that ever was. He yearned till he all but swooned to go and embrace her, but refrained, for bashfulness, in the lady's presence. And overjoyed as he was, the joy of the damsel was no less. The lady received him with great cheer, and though, when she had heard the story of his adventures from his own lips, she chid him not a little for having set at nought the wishes of his kinsfolk; yet, seeing that he was still of the same mind, and that the damsel was also constant, she said to herself: – To what purpose give I myself all this trouble? they love one another, they know one another; they love with equal ardour; their love is honourable, and I doubt not is well pleasing to God, seeing that the one has escaped the gallows and the other the lance, and both the wild beasts: wherefore be it as they would have it. Then, turning to them, she said: – "If 'tis your will to be joined in wedlock as man and wife, mine jumps with it: here shall your nuptials be solemnized and at Liello's charges, and for the rest I will see that your peace is made with your kinsfolk." So in the castle the pair were wedded, Pietro only less blithe than Agnolella, the lady ordering the nuptials as honourably as might be in her mountain-home, and there they had most sweet joyance of the first fruits of their love. So some days they tarried there, and then accompanied by the lady with a strong escort, they took horse and returned to Rome, where, very wroth though she found Pietro's kinsfolk for what he had done, the lady re-established solid peace between him and them; and so at Rome Pietro and Agnolella lived together to a good old age in great tranquillity and happiness.

Fifth Day
Novel IV

— Ricciardo Manardi is found by Messer Lizio da Valbona with his daughter, whom he marries, and remains at peace with her father. —

IN SILENCE Elisa received the praise bestowed on her story by her fair companions; and then the queen called for a story from Filostrato, who with a laugh began on this wise: –

Chidden have I been so often and by so many of you for the sore burden, which I laid upon you, of discourse harsh and meet for tears, that, as some compensation for such annoy, I deem myself bound to tell you somewhat that may cause you to laugh a little: wherefore my story, which will be of the briefest, shall be of a love, the course whereof, save for sighs and a brief passage of fear mingled with shame, ran smooth to a happy consummation.

Know then, noble ladies, that 'tis no long time since there dwelt in Romagna a right worthy and courteous knight, Messer Lizio da Valbona by name, who was already verging upon old age, when, as it happened, there was born to him of his wife, Madonna Giacomina, a daughter, who, as she grew up, became the fairest and most debonair of all the girls of those parts, and, for that she was the only daughter left to them, was most dearly loved and cherished by her father and mother, who guarded her with most jealous care, thinking to arrange some great match for her. Now there was frequently in Messer Lizio's house, and much in his company, a fine, lusty young man, one Ricciardo de' Manardi da Brettinoro, whom Messer Lizio and his wife would as little have thought of mistrusting as if he had been their own son: who, now and again taking note of the damsel, that she was very fair and graceful, and in bearing and behaviour most commendable, and of marriageable age, fell vehemently in love with her, which love he was very careful to conceal. The damsel detected it, however, and in like manner plunged headlong into love with him, to Ricciardo's no small satisfaction. Again and again he was on the point of speaking to her, but refrained for fear; at length, however, he summoned up his courage, and seizing his opportunity, thus addressed her: – "Caterina, I implore thee, suffer me not to die for love of thee." Whereto the damsel forthwith responded: – "Nay, God grant that it be not rather that I die for love of thee." Greatly exhilarated and encouraged, Ricciardo made answer: – "'Twill never be by default of mine that thou lackest aught that may pleasure thee; but it rests with thee to find the means to save thy life and mine." Then said the damsel: – "Thou seest, Ricciardo, how closely watched I am, insomuch that I see not how 'twere possible for thee to come to me; but if thou seest aught that I may do without dishonour, speak the word, and I will do it." Ricciardo was silent a while, pondering many matters: then, of a sudden, he said: – "Sweet my Caterina, there is but one way that I can see, to wit, that thou shouldst sleep either on or where thou mightst have access to the terrace by thy father's garden, where, so I but knew that thou wouldst be there at night, I would without fail contrive to meet thee, albeit 'tis very high." "As for my sleeping there," replied Caterina, "I doubt not that it may be managed, if thou art sure that thou canst join me." Ricciardo answered in the affirmative. Whereupon they exchanged a furtive kiss, and parted.

On the morrow, it being now towards the close of May, the damsel began complaining to her mother that by reason of the excessive heat she had not been able to get any sleep during the night. "Daughter," said the lady, "what heat was there? Nay, there was no heat at all." "Had you said, 'to my thinking,' mother," rejoined Caterina, "you would perhaps have said sooth; but you should bethink you how much more heat girls have in them than ladies that are advanced in years." "True, my daughter," returned the lady, "but I cannot order that it shall be hot and cold, as thou perchance wouldst like; we must take the weather as we find it, and as the seasons provide it: perchance to-night it will be cooler, and thou wilt sleep better." "God grant it be so," said Caterina, "but 'tis not wonted for the nights to grow cooler as the summer comes on." "What then," said the lady, "wouldst thou have me do?" "With your leave and my father's," answered Caterina, "I should like to have a little bed made up on the terrace by his room and over his garden, where, hearing the nightingales sing, and being in a much cooler place, I should sleep much better than in your room." Whereupon: – "Daughter, be of good cheer," said the mother; "I will speak to thy father, and we will do as he shall decide." So the lady told Messer Lizio what had passed between her and the damsel; but he, being old and perhaps for that reason a little morose, said: – "What nightingale is this, to whose chant she would fain sleep? I will see to it that the cicalas shall yet lull her to sleep." Which speech, coming to Caterina's ears, gave her such offence, that for anger, rather than by reason of the heat, she not only slept not herself that night, but suffered not her mother to sleep, keeping up a perpetual complaint of the great heat. Wherefore her mother hied her in the morning to Messer Lizio, and said to him: – "Sir, you hold your daughter none too dear; what difference can it make to you that she lie on the terrace? She has tossed about all night long by reason of the heat; and besides, can you wonder that she, girl that she is, loves to hear the nightingale sing? Young folk naturally affect their likes." Whereto Messer Lizio made answer: – "Go, make her a bed there to your liking, and set a curtain round it, and let her sleep there, and hear the nightingale sing to her heart's content." Which the damsel no sooner learned, than she had a bed made there with intent to sleep there that same night; wherefore she watched until she saw Ricciardo, whom by a concerted sign she gave to understand what he was to do. Messer Lizio, as soon as he had heard the damsel go to bed, locked a door that led from his room to the terrace, and went to sleep himself. When all was quiet, Ricciardo with the help of a ladder got upon a wall, and standing thereon laid hold of certain toothings of another wall, and not without great exertion and risk, had he fallen, clambered up on to the terrace, where the damsel received him quietly with the heartiest of cheer. Many a kiss they exchanged; and then got them to bed, where well-nigh all night long they had solace and joyance of one another, and made the nightingale sing not a few times. But, brief being the night and great their pleasure, towards dawn, albeit they wist it not, they fell asleep, Caterina's right arm encircling Ricciardo's neck, while with her left hand she held him by that part of his person which your modesty, my ladies, is most averse to name in the company of men. So, peacefully they slept, and were still asleep when day broke and Messer Lizio rose; and calling to mind that his daughter slept on the terrace, softly opened the door, saying to himself: – Let me see what sort of night's rest the nightingale has afforded our Caterina? And having entered, he gently raised the curtain that screened the bed, and saw Ricciardo asleep with her and in her embrace as described, both being quite naked and uncovered; and having taken note of Ricciardo, he went away, and hied him to his lady's room, and called her, saying: – "Up, up, wife, come and see; for thy daughter has fancied the nightingale to such purpose that she has caught him, and holds him in her hand." "How can this be?" said the lady. "Come quickly, and thou shalt see," replied Messer Lizio. So the lady huddled on her clothes, and silently followed Messer Lizio, and when they were come to the bed, and had raised the curtain, Madonna Giacomina saw plainly enough how her daughter had caught, and did hold the nightingale, whose song she had so longed to hear. Whereat the lady, deeming that Ricciardo had played her a cruel trick, would have cried out and upbraided him; but Messer Lizio said to her: – "Wife, as thou valuest my love, say not a word; for in good sooth, seeing that she has caught him, he shall be hers. Ricciardo is a gentleman and wealthy; an alliance with him cannot but be to our advantage: if he would part from me on good terms, he must first marry her, so that the nightingale shall prove to have been put in his own cage and not in that of another." Whereby the lady was reassured, seeing that her husband took the affair so quietly, and that her daughter had had a good night, and was rested, and had caught the nightingale. So she kept silence; nor had they long to wait before Ricciardo awoke; and, seeing that 'twas broad day, deemed that 'twas as much as his life was worth, and aroused Caterina, saying: – "Alas! my soul, what shall we do, now that day has come and surprised me here?" Which question Messer Lizio answered by coming forward, and saying: – "We shall do well." At sight of him Ricciardo felt as if his heart were torn out of his body, and sate up in the bed, and said: – "My lord, I cry you mercy for God's sake. I wot that my disloyalty and delinquency have merited death; wherefore deal with me even as it may seem best to you: however, I pray you, if so it may be, to spare my life, that I die not." "Ricciardo," replied Messer Lizio, "the love I bore thee, and the faith I reposed in thee, merited a better return; but still, as so it is, and youth has seduced thee into such a transgression, redeem thy life, and preserve my honour, by making Caterina thy lawful spouse, that thine, as she has been for this past night, she may remain for the rest of her life. In this way thou mayst secure my peace and thy safety; otherwise commend thy soul to God." Pending this colloquy, Caterina let go the nightingale, and having covered herself, began with many a tear to implore her father to forgive Ricciardo, and Ricciardo to do as Messer Lizio required, that thereby they might securely count upon a long continuance of such nights of delight. But there needed not much supplication; for, what with remorse for the wrong done, and the wish to make amends, and the fear of death, and the desire to escape it, and above all ardent love, and the craving to possess the beloved one, Ricciardo lost no time in making frank avowal of his readiness to do as Messer Lizio would have him. Wherefore Messer Lizio, having borrowed a ring from Madonna Giacomina, Ricciardo did there and then in their presence wed Caterina. Which done, Messer Lizio and the lady took their leave, saying: – "Now rest ye a while; for so perchance 'twere better for you than if ye rose." And so they left the young folks, who forthwith embraced, and not having travelled more than six miles during the night, went two miles further before they rose, and so concluded their first day. When they were risen, Ricciardo and Messer Lizio discussed the matter with more formality; and some days afterwards Ricciardo, as was meet, married the damsel anew in presence of their friends and kinsfolk, and brought her home with great pomp, and celebrated his nuptials with due dignity and splendour. And so for many a year thereafter he lived with her in peace and happiness, and snared the nightingales day and night to his heart's content.

Fifth Day

Novel V

— *Guidotto da Cremona dies leaving a girl to Giacomino da Pavia. She has two lovers in Faenza, to wit, Giannole di Severino and Minghino di Mingole, who fight about her. She is discovered to be Giannole's sister, and is given to Minghino to wife.* —

ALL THE LADIES laughed so heartily over the story of the nightingale, that, even when Filostrato had finished, they could not control their merriment. However, when the laughter was somewhat abated, the queen said: – "Verily if thou didst yesterday afflict us, to-day thou hast tickled us to such purpose that none of us may justly complain of thee." Then, as the turn had now come round to Neifile, she bade her give them a story. And thus, blithely, Neifile began: –

As Filostrato went to Romagna for the matter of his discourse, I too am fain to make a short journey through the same country in what I am about to relate to you.

I say, then, that there dwelt of yore in the city of Fano two Lombards, the one ycleped Guidotto da Cremona and the other Giacomino da Pavia, men advanced in life, who, being soldiers, had spent the best part of their youth in feats of arms. Now Guidotto, being at the point of death, and having no son or any friend or kinsman in whom he placed more trust than in Giacomino, left him a girl of about ten years, and all that he had in the world, and so, having given him to know not a little of his affairs, he died. About the same time the city of Faenza, which had long been at war and in a most sorry plight, began to recover some measure of prosperity; and thereupon liberty to return thither on honourable terms was accorded to all that were so minded. Whither, accordingly, Giacomino, who had dwelt there aforetime, and liked the place, returned with all his goods and chattels, taking with him the girl left him by Guidotto, whom he loved and entreated as his daughter. The girl grew up as beautiful a maiden as was to be found in the city; and no less debonair and modest was she than fair. Wherefore she lacked not admirers; but above all two young men, both very gallant and of equal merit, the one Giannole di Severino, the other Minghino di Mingole, affected her with so ardent a passion, that, growing jealous, they came to hate one another with an inordinate hatred. Right gladly would each have espoused her, she being now fifteen years old, but that his kinsmen forbade it; wherefore seeing that neither might have her in an honourable way, each determined to compass his end as best he might.

Now Giacomino had in his house an ancient maid, and a man, by name Crivello, a very pleasant and friendly sort of fellow, with whom Giannole grew familiar, and in due time confided to him all his love, praying him to further the attainment of his desire, and promising to reward him handsomely, if he did so. Crivello made answer: – "Thou must know that there is but one way in which I might be of service to thee in this affair: I might contrive that thou shouldst be where she is when Giacomino is gone off to supper; but, were I to presume to say aught to her on thy behalf, she would never listen to me. This, if it please thee, I promise to do for thee, and will be as good as my word; and then thou canst do whatever thou mayst deem most expedient." Giannole said that he asked no more; and so 'twas arranged.

Meanwhile Minghino on his part had made friends with the maid, on whom he had so wrought that she had carried several messages to the girl, and had gone far to kindle her to his love, and furthermore had promised to contrive that he should meet her when for any cause Giacomino should be from home in the evening. And so it befell that no long time after these parleys, Giacomino, by Crivello's management, was to go sup at the house of a friend, and by preconcert between Crivello and Giannole, upon signal given, Giannole was to come to Giacomino's house and find the door open. The maid, on her part, witting nought of the understanding between Crivello and Giannole, let Minghino know that Giacomino would not sup at home, and bade him be near the house, so that he might come and enter it on sight of a signal from her. The evening came; neither of the lovers knew aught of what the other was about; but, being suspicious of one another, they came to take possession, each with his own company of armed friends. Minghino, while awaiting the signal, rested with his company in the house of one of his friends hard by the girl's house: Giannole with his company was posted a little farther off. Crivello and the maid, when Giacomino was gone, did each their endeavour to get the other out of the way. Crivello said to the maid: – "How is it thou takest not thyself off to bed, but goest still hither and thither about the house?" And the maid said to Crivello: – "Nay, but why goest thou not after thy master? Thou hast supped; what awaitest thou here?" And so, neither being able to make the other quit the post, Crivello, the hour concerted with Giannole being come, said to himself: – What care I for her? If she will not keep quiet, 'tis like to be the worse for her. Whereupon he gave the signal, and hied him to the door, which he had no sooner opened, than Giannole entered with two of his companions, and finding the girl in the saloon, laid hands on her with intent to carry her off. The girl struggled, and shrieked amain, as did also the maid. Minghino, fearing the noise, hasted to the spot with his companions; and, seeing that the girl was already being borne across the threshold, they drew their swords, and cried out in chorus: – "Ah! Traitors that ye are, ye are all dead men! 'Twill go otherwise than ye think for. What means this force?" Which said, they fell upon them with their swords, while the neighbours, alarmed by the noise, came hurrying forth with lights and arms, and protested that 'twas an outrage, and took Minghino's part. So, after a prolonged struggle, Minghino wrested the girl from Giannole, and set her again in Giacomino's house. Nor were the combatants separated before the officers of the Governor of the city came up and arrested not a few of them; among them Minghino and Giannole and Crivello, whom they marched off to prison. However, peace being restored and Giacomino returned, 'twas with no little chagrin that he heard of the affair; but finding upon investigation that the girl was in no wise culpable, he was somewhat reassured; and determined, lest the like should again happen, to bestow the girl in marriage as soon as might be.

On the morrow the kinsfolk of the two lovers, having learned the truth of the matter, and knowing what evil might ensue to the captives, if Giacomino should be minded to take the course which he reasonably might, came and gave him good words, beseeching him to let the kindly feeling, the love, which they believed he bore to them, his suppliants, count for more with him than the wrong that the hare-brained gallants had done him, and on their part and their own offering to make any amend that he might require. Giacomino, who had seen many things in his time, and lacked not sound sense, made answer briefly: – "Gentlemen, were I in my own country, as I am in yours, I hold myself in such sort your friend that nought would I do in this matter, or in any other, save what might be agreeable to you: besides which, I have the more reason to consider your wishes, because 'tis against you yourselves that you have offended, inasmuch as this damsel, whatever many folk may suppose, is neither of Cremona nor of Pavia, but is of Faenza, albeit neither I nor she, nor he from whom I had her, did ever wot whose daughter she was: wherefore, touching that you ask of me, I will even do just as you bid me." The worthy men found it passing strange that the girl should be of Faenza; and having thanked Giacomino for his handsome answer, they besought him that he would be pleased to tell them how she had come into his hands, and how he knew that she was of Faenza. To whom Giacomino replied on this wise: – "A comrade and friend I had, Guidotto da Cremona, who, being at the point of death, told me that, when this city of Faenza was taken by the Emperor Frederic, he and his comrades, entering one of the houses during the sack, found there good store of booty, and never a soul save this girl, who, being two years old or thereabouts, greeted him as father as he came up the stairs; wherefore he took pity on her, and carried her with whatever else was in the house away with him to Fano; where on his deathbed he left her to me, charging me in due time to bestow her in marriage, and give her all his goods and chattels by way of dowry: but, albeit she is now of marriageable age, I have not been able to provide her with a husband to my mind; though right glad should I be to do so, that nought like the event of yesterday may again befall me."

Now among the rest of those present was one Guglielmo da Medicina, who had been with Guidotto on that occasion, and knew well whose house it was that Guidotto had sacked; and seeing the owner there among the rest, he went up to him, and said: – "Dost hear, Bernabuccio, what Giacomino says?" "Ay," answered Bernabuccio, "and I gave the more heed thereto, for that I call to mind that during those disorders I lost a little daughter of just the age that Giacomino speaks of." "'Tis verily she then," said Guglielmo, "for once when I was with Guidotto I heard him describe what house it was that he had sacked, and I wist that 'twas thine. Wherefore search thy memory if there be any sign by which thou thinkest to recognize her, and let her be examined that thou mayst be assured that she is thy daughter." So Bernabuccio pondered a while, and then recollected that she ought to have a scar, shewing like a tiny cross, above her left ear, being where he had excised a tumour a little while before that affair: wherefore without delay he went up to Giacomino, who was still there, and besought him to let him go home with him and see the damsel. Giacomino gladly did so, and no sooner was the girl brought into Bernabuccio's presence, than, as he beheld her, 'twas as if he saw the face of her mother, who was still a beautiful woman. However, he would not rest there, but besought Giacomino of his grace to permit him to lift a lock or two of hair above her left ear; whereto Giacomino consented. So Bernabuccio approached her where she stood somewhat shamefast, and with his right hand lifted her locks, and, seeing the cross, wist that in very truth she was his daughter, and tenderly wept and embraced her, albeit she withstood him; and then, turning to Giacomino, he said: – "My brother, the girl is my daughter; 'twas my house that Guidotto sacked, and so sudden was the assault that my wife, her mother, forgot her, and we have always hitherto supposed that, my house being burned that same day, she perished in the flames." Catching his words, and seeing that he was advanced in years, the girl inclined to believe him, and impelled by some occult instinct, suffered his embraces, and melting, mingled her tears with his. Bernabuccio forthwith sent for her mother and her sisters and other kinswomen and her brothers, and having shewn her to them all, and told the story, after they had done her great cheer and embraced her a thousand times, to Giacomino's no small delight, he brought her home with him. Which coming to the ears of the Governor of the city, the worthy man, knowing that Giannole, whom he had in ward, was Bernabuccio's son and the girl's brother, made up his mind to deal leniently with Giannole: wherefore he took upon himself the part of mediator in the affair, and having made peace between Bernabuccio and Giacomino and Giannole and Minghino, gave Agnesa – such was the damsel's name – to Minghino to wife, to the great delight of all Minghino's kinsfolk, and set at liberty not only Giannole and Minghino but Crivello, and the others their confederates in the affair. Whereupon Minghino with the blithest of hearts wedded Agnesa with all due pomp and circumstance, and brought her home, where for many a year thereafter he lived with her in peace and prosperity.

Fifth Day

Novel VI

— *Gianni di Procida, being found with a damsel that he loves, and who had been given to King Frederic, is bound with her to a stake, so to be burned. He is recognized by Ruggieri dell' Oria, is delivered, and marries her.* —

NEIFILE'S STORY, with which the ladies were greatly delighted, being ended, the queen called for one from Pampinea; who forthwith raised her noble countenance, and thus began: –

Mighty indeed, gracious ladies, are the forces of Love, and great are the labours and excessive and unthought of the perils which they induce lovers to brave; as is manifest enough by what we have heard to-day and on other occasions: howbeit I mean to shew you the same once more by a story of an enamoured youth.

Hard by Naples is the island of Ischia, in which there dwelt aforetime with other young damsels one, Restituta by name, daughter of one Marin Bolgaro, a gentleman of the island. Very fair was she, and blithe of heart, and by a young gallant, Gianni by name, of the neighbouring islet of Procida, was beloved more dearly than life, and in like measure returned his love. Now, not to mention his daily resort to Ischia to see her, there were times not a few when Gianni, not being able to come by a boat, would swim across from Procida by night, that he might have sight, if of nought else, at least of the walls of her house. And while their love burned thus fervently, it so befell that one summer's day, as the damsel was all alone on the seashore, picking her way from rock to rock, detaching, as she went, shells from their beds with a knife, she came to a recess among the rocks, where for the sake, as well of the shade as of the comfort afforded by a spring of most cool water that was there, some Sicilian gallants, that were come from Naples, had put in with their felucca. Who, having taken note of the damsel, that she was very fair, and that she was not yet ware of them, and was alone, resolved to capture her, and carry her away; nor did they fail to give effect to their resolve; but, albeit she shrieked amain, they laid hands on her, and set her aboard their boat, and put to sea. Arrived at Calabria, they fell a wrangling as to whose the damsel should be, and in brief each claimed her for his own: wherefore, finding no means of coming to an agreement, and fearing that worse might befall them, and she bring misfortune upon them, they resolved with one accord to give her to Frederic, King of Sicily, who was then a young man, and took no small delight in commodities of that quality; and so, being come to Palermo, they did.

Marking her beauty, the King set great store by her; but as she was somewhat indisposed, he commanded that, till she was stronger, she should be lodged and tended in a very pretty villa that was in one of his gardens, which he called Cuba; and so 'twas done. The purloining of the damsel caused no small stir in Ischia, more especially because 'twas impossible to discover by whom she had been carried off. But Gianni, more concerned than any other, despairing of finding her in Ischia, and being apprised of the course the felucca had taken, equipped one himself, and put to sea, and in hot haste scoured the whole coast from Minerva to Scalea in Calabria, making everywhere diligent search for the damsel, and in Scalea learned that she had been taken by Sicilian mariners to Palermo. Whither, accordingly, he hied him with all speed; and there after long search discovering that she had been given to the King, who kept her at Cuba, he was sore troubled, insomuch that he now scarce ventured to hope that he should ever set eyes on her, not to speak of having her for his own, again. But still, holden by Love, and seeing that none there knew him, he sent the felucca away, and tarried there, and frequently passing by Cuba, he chanced one day to catch sight of her at a window, and was seen of her, to their great mutual satisfaction. And Gianni, taking note that the place was lonely, made up to her, and had such speech of her as he might, and being taught by her after what fashion he must proceed, if he would have further speech of her, he departed, but not till he had made himself thoroughly acquainted with the configuration of the place; and having waited until night was come and indeed far spent, he returned thither, and though the ascent was such that 'twould scarce have afforded lodgment to a woodpecker, won his way up and entered the garden, where, finding a pole, he set it against the window which the damsel had pointed out as hers, and thereby swarmed up easily enough.

The damsel had aforetime shewn herself somewhat distant towards him, being careful of her honour, but now deeming it already lost, she had bethought her that there was none to whom she might more worthily give herself than to him; and reckoning upon inducing him to carry her off, she had made up her mind to gratify his every desire; and to that end had left the window open that his ingress might be unimpeded. So, finding it open, Gianni softly entered, lay down beside the damsel, who was awake, and before they went further, opened to him all her mind, beseeching him most earnestly to take her thence, and carry her off. Gianni replied that there was nought that would give him so much pleasure, and that without fail, upon leaving her, he would make all needful arrangements for bringing her away when he next came. Whereupon with exceeding great delight they embraced one another, and plucked that boon than which Love has no greater to bestow; and having so done divers times, they unwittingly fell asleep in one another's arms.

Now towards daybreak the King, who had been greatly charmed with the damsel at first sight, happened to call her to mind, and feeling himself fit, resolved, notwithstanding the hour, to go lie with her a while; and so, attended by a few of his servants, he hied him privily to Cuba. Having entered the house, he passed (the door being softly opened) into the room in which he knew the damsel slept. A great blazing torch was borne before him, and so, as he bent his glance on the bed, he espied the damsel and Gianni lying asleep, naked and in one another's arms. Whereat he was seized with a sudden and vehement passion of wrath, insomuch that, albeit he said never a word, he could scarce refrain from slaying both of them there and then with a dagger that he had with him. Then, bethinking him that 'twere the depth of baseness in any man – not to say a king – to slay two naked sleepers, he mastered himself, and determined to do them to death in public and by fire. Wherefore, turning to a single companion that he had with him, he said: – "What thinkest thou of this base woman, in whom I had placed my hope?" And then he asked whether he knew the gallant, that had presumed to enter his house to do him such outrage and despite. Whereto the other replied that he minded not ever to have seen him. Thereupon the King hied him out of the room in a rage, and bade take the two lovers, naked as they were, and bind them, and, as soon as 'twas broad day, bring them to Palermo, and bind them back to back to a stake in the piazza, there to remain until tierce, that all might see them, after which they were to be burned, as they had deserved. And having so ordered, he went back to Palermo, and shut himself up in his room, very wroth.

No sooner was he gone than there came unto the two lovers folk not a few, who, having awakened them, did forthwith ruthlessly take and bind them: whereat, how they did grieve and tremble for their lives, and weep and bitterly bewail their fate, may readily be understood.

Pursuant to the King's commandment they were brought to Palermo, and bound to a stake in the piazza; and before their eyes faggots and fire were made ready to burn them at the hour appointed by the King. Great was the concourse of the folk of Palermo, both men and women, that came to see the two lovers, the men all agog to feast their eyes on the damsel, whom they lauded for shapeliness and loveliness, and no less did the women commend the gallant, whom in like manner they crowded to see, for the same qualities. Meanwhile the two hapless lovers, both exceeding shamefast, stood with bent heads bitterly bewailing their evil fortune, and momently expecting their death by the cruel fire. So they awaited the time appointed by the King; but their offence being bruited abroad, the tidings reached the ears of Ruggieri dell' Oria, a man of peerless worth, and at that time the King's admiral, who, being likewise minded to see them, came to the place where they were bound, and after gazing on the damsel and finding her very fair, turned to look at the gallant, whom with little trouble he recognized, and drawing nearer to him, he asked him if he were Gianni di Procida. Gianni raised his head, and recognizing the admiral, made answer: – "My lord, he, of whom you speak, I was; but I am now as good as no more." The admiral then asked him what it was that had brought him to such a pass. Whereupon: – "Love and the King's wrath," quoth Gianni. The admiral induced him to be more explicit, and having learned from him exactly how it had come about, was turning away, when Gianni called him back, saying: – "Oh! my lord, if so it may be, procure me one favour of him by whose behest I thus stand here." "What favour?" demanded Ruggieri. "I see," returned Gianni, "that die I must, and that right soon. I crave, then, as a favour, that, whereas this damsel and I, that have loved one another more dearly than life, are here set back to back, we may be set face to face, that I may have the consolation of gazing on her face as I depart." Ruggieri laughed as he replied: – "With all my heart. I will so order it that thou shalt see enough of her to tire of her." He then left him and charged the executioners to do nothing more without further order of the King; and being assured of their obedience, he hied him forthwith to the King, to whom, albeit he found him in a wrathful mood, he spared not to speak his mind, saying: – "Sire, wherein have they wronged thee, those two young folk, whom thou hast ordered to be burned down there in the piazza?" The King told him. Whereupon Ruggieri continued: – "Their offence does indeed merit such punishment, but not at thy hands, and if misdeeds should not go unpunished, services should not go unrewarded; nay, may warrant indulgence and mercy. Knowest thou who they are whom thou wouldst have burned?" The King signified that he did not. Whereupon Ruggieri: – "But I," quoth he, "am minded that thou shouldest know them, to the end that thou mayst know with what discretion thou surrenderest thyself to a transport of rage. The young man is the son of Landolfo di Procida, brother of Messer Gianni di Procida, to whom thou owest it that thou art lord and king of this island. The damsel is a daughter of Marin Bolgaro, whose might alone to-day prevents Ischia from throwing off thy yoke. Moreover, these young folk have long been lovers, and 'tis for that the might of Love constrained them, and not that they would do despite to thy lordship, that they have committed this offence, if indeed 'tis meet to call that an offence which young folk do for Love's sake. Wherefore, then, wouldst thou do them to death, when thou shouldest rather do them all cheer, and honour them with lordly gifts?" The King gave ear to Ruggieri's words, and being satisfied that he spoke sooth, repented him, not only of his evil purpose, but of what he had already done, and forthwith gave order to loose the two young folk from the stake, and bring them before him; and so 'twas done. And having fully apprised himself of their case, he saw fit to make them amends of the wrong he had done them with honours and largess. Wherefore he caused them to be splendidly arrayed, and being assured that they were both minded to wed, he himself gave Gianni his bride, and loading them with rich presents, sent them well content back to Ischia, where they were welcomed with all festal cheer, and lived long time thereafter to their mutual solace and delight.

Fifth Day

Novel VII

— Teodoro, being enamoured of Violante, daughter of Messer Amerigo, his lord, gets her with child, and is sentenced to the gallows; but while he is being scourged thither, he is recognized by his father, and being set at large, takes Violante to wife. —

WHILE THEY doubted whether the two lovers would be burned, the ladies were all fear and suspense; but when they heard of their deliverance, they all with one accord put on a cheerful countenance, praising God. The story ended, the queen ordained that the next should be told by Lauretta, who blithely thus began: –

Fairest ladies, what time good King Guglielmo ruled Sicily there dwelt on the island a gentleman, Messer Amerigo Abate da Trapani by name, who was well provided, as with other temporal goods, so also with children. For which cause being in need of servants, he took occasion of the appearance in Trapani waters of certain Genoese corsairs from the Levant, who, scouring the coast of Armenia, had captured not a few boys, to purchase of them some of these youngsters, supposing them to be Turks; among whom, albeit most shewed as mere shepherd boys, there was one, Teodoro, by name, whose less rustic mien seemed to betoken gentle blood. Who, though still treated as a slave, was suffered to grow up in the house with Messer Amerigo's children, and, nature getting the better of circumstance, bore himself with such grace and dignity that Messer Amerigo gladly gave him his freedom, and still deeming him to be a Turk, had him baptized and named Pietro, and made him his majordomo, and placed much trust in him. Now among the other children that grew up in Messer Amerigo's house was his fair and dainty daughter, Violante; and, as her father was in no hurry to give her in marriage, it so befell that she became enamoured of Pietro, but, for all her love and the great conceit she had of his qualities and conduct, she nevertheless was too shamefast to discover her passion to him. However, Love spared her the pains, for Pietro had cast many a furtive glance in her direction, and had grown so enamoured of her that 'twas never well with him except he saw her; but great was his fear lest any should detect his passion, for he deemed 'twould be the worse for him. The damsel, who was fain indeed of the sight of him, understood his case; and to encourage him dissembled not her exceeding great satisfaction. On which footing they remained a great while, neither venturing to say aught to the other, much as both longed to do so. But, while they both burned with a mutual flame, Fortune, as if their entanglement were of her preordaining, found means to banish the fear and hesitation that kept them tongue-tied.

Messer Amerigo possessed, a mile or so from Trapani, a goodly estate, to which he was wont not seldom to resort with his daughter and other ladies by way of recreation; and on one of these days, while there they tarried with Pietro, whom they had brought with them, suddenly, as will sometimes happen in summer, the sky became overcast with black clouds, insomuch that the lady and her companions, lest the storm should surprise them there, set out on their return to Trapani, making all the haste they might. But Pietro and the girl being young, and sped perchance by Love no less than by fear of the storm, completely outstripped her mother and the other ladies; and when they were gotten so far ahead as to be well-nigh out of sight of the lady and all the rest, the thunder burst upon them peal upon peal, hard upon which came a fall of hail very thick and close, from which the lady sought shelter in the house of a husbandman. Pietro and the damsel, finding no more convenient refuge, betook them to an old, and all but ruinous, and now deserted, cottage, which, however, still had a bit of roof left, whereunder they both took their stand in such close quarters, owing to the exiguity of the shelter, that they perforce touched one another. Which contact was the occasion that they gathered somewhat more courage to disclose their love; and so it was that Pietro began on this wise: – "Now would to God that this hail might never cease, that so I might stay here for ever!" "And well content were I," returned the damsel. And by and by their hands met, not without a tender pressure, and then they fell to embracing and so to kissing one another, while the hail continued. And not to dwell on every detail, the sky was not clear before they had known the last degree of love's felicity, and had taken thought how they might secretly enjoy one another in the future. The cottage being close to the city gate, they hied them thither, as soon as the storm was overpast, and having there awaited the lady, returned home with her. Nor, using all discretion, did they fail thereafter to meet from time to time in secret, to their no small solace; and the affair went so far that the damsel conceived, whereby they were both not a little disconcerted; insomuch that the damsel employed many artifices to arrest the course of nature, but to no effect. Wherefore Pietro, being in fear of his life, saw nothing for it but flight, and told her so. Whereupon: – "If thou leave me," quoth she, "I shall certainly kill myself." Much as he loved her, Pietro answered: – "Nay but, my lady, wherefore wouldst thou have me tarry here? Thy pregnancy will discover our offence: thou wilt be readily forgiven; but 'twill be my woeful lot to bear the penalty of thy sin and mine." "Pietro," returned the damsel, "too well will they wot of my offence, but be sure that, if thou confess not, none will ever wot of thine." Then quoth he: – "Since thou givest me this promise, I will stay; but mind thou keep it."

The damsel, who had done her best to keep her condition secret, saw at length by the increase of her bulk that 'twas impossible: wherefore one day most piteously bewailing herself, she made her avowal to her mother, and besought her to shield her from the consequences. Distressed beyond measure, the lady chid her severely, and then asked her how it had come to pass. The damsel, to screen Pietro, invented a story by which she put another complexion on the affair. The lady believed her, and, that her fall might not be discovered, took her off to one of their estates; where, the time of her delivery being come, and she, as women do in such a case, crying out for pain, it so befell that Messer Amerigo, whom the lady expected not, as indeed he was scarce ever wont, to come there, did so, having been out a hawking, and passing by the chamber where the damsel lay, marvelled to hear her cries, and forthwith entered, and asked what it meant. On sight of whom the lady rose and sorrowfully gave him her daughter's version of what had befallen her. But he, less credulous than his wife, averred that it could not be true that she knew not by whom she was pregnant, and was minded to know the whole truth: let the damsel confess and she might regain his favour; otherwise she must expect no mercy and prepare for death.

The lady did all she could to induce her husband to rest satisfied with what she had told him; but all to no purpose. Mad with rage, he rushed, drawn sword in hand, to his daughter's bedside (she, pending the parley, having given birth to a boy) and cried out: – "Declare whose this infant is, or forthwith thou diest." Overcome by fear of death, the damsel broke her promise to Pietro, and made a clean breast of all that had passed between him and her. Whereat the knight, grown fell with rage, could scarce refrain from slaying her. However, having given vent to his wrath in such words as it dictated, he remounted his horse and rode to Trapani, and there before one

Messer Currado, the King's lieutenant, laid information of the wrong done him by Pietro, in consequence whereof Pietro, who suspected nothing, was forthwith taken, and being put to the torture, confessed all. Some days later the lieutenant sentenced him to be scourged through the city, and then hanged by the neck; and Messer Amerigo, being minded that one and the same hour should rid the earth of the two lovers and their son (for to have compassed Pietro's death was not enough to appease his wrath), mingled poison and wine in a goblet, and gave it to one of his servants with a drawn sword, saying: – "Get thee with this gear to Violante, and tell her from me to make instant choice of one of these two deaths, either the poison or the steel; else, I will have her burned, as she deserves, in view of all the citizens; which done, thou wilt take the boy that she bore a few days ago, and beat his brains out against the wall, and cast his body for a prey to the dogs."

Hearing the remorseless doom thus passed by the angry father upon both his daughter and his grandson, the servant, prompt to do evil rather than good, hied him thence.

Now, as Pietro in execution of his sentence was being scourged to the gallows by the serjeants, 'twas so ordered by the leaders of the band that he passed by an inn, where were three noblemen of Armenia, sent by the king of that country as ambassadors to Rome, to treat with the Pope of matters of the highest importance, touching a crusade that was to be; who, having there alighted to rest and recreate them for some days, had received not a few tokens of honour from the nobles of Trapani, and most of all from Messer Amerigo. Hearing the tramp of Pietro's escort, they came to a window to see what was toward; and one of them, an aged man, and of great authority, Fineo by name, looking hard at Pietro, who was stripped from the waist up, and had his hands bound behind his back, espied on his breast a great spot of scarlet, not laid on by art, but wrought in the skin by operation of Nature, being such as the ladies here call a rose. Which he no sooner saw, than he was reminded of a son that had been stolen from him by corsairs on the coast of Lazistan some fifteen years before, nor had he since been able to hear tidings of him; and guessing the age of the poor wretch that was being scourged, he set it down as about what his son's would be, were he living, and, what with the mark and the age, he began to suspect that 'twas even his son, and bethought him that, if so, he would scarce as yet have forgotten his name or the speech of Armenia. Wherefore, as he was within earshot he called to him: – "Teodoro!" At the word Pietro raised his head: whereupon Fineo, speaking in Armenian, asked him: – "Whence and whose son art thou?" The serjeants, that were leading him, paused in deference to the great man, and so Pietro answered: – "Of Armenia was I, son of one Fineo, brought hither by folk I wot not of, when I was but a little child." Then Fineo, witting that in very truth 'twas the boy that he had lost, came down with his companions, weeping; and, all the serjeants making way, he ran to him, and embraced him, and doffing a mantle of richest texture that he wore, he prayed the captain of the band to be pleased to tarry there until he should receive orders to go forward, and was answered by the captain that he would willingly so wait.

Fineo already knew, for 'twas bruited everywhere, the cause for which Pietro was being led to the gallows; wherefore he straightway hied him with his companions and their retinue to Messer Currado, and said to him: – "Sir, this lad, whom you are sending to the gallows like a slave, is freeborn, and my son, and is ready to take to wife her whom, as 'tis said, he has deflowered; so please you, therefore, delay the execution until such time as it may be understood whether she be minded to have him for husband, lest, should she be so minded, you be found to have broken the law." Messer Currado marvelled to hear that Pietro was Fineo's son, and not without shame, albeit 'twas not his but Fortune's fault, confessed that 'twas even as Fineo said: and having caused Pietro to be taken home with all speed, and Messer Amerigo to be brought before him, told him the whole matter. Messer Amerigo, who supposed that by this time his daughter and grandson must be dead, was the saddest man in the world to think that 'twas by his deed, witting that, were the damsel still alive, all might very easily be set right: however, he sent post haste to his daughter's abode, revoking his orders, if they were not yet carried out. The servant, whom he had earlier despatched, had laid the sword and poison before the damsel, and, for that she was in no hurry to make her choice, was giving her foul words, and endeavouring to constrain her thereto, when the messenger arrived; but on hearing the injunction laid upon him by his lord, he desisted, and went back, and told him how things stood. Whereupon Messer Amerigo, much relieved, hied him to Fineo, and well-nigh weeping, and excusing himself for what had befallen, as best he knew how, craved his pardon, and professed himself well content to give Teodoro, so he were minded to have her, his daughter to wife. Fineo readily accepted his excuses, and made answer: – "'Tis my will that my son espouse your daughter, and, so he will not, let thy sentence passed upon him be carried out."

So Fineo and Messer Amerigo being agreed, while Teodoro still languished in fear of death, albeit he was glad at heart to have found his father, they questioned him of his will in regard of this matter.

When he heard that, if he would, he might have Violante to wife, Teodoro's delight was such that he seemed to leap from hell to paradise, and said that, if 'twas agreeable to them all, he should deem it the greatest of favours. So they sent to the damsel to learn her pleasure: who, having heard how it had fared, and was now like to fare, with Teodoro, albeit, saddest of women, she looked for nought but death, began at length to give some credence to their words, and to recover heart a little, and answered that, were she to follow the bent of her desire, nought that could happen would delight her more than to be Teodoro's wife; but nevertheless she would do as her father bade her.

So, all agreeing, the damsel was espoused with all pomp and festal cheer, to the boundless delight of all the citizens, and was comforted, and nurtured her little boy, and in no long time waxed more beautiful than ever before; and, her confinement being ended, she presented herself before Fineo, who was then about to quit Rome on his homeward journey, and did him such reverence as is due to a father. Fineo, mighty well pleased to have so fair a daughter-in-law, caused celebrate her nuptials most bravely and gaily, and received, and did ever thereafter entreat, her as his daughter.

And so he took her, not many days after the festivities were ended, with his son and little grandson, aboard a galley, and brought them to Lazistan, and there thenceforth the two lovers dwelt with him in easeful and lifelong peace.

Fifth Day
Novel VIII

— *Nastagio degli Onesti, loving a damsel of the Traversari family, by lavish expenditure gains not her love. At the instance of his kinsfolk he hies him to Chiassi, where he sees a knight hunt a damsel and slay her and cause her to be devoured by two dogs. He bids his kinsfolk and the lady that he loves to breakfast. During the meal the said damsel is torn in pieces before the eyes of the lady, who, fearing a like fate, takes Nastagio to husband.* —

LAURETTA WAS no sooner silent than thus at the queen's behest began Filomena: –
Sweet ladies, as in us pity has ever its meed of praise, even so Divine justice suffers not our cruelty to escape severe chastisement: the which that I may shew you, and thereby dispose you utterly to banish that passion from your souls, I am minded to tell you a story no less touching than delightsome.

In Ravenna, that most ancient city of Romagna, there dwelt of yore noblemen and gentlemen not a few, among whom was a young man, Nastagio degli Onesti by name, who by the death of his father and one of his uncles inherited immense wealth. Being without a wife, Nastagio, as 'tis the way with young men, became enamoured of a daughter of Messer Paolo Traversaro, a damsel of much higher birth than his, whose love he hoped to win by gifts and the like modes of courting, which, albeit they were excellent and fair and commendable, not only availed him not, but seemed rather to have the contrary effect, so harsh and ruthless and unrelenting did the beloved damsel shew herself towards him; for whether it was her uncommon beauty or her noble lineage that puffed her up, so haughty and disdainful was she grown that pleasure she had none either in him or in aught that pleased him. The burden of which disdain Nastagio found so hard to bear, that many a time, when he had made his moan, he longed to make away with himself. However he refrained therefrom, and many a time resolved to give her up altogether, or, if so he might, to hold her in despite, as she did him: but 'twas all in vain, for it seemed as if, the more his hope dwindled, the greater grew his love. And, as thus he continued, loving and spending inordinately, certain of his kinsfolk and friends, being apprehensive lest he should waste both himself and his substance, did many a time counsel and beseech him to depart Ravenna, and go tarry for a time elsewhere, that so he might at once cool his flame and reduce his charges. For a long while Nastagio answered their admonitions with banter; but as they continued to ply him with them, he grew weary of saying no so often, and promised obedience. Whereupon he equipped himself as if for a journey to France or Spain, or other distant parts, got on horseback and sallied forth of Ravenna, accompanied by not a few of his friends, and being come to a place called Chiassi, about three miles from Ravenna, he halted, and having sent for tents and pavilions, told his companions that there he meant to stay, and they might go back to Ravenna. So Nastagio pitched his camp, and there commenced to live after as fine and lordly a fashion as did ever any man, bidding divers of his friends from time to time to breakfast or sup with him, as he had been wont to do. Now it so befell that about the beginning of May, the season being very fine, he fell a brooding on the cruelty of his mistress, and, that his meditations might be the less disturbed, he bade all his servants leave him, and sauntered slowly, wrapt in thought, as far as the pinewood. Which he had threaded for a good half-mile, when, the fifth hour of the day being well-nigh past, yet he recking neither of food nor of aught else, 'twas as if he heard a woman wailing exceedingly and uttering most piercing shrieks: whereat, the train of his sweet melancholy being broken, he raised his head to see what was toward, and wondered to find himself in the pinewood; and saw, moreover, before him running through a grove, close set with underwood and brambles, towards the place where he was, a damsel most comely, stark naked, her hair dishevelled, and her flesh all torn by the briers and brambles, who wept and cried piteously for mercy; and at her flanks he saw two mastiffs, exceeding great and fierce, that ran hard upon her track, and not seldom came up with her and bit her cruelly; and in the rear he saw, riding a black horse, a knight sadly accoutred, and very wrathful of mien, carrying a rapier in his hand, and with despiteful, blood-curdling words threatening her with death. Whereat he was at once amazed and appalled, and then filled with compassion for the hapless lady, whereof was bred a desire to deliver her, if so he might, from such anguish and peril of death. Wherefore, as he was unarmed, he ran and took in lieu of a cudgel a branch of a tree, with which he prepared to encounter the dogs and the knight. Which the knight observing, called to him before he was come to close quarters, saying: – "Hold off, Nastagio, leave the dogs and me alone to deal with this vile woman as she has deserved." And, even as he spoke, the dogs gripped the damsel so hard on either flank that they arrested her flight, and the knight, being come up, dismounted. Whom Nastagio approached, saying: – "I know not who thou art, that knowest me so well, but thus much I tell thee: 'tis a gross outrage for an armed knight to go about to kill a naked woman, and set his dogs upon her as if she were a wild beast: rest assured that I shall do all I can to protect her." Whereupon: – "Nastagio," replied the knight, "of the same city as thou was I, and thou wast yet a little lad when I, Messer Guido degli Anastagi by name, being far more enamoured of this damsel than thou art now of her of the Traversari, was by her haughtiness and cruelty brought to so woeful a pass that one day in a fit of despair I slew myself with this rapier which thou seest in my hand; for which cause I am condemned to the eternal pains. Nor was it long after my death that she, who exulted therein over measure, also died, and for that she repented her not of her cruelty and the joy she had of my sufferings, for which she took not blame to herself, but merit, was likewise condemned to the pains of hell. Nor had she sooner made her descent, than for her pain and mine 'twas ordained, that she should flee before me, and that I, who so loved her, should pursue her, not as my beloved lady, but as my mortal enemy, and so, as often as I come up with her, I slay her with this same rapier with which I slew myself, and having ripped her up by the back, I take out that hard and cold heart, to which neither love nor pity had ever access, and therewith her other inward parts, as thou shalt forthwith see, and cast them to these dogs to eat. And in no long time, as the just and mighty God decrees, she rises even as if she had not died, and recommences her dolorous flight, I and the dogs pursuing her. And it so falls out that every Friday about this hour I here come up with her, and slaughter her as thou shalt see; but ween not that we rest on other days; for there are other places in which I overtake her, places in which she used, or devised how she might use, me cruelly; on which wise, changed as thou seest from her lover into her foe, I am to pursue her for years as many as the months during which she shewed herself harsh to me. Wherefore leave me to execute the decree of the Divine justice, and presume not to oppose that which thou mayst not avail to withstand."

Affrighted by the knight's words, insomuch that there was scarce a hair on his head but stood on end, Nastagio shrank back, still gazing on the hapless damsel, and waited all a tremble to see what the knight would do. Nor had he long to wait; for the knight, as soon as he had done speaking, sprang, rapier in hand, like a mad dog upon the damsel, who, kneeling, while the two mastiffs gripped her tightly, cried him mercy; but the knight, thrusting with all his force, struck her between the breasts, and ran her clean through the body. Thus stricken, the damsel fell forthwith prone on the ground sobbing and shrieking: whereupon the knight drew forth a knife, and having therewith opened her in the back, took out the heart and all the circumjacent parts, and threw them to the two mastiffs, who, being famished, forthwith devoured them. And in no long time the damsel, as if nought thereof had happened, started to her feet, and took to flight towards the sea, pursued, and ever and anon bitten, by the dogs, while the knight, having gotten him to horse again, followed them as before, rapier in hand; and so fast sped they that they were quickly lost to Nastagio's sight.

Long time he stood musing on what he had seen, divided between pity and terror, and then it occurred to him that, as this passed every Friday, it might avail him not a little. So, having marked the place, he rejoined his servants, and in due time thereafter sent for some of his kinsfolk and friends, and said to them: – "'Tis now a long while that you urge me to give up loving this lady that is no friend to me, and therewith make an end of my extravagant way of living; and I am now ready so to do, provided you procure me one favour, to wit, that next Friday Messer Paolo Traversaro, and his wife and daughter, and all the ladies, their kinswomen, and as many other ladies as you may be pleased to bid, come hither to breakfast with me: when you will see for yourselves the reason why I so desire." A small matter this seemed to them; and so, on their return to Ravenna, they lost no time in conveying Nastagio's message to his intended guests: and, albeit she was hardly persuaded, yet in the end the damsel that Nastagio loved came with the rest.

Nastagio caused a lordly breakfast to be prepared, and had the tables set under the pines about the place where he had witnessed the slaughter of the cruel lady; and in ranging the ladies and gentlemen at table he so ordered it, that the damsel whom he loved was placed opposite the spot where it should be enacted. The last course was just served, when the despairing cries of the hunted damsel became audible to all, to their no small amazement; and each asking, and none knowing, what it might import, up they all started intent to see what was toward; and perceived the suffering damsel, and the knight and the dogs, who in a trice were in their midst. They hollaed amain to dogs and knight, and not a few advanced to succour the damsel: but the words of the knight, which were such as he had used to Nastagio, caused them to fall back, terror-stricken and lost in amazement. And when the knight proceeded to do as he had done before, all the ladies that were there, many of whom were of kin to the suffering damsel and to the knight, and called to mind his love and death, wept as bitterly as if 'twere their own case.

When 'twas all over, and the lady and the knight had disappeared, the strange scene set those that witnessed it pondering many and divers matters: but among them all none was so appalled as the cruel damsel that Nastagio loved, who, having clearly seen and heard all that had passed, and being ware that it touched her more nearly than any other by reason of the harshness that she had ever shewn to Nastagio, seemed already to be fleeing from her angered lover, and to have the mastiffs on her flanks. And so great was her terror that, lest a like fate should befall her, she converted her aversion into affection, and as soon as occasion served, which was that very night, sent a trusty chambermaid privily to Nastagio with a request that he would be pleased to come to her, for that she was ready in all respects to pleasure him to the full. Nastagio made answer that he was greatly flattered, but that he was minded with her consent to have his pleasure of her in an honourable way, to wit, by marrying her. The damsel, who knew that none but herself was to blame that she was not already Nastagio's wife, made answer that she consented. Wherefore by her own mouth she acquainted her father and mother that she agreed to marry Nastagio; and, they heartily approving her choice, Nastagio wedded her on the ensuing Sunday, and lived happily with her many a year. Nor was it in her instance alone that this terror was productive of good: on the contrary, it so wrought among the ladies of Ravenna that they all became, and have ever since been, much more compliant with men's desires than they had been wont to be.

Fifth Day

Novel IX

— Federigo degli Alberighi loves and is not loved in return: he wastes his substance by lavishness until nought is left but a single falcon, which, his lady being come to see him at his house, he gives her to eat: she, knowing his case, changes her mind, takes him to husband and makes him rich. —

SO ENDED FILOMENA; and the queen, being ware that besides herself only Dioneo (by virtue of his privilege) was left to speak, said with gladsome mien: –

'Tis now for me to take up my parable; which, dearest ladies, I will do with a story like in some degree to the foregoing, and that, not only that you may know how potent are your charms to sway the gentle heart, but that you may also learn how upon fitting occasions to make bestowal of your guerdons of your own accord, instead of always waiting for the guidance of Fortune, which most times, not wisely, but without rule or measure, scatters her gifts.

You are then to know, that Coppo di Borghese Domenichi, a man that in our day was, and perchance still is, had in respect and great reverence in our city, being not only by reason of his noble lineage, but, and yet more, for manners and merit most illustrious and worthy of eternal renown, was in his old age not seldom wont to amuse himself by discoursing of things past with his neighbours and other folk; wherein he had not his match for accuracy and compass of memory and concinnity of speech. Among other good stories, he would tell, how that there was of yore in Florence a gallant named Federigo di Messer Filippo Alberighi, who for feats of arms and courtesy had not his peer in Tuscany; who, as is the common lot of gentlemen, became enamoured of a lady named Monna Giovanna, who in her day held rank among the fairest and most elegant ladies of Florence; to gain whose love he jousted, tilted, gave entertainments, scattered largess, and in short set no bounds to his expenditure. However the lady, no less virtuous than fair, cared not a jot for what he did for her sake, nor yet for him.

Spending thus greatly beyond his means, and making nothing, Federigo could hardly fail to come to lack, and was at length reduced to such poverty that he had nothing left but a little estate, on the rents of which he lived very straitly, and a single falcon, the best in the world. The estate was at Campi, and thither, deeming it no longer possible for him to live in the city as he desired, he repaired, more in love than ever before; and there, in complete seclusion, diverting himself with hawking, he bore his poverty as patiently as he might.

Now, Federigo being thus reduced to extreme poverty, it so happened that one day Monna Giovanna's husband, who was very rich, fell ill, and, seeing that he was nearing his end, made his will, whereby he left his estate to his son, who was now growing up, and in the event of his death without lawful heir named Monna Giovanna, whom he dearly loved, heir in his stead; and having made these dispositions he died.

Monna Giovanna, being thus left a widow, did as our ladies are wont, and repaired in the summer to one of her estates in the country which lay very near to that of Federigo. And so it befell that the urchin began to make friends with Federigo, and to shew a fondness for hawks and dogs, and having seen Federigo's falcon fly not a few times, took a singular fancy to him, and greatly longed to have him for his own, but still did not dare to ask him of Federigo, knowing that Federigo prized him so much. So the matter stood when by chance the boy fell sick; whereby the mother was sore distressed, for he was her only son, and she loved him as much as might be, insomuch that all day long she was beside him, and ceased not to comfort him, and again and again asked him if there were aught that he wished for, imploring him to say the word, and, if it might by any means be had, she would assuredly do her utmost to procure it for him. Thus repeatedly exhorted, the boy said: – "Mother mine, do but get me Federigo's falcon, and I doubt not I shall soon be well." Whereupon the lady was silent a while, bethinking her what she should do. She knew that Federigo had long loved her, and had never had so much as a single kind look from her: wherefore she said to herself: – How can I send or go to beg of him this falcon, which by what I hear is the best that ever flew, and moreover is his sole comfort? And how could I be so unfeeling as to seek to deprive a gentleman of the one solace that is now left him? And so, albeit she very well knew that she might have the falcon for the asking, she was perplexed, and knew not what to say, and gave her son no answer. At length, however, the love she bore the boy carried the day, and she made up her mind, for his contentment, come what might, not to send, but to go herself and fetch him the falcon. So: – "Be of good cheer, my son," she said, "and doubt not thou wilt soon be well; for I promise thee that the very first thing that I shall do tomorrow morning will be to go and fetch thee the falcon." Whereat the child was so pleased that he began to mend that very day.

On the morrow the lady, as if for pleasure, hied her with another lady to Federigo's little house, and asked to see him. 'Twas still, as for some days past, no weather for hawking, and Federigo was in his garden, busy about some small matters which needed to be set right there. When he heard that Monna Giovanna was at the door, asking to see him, he was not a little surprised and pleased, and hied him to her with all speed. As soon as she saw him, she came forward to meet him with womanly grace, and having received his respectful salutation, said to him: – "Good morrow, Federigo," and continued: – "I am come to requite thee for what thou hast lost by loving me more than thou shouldst: which compensation is this, that I and this lady that accompanies me will breakfast with thee without ceremony this morning." "Madam," Federigo replied with all humility, "I mind not ever to have lost aught by loving you, but rather to have been so much profited that, if I ever deserved well in aught, 'twas to your merit that I owed it, and to the love that I bore you. And of a surety had I still as much to spend as I have spent in the past, I should not prize it so much as this visit you so frankly pay me, come as you are to one who can afford you but a sorry sort of hospitality." Which said, with some confusion, he bade her welcome to his house, and then led her into his garden, where, having none else to present to her by way of companion, he said: – "Madam, as there is none other here, this good woman, wife of this husbandman, will bear you company, while I go to have the table set." Now, albeit his poverty was extreme, yet he had not known as yet how sore was the need to which his extravagance had reduced him; but this morning 'twas brought home to him, for that he could find nought wherewith to do honour to the lady, for love of whom he had done the honours of his house to men without number: wherefore, distressed beyond measure, and inwardly cursing his evil fortune, he sped hither and thither like one beside himself, but never a coin found he, nor yet aught to pledge. Meanwhile it grew late, and sorely he longed that the lady might not leave his house altogether unhonoured, and yet to crave help of his own husbandman was more than his pride could brook. In these desperate straits his glance happened to fall on his brave falcon on his perch in his little parlour. And so, as a last resource, he took him, and finding him plump, deemed that he would make a dish meet for such a lady. Wherefore, without thinking twice about it, he wrung the bird's neck, and caused his maid forthwith pluck him and set him on a spit, and roast him carefully; and having still some spotless table linen, he had the table laid therewith, and with a cheerful countenance hied him back to his lady in the garden, and told her that such breakfast as he could give her was ready. So the lady and her companion rose and came to table, and there, with Federigo, who waited on them most faithfully, ate the brave falcon, knowing not what they ate.

When they were risen from table, and had dallied a while in gay converse with him, the lady deemed it time to tell the reason of her visit: wherefore, graciously addressing Federigo, thus began she: – "Federigo, by what thou rememberest of thy past life and my virtue, which, perchance, thou hast deemed harshness and cruelty, I doubt not thou must marvel at my presumption, when thou hearest the main purpose of my visit; but if thou hadst sons, or hadst had them, so that thou mightest know the full force of the love that is borne them, I should make no doubt that thou wouldst hold me in part excused. Nor, having a son, may I, for that thou hast none, claim exemption from the laws to which all other mothers are subject, and, being thus bound to own their sway, I must, though fain were I not, and though 'tis neither meet nor right, crave of thee that which I know thou dost of all things and with justice prize most highly, seeing that this extremity of thy adverse fortune has left thee nought else wherewith to delight, divert and console thee; which gift is no other than thy falcon, on which my boy has so set his heart that, if I bring him it not, I fear lest he grow so much worse of the malady that he has, that thereby it may come to pass that I lose him. And so, not for the love which thou dost bear me, and which may nowise bind thee, but for that nobleness of temper, whereof in courtesy more conspicuously than in aught else thou hast given proof, I implore thee that thou be pleased to give me the bird, that thereby I may say that I have kept my son alive, and thus made him for aye thy debtor."

No sooner had Federigo apprehended what the lady wanted, than, for grief that 'twas not in his power to serve her, because he had given her the falcon to eat, he fell a weeping in her presence, before he could so much as utter a word. At first the lady supposed that 'twas only because he was loath to part with the brave falcon that he wept, and as good as made up her mind that he would refuse her: however, she awaited with patience Federigo's answer, which was on this wise: – "Madam, since it pleased God that I should set my affections upon you there have been matters not a few, in which to my sorrow I have deemed Fortune adverse to me; but they have all been trifles in comparison of the trick that she now plays me: the which I shall never forgive her, seeing that you are come here to my poor house, where, while I was rich, you deigned not to come, and ask a trifling favour of me, which she has put it out of my power to grant: how 'tis so, I will briefly tell you. When I learned that you, of your grace, were minded to breakfast with me, having respect to your high dignity and desert, I deemed it due and seemly that in your honour I should regale you, to the best of my power, with fare of a more excellent quality than is commonly set before others; and, calling to mind the falcon which you now ask of me, and his excellence, I judged him meet food for you, and so you have had him roasted on the trencher this morning; and well indeed I thought I had bestowed him; but, as now I see that you would fain have had him in another guise, so mortified am I that I am not able to serve you, that I doubt I shall never know peace of mind more." In witness whereof he had the feathers and feet and beak of the bird brought in and laid before her.

The first thing the lady did, when she had heard Federigo's story, and seen the relics of the bird, was to chide him that he had killed so fine a falcon to furnish a woman with a breakfast; after which the magnanimity of her host, which poverty had been and was powerless to impair, elicited no small share of inward commendation. Then, frustrate of her hope of possessing the falcon, and doubting of her son's recovery, she took her leave with the heaviest of hearts, and hied her back to the boy: who, whether for fretting, that he might not have the falcon, or by the unaided energy of his disorder, departed this life not many days after, to the exceeding great grief of his mother. For a while she would do nought but weep and bitterly bewail herself; but being still young, and left very wealthy, she was often urged by her brothers to marry again, and though she would rather have not done so, yet being importuned, and remembering Federigo's high desert, and the magnificent generosity with which he had finally killed his falcon to do her honour, she said to her brothers: – "Gladly, with your consent, would I remain a widow, but if you will not be satisfied except I take a husband, rest assured that none other will I ever take save Federigo degli Alberighi." Whereupon her brothers derided her, saying: – "Foolish woman, what is't thou sayst? How shouldst thou want Federigo, who has not a thing in the world?" To whom she answered: – "My brothers, well wot I that 'tis as you say; but I had rather have a man without wealth than wealth without a man." The brothers, perceiving that her mind was made up, and knowing Federigo for a good man and true, poor though he was, gave her to him with all her wealth. And so Federigo, being mated with such a wife, and one that he had so much loved, and being very wealthy to boot, lived happily, keeping more exact accounts, to the end of his days.

Fifth Day
Novel X

— *Pietro di Vinciolo goes from home to sup: his wife brings a boy into the house to bear her company: Pietro returns, and she hides her gallant under a hen-coop: Pietro explains that in the house of Ercolano, with whom he was to have supped, there was discovered a young man bestowed there by Ercolano's wife: the lady thereupon censures Ercolano's wife: but unluckily an ass treads on the fingers of the boy that is hidden under the hen-coop, so that he cries for pain: Pietro runs to the place, sees him, and apprehends the trick played on him by his wife, which nevertheless he finally condones, for that he is not himself free from blame. —*

WHEN THE QUEEN had done speaking, and all had praised God that He had worthily rewarded Federigo, Dioneo, who never waited to be bidden, thus began: –

I know not whether I am to term it a vice accidental and superinduced by bad habits in us mortals, or whether it be a fault seated in nature, that we are more prone to laugh at things dishonourable than at good deeds, and that more especially when they concern not ourselves. However, as the sole scope of all my efforts has been and still shall be to dispel your melancholy, and in lieu thereof to minister to you laughter and jollity; therefore, enamoured my damsels, albeit the ensuing story is not altogether free from matter that is scarce seemly, yet, as it may afford you pleasure, I shall not fail to relate it; premonishing you my hearers, that you take it with the like discretion as when, going into your gardens, you stretch forth your delicate hands and cull the roses, leaving the thorns alone: which, being interpreted, means that you will leave the caitiff husband to abide in sorry plight with his dishonour, and will gaily laugh at the amorous wiles or his wife, and commiserate her unfortunate gallant, when occasion requires.

'Tis no great while since there dwelt at Perugia a rich man named Pietro di Vinciolo, who rather, perchance, to blind others and mitigate the evil repute in which he was held by the citizens of Perugia, than for any desire to wed, took a wife: and such being his motive, Fortune provided him with just such a spouse as he merited. For the wife of his choice was a stout, red-haired young woman, and so hot-blooded that two husbands would have been more to her mind than one, whereas one fell to her lot that gave her only a subordinate place in his regard. Which she perceiving, while she knew herself to be fair and lusty, and felt herself to be gamesome and fit, waxed very wroth, and now and again had high words with her husband, and led but a sorry life with him at most times. Then, seeing that thereby she was more like to fret herself than to dispose her husband to conduct less base, she said to herself: – This poor creature deserts me to go walk in pattens in the dry; wherefore it shall go hard but I will bring another aboard the ship for the wet weather. I married him, and brought him a great and goodly dowry, knowing that he was a man, and supposing him to have the desires which men have and ought to have; and had I not deemed him to be a man, I should never have married him. He knew me to be a woman: why then took he me to wife, if women were not to his mind? 'Tis not to be endured. Had I not been minded to live in the world, I had become a nun; and being minded there to live, as I am, if I am to wait until I have pleasure or solace of him, I shall wait perchance until I am old; and then, too late, I shall bethink me to my sorrow that I have wasted my youth; and as to the way in which I should seek its proper solace I need no better teacher and guide than him, who finds his delight where I should find mine, and finds it to his own condemnation, whereas in me 'twere commendable. 'Tis but the laws that I shall set at nought, whereas he sets both them and Nature herself at nought.

So the good lady reasoned, and peradventure more than once; and then, casting about how she might privily compass her end, she made friends with an old beldam, that shewed as a veritable Santa Verdiana, foster-mother of vipers, who was ever to be seen going to pardonings with a parcel of paternosters in her hand, and talked of nothing but the lives of the holy Fathers, and the wounds of St. Francis, and was generally reputed a saint; to whom in due time she opened her whole mind. "My daughter," replied the beldam, "God, who knows all things, knows that thou wilt do very rightly indeed: were it for no other reason, 'twould be meet for thee and every other young woman so to do, that the heyday of youth be not wasted; for there is no grief like that of knowing that it has been wasted. And what the devil are we women fit for when we are old except to pore over the cinders on the hearth? The which if any know, and may attest it, 'tis I, who, now that I am old, call to mind the time that I let slip from me, not without most sore and bitter and fruitless regret: and albeit 'twas not all wasted, for I would not have thee think that I was entirely without sense, yet I did not make the best use of it: whereof when I bethink me, and that I am now, even as thou seest me, such a hag that never a spark of fire may I hope to get from any, God knows how I rue it. Now with men 'tis otherwise: they are born meet for a thousand uses, not for this alone; and the more part of them are of much greater consequence in old age than in youth: but women are fit for nought but this, and 'tis but for that they bear children that they are cherished. Whereof, if not otherwise, thou mayst assure thyself, if thou do but consider that we are ever ready for it; which is not the case with men; besides which, one woman will tire out many men without being herself tired out. Seeing then that 'tis for this we are born, I tell thee again that thou wilt do very rightly to give thy husband thy loaf for his cake, that in thy old age thy soul may have no cause of complaint against thy flesh. Every one has just as much of this life as he appropriates: and this is especially true of women, whom therefore it behoves, much more than men, to seize the moment as it flies: indeed, as thou mayst see for thyself, when we grow old neither husband, nor any other man will spare us a glance; but, on the contrary, they banish us to the kitchen, there to tell stories to the cat, and to count the pots and pans; or, worse, they make rhymes about us: – 'To the damsel dainty bits; to the beldam ague-fits;' and such-like catches. But to make no more words about it, I tell thee at once that there is no person in the world to whom thou couldst open thy mind with more advantage than to me; for there is no gentleman so fine but I dare speak my mind to him, nor any so harsh and forbidding but I know well how to soften him and fashion him to my will. Tell me only what thou wouldst have, and leave the rest to me: but one word more: I pray thee to have me in kindly remembrance, for that I am poor; and thou shalt henceforth go shares with me in all my indulgences and every paternoster that I say, that God may make thereof light and tapers for thy dead:" wherewith she ended.

So the lady came to an understanding with the beldam, that, as soon as she set eyes on a boy that often came along that street, and of whom the lady gave her a particular description, she would know what she was to do: and thereupon the lady gave her a chunk of salt meat, and bade her God-speed. The beldam before long smuggled into the lady's chamber the boy of whom she had spoken, and not long after another, such being the humour of the lady, who, standing in perpetual dread of her husband, was disposed, in this particular, to make the most of her opportunities. And one of these days, her husband being to sup in the evening with a friend named Ercolano, the lady bade the beldam bring her a boy as pretty and dainty as was to be found in Perugia; and so the beldam forthwith did. But the lady and the boy being set at table to sup, lo, Pietro's voice was heard at the door, bidding open to him. Whereupon the lady gave herself up for dead; but being fain, if she might, to screen the boy, and knowing not where else to convey or conceal him, bestowed him under a hen-coop that stood in a veranda hard by the chamber in which they were supping, and threw over it a sorry mattress that she had that day emptied of its straw; which done she hastened to open the door to her husband; saying to him as he entered: – "You have gulped your supper mighty quickly to-night." Whereto Pietro replied: – "We have not so much as tasted it." "How so?" enquired the lady. "I will tell thee," said Pietro. "No sooner were we set at table, Ercolano, his wife, and I, than we heard a sneeze close to us, to which, though 'twas repeated, we paid no heed; but as the sneezer continued to sneeze a third, a fourth, a fifth, and many another time to boot, we all began to wonder, and Ercolano, who was somewhat out of humour with his wife, because she had kept us a long time at the door before she opened it, burst out in a sort of rage with: – 'What means this? Who is't that thus sneezes?' and made off to a stair hard by, beneath which and close to its foot was a wooden closet, of the sort which, when folk are furnishing their houses, they commonly cause to be placed there, to stow things in upon occasion. And as it seemed to him that the sneezing proceeded thence, he undid the wicket, and no sooner had he opened it than out flew never so strong a stench of brimstone; albeit we had already been saluted by a whiff of it, and complained thereof, but had been put off by the lady with: – "Tis but that a while ago I bleached my veils with brimstone, having sprinkled it on a dish, that they might catch its fumes, which dish I then placed under the stair, so that it still smells a little.'

"However the door being now, as I have said, open, and the smoke somewhat less dense, Ercolano, peering in, espied the fellow that had sneezed, and who still kept sneezing, being thereto constrained by the pungency of the brimstone. And for all he sneezed, yet was he by this time so well-nigh choked with the brimstone that he was like neither to sneeze nor to do aught else again. As soon as he caught sight of him, Ercolano bawled out: – 'Now see I, Madam, why it was that a while ago, when we came here, we were kept waiting so long at the gate before 'twas opened; but woe betide me for the rest of my days, if I pay you not out.' Whereupon the lady, perceiving that her offence was discovered, ventured no excuse, but fled from the table, whither I know not. Ercolano, ignoring his wife's flight, bade the sneezer again and again to come forth; but he, being by this time fairly spent, budged not an inch for aught that Ercolano said. Wherefore Ercolano caught him by one of his feet, and dragged him forth, and ran off for a knife with intent to kill him; but I, standing in fear of the Signory on my own account, got up and would not suffer him to kill the fellow or do him any hurt, and for his better protection raised the alarm, whereby some of the neighbours came up and took the lad, more dead than alive, and bore him off, I know not whither. However, our supper being thus rudely interrupted, not only have not gulped it, but I have not so much as tasted it, as I said before!"

Her husband's story shewed his wife that there were other ladies as knowing as she, albeit misfortune might sometimes overtake them and gladly would she have spoken out in defence of Ercolano's wife, but, thinking that, by censuring another's sin, she would secure more scope for her own, she launched out on this wise: – "Fine doings indeed, a right virtuous and saintly lady she must be: here is the loyalty of an honest woman, and one to whom I had lief have confessed, so spiritual I deemed her; and the worst of it is that, being no longer young, she sets a rare example to those that are so. Curses on the hour that she came into the world: curses upon her that she make not away with herself, basest, most faithless of women that she must needs be, the reproach of her sex, the opprobrium of all the ladies of this city, to cast aside all regard for her honour, her marriage vow, her reputation before the world, and, lost to all sense of shame, to scruple not to bring disgrace upon a man so worthy, a citizen so honourable, a husband by whom she was so well treated, ay, and upon herself to boot! By my hope of salvation no mercy should be shewn to such women; they should pay the penalty with their lives; to the fire with them while they yet live, and let them be burned to ashes." Then, calling to mind the lover that she had close at hand in the hen-coop, she fell to coaxing Pietro to get him to bed, for the hour grew late. Pietro, who was more set on eating than sleeping, only asked whether there was aught he might have by way of supper. "Supper, forsooth!" replied the lady. "Ay, of course 'tis our way to make much of supper when thou art not at home. As if I were Ercolano's wife! Now, wherefore tarry longer? Go, get thy night's rest: 'twere far better for thee."

Now so it was that some of Pietro's husbandmen had come to the house that evening with divers things from the farm, and had put up their asses in a stable that adjoined the veranda, but had neglected to water them; and one of the asses being exceeding thirsty, got his head out of the halter and broke loose from the stable, and went about nosing everything, if haply he might come by water: whereby he came upon the hen-coop, beneath which was the boy; who, being constrained to stand on all fours, had the fingers of one hand somewhat protruding from under the hen-coop; and so as luck or rather ill-luck would have it, the ass trod on them; whereat, being sorely hurt, he set up a great howling, much to the surprise of Pietro, who perceived that 'twas within his house. So forth he came, and hearing the boy still moaning and groaning, for the ass still kept his hoof hard down on the fingers, called out: – "Who is there?" and ran to the hen-coop and raised it, and espied the fellow, who, besides the pain that the crushing of his fingers by the ass's hoof occasioned him, trembled in every limb for fear that Pietro should do him a mischief. He was one that Pietro had long been after for his foul purposes: so Pietro, recognizing him, asked him: – "What dost thou here?" The boy making no answer, save to beseech him for the love of God to do him no hurt, Pietro continued: – "Get up, have no fear that I shall hurt thee; but tell me: – How, and for what cause comest thou to be here?" The boy then confessed everything. Whereupon Pietro, as elated by the discovery as his wife was distressed, took him by the hand; and led him into the room where the lady in the extremity of terror awaited him; and, having seated himself directly in front of her, said: – "'Twas but a moment ago that thou didst curse Ercolano's wife, and averred that she ought to be burned, and that she was the reproach of your sex: why saidst thou not, of thyself? Or, if thou wast not minded to accuse thyself, how hadst thou the effrontery to censure her, knowing that thou hadst done even as she? Verily 'twas for no other reason than that ye are all fashioned thus, and study to cover your own misdeeds with the delinquencies of others: would that fire might fall from heaven and burn you all, brood of iniquity that ye are!"

The lady, marking that in the first flush of his wrath he had given her nothing worse than hard words, and discerning, as she thought, that he was secretly overjoyed to hold so beautiful a boy by the hand, took heart of grace and said: – "I doubt not indeed that thou wouldst be well pleased that fire should fall from heaven and devour us all, seeing that thou art as fond of us as a dog is of the stick, though by the Holy Rood thou wilt be disappointed; but I would fain have a little argument with thee, to know whereof thou complainest. Well indeed were it with me, didst thou but place me on an equality with Ercolano's wife, who is an old sanctimonious hypocrite, and has of him all that she wants, and is cherished by him as a wife should be:

but that is not my case. For, granted that thou givest me garments and shoes to my mind, thou knowest how otherwise ill bested I am, and how long it is since last thou didst lie with me; and far liefer had I go barefoot and in rags, and have thy benevolence abed, than have all that I have, and be treated as thou dost treat me. Understand me, Pietro, be reasonable; consider that I am a woman like other women, with the like craving; whereof if thou deny me the gratification, 'tis no blame to me that I seek it elsewhere; and at least I do thee so much honour as not forgather with stable-boys or scurvy knaves."

Pietro perceived that she was like to continue in this vein the whole night: wherefore, indifferent as he was to her, he said: – "Now, Madam, no more of this; in the matter of which thou speakest I will content thee; but of thy great courtesy let us have something to eat by way of supper; for, methinks, the boy, as well as I, has not yet supped." "Ay, true enough," said the lady, "he has not supped; for we were but just sitting down to table to sup, when, beshrew thee, thou madest thy appearance." "Go then," said Pietro, "get us some supper; and by and by I will arrange this affair in such a way that thou shalt have no more cause of complaint." The lady, perceiving that her husband was now tranquil, rose, and soon had the table laid again and spread with the supper which she had ready; and so they made a jolly meal of it, the caitiff husband, the lady and the boy. What after supper Pietro devised for their mutual satisfaction has slipped from my memory. But so much as this I know, that on the morrow as he wended his way to the piazza, the boy would have been puzzled to say, whether of the twain, the wife or the husband, had had the most of his company during the night. But this I would say to you, dear my ladies, that whoso gives you tit, why, just give him tat; and if you cannot do it at once, why, bear it in mind until you can, that even as the ass gives, so he may receive.

Dioneo's story, whereat the ladies laughed the less for shamefastness rather than for disrelish, being ended, the queen, taking note that the term of her sovereignty was come, rose to her feet, and took off the laurel wreath and set it graciously upon Elisa's head, saying: – "Madam, 'tis now your turn to bear sway." The dignity accepted, Elisa followed in all respects the example of her predecessors: she first conferred with the seneschal, and directed him how meetly to order all things during the time of her sovereignty; which done to the satisfaction of the company: – "Ofttimes," quoth she, "have we heard how with bright sallies, and ready retorts, and sudden devices, not a few have known how to repugn with apt checks the bites of others, or to avert imminent perils; and because 'tis an excellent argument, and may be profitable, I ordain that to-morrow, God helping us, the following be the rule of our discourse; to wit, that it be of such as by some sprightly sally have repulsed an attack, or by some ready retort or device have avoided loss, peril or scorn." The rule being heartily approved by all, the queen rose and dismissed them till supper-time. So the honourable company, seeing the queen risen, rose all likewise, and as their wont was, betook them to their diversions as to each seemed best. But when the cicalas had hushed their chirping, all were mustered again for supper; and having blithely feasted, they all addressed them to song and dance. And the queen, while Emilia led a dance, called for a song from Dioneo, who at once came out with: – 'Monna Aldruda, come perk up thy mood, a piece of glad tidings I bring thee.' Whereat all the ladies fell a laughing, and most of all the queen, who bade him give them no more of that, but sing another. Quoth Dioneo: – "Madam, had I a tabret, I would sing: – 'Up with your smock, Monna Lapa!' or: – 'Oh! the greensward under the olive!' Or perchance you had liefer I should give you: – 'Woe is me, the wave of the sea!' But no tabret have I: wherefore choose which of these others you will have. Perchance you would like: – 'Now hie thee to us forth, that so it may be cut, as May the fields about.'" "No," returned the queen, "give us another." "Then," said Dioneo, "I will sing: – 'Monna Simona, embarrel, embarrel. Why, 'tis not the month of

October.'" "Now a plague upon thee," said the queen, with a laugh; "give us a proper song, wilt thou? for we will have none of these." "Never fear, Madam," replied Dioneo; "only say which you prefer. I have more than a thousand songs by heart. Perhaps you would like: – 'This my little covert, make I ne'er it overt'; or: – 'Gently, gently, husband mine'; or: – 'A hundred pounds were none too high a price for me a cock to buy.'" The queen now shewed some offence, though the other ladies laughed, and: – "A truce to thy jesting, Dioneo," said she, "and give us a proper song: else thou mayst prove the quality of my ire." Whereupon Dioneo forthwith ceased his fooling, and sang on this wise: –

> So ravishing a light
> Doth from the fair eyes of my mistress move
> As keeps me slave to her and thee, O Love.
>
> A beam from those bright orbs did radiate
> That flame that through mine own eyes to my breast
> Did whilom entrance gain.
> Thy majesty, O Love, thy might, how great
> They be, 'twas her fair face did manifest:
> Whereon to brood still fain,
> I felt thee take and chain
> Each sense, my soul enthralling on such wise
> That she alone henceforth evokes my sighs.
>
> Wherefore, O dear my Lord, myself I own
> Thy slave, and, all obedience, wait and yearn,
> Till thy might me console.
> Yet wot I not if it be throughly known
> How noble is the flame wherewith I burn,
> My loyalty how whole
> To her that doth control
> Ev'n in such sort my mind that shall I none,
> Nor would I, peace receive, save hers alone.
>
> And so I pray thee, sweet my Lord, that thou
> Give her to feel thy fire, and shew her plain
> How grievous my disease.
> This service deign to render; for that now
> Thou seest me waste for love, and in the pain
> Dissolve me by degrees:
> And then the apt moment seize
> My cause to plead with her, as is but due
> From thee to me, who fain with thee would sue.

When Dioneo's silence shewed that his song was ended, the queen accorded it no stinted meed of praise; after which she caused not a few other songs to be sung. Thus passed some part of the night; and then the queen, taking note that its freshness had vanquished the heat of the day, bade all go rest them, if they would, till the morning.

— *Endeth here the fifth day of the Decameron, beginneth the sixth, wherein, under the rule of Elisa, discourse is had of such as by some sprightly sally have repulsed an attack, or by some ready retort or device have avoided loss, peril or scorn.* —

STILL IN MID HEAVEN, the moon had lost her radiance, nor was any part of our world unillumined by the fresh splendour of the dawn, when, the queen being risen and having mustered her company, they hied them, gently sauntering, across the dewy mead some distance from the beautiful hill, conversing now of this, now of the other matter, canvassing the stories, their greater or less degree of beauty, and laughing afresh at divers of their incidents, until, the sun being now in his higher ascendant, they began to feel his heat, and turning back by common consent, retraced their steps to the palace, where, the tables being already set, and fragrant herbs and fair flowers strewn all about, they by the queen's command, before it should grow hotter, addressed themselves to their meal. So, having blithely breakfasted, they first of all sang some dainty and jocund ditties, and then, as they were severally minded, composed them to sleep or sat them down to chess or dice, while Dioneo and Lauretta fell a singing of Troilus and Cressida.

The hour of session being come, they took their places, at the queen's summons, in their wonted order by the fountain; but, when the queen was about to call for the first story, that happened which had not happened before; to wit, there being a great uproar in the kitchen among the maids and men, the sound thereof reached the ears of the queen and all the company. Whereupon the queen called the seneschal and asked him who bawled so loud, and what was the occasion of the uproar. The seneschal made answer that 'twas some contention between Licisca and Tindaro; but the occasion he knew not, having but just come to quiet them, when he received her summons. The queen then bade him cause Licisca and Tindaro to come thither forthwith: so they came, and the queen enquired of them the cause of the uproar. Tindaro was about to make answer, when Licisca, who was somewhat advanced in years, and disposed to give herself airs, and heated to the strife of words, turned to Tindaro, and scowling upon him said: – "Unmannerly varlet that makest bold to speak before me; leave me to tell the story." Then, turning to the queen, she said: – "Madam, this fellow would fain instruct me as to Sicofante's wife, and – neither more or less – as if I had not known her well – would have me believe that, the first night that Sicofante lay with her, 'twas by force and not without effusion of blood that Master Yard made his way into Dusky Hill; which I deny, averring that he met with no resistance, but, on the contrary, with a hearty welcome on the part of the garrison. And such a numskull is he as fondly to believe that the girls are so simple as to let slip their opportunities, while they wait on the caprice of father or brothers, who six times out of seven delay to marry them for three or four years after they should. Ay, ay indeed, doubtless they were well advised to tarry so long! Christ's faith! I should know the truth of what I swear; there is never a woman in my neighbourhood whose husband had her virginity; and well I know how many and what manner of tricks our married dames play their husbands; and yet this booby would fain teach me to know women as if I were but born yesterday."

While Licisca thus spoke, the ladies laughed till all their teeth were ready to start from their heads. Six times at least the queen bade her be silent: but all in vain; she halted not till she had said all that she had a mind to. When she had done, the queen turned with a smile to Dioneo saying: – "This is a question for thee to deal with, Dioneo; so hold thyself in readiness to give final judgment upon it, when our stories are ended." "Madam," replied Dioneo forthwith, "I give judgment without more ado: I say that Licisca is in the right; I believe that 'tis even as she says, and that Tindaro is a fool." Whereupon Licisca burst out laughing, and turning to Tindaro:

– "Now did I not tell thee so?" quoth she. "Begone in God's name: dost think to know more than I, thou that art but a sucking babe? Thank God, I have not lived for nothing, not I." And had not the queen sternly bade her be silent, and make no more disturbance, unless she had a mind to be whipped, and sent both her and Tindaro back to the kitchen, the whole day would have been spent in nought but listening to her. So Licisca and Tindaro having withdrawn, the queen charged Filomena to tell the first story: and gaily thus Filomena began.

The
DECAMERON

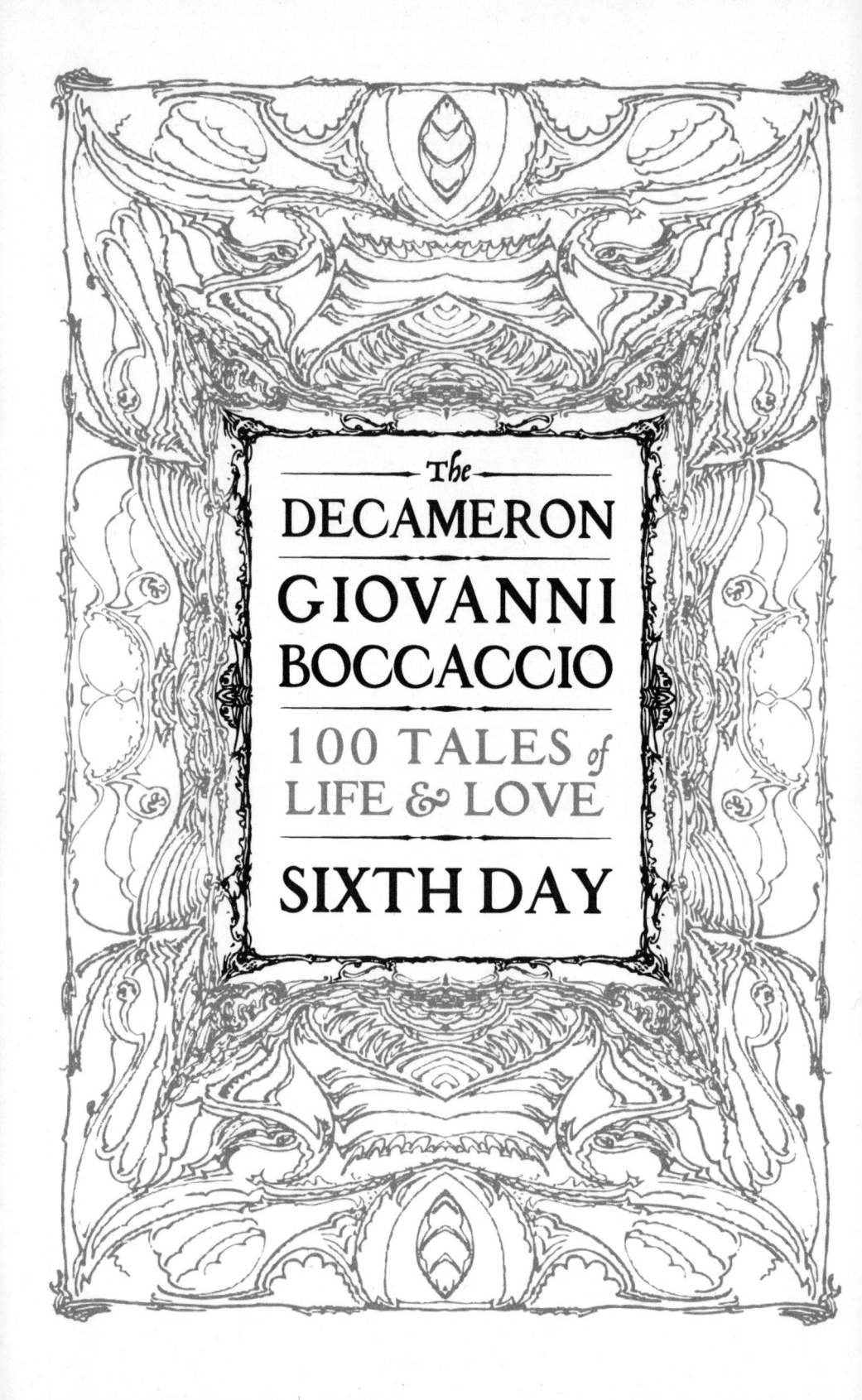

GIOVANNI
BOCCACCIO

100 TALES of
LIFE & LOVE

SIXTH DAY

Sixth Day

Novel I

— *A knight offers to carry Madonna Oretta a horseback with a story, but tells it so ill that she prays him to dismount her.* —

AS STARS ARE set for an ornament in the serene expanse of heaven, and likewise in springtime flowers and leafy shrubs in the green meadows, so, damsels, in the hour of rare and excellent discourse, is wit with its bright sallies. Which, being brief, are much more proper for ladies than for men, seeing that prolixity of speech, where brevity is possible, is much less allowable to them. But for whatever cause, be it the sorry quality of our understanding, or some especial enmity that heaven bears to our generation, few ladies or none are left to-day that, when occasion prompts, are able to meet it with apt speech, ay, or if aught of the kind they hear, can understand it aright: to our common shame be it spoken! But as, touching this matter, enough has already been said by Pampinea, I purpose not to enlarge thereon; but, that you may know what excellence resides in speech apt for the occasion, I am minded to tell you after how courteous a fashion a lady imposed silence upon a gentleman.

'Tis no long time since there dwelt in our city a lady, noble, debonair and of excellent discourse, whom not a few of you may have seen or heard of, whose name – for such high qualities merit not oblivion – was Madonna Oretta, her husband being Messer Geri Spina. Now this lady, happening to be, as we are, in the country, moving from place to place for pleasure with a company of ladies and gentlemen, whom she had entertained the day before at breakfast at her house, and the place of their next sojourn, whither they were to go afoot, being some considerable distance off, one of the gentlemen of the company said to her: – "Madonna Oretta, so please you, I will carry you great part of the way a horseback with one of the finest stories in the world." "Indeed, Sir," replied the lady, "I pray you do so; and I shall deem it the greatest of favours." Whereupon the gentleman, who perhaps was no better master of his weapon than of his story, began a tale, which in itself was indeed excellent, but which, by repeating the same word three, four or six times, and now and again harking back, and saying: – "I said not well"; and erring not seldom in the names, setting one in place of another, he utterly spoiled; besides which, his mode of delivery accorded very ill with the character of the persons and incidents: insomuch that Madonna Oretta, as she listened, did oft sweat, and was like to faint, as if she were ill and at the point of death. And being at length able to bear no more of it, witting that the gentleman had got into a mess and was not like to get out of it, she said pleasantly to him: – "Sir, this horse of yours trots too hard; I pray you be pleased to set me down." The gentleman, being perchance more quick of apprehension than he was skilful in narration, missed not the meaning of her sally, and took it in all good and gay humour. So, leaving unfinished the tale which he had begun, and so mishandled, he addressed himself to tell her other stories.

Sixth Day
Novel II

— *Cisti, a baker, by an apt speech gives Messer Geri Spina to know that he has by inadvertence asked that of him which he should not.* —

ALL THE LADIES and the men alike having greatly commended Madonna Oretta's apt saying, the queen bade Pampinea follow suit, and thus she began: –

Fair ladies, I cannot myself determine whether Nature or Fortune be the more at fault, the one in furnishing a noble soul with a vile body, or the other in allotting a base occupation to a body endowed with a noble soul, whereof we may have seen an example, among others, in our fellow-citizen, Cisti; whom, furnished though he was with a most lofty soul, Fortune made a baker. And verily I should curse Nature and Fortune alike, did I not know that Nature is most discreet, and that Fortune, albeit the foolish imagine her blind, has a thousand eyes. For 'tis, I suppose, that, being wise above a little, they do as mortals ofttimes do, who, being uncertain as to their future, provide against contingencies by burying their most precious treasures in the basest places in their houses, as being the least likely to be suspected; whence, in the hour of their greatest need, they bring them forth, the base place having kept them more safe than the dainty chamber would have done. And so these two arbitresses of the world not seldom hide their most precious commodities in the obscurity of the crafts that are reputed most base, that thence being brought to light they may shine with a brighter splendour. Whereof how in a trifling matter Cisti, the baker, gave proof, restoring the eyes of the mind to Messer Geri Spina, whom the story of his wife, Madonna Oretta, has brought to my recollection, I am minded to shew you in a narrative which shall be of the briefest.

I say then that Pope Boniface, with whom Messer Geri Spina stood very high in favour and honour, having sent divers of his courtiers to Florence as ambassadors to treat of certain matters of great moment, and they being lodged in Messer Geri's house, where he treated with them of the said affairs of the Pope, 'twas, for some reason or another, the wont of Messer Geri and the ambassadors of the Pope to pass almost every morning by Santa Maria Ughi, where Cisti, the baker, had his bakehouse, and plied his craft in person. Now, albeit Fortune had allotted him a very humble occupation, she had nevertheless prospered him therein to such a degree that he was grown most wealthy, and without ever aspiring to change it for another, lived in most magnificent style, having among his other good things a cellar of the best wines, white and red, that were to be found in Florence, or the country parts; and marking Messer Geri and the ambassadors of the Pope pass every morning by his door, he bethought him that, as 'twas very hot, 'twould be a very courteous thing to give them to drink of his good wine; but comparing his rank with that of Messer Geri, he deemed it unseemly to presume to invite him, and cast about how he might lead Messer Geri to invite himself. So, wearing always the whitest of doublets and a spotless apron, that denoted rather the miller, than the baker, he let bring, every morning about the hour that he expected Messer Geri and the ambassadors to pass by his door, a spick-and-span bucket of fresh and cool spring water, and a small Bolognese flagon of his good white wine, and two beakers that shone like silver, so bright were they: and there down he sat him, as they came by, and after hawking once or twice, fell a drinking his wine with such gusto that 'twould have raised a thirst in a corpse. Which Messer Geri having observed on two successive mornings, said on the third: – "What is't, Cisti? Is't good?" Whereupon Cisti jumped up, and answered: – "Ay, Sir, good it is; but in what degree I might by no means make you understand, unless you tasted it." Messer Geri, in whom either the heat of the weather, or unwonted fatigue, or, perchance, the gusto with which he had seen Cisti drink, had bred a thirst, turned to the ambassadors and said with a smile: – "Gentlemen, 'twere well to test the quality of this worthy man's wine: it may be such that we shall not repent us." And so in a body they came up to where Cisti stood; who, having caused a goodly bench to be brought out of the bakehouse, bade them be seated, and to their servants, who were now coming forward to wash the beakers, said: – "Stand back, comrades, and leave this office to me, for I know as well how to serve wine as to bake bread; and expect not to taste a drop yourselves." Which said, he washed four fine new beakers with his own hands, and having sent for a small flagon of his good wine, he heedfully filled the beakers, and presented them to Messer Geri and his companions; who deemed the wine the best that they had drunk for a great while. So Messer Geri, having praised the wine not a little, came there to drink every morning with the ambassadors as long as they tarried with him.

Now when the ambassadors had received their conge, and were about to depart, Messer Geri gave a grand banquet, to which he bade some of the most honourable of the citizens, and also Cisti, who could by no means be induced to come. However, Messer Geri bade one of his servants go fetch a flask of Cisti's wine, and serve half a beaker thereof to each guest at the first course. The servant, somewhat offended, perhaps, that he had not been suffered to taste any of the wine, took with him a large flask, which Cisti no sooner saw, than: – "Son," quoth he, "Messer Geri does not send thee to me": and often as the servant affirmed that he did, he could get no other answer: wherewith he was fain at last to return to Messer Geri. "Go, get thee back, said Messer Geri, and tell him that I do send thee to him, and if he answers thee so again, ask him, to whom then I send thee." So the servant came back, and said: – "Cisti, Messer Geri does, for sure, send me to thee." "Son," answered Cisti, "Messer Geri does, for sure, not send thee to me." "To whom then," said the servant, "does he send me?" "To Arno," returned Cisti. Which being reported by the servant to Messer Geri, the eyes of his mind were straightway opened, and: – "Let me see," quoth he to the servant, "what flask it is thou takest there." And when he had seen it: – "Cisti says sooth," he added; and having sharply chidden him, he caused him take with him a suitable flask, which when Cisti saw: – "Now know I," quoth he, "that 'tis indeed Messer Geri that sends thee to me," and blithely filled it. And having replenished the rundlet that same day with wine of the same quality, he had it carried with due care to Messer Geri's house, and followed after himself; where finding Messer Geri he said: – "I would not have you think, Sir, that I was appalled by the great flask your servant brought me this morning; 'twas but that I thought you had forgotten that which by my little beakers I gave you to understand, when you were with me of late; to wit, that this is no table wine; and so wished this morning to refresh your memory. Now, however, being minded to keep the wine no longer, I have sent you all I have of it, to be henceforth entirely at your disposal." Messer Geri set great store by Cisti's gift, and thanked him accordingly, and ever made much of him and entreated him as his friend.

Sixth Day

Novel III

— *Monna Nonna de' Pulci by a ready retort silences the scarce seemly jesting of the Bishop of Florence.* —

PAMPINEA'S STORY ended, and praise not a little bestowed on Cisti alike for his apt speech and for his handsome present, the queen was pleased to call forthwith for a story from Lauretta, who blithely thus began: –

Debonair my ladies, the excellency of wit, and our lack thereof, have been noted with no small truth first by Pampinea and after her by Filomena. To which topic 'twere bootless to return: wherefore to that which has been said touching the nature of wit I purpose but to add one word, to remind you that its bite should be as a sheep's bite and not as a dog's; for if it bite like a dog, 'tis no longer wit but discourtesy. With which maxim the words of Madonna Oretta, and the apt reply of Cisti, accorded excellently. True indeed it is that if 'tis by way of retort, and one that has received a dog's bite gives the biter a like bite in return, it does not seem to be reprehensible, as otherwise it would have been. Wherefore one must consider how and when and on whom and likewise where one exercises one's wit. By ill observing which matters one of our prelates did once upon a time receive no less shrewd a bite than he gave; as I will shew you in a short story.

While Messer Antonio d'Orso, a prelate both worthy and wise, was Bishop of Florence, there came thither a Catalan gentleman, Messer Dego della Ratta by name, being King Ruberto's marshal. Now Dego being very goodly of person, and inordinately fond of women, it so befell that of the ladies of Florence she that he regarded with especial favour was the very beautiful niece of a brother of the said bishop. And having learned that her husband, though of good family, was but a caitiff, and avaricious in the last degree, he struck a bargain with him that he should lie one night with the lady for five hundred florins of gold: whereupon he had the same number of popolins of silver, which were then current, gilded, and having lain with the lady, albeit against her will, gave them to her husband. Which coming to be generally known, the caitiff husband was left with the loss and the laugh against him; and the bishop, like a wise man, feigned to know nought of the affair. And so the bishop and the marshal being much together, it befell that on St. John's day, as they rode side by side down the street whence they start to run the palio, and took note of the ladies, the bishop espied a young gentlewoman, whom this present pestilence has reft from us, Monna Nonna de' Pulci by name, a cousin of Messer Alesso Rinucci, whom you all must know; whom, for that she was lusty and fair, and of excellent discourse and a good courage, and but just settled with her husband in Porta San Piero, the bishop presented to the marshal; and then, being close beside her, he laid his hand on the marshal's shoulder and said to her: – "Nonna, what thinkest thou of this gentleman? That thou mightst make a conquest of him?" Which words the lady resented as a jibe at her honour, and like to tarnish it in the eyes of those, who were not a few, in whose hearing they were spoken. Wherefore without bestowing a thought upon the vindication of her honour, but being minded to return blow for blow, she retorted hastily: – "Perchance, Sir, he might not make a conquest of me; but if he did so, I should want good money." The answer stung both the marshal and the bishop to the quick, the one as contriver of the scurvy trick played upon the bishop's brother in regard of his niece, the other as thereby outraged in the person of his brother's niece; insomuch that they dared not look one another in the face, but took themselves off in shame and silence, and said never a word more to her that day.

In such a case, then, the lady having received a bite, 'twas allowable in her wittily to return it.

Sixth Day

Novel IV

— *Chichibio, cook to Currado Gianfigliazzi, owes his safety to a ready answer, whereby he converts Currado's wrath into laughter, and evades the evil fate with which Currado had threatened him.* —

LAURETTA BEING now silent, all lauded Nonna to the skies; after which Neifile received the queen's command to follow suit, and thus began: –

Albeit, loving ladies, ready wit not seldom ministers words apt and excellent and congruous with the circumstances of the speakers, 'tis also true that Fortune at times comes to the aid of the timid, and unexpectedly sets words upon the tongue, which in a quiet hour the speaker could never have found for himself: the which 'tis my purpose to shew you by my story.

Currado Gianfigliazzi, as the eyes and ears of each of you may bear witness, has ever been a noble citizen of our city, open-handed and magnificent, and one that lived as a gentleman should with hounds and hawks, in which, to say nothing at present of more important matters, he found unfailing delight. Now, having one day hard by Peretola despatched a crane with one of his falcons, finding it young and plump, he sent it to his excellent cook, a Venetian, Chichibio by name, bidding him roast it for supper and make a dainty dish of it. Chichibio, who looked, as he was, a very green-head, had dressed the crane, and set it to the fire and was cooking it carefully, when, the bird being all but roasted, and the fumes of the cooking very strong, it so chanced that a girl, Brunetta by name, that lived in the same street, and of whom Chichibio was greatly enamoured, came into the kitchen, and perceiving the smell and seeing the bird, began coaxing Chichibio to give her a thigh. By way of answer Chichibio fell a singing: – "You get it not from me, Madam Brunetta, you get it not from me." Whereat Madam Brunetta was offended, and said to him: – "By God, if thou givest it me not, thou shalt never have aught from me to pleasure thee." In short there was not a little altercation; and in the end Chichibio, fain not to vex his mistress, cut off one of the crane's thighs, and gave it to her. So the bird was set before Currado and some strangers that he had at table with him, and Currado, observing that it had but one thigh, was surprised, and sent for Chichibio, and demanded of him what was become of the missing thigh. Whereto the mendacious Venetian answered readily: – "The crane, Sir, has but one thigh and one leg." "What the devil?" rejoined Currado in a rage: "so the crane has but one thigh and one leg? thinkst thou I never saw crane before this?" But Chichibio continued: – "'Tis even so as I say, Sir; and, so please you, I will shew you that so it is in the living bird." Currado had too much respect for his guests to pursue the topic; he only said: – "Since thou promisest to shew me in the living bird what I have never seen or heard tell of, I bid thee do so to-morrow, and I shall be satisfied, but if thou fail, I swear to thee by the body of Christ that I will serve thee so that thou shalt ruefully remember my name for the rest of thy days."

No more was said of the matter that evening, but on the morrow, at daybreak, Currado, who had by no means slept off his wrath, got up still swelling therewith, and ordered his horses, mounted Chichibio on a hackney, and saying to him: – "We shall soon see which of us lied yesternight, thou or I," set off with him for a place where there was much water, beside which there were always cranes to be seen about dawn. Chichibio, observing that Currado's ire was unabated, and knowing not how to bolster up his lie, rode by Currado's side in a state of the utmost trepidation, and would gladly, had he been able, have taken to flight; but, as he might not, he glanced, now ahead, now aback, now aside, and saw everywhere nought but cranes standing on two feet. However, as they approached the river, the very first thing they saw upon the bank was a round dozen of cranes standing each and all on one foot, as is their wont, when asleep. Which Chichibio presently pointed out to Currado, saying: – "Now may you see well enough, Sir, that 'tis true as I said yesternight, that the crane has but one thigh and one leg; mark but how they stand over there." Whereupon Currado: – "Wait," quoth he, "and I will shew thee that they have each thighs and legs twain." So, having drawn a little nigher to them, he ejaculated, "Oho!" Which caused the cranes to bring each the other foot to the ground, and, after hopping a step or two, to take to flight. Currado then turned to Chichibio, saying: – "How now, rogue? art satisfied that the bird has thighs and legs twain?" Whereto Chichibio, all but beside himself with fear, made answer: – "Ay, Sir; but you cried not, oho! to our crane of yestereve: had you done so, it would have popped its other thigh and foot forth, as these have done." Which answer Currado so much relished, that, all his wrath changed to jollity and laughter: – "Chichibio," quoth he, "thou art right, indeed I ought to have so done."

Thus did Chichibio by his ready and jocund retort arrest impending evil, and make his peace with his master.

Sixth Day
Novel V

— *Messer Forese da Rabatta and Master Giotto, the painter, journeying together from Mugello, deride one another's scurvy appearance.* —

NEIFILE BEING silent, and the ladies having made very merry over Chichibio's retort, Pamfilo at the queen's command thus spoke: –

Dearest ladies, if Fortune, as Pampinea has shewn us, does sometimes bide treasures most rich of native worth in the obscurity of base occupations, so in like manner 'tis not seldom found that Nature has enshrined prodigies of wit in the most ignoble of human forms. Whereof a notable example is afforded by two of our citizens, of whom I purpose for a brief while to discourse. The one, Messer Forese da Rabatta by name, was short and deformed of person and withal flat-cheeked and flat-nosed, insomuch that never a Baroncio had a visage so misshapen but his would have shewed as hideous beside it; yet so conversant was this man with the laws, that by not a few of those well able to form an opinion he was reputed a veritable storehouse of civil jurisprudence. The other, whose name was Giotto, was of so excellent a wit that, let Nature, mother of all, operant ever by continual revolution of the heavens, fashion what she would, he with his style and pen and pencil would depict its like on such wise that it shewed not as its like, but rather as the thing itself, insomuch that the visual sense of men did often err in regard thereof, mistaking for real that which was but painted. Wherefore, having brought back to light that art which had for many ages lain buried beneath the blunders of those who painted rather to delight the eyes of the ignorant than to satisfy the intelligence of the wise, he may deservedly be called one of the lights that compose the glory of Florence, and the more so, the more lowly was the spirit in which he won that glory, who, albeit he was, while he yet lived, the master of others, yet did ever refuse to be called their master. And this title that he rejected adorned him with a lustre the more splendid in proportion to the avidity with which it was usurped by those who were less knowing than he, or were his pupils. But for all the exceeding greatness of his art, yet in no particular had he the advantage of Messer Forese either in form or in feature. But to come to the story: – 'Twas in Mugello that Messer Forese, as likewise Giotto, had his country-seat, whence returning from a sojourn that he had made there during the summer vacation of the courts, and being, as it chanced, mounted on a poor jade of a draught horse, he fell in with the said Giotto, who was also on his way back to Florence after a like sojourn on his own estate, and was neither better mounted, nor in any other wise better equipped, than Messer Forese. And so, being both old men, they jogged on together at a slow pace: and being surprised by a sudden shower, such as we frequently see fall in summer, they presently sought shelter in the house of a husbandman that was known to each of them, and was their friend. But after a while, as the rain gave no sign of ceasing, and they had a mind to be at Florence that same day, they borrowed of the husbandman two old cloaks of Romagnole cloth, and two hats much the worse for age (there being no better to be had), and resumed their journey. Whereon they had not proceeded far, when, taking note that they were soaked through and through, and liberally splashed with the mud cast up by their nags' hooves (circumstances which are not of a kind to add to one's dignity), they, after long silence, the sky beginning to brighten a little, began to converse. And Messer Forese, as he rode and hearkened to Giotto, who was an excellent talker, surveyed him sideways, and from head to foot, and all over, and seeing him in all points in so sorry and scurvy a trim, and recking nought of his own appearance, broke into a laugh and said: – "Giotto, would e'er a stranger that met us, and had not seen thee before, believe, thinkst thou, that thou wert, as thou art, the greatest painter in the world." Whereto Giotto answered promptly: – "Methinks, Sir, he might, if, scanning you, he gave you credit for knowing the A B C." Which hearing, Messer Forese recognized his error, and perceived that he had gotten as good as he brought.

Sixth Day

Novel VI

— *Michele Scalza proves to certain young men that the Baronci are the best gentlemen in the world and the Maremma, and wins a supper.* —

THE LADIES were still laughing over Giotto's ready retort, when the queen charged Fiammetta to follow suit; wherefore thus Fiammetta began: –

Pamfilo's mention of the Baronci, who to you, Damsels, are perchance not so well known as to him, has brought to my mind a story in which 'tis shewn how great is their nobility; and, for that it involves no deviation from our rule of discourse, I am minded to tell it you.

'Tis no long time since there dwelt in our city a young man, Michele Scalza by name, the pleasantest and merriest fellow in the world, and the best furnished with quaint stories: for which reason the Florentine youth set great store on having him with them when they forgathered in company. Now it so befell that one day, he being with a party of them at Mont' Ughi, they fell a disputing together on this wise; to wit, who were the best gentlemen and of the longest descent in Florence. One said, the Uberti, another, the Lamberti, or some other family, according to the predilection of the speaker. Whereat Scalza began to smile, and said: – "Now out upon you, out upon you, blockheads that ye are: ye know not what ye say. The best gentlemen and of longest descent in all the world and the Maremma (let alone Florence) are the Baronci by the common consent of all phisopholers, and all that know them as I do; and lest you should otherwise conceive me, I say that 'tis of your neighbours the Baronci of Santa Maria Maggiore that I speak." Whereupon the young men, who had looked for somewhat else from him, said derisively: – "Thou dost but jest with us; as if we did not know the Baronci as well as thou!" Quoth Scalza: – "By the Gospels I jest not, but speak sooth; and if there is any of you will wager a supper to be given to the winner and six good fellows whom he shall choose, I will gladly do the like, and – what is more – I will abide by the decision of such one of you as you may choose." Then said one of them whose name was Neri Mannini: – "I am ready to adventure this supper;" and so they agreed together that Piero di Fiorentino, in whose house they were, should be judge, and hied them to him followed by all the rest, eager to see Scalza lose, and triumph in his discomfiture, and told Piero all that had been said. Piero, who was a young man of sound sense, heard what Neri had to say; and then turning to Scalza: – "And how," quoth he, "mayst thou make good what thou averrest?" "I will demonstrate it," returned Scalza, "by reasoning so cogent that not only you, but he that denies it shall acknowledge that I say sooth. You know, and so they were saying but now, that the longer men's descent, the better is their gentility, and I say that the Baronci are of longer descent, and thus better gentlemen than any other men. If, then, I prove to you that they are of longer descent than any other men, without a doubt the victory in this dispute will rest with me. Now you must know that when God made the Baronci, He was but a novice in His art, of which, when He made the rest of mankind, He was already master. And to assure yourself that herein I say sooth, you have but to consider the Baronci, how they differ from the rest of mankind, who all have faces well composed and duly proportioned, whereas of the Baronci you will see one with a face very long and narrow, another with a face inordinately broad, one with a very long nose, another with a short one, one with a protruding and upturned chin, and great jaws like an ass's; and again there will be one that has one eye larger than its fellow, or set on a lower plane; so that their faces resemble those that children make when they begin to learn to draw. Whereby, as I said, 'tis plainly manifest that, when God made them, He was but novice in His art; and so they are of longer descent than the rest of mankind, and by consequence better gentlemen." By which entertaining argument Piero, the judge, and Neri who had wagered the supper, and all the rest, calling to mind the Baronci's ugliness, were so tickled, that they fell a laughing, and averred that Scalza was in the right, and that he had won the wager, and that without a doubt the Baronci were the best gentlemen, and of the longest descent, not merely in Florence, but in the world and the Maremma to boot. Wherefore 'twas not without reason that Pamfilo, being minded to declare Messer Forese's ill-favouredness, said that he would have been hideous beside a Baroncio.

Sixth Day
Novel VII

— Madonna Filippa, being found by her husband with her lover, is cited before the court, and by a ready and jocund answer acquits herself, and brings about an alteration of the statute. —

FIAMMETTA HAD been silent some time, but Scalza's novel argument to prove the pre-eminent nobility of the Baronci kept all still laughing, when the queen called for a story from Filostrato, who thus began: –

Noble ladies, an excellent thing is apt speech on all occasions, but to be proficient therein I deem then most excellent when the occasion does most imperatively demand it. As was the case with a gentlewoman, of whom I purpose to speak to you, who not only ministered gaiety and merriment to her hearers, but extricated herself, as you shall hear, from the toils of an ignominious death.

There was aforetime in the city of Prato a statute no less censurable than harsh, which, making no distinction between the wife whom her husband took in adultery with her lover, and the woman found pleasuring a stranger for money, condemned both alike to be burned. While this statute was in force, it befell that a gentlewoman, fair and beyond measure enamoured, Madonna Filippa by name, was by her husband, Rinaldo de' Pugliesi, found in her own chamber one night in the arms of Lazzarino de' Guazzagliotri, a handsome young noble of the same city, whom she loved even as herself. Whereat Rinaldo, very wroth, scarce refrained from falling upon them and killing them on the spot; and indeed, but that he doubted how he should afterwards fare himself, he had given way to the vehemence of his anger, and so done. Nor, though he so far mastered himself, could he forbear recourse to the statute, thereby to compass that which he might not otherwise lawfully compass, to wit, the death of his lady. Wherefore, having all the evidence needful to prove her guilt, he took no further counsel; but, as soon as 'twas day, he charged the lady and had her summoned. Like most ladies that are veritably enamoured, the lady was of a high courage; and, though not a few of her friends and kinsfolk sought to dissuade her, she resolved to appear to the summons, having liefer die bravely confessing the truth than basely flee and for defiance of the law live in exile, and shew herself unworthy of such a lover as had had her in his arms that night. And so, attended by many ladies and gentlemen, who all exhorted her to deny the charge, she came before the Podesta, and with a composed air and unfaltering voice asked whereof he would interrogate her. The Podesta, surveying her, and taking note of her extraordinary beauty, and exquisite manners, and the high courage that her words evinced, was touched with compassion for her, fearing she might make some admission, by reason whereof, to save his honour, he must needs do her to death. But still, as he could not refrain from examining her of that which was laid to her charge, he said: – "Madam, here, as you see, is your husband, Rinaldo, who prefers a charge against you, alleging that he has taken you in adultery, and so he demands that, pursuant to a statute which is in force here, I punish you with death: but this I may not do, except you confess; wherefore be very careful what you answer, and tell me if what your husband alleges against you be true." The lady, no wise dismayed, and in a tone not a little jocund, thus made answer: – "True it is, Sir, that Rinaldo is my husband, and that last night he found me in the arms of Lazzarino, in whose arms for the whole-hearted love that I bear him I have ofttimes lain; nor shall I ever deny it; but, as well I wot you know, the laws ought to be common and enacted with the common consent of all that they affect; which conditions are wanting to this law, inasmuch as it binds only us poor women, in whom to be liberal is much less reprehensible than it were in men; and furthermore the consent of no woman was – I say not had, but – so much as asked before 'twas made; for which reasons it justly deserves to be called a bad law. However, if in scathe of my body and your own soul, you are minded to put it in force, 'tis your affair; but, I pray you, go not on to try this matter in any wise, until you have granted me this trifling grace, to wit, to ask my husband if I ever gainsaid him, but did not rather accord him, when and so often as he craved it, complete enjoyment of myself." Whereto Rinaldo, without awaiting the Podesta's question, forthwith answered, that assuredly the lady had ever granted him all that he had asked of her for his gratification. "Then," promptly continued the lady, "if he has ever had of me as much as sufficed for his solace, what was I or am I to do with the surplus? Am I to cast it to the dogs? Is it not much better to bestow it on a gentleman that loves me more dearly than himself, than to suffer it to come to nought or worse?" Which jocund question being heard by well-nigh all the folk of Prato, who had flocked thither all agog to see a dame so fair and of such quality on her trial for such an offence, they laughed loud and long, and then all with one accord, and as with one voice, exclaimed that the lady was in the right and said well; nor left they the court until in concert with the Podesta they had so altered the harsh statute as that thenceforth only such women as should wrong their husbands for money should be within its purview.

Wherefore Rinaldo left the court, discomfited of his foolish enterprise; and the lady blithe and free, as if rendered back to life from the burning, went home triumphant.

Sixth Day

Novel VIII

— *Fresco admonishes his niece not to look at herself in the glass, if 'tis, as she says, grievous to her to see nasty folk.* —

'TWAS NOT at first without some flutterings of shame, evinced by the modest blush mantling on their cheeks, that the ladies heard Filostrato's story; but afterwards, exchanging glances, they could scarce forbear to laugh, and hearkened tittering. However, when he had done, the queen turning to Emilia bade her follow suit. Whereupon Emilia, fetching a deep breath as if she were roused from sleep, thus began: –

Loving ladies, brooding thought has kept my spirit for so long time remote from here that perchance I may make a shift to satisfy our queen with a much shorter story than would have been forthcoming but for my absence of mind, wherein I purpose to tell you how a young woman's folly was corrected by her uncle with a pleasant jest, had she but had the sense to apprehend it. My story, then, is of one, Fresco da Celatico by name, that had a niece, Ciesca, as she was playfully called, who, being fair of face and person, albeit she had none of those angelical charms that we ofttimes see, had so superlative a conceit of herself, that she had contracted a habit of disparaging both men and women and all that she saw, entirely regardless of her own defects, though for odiousness, tiresomeness, and petulance she had not her match among women, insomuch that there was nought that could be done to her mind: besides which, such was her pride that had she been of the blood royal of France, 'twould have been inordinate. And when she walked abroad, so fastidious was her humour, she was ever averting her head, as if there was never a soul she saw or met but reeked with a foul smell. Now one day – not to speak of other odious and tiresome ways that she had – it so befell that being come home, where Fresco was, she sat herself down beside him with a most languishing air, and did nought but fume and chafe. Whereupon: – "Ciesca," quoth he, "what means this, that, though 'tis a feast-day, yet thou art come back so soon?" She, all but dissolved with her vapourish humours, made answer: – "Why, the truth is, that I am come back early because never, I believe, were there such odious and tiresome men and women in this city as there are to-day. I cannot pass a soul in the street that I loathe not like ill-luck; and I believe there is not a woman in the world that is so distressed by the sight of odious people as I am; and so I am come home thus soon to avoid the sight of them." Whereupon Fresco, to, whom his niece's bad manners were distasteful in the extreme: – "Daughter," quoth he, "if thou loathe odious folk as much as thou sayest, thou wert best, so thou wouldst live happy, never to look at thyself in the glass." But she, empty as a reed, albeit in her own conceit a match for Solomon in wisdom, was as far as any sheep from apprehending the true sense of her uncle's jest; but answered that on the contrary she was minded to look at herself in the glass like other women. And so she remained, and yet remains, hidebound in her folly.

Sixth Day
Novel IX

— Guido Cavalcanti by a quip meetly rebukes certain Florentine gentlemen who had taken him at a disadvantage. —

THE QUEEN, perceiving that Emilia had finished her story, and that none but she, and he who had the privilege of speaking last, now remained to tell, began on this wise: –

Albeit, debonair my ladies, you have forestalled me to-day of more than two of the stories, of which I had thought to tell one, yet one is still left me to recount, which carries at the close of it a quip of such a sort, that perhaps we have as yet heard nought so pregnant.

You are to know, then, that in former times there obtained in our city customs excellent and commendable not a few, whereof today not one is left to us, thanks to the greed which, growing with the wealth of our folk, has banished them all from among us. One of which customs was that in divers quarters of Florence the gentlemen that there resided would assemble together in companies of a limited number, taking care to include therein only such as might conveniently bear the expenses, and to-day one, another to-morrow, each in his turn for a day, would entertain the rest of the company; and so they would not seldom do honour to gentlemen from distant parts when they visited the city, and also to their fellow-citizens; and in like manner they would meet together at least once a year all in the same trim, and on the most notable days would ride together through the city, and now and again they would tilt together, more especially on the greater feasts, or when the city was rejoiced by tidings of victory or some other glad event. Among which companies was one of which Messer Betto Brunelleschi was the leading spirit, into which Messer Betto and his comrades had striven hard to bring Guido, son of Cavalcante de' Cavalcanti, and not without reason, inasmuch as, besides being one of the best logicians in the world, and an excellent natural philosopher (qualities of which the company made no great account), he was without a peer for gallantry and courtesy and excellence of discourse and aptitude for all matters which he might set his mind to, and that belonged to a gentleman; and therewithal he was very rich, and, when he deemed any worthy of honour, knew how to bestow it to the uttermost. But, as Messer Betto had never been able to gain him over, he and his comrades supposed that 'twas because Guido, being addicted to speculation, was thereby estranged from men. And, for that he was somewhat inclined to the opinion of the Epicureans, the vulgar averred that these speculations of his had no other scope than to prove that God did not exist. Now one day it so befell that, Guido being come, as was not seldom his wont, from Or San Michele by the Corso degli Adimari as far as San Giovanni, around which were then the great tombs of marble that are to-day in Santa Reparata, besides other tombs not a few, and Guido being between the columns of porphyry, that are there, and the tombs and the door of San Giovanni, which was locked, Messer Betto and his company came riding on to the piazza of Santa Reparata, and seeing him among the tombs, said: – "Go we and flout him." So they set spurs to their horses, and making a mock onset, were upon him almost before he saw them. Whereupon: – "Guido," they began, "thou wilt be none of our company; but, lo now, when thou hast proved that God does not exist, what wilt thou have achieved?" Guido, seeing that he was surrounded, presently answered: – "Gentlemen, you may say to me what you please in your own house." Thereupon he laid his hand on one of the great tombs, and being very nimble, vaulted over it, and so evaded them, and went his way, while they remained gazing in one another's faces, and some said that he had taken leave of his wits, and that his answer was but nought, seeing that the ground on which they stood was common to them with the rest of the citizens, and among them Guido himself. But Messer Betto, turning to them: – "Nay but," quoth he, "'tis ye that have taken leave of your wits, if ye have not understood him; for meetly and in few words he has given us never so shrewd a reprimand; seeing that, if you consider it well, these tombs are the houses of the dead, that are laid and tarry therein; which he calls our house, to shew us that we, and all other simple, unlettered men, are, in comparison of him and the rest of the learned, in sorrier case than dead men, and so being here, we are in our own house." Then none was there but understood Guido's meaning and was abashed, insomuch that they flouted him no more, and thenceforth reputed Messer Betto a gentleman of a subtle and discerning wit.

Sixth Day

Novel X

— Fra Cipolla promises to shew certain country-folk a feather of the Angel Gabriel, in lieu of which he finds coals, which he avers to be of those with which St. Lawrence was roasted. —

ALL THE COMPANY save Dioneo being delivered of their several stories, he wist that 'twas his turn to speak. Wherefore, without awaiting any very express command, he enjoined silence on those that were commending Guido's pithy quip, and thus began: –

Sweet my ladies, albeit 'tis my privilege to speak of what likes me most, I purpose not to-day to deviate from that theme whereon you have all discoursed most appositely; but, following in your footsteps, I am minded to shew you with what adroitness and readiness of resource one of the Friars of St. Antony avoided a pickle that two young men had in readiness for him. Nor, if, in order to do the story full justice, I be somewhat prolix of speech, should it be burdensome to you, if you will but glance at the sun, which is yet in mid-heaven.

Certaldo, as perchance you may have heard, is a town of Val d'Elsa within our country-side, which, small though it is, had in it aforetime people of rank and wealth. Thither, for that there he found good pasture, 'twas long the wont of one of the Friars of St. Antony to resort once every year, to collect the alms that fools gave them. Fra Cipolla – so hight the friar – met with a hearty welcome, no less, perchance, by reason of his name than for other cause, the onions produced in that district being famous throughout Tuscany. He was little of person, red-haired, jolly-visaged, and the very best of good fellows; and therewithal, though learning he had none, he was so excellent and ready a speaker that whoso knew him not would not only have esteemed him a great rhetorician, but would have pronounced him Tully himself or, perchance, Quintilian; and in all the country-side there was scarce a soul to whom he was not either gossip or friend or lover. Being thus wont from time to time to visit Certaldo, the friar came there once upon a time in the month of August, and on a Sunday morning, all the good folk of the neighbouring farms being come to mass in the parish church, he took occasion to come forward and say: – "Ladies and gentlemen, you wot 'tis your custom to send year by year to the poor of Baron Master St. Antony somewhat of your wheat and oats, more or less, according to the ability and the devoutness of each, that blessed St. Antony may save your oxen and asses and pigs and sheep from harm; and you are also accustomed, and especially those whose names are on the books of our confraternity, to pay your trifling annual dues. To collect which offerings, I am hither sent by my superior, to wit, Master Abbot; wherefore, with the blessing of God, after none, when you hear the bells ring, you will come out of the church to the place where in the usual way I shall deliver you my sermon, and you will kiss the cross; and therewithal, knowing, as I do, that you are one and all most devoted to Baron Master St. Antony, I will by way of especial grace shew you a most holy and goodly relic, which I brought myself from the Holy Land overseas, which is none other than one of the feathers of the Angel Gabriel, which he left behind him in the room of the Virgin Mary, when he came to make her the annunciation in Nazareth." And having said thus much, he ceased, and went on with the mass. Now among the many that were in the church, while Fra Cipolla made this speech, were two very wily young wags, the one Giovanni del Bragoniera by name, the other Biagio Pizzini; who, albeit they were on the best of terms with Fra Cipolla and much in his company, had a sly laugh together over the relic, and resolved to make game of him and his feather. So, having learned that Fra Cipolla was to breakfast that morning in the town with one of his friends, as soon as they knew that he was at table, down they hied them into the street, and to the inn where the friar lodged, having complotted that Biagio should keep the friar's servant in play, while Giovanni made search among the friar's goods and chattels for this feather, whatever it might be, to carry it off, that they might see how the friar would afterwards explain the matter to the people. Now Fra Cipolla had for servant one Guccio, whom some called by way of addition Balena, others Imbratta, others again Porco, and who was such a rascallion that sure it is that Lippo Topo himself never painted his like. Concerning whom Fra Cipolla would ofttimes make merry with his familiars, saying: – "My servant has nine qualities, any one of which in Solomon, Aristotle, or Seneca, would have been enough to spoil all their virtue, wisdom and holiness. Consider, then, what sort of a man he must be that has these nine qualities, and yet never a spark of either virtue or wisdom or holiness." And being asked upon divers occasions what these nine qualities might be, he strung them together in rhyme, and answered: – "I will tell you. Lazy and uncleanly and a liar he is, Negligent, disobedient and foulmouthed, iwis, And reckless and witless and mannerless: and therewithal he has some other petty vices, which 'twere best to pass over. And the most amusing thing about him is, that, wherever he goes, he is for taking a wife and renting a house, and on the strength of a big, black, greasy beard he deems himself so very handsome a fellow and seductive, that he takes all the women that see him to be in love with him, and, if he were left alone, he would slip his girdle and run after them all. True it is that he is of great use to me, for that, be any minded to speak with me never so secretly, he must still have his share of the audience; and, if perchance aught is demanded of me, such is his fear lest I should be at a loss what answer to make, that he presently replies, ay or no, as he deems meet."

Now, when he left this knave at the inn, Fra Cipolla had strictly enjoined him on no account to suffer any one to touch aught of his, and least of all his wallet, because it contained the holy things. But Guccio Imbratta, who was fonder of the kitchen than any nightingale of the green boughs, and most particularly if he espied there a maid, and in the host's kitchen had caught sight of a coarse fat woman, short and misshapen, with a pair of breasts that shewed as two buckets of muck and a face that might have belonged to one of the Baronci, all reeking with sweat and grease and smoke, left Fra Cipolla's room and all his things to take care of themselves, and like a vulture swooping down upon the carrion, was in the kitchen in a trice. Where, though 'twas August, he sat him down by the fire, and fell a gossiping with Nuta – such was the maid's name – and told her that he was a gentleman by procuration, and had more florins than could be reckoned, besides those that he had to give away, which were rather more than less, and that he could do and say such things as never were or might be seen or heard forever, good Lord! and a day. And all heedless of his cowl, which had as much grease upon it as would have furnished forth the caldron of Altopascio, and of his rent and patched doublet, inlaid with filth about the neck and under the armpits, and so stained that it shewed hues more various than ever did silk from Tartary or the Indies, and of his shoes that were all to pieces, and of his hose that were all in tatters, he told her in a tone that would have become the Sieur de Chatillon, that he was minded to rehabit her and put her in trim, and raise her from her abject condition, and place her where, though she would not have much to call her own, at any rate she would have hope of better things, with much more to the like effect; which professions, though made with every appearance of good will, proved, like most of his schemes, insubstantial as air, and came to nothing.

Finding Guccio Porco thus occupied with Nuta, the two young men gleefully accounted their work half done, and, none gainsaying them, entered Fra Cipolla's room, which was open, and lit at once upon the wallet, in which was the feather. The wallet opened, they found, wrapt up in many folds of taffeta, a little casket, on opening which they discovered one of the tail-feathers of a parrot, which they deemed must be that which the friar had promised to shew the good folk of Certaldo. And in sooth he might well have so imposed upon them, for in those days the luxuries of Egypt had scarce been introduced into Tuscany, though they have since been brought over in prodigious abundance, to the grave hurt of all Italy. And though some conversance with them there was, yet in those parts folk knew next to nothing of them; but, adhering to the honest, simple ways of their forefathers, had not seen, nay for the most part had not so much as heard tell of, a parrot.

So the young men, having found the feather, took it out with great glee; and looking around for something to replace it, they espied in a corner of the room some pieces of coal, wherewith they filled the casket; which they then closed, and having set the room in order exactly as they had found it, they quitted it unperceived, and hied them merrily off with the feather, and posted themselves where they might hear what Fra Cipolla would say when he found the coals in its stead. Mass said, the simple folk that were in the church went home with the tidings that the feather of the Angel Gabriel was to be seen after none; and this goodman telling his neighbour, and that goodwife her gossip, by the time every one had breakfasted, the town could scarce hold the multitude of men and women that flocked thither all agog to see this feather.

Fra Cipolla, having made a hearty breakfast and had a little nap, got up shortly after none, and marking the great concourse of country-folk that were come to see the feather, sent word to Guccio Imbratta to go up there with the bells, and bring with him the wallet. Guccio, though 'twas with difficulty that he tore himself away from the kitchen and Nuta, hied him up with the things required; and though, when he got up, he was winded, for he was corpulent with drinking nought but water, he did Fra Cipolla's bidding by going to the church door and ringing the bells amain. When all the people were gathered about the door, Fra Cipolla, all unwitting that aught of his was missing, began his sermon, and after much said in glorification of himself, caused the confiteor to be recited with great solemnity, and two torches to be lit by way of preliminary to the shewing of the feather of the Angel Gabriel: he then bared his head, carefully unfolded the taffeta, and took out the casket, which, after a few prefatory words in praise and laudation of the Angel Gabriel and his relic, he opened. When he saw that it contained nought but coals, he did not suspect Guccio Balena of playing the trick, for he knew that he was not clever enough, nor did he curse him, that his carelessness had allowed another to play it, but he inly imprecated himself, that he had committed his things to the keeping of one whom he knew to be "negligent and disobedient, reckless and witless." Nevertheless, he changed not colour, but with face and hands upturned to heaven, he said in a voice that all might hear: – "O God, blessed be Thy might for ever and ever." Then, closing the casket, and turning to the people: – "Ladies and gentlemen," he said, "you are to know, that when I was yet a very young man, I was sent by my superior into those parts where the sun rises, and I was expressly bidden to search until I should find the Privileges of Porcellana, which, though they cost nothing to seal, are of much more use to others than to us. On which errand I set forth, taking my departure from Venice, and traversing the Borgo de' Greci, and thence on horseback the realm of Algarve, and so by Baldacca I came to Parione, whence, somewhat athirst, I after a while got on to Sardinia. But wherefore go I about to enumerate all the lands in which I pursued my quest? Having passed the straits of San Giorgio, I arrived at Truffia and Buffia, countries thickly populated and with great nations, whence I pursued my journey to Menzogna, where I met with many of our own brethren, and of other religious not a few, intent one and all on eschewing hardship for the love of God, making little account of others!' toil, so they might ensue their own advantage, and paying in nought but unminted coin throughout the length and breadth of the country; and so I came to the land of Abruzzi, where the men and women go in pattens on the mountains, and clothe the hogs with their own entrails; and a little further on I found folk that carried bread in staves and wine in sacks. And leaving them, I arrived at the mountains of the Bachi, where all the waters run downwards. In short I penetrated so far that I came at last to India Pastinaca, where I swear to you by the habit that I wear, that I saw pruning-hooks fly: a thing that none would believe that had not seen it. Whereof be my witness that I lie not Maso del Saggio, that great merchant, whom I found there cracking nuts, and selling the shells by retail! However, not being able to find that whereof I was in quest, because from thence one must travel by water, I turned back, and so came at length to the Holy Land, where in summer cold bread costs four deniers, and hot bread is to be had for nothing. And there I found the venerable father Nonmiblasmetesevoipiace, the most worshipful Patriarch of Jerusalem; who out of respect for the habit that I have ever worn, to wit, that of Baron Master St. Antony, was pleased to let me see all the holy relics that he had by him, which were so many, that, were I to enumerate them all, I should not come to the end of them in some miles. However, not to disappoint you, I will tell you a few of them. In the first place, then, he shewed me the finger of the Holy Spirit, as whole and entire as it ever was, and the tuft of the Seraph that appeared to St. Francis, and one of the nails of the Cherubim, and one of the ribs of the Verbum Caro hie thee to the casement, and some of the vestments of the Holy Catholic Faith, and some of the rays of the star that appeared to the Magi in the East, and a phial of the sweat of St. Michael a battling with the Devil and the jaws of death of St. Lazarus, and other relics. And for that I gave him a liberal supply of the acclivities of Monte Morello in the vulgar and some chapters of Caprezio, of which he had long been in quest, he was pleased to let me participate in his holy relics, and gave me one of the teeth of the Holy Cross, and in a small phial a bit of the sound of the bells of Solomon's temple, and this feather of the Angel Gabriel, whereof I have told you, and one of the pattens of San Gherardo da Villa Magna, which, not long ago, I gave at Florence to Gherardo di Bonsi, who holds him in prodigious veneration. He also gave me some of the coals with which the most blessed martyr, St. Lawrence, was roasted. All which things I devoutly brought thence, and have them all safe. True it is that my superior has not hitherto permitted me to shew them, until he should be certified that they are genuine. However, now that this is avouched by certain miracles wrought by them, of which we have tidings by letter from the Patriarch, he has given me leave to shew them. But, fearing to trust them to another, I always carry them with me; and to tell you the truth I carry the feather of the Angel Gabriel, lest it should get spoiled, in a casket, and the coals, with which St. Lawrence was roasted, in another casket; which caskets are so like the one to the other, that not seldom I mistake one for the other, which has befallen me on this occasion; for, whereas I thought to have brought with me the casket wherein is the feather, I have brought instead that which contains the coals. Nor deem I this a mischance; nay, methinks, 'tis by interposition, of God, and that He Himself put the casket of coals in my hand, for I mind me that the feast of St. Lawrence falls but two days hence. Wherefore God, being minded that by shewing you the coals, with which he was roasted, I should rekindle in your souls the devotion that you ought to feel towards him, guided my hand, not to the feather which I meant to take, but to the blessed coals that were extinguished by the humours that exuded from that most holy body. And so, blessed children, bare your heads and devoutly draw nigh to see them. But first of all I would have you know, that whoso has the sign of the cross made upon him with these coals, may live secure for the whole of the ensuing year, that fire shall not touch him, that he feel it not."

Having so said, the friar, chanting a hymn in praise of St. Lawrence, opened the casket, and shewed the coals. Whereon the foolish crowd gazed a while in awe and reverent wonder, and then came pressing forward in a mighty throng about Fra Cipolla with offerings beyond their wont, each and all praying him to touch them with the coals. Wherefore Fra Cipolla took the coals in his hand, and set about making on their white blouses, and on their doublets, and on the veils of the women crosses as big as might be, averring the while that whatever the coals might thus lose would be made good to them again in the casket, as he had often proved. On this wise, to his exceeding great profit, he marked all the folk of Certaldo with the cross, and, thanks to his ready wit and resource, had his laugh at those, who by robbing him of the feather thought to make a laughing-stock of him. They, indeed, being among his hearers, and marking his novel expedient, and how voluble he was, and what a long story he made of it, laughed till they thought their jaws would break; and, when the congregation was dispersed, they went up to him, and never so merrily told him what they had done, and returned him his feather; which next year proved no less lucrative to him than that day the coals had been.

Immense was the delight and diversion which this story afforded to all the company alike, and great and general was the laughter over Fra Cipolla, and more especially at his pilgrimage, and the relics, as well those that he had but seen as those that he had brought back with him. Which being ended, the queen, taking note that therewith the close of her sovereignty was come, stood up, took off the crown, and set it on Dioneo's head, saying with a laugh: – "'Tis time, Dioneo, that thou prove the weight of the burden of having ladies to govern and guide. Be thou king then; and let thy rule be such that, when 'tis ended, we may have cause to commend it." Dioneo took the crown, and laughingly answered: – "Kings worthier far than I you may well have seen many a time ere now – I speak of the kings in chess; but let me have of you that obedience which is due to a true king, and of a surety I will give you to taste of that solace, without which perfection of joy there may not be in any festivity. But enough of this: I will govern as best I may." Then, as was the wont, he sent for the seneschal, and gave him particular instruction how to order matters during the term of his sovereignty; which done, he said: – "Noble ladies, such and so diverse has been our discourse of the ways of men and their various fortunes, that but for the visit that we had a while ago from Madam Licisca, who by what she said has furnished me with matter of discourse for to-morrow, I doubt I had been not a little put to it to find a theme. You heard how she said that there was not a woman in her neighbourhood whose husband had her virginity; adding that well she knew how many and what manner of tricks they, after marriage, played their husbands. The first count we may well leave to the girls whom it concerns; the second, methinks, should prove a diverting topic: wherefore I ordain that, taking our cue from Madam Licisca, we discourse to-morrow of the tricks that, either for love or for their deliverance from peril, ladies have heretofore played their husbands, and whether they were by the said husbands detected or no." To discourse of such a topic some of the ladies deemed unmeet for them, and besought the king to find another theme. But the king made answer: – "Ladies, what manner of theme I have prescribed I know as well as you, nor was I to be diverted from prescribing it by that which you now think to declare unto me, for I wot the times are such that, so only men and women have a care to do nought that is unseemly, 'tis allowable to them to discourse of what they please. For in sooth, as you must know, so out of joint are the times that the judges have deserted the judgment-seat, the laws are silent, and ample licence to preserve his life as best he may is accorded to each and all. Wherefore, if you are somewhat less strict of speech than is your wont, not that aught unseemly in act may follow, but that you may afford solace to yourselves and others, I see not how you can be open to reasonable censure on the part of any. Furthermore, nought that has been said from the first day to the present moment has, methinks, in any degree sullied the immaculate honour of your company, nor, God helping us, shall aught ever sully it. Besides, who is there that knows not the quality of your honour? which were proof, I make no doubt, against not only the seductive influence of diverting discourse, but even the terror of death. And, to tell you the truth, whoso wist that you refused to discourse of these light matters for a while, would be apt to suspect that 'twas but for that you had yourselves erred in like sort. And truly a goodly honour would you confer upon me, obedient as I have ever been to you, if after making me your king and your lawgiver, you were to refuse to discourse of the theme which I prescribe. Away, then, with this scruple fitter for low minds than yours, and let each study how she may give us a goodly story, and Fortune prosper her therein."

So spake the king, and the ladies, hearkening, said that, even as he would, so it should be: whereupon he gave all leave to do as they might be severally minded until the supper-hour. The sun was still quite high in the heaven, for they had not enlarged in their discourse: wherefore, Dioneo with the other gallants being set to play at dice, Elisa called the other ladies apart, and said: – "There is a nook hard by this place, where I think none of you has ever been: 'tis called the Ladies' Vale: whither, ever since we have been here, I have desired to take you, but time meet I have not found until today, when the sun is still so high: if, then, you are minded to visit it, I have no manner of doubt that, when you are there, you will be very glad you came." The ladies answered that they were ready, and so, saying nought to the young men, they summoned one of their maids, and set forth; nor had they gone much more than a mile, when they arrived at the Vale of Ladies. They entered it by a very strait gorge, through which there issued a rivulet, clear as crystal, and a sight, than which nought more fair and pleasant, especially at that time when the heat was great, could be imagined, met their eyes. Within the valley, as one of them afterwards told me, was a plain about half-a-mile in circumference, and so exactly circular that it might have been fashioned according to the compass, though it seemed a work of Nature's art, not man's: 'twas girdled about by six hills of no great height, each crowned with a palace that shewed as a goodly little castle. The slopes of the hills were graduated from summit to base after the manner of the successive tiers, ever abridging their circle, that we see in our theatres; and as many as fronted the southern rays were all planted so close with vines, olives, almond-trees, cherry-trees, fig-trees and other fruitbearing trees not a few, that there was not a hand's-breadth of vacant space. Those that fronted the north were in like manner covered with copses of oak saplings, ashes and other trees, as green and straight as might be. Besides which, the plain, which was shut in on all sides save that on which the ladies had entered, was full of firs, cypresses, and bay-trees, with here and there a pine, in order and symmetry so meet and excellent as had they been planted by an artist, the best that might be found in that kind; wherethrough, even when the sun was in the zenith, scarce a ray of light might reach the ground, which was all one lawn of the finest turf, pranked with the hyacinth and divers other flowers. Add to which – nor was there aught there more delightsome – a rivulet that, issuing from one of the gorges between two of the hills, descended over ledges of living rock, making, as it fell, a murmur most gratifying to the ear, and, seen from a distance, shewed as a spray of finest, powdered quick-silver, and no sooner reached the little plain, than 'twas gathered into a tiny channel, by which it sped with great velocity to the middle of the plain, where it formed a diminutive lake, like the fishponds that townsfolk sometimes make in their gardens, when they have occasion for them. The lake was not so deep but that a man might stand therein with his breast above the water; and so clear, so pellucid was the water that the bottom, which was of the finest gravel, shewed so distinct, that one, had he wished, who had nought better to do, might have counted the stones. Nor was it only the bottom that was to be seen, but such a multitude of fishes, glancing to and fro, as was at once a delight and a marvel to behold. Bank it had none, but its margin was the lawn, to which it imparted a goodlier freshness. So much of the water as it might not contain was received by another tiny channel, through which, issuing from the vale, it glided swiftly to the plain below.

To which pleasaunce the damsels being come surveyed it with roving glance, and finding it commendable, and marking the lake in front of them, did, as 'twas very hot, and they deemed themselves secure from observation, resolve to take a bath. So, having bidden their maid wait and keep watch over the access to the vale, and give them warning, if haply any should approach it, they all seven undressed and got into the water, which to the whiteness of their flesh was even such a veil as fine glass is to the vermeil of the rose. They, being thus in the water, the clearness of which was thereby in no wise affected, did presently begin to go hither and thither after the fish, which had much ado where to bestow themselves so as to escape out of their hands. In which diversion they spent some time, and caught a few, and then they hied them out of the water and dressed them again, and bethinking them that 'twas time to return to the palace, they began slowly sauntering thither, dilating much as they went upon the beauty of the place, albeit they could not extol it more than they had already done. 'Twas still quite early when they reached the palace, so that they found the gallants yet at play where they had left them. To whom quoth Pampinea with a smile: – "We have stolen a march upon you to-day." "So," replied Dioneo, "'tis with you do first and say after?" "Ay, my lord," returned Pampinea, and told him at large whence they came, and what the place was like, and how far 'twas off, and what they had done. What she said of the beauty of the spot begat in the king a desire to see it: wherefore he straightway ordered supper, whereof when all had gaily partaken, the three gallants parted from the ladies and hied them with their servants to the vale, where none of them had ever been before, and, having marked all its beauties, extolled it as scarce to be matched in all the world. Then, as the hour was very late, they did but bathe, and as soon as they had resumed their clothes, returned to the ladies, whom they found dancing a carol to an air that Fiammetta sang, which done, they conversed of the Ladies' Vale, waxing eloquent in praise thereof: insomuch that the king called the seneschal, and bade him have some beds made ready and carried thither on the morrow, that any that were so minded might there take their siesta. He then had lights and wine and comfits brought; and when they had taken a slight refection, he bade all address them to the dance. So at his behest Pamfilo led a dance, and then the king, turning with gracious mien to Elisa: – "Fair damsel," quoth he, "'twas thou to-day didst me this honour of the crown; and 'tis my will that thine to-night be the honour of the song; wherefore sing us whatsoever thou hast most lief." "That gladly will I," replied Elisa smiling; and thus with dulcet voice began: –

>*If of thy talons, Love, be quit I may,*
>*I deem it scarce can be*
>*But other fangs I may elude for aye.*
>
>*Service I took with thee, a tender maid,*
>*In thy war thinking perfect peace to find,*
>*And all my arms upon the ground I laid,*
>*Yielding myself to thee with trustful mind:*
>*Thou, harpy-tyrant, whom no faith may bind,*

> *Eftsoons didst swoop on me,*
> *And with thy cruel claws mad'st me thy prey.*
>
> *Then thy poor captive, bound with many a chain,*
>   *Thou tookst, and gav'st to him, whom fate did call*
>   *Hither my death to be; for that in pain*
>   *And bitter tears I waste away, his thrall:*
>   *Nor heave I e'er a sigh, or tear let fall,*
>   *So harsh a lord is he,*
>   *That him inclines a jot my grief to allay.*
>
> *My prayers upon the idle air are spent:*
>   *He hears not, will not hear; wherefore in vain*
>   *The more each hour my soul doth her torment;*
>   *Nor may I die, albeit to die were gain.*
>   *Ah! Lord, have pity of my bitter pain!*
>   *Help have I none but thee;*
>   *Then take and bind and at my feet him lay.*
>
> *But if thou wilt not, do my soul but loose*
>   *From hope, that her still binds with triple chain.*
>   *Sure, O my Lord, this prayer thou'lt not refuse:*
>   *The which so thou to grant me do but deign,*
>   *I look my wonted beauty to regain,*
>   *And banish misery*
>   *With roses white and red bedecked and gay.*

So with a most piteous sigh ended Elisa her song, whereat all wondered exceedingly, nor might any conjecture wherefore she so sang. But the king, who was in a jolly humour, sent for Tindaro, and bade him out with his cornemuse, and caused them tread many a measure thereto, until, no small part of the night being thus spent, he gave leave to all to betake them to rest.

— *Endeth here the sixth day of the Decameron, beginneth the seventh, in which, under the rule of Dioneo, discourse is had of the tricks which, either for love or for their deliverance from peril, ladies have heretofore played their husbands, and whether they were by the said husbands detected, or no.* —

FLED WAS NOW each star from the eastern sky, save only that which we call Lucifer, which still glowed in the whitening dawn, when uprose the seneschal, and with a goodly baggage-train hied him to the Ladies' Vale, there to make all things ready according to the ordinance and commandment of the king. Nor was it long after his departure that the king rose, being awaked by the stir and bustle that the servants made in lading the horses, and being risen he likewise roused all the ladies and the other gallants; and so, when as yet 'twas scarce clear daybreak, they all took the road; nor seemed it to them that the nightingales and the other birds had ever chanted so blithely as that morning. By which choir they were attended to the Ladies' Vale, where they were greeted by other warblers not a few, that seemed rejoiced at their arrival. Roving about the vale, and surveying its beauties afresh, they rated them higher than on the previous day, as indeed the hour was more apt to shew them forth. Then with good wine and comfits they broke their fast, and, that they might not lag behind the songsters, they fell a singing, whereto the vale responded, ever echoing their strains; nor did the birds, as minded not to be beaten, fail to swell the chorus with notes of unwonted sweetness. However, breakfast-time came, and then, the tables being laid under a living canopy of trees, and beside other goodly trees that fringed the little lake, they sat them down in order as to the king seemed meet. So they took their meal, glancing from time to time at the lake, where the fish darted to and fro in multitudinous shoals, which afforded not only delight to their eyes but matter for converse. Breakfast ended, and the tables removed, they fell a singing again more blithely than before. After which, there being set, in divers places about the little vale, beds which the discreet seneschal had duly furnished and equipped within and without with store of French coverlets, and other bedgear, all, that were so minded, had leave of the king to go to sleep, and those that cared not to sleep might betake them, as each might choose, to any of their wonted diversions. But, all at length being risen, and the time for addressing them to the story-telling being come, the king had carpets spread on the sward no great way from the place where they had breakfasted; and, all having sat them down beside the lake, he bade Emilia begin; which, blithe and smiling, Emilia did on this wise.

The DECAMERON
GIOVANNI BOCCACCIO
100 TALES of LIFE & LOVE
SEVENTH DAY

Seventh Day

Novel I

— *Gianni Lotteringhi hears a knocking at his door at night: he awakens his wife, who persuades him that 'tis the bogey, which they fall to exorcising with a prayer; whereupon the knocking ceases.* —

MY LORD, glad indeed had I been, that, saving your good pleasure, some other than I had had precedence of discourse upon so goodly a theme as this of which we are to speak – I doubt I am but chosen to teach others confidence; but, such being your will, I will gladly obey it. And my endeavour shall be, dearest ladies, to tell you somewhat that may be serviceable to you in the future: for, if you are, as I am, timorous, and that most especially of the bogey, which, God wot, I know not what manner of thing it may be, nor yet have found any that knew, albeit we are all alike afraid of it, you may learn from this my story how to put it to flight, should it intrude upon you, with a holy, salutary and most efficacious orison.

There dwelt of yore at Florence, in the quarter of San Pancrazio, a master-spinner, Gianni Lotteringhi by name, one that had prospered in his business, but had little understanding of aught else; insomuch that being somewhat of a simpleton, he had many a time been chosen leader of the band of laud-singers of Santa Maria Novella, and had charge of their school; and not a few like offices had he often served, upon which he greatly plumed himself. Howbeit, 'twas all for no other reason than that, being a man of substance, he gave liberal doles to the friars; who, for that they got thereof, this one hose, another a cloak, and a third a hood, would teach him good orisons, or give him the paternoster in the vernacular, or the chant of St. Alexis, or the lament of St. Bernard, or the laud of Lady Matilda, or the like sorry stuff, which he greatly prized, and guarded with jealous care, deeming them all most conducive to the salvation of his soul.

Now our simple master-spinner had a most beautiful wife, and amorous withal, her name Monna Tessa. Daughter she was of Mannuccio dalla Cuculla, and not a little knowing and keen-witted; and being enamoured of Federigo di Neri Pegolotti, a handsome and lusty gallant, as he also of her, she, knowing her husband's simplicity, took counsel with her maid, and arranged that Federigo should come to chat with her at a right goodly pleasure-house that the said Gianni had at Camerata, where she was wont to pass the summer, Gianni coming now and again to sup and sleep, and going back in the morning to his shop, or, maybe, to his laud-singers. Federigo, who desired nothing better, went up there punctually on the appointed day about vespers, and as the evening passed without Gianni making his appearance, did most comfortably, and to his no small satisfaction, sup and sleep with the lady, who lying in his arms taught him that night some six of her husband's lauds. But, as neither she nor Federigo was minded that this beginning should also be the end of their intercourse, and that it might not be needful for the maid to go each time to make the assignation with him, they came to the following understanding; to wit, that as often as he came and went between the house and an estate that he had a little higher up, he should keep an eye on a vineyard that was beside the house, where he would see an ass's head stuck on one of the poles of the vineyard, and as often as he observed the muzzle turned towards Florence, he might visit her without any sort of misgiving; and if he found not the door open, he was to tap it thrice, and she would open it; and when he saw the muzzle of the ass's head turned towards Fiesole, he was to keep away, for then Gianni would be there. Following which plan, they forgathered not seldom: but on one of these evenings, when Federigo was to sup with Monna Tessa on two fat capons that she bad boiled, it so chanced that Gianni arrived there unexpectedly and very late, much to the lady's chagrin: so she had a little salt meat boiled apart, on which she supped with her husband; and the maid by her orders carried the two boiled capons laid in a spotless napkin with plenty of fresh eggs and a bottle of good wine into the garden, to which there was access otherwise than from the house, and where she was wont at times to sup with Federigo; and there the maid set them down at the foot of a peach-tree, that grew beside a lawn. But in her vexation she forgot to tell the maid to wait till Federigo should come, and let him know that Gianni was there, and he must take his supper in the garden: and she and Gianni and the maid were scarce gone to bed, when Federigo came and tapped once at the door, which being hard by the bedroom, Gianni heard the tap, as did also the lady, albeit, that Gianni might have no reason to suspect her, she feigned to be asleep. Federigo waited a little, and then gave a second tap; whereupon, wondering what it might mean, Gianni nudged his wife, saying: – "Tessa, dost hear what I hear? Methinks some one has tapped at our door." The lady, who had heard the noise much better than he, feigned to wake up, and: – "How? what sayst thou?" quoth she. "I say," replied Gianni, "that, meseems, some one has tapped at our door." "Tapped at it?" quoth the lady. "Alas, my Gianni, wottest thou not what that is? 'Tis the bogey, which for some nights past has so terrified me as never was, insomuch that I never hear it but I pop my head under the clothes and venture not to put it out again until 'tis broad day." "Come, come, wife," quoth Gianni, "if such it is, be not alarmed; for before we got into bed I repeated the Te lucis, the Intemerata, and divers other good orisons, besides which I made the sign of the cross in the name of the Father, Son and Holy Spirit at each corner of the bed; wherefore we need have no fear that it may avail to hurt us, whatever be its power." The lady, lest Federigo, perchance suspecting a rival, should take offence, resolved to get up, and let him understand that Gianni was there: so she said to her husband: – "Well well; so sayst thou; but I for my part shall never deem myself safe and secure, unless we exorcise it, seeing that thou art here." "Oh!" said Gianni, "and how does one exorcise it?" "That," quoth the lady, "I know right well; for t'other day, when I went to Fiesole for the pardoning, one of those anchoresses, the saintliest creature, my Gianni, God be my witness, knowing how much afraid I am of the bogey, taught me a holy and salutary orison, which she said she had tried many a time before she was turned anchoress, and always with success. God wot, I should never have had courage to try it alone; but as thou art here, I propose that we go exorcise it together." Gianni made answer that he was quite of the same mind; so up they got, and stole to the door, on the outside of which Federigo, now suspicious, was still waiting. And as soon as they were there: – "Now," quoth the lady to Gianni, "thou wilt spit, when I tell thee." "Good," said Gianni. Whereupon the lady began her orison, saying: –

> "Bogey, bogey that goest by night,
> Tail erect, thou cam'st, tail erect, take thy flight
> Hie thee to the garden, and the great peach before,
> Grease upon grease, and droppings five score
> Of my hen shalt thou find:
> Set the flask thy lips to,

> *Then away like the wind,*
> *And no scathe unto me or my Gianni do."*

And when she had done: – "Now, Gianni," quoth she, "spit": and Gianni spat.

There was no more room for jealousy in Federigo's mind as he heard all this from without; nay, for all his disappointment, he was like to burst with suppressed laughter, and when Gianni spat, he muttered under his breath: – "Now out with thy teeth." The lady, having after this fashion thrice exorcised the bogey, went back to bed with her husband. Federigo, disappointed of the supper that he was to have had with her, and apprehending the words of the orison aright, hied him to the garden, and having found the two capons and the wine and the eggs at the foot of the peach-tree, took them home with him, and supped very comfortably. And many a hearty laugh had he and the lady over the exorcism during their subsequent intercourse.

Now, true it is that some say that the lady had in fact turned the ass's head towards Fiesole, but that a husbandman, passing through the vineyard, had given it a blow with his stick, whereby it had swung round, and remained fronting Florence, and so it was that Federigo thought that he was invited, and came to the house, and that the lady's orison was on this wise: –

> *"Bogey, a God's name, away thee hie,*
> *For whoe'er turned the ass's head, 'twas not I:*
> *Another it was, foul fall his eyne;*
> *And here am I with Gianni mine."*

Wherefore Federigo was fain to take himself off, having neither slept nor supped.

But a neighbour of mine, a lady well advanced in years, tells me that, by what she heard when she was a girl, both stories are true; but that the latter concerned not Gianni Lotteringhi but one Gianni di Nello, that lived at Porta San Piero, and was no less a numskull than Gianni Lotteringhi. Wherefore, dear my ladies, you are at liberty to choose which exorcism you prefer, or take both if you like. They are both of extraordinary and approved virtue in such cases, as you have heard: get them by heart, therefore, and they may yet stand you in good stead.

Seventh Day
Novel II

— Her husband returning home, Peronella bestows her lover in a tun; which, being sold by her husband, she avers to have been already sold by herself to one that is inside examining it to see if it be sound. Whereupon the lover jumps out, and causes the husband to scour the tun for him, and afterwards to carry it to his house. —

GREAT INDEED was the laughter with which Emilia's story was received; which being ended, and her orison commended by all as good and salutary, the king bade Filostrato follow suit; and thus Filostrato began: –

Dearest my ladies, so many are the tricks that men play you, and most of all your husbands, that, when from time to time it so befalls that some lady plays her husband a trick, the circumstance, whether it come within your own cognizance or be told you by another, should not only give you joy but should incite you to publish it on all hands, that men may be ware, that, knowing as they are, their ladies also, on their part, know somewhat: which cannot but be serviceable to you, for that one does not rashly essay to take another with guile whom one wots not to lack that quality. Can we doubt, then, that, should but the converse that we shall hold to-day touching this matter come to be bruited among men, 'twould serve to put a most notable check upon the tricks they play you, by doing them to wit of the tricks, which you, in like manner, when you are so minded, may play them? Wherefore 'tis my intention to tell you in what manner a young girl, albeit she was but of low rank, did, on the spur of the moment, beguile her husband to her own deliverance.

'Tis no long time since at Naples a poor man, a mason by craft, took to wife a fair and amorous maiden – Peronella was her name – who eked out by spinning what her husband made by his craft; and so the pair managed as best they might on very slender means. And as chance would have it, one of the gallants of the city, taking note of this Peronella one day, and being mightily pleased with her, fell in love with her, and by this means and that so prevailed that he won her to accord him her intimacy. Their times of forgathering they concerted as follows: – to wit, that, her husband being wont to rise betimes of a morning to go to work or seek for work, the gallant was to be where he might see him go forth, and, the street where she dwelt, which is called Avorio, being scarce inhabited, was to come into the house as soon as her husband was well out of it; and so times not a few they did. But on one of these occasions it befell that, the good man being gone forth, and Giannello Sirignario – such was the gallant's name – being come into the house, and being with Peronella, after a while, back came the good man, though 'twas not his wont to return until the day was done; and finding the door locked, he knocked, and after knocking, he fell a saying to himself: – O God, praised be Thy name forever; for that, albeit Thou hast ordained that I be poor, at least Thou hast accorded me the consolation of a good and honest girl for wife. Mark what haste she made to shut the door when I was gone forth, that none else might enter to give her trouble.

Now Peronella knew by his knock that 'twas her husband; wherefore: – "Alas, Giannello mine," quoth she, "I am a dead woman, for lo, here is my husband, foul fall him! come back!

What it may import, I know not, for he is never wont to come back at this hour; perchance he caught sight of thee as thou camest in. However, for the love of God, be it as it may, get thee into this tun that thou seest here, and I will go open to him, and we shall see what is the occasion of this sudden return this morning." So Giannello forthwith got into the tun, and Peronella went to the door, and let in her husband, and gave him black looks, saying: – "This is indeed a surprise that thou art back so soon this morning! By what I see thou hast a mind to make this a holiday, that thou returnest tools in hand; if so, what are we to live on? whence shall we get bread to eat? Thinkest thou I will let thee pawn my gown and other bits of clothes? Day and night I do nought else but spin, insomuch that the flesh is fallen away from my nails, that at least I may have oil enough to keep our lamp alight. Husband, husband, there is never a woman in the neighbourhood but marvels and mocks at me, that I am at such labour and pains; and thou comest home to me with thy hands hanging idle, when thou shouldst be at work." Which said, she fell a weeping and repeating: – "Alas, alas, woe 's me, in what evil hour was I born? in what luckless moment came I hither, I, that might have had so goodly a young man, and I would not, to take up with one that bestows never a thought on her whom he has made his wife? Other women have a good time with their lovers, and never a one have we here but has two or three; they take their pleasure, and make their husbands believe that the moon is the sun; and I, alas! for that I am an honest woman, and have no such casual amours, I suffer, and am hard bested. I know not why I provide not myself with one of these lovers, as others do. Give good heed, husband, to what I say: were I disposed to dishonour thee, I were at no loss to find the man: for here are gallants enough, that love me, and court me, and have sent me many an offer of money – no stint – or dresses or jewels, should I prefer them; but my pride would never suffer it, because I was not born of a woman of that sort: and now thou comest home to me when thou oughtest to be at work."

Whereto the husband: – "Wife, wife, for God's sake distress not thyself: thou shouldst give me credit for knowing what manner of woman thou art, as indeed I have partly seen this morning. True it is that I went out to work; but 'tis plain that thou knowest not, as indeed I knew not, that to-day 'tis the feast of San Galeone, and a holiday, and that is why I am come home at this hour; but nevertheless I have found means to provide us with bread for more than a month; for I have sold to this gentleman, whom thou seest with me, the tun, thou wottest of, seeing that it has encumbered the house so long, and he will give me five gigliats for it." Quoth then Peronella: – "And all this but adds to my trouble: thou, that art a man, and goest abroad, and shouldst know affairs, hast sold for five gigliats a tun, which I, that am but a woman, and was scarce ever out of doors, have, for that it took up so much room in the house, sold for seven gigliats to a good man, that but now, as thou cam'st back, got therein, to see if 'twere sound." So hearing, the husband was overjoyed, and said to the man that was come to take it away: – "Good man, I wish thee Godspeed; for, as thou hearest, my wife has sold the tun for seven gigliats, whereas thou gavest me only five." Whereupon: – "So be it," said the good man, and took himself off. Then said Peronella to her husband: – "Now, as thou art here, come up, and arrange the matter with the good man."

Now Giannello, who, meanwhile, had been all on the alert to discover if there were aught he had to fear or be on his guard against, no sooner heard Peronella's last words, than he sprang out of the tun, and feigning to know nought of her husband's return, began thus: – "Where art thou, good dame?" Whereto the husband, coming up, answered: – "Here am I: what wouldst thou of me?" Quoth Giannello: – "And who art thou? I would speak with the lady with whom I struck the bargain for this tun." Then said the good man: – "Have no fear, you can deal with me; for I am her husband." Quoth then Giannello: – "The tun seems to me sound enough; but

I think you must have let the lees remain in it; for 'tis all encrusted with I know not what that is so dry, that I cannot raise it with the nail; wherefore I am not minded to take it unless I first see it scoured." Whereupon Peronella: – "To be sure: that shall not hinder the bargain; my husband will scour it clean." And: – "Well and good," said the husband.

So he laid down his tools, stripped himself to his vest, sent for a light and a rasp, and was in the tun, and scraping away, in a trice. Whereupon Peronella, as if she were curious to see what he did, thrust her head into the vent of the tun, which was of no great size, and therewithal one of her arms up to the shoulder, and fell a saying: – "Scrape here, and here, and there too, and look, there is a bit left here." So, she being in this posture, directing and admonishing her husband, Giannello, who had not, that morning, fully satisfied his desire, when the husband arrived, now seeing that as he would, he might not, brought his mind to his circumstances, and resolved to take his pleasure as he might: wherefore he made up to the lady, who completely blocked the vent of the tun; and even on such wise as on the open champaign the wild and lusty horses do amorously assail the mares of Parthia, he sated his youthful appetite; and so it was that almost at the same moment that he did so, and was off, the tun was scoured, the husband came forth of it, and Peronella withdrew her head from the vent, and turning to Giannello, said: – "Take this light, good man, and see if 'tis scoured to thy mind." Whereupon Giannello, looking into the tun, said that 'twas in good trim, and that he was well content, and paid the husband the seven gigliats, and caused him carry the tun to his house.

Seventh Day
Novel III

— *Fra Rinaldo lies with his gossip: her husband finds him in the room with her; and they make him believe that he was curing his godson of worms by a charm.* —

FILOSTRATO KNEW not how so to veil what he said touching the mares of Parthia, but that the keen-witted ladies laughed thereat, making as if 'twas at somewhat else. However, his story being ended, the king called for one from Elisa, who, all obedience, thus began: –

Debonair my ladies, we heard from Emilia how the bogey is exorcised, and it brought to my mind a story of another incantation: 'tis not indeed so good a story as hers; but, as no other, germane to our theme, occurs to me at present, I will relate it.

You are to know, then, that there dwelt aforetime at Siena a young man, right gallant and of honourable family, his name Rinaldo; who, being in the last degree enamoured of one of his neighbours, a most beautiful gentlewoman and the wife of a rich man, was not without hopes that, if he could but find means to speak with her privately, he might have of her all that he desired; but seeing no way, and the lady being pregnant, he cast about how he might become her child's godfather. Wherefore, having ingratiated himself with her husband, he broached the matter to him in as graceful a manner as he might; and 'twas arranged. So Rinaldo, being now godfather to Madonna Agnesa's child, and having a more colourable pretext for speaking to her, took courage, and told her in words that message of his heart which she had long before read in his eyes; but though 'twas not displeasing to the lady to hear, it availed him but little.

Now not long afterwards it so befell that, whatever may have been his reason, Rinaldo betook him to friarage; and whether it was that he found good pasture therein, or what not, he persevered in that way of life. And though for a while after he was turned friar, he laid aside the love he bore his gossip, and certain other vanities, yet in course of time, without putting off the habit, he resumed them, and began to take a pride in his appearance, and to go dressed in fine clothes, and to be quite the trim gallant, and to compose songs and sonnets and ballades, and to sing them, and to make a brave shew in all else that pertained to his new character. But why enlarge upon our Fra Rinaldo, of whom we speak? what friars are there that do not the like? Ah! opprobrium of a corrupt world! Sleek-faced and sanguine, daintily clad, dainty in all their accessories, they ruffle it shamelessly before the eyes of all, shewing not as doves but as insolent cocks with raised crest and swelling bosom, and, what is worse (to say nought of the vases full of electuaries and unguents, the boxes packed with divers comfits, the pitchers and phials of artificial waters, and oils, the flagons brimming with Malmsey and Greek and other wines of finest quality, with which their cells are so packed that they shew not as the cells of friars, but rather as apothecaries' or perfumers' shops), they blush not to be known to be gouty, flattering themselves that other folk wot not that long fasts and many of them, and coarse fare and little of it, and sober living, make men lean and thin and for the most part healthy; or if any malady come thereof, at any rate 'tis not the gout, the wonted remedy for which is chastity and all beside that belongs to the regimen of a humble friar. They flatter themselves, too, that others wot not that over and above the meagre diet, long vigils and orisons and strict discipline ought to mortify men and make them pale, and that neither St. Dominic nor St. Francis went clad in stuff dyed in grain or any other goodly garb, but in coarse woollen habits innocent of the dyer's art, made to keep out the cold, and not for shew. To which matters 'twere well God had a care, no less than to the souls of the simple folk by whom our friars are nourished.

Fra Rinaldo, then, being come back to his first affections, took to visiting his gossip very frequently; and gaining confidence, began with more insistence than before to solicit her to that which he craved of her. So, being much urged, the good lady, to whom Fra Rinaldo, perhaps, seemed now more handsome than of yore, had recourse one day, when she felt herself unusually hard pressed by him, to the common expedient of all that would fain concede what is asked of them, and said: – "Oh! but Fra Rinaldo, do friars then do this sort of thing?" "Madam," replied Fra Rinaldo, "when I divest myself of this habit, which I shall do easily enough, you will see that I am a man furnished as other men, and no friar." Whereto with a truly comical air the lady made answer: – "Alas! woe's me! you are my child's godfather: how might it be? nay, but 'twere a very great mischief; and many a time I have heard that 'tis a most heinous sin; and without a doubt, were it not so, I would do as you wish." "If," said Fra Rinaldo, "you forego it for such a scruple as this, you are a fool for your pains. I say not that 'tis no sin; but there is no sin so great but God pardons it, if one repent. Now tell me: whether is more truly father to your son, I that held him at the font, or your husband that begot him?" "My husband," replied the lady. "Sooth say you," returned the friar, "and does not your husband lie with you?" "Why, yes," said the lady. "Then," rejoined the friar, "I that am less truly your son's father than your husband, ought also to lie with you, as does your husband." The lady was no logician, and needed little to sway her: she therefore believed or feigned to believe that what the friar said was true. So: – "Who might avail to answer your words of wisdom?" quoth she; and presently forgot the godfather in the lover, and complied with his desires. Nor had they begun their course to end it forthwith: but under cover of the friar's sponsorship, which set them more at ease, as it rendered them less open to suspicion, they forgathered again and again.

But on one of these occasions it so befell that Fra Rinaldo, being come to the lady's house, where he espied none else save a very pretty and dainty little maid that waited on the lady, sent his companion away with her into the pigeon-house, there to teach her the paternoster, while he and the lady, holding her little boy by the hand, went into the bedroom, locked themselves in, got them on to a divan that was there, and began to disport them. And while thus they sped the time, it chanced that the father returned, and, before any was ware of him, was at the bedroom door, and knocked, and called the lady by her name. Whereupon: – "'Tis as much as my life is worth," quoth Madonna Agnesa; "lo, here is my husband; and the occasion of our intimacy cannot but be now apparent to him." "Sooth say you," returned Fra Rinaldo, who was undressed, that is to say, had thrown off his habit and hood, and was in his tunic; "if I had but my habit and hood on me in any sort, 'twould be another matter; but if you let him in, and he find me thus, 'twill not be possible to put any face on it." But with an inspiration as happy as sudden: – "Now get them on you," quoth the lady; "and when you have them on, take your godson in your arms, and give good heed to what I shall say to him, that your words may accord with mine; and leave the rest to me."

The good man was still knocking, when his wife made answer: – "Coming, coming." And so up she got, and put on a cheerful countenance and hied her to the door, and opened it and said: – "Husband mine: well indeed was it for us that in came Fra Rinaldo, our sponsor;

'twas God that sent him to us; for in sooth, but for that, we had to-day lost our boy." Which the poor simpleton almost swooned to hear; and: – "How so?" quoth he. "O husband mine," replied the lady, "he was taken but now, all of a sudden, with a fainting fit, so that I thought he was dead: and what to do or say I knew not, had not Fra Rinaldo, our sponsor, come just in the nick of time, and set him on his shoulder, and said: – 'Gossip, 'tis that he has worms in his body, and getting, as they do, about the heart, they might only too readily be the death of him; but fear not; I will say a charm that will kill them all; and before I take my leave, you will see your boy as whole as you ever saw him.' And because to say certain of the prayers thou shouldst have been with us, and the maid knew not where to find thee, he caused his companion to say them at the top of the house, and he and I came in here. And for that 'tis not meet for any but the boy's mother to assist at such a service, that we might not be troubled with any one else, we locked the door; and he yet has him in his arms; and I doubt not that he only waits till his companion have said his prayers, and then the charm will be complete; for the boy is already quite himself again."

The good simple soul, taking all this for sooth, and overwrought by the love he bore his son, was entirely without suspicion of the trick his wife was playing him, and heaving a great sigh, said: – "I will go look for him." "Nay," replied the wife, "go not: thou wouldst spoil the efficacy of the charm: wait here; I will go see if thou mayst safely go; and will call thee."

Whereupon Fra Rinaldo, who had heard all that passed, and was in his canonicals, and quite at his ease, and had the boy in his arms, having made sure that all was as it should be, cried out: – "Gossip, do I not hear the father's voice out there?" "Ay indeed, Sir," replied the simpleton. "Come in then," said Fra Rinaldo. So in came the simpleton. Whereupon quoth Fra Rinaldo: – "I restore to you your boy made whole by the grace of God, whom but now I scarce thought you would see alive at vespers. You will do well to have his image fashioned in wax, not less than life-size, and set it for a thanksgiving to God, before the statue of Master St. Ambrose, by whose merits you have this favour of God."

The boy, catching sight of his father, ran to him with joyous greetings, as little children are wont; and the father, taking him in his arms, and weeping as if he were restored to him from the grave, fell by turns a kissing him and thanking his godfather, that he had cured him. Fra Rinaldo's companion, who had taught the maid not one paternoster only, but peradventure four or more, and by giving her a little purse of white thread that a nun had given him, had made her his devotee, no sooner heard Fra Rinaldo call the simpleton into his wife's room, than he stealthily got him to a place whence he might see and hear what was going on. Observing that the affair was now excellently arranged, he came down, and entered the chamber, saying: – "Fra Rinaldo, those four prayers that you bade me say, I have said them all." "Then well done, my brother," quoth Fra Rinaldo, "well-breathed must thou be. For my part, I had but said two, when my gossip came in; but what with thy travail and mine, God of His grace has vouchsafed-us the healing or the boy." The simpleton then had good wine and comfits brought in, and did the honours to the godfather and his companion in such sort as their occasions did most demand. He then ushered them forth of the house, commending them to God; and without delay had the waxen image made, and directed it to be set up with the others in front of the statue of St. Ambrose, not, be it understood, St. Ambrose of Milan.

Seventh Day
Novel IV

— Tofano one night locks his wife out of the house: she, finding that by no entreaties may she prevail upon him to let her in, feigns to throw herself into a well, throwing therein a great stone. Tofano hies him forth of the house, and runs to the spot: she goes into the house, and locks him out, and hurls abuse at him from within. —

THE KING no sooner wist that Elisa's story was ended, than, turning to Lauretta, he signified his will that she should tell somewhat: wherefore without delay she began: –

O Love, how great and signal is thy potency! how notable thy stratagems, thy devices! Was there ever, shall there ever be, philosopher or adept competent to inspire, counsel and teach in such sort as thou by thine unpremeditated art dost tutor those that follow thy lead? Verily laggard teachers are they all in comparison of thee, as by the matters heretofore set forth may very well be understood. To which store I will add, loving ladies, a stratagem used by a woman of quite ordinary understanding, and of such a sort that I know not by whom she could have been taught it save by Love.

Know, then, that there dwelt aforetime at Arezzo a rich man, Tofano by name, who took to wife Monna Ghita, a lady exceeding fair, of whom, for what cause he knew not, he presently grew jealous. Whereof the lady being ware, waxed resentful, and having on divers occasions demanded of him the reason of his jealousy, and gotten from him nought precise, but only generalities and trivialities, resolved at last to give him cause enough to die of that evil which without cause he so much dreaded. And being ware that a gallant, whom she deemed well worthy of her, was enamoured of her, she, using due discretion, came to an understanding with him; which being brought to the point that it only remained to give effect to their words in act, the lady cast about to devise how this might be. And witting that, among other bad habits that her husband had, he was too fond of his cups, she would not only commend indulgence, but cunningly and not seldom incite him thereto; insomuch that, well-nigh as often as she was so minded, she led him to drink to excess; and when she saw that he was well drunken, she would put him to bed; and so not once only but divers times without any manner of risk she forgathered with her lover; nay, presuming upon her husband's intoxication, she grew so bold that, not content with bringing her lover into her house, she would at times go spend a great part of the night with him at his house, which was not far off.

Now such being the enamoured lady's constant practice, it so befell that the dishonoured husband took note that, while she egged him on to drink, she herself drank never a drop; whereby he came to suspect the truth, to wit, that the lady was making him drunk, that afterwards she might take her pleasure while he slept. And being minded to put his surmise to the proof, one evening, having drunken nought all day, he mimicked never so drunken a sot both in speech and in carriage. The lady, deeming him to be really as he appeared, and that 'twas needless to ply him with liquor, presently put him to bed. Which done, she, as she at times was wont, hied her forth to her lover's house, where she tarried until midnight. Tofano no sooner perceived that his wife was gone, than up he got, hied him to the door, locked it, and then posted himself at the window to observe her return, and let her know that he was ware of her misconduct. So there he stood until the lady returned, and finding herself locked out, was annoyed beyond measure, and sought to force the door open. Tofano let her try her strength upon it a while, and then: – "Madam," quoth he, "'tis all to no purpose: thou canst not get in. Go get thee back thither where thou hast tarried all this while, and rest assured that thou shalt never recross this threshold, until I have done thee such honour as is meet for thee in the presence of thy kinsfolk and neighbours." Thereupon the lady fell entreating him to be pleased to open to her for the love of God, for that she was not come whence he supposed, but had only been passing the time with one of her gossips, because the nights were long, and she could not spend the whole time either in sleep or in solitary watching. But her supplications availed her nothing, for the fool was determined that all Arezzo should know their shame, whereof as yet none wist aught. So as 'twas idle to entreat, the lady assumed a menacing tone, saying: – "So thou open not to me, I will make thee the saddest man alive." Whereto Tofano made answer: – "And what then canst thou do?" The lady, her wits sharpened by Love, rejoined: – "Rather than endure the indignity to which thou wouldst unjustly subject me, I will cast myself into the well hard by here, and when I am found dead there, all the world will believe that 'twas thou that didst it in thy cups, and so thou wilt either have to flee and lose all that thou hast and be outlawed, or forfeit thy head as guilty of my death, as indeed thou wilt be." But, for all she said, Tofano wavered not a jot in his foolish purpose. So at last: – "Lo, now," quoth the lady, "I can no more abide thy surly humour: God forgive thee: I leave thee my distaff here, which be careful to bestow in a safe place." So saying, away she hied her to the well, and, the night being so dark that wayfarers could scarce see one another as they passed, she took up a huge stone that was by the well, and ejaculating, "God forgive me!" dropped it therein. Tofano, hearing the mighty splash that the stone made as it struck the water, never doubted that she had cast herself in: so, bucket and rope in hand, he flung himself out of the house, and came running to the well to her rescue. The lady had meanwhile hidden herself hard by the door, and seeing him make for the well, was in the house in a trice, and having locked the door, hied her to the window, and greeted him with: – "'Tis while thou art drinking, not now, when the night is far spent, that thou shouldst temper thy wine with water." Thus derided, Tofano came back to the door, and finding his ingress barred, began adjuring her to let him in. Whereupon, changing the low tone she had hitherto used for one so shrill that 'twas well-nigh a shriek, she broke out with: – "By the Holy Rood, tedious drunken sot that thou art, thou gettest no admittance here to-night; thy ways are more than I can endure: 'tis time I let all the world know what manner of man thou art, and at what hour of the night thou comest home." Tofano, on his part, now grew angry, and began loudly to upbraid her; insomuch that the neighbours, aroused by the noise, got up, men and women alike, and looked out of the windows, and asked what was the matter. Whereupon the lady fell a weeping and saying: – "'Tis this wicked man, who comes home drunk at even, or falls asleep in some tavern, and then returns at this hour. Long and to no purpose have I borne with him; but 'tis now past endurance, and I have done him this indignity of locking him out of the house in the hope that perchance it may cause him to mend his ways."

Tofano, on his part, told, dolt that he was, just what had happened, and was mighty menacing. Whereupon: – "Now mark," quoth the lady to the neighbours, "the sort of man he is! What would you say if I were, as he is, in the street, and he were in the house, as I am? God's faith, I doubt you would believe what he said. Hereby you may gauge his sense. He tells you that I have done just what, I doubt not, he has done himself. He thought to terrify me by throwing I know not what into the well, wherein would to God he had thrown himself indeed, and drowned himself, whereby the wine of which he has taken more than enough, had been watered to some purpose!" The neighbours, men and women alike, now with one accord gave tongue, censuring Tofano, throwing all the blame upon him, and answering what he alleged against the lady with loud recrimination; and in short the bruit, passing from neighbour to neighbour, reached at last the ears of the lady's kinsfolk; who hied them to the spot, and being apprised of the affair from this, that and the other of the neighbours, laid hands on Tofano, and beat him till he was black and blue from head to foot. Which done, they entered his house, stripped it of all that belonged to the lady, and took her home with them, bidding Tofano look for worse to come. Thus hard bested, and ruing the plight in which his jealousy had landed him, Tofano, who loved his wife with all his heart, set some friends to work to patch matters up, whereby he did in fact induce his lady to forgive him and live with him again, albeit he was fain to promise her never again to be jealous, and to give her leave to amuse herself to her heart's content, provided she used such discretion that he should not be ware of it. On such wise, like the churl and booby that he was, being despoiled, he made terms. Now long live Love, and perish war, and all that wage it!

Seventh Day

Novel V

— A jealous husband disguises himself as a priest, and hears his own wife's confession: she tells him that she loves a priest, who comes to her every night. The husband posts himself at the door to watch for the priest, and meanwhile the lady brings her lover in by the roof, and tarries with him. —

WHEN LAURETTA had done speaking, and all had commended the lady, for that she had done well, and treated her caitiff husband as he had deserved, the king, not to lose time, turned to Fiammetta, and graciously bade her take up her parable; which she did on this wise:

Most noble ladies, the foregoing story prompts me likewise to discourse of one of these jealous husbands, deeming that they are justly requited by their wives, more especially when they grow jealous without due cause. And had our legislators taken account of everything, I am of opinion that they would have visited ladies in such a case with no other penalty than such as they provide for those that offend in self-defence, seeing that a jealous husband does cunningly practise against the life of his lady, and most assiduously machinate her death. All the week the wife stays at home, occupied with her domestic duties; after which, on the day that is sacred to joy, she, like every one else, craves some solace, some peace, some recreation, not unreasonably, for she craves but what the husbandmen take in the fields, the craftsmen in the city, the magistrates in the courts, nay what God Himself took, when He rested from all His labours on the seventh day, and which laws human and Divine, mindful alike of the honour of God and the common well-being, have ordained, appropriating certain days to work, and others to repose. To which ordinance these jealous husbands will in no wise conform; on the contrary by then most sedulously secluding their wives, they make those days which to all other women are gladsome, to them most grievous and dolorous. And what an affliction it is to the poor creatures, they alone know, who have proved it; for which reason, to sum up, I say that a wife is rather to be commended than censured, if she take her revenge upon a husband that is jealous without cause.

Know then that at Rimini there dwelt a merchant, a man of great substance in lands and goods and money, who, having a most beautiful woman to wife, waxed inordinately jealous of her, and that for no better reason than that, loving her greatly, and esteeming her exceeding fair, and knowing that she did her utmost endeavour to pleasure him, he must needs suppose that every man loved her, and esteemed her fair, and that she, moreover, was as zealous to stand well with every other man as with himself; whereby you may see that he was a poor creature, and of little sense. Being thus so deeply infected with jealousy, he kept so strict and close watch over her, that some, maybe, have lain under sentence of death and been less rigorously confined by their warders. 'Twas not merely that the lady might not go to a wedding, or a festal gathering, or even to church, or indeed set foot out of doors in any sort; but she dared not so much as shew herself at a window, or cast a glance outside the house, no matter for what purpose. Wherefore she led a most woeful life of it, and found it all the harder to bear because she knew herself to be innocent. Accordingly, seeing herself evilly entreated by her husband without good cause, she cast about how for her own consolation she might devise means to justify his usage of her. And for that, as she might not shew herself at the window, there could be no interchange of amorous glances between her and any man that passed along the street, but she wist that in the next house there was a goodly and debonair gallant, she bethought her, that, if there were but a hole in the wall that divided the two houses, she might watch thereat, until she should have sight of the gallant on such wise that she might speak to him, and give him her love, if he cared to have it, and, if so it might be contrived, forgather with him now and again, and after this fashion relieve the burden of her woeful life, until such time as the evil spirit should depart from her husband. So peering about, now here, now there, when her husband was away, she found in a very remote part of the house a place, where, by chance, the wall had a little chink in it. Peering through which, she made out, though not without great difficulty, that on the other side was a room, and said to herself: – If this were Filippo's room – Filippo was the name of the gallant, her neighbour – I should be already halfway to my goal. So cautiously, through her maid, who was grieved to see her thus languish, she made quest, and discovered that it was indeed the gallant's room, where he slept quite alone. Wherefore she now betook her frequently to the aperture, and whenever she was ware that the gallant was in the room, she would let fall a pebble or the like trifle; whereby at length she brought the gallant to the other side of the aperture to see what the matter was. Whereupon she softly called him, and he knowing her voice, answered; and so, having now the opportunity she had sought, she in few words opened to him all her mind. The gallant, being overjoyed, wrought at the aperture on such wise that albeit none might be ware thereof, he enlarged it; and there many a time they held converse together, and touched hands, though further they might not go by reason of the assiduous watch that the jealous husband kept.

Now towards Christmas the lady told her husband that, if he approved, she would fain go on Christmas morning to church, and confess and communicate, like other Christians. "And what sins," quoth he, "hast thou committed, that wouldst be shriven?" "How?" returned the lady; "dost thou take me for a saint? For all thou keepest me so close, thou must know very well that I am like all other mortals. However, I am not minded to confess to thee, for that thou art no priest." Her husband, whose suspicions were excited by what she had said, cast about how he might discover these sins of hers, and having bethought him of what seemed an apt expedient, made answer that she had his consent, but he would not have her go to any church but their own chapel, where she might hie her betimes in the morning, and confess either to their own chaplain or some other priest that the chaplain might assign her, but to none other, and presently return to the house. The lady thought she half understood him, but she answered only that she would do as he required. Christmas morning came, and with the dawn the lady rose, dressed herself, and hied her to the church appointed by her husband, who also rose, and hied him to the same church, where he arrived before her; and having already concerted matters with the priest that was in charge, he forthwith put on one of the priest's robes with a great hood, overshadowing the face, such as we see priests wear, and which he pulled somewhat forward; and so disguised he seated himself in the choir.

On entering the church the lady asked for the priest, who came, and learning that she was minded to confess, said that he could not hear her himself, but would send her one of his brethren; so away he hied him and sent her, in an evil hour for him, her husband. For though he wore an air of great solemnity, and 'twas not yet broad day, and he had pulled the hood well over his eyes, yet all did not avail, but that his lady forthwith recognized him, and said to herself: – God be praised! why, the jealous rogue is turned priest: but leave it me to give him that whereof he is in quest. So she feigned not to know him, and seated herself at his feet. (I should tell you that he had put some pebbles in his mouth, that his speech, being impeded, might not betray him to his wife, and in all other respects he deemed himself so thoroughly disguised that there was nought whereby she might recognize him.) Now, to come to the confession, the lady, after informing him that she was married, told him among other matters that she was enamoured of a priest, who came every night to lie with her. Which to hear was to her husband as if he were stricken through the heart with a knife; and had it not been that he was bent on knowing more, he would have forthwith given over the confession, and taken himself off. However he kept his place, and: – "How?" said he to the lady, "does not your husband lie with you?" The lady replied in the affirmative. "How, then," quoth the husband, "can the priest also lie with you?" "Sir," replied she, "what art the priest employs I know not; but door there is none, however well locked, in the house, that comes not open at his touch; and he tells me that, being come to the door of my room, before he opens it, he says certain words, whereby my husband forthwith falls asleep; whereupon he opens the door, and enters the room, and lies with me; and so 'tis always, without fail." "Then 'tis very wrong, Madam, and you must give it up altogether," said the husband. "That, Sir," returned the lady, "I doubt I can never do; for I love him too much." "In that case," quoth the husband, "I cannot give you absolution." "The pity of it!" ejaculated the lady; "I came not hither to tell you falsehoods: if I could give it up, I would." "Madam," replied the husband, "indeed I am sorry for you; for I see that you are in a fair way to lose your soul. However, this I will do for you; I will make special supplication to God on your behalf; and perchance you may be profited thereby. And from time to time I will send you one of my young clerks; and you will tell him whether my prayers have been of any help to you, or no, and if they have been so, I shall know what to do next." "Nay, Sir," quoth the lady, "do not so; send no man to me at home; for, should my husband come to know it, he is so jealous that nothing in the world would ever disabuse him of the idea that he came but for an evil purpose, and so I should have no peace with him all the year long." Madam, returned the husband, "have no fear; rest assured that I will so order matters that you shall never hear a word about it from him." "If you can make sure of that," quoth the lady, "I have no more to say." And so, her confession ended, and her penance enjoined, she rose, and went to mass, while the luckless husband, fuming and fretting, hasted to divest himself of his priest's trappings, and then went home bent upon devising some means to bring the priest and his wife together, and take his revenge upon them both.

When the lady came home from church she read in her husband's face that she had spoiled his Christmas for him, albeit he dissembled to the uttermost, lest she should discover what he had done, and supposed himself to have learned. His mind was made up to keep watch for the priest that very night by his own front door. So to the lady he said: – "I have to go out to-night to sup and sleep; so thou wilt take care that the front door, and the mid-stair door, and the bedroom door are well locked; and for the rest thou mayst go to bed, at thine own time." "Well and good," replied the lady: and as soon as she was able, off she hied her to the aperture, and gave the wonted signal, which Filippo no sooner heard, than he was at the spot. The lady then told him what she had done in the morning, and what her husband had said to her after breakfast, adding: – "Sure I am that he will not stir out of the house, but will keep watch beside the door; wherefore contrive to come in to-night by the roof, that we may be together." "Madam," replied the gallant, nothing loath, "trust me for that."

Night came, the husband armed, and noiselessly hid himself in a room on the ground floor: the lady locked all the doors, being especially careful to secure the mid-stair door, to bar her husband's ascent; and in due time the gallant, having found his way cautiously enough over the roof, they got them to bed, and there had solace of one another and a good time; and at daybreak the gallant hied him back to his house. Meanwhile the husband, rueful and supperless, half dead with cold, kept his armed watch beside his door, momently expecting the priest, for the best part of the night; but towards daybreak, his powers failing him, he lay down and slept in the ground-floor room. 'Twas hard upon tierce when he awoke, and the front door was then open; so, making as if he had just come in, he went upstairs and breakfasted. Not long afterwards he sent to his wife a young fellow, disguised as the priest's underling, who asked her if he of whom she wist had been with her again. The lady, who quite understood what that meant, made answer that he had not come that night, and that, if he continued to neglect her so, 'twas possible he might be forgotten, though she had no mind to forget him.

Now, to make a long story short, the husband passed many a night in the same way, hoping to catch the priest as he came in, the lady and her gallant meanwhile having a good time. But at last the husband, being able to stand it no longer, sternly demanded of his wife what she had said to the priest the morning when she was confessed. The lady answered that she was not minded to tell him, for that 'twas not seemly or proper so to do. Whereupon: – "Sinful woman," quoth the husband, "in thy despite I know what thou saidst to him, and know I must and will who this priest is, of whom thou art enamoured, and who by dint of his incantations lies with thee a nights, or I will sluice thy veins for thee." "'Tis not true," replied the lady, "that I am enamoured of a priest." "How?" quoth the husband, "saidst thou not as much to the priest that confessed thee?" "Thou canst not have had it from him," rejoined the lady. "Wast thou then present thyself? For sure I never told him so." "Then tell me," quoth the husband, "who this priest is; and lose no time about it." Whereat the lady began to smile, and: – "I find it not a little diverting," quoth she, "that a wise man should suffer himself to be led by a simple woman as a ram is led by the horns to the shambles; albeit no wise man art thou: not since that fatal hour when thou gavest harbourage in thy breast, thou wist not why, to the evil spirit of jealousy; and the more foolish and insensate thou art, the less glory have I. Deemest thou, my husband, that I am as blind of the bodily eye as thou art of the mind's eye? Nay, but for sure I am not so. I knew at a glance the priest that confessed me, and that 'twas even thyself. But I was minded to give thee that of which thou wast in quest, and I gave it thee. Howbeit, if thou hadst been the wise man thou takest thyself to be, thou wouldst not have chosen such a way as that to worm out thy good lady's secrets, nor wouldst thou have fallen a prey to a baseless suspicion, but wouldst have understood that what she confessed was true, and she all the while guiltless. I told thee that I loved a priest; and wast not thou, whom I love, though ill enough dost thou deserve it, turned priest? I told thee that there was no door in my house but would open when he was minded to lie with me: and when thou wouldst fain have access to me, what door was ever closed against thee? I told thee that the priest lay nightly with me: and what night was there that thou didst not lie with me? Thou sentest thy young clerk to me: and thou knowest that, as often as thou hadst not been with me, I sent word that the priest had not been with me. Who but thou, that hast suffered jealousy to blind thee, would have been so witless as not to read such a riddle? But thou must needs mount guard at night beside the door, and think to make me believe that thou hadst gone out to sup and sleep. Consider thy ways, and court not the mockery of those that know them as I do, but turn a man again as thou wast wont to be: and let there be no more of this strict restraint in which thou keepest me; for I swear to thee by God that, if I were minded to set horns on thy brow, I should not fail so to take my pastime that thou wouldst never find it out, though thou hadst a hundred eyes, as thou hast but two."

Thus admonished, the jealous caitiff, who had flattered himself that he had very cunningly discovered his wife's secret, was ashamed, and made no answer save to commend his wife's wit and honour; and thus, having cause for jealousy, he discarded it, as he had erstwhile been jealous without cause. And so the adroit lady had, as it were, a charter of indulgence, and needed no more to contrive for her lover to come to her over the roof like a cat, but admitted him by the door, and using due discretion, had many a good time with him, and sped her life gaily.

Seventh Day

Novel VI

— Madonna Isabella has with her Leonetto, her accepted lover, when she is surprised by one Messer Lambertuccio, by whom she is beloved: her husband coming home about the same time, she sends Messer Lambertuccio forth of the house drawn sword in hand, and the husband afterwards escorts Leonetto home. —

WONDROUS WAS the delight that all the company had of Fiammetta's story, nor was there any but affirmed that the lady had done excellent well, and dealt with her insensate husband as he deserved. However, it being ended, the king bade Pampinea follow suit; which she did on this wise: –

Not a few there are that in their simplicity aver that Love deranges the mind, insomuch that whoso loves becomes as it were witless: the folly of which opinion, albeit I doubt it not, and deem it abundantly proven by what has been already said, I purpose once again to demonstrate.

In our city, rich in all manner of good things, there dwelt a young gentlewoman, fair exceedingly, and wedded to a most worthy and excellent gentleman. And as it not seldom happens that one cannot keep ever to the same diet, but would fain at times vary it, so this lady, finding her husband not altogether to her mind, became enamoured of a gallant, Leonetto by name, who, though of no high rank, was not a little debonair and courteous, and he in like manner fell in love with her; and (as you know that 'tis seldom that what is mutually desired fails to come about) 'twas not long before they had fruition of their love. Now the lady being, as I said, fair and winsome, it so befell that a gentleman, Messer Lambertuccio by name, grew mightily enamoured of her, but so tiresome and odious did she find him, that for the world she could not bring herself to love him. So, growing tired of fruitlessly soliciting her favour by ambassage, Messer Lambertuccio, who was a powerful signior, sent her at last another sort of message in which he threatened to defame her if she complied not with his wishes. Wherefore the lady, knowing her man, was terrified, and disposed herself to pleasure him.

Now it so chanced that Madonna Isabella, for such was the lady's name, being gone, as is our Florentine custom in the summer, to spend some time on a very goodly estate that she had in the contado, one morning finding herself alone, for her husband had ridden off to tarry some days elsewhere, she sent for Leonetto to come and keep her company; and Leonetto came forthwith in high glee. But while they were together, Messer Lambertuccio, who, having got wind that the husband was away, had mounted his horse and ridden thither quite alone, knocked at the door. Whereupon the lady's maid hied her forthwith to her mistress, who was alone with Leonetto, and called her, saying: – "Madam, Messer Lambertuccio is here below, quite alone." Whereat the lady was vexed beyond measure; and being also not a little dismayed, she said to Leonetto: – "Prithee, let it not irk thee to withdraw behind the curtain, and there keep close until Messer Lambertuccio be gone." Leonetto, who stood in no less fear of Messer Lambertuccio than did the lady, got into his hiding-place; and the lady bade the maid go open to Messer Lambertuccio: she did so; and having dismounted and fastened his palfrey to a pin, he ascended the stairs; at the head of which the lady received him with a smile and as gladsome a greeting as she could find words for, and asked him on what errand he was come. The gentleman embraced and kissed her, saying: – "My soul, I am informed that your husband is not here, and therefore I am come to stay a while with you." Which said, they went into the room, and locked them in, and Messer Lambertuccio fell a toying with her.

Now, while thus he sped the time with her, it befell that the lady's husband, albeit she nowise expected him, came home, and, as he drew nigh the palace, was observed by the maid, who forthwith ran to the lady's chamber, and said: – "Madam, the master will be here anon; I doubt he is already in the courtyard." Whereupon, for that she had two men in the house, and the knight's palfrey, that was in the courtyard, made it impossible to hide him, the lady gave herself up for dead. Nevertheless she made up her mind on the spur of the moment, and springing out of bed "Sir," quoth she to Messer Lambertuccio, "if you have any regard for me, and would save my life, you will do as I bid you: that is to say, you will draw your blade, and put on a fell and wrathful countenance, and hie you downstairs, saying: – 'By God, he shall not escape me elsewhere.' And if my husband would stop you, or ask you aught, say nought but what I have told you, and get you on horseback and tarry with him on no account." "To hear is to obey," quoth Messer Lambertuccio, who, with the flush of his recent exertion and the rage that he felt at the husband's return still on his face, and drawn sword in hand, did as she bade him. The lady's husband, being now dismounted in the courtyard, and not a little surprised to see the palfrey there, was about to go up the stairs, when he saw Messer Lambertuccio coming down them, and marvelling both at his words and at his mien: – "What means this, Sir?" quoth he. But Messer Lambertuccio clapped foot in stirrup, and mounted, saying nought but: – "Zounds, but I will meet him elsewhere;" and so he rode off.

The gentleman then ascended the stairs, at the head of which he found his lady distraught with terror, to whom he said: – "What manner of thing is this? After whom goes Messer Lambertuccio, so wrathful and menacing?" Whereto the lady, drawing nigher the room, that Leonetto might hear her, made answer: – "Never, Sir, had I such a fright as this. There came running in here a young man, who to me is quite a stranger, and at his heels Messer Lambertuccio with a drawn sword in his hand; and as it happened the young man found the door of this room open, and trembling in every limb, cried out: – 'Madam, your succour, for God's sake, that I die not in your arms.' So up I got, and would have asked him who he was, and how bested, when up came Messer Lambertuccio, exclaiming: – 'Where art thou, traitor?' I planted myself in the doorway, and kept him from entering, and seeing that I was not minded to give him admittance, he was courteous enough, after not a little parley, to take himself off, as you saw." Whereupon: – "Wife," quoth the husband, "thou didst very right. Great indeed had been the scandal, had some one been slain here, and 'twas a gross affront on Messer Lambertuccio's part to pursue a fugitive within the house." He then asked where the young man was. Whereto the lady answered: – "Nay, where he may be hiding, Sir, I wot not." So: – "Where art thou?" quoth the knight. "Fear not to shew thyself." Then forth of his hiding-place, all of a tremble, for in truth he had been thoroughly terrified, crept Leonetto, who had heard all that had passed. To whom: – "What hast thou to do with Messer Lambertuccio?" quoth the knight. "Nothing in the world," replied the young man: "wherefore, I doubt he must either be out of his mind, or have mistaken me for another; for no sooner had he sight of me in the street hard by the palace, than he laid his hand on his sword, and exclaimed: – 'Traitor, thou art a dead man.' Whereupon I sought not to know why, but fled with all speed, and got me here, and so, thanks to God and this gentlewoman, I escaped his hands." "Now away with thy fears," quoth the knight; "I will see thee home safe and sound; and then 'twill be for thee to determine how thou shalt deal with him." And so, when they had supped, he set him on horseback, and escorted him to Florence, and left him not until he was safe in his own house. And the very same evening, following the lady's instructions, Leonetto spoke privily with Messer Lambertuccio, and so composed the affair with him, that, though it occasioned not a little talk, the knight never wist how he had been tricked by his wife.

Seventh Day
Novel VII

— Lodovico discovers to Madonna Beatrice the love that he bears her: she sends Egano, her husband, into a garden disguised as herself, and lies with Lodovico; who thereafter, being risen, hies him to the garden and cudgels Egano. —

THIS DEVICE of Madonna Isabella, thus recounted by Pampinea, was held nothing short of marvellous by all the company. But, being bidden by the king to tell the next story, thus spake Filomena: –

Loving ladies, if I mistake not, the device, of which you shall presently hear from me, will prove to be no less excellent than the last.

You are to know, then, that there dwelt aforetime at Paris a Florentine gentleman, who, being by reason of poverty turned merchant, had prospered so well in his affairs that he was become very wealthy; and having by his lady an only son, Lodovico by name, whose nobility disrelished trade, he would not put him in any shop; but that he might be with other gentlemen, he caused him to enter the service of the King of France, whereby he acquired very fine manners and other accomplishments. Being in this service, Lodovico was one day with some other young gallants that talked of the fair ladies of France, and England, and other parts of the world, when they were joined by certain knights that were returned from the Holy Sepulchre; and hearing their discourse, one of the knights fell a saying, that of a surety in the whole world, so far as he had explored it, there was not any lady, of all that he had ever seen, that might compare for beauty with Madonna Beatrice, the wife of Egano de' Galluzzi, of Bologna: wherein all his companions, who in common with him had seen the lady at Bologna, concurred. Which report Lodovico, who was as yet fancy-free, no sooner heard, than he burned with such a yearning to see the lady that he was able to think of nought else: insomuch that he made up his mind to betake him to Bologna to see her, and if she pleased him, to remain there; to which end he gave his father to understand that he would fain visit the Holy Sepulchre, whereto his father after no little demur consented.

So to Bologna Anichino – for so he now called himself – came; and, as Fortune would have it, the very next day, he saw the lady at a festal gathering, and deemed her vastly more beautiful than he had expected: wherefore he waxed most ardently enamoured of her, and resolved never to quit Bologna, until he had gained her love. So, casting about how he should proceed, he could devise no other way but to enter her husband's service, which was the more easy that he kept not a few retainers: on this wise Lodovico surmised that, peradventure, he might compass his end. He therefore sold his horses and meetly bestowed his servants, bidding them make as if they knew him not; and being pretty familiar with his host, he told him that he was minded to take service with some worthy lord, it any such he might find. "Thou wouldst make," quoth the host, "the very sort of retainer to suit a gentleman of this city, Egano by name, who keeps not a few of them, and will have all of them presentable like thee: I will mention the matter to him." And so he accordingly did, and before he took leave of Egano had placed Anichino with him, to Egano's complete satisfaction.

Being thus resident with Egano, and having abundant opportunities of seeing the fair lady, Anichino set himself to serve Egano with no little zeal; wherein he succeeded so well, that Egano was more than satisfied, insomuch that by and by there was nought he could do without his advice, and he entrusted to him the guidance not only of himself, but of all his affairs. Now it so befell that one day when Egano was gone a hawking, having left Anichino at home, Madonna Beatrice, who as yet wist not of his love, albeit she had from time to time taken note of him and his manners, and had not a little approved and commended them, sat herself down with him to a game of chess, which, to please her, Anichino most dexterously contrived to lose, to the lady's prodigious delight. After a while, the lady's women, one and all, gave over watching their play, and left them to it; whereupon Anichino heaved a mighty sigh. The lady, looking hard at him, said: – "What ails thee, Anichino? Is it, then, such a mortification to thee to be conquered by me?" "Nay, Madam," replied Anichino, "my sigh was prompted by a much graver matter." "Then, if thou hast any regard for me," quoth the lady, "tell me what it is." Hearing himself thus adjured by "any regard" he had for her whom he loved more than aught else, Anichino heaved a yet mightier sigh, which caused the lady to renew her request that he would be pleased to tell her the occasion of his sighs. Whereupon: – "Madam," said Anichino, "I greatly fear me, that, were I to tell it you, 'twould but vex you; and, moreover, I doubt you might repeat it to some one else." "Rest assured," returned the lady, "that I shall neither be annoyed, nor, without thy leave, ever repeat to any other soul aught that thou mayst say." "Then," said Anichino, "having this pledge from you, I will tell it you." And, while the tears all but stood in his eyes, he told her, who he was, the report he had heard of her, and where and how he had become enamoured of her, and with what intent he had taken service with her husband: after which, he humbly besought her, that, if it might be, she would have pity on him, and gratify this his secret and ardent desire; and that, if she were not minded so to do, she would suffer him to retain his place there, and love her. Ah! Bologna! how sweetly mixed are the elements in thy women! How commendable in such a case are they all! No delight have they in sighs and tears, but are ever inclinable to prayers, and ready to yield to the solicitations of Love. Had I but words apt to praise them as they deserve, my eloquence were inexhaustible.

The gentlewoman's gaze was fixed on Anichino as he spoke; she made no doubt that all he said was true, and yielding to his appeal, she entertained his love within her heart in such measure that she too began to sigh, and after a sigh or two made answer: – "Sweet my Anichino, be of good cheer; neither presents nor promises, nor any courting by gentleman, or lord, or whoso else (for I have been and am still courted by not a few) was ever able to sway my soul to love any of them: but thou, by the few words that thou hast said, hast so wrought with me that, brief though the time has been, I am already in far greater measure thine than mine. My love I deem thee to have won right worthily; and so I give it thee, and vow to give thee joyance thereof before the coming night be past. To which end thou wilt come to my room about midnight; I will leave the door open; thou knowest the side of the bed on which I sleep; thou wilt come there; should I be asleep, thou hast but to touch me, and I shall awake, and give thee solace of thy long-pent desire. In earnest whereof I will even give thee a kiss." So saying, she threw her arms about his neck, and lovingly kissed him, as Anichino her.

Their colloquy thus ended, Anichino betook him elsewhere about some matters which he had to attend to, looking forward to midnight with boundless exultation. Egano came in from his hawking; and after supper, being weary, went straight to bed, whither the lady soon followed him, leaving, as she had promised, the door of the chamber open. Thither accordingly, at the appointed hour, came Anichino, and having softly entered the chamber, and closed the door behind him, stole up to where the lady lay, and laying his hand upon her breast, found that she was awake. Now, as soon as she wist that Anichino was come, she took his hand in both her own; and keeping fast hold of him, she turned about in the bed, until she awoke Egano; whereupon: – "Husband," quoth she, "I would not say aught of this to thee, yestereve, because I judged thou wast weary; but tell me, upon thy hope of salvation, Egano, whom deemest thou thy best and most loyal retainer, and the most attached to thee, of all that thou hast in the house?" "What a question is this, wife?" returned Egano. "Dost not know him? Retainer I have none, nor ever had, so trusted, or loved, as Anichino. But wherefore put such a question?"

Now, when Anichino wist that Egano was awake, and heard them talk of himself, he more than once tried to withdraw his hand, being mightily afraid lest the lady meant to play him false; but she held it so tightly that he might not get free, while thus she made answer to Egano: – "I will tell thee what he is. I thought that he was all thou sayst, and that none was so loyal to thee as he, but he has undeceived me, for that yesterday, when thou wast out a hawking, he, being here, chose his time, and had the shamelessness to crave of me compliance with his wanton desires: and I, that I might not need other evidence than that of thine own senses to prove his guilt to thee, I made answer, that I was well content, and that to-night, after midnight, I would get me into the garden, and await him there at the foot of the pine. Now go thither I shall certainly not; but, if thou wouldst prove the loyalty of thy retainer, thou canst readily do so, if thou but slip on one of my loose robes, and cover thy face with a veil, and go down and attend his coming, for come, I doubt not, he will." Whereto Egano: – "Meet indeed it is," quoth he, "that I should go see;" and straightway up he got, and, as best he might in the dark, he put on one of the lady's loose robes and veiled his face, and then hied him to the garden, and sate down at the foot of the pine to await Anichino. The lady no sooner wist that he was out of the room, than she rose, and locked the door. Anichino, who had never been so terrified in all his life, and had struggled with all his might to disengage his hand from the lady's clasp, and had inwardly cursed her and his love, and himself for trusting her, a hundred thousand times, was overjoyed beyond measure at this last turn that she had given the affair. And so, the lady having got her to bed again, and he, at her bidding, having stripped and laid him down beside her, they had solace and joyance of one another for a good while. Then, the lady, deeming it unmeet for Anichino to tarry longer with her, caused him to get up and resume his clothes, saying to him: – "Sweet my mouth, thou wilt take a stout cudgel, and get thee to the garden, and making as if I were there, and thy suit to me had been but to try me, thou wilt give Egano a sound rating with thy tongue and a sound belabouring with thy cudgel, the sequel whereof will be wondrously gladsome and delightful." Whereupon Anichino hied him off to the garden, armed with a staff of wild willow; and as he drew nigh the pine, Egano saw him, and rose and came forward to meet him as if he would receive him with the heartiest of cheer. But: – "Ah! wicked woman!" quoth Anichino; "so thou art come! Thou didst verily believe, then, that I was, that I am, minded thus to wrong my lord? Foul fall thee a thousand times!" And therewith he raised his cudgel, and began to lay about him. Egano, however, had heard and seen enough, and without a word took to flight, while Anichino pursued him, crying out: – "Away with thee! God send thee a bad year, lewd woman that thou art; nor doubt that Egano shall hear of this to-morrow." Egano, having received sundry round knocks, got him back to his chamber with what speed he might; and being asked by the lady, whether Anichino had come into the garden: – "Would to God he had not!" quoth he, "for that, taking me for thee, he has beaten me black and blue with his cudgel, and rated me like the vilest woman that ever was: passing strange, indeed, it had seemed to me that he should have said those words to thee with intent to dishonour me; and now 'tis plain that 'twas but that, seeing thee so blithe and frolicsome, he was minded to prove thee." Whereto: – "God be praised," returned the lady, "that he proved me by words, as thee by acts: and I doubt not he may say that I bear his words with more patience than thou his acts. But since he is so loyal to thee, we must make much of him and do him honour." "Ay, indeed," quoth Egano, "thou sayst sooth."

Thus was Egano fortified in the belief that never had any gentleman wife so true, or retainer so loyal, as he; and many a hearty laugh had he with Anichino and his lady over this affair, which to them was the occasion that, with far less let than might else have been, they were able to have solace and joyance of one another, so long as it pleased Anichino to tarry at Bologna.

Seventh Day
Novel VIII

— *A husband grows jealous of his wife, and discovers that she has warning of her lover's approach by a piece of pack-thread, which she ties to her great toe a nights. While he is pursuing her lover, she puts another woman in bed in her place. The husband, finding her there, beats her, and cuts off her hair. He then goes and calls his wife's brothers, who, holding his accusation to be false, give him a rating.* —

RARE INDEED was deemed by common consent the subtlety shewn by Madonna Beatrice in the beguilement of her husband, and all affirmed that the terror of Anichino must have been prodigious, when, the lady still keeping fast hold of him, he had heard her say that he had made suit of love to her. However, Filomena being silent, the king turned to Neifile, saying: – "'Tis now for you to tell." Whereupon Neifile, while a slight smile died away upon her lips, thus began: –

Fair ladies, to entertain you with a goodly story, such as those which my predecessors have delighted you withal, is indeed a heavy burden, but, God helping me, I trust fairly well to acquit myself thereof.

You are to know, then, that there dwelt aforetime in our city a most wealthy merchant, Arriguccio Berlinghieri by name, who foolishly, as we wot by daily experience is the way of merchants, thinking to compass gentility by matrimony, took to wife a young gentlewoman, by no means suited to him, whose name was Monna Sismonda. Now Monna Sismonda, seeing that her husband was much abroad, and gave her little of his company, became enamoured of a young gallant, Ruberto by name, who had long courted her: and she being grown pretty familiar with him, and using, perchance, too little discretion, for she affected him extremely, it so befell that Arriguccio, whether it was that he detected somewhat, or howsoever, waxed of all men the most jealous, and gave up going abroad, and changed his way of life altogether, and made it his sole care to watch over his wife, insomuch that he never allowed himself a wink of sleep until he had seen her to bed: which occasioned the lady the most grievous dumps, because 'twas on no wise possible for her to be with her Ruberto. So, casting about in many ways how she might contrive to meet him, and being thereto not a little plied by Ruberto himself, she bethought her at last of the following expedient: to wit, her room fronting the street, and Arriguccio, as she had often observed, being very hard put to it to get him to sleep, but thereafter sleeping very soundly, she resolved to arrange with Ruberto that he should come to the front door about midnight, whereupon she would get her down, and open the door, and stay some time with him while her husband was in his deep sleep. And that she might have tidings of his arrival, yet so as that none else might wot aught thereof, she adopted the device of lowering a pack-thread from the bedroom window on such wise that, while with one end it should all but touch the ground, it should traverse the floor of the room, until it reached the bed, and then be brought under the clothes, so that, when she was abed, she might attach it to her great toe. Having so done, she sent word to Ruberto, that when he came, he must be sure to jerk the pack-thread, and, if her husband were asleep, she would loose it, and go open to him; but, if he were awake, she would hold it taut and draw it to herself, to let him know that he must not expect her. Ruberto fell in with the idea, came there many times, and now forgathered with her and again did not. But at last, they still using this cunning practice, it so befell that one night, while the lady slept, Arriguccio, letting his foot stray more than he was wont about the bed, came upon the pack-thread, and laying his hand upon it, found that it was attached to his lady's great toe, and said to himself: – This must be some trick: and afterwards discovering that the thread passed out of the window, was confirmed in his surmise. Wherefore, he softly severed it from the lady's toe, and affixed it to his own; and waited, all attention, to learn the result of his experiment. Nor had he long to wait before Ruberto came, and Arriguccio felt him jerk the thread according to his wont: and as Arriguccio had not known how to attach the thread securely, and Ruberto jerked it with some force, it gave way, whereby he understood that he was to wait, and did so. Arriguccio straightway arose, caught up his arms, and hasted to the door to see who might be there, intent to do him a mischief. Now Arriguccio, for all he was a merchant, was a man of spirit, and of thews and sinews; and being come to the door, he opened it by no means gingerly, as the lady was wont; whereby Ruberto, who was in waiting, surmised the truth, to wit, that 'twas Arriguccio by whom the door was opened. Wherefore he forthwith took to flight, followed by Arriguccio. But at length, when he had run a long way, as Arriguccio gave not up the pursuit, he being also armed, drew his sword, and faced about; and so they fell to, Arriguccio attacking, and Ruberto defending himself.

Now when Arriguccio undid the bedroom door, the lady awoke, and finding the pack-thread cut loose from her toe, saw at a glance that her trick was discovered; and hearing Arriguccio running after Ruberto, she forthwith got up, foreboding what the result was like to be, and called her maid, who was entirely in her confidence: whom she so plied with her obsecrations that at last she got her into bed in her room, beseeching her not to say who she was, but to bear patiently all the blows that Arriguccio might give her; and she would so reward her that she should have no reason to complain. Then, extinguishing the light that was in the room, forth she hied her, and having found a convenient hiding-place in the house, awaited the turn of events. Now Arriguccio and Ruberto being hotly engaged in the street, the neighbours, roused by the din of the combat, got up and launched their curses upon them. Wherefore Arriguccio, fearing lest he should be recognized, drew off before he had so much as discovered who the young gallant was, or done him any scathe, and in a fell and wrathful mood betook him home. Stumbling into the bedroom, he cried out angrily: – "Where art thou, lewd woman? Thou hast put out the light, that I may not be able to find thee; but thou hast miscalculated." And going to the bedside, he laid hold of the maid, taking her to be his wife, and fell a pummelling and kicking her with all the strength he had in his hands and feet, insomuch that he pounded her face well-nigh to pulp, rating her the while like the vilest woman that ever was; and last of all he cut off her hair. The maid wept bitterly, as indeed she well might; and though from time to time she ejaculated an "Alas! Mercy, for God's sake!" or "Spare me, spare me;" yet her voice was so broken by her sobs, and Arriguccio's hearing so dulled by his wrath, that he was not able to discern that 'twas not his wife's voice but that of another woman. So, having soundly thrashed her, and cut off her hair, as we said: – "Wicked woman," quoth he, "I touch thee no more; but I go to find thy brothers, and shall do them to wit of thy good works; and then they may come here, and deal with thee as they may deem their honour demands, and take thee hence, for be sure thou shalt no more abide in this house." With this he was gone, locking the door of the room behind him, and quitted the house alone.

Now no sooner did Monna Sismonda, who had heard all that passed, perceive that her husband was gone, than she opened the door of the bedroom, rekindled the light, and finding her maid all bruises and tears, did what she could to comfort her, and carried her back to her own room, where, causing her to be privily waited on and tended, she helped her so liberally from Arriguccio's own store, that she confessed herself content. The maid thus bestowed in her room, the lady presently hied her back to her own, which she set all in neat and trim order, remaking the bed, so that it might appear as if it had not been slept in, relighting the lamp, and dressing and tiring herself, until she looked as if she had not been abed that night; then, taking with her a lighted lamp and some work, she sat her down at the head of the stairs, and began sewing, while she waited to see how the affair would end.

Arriguccio meanwhile had hied him with all speed straight from the house to that of his wife's brothers, where by dint of much knocking he made himself heard, and was admitted. The lady's three brothers, and her mother, being informed that 'twas Arriguccio, got up, and having set lights a burning, came to him and asked him on what errand he was come there at that hour, and alone. Whereupon Arriguccio, beginning with the discovery of the pack-thread attached to his lady's great toe, gave them the whole narrative of his discoveries and doings down to the very end; and to clinch the whole matter, he put in their hands the locks which he had cut, as he believed, from his wife's head, adding that 'twas now for them to come for her and deal with her on such wise as they might deem their honour required, seeing that he would nevermore have her in his house. Firmly believing what he told them, the lady's brothers were very wroth with her, and having provided themselves with lighted torches, set out with Arriguccio, and hied them to his house with intent to scorn her, while their mother followed, weeping and beseeching now one, now another, not to credit these matters so hastily, until they had seen or heard somewhat more thereof; for that the husband might have some other reason to be wroth with her, and having ill-treated her, might have trumped up this charge by way of exculpation, adding that, if true, 'twas passing strange, for well she knew her daughter, whom she had brought up from her tenderest years, and much more to the like effect.

However, being come to Arriguccio's house, they entered, and were mounting the stairs, when Monna Sismonda, hearing them, called out: – "Who is there?" Whereto one of the brothers responded: – "Lewd woman, thou shalt soon have cause enough to know who it is." "Now Lord love us!" quoth Monna Sismonda, "what would he be at?" Then, rising, she greeted them with: – "Welcome, my brothers but what seek ye abroad at this hour, all three of you?" They had seen her sitting and sewing with never a sign of a blow on her face, whereas Arriguccio had averred that he had pummelled her all over: wherefore their first impression was one of wonder, and refraining the vehemence of their wrath, they asked her what might be the truth of the matter which Arriguccio laid to her charge, and threatened her with direful consequences, if she should conceal aught. Whereto the lady: – "What you would have me tell you," quoth she, "or what Arriguccio may have laid to my charge, that know not I." Arriguccio could but gaze upon her, as one that had taken leave of his wits, calling to mind how he had pummelled her about the face times without number, and scratched it for her, and mishandled her in all manner of ways, and there he now saw her with no trace of aught of it all upon her. However, to make a long story short, the lady's brothers told her what Arriguccio had told them touching the pack-thread and the beating and all the rest of it. Whereupon the lady turned to him with: – "Alas, my husband, what is this that I hear? Why givest thou me, to thy own great shame, the reputation of a lewd woman, when such I am not, and thyself the reputation of a wicked and cruel man, which thou art not? Wast thou ever to-night, I say not in my company, but so much as in the house until now? Or when didst thou beat me? For my part I mind me not of it." Arriguccio began: – "How sayst thou, lewd woman? Did we not go to bed together? Did I not come back, after chasing thy lover? Did I not give thee bruises not a few, and cut thy hair for thee?" But the lady interrupted him, saying: – "Nay, thou didst not lie here to-night. But leave we this, of which my true words are my sole witness, and pass we to this of the beating thou sayst thou gavest me, and how thou didst cut my hair. Never a beating had I from thee, and I bid all that are here, and thee among them, look at me, and say if I have any trace of a beating on my person; nor should I advise thee to dare lay hand upon me; for, by the Holy Rood, I would spoil thy beauty for thee. Nor didst thou cut my hair, for aught that I saw or felt: however, thou didst it, perchance, on such wise that I was not ware thereof: so let me see whether 'tis cut or no." Then, unveiling herself, she shewed that her hair was uncut and entire. Wherefore her brothers and mother now turned to Arriguccio with: – "What means this, Arriguccio? This accords not with what thou gavest us to understand thou hadst done; nor know we how thou wilt prove the residue."

Arriguccio was lost, as it were, in a dream, and yet he would fain have spoken; but, seeing that what he had thought to prove was otherwise, he essayed no reply. So the lady turning to her brothers: – "I see," quoth she, "what he would have: he will not be satisfied unless I do what I never would otherwise have done, to wit, give you to know what a pitiful caitiff he is; as now I shall not fail to do. I make no manner of doubt that, as he has said, even so it befell, and so he did. How, you shall hear. This worthy man, to whom, worse luck! you gave me to wife, a merchant, as he calls himself, and as such would fain have credit, and who ought to be more temperate than a religious, and more continent than a girl, lets scarce an evening pass but he goes a boozing in the taverns, and consorting with this or the other woman of the town; and 'tis for me to await his return until midnight or sometimes until matins, even as you now find me. I doubt not that, being thoroughly well drunk, he got him to bed with one of these wantons, and, awaking, found the pack-thread on her foot, and afterwards did actually perform all these brave exploits of which he speaks, and in the end came back to her, and beat her, and cut her hair off, and being not yet quite recovered from his debauch, believed, and, I doubt not, still believes, that 'twas I that he thus treated; and if you will but scan his face closely, you will see that he is still half drunk. But, whatever he may have said about me, I would have you account it as nothing more than the disordered speech of a tipsy man; and forgive him as I do." Whereupon the lady's mother raised no small outcry, saying: – "By the Holy Rood, my daughter, this may not be! A daughter, such as thou, to be mated with one so unworthy of thee! The pestilent, insensate cur should be slain on the spot! A pretty state of things, indeed! Why, he might have picked thee up from the gutter! Now foul fall him! but thou shalt no more be vexed with the tedious drivel of a petty dealer in ass's dung, some blackguard, belike, that came hither from the country because he was dismissed the service of some petty squire, clad in romagnole, with belfry-breeches, and a pen in his arse, and for that he has a few pence, must needs have a gentleman's daughter and a fine lady to wife, and set up a coat of arms, and say: – 'I am of the such and such,' and 'my ancestors did thus and thus.' Ah! had my sons but followed my advice! Thy honour were safe in the house of the Counts Guidi, where they might have bestowed thee, though thou hadst but a morsel of bread to thy dowry: but they must needs give thee to this rare treasure, who, though better daughter and more chaste there is none than thou in Florence, has not blushed this very midnight and in our presence to call thee a strumpet, as if we knew thee not. God's faith! so I were hearkened to, he should shrewdly smart for it." Then, turning to her sons, she said: – "My sons, I told you plainly enough that this ought not to be. Now, have you heard how your worthy brother-in-law treats your sister? Petty twopenny trader that he is: were it for me to act, as it is for you, after what he has said of her and done to her, nought would satisfy or appease me, till I had rid the earth of him. And were I a man, who am but a woman, none other but myself should meddle with the affair. God's curse upon him, the woeful, shameless sot!" Whereupon the young men, incensed by what they had seen and heard, turned to Arriguccio, and after giving him the soundest rating that ever was bestowed upon caitiff, concluded as follows: – "This once we pardon thee, witting thee to be a drunken knave – but as thou holdest thy life dear, have a care that henceforth we hear no such tales of thee; for rest assured that if aught of the kind do reach our ears, we will requite thee for both turns." Which said, they departed. Arriguccio, standing there like one dazed, not witting whether his late doings were actual fact or but a dream, made no more words about the matter, but left his wife in peace. Thus did she by her address not only escape imminent peril, but open a way whereby in time to come she was able to gratify her passion to the full without any farther fear of her husband.

Seventh Day

Novel IX

— Lydia, wife of Nicostratus, loves Pyrrhus, who to assure himself thereof, asks three things of her, all of which she does, and therewithal enjoys him in presence of Nicostratus, and makes Nicostratus believe that what he saw was not real. —

SO DIVERTING did the ladies find Neifile's story that it kept them still laughing and talking, though the king, having bidden Pamfilo tell his story, had several times enjoined silence upon them. However, as soon as they had done, Pamfilo thus began: –

Methinks, worshipful ladies, there is no venture, though fraught with gravest peril, that whoso loves ardently will not make: of which truth, exemplified though it has been in stories not a few, I purpose to afford you yet more signal proof in one which I shall tell you; wherein you will hear of a lady who in her enterprises owed far more to the favour of Fortune than to the guidance of reason: wherefore I should not advise any of you rashly to follow in her footsteps, seeing that Fortune is not always in a kindly mood, nor are the eyes of all men equally holden.

In Argos, that most ancient city of Achaia, the fame of whose kings of old time is out of all proportion to its size, there dwelt of yore Nicostratus, a nobleman, to whom, when he was already verging on old age, Fortune gave to wife a great lady, Lydia by name, whose courage matched her charms. Nicostratus, as suited with his rank and wealth, kept not a few retainers and hounds and hawks, and was mightily addicted to the chase. Among his dependants was a young man named Pyrrhus, a gallant of no mean accomplishment, and goodly of person and beloved and trusted by Nicostratus above all other. Of whom Lydia grew mighty enamoured, insomuch that neither by day nor by night might her thoughts stray from him: but, whether it was that Pyrrhus wist not her love, or would have none of it, he gave no sign of recognition; whereby the lady's suffering waxing more than she could bear, she made up her mind to declare her love to him; and having a chambermaid, Lusca by name, in whom she placed great trust, she called her, and said: – "Lusca, tokens thou hast had from me of my regard that should ensure thy obedience and loyalty; wherefore have a care that what I shall now tell thee reach the ears of none but him to whom I shall bid thee impart it. Thou seest, Lusca, that I am in the prime of my youth and lustihead, and have neither lack nor stint of all such things as folk desire, save only, to be brief, that I have one cause to repine, to wit, that my husband's years so far outnumber my own. Wherefore with that wherein young ladies take most pleasure I am but ill provided, and, as my desire is no less than theirs, 'tis now some while since I determined that, if Fortune has shewn herself so little friendly to me by giving me a husband so advanced in years, at least I will not be mine own enemy by sparing to devise the means whereby my happiness and health may be assured; and that herein, as in all other matters, my joy may be complete, I have chosen, thereto to minister by his embraces, our Pyrrhus, deeming him more worthy than any other man, and have so set my heart upon him that I am ever ill at ease save when he is present either to my sight or to my mind, insomuch that, unless I forgather with him without delay, I doubt not that 'twill be the death of me. And so, if thou holdest my life dear, thou wilt shew him my love on such wise as thou mayst deem best, and make my suit to him that he be pleased to come to me, when thou shalt go to fetch him." "That gladly will I," replied the chambermaid; and as soon as she found convenient time and place, she drew Pyrrhus apart, and, as best she knew how, conveyed her lady's message to him. Which Pyrrhus found passing strange to hear, for 'twas in truth a complete surprise to him, and he doubted the lady did but mean to try him. Wherefore he presently, and with some asperity, answered thus: – "Lusca, believe I cannot that this message comes from my lady: have a care, therefore, what thou sayst, and if, perchance, it does come from her, I doubt she does not mean it; and if perchance, she does mean it, why, then I am honoured by my lord above what I deserve, and I would not for my life do him such a wrong: so have a care never to speak of such matters to me again." Lusca, nowise disconcerted by his uncompliant tone, rejoined: – "I shall speak to thee, Pyrrhus, of these and all other matters, wherewith I may be commissioned by my lady, as often as she shall bid me, whether it pleases or irks thee; but thou art a blockhead."

So, somewhat chafed, Lusca bore Pyrrhus' answer back to her lady, who would fain have died, when she heard it, and some days afterwards resumed the topic, saying: – "Thou knowest, Lusca, that 'tis not the first stroke that fells the oak; wherefore, methinks, thou wert best go back to this strange man, who is minded to evince his loyalty at my expense, and choosing a convenient time, declare to him all my passion, and do thy best endeavour that the affair be carried through; for if it should thus lapse, 'twould be the death of me; besides which, he would think we had but trifled with him, and, whereas 'tis his love we would have, we should earn his hatred." So, after comforting the lady, the maid hied her in quest of Pyrrhus, whom she found in a gladsome and propitious mood, and thus addressed: – "'Tis not many days, Pyrrhus, since I declared to thee how ardent is the flame with which thy lady and mine is consumed for love of thee, and now again I do thee to wit thereof, and that, if thou shalt not relent of the harshness that thou didst manifest the other day, thou mayst rest assured that her life will be short: wherefore I pray thee to be pleased to give her solace of her desire, and shouldst thou persist in thy obduracy, I, that gave thee credit for not a little sense, shall deem thee a great fool. How flattered thou shouldst be to know thyself beloved above all else by a lady so beauteous and high-born! And how indebted shouldst thou feel thyself to Fortune, seeing that she has in store for thee a boon so great and so suited to the cravings of thy youth, ay, and so like to be of service to thee upon occasion of need! Bethink thee, if there be any of thine equals whose life is ordered more agreeably than thine will be if thou but be wise. Which of them wilt thou find so well furnished with arms and horses, clothes and money as thou shalt be, if thou but give my lady thy love? Receive, then, my words with open mind; be thyself again; bethink thee that 'tis Fortune's way to confront a man but once with smiling mien and open lap, and, if he then accept not her bounty, he has but himself to blame, if afterward he find himself in want, in beggary. Besides which, no such loyalty is demanded between servants and their masters as between friends and kinsfolk; rather 'tis for servants, so far as they may, to behave towards their masters as their masters behave towards them. Thinkest thou, that, if thou hadst a fair wife or mother or daughter or sister that found favour in Nicostratus' eyes, he would be so scrupulous on the point of loyalty as thou art disposed to be in regard of his lady? Thou art a fool, if so thou dost believe. Hold it for certain, that, if blandishments and supplications did not suffice, he would, whatever thou mightest think of it, have recourse to force. Observe we, then, towards them and theirs the same rule which they observe towards us and ours. Take the boon that Fortune offers thee; repulse her not; rather go thou to meet her, and hail her advance; for be sure that, if thou do not so, to say nought of thy lady's death, which will certainly ensue, thou thyself wilt repent thee thereof so often that thou wilt be fain of death."

Since he had last seen Lusca, Pyrrhus had repeatedly pondered what she had said to him, and had made his mind up that, should she come again, he would answer her in another sort, and comply in all respects with the lady's desires, provided he might be assured that she was not merely putting him to the proof; wherefore he now made answer: – "Lo, now, Lusca, I acknowledge the truth of all that thou sayst; but, on the other hand, I know that my lord is not a little wise and wary, and, as he has committed all his affairs to my charge, I sorely misdoubt me that 'tis with his approbation, and by his advice, and but to prove me, that Lydia does this: wherefore let her do three things which I shall demand of her for my assurance, and then there is nought that she shall crave of me, but I will certainly render her prompt obedience. Which three things are these: – first, let her in Nicostratus' presence kill his fine sparrow-hawk: then she must send me a lock of Nicostratus' beard, and lastly one of his best teeth." Hard seemed these terms to Lusca, and hard beyond measure to the lady, but Love, that great fautor of enterprise, and master of stratagem, gave her resolution to address herself to their performance: wherefore through the chambermaid she sent him word that what he required of her she would do, and that without either reservation or delay; and therewithal she told him, that, as he deemed Nicostratus so wise, she would contrive that they should enjoy one another in Nicostratus' presence, and that Nicostratus should believe that 'twas a mere show. Pyrrhus, therefore, anxiously expected what the lady would do. Some days thus passed, and then Nicostratus gave a great breakfast, as was his frequent wont, to certain gentlemen, and when the tables were removed, the lady, robed in green samite, and richly adorned, came forth of her chamber into the hall wherein they sate, and before the eyes of Pyrrhus and all the rest of the company hied her to the perch, on which stood the sparrow-hawk that Nicostratus so much prized, and loosed him, and, as if she were minded to carry him on her hand, took him by the jesses and dashed him against the wall so that he died. Whereupon: – "Alas! my lady, what hast thou done?" exclaimed Nicostratus: but she vouchsafed no answer, save that, turning to the gentlemen that had sate at meat with him, she said: – "My lords, ill fitted were I to take vengeance on a king that had done me despite, if I lacked the courage to be avenged on a sparrow-hawk. You are to know that by this bird I have long been cheated of all the time that ought to be devoted by gentlemen to pleasuring their ladies; for with the first streaks of dawn Nicostratus has been up and got him to horse, and hawk on hand hied him to the champaign to see him fly, leaving me, such as you see me, alone and ill content abed. For which cause I have oftentimes been minded to do that which I have now done, and have only refrained therefrom, that, biding my time, I might do it in the presence of men that should judge my cause justly, as I trust you will do." Which hearing, the gentlemen, who deemed her affections no less fixed on Nicostratus than her words imported, broke with one accord into a laugh, and turning to Nicostratus, who was sore displeased, fell a saying: – "Now well done of the lady to avenge her wrongs by the death of the sparrow-hawk!" and so, the lady being withdrawn to her chamber, they passed the affair off with divers pleasantries, turning the wrath of Nicostratus to laughter.

Pyrrhus, who had witnessed what had passed, said to himself: – Nobly indeed has my lady begun, and on such wise as promises well for the felicity of my love. God grant that she so continue. And even so Lydia did: for not many days after she had killed the sparrow-hawk, she, being with Nicostratus in her chamber, from caressing passed to toying and trifling with him, and he, sportively pulling her by the hair, gave her occasion to fulfil the second of Pyrrhus' demands; which she did by nimbly laying hold of one of the lesser tufts of his beard, and, laughing the while, plucking it so hard that she tore it out of his chin. Which Nicostratus somewhat resenting: – "Now what cause hast thou," quoth she, "to make such a wry face? 'Tis but that I have plucked some half-dozen hairs from thy beard. Thou didst not feel it as much as did I but now thy tugging of my hair." And so they continued jesting and sporting with one another, the lady jealously guarding the tuft that she had torn from the beard, which the very same day she sent to her cherished lover. The third demand caused the lady more thought; but, being amply endowed with wit, and powerfully seconded by Love, she failed not to hit upon an apt expedient.

Nicostratus had in his service two lads, who, being of gentle birth, had been placed with him by their kinsfolk, that they might learn manners, one of whom, when Nicostratus sate at meat, carved before him, while the other gave him to drink. Both lads Lydia called to her, and gave them to understand that their breath smelt, and admonished them that, when they waited on Nicostratus, they should hold their heads as far back as possible, saying never a word of the matter to any. The lads believing her, did as she bade them. Whereupon she took occasion to say to Nicostratus: – "Hast thou marked what these lads do when they wait upon thee?" "Troth, that have I," replied Nicostratus; "indeed I have often had it in mind to ask them why they do so." "Nay," rejoined the lady, "spare thyself the pains; for I can tell thee the reason, which I have for some time kept close, lest it should vex thee; but as I now see that others begin to be ware of it, it need no longer be withheld from thee. 'Tis for that thy breath stinks shrewdly that they thus avert their heads from thee: 'twas not wont to be so, nor know I why it should be so; and 'tis most offensive when thou art in converse with gentlemen; and therefore 'twould be well to find some way of curing it." "I wonder what it could be," returned Nicostratus; "is it perchance that I have a decayed tooth in my jaw?" "That may well be," quoth Lydia: and taking him to a window, she caused him open his mouth, and after regarding it on this side and that: – "Oh! Nicostratus," quoth she, "how couldst thou have endured it so long? Thou hast a tooth here, which, by what I see, is not only decayed, but actually rotten throughout; and beyond all manner of doubt, if thou let it remain long in thy head, 'twill infect its neighbours; so 'tis my advice that thou out with it before the matter grows worse." "My judgment jumps with thine," quoth Nicostratus; "wherefore send without delay for a chirurgeon to draw it." "God forbid," returned the lady, "that chirurgeon come hither for such a purpose; methinks, the case is such that I can very well dispense with him, and draw the tooth myself. Besides which, these chirurgeons do these things in such a cruel way, that I could never endure to see thee or know thee under the hands of any of them: wherefore my mind is quite made up to do it myself, that, at least, if thou shalt suffer too much, I may give it over at once, as a chirurgeon would not do." And so she caused the instruments that are used on such occasions to be brought her, and having dismissed all other attendants save Lusca from the chamber, and locked the door, made Nicostratus lie down on a table, set the pincers in his mouth, and clapped them on one of his teeth, which, while Lusca held him, so that, albeit he roared for pain, he might not move, she wrenched by main force from his jaw, and keeping it close, took from Lusca's hand another and horribly decayed tooth, which she shewed him, suffering and half dead as he was, saying: – "See what thou hadst in thy jaw; mark how far gone it is." Believing what she said, and deeming that, now the tooth was out, his breath would no more be offensive, and being somewhat eased of the pain, which had been extreme, and still remained, so that he murmured not little, by divers comforting applications, he quitted the chamber: whereupon the lady forthwith sent the tooth to her lover, who, having now full assurance of her love, placed himself entirely at her service. But the lady being minded to make his assurance yet more sure, and deeming each hour a thousand till she might be with him, now saw fit, for the more ready performance of the promise she had given him, to feign sickness; and Nicostratus, coming to see her one day after breakfast, attended only by Pyrrhus, she besought him for her better solacement, to help her down to the garden. Wherefore Nicostratus on one side, and Pyrrhus on the other, took her and bore her down to the garden, and set her on a lawn at the foot of a beautiful pear-tree: and after they had sate there a while, the lady, who had already given Pyrrhus to understand what he must do, said to him: – "Pyrrhus, I should greatly like to have some of those pears; get thee up the tree, and shake some of them down." Pyrrhus climbed the tree in a trice, and began to shake down the pears, and while he did so: – "Fie! Sir," quoth he, "what is this you do? And you, Madam, have you no shame, that you suffer him to do so in my presence? Think you that I am blind? 'Twas but now that you were gravely indisposed. Your cure has been speedy indeed to permit of your so behaving: and as for such a purpose you have so many goodly chambers, why betake you not yourselves to one of them, if you must needs so disport yourselves? 'Twould be much more decent than to do so in my presence." Whereupon the lady, turning to her husband: – "Now what can Pyrrhus mean?" said she. "Is he mad?" "Nay, Madam," quoth Pyrrhus; "mad am not I. Think you I see you not?" Whereat Nicostratus marvelled not a little; and: – "Pyrrhus," quoth he, "I verily believe thou dreamest." "Nay, my lord," replied Pyrrhus, "not a whit do I dream; neither do you; rather you wag it with such vigour, that, if this pear-tree did the like, there would be never a pear left on it." Then the lady: – "What can this mean?" quoth she: "can it be that it really seems to him to be as he says? Upon my hope of salvation, were I but in my former health, I would get me up there to judge for myself what these wonders are which he professes to see." Whereupon, as Pyrrhus in the pear-tree continued talking in the same strange strain: – "Come down," quoth Nicostratus; and when he was down: – "Now what," said Nicostratus, "is it thou sayst thou seest up there?" "I suppose," replied Pyrrhus, "that you take me to be deluded or dreaming: but as I must needs tell you the truth, I saw you lying upon your wife, and then, when I came down, I saw you get up and sit you down here where you now are." "Therein," said Nicostratus, "thou wast certainly deluded, for, since thou clombest the pear-tree, we have not budged a jot, save as thou seest." Then said Pyrrhus: – "Why make more words about the matter? See you I certainly did; and, seeing you, I saw you lying upon your own." Nicostratus' wonder now waxed momently, insomuch that he said: – "I am minded to see if this pear-tree be enchanted, so that whoso is in it sees marvels;" and so he got him up into it. Whereupon the lady and Pyrrhus fell to disporting them, and Nicostratus, seeing what they were about, exclaimed: – "Ah! lewd woman, what is this thou doest? And thou, Pyrrhus, in whom I so much trusted!" And so saying, he began to climb down. Meanwhile the lady and Pyrrhus had made answer: – "We are sitting here:" and seeing him descending, they placed themselves as they had been when he had left them, whom Nicostratus, being come down, no sooner saw, than he fell a rating them. Then quoth Pyrrhus: – "Verily, Nicostratus, I now acknowledge, that, as you said a while ago, what I saw when I was in the pear-tree was but a false show, albeit I had never understood that so it was but that I now see and know that thou hast also seen a false show. And that I speak truth, you may sufficiently assure yourself, if you but reflect whether 'tis likely that your wife, who for virtue and discretion has not her peer among women, would, if she were minded so to dishonour you, see fit to do so before your very eyes. Of myself I say nought, albeit I had liefer be hewn in pieces than that I should so much as think of such a thing, much less do it in your presence. Wherefore 'tis evident that 'tis some illusion of sight that is propagated from the pear-tree; for nought in the world would have made me believe that I saw not you lying there in carnal intercourse with your wife, had I not heard you say that you saw me doing that which most assuredly, so far from doing, I never so much as thought of." The lady then started up with a most resentful mien, and burst out with: – "Foul fall thee, if thou knowest so little of me as to suppose that, if I were minded to do thee such foul dishonour as thou sayst thou didst see me do, I would come hither to do it before thine eyes! Rest assured that for such a purpose, were it ever mine, I should deem one of our chambers more meet, and it should go hard but I would so order the matter that thou shouldst never know aught of it." Nicostratus, having heard both, and deeming that what they both averred must be true, to wit, that they would never have ventured upon such an act in his presence, passed from chiding to talk of the singularity of the thing, and how marvellous it was that the vision should reshape itself for every one that clomb the tree. The lady, however, made a show of being distressed that Nicostratus should so have thought of her, and: – "Verily," quoth she, "no woman, neither I nor another, shall again suffer loss of honour by this pear-tree: run, Pyrrhus, and bring hither an axe, and at one and the same time vindicate thy honour and mine by felling it, albeit 'twere better far Nicostratus' skull should feel the weight of the axe, seeing that in utter heedlessness he so readily suffered the eyes of his mind to be blinded; for, albeit this vision was seen by the bodily eye, yet ought the understanding by no means to have entertained and affirmed it as real."

So Pyrrhus presently hied him to fetch the axe, and returning therewith felled the pear; whereupon the lady, turning towards Nicostratus: – "Now that this foe of my honour is fallen," quoth she, "my wrath is gone from me." Nicostratus then craving her pardon, she graciously granted it him, bidding him never again to suffer himself to be betrayed into thinking such a thing of her, who loved him more dearly than herself. So the poor duped husband went back with her and her lover to the palace, where not seldom in time to come Pyrrhus and Lydia took their pastime together more at ease. God grant us the like.

Seventh Day
Novel X

— *Two Sienese love a lady, one of them being her gossip: the gossip dies, having promised his comrade to return to him from the other world; which he does, and tells him what sort of life is led there.* —

NONE NOW was left to tell, save the king, who, as soon as the ladies had ceased mourning over the fall of the pear-tree, that had done no wrong, and were silent, began thus: –

Most manifest it is that 'tis the prime duty of a just king to observe the laws that he has made; and, if he do not so, he is to be esteemed no king, but a slave that has merited punishment, into which fault, and under which condemnation, I, your king, must, as of necessity, fall. For, indeed, when yesterday I made the law which governs our discourse of to-day, I thought not to-day to avail myself of my privilege, but to submit to the law, no less than you, and to discourse of the same topic whereof you all have discoursed; but not only has the very story been told which I had intended to tell, but therewithal so many things else, and so very much goodlier have been said, that, search my memory as I may, I cannot mind me of aught, nor wot I that touching such a matter there is indeed aught, for me to say, that would be comparable with what has been said; wherefore, as infringe I must the law that I myself have made, I confess myself worthy of punishment, and instantly declaring my readiness to pay any forfeit that may be demanded of me, am minded to have recourse to my wonted privilege. And such, dearest ladies, is the potency of Elisa's story of the godfather and his gossip, and therewith of the simplicity of the Sienese, that I am prompted thereby to pass from this topic of the beguilement of foolish husbands by their cunning wives to a little story touching these same Sienese, which, albeit there is not a little therein which you were best not to believe, may yet be in some degree entertaining to hear.

Know, then, that at Siena there dwelt in Porta Salaia two young men of the people, named, the one, Tingoccio Mini, the other Meuccio di Tura, who, by what appeared, loved one another not a little, for they were scarce ever out of one another's company; and being wont, like other folk, to go to church and listen to sermons, they heard from time to time of the glory and the woe, which in the other world are allotted, according to merit, to the souls of the dead. Of which matters craving, but being unable to come by, more certain assurance, they agreed together that, whichever of them should die first, should, if he might, return to the survivor, and certify him of that which he would fain know; and this agreement they confirmed with an oath. Now, after they had made this engagement, and while they were still constantly together, Tingoccio chanced to become sponsor to one Ambruogio Anselmini, that dwelt in Campo Reggi, who had had a son by his wife, Monna Mita. The lady was exceeding fair, and amorous withal, and Tingoccio being wont sometimes to visit her as his gossip, and to take Meuccio with him, he, notwithstanding his sponsorship, grew enamoured of her, as did also Meuccio, for she pleased him not a little, and he heard her much commended by Tingoccio. Which love each concealed from the other; but not for the same reason. Tingoccio was averse to discover it to Meuccio, for that he deemed it an ignominious thing to love his gossip, and was ashamed to let any one know it. Meuccio was on his guard for a very different reason, to wit, that he was already ware that the lady was in Tingoccio's good graces. Wherefore he said to himself: – If I avow my love to him, he will be jealous of me, and as, being her gossip, he can speak with her as often as he pleases, he will do all he can to make her hate me, and so I shall never have any favour of her.

Now, the two young men being thus, as I have said, on terms of most familiar friendship, it befell that Tingoccio, being the better able to open his heart to the lady, did so order his demeanour and discourse that he had from her all that he desired. Nor was his friend's success hidden from Meuccio; though, much as it vexed him, yet still cherishing the hope of eventually attaining his end, and fearing to give Tingoccio occasion to baulk or hamper him in some way, he feigned to know nought of the matter. So Tingoccio, more fortunate than his comrade, and rival in love, did with such assiduity till his gossip's good land that he got thereby a malady, which in the course of some days waxed so grievous that he succumbed thereto, and departed this life. And on the night of the third day after his decease (perchance because earlier he might not) he made his appearance, according to his promise, in Meuccio's chamber, and called Meuccio, who was fast asleep, by his name. Whereupon: – "Who art thou?" quoth Meuccio, as he awoke. "'Tis I, Tingoccio," replied he, "come back, in fulfilment of the pledge I gave thee, to give thee tidings of the other world." For a while Meuccio saw him not without terror: then, his courage reviving: – "Welcome, my brother," quoth he: and proceeded to ask him if he were lost. "Nought is lost but what is irrecoverable," replied Tingoccio: "how then should I be here, if I were lost?" "Nay," quoth then Meuccio; "I mean it not so: I would know of thee, whether thou art of the number of the souls that are condemned to the penal fire of hell." "Why no," returned Tingoccio, "not just that; but still for the sins that I did I am in most sore and grievous torment." Meuccio then questioned Tingoccio in detail of the pains there meted out for each of the sins done here; and Tingoccio enumerated them all. Whereupon Meuccio asked if there were aught he might do for him here on earth. Tingoccio answered in the affirmative; to wit, that he might have masses and prayers said and alms-deeds done for him, for that such things were of great service to the souls there. "That gladly will I," replied Meuccio; and then, as Tingoccio was about to take his leave, he bethought him of the gossip, and raising his head a little, he said: – "I mind me, Tingoccio, of the gossip, with whom thou wast wont to lie when thou wast here. Now what is thy punishment for that?" "My brother," returned Tingoccio, "as soon as I got down there, I met one that seemed to know all my sins by heart, who bade me betake me to a place, where, while in direst torment I bewept my sins, I found comrades not a few condemned to the same pains; and so, standing there among them, and calling to mind what I had done with the gossip, and foreboding in requital thereof a much greater torment than had yet been allotted me, albeit I was in a great and most vehement flame, I quaked for fear in every part of me. Which one that was beside me observing: – 'What,' quoth he, 'hast thou done more than the rest of us that are here, that thou quakest thus as thou standest in the fire?' 'My friend,' quoth I, 'I am in mortal fear of the doom that I expect for a great sin that I once committed.' He then asked what sin it might be. ''Twas on this wise,' replied I: 'I lay with my gossip, and that so much that I died thereof.' Whereat, he did but laugh, saying: – 'Go to, fool, make thy mind easy; for here there is no account taken of gossips.' Which completely revived my drooping spirits."

'Twas now near daybreak: wherefore: – "Adieu! Meuccio," quoth his friend: "for longer tarry with thee I may not;" and so he vanished. As for Meuccio, having learned that no account was taken of gossips in the other world, he began to laugh at his own folly in that he had already spared divers such; and so, being quit of his ignorance, he in that respect in course of time waxed wise. Which matters had Fra Rinaldo but known, he would not have needed to go about syllogizing in order to bring his fair gossip to pleasure him.

The sun was westering, and a light breeze blew, when the king, his story ended, and none else being left to speak, arose, and taking off the crown, set it on Lauretta's head, saying: – "Madam, I crown you with yourself queen of our company: 'tis now for you, as our sovereign lady, to make such ordinances as you shall deem meet for our common solace and delectation;" and having so said, he sat him down again. Queen Lauretta sent for the seneschal, and bade him have a care that the tables should be set in the pleasant vale somewhat earlier than had been their wont, that their return to the palace might be more leisurely; after which she gave him to know what else he had to do during her sovereignty. Then turning to the company: – "Yesterday," quoth she, "Dioneo would have it that to-day we should discourse of the tricks that wives play their husbands; and but that I am minded not to shew as of the breed of yelping curs, that are ever prompt to retaliate, I would ordain that to-morrow we discourse of the tricks that husbands play their wives. However, in lieu thereof, I will have every one take thought to tell of those tricks that, daily, woman plays man, or man woman, or one man another; wherein, I doubt not, there will be matter of discourse no less agreeable than has been that of to-day." So saying, she rose and dismissed the company until supper-time. So the ladies and the men being risen, some bared their feet and betook them to the clear water, there to disport them, while others took their pleasure upon the green lawn amid the trees that there grew goodly and straight. For no brief while Dioneo and Fiammetta sang in concert of Arcite and Palamon. And so, each and all taking their several pastimes, they sped the hours with exceeding great delight until supper-time. Which being come, they sat them down at table beside the little lake, and there, while a thousand songsters charmed their ears, and a gentle breeze, that blew from the environing hills, fanned them, and never a fly annoyed them, reposefully and joyously they supped. The tables removed, they roved a while about the pleasant vale, and then, the sun being still high, for 'twas but half vespers, the queen gave the word, and they wended their way back to their wonted abode, and going slowly, and beguiling the way with quips and quirks without number upon divers matters, nor those alone of which they had that day discoursed, they arrived, hard upon nightfall, at the goodly palace. There, the short walk's fatigue dispelled by wines most cool and comfits, they presently gathered for the dance about the fair fountain, and now they footed it to the strains of Tindaro's cornemuse, and now to other music. Which done, the queen bade Filomena give them a song; and thus Filomena sang: –

>   *Ah! woe is me, my soul!*
>   *Ah! shall I ever thither fare again*
>   *Whence I was parted to my grievous dole?*
>
>   *Full sure I know not; but within my breast*
>   *Throbs ever the same fire*
>   *Of yearning there where erst I was to be.*
>   *O thou in whom is all my weal, my rest,*
>   *Lord of my heart's desire,*
>   *Ah! tell me thou! for none to ask save thee*
>   *Neither dare I, nor see.*
>   *Ah! dear my Lord, this wasted heart disdain*
>   *Thou wilt not, but with hope at length console.*
>
>   *Kindled the flame I know not what delight,*
>   *Which me doth so devour,*
>   *That day and night alike I find no ease;*

For whether it was by hearing, touch, or sight,
  Unwonted was the power,
And fresh the fire that me each way did seize;
Wherein without release
I languish still, and of thee, Lord, am fain,
For thou alone canst comfort and make whole.

Ah! tell me if it shall be, and how soon,
  That I again thee meet
Where those death-dealing eyes I kissed. Thou, chief
Weal of my soul, my very soul, this boon
  Deny not; say that fleet
Thou hiest hither: comfort thus my grief.
  Ah! let the time be brief
Till thou art here, and then long time remain;
For I, Love-stricken, crave but Love's control.

Let me but once again mine own thee call,
  No more so indiscreet
As erst, I'll be, to let thee from me part:
Nay, I'll still hold thee, let what may befall,
  And of thy mouth so sweet
Such solace take as may content my heart
  So this be all my art,
Thee to entice, me with thine arms to enchain:
Whereon but musing inly chants my soul.

This song set all the company conjecturing what new and delightsome love might now hold Filomena in its sway; and as its words imported that she had had more joyance thereof than sight alone might yield, some that were there grew envious of her excess of happiness. However, the song being ended, the queen, bethinking her that the morrow was Friday, thus graciously addressed them all: – "Ye wot, noble ladies, and ye also, my gallants, that to-morrow is the day that is sacred to the passion of our Lord, which, if ye remember, we kept devoutly when Neifile was queen, intermitting delectable discourse, as we did also on the ensuing Saturday. Wherefore, being minded to follow Neifile's excellent example, I deem that now, as then, 'twere a seemly thing to surcease from this our pastime of story-telling for those two days, and compose our minds to meditation on what was at that season accomplished for the weal of our souls." All the company having approved their queen's devout speech, she, as the night was now far spent, dismissed them; and so they all betook them to slumber.

— Endeth here the seventh day of the Decameron, beginneth the eighth, in which, under the rule of Lauretta, discourse is had of those tricks that, daily, woman plays man, or man woman, or one man another. —

THE SUMMITS of the loftiest mountains were already illumined by the rays of the rising sun, the shades of night were fled, and all things plainly visible, when the queen and her company arose, and hied them first to the dewy mead, where for a while they walked: then, about half tierce, they wended their way to a little church that was hard by, where they heard Divine service; after which, they returned to the palace, and having breakfasted with gay and gladsome cheer, and sung and danced a while, were dismissed by the queen, to rest them as to each might seem good. But when the sun was past the meridian, the queen mustered them again for their wonted pastime; and, all being seated by the fair fountain, thus, at her command, Neifile began.

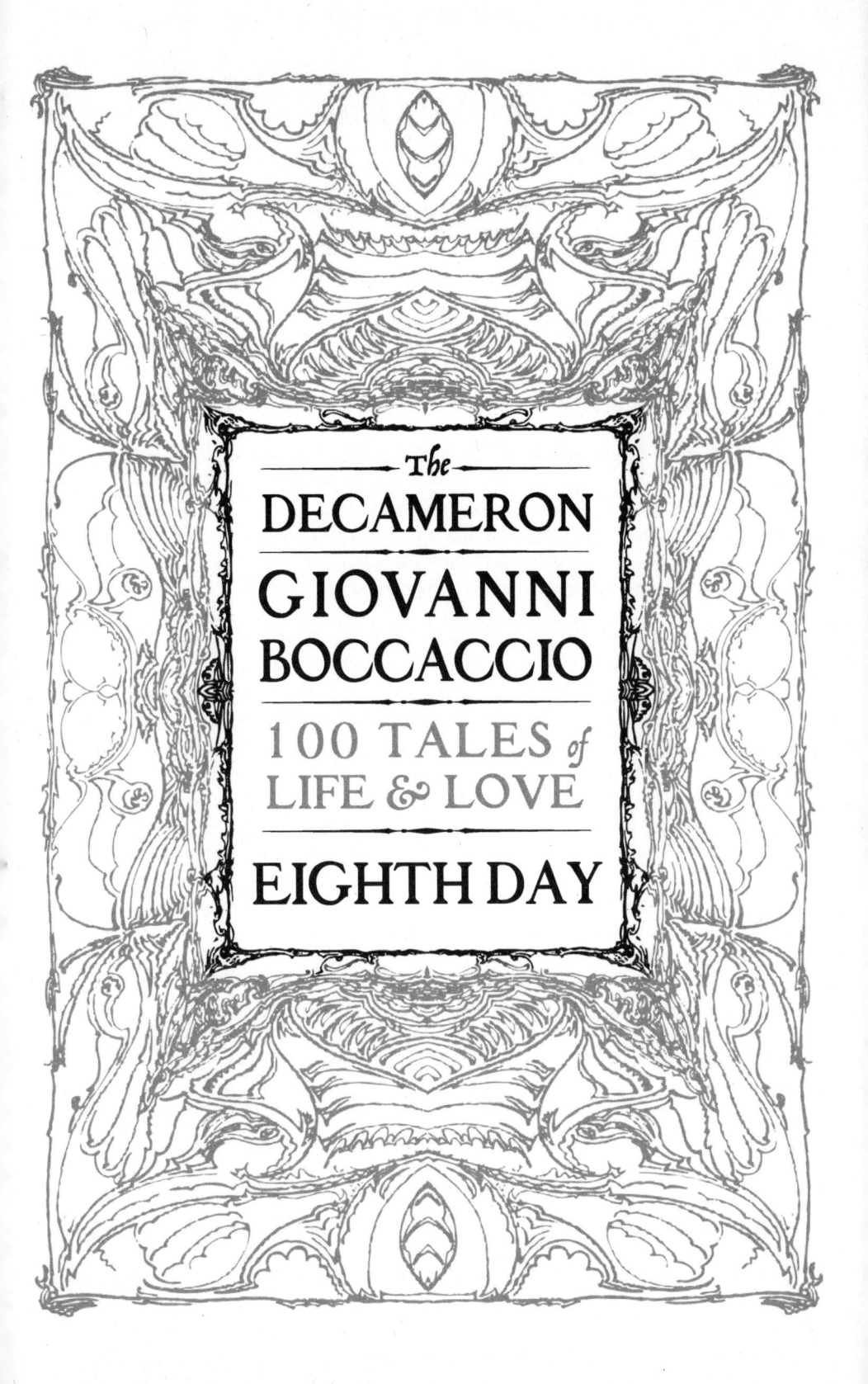

The DECAMERON
GIOVANNI BOCCACCIO
100 TALES of LIFE & LOVE
EIGHTH DAY

Eighth Day

Novel I

— *Gulfardo borrows moneys of Guasparruolo, which he has agreed to give Guasparruolo's wife, that he may lie with her. He gives them to her, and in her presence tells Guasparruolo that he has done so, and she acknowledges that 'tis true.* —

SITH GOD HAS ordained that 'tis for me to take the lead to-day with my story, well pleased am I. And for that, loving ladies, much has been said touching the tricks that women play men, I am minded to tell you of one that a man played a woman, not because I would censure what the man did, or say that 'twas not merited by the woman, but rather to commend the man and censure the woman, and to shew that men may beguile those that think to beguile them, as well as be beguiled by those they think to beguile; for peradventure what I am about to relate should in strictness of speech not be termed beguilement, but rather retaliation; for, as it behoves woman to be most strictly virtuous, and to guard her chastity as her very life, nor on any account to allow herself to sully it, which notwithstanding, 'tis not possible by reason of our frailty that there should be as perfect an observance of this law as were meet, I affirm, that she that allows herself to infringe it for money merits the fire; whereas she that so offends under the prepotent stress of Love will receive pardon from any judge that knows how to temper justice with mercy: witness what but the other day we heard from Filostrato touching Madonna Filippa at Prato.

Know, then, that there was once at Milan a German mercenary, Gulfardo by name, a doughty man, and very loyal to those with whom he took service; a quality most uncommon in Germans. And as he was wont to be most faithful in repaying whatever moneys he borrowed, he would have had no difficulty in finding a merchant to advance him any amount of money at a low rate of interest. Now, tarrying thus at Milan, Gulfardo fixed his affection on a very fine woman, named Madonna Ambruogia, the wife of a wealthy merchant, one Guasparruolo Cagastraccio, with whom he was well acquainted and on friendly terms: which amour he managed with such discretion that neither the husband nor any one else wist aught of it. So one day he sent her a message, beseeching her of her courtesy to gratify his passion, and assuring her that he on his part was ready to obey her every behest.

The lady made a great many words about the affair, the upshot of which was that she would do as Gulfardo desired upon the following terms: to wit, that, in the first place, he should never discover the matter to a soul, and, secondly, that, as for some purpose or another she required two hundred florins of gold, he out of his abundance should supply her necessity; these conditions being satisfied she would be ever at his service. Offended by such base sordidness in one whom he had supposed to be an honourable woman, Gulfardo passed from ardent love to something very like hatred, and cast about how he might flout her. So he sent her word that he would right gladly pleasure her in this and in any other matter that might be in his power; let her but say when he was to come to see her, and he would bring the moneys with him, and none should know of the matter except a comrade of his, in whom he placed much trust, and who was privy to all that he did. The lady, if she should not rather be called the punk, gleefully made answer that in the course of a few days her husband, Guasparruolo, was to go to Genoa on business, and that, when he was gone, she would let Gulfardo know, and appoint a time for him to visit her. Gulfardo thereupon chose a convenient time, and hied him to Guasparruolo, to whom: – "I am come," quoth he, "about a little matter of business which I have on hand, for which I require two hundred florins of gold, and I should be glad if thou wouldst lend them me at the rate of interest which thou art wont to charge me." "That gladly will I," replied Guasparruolo, and told out the money at once. A few days later Guasparruolo being gone to Genoa, as the lady had said, she sent word to Gulfardo that he should bring her the two hundred florins of gold. So Gulfardo hied him with his comrade to the lady's house, where he found her expecting him, and lost no time in handing her the two hundred florins of gold in his comrade's presence, saying: – "You will keep the money, Madam, and give it to your husband when he returns." Witting not why Gulfardo so said, but thinking that 'twas but to conceal from his comrade that it was given by way of price, the lady made answer: – "That will I gladly; but I must first see whether the amount is right;" whereupon she told the florins out upon a table, and when she found that the two hundred were there, she put them away in high glee, and turning to Gulfardo, took him into her chamber, where, not on that night only but on many another night, while her husband was away, he had of her all that he craved. On Guasparruolo's return Gulfardo presently paid him a visit, having first made sure that the lady would be with him, and so in her presence: – "Guasparruolo," quoth he, "I had after all no occasion for the money, to wit, the two hundred florins of gold that thou didst lend me the other day, being unable to carry through the transaction for which I borrowed them, and so I took an early opportunity of bringing them to thy wife, and gave them to her: thou wilt therefore cancel the account." Whereupon Guasparruolo turned to the lady, and asked her if she had had them. She, not daring to deny the fact in presence of the witness, answered: – "Why, yes, I had them, and quite forgot to tell thee." "Good," quoth then Guasparruolo, "we are quits, Gulfardo; make thy mind easy; I will see that thy account is set right." Gulfardo then withdrew, leaving the flouted lady to hand over her ill-gotten gains to her husband; and so the astute lover had his pleasure of his greedy mistress for nothing.

Eighth Day
Novel II

— The priest of Varlungo lies with Monna Belcolore: he leaves with her his cloak by way of pledge, and receives from her a mortar. He returns the mortar, and demands of her the cloak that he had left in pledge, which the good lady returns him with a gibe. —

LADIES AND MEN alike commended Gulfardo for the check that he gave to the greed of the Milanese lady; but before they had done, the queen turned to Pamfilo, and with a smile bade him follow suit: wherefore thus Pamfilo began: –

Fair my ladies, it occurs to me to tell you a short story, which reflects no credit on those by whom we are continually wronged without being able to retaliate, to wit, the priests, who have instituted a crusade against our wives, and deem that, when they have made conquest of one of them, they have done a work every whit as worthy of recompense by remission of sin and punishment as if they had brought the Soldan in chains to Avignon: in which respect 'tis not possible for the hapless laity to be even with them: howbeit they are as hot to make reprisals on the priests' mothers, sisters, mistresses, and daughters as the priests to attack their wives. Wherefore I am minded to give you, as I may do in few words, the history of a rustic amour, the conclusion whereof was not a little laughable, nor barren of moral, for you may also gather therefrom, that 'tis not always well to believe everything that a priest says.

I say then, that at Varlungo, a village hard by here, as all of you, my ladies, should wot either of your own knowledge or by report, there dwelt a worthy priest, and doughty of body in the service of the ladies: who, albeit he was none too quick at his book, had no lack of precious and blessed solecisms to edify his flock withal of a Sunday under the elm. And when the men were out of doors, he would visit their wives as never a priest had done before him, bringing them feast-day gowns and holy water, and now and again a bit of candle, and giving them his blessing. Now it so befell that among those of his fair parishioners whom he most affected the first place was at length taken by one Monna Belcolore, the wife of a husbandman that called himself Bentivegna del Mazzo. And in good sooth she was a winsome and lusty country lass, brown as a berry and buxom enough, and fitter than e'er another for his mill. Moreover she had not her match in playing the tabret and singing: – The borage is full sappy,[1] and in leading a brawl or a breakdown, no matter who might be next her, with a fair and dainty kerchief in her hand. Which spells so wrought upon Master Priest, that for love of her he grew distracted, and did nought all day long but loiter about the village on the chance of catching sight of her. And if of a Sunday morning he espied her in church, he strove might and main to acquit himself of his Kyrie and Sanctus in the style of a great singer, albeit his performance was liker to the braying of an ass: whereas, if he saw her not, he scarce exerted himself at all. However, he managed with such discretion that neither Bentivegna del Mazzo nor any of the neighbours wist aught of his love. And hoping thereby to ingratiate himself with Monna Belcolore, he from time to time would send her presents, now a clove of fresh garlic, the best in all the country-side, from his own garden, which he tilled with his own hands, and anon a basket of beans or a bunch of chives or shallots; and, when he thought it might serve his turn, he would give her a sly glance, and follow it up with a little amorous mocking and mowing, which she, with rustic awkwardness, feigned not to understand, and ever maintained her reserve, so that Master Priest made no headway.

Now it so befell that one day, when the priest at high noon was aimlessly gadding about the village, he encountered Bentivegna del Mazzo at the tail of a well laden ass; and greeted him, asking him whither he was going. "I'faith, Sir," quoth Bentivegna, "for sure 'tis to town I go, having an affair or two to attend to there; and I am taking these things to Ser Buonaccorri da Ginestreto, to get him to stand by me in I wot not what matter, whereof the justice o' th' coram has by his provoker served me with a pertrumpery summons to appear before him." Whereupon: – "'Tis well, my son," quoth the priest, overjoyed, "my blessing go with thee: good luck to thee and a speedy return; and harkye, shouldst thou see Lapuccio or Naldino, do not forget to tell them to send me those thongs for my flails." "It shall be done," quoth Bentivegna, and jogged on towards Florence, while the priest, thinking that now was his time to hie him to Belcolore and try his fortune, put his best leg forward, and stayed not till he was at the house, which entering, he said: – "God be gracious to us! Who is within?" Belcolore, who was up in the loft, made answer: – "Welcome, Sir; but what dost thou, gadding about in the heat?" "Why, as I hope for God's blessing," quoth he, "I am just come to stay with thee a while, having met thy husband on his way to town." Whereupon down came Belcolore, took a seat, and began sifting cabbage-seed that her husband had lately threshed. By and by the priest began: – "So, Belcolore, wilt thou keep me ever a dying thus?" Whereat Belcolore tittered, and said: – "Why, what is't I do to you?" "Truly, nothing at all," replied the priest: "but thou sufferest me not to do to thee that which I had lief, and which God commands." "Now away with you!" returned Belcolore, "do priests do that sort of thing?" "Indeed we do," quoth the priest, "and to better purpose than others: why not? I tell you our grinding is far better; and wouldst thou know why? 'tis because 'tis intermittent. And in truth 'twill be well worth thy while to keep thine own counsel, and let me do it." "Worth my while!" ejaculated Belcolore. "How may that be? There is never a one of you but would overreach the very Devil." "'Tis not for me to say," returned the priest; "say but what thou wouldst have: shall it be a pair of dainty shoes? Or wouldst thou prefer a fillet? Or perchance a gay riband? What's thy will?" "Marry, no lack have I," quoth Belcolore, "of such things as these. But, if you wish me so well, why do me not a service? and I would then be at your command." "Name but the service," returned the priest, "and gladly will I do it." Quoth then Belcolore: – "On Saturday I have to go to Florence to deliver some wool that I have spun, and to get my spinning-wheel put in order: lend me but five pounds – I know you have them – and I will redeem my perse petticoat from the pawnshop, and also the girdle that I wear on saints' days, and that I had when I was married – you see that without them I cannot go to church or anywhere else, and then I will do just as you wish thenceforth and forever." Whereupon: – "So God give me a good year," quoth he, "as I have not the money with me: but never fear that I will see that thou hast it before Saturday with all the pleasure in life." "Ay, ay," rejoined Belcolore, "you all make great promises, but then you never keep them. Think you to serve me as you served Biliuzza, whom you left in the lurch at last? God's faith, you do not so. To think that she turned woman of the world just for that! If you have not the money with you, why, go and get it." "Prithee," returned the priest, "send me not home just now. For, seest thou, 'tis the very nick of time with me, and the coast is clear, and perchance it might not be so on my return, and in short I know not when it would be likely to go so well as now." Whereto she did but rejoin: – "Good; if you are minded to go, get you gone; if not, stay where you are." The priest, therefore, seeing that she was not disposed to give him what he wanted, as he was fain, to wit, on his own terms, but was bent upon having a quid pro quo, changed his tone; and: – "Lo, now," quoth he, "thou doubtest I will not bring thee the money; so to set thy mind at rest, I will leave thee this cloak – thou seest 'tis good sky-blue silk – in pledge." So raising her head and glancing at the cloak: – "And what may the cloak be worth?" quoth Belcolore. "Worth!" ejaculated the priest: "I would have thee know that 'tis all Douai, not to say Trouai, make: nay, there are some of our folk here that say 'tis Quadrouai; and 'tis not a fortnight since I bought it of Lotto, the secondhand dealer, for seven good pounds, and then had it five good soldi under value, by what I hear from Buglietto, who, thou knowest, is an excellent judge of these articles." "Oh! say you so?" exclaimed Belcolore. "So help me God, I should not have thought it; however, let me look at it." So Master Priest, being ready for action, doffed the cloak and handed it to her. And she, having put it in a safe place, said to him: – "Now, Sir, we will away to the hut; there is never a soul goes there;" and so they did. And there Master Priest, giving her many a mighty buss and straining her to his sacred person, solaced himself with her no little while.

Which done, he hied him away in his cassock, as if he were come from officiating at a wedding; but, when he was back in his holy quarters, he bethought him that not all the candles that he received by way of offering in the course of an entire year would amount to the half of five pounds, and saw that he had made a bad bargain, and repented him that he had left the cloak in pledge, and cast about how he might recover it without paying anything. And as he did not lack cunning, he hit upon an excellent expedient, by which he compassed his end. So on the morrow, being a saint's day, he sent a neighbour's lad to Monna Belcolore with a request that she would be so good as to lend him her stone mortar, for that Binguccio dal Poggio and Nuto Buglietti were to breakfast with him that morning, and he therefore wished to make a sauce. Belcolore having sent the mortar, the priest, about breakfast time, reckoning that Bentivegna del Mazzo and Belcolore would be at their meal, called his clerk, and said to him: – "Take the mortar back to Belcolore, and say: – 'My master thanks you very kindly, and bids you return the cloak that the lad left with you in pledge.'" The clerk took the mortar to Belcolore's house, where, finding her at table with Bentivegna, he set the mortar down and delivered the priest's message. Whereto Belcolore would fain have demurred; but Bentivegna gave her a threatening glance, saying: – "So, then, thou takest a pledge from Master Priest? By Christ, I vow, I have half a mind to give thee a great clout o' the chin. Go, give it back at once, a murrain on thee! And look to it that whatever he may have a mind to, were it our very ass, he be never denied." So, with a very bad grace, Belcolore got up, and went to the wardrobe, and took out the cloak, and gave it to the clerk, saying: – "Tell thy master from me: – Would to God he may never ply pestle in my mortar again, such honour has he done me for this turn!" So the clerk returned with the cloak, and delivered the message to Master Priest; who, laughing, made answer: – "Tell her, when thou next seest her, that, so she lend us not the mortar, I will not lend her the pestle: be it tit for tat."

Bentivegna made no account of his wife's words, deeming that 'twas but his chiding that had provoked them. But Belcolore was not a little displeased with Master Priest, and had never a word to say to him till the vintage; after which, what with the salutary fear in which she stood of the mouth of Lucifer the Great, to which he threatened to consign her, and the must and roast chestnuts that he sent her, she made it up with him, and many a jolly time they had together. And though she got not the five pounds from him, he put a new skin on her tabret, and fitted it with a little bell, wherewith she was satisfied.

Footnote 1: For this folk-song see *Cantilene e Ballate, Strambotti e Madrigali*, ed. Carducci (1871), p. 60. The fragment there printed maybe freely rendered as follows: –

The borage is full sappy,
And clusters red we see,

And my love would make me happy;
  So that maiden give to me.

Ill set I find this dance,
  And better might it be:
So, comrade mine, advance,
  And, changing place with me,
Stand thou thy love beside.

Eighth Day
Novel III

— *Calandrino, Bruno and Buffalmacco go in quest of the heliotrope beside the Mugnone. Thinking to have found it, Calandrino gets him home laden with stones. His wife chides him: whereat he waxes wroth, beats her, and tells his comrades what they know better than he.* —

ENDED PAMFILO'S STORY, which moved the ladies to inextinguishable laughter, the queen bade Elisa follow suit: whereupon, laughing, she thus began: –

I know not, debonair my ladies, whether with my little story, which is no less true than entertaining, I shall give you occasion to laugh as much as Pamfilo has done with his, but I will do my best.

In our city, where there has never been lack of odd humours and queer folk, there dwelt, no long time ago, a painter named Calandrino, a simple soul, of uncouth manners, that spent most of his time with two other painters, the one Bruno, the other Buffalmacco, by name, pleasant fellows enough, but not without their full share of sound and shrewd sense, and who kept with Calandrino for that they not seldom found his singular ways and his simplicity very diverting. There was also at the same time at Florence one Maso del Saggio, a fellow marvellously entertaining by his cleverness, dexterity and unfailing resource; who having heard somewhat touching Calandrino's simplicity, resolved to make fun of him by playing him a trick, and inducing him to believe some prodigy. And happening one day to come upon Calandrino in the church of San Giovanni, where he sate intently regarding the paintings and intaglios of the tabernacle above the altar, which had then but lately been set there, he deemed time and place convenient for the execution of his design; which he accordingly imparted to one of his comrades: whereupon the two men drew nigh the place where Calandrino sate alone, and feigning not to see him fell a talking of the virtues of divers stones, of which Maso spoke as aptly and pertinently as if he had been a great and learned lapidary. Calandrino heard what passed between them, and witting that 'twas no secret, after a while got up, and joined them, to Maso's no small delight. He therefore continued his discourse, and being asked by Calandrino, where these stones of such rare virtues were to be found, made answer: – "Chiefly in Berlinzone, in the land of the Basques. The district is called Bengodi, and there they bind the vines with sausages, and a denier will buy a goose and a gosling into the bargain; and on a mountain, all of grated Parmesan cheese, dwell folk that do nought else but make macaroni and raviuoli, and boil them in capon's broth, and then throw them down to be scrambled for; and hard by flows a rivulet of Vernaccia, the best that ever was drunk, and never a drop of water therein." "Ah! 'tis a sweet country!" quoth Calandrino; "but tell me, what becomes of the capons that they boil?" "They are all eaten by the Basques," replied Maso. Then: – "Wast thou ever there?" quoth Calandrino. Whereupon: – "Was I ever there, sayst thou?" replied Maso. "Why, if I have been there once, I have been there a thousand times." "And how many miles is't from here?" quoth Calandrino. "Oh!" returned Maso, "more than thou couldst number in a night without slumber." "Farther off, then, than the Abruzzi?" said Calandrino. "Why, yes, 'tis a bit farther," replied Maso.

Now Calandrino, like the simple soul that he was, marking the composed and grave countenance with which Maso spoke, could not have believed him more thoroughly, if he had uttered the most patent truth, and thus taking his words for gospel: – "'Tis a trifle too far for my purse," quoth he; "were it nigher, I warrant thee, I would go with thee thither one while, just to see the macaroni come tumbling down, and take my fill thereof. But tell me, so good luck befall thee, are none of these stones, that have these rare virtues, to be found in these regions?" "Ay," replied Maso, "two sorts of stone are found there, both of virtues extraordinary. The one sort are the sandstones of Settignano and Montisci, which being made into millstones, by virtue thereof flour is made; wherefore 'tis a common saying in those countries that blessings come from God and millstones from Montisci: but, for that these sandstones are in great plenty, they are held cheap by us, just as by them are emeralds, whereof they have mountains, bigger than Monte Morello, that shine at midnight, a God's name! And know this, that whoso should make a goodly pair of millstones, and connect them with a ring before ever a hole was drilled in them, and take them to the Soldan, should get all he would have thereby. The other sort of stone is the heliotrope, as we lapidaries call it, a stone of very great virtue, inasmuch as whoso carries it on his person is seen, so long as he keep it, by never another soul, where he is not." "These be virtues great indeed," quoth Calandrino; "but where is this second stone to be found?" Whereto Maso made answer that there were usually some to be found in the Mugnone. "And what are its size and colour?" quoth Calandrino. "The size varies," replied Maso, "for some are bigger and some smaller than others; but all are of the same colour, being nearly black." All these matters duly marked and fixed in his memory, Calandrino made as if he had other things to attend to, and took his leave of Maso with the intention of going in quest of the stone, but not until he had let his especial friends, Bruno and Buffalmacco, know of his project. So, that no time might be lost, but, postponing everything else, they might begin the quest at once, he set about looking for them, and spent the whole morning in the search. At length, when 'twas already past none, he called to mind that they would be at work in the Faentine women's convent, and though 'twas excessively hot, he let nothing stand in his way, but at a pace that was more like a run than a walk, hied him thither; and so soon as he had made them ware of his presence, thus he spoke: – "Comrades, so you are but minded to hearken to me, 'tis in our power to become the richest men in Florence; for I am informed by one that may be trusted that there is a kind of stone in the Mugnone which renders whoso carries it invisible to every other soul in the world. Wherefore, methinks, we were wise to let none have the start of us, but go search for this stone without any delay. We shall find it without a doubt, for I know what 'tis like, and when we have found it, we have but to put it in the purse, and get us to the moneychangers, whose counters, as you know, are always laden with groats and florins, and help ourselves to as many as we have a mind to. No one will see us, and so, hey presto! we shall be rich folk in the twinkling of an eye, and have no more need to go besmearing the walls all day long like so many snails." Whereat Bruno and Buffalmacco began only to laugh, and exchanging glances, made as if they marvelled exceedingly, and expressed approval of Calandrino's project. Then Buffalmacco asked, what might be the name of the stone. Calandrino, like the numskull that he was, had already forgotten the name: so he made answer: – "Why need we concern ourselves with the name, since we know the stone's virtue? methinks, we were best to go look for it, and waste no more time." "Well, well," said Bruno, "but what are the size and shape of the stone?" "They are of all sizes and shapes," said Calandrino, "but they are all pretty nearly black; wherefore, methinks, we were best to collect all the black stones that we see until we hit upon it: and so, let us be off, and lose no more time." "Nay, but," said Bruno, "wait a bit." And turning to Buffalmacco: – "Methinks," quoth he, "that Calandrino says well: but I doubt this is not the time for such work, seeing that the sun is high, and his rays so flood the Mugnone as to dry all the stones; insomuch that stones will now shew as white that in the morning, before the sun had dried them, would shew as black: besides which, to-day being a working-day, there will be for one cause or another folk not a few about the Mugnone, who, seeing us, might guess what we were come for, and peradventure do the like themselves; whereby it might well be that they found the stone, and we might miss the trot by trying after the amble. Wherefore, so you agree, methinks we were best to go about it in the morning, when we shall be better able to distinguish the black stones from the white, and on a holiday, when there will be none to see us."

Buffalmacco's advice being approved by Bruno, Calandrino chimed in; and so 'twas arranged that they should all three go in quest of the stone on the following Sunday. So Calandrino, having besought his companions above all things to let never a soul in the world hear aught of the matter, for that it had been imparted to him in strict confidence, and having told them what he had heard touching the land of Bengodi, the truth of which he affirmed with oaths, took leave of them; and they concerted their plan, while Calandrino impatiently expected the Sunday morning. Whereon, about dawn, he arose, and called them; and forth they issued by the Porta a San Gallo, and hied them to the Mugnone, and following its course, began their quest of the stone, Calandrino, as was natural, leading the way, and jumping lightly from rock to rock, and wherever he espied a black stone, stooping down, picking it up and putting it in the fold of his tunic, while his comrades followed, picking up a stone here and a stone there. Thus it was that Calandrino had not gone far, before, finding that there was no more room in his tunic, he lifted the skirts of his gown, which was not cut after the fashion of Hainault, and gathering them under his leathern girdle and making them fast on every side, thus furnished himself with a fresh and capacious lap, which, however, taking no long time to fill, he made another lap out of his cloak, which in like manner he soon filled with stones. Wherefore, Bruno and Buffalmacco seeing that Calandrino was well laden, and that 'twas nigh upon breakfast-time, and the moment for action come: – "Where is Calandrino?" quoth Bruno to Buffalmacco. Whereto Buffalmacco, who had Calandrino full in view, having first turned about and looked here, there and everywhere, made answer: – "That wot not I; but not so long ago he was just in front of us." "Not so long ago, forsooth," returned Bruno; "'tis my firm belief that at this very moment he is at breakfast at home, having left to us this wild-goose chase of black stones in the Mugnone." "Marry," quoth Buffalmacco, "he did but serve us right so to trick us and leave, seeing that we were so silly as to believe him. Why, who could have thought that any but we would have been so foolish as to believe that a stone of such rare virtue was to be found in the Mugnone?" Calandrino, hearing their colloquy, forthwith imagined that he had the stone in his hand, and by its virtue, though present, was invisible to them; and overjoyed by such good fortune, would not say a word to undeceive them, but determined to hie him home, and accordingly faced about, and put himself in motion. Whereupon: – "Ay!" quoth Buffalmacco to Bruno, "what are we about that we go not back too?" "Go we then," said Bruno; "but by God I swear that Calandrino shall never play me another such trick; and as to this, were I nigh him, as I have been all the morning, I would teach him to remember it for a month or so, such a reminder would I give him in the heel with this stone." And even as he spoke he threw back his arm, and launched the stone against Calandrino's heel. Galled by the blow, Calandrino gave a great hop and a slight gasp, but said nothing, and halted not. Then, picking out one of the stones that he had collected: – "Bruno," quoth Buffalmacco, "see what a goodly stone I have here, would it might but catch Calandrino in the back;" and forthwith he discharged it with main force upon the said back. And in short, suiting action to word, now in this way, now in that, they stoned him all the way up the Mugnone as far as the Porta a San Gallo. There they threw away the stones they had picked up, and tarried a while with the customs' officers, who, being primed by them, had let Calandrino pass unchallenged, while their laughter knew no bounds.

So Calandrino, halting nowhere, betook him to his house, which was hard by the corner of the Macina. And so well did Fortune prosper the trick, that all the way by the stream and across the city there was never a soul that said a word to Calandrino, and indeed he encountered but few, for most folk were at breakfast. But no sooner was Calandrino thus gotten home with his stones, than it so happened that his good lady, Monna Tessa, shewed her fair face at the stair's head, and catching sight of him, and being somewhat annoyed by his long delay, chid him, saying: – "What the Devil brings thee here so late? Must breakfast wait thee until all other folk have had it?" Calandrino caught the words, and angered and mortified to find that he was not invisible, broke out with: – "Alas! curst woman! so 'twas thou! Thou hast undone me: but, God's faith, I will pay thee out." Whereupon he was upstairs in a trice, and having discharged his great load of stones in a parlour, rushed with fell intent upon his wife, and laid hold of her by the hair, and threw her down at his feet, and beat and kicked her in every part of her person with all the force he had in his arms and legs, insomuch that he left never a hair of her head or bone of her body unscathed, and 'twas all in vain that she laid her palms together and crossed her fingers and cried for mercy.

Now Buffalmacco and Bruno, after making merry a while with the warders of the gate, had set off again at a leisurely pace, keeping some distance behind Calandrino. Arrived at his door, they heard the noise of the sound thrashing that he was giving his wife; and making as if they were but that very instant come upon the scene, they called him. Calandrino, flushed, all of a sweat, and out of breath, shewed himself at the window, and bade them come up. They, putting on a somewhat angry air, did so; and espied Calandrino sitting in the parlour, amid the stones which lay all about, untrussed, and puffing with the air of a man spent with exertion, while his lady lay in one of the corners, weeping bitterly, her hair all dishevelled, her clothes torn to shreds, and her face livid, bruised and battered. So after surveying the room a while: – "What means this, Calandrino?" quoth they. "Art thou minded to build thee a wall, that we see so many stones about?" And then, as they received no answer, they continued: – "And how's this? How comes Monna Tessa in this plight? 'Twould seem thou hast given her a beating! What unheard-of doings are these?" What with the weight of the stones that he had carried, and the fury with which he had beaten his wife, and the mortification that he felt at the miscarriage of his enterprise, Calandrino was too spent to utter a word by way of reply. Wherefore in a menacing tone Buffalmacco began again: – "However out of sorts thou mayst have been, Calandrino, thou shouldst not have played us so scurvy a trick as thou hast. To take us with thee to the Mugnone in quest of this stone of rare virtue, and then, without so much as saying either God-speed or Devil-speed, to be off, and leave us there like a couple of gowks! We take it not a little unkindly: and rest assured that thou shalt never so fool us again." Whereto with an effort Calandrino replied: – "Comrades, be not wroth with me: 'tis not as you think. I, luckless wight! found the stone: listen, and you will no longer doubt that I say sooth. When you began saying one to the other: – 'Where is Calandrino?' I was within ten paces of you, and marking that you came by without seeing me, I went before, and so, keeping ever a little ahead of you, I came hither." And then he told them the whole story of what they had said and done from beginning to end, and shewed them his back and heel, how they had been mauled by the stones; after which: – "And I tell you," he went on, "that, laden though I was with all these stones, that you see here, never a word was said to me by the warders of the gate as I passed in, though you know how vexatious and grievous these warders are wont to make themselves in their determination to see everything: and moreover I met by the way several of my gossips and friends that are ever wont to greet me, and ask me to drink, and never a word said any of them to me, no, nor half a word either; but they passed me by as men that saw me not. But at last, being come home, I was met and seen by this devil of a woman, curses upon her, forasmuch as all things, as you know, lose their virtue in the presence of a woman; whereby I from being the most lucky am become the most luckless man in Florence: and therefore I thrashed her as long as I could stir a hand, nor know I wherefore I forbear to sluice her veins for her, cursed be the hour that first I saw her, cursed be the hour that I brought her into the house!" And so, kindling with fresh wrath, he was about to start up and give her another thrashing; when Buffalmacco and Bruno, who had listened to his story with an air of great surprise, and affirmed its truth again and again, while they all but burst with suppressed laughter, seeing him now frantic to renew his assault upon his wife, got up and withstood and held him back, averring that the lady was in no wise to blame for what had happened, but only he, who, witting that things lost their virtue in the presence of women, had not bidden her keep aloof from him that day; which precaution God had not suffered him to take, either because the luck was not to be his, or because he was minded to cheat his comrades, to whom he should have shewn the stone as soon as he found it. And so, with many words they hardly prevailed upon him to forgive his injured wife, and leaving him to rue the ill-luck that had filled his house with stones, went their way.

Eighth Day

Novel IV

— *The rector of Fiesole loves a widow lady, by whom he is not loved, and thinking to lie with her, lies with her maid, with whom the lady's brothers cause him to be found by his Bishop.* —

ELISA BEING come to the end of her story, which in the telling had yielded no small delight to all the company, the queen, turning to Emilia, signified her will, that her story should ensue at once upon that of Elisa. And thus with alacrity Emilia began: –

Noble ladies, how we are teased and tormented by these priests and friars, and indeed by clergy of all sorts, I mind me to have been set forth in more than one of the stories that have been told; but as 'twere not possible to say so much thereof but that more would yet remain to say, I purpose to supplement them with the story of a rector, who, in defiance of all the world, was bent upon having the favour of a gentlewoman, whether she would or no. Which gentlewoman, being discreet above a little, treated him as he deserved.

Fiesole, whose hill is here within sight, is, as each of you knows, a city of immense antiquity, and was aforetime great, though now 'tis fallen into complete decay; which notwithstanding, it always was, and still is the see of a bishop. Now there was once a gentlewoman, Monna Piccarda by name, a widow, that had an estate at Fiesole, hard by the cathedral, on which, for that she was not in the easiest circumstances, she lived most part of the year, and with her her two brothers, very worthy and courteous young men, both of them. And the lady being wont frequently to resort to the cathedral, and being still quite young and fair and debonair withal, it so befell that the rector grew in the last degree enamoured of her, and waxed at length so bold, that he himself avowed his passion to the lady, praying her to entertain his love, and requite it in like measure. The rector was advanced in years, but otherwise the veriest springald, being bold and of a high spirit, of a boundless conceit of himself, and of mien and manners most affected and in the worst taste, and withal so tiresome and insufferable that he was on bad terms with everybody, and, if with one person more than another, with this lady, who not only cared not a jot for him, but had liefer have had a headache than his company. Wherefore the lady discreetly made answer: – "I may well prize your love, Sir, and love you I should and will right gladly; but such love as yours and mine may never admit of aught that is not honourable. You are my spiritual father and a priest, and now verging towards old age, circumstances which should ensure your honour and chastity; and I, on my part, am no longer a girl, such as these love affairs might beseem, but a widow, and well you wot how it behoves widows to be chaste. Wherefore I pray you to have me excused; for, after the sort you crave, you shall never have my love, nor would I in such sort be loved by you." With this answer the rector was for the nonce fain to be content; but he was not the man to be dismayed and routed by a first repulse; and with his wonted temerity and effrontery he plied her again and again with letters and ambassages, and also by word of mouth, when he espied her entering the church. Wherefore the lady finding this persecution more grievous and harassing than she could well bear, cast about how she might be quit thereof in such fashion as he deserved, seeing that he left her no choice; howbeit she would do nought in the matter until she had conferred with her brothers. She therefore told them how the rector pursued her, and how she meant to foil him; and, with their full concurrence, some few days afterwards she went, as she was wont, to church. The rector no sooner saw her, than he approached and accosted her, as he was wont, in a tone of easy familiarity. The lady greeted him, as he came up, with a glance of gladsome recognition; and when he had treated her to not a little of his wonted eloquence, she drew him aside, and heaving a great sigh, said: – "I have oftentimes heard it said, Sir, that there is no castle so strong, but that, if the siege be continued day by day, it will sooner or later be taken; which I now plainly perceive is my own case. For so fairly have you hemmed me in with this, that, and the other pretty speech or the like blandishments, that you have constrained me to make nought of my former resolve, and, seeing that I find such favour with you, to surrender myself unto you." Whereto, overjoyed, the rector made answer: – "Madam, I am greatly honoured; and, sooth to say, I marvelled not a little how you should hold out so long, seeing that I have never had the like experience with any other woman, insomuch that I have at times said: – 'Were women of silver, they would not be worth a denier, for there is none but would give under the hammer!' But no more of this: when and where may we come together?" "Sweet my lord," replied the lady, "for the when, 'tis just as we may think best, for I have no husband to whom to render account of my nights, but the where passes my wit to conjecture." "How so?" quoth the rector. "Why not in your own house?" "Sir," replied the lady, "you know that I have two brothers, both young men, who day and night bring their comrades into the house, which is none too large: for which reason it might not be done there, unless we were minded to make ourselves, as it were, dumb and blind, uttering never a word, not so much as a monosyllable, and abiding in the dark: in such sort indeed it might be, because they do not intrude upon my chamber; but theirs is so near to mine that the very least whisper could not but be heard." "Nay but, Madam," returned the rector, "let not this stand in our way for a night or two, until I may bethink me where else we might be more at our ease." "Be that as you will, Sir," quoth the lady, "I do but entreat that the affair be kept close, so that never a word of it get wind." "Have no fear on that score, Madam," replied the priest; "and if so it may be, let us forgather to-night." "With pleasure," returned the lady; and having appointed him how and when to come, she left him and went home.

Now the lady had a maid, that was none too young, and had a countenance the ugliest and most misshapen that ever was seen; for indeed she was flat-nosed, wry-mouthed, and thick-lipped, with huge, ill-set teeth, eyes that squinted and were ever bleared, and a complexion betwixt green and yellow, that shewed as if she had spent the summer not at Fiesole but at Sinigaglia: besides which she was hip-shot and somewhat halting on the right side. Her name was Ciuta, but, for that she was such a scurvy bitch to look upon, she was called by all folk Ciutazza. And being thus misshapen of body, she was also not without her share of guile. So the lady called her and said: – "Ciutazza, so thou wilt do me a service to-night, I will give thee a fine new shift." At the mention of the shift Ciutazza made answer: – "So you give me a shift, Madam, I will throw myself into the very fire." "Good," said the lady; "then I would have thee lie to-night in my bed with a man, whom thou wilt caress; but look thou say never a word, that my brothers, who, as thou knowest, sleep in the next room, hear thee not; and afterwards I will give thee the shift." "Sleep with a man!" quoth Ciutazza: "why, if need be, I will sleep with six." So in the evening Master Rector came, as he had been bidden; and the two young men, as the lady had arranged, being in their room, and making themselves very audible, he stole noiselessly, and in the dark, into the lady's room, and got him on to the bed, which Ciutazza, well advised by the lady how to behave, mounted from the other side. Whereupon Master Rector, thinking to have the lady by his side, took Ciutazza in his arms, and fell a kissing her, saying never a word the while, and Ciutazza did the like; and so he enjoyed her, plucking the boon which he had so long desired.

The rector and Ciutazza thus closeted, the lady charged her brothers to execute the rest of her plan. They accordingly stole quietly out of their room, and hied them to the piazza, where Fortune proved propitious beyond what they had craved of her; for, it being a very hot night, the bishop had been seeking them, purposing to go home with them, and solace himself with their society, and quench his thirst. With which desire he acquainted them, as soon as he espied them coming into the piazza; and so they escorted him to their house, and there in the cool of their little courtyard, which was bright with many a lamp, he took, to his no small comfort, a draught of their good wine. Which done: – "Sir," said the young men, "since of your great courtesy you have deigned to visit our poor house, to which we were but now about to invite you, we should be gratified if you would be pleased to give a look at somewhat, a mere trifle though it be, which we have here to shew you." The bishop replied that he would do so with pleasure. Whereupon one of the young men took a lighted torch and led the way, the bishop and the rest following, to the chamber where Master Rector lay with Ciutazza.

Now the rector, being in hot haste, had ridden hard, insomuch that he was already gotten above three miles on his way when they arrived; and so, being somewhat tired, he was resting, but, hot though the night was, he still held Ciutazza in his arms. In which posture he was shewn to the bishop, when, preceded by the young man bearing the light, and followed by the others, he entered the chamber. And being roused, and observing the light and the folk that stood about him, Master Rector was mighty ashamed and affrighted, and popped his head under the clothes. But the bishop, reprimanding him severely, constrained him to thrust his head out again, and take a view of his bed-fellow. Thus made aware of the trick which the lady had played him, the rector was now, both on that score and by reason of his signal disgrace, the saddest man that ever was; and his discomfiture was complete, when, having donned his clothes, he was committed by the bishop's command to close custody and sent to prison, there to expiate his offence by a rigorous penance.

The bishop was then fain to know how it had come about that he had forgathered there with Ciutazza. Whereupon the young men related the whole story; which ended, the bishop commended both the lady and the young men not a little, for that they had taken condign vengeance upon him without imbruing their hands in the blood of a priest. The bishop caused him to bewail his transgression forty days; but what with his love, and the scornful requital which it had received, he bewailed it more than forty and nine days, not to mention that for a great while he could not shew himself in the street but the boys would point the finger at him and say: – "There goes he that lay with Ciutazza." Which was such an affliction to him that he was like to go mad. On this wise the worthy lady rid herself of the rector's vexatious importunity, and Ciutazza had a jolly night and earned her shift.

Eighth Day

Novel V

— Three young men pull down the breeches of a judge from the Marches, while he is administering justice on the bench. —

SO ENDED Emilia her story; and when all had commended the widow lady: – "'Tis now thy turn to speak," quoth the queen, fixing her gaze upon Filostrato, who answered that he was ready, and forthwith thus began: –

Sweet my ladies, by what I remember of that young man, to wit, Maso del Saggio, whom Elisa named a while ago, I am prompted to lay aside a story that I had meant to tell you, and to tell you another, touching him and some of his comrades, which, notwithstanding there are in it certain words (albeit 'tis not unseemly) which your modesty forbears to use, is yet so laughable that I shall relate it.

As you all may well have heard, there come not seldom to our city magistrates from the Marches, who for the most part are men of a mean spirit, and in circumstances so reduced and beggarly, that their whole life seems to be but a petty-foggery; and by reason of this their inbred sordidness and avarice they bring with them judges and notaries that have rather the air of men taken from the plough or the last than trained in the schools of law. Now one of these Marchers, being come hither as Podesta, brought with him judges not a few, and among them one that called himself Messer Niccola da San Lepidio, and looked liker to a locksmith than aught else. However, this fellow was assigned with the rest of the judges to hear criminal causes. And as folk will often go to the court, though they have no concern whatever there, it so befell that Maso del Saggio went thither one morning in quest of one of his friends, and there chancing to set eyes on this Messer Niccola, where he sate, deemed him a fowl of no common feather, and surveyed him from head to foot, observing that the vair which he wore on his head was all begrimed, that he carried an ink-horn at his girdle, that his gown was longer than his robe, and many another detail quite foreign to the appearance of a man of birth and breeding, of which that which he deemed most notable was a pair of breeches, which, as he saw (for the judge's outer garments being none too ample were open in front, as he sate), reached half-way down his legs. By which sight his mind was presently diverted from the friend whom he came there to seek; and forth he hied him in quest of other two of his comrades, the one Ribi, the other Matteuzzo by name, fellows both of them not a whit less jolly than Maso himself; and having found them, he said to them: – "An you love me, come with me to the court, and I will shew you the queerest scarecrow that ever you saw." So the two men hied them with him to the court; and there he pointed out to them the judge and his breeches. What they saw from a distance served to set them laughing: then drawing nearer to the dais on which Master Judge was seated, they observed that 'twas easy enough to get under the dais, and moreover that the plank, on which the judge's feet rested, was broken, so that there was plenty of room for the passage of a hand and arm. Whereupon quoth Maso to his comrades: – "'Twere a very easy matter to pull these breeches right down: wherefore I propose that we do so." Each of the men had marked how it might be done; and so, having concerted both what they should do and what they should say, they came to the court again next morning; and, the court being crowded, Matteuzzo, observed by never a soul, slipped beneath the dais, and posted himself right under the spot where the judge's feet rested, while the other two men took their stand on either side of the judge, each laying hold of the hem of his robe. Then: – "Sir, sir, I pray you for God's sake," began Maso, "that, before the pilfering rascal that is there beside you can make off, you constrain him to give me back a pair of jack boots that he has stolen from me, which theft he still denies, though 'tis not a month since I saw him getting them resoled." Meanwhile Ribi, at the top of his voice, shouted: – "Believe him not, Sir, the scurvy knave! 'Tis but that he knows that I am come to demand restitution of a valise that he has stolen from me that he now for the first time trumps up this story about a pair of jack boots that I have had in my house down to the last day or two; and if you doubt what I say, I can bring as witness Trecca, my neighbour, and Grassa, the tripe-woman, and one that goes about gathering the sweepings of Santa Maria a Verzaia, who saw him when he was on his way back from the farm." But shout as he might, Maso was still even with him, nor for all that did Ribi bate a jot of his clamour. And while the judge stood, bending now towards the one, now towards the other, the better to hear them, Matteuzzo seized his opportunity, and thrusting his hand through the hole in the plank caught hold of the judge's breeches, and tugged at them amain. Whereby down they came straightway, for the judge was a lean man, and shrunk in the buttocks. The judge, being aware of the accident, but knowing not how it had come about, would have gathered his outer garments together in front, so as to cover the defect, but Maso on the one side, and Ribi on the other, held him fast, shouting amain and in chorus: – "You do me a grievous wrong, Sir, thus to deny me justice, nay, even a hearing, and to think of quitting the court: there needs no writ in this city for such a trifling matter as this." And thus they held him by the clothes and in parley, until all that were in the court perceived that he had lost his breeches. However, after a while, Matteuzzo dropped the breeches, and slipped off, and out of the court, without being observed, and Ribi, deeming that the joke had gone far enough, exclaimed: – "By God, I vow, I will appeal to the Syndics;" while Maso, on the other side, let go the robe, saying: – "Nay, but for my part, I will come here again and again and again, until I find you less embarrassed than you seem to be to-day." And so the one this way, the other that way, they made off with all speed. Whereupon Master Judge, disbreeched before all the world, was as one that awakens from sleep, albeit he was ware of his forlorn condition, and asked whither the parties in the case touching the jack boots and the valise were gone. However, as they were not to be found, he fell a swearing by the bowels of God, that 'twas meet and proper that he should know and wit, whether 'twas the custom at Florence to disbreech judges sitting in the seat of justice.

When the affair reached the ears of the Podesta, he made no little stir about it; but, being informed by some of his friends, that 'twould not have happened, but that the Florentines were minded to shew him, that, in place of the judges he should have brought with him, he had brought but gowks, to save expense, he deemed it best to say no more about it, and so for that while the matter went no further.

Eighth Day

Novel VI

— *Bruno and Buffalmacco steal a pig from Calandrino, and induce him to essay its recovery by means of pills of ginger and vernaccia. Of the said pills they give him two, one after the other, made of dog-ginger compounded with aloes; and it then appearing as if he had had the pig himself, they constrain him to buy them off, if he would not have them tell his wife.* —

FILOSTRATO'S STORY, which elicited not a little laughter, was no sooner ended, than the queen bade Filomena follow suit. Wherefore thus Filomena began: –

As, gracious ladies, 'twas the name of Maso del Saggio that prompted Filostrato to tell the story that you have but now heard, even so 'tis with me in regard of Calandrino and his comrades, of whom I am minded to tell you another story, which you will, I think, find entertaining. Who Calandrino, Bruno and Buffalmacco were, I need not explain; you know them well enough from the former story; and therefore I will tarry no longer than to say that Calandrino had a little estate not far from Florence, which his wife had brought him by way of dowry, and which yielded them yearly, among other matters, a pig; and 'twas his custom every year in the month of December to resort to the farm with his wife, there to see to the killing and salting of the said pig. Now, one of these years it so happened that his wife being unwell, Calandrino went thither alone to kill the pig. And Bruno and Buffalmacco learning that he was gone to the farm, and that his wife was not with him, betook them to the house of a priest that was their especial friend and a neighbour of Calandrino, there to tarry a while. Upon their arrival Calandrino, who had that very morning killed the pig, met them with the priest, and accosted them, saying: – "A hearty welcome to you. I should like you to see what an excellent manager I am;" and so he took them into his house, and shewed them the pig. They observed that 'twas a very fine pig; and learned from Calandrino that he was minded to salt it for household consumption. "Then thou art but a fool," quoth Bruno. "Sell it, man, and let us have a jolly time with the money; and tell thy wife that 'twas stolen." "Not I," replied Calandrino: "she would never believe me, and would drive me out of the house. Urge me no further, for I will never do it." The others said a great deal more, but to no purpose; and Calandrino bade them to supper, but so coldly that they declined, and left him.

Presently: – "Should we not steal this pig from him to-night?" quoth Bruno to Buffalmacco. "Could we so?" returned Buffalmacco. "How?" "Why, as to that," rejoined Bruno, "I have already marked how it may be done, if he bestow not the pig elsewhere." "So be it, then," said Buffalmacco: "we will steal it; and then, perchance, our good host, Master Priest, will join us in doing honour to such good cheer?" "That right gladly will I," quoth the priest. Whereupon: – "Some address, though," quoth Bruno, "will be needful: thou knowest, Buffalmacco, what a niggardly fellow Calandrino is, and how greedily he drinks at other folk's expense. Go we, therefore, and take him to the tavern, and there let the priest make as if, to do us honour, he would pay the whole score, and suffer Calandrino to pay never a soldo, and he will grow tipsy, and then we shall speed excellent well, because he is alone in the house."

As Bruno proposed, so they did: and Calandrino, finding that the priest would not suffer him to pay, drank amain, and took a great deal more aboard than he had need of; and the night being far spent when he left the tavern, he dispensed with supper, and went home, and thinking to have shut the door, got him to bed, leaving it open. Buffalmacco and Bruno went to sup with the priest; and after supper, taking with them certain implements with which to enter Calandrino's house, where Bruno thought it most feasible, they stealthily approached it; but finding the door open, they entered, and took down the pig, and carried it away to the priest's house, and having there bestowed it safely, went to bed. In the morning when Calandrino, his head at length quit of the fumes of the wine, got up, and came downstairs and found that his pig was nowhere to be seen, and that the door was open, he asked this, that, and the other man, whether they wist who had taken the pig away, and getting no answer, he began to make a great outcry: – "Alas, alas! luckless man that I am, that my pig should have been stolen from me!" Meanwhile Bruno and Buffalmacco, being also risen, made up to him, to hear what he would say touching the pig. Whom he no sooner saw, than well-nigh weeping he called them, saying: – "Alas! my friends! my pig is stolen from me." Bruno stepped up to him and said in a low tone: – "'Tis passing strange if thou art in the right for once." "Alas!" returned Calandrino, "what I say is but too true." "Why, then, out with it, man," quoth Bruno, "cry aloud, that all folk may know that 'tis so." Calandrino then raised his voice and said: – "By the body o' God I say of a truth that my pig has been stolen from me." "So!" quoth Bruno, "but publish it, man, publish it; lift up thy voice, make thyself well heard, that all may believe thy report." "Thou art enough to make me give my soul to the Enemy," replied Calandrino. "I say – dost not believe me? – that hang me by the neck if the pig is not stolen from me!" "Nay, but," quoth Bruno, "how can it be? I saw it here but yesterday. Dost think to make me believe that it has taken to itself wings and flown away?" "All the same 'tis as I tell thee," returned Calandrino. "Is it possible?" quoth Bruno. "Ay indeed," replied Calandrino; "'tis even so: and I am undone, and know not how to go home. Never will my wife believe me; or if she do so, I shall know no peace this year." "Upon my hope of salvation," quoth Bruno, "'tis indeed a bad business, if so it really is. But thou knowest, Calandrino, that 'twas but yesterday I counselled thee to make believe that 'twas so. I should be sorry to think thou didst befool thy wife and us at the same time." "Ah!" vociferated Calandrino, "wilt thou drive me to despair and provoke me to blaspheme God and the saints and all the company of heaven? I tell thee that the pig has been stolen from me in the night." Whereupon: – "If so it be," quoth Buffalmacco, "we must find a way, if we can, to recover it." "Find a way?" said Calandrino: "how can we compass that?" "Why," replied Buffalmacco, "'tis certain that no one has come from India to steal thy pig: it must have been one of thy neighbours, and if thou couldst bring them together, I warrant thee, I know how to make the assay with bread and cheese, and we will find out in a trice who has had the pig." "Ay," struck in Bruno, "make thy assay with bread and cheese in the presence of these gentry hereabout, one of whom I am sure has had the pig! why, the thing would be seen through: and they would not come." "What shall we do, then?" said Buffalmacco. Whereto Bruno made answer: – "It must be done with good pills of ginger and good vernaccia; and they must be bidden come drink with us. They will suspect nothing, and will come; and pills of ginger can be blessed just as well as bread and cheese." "Beyond a doubt, thou art right," quoth Buffalmacco; "and thou Calandrino, what sayst thou? Shall we do as Bruno says?" "Nay, I entreat you for the love of God," quoth Calandrino, "do even so: for if I knew but who had had the pig, I should feel myself half consoled for my loss." "Go to, now," quoth Bruno, "I am willing to do thy errand to Florence for these commodities, if thou givest me the money."

Calandrino had some forty soldi upon him, which he gave to Bruno, who thereupon hied him to Florence to a friend of his that was an apothecary, and bought a pound of good pills of ginger, two of which, being of dog-ginger, he caused to be compounded with fresh hepatic aloes, and then to be coated with sugar like the others; and lest they should be lost, or any of the others mistaken for them, he had a slight mark set upon them by which he might readily recognize them. He also bought a flask of good vernaccia, and, thus laden, returned to the farm, and said to Calandrino: – "To-morrow morning thou wilt bid those whom thou suspectest come hither to drink with thee: as 'twill be a saint's day, they will all come readily enough; and to-night I and Buffalmacco will say the incantation over the pills, which in the morning I will bring to thee here, and for our friendship's sake will administer them myself, and do and say all that needs to be said and done." So Calandrino did as Bruno advised, and on the morrow a goodly company, as well of young men from Florence, that happened to be in the village, as of husbandmen, being assembled in front of the church around the elm, Bruno and Buffalmacco came, bearing a box containing the ginger, and the flask of wine, and ranged the folk in a circle. Whereupon: "Gentlemen," said Bruno, "'tis meet I tell you the reason why you are gathered here, that if aught unpleasant to you should befall, you may have no ground for complaint against me. Calandrino here was the night before last robbed of a fine pig, and cannot discover who has had it; and, for that it must have been stolen by some one of us here, he would have each of you take and eat one of these pills and drink of this vernaccia. Wherefore I forthwith do you to wit, that whoso has had the pig will not be able to swallow the pill, but will find it more bitter than poison, and will spit it out; and so, rather than he should suffer this shame in presence of so many, 'twere perhaps best that he that has had the pig should confess the fact to the priest, and I will wash my hands of the affair."

All professed themselves ready enough to eat the pills; and so, having set them in a row with Calandrino among them, Bruno, beginning at one end, proceeded to give each a pill, and when he came to Calandrino he chose one of the pills of dog-ginger and put it in his hand. Calandrino thrust it forthwith between his teeth and began to chew it; but no sooner was his tongue acquainted with the aloes, than, finding the bitterness intolerable, he spat it out. Now, the eyes of all the company being fixed on one another to see who should spit out his pill, Bruno, who, not having finished the distribution, feigned to be concerned with nought else, heard some one in his rear say: – "Ha! Calandrino, what means this?" and at once turning round, and marking that Calandrino had spit out his pill: – "Wait a while," quoth he, "perchance 'twas somewhat else that caused thee to spit: take another;" and thereupon whipping out the other pill of dog-ginger, he set it between Calandrino's teeth, and finished the distribution. Bitter as Calandrino had found the former pill, he found this tenfold more so; but being ashamed to spit it out, he kept it a while in his mouth and chewed it, and, as he did so, tears stood in his eyes that shewed as large as filberts, and at length, being unable to bear it any longer, he spat it out, as he had its predecessor. Which being observed by Buffalmacco and Bruno, who were then administering the wine, and by all the company, 'twas averred by common consent that Calandrino had committed the theft himself; for which cause certain of them took him severely to task.

However, the company being dispersed, and Bruno and Buffalmacco left alone with Calandrino, Buffalmacco began on this wise: – "I never doubted but that thou hadst had it thyself, and wast minded to make us believe that it had been stolen from thee, that we might not have of thee so much as a single drink out of the price which thou gottest for it." Calandrino, with the bitterness of the aloes still on his tongue, fell a swearing that he had not had it. Whereupon: – "Nay, but, comrade," quoth Buffalmacco, "upon thy honour, what did it fetch? Six florins?" Whereto, Calandrino being now on the verge of desperation, Bruno added: – "Now be reasonable, Calandrino; among the company that ate and drank with us there was one that told me that thou hadst up there a girl that thou didst keep for thy pleasure, giving her what by hook or by crook thou couldst get together, and that he held it for certain that thou hadst sent her this pig. And thou art grown expert in this sort of cozenage. Thou tookest us one while adown the Mugnone a gathering black stones, and having thus started us on a wild-goose chase, thou madest off; and then wouldst fain have us believe that thou hadst found the stone: and now, in like manner, thou thinkest by thine oaths to persuade us that this pig which thou hast given away or sold, has been stolen from thee. But we know thy tricks of old; never another couldst thou play us; and, to be round with thee, this spell has cost us some trouble: wherefore we mean that thou shalt give us two pair of capons, or we will let Monna Tessa know all." Seeing that he was not believed, and deeming his mortification ample without the addition of his wife's resentment, Calandrino gave them the two pair of capons, with which, when the pig was salted, they returned to Florence, leaving Calandrino with the loss and the laugh against him.

Eighth Day
Novel VII

— A scholar loves a widow lady, who, being enamoured of another, causes him to spend a winter's night awaiting her in the snow. He afterwards by a stratagem causes her to stand for a whole day in July, naked upon a tower, exposed to the flies, the gadflies, and the sun. —

OVER THE WOES of poor Calandrino the ladies laughed not a little, and had laughed yet more, but that it irked them that those that had robbed him of the pig should also take from him the capons. However, the story being ended, the queen bade Pampinea give them hers: and thus forthwith Pampinea began: –

Dearest ladies, it happens oftentimes that the artful scorner meets his match; wherefore 'tis only little wits that delight to scorn. In a series of stories we have heard tell of tricks played without aught in the way of reprisals following: by mine I purpose in some degree to excite your compassion for a gentlewoman of our city (albeit the retribution that came upon her was but just) whose flout was returned in the like sort, and to such effect that she well-nigh died thereof. The which to hear will not be unprofitable to you, for thereby you will learn to be more careful how you flout others, and therein you will do very wisely.

'Tis not many years since there dwelt at Florence a lady young and fair, and of a high spirit, as also of right gentle lineage, and tolerably well endowed with temporal goods. Now Elena – such was the lady's name – being left a widow, was minded never to marry again, being enamoured of a handsome young gallant of her own choosing, with whom she, recking nought of any other lover, did, by the help of a maid in whom she placed much trust, not seldom speed the time gaily and with marvellous delight. Meanwhile it so befell that a young nobleman of our city, Rinieri by name, who had spent much time in study at Paris, not that he might thereafter sell his knowledge by retail, but that he might learn the reasons and causes of things, which accomplishment shews to most excellent advantage in a gentleman, returned to Florence, and there lived as a citizen in no small honour with his fellows, both by reason of his rank and of his learning. But as it is often the case that those who are most versed in deep matters are the soonest mastered by Love, so was it with Rinieri. For at a festal gathering, to which one day he went, there appeared before his eyes this Elena, of whom we spoke, clad in black, as is the wont of our Florentine widows, and shewing to his mind so much fairer and more debonair than any other woman that he had ever seen, that happy indeed he deemed the man might call himself, to whom God in His goodness should grant the right to hold her naked in his arms. So now and again he eyed her stealthily, and knowing that boons goodly and precious are not to be gotten without trouble, he made up his mind to study and labour with all assiduity how best to please her, that so he might win her love, and thereby the enjoyment of her.

The young gentlewoman was not used to keep her eyes bent ever towards the infernal regions; but, rating herself at no less, if not more, than her deserts, she was dexterous to move them to and fro, and thus busily scanning her company, soon detected the men who regarded her with pleasure. By which means having discovered Rinieri's passion, she inly laughed, and said: – 'Twill turn out that 'twas not for nothing that I came here to-day, for, if I mistake not, I have caught a gander by the bill. So she gave him an occasional sidelong glance, and sought as best she might to make him believe that she was not indifferent to him, deeming that the more men she might captivate by her charms, the higher those charms would be rated, and most especially by him whom she had made lord of them and her love. The erudite scholar bade adieu to philosophical meditation, for the lady entirely engrossed his mind; and, having discovered her house, he, thinking to please her, found divers pretexts for frequently passing by it. Whereon the lady, her vanity flattered for the reason aforesaid, plumed herself not a little, and shewed herself pleased to see him. Thus encouraged, the scholar found means to make friends with her maid, to whom he discovered his love, praying her to do her endeavour with her mistress, that he might have her favour. The maid was profuse of promises, and gave her mistress his message, which she no sooner heard, than she was convulsed with laughter, and replied: – "He brought sense enough hither from Paris: knowest thou where he has since been to lose it? Go to, now; let us give him that which he seeks. Tell him, when he next speaks to you of the matter, that I love him vastly more than he loves me, but that I must have regard to my reputation, so that I may be able to hold my head up among other ladies; which, if he is really the wise man they say, will cause him to affect me much more." Ah! poor woman! poor woman! she little knew, my ladies, how rash it is to try conclusions with scholars.

The maid found the scholar, and did her mistress's errand. The scholar, overjoyed, proceeded to urge his suit with more ardour, to indite letters, and send presents. The lady received all that he sent her, but vouchsafed no answers save such as were couched in general terms: and on this wise she kept him dangling a long while. At last, having disclosed the whole affair to her lover, who evinced some resentment and jealousy, she, to convince him that his suspicions were groundless, and for that she was much importuned by the scholar, sent word to him by her maid, that never since he had assured her of his love, had occasion served her to do him pleasure, but that next Christmastide she hoped to be with him; wherefore, if he were minded to await her in the courtyard of her house on the night of the day next following the feast, she would meet him there as soon as she could. Elated as ne'er another, the scholar hied him at the appointed time to the lady's house, and being ushered into a courtyard by the maid, who forthwith turned the key upon him, addressed himself there to await the lady's coming.

Now the lady's lover, by her appointment, was with her that evening; and, when they had gaily supped, she told him what she had in hand that night, adding: – "And so thou wilt be able to gauge the love which I have borne and bear this scholar, whom thou hast foolishly regarded as a rival." The lover heard the lady's words with no small delight, and waited in eager expectancy to see her make them good. The scholar, hanging about there in the courtyard, began to find it somewhat chillier than he would have liked, for it had snowed hard all day long, so that the snow lay everywhere thick on the ground; however, he bore it patiently, expecting to be recompensed by and by. After a while the lady said to her lover: – "Go we to the chamber and take a peep through a lattice at him of whom thou art turned jealous, and mark what he does, and how he will answer the maid, whom I have bidden go speak with him." So the pair hied them to a lattice, wherethrough they could see without being seen, and heard the maid call from another lattice to the scholar, saying: – "Rinieri, my lady is distressed as never woman was, for that one of her brothers is come here to-night, and after talking a long while with her, must needs sup with her, and is not yet gone, but, I think, he will soon be off; and that is the reason why she has not been able to come to thee, but she will come soon now. She trusts it does not irk thee to wait so long." Whereto the scholar, supposing that 'twas true, made answer: – "Tell my lady to give herself no anxiety on my account, until she can conveniently come to me, but to do so as soon as she may." Whereupon the maid withdrew from the window, and went to bed; while the lady said to her lover: – "Now, what sayst thou? Thinkst thou that, if I had that regard for him, which thou fearest, I would suffer him to tarry below there to get frozen?" Which said, the lady and her now partly reassured lover got them to bed, where for a great while they disported them right gamesomely, laughing together and making merry over the luckless scholar.

The scholar, meanwhile, paced up and down the courtyard to keep himself warm, nor indeed had he where to sit, or take shelter: in this plight he bestowed many a curse upon the lady's brother for his long tarrying, and never a sound did he hear but he thought that 'twas the lady opening the door. But vain indeed were his hopes: the lady, having solaced herself with her lover until hard upon midnight, then said to him: – "How ratest thou our scholar, my soul? whether is the greater his wit, or the love I bear him, thinkst thou? Will the cold, that, of my ordaining, he now suffers, banish from thy breast the suspicion which my light words the other day implanted there?" "Ay, indeed, heart of my body!" replied the lover, "well wot I now that even as thou art to me, my weal, my consolation, my bliss, so am I to thee." "So:" quoth the lady, "then I must have full a thousand kisses from thee, to prove that thou sayst sooth." The lover's answer was to strain her to his heart, and give her not merely a thousand but a hundred thousand kisses. In such converse they dallied a while longer, and then: – "Get we up, now," quoth the lady, "that we may go see if 'tis quite spent, that fire, with which, as he wrote to me daily, this new lover of mine used to burn." So up they got and hied them to the lattice which they had used before, and peering out into the courtyard, saw the scholar dancing a hornpipe to the music that his own teeth made, a chattering for extremity of cold; nor had they ever seen it footed so nimbly and at such a pace. Whereupon: – "How sayst thou, sweet my hope?" quoth the lady. "Know I not how to make men dance without the aid of either trumpet or cornemuse?" "Indeed thou dost my heart's delight," replied the lover. Quoth then the lady: – "I have a mind that we go down to the door. Thou wilt keep quiet, and I will speak to him, and we shall hear what he says, which, peradventure, we shall find no less diverting than the sight of him."

So they stole softly out of the chamber and down to the door, which leaving fast closed, the lady set her lips to a little hole that was there, and with a low voice called the scholar, who, hearing her call him, praised God, making too sure that he was to be admitted, and being come to the door, said: – "Here am I, Madam; open for God's sake; let me in, for I die of cold." "Oh! ay," replied the lady, "I know thou hast a chill, and of course, there being a little snow about, 'tis mighty cold; but well I wot the nights are colder far at Paris. I cannot let thee in as yet, because my accursed brother, that came to sup here this evening, is still with me; but he will soon take himself off, and then I will let thee in without a moment's delay. I have but now with no small difficulty given him the slip, to come and give thee heart that the waiting irk thee not." "Nay but, Madam," replied the scholar, "for the love of God, I entreat you, let me in, that I may have a roof over my head, because for some time past there has been never so thick a fall of snow, and 'tis yet snowing; and then I will wait as long as you please." "Alas! sweet my love," quoth the lady, "that I may not, for this door makes such a din, when one opens it, that my brother would be sure to hear, were I to let thee in; but I will go tell him to get him gone, and so come back and admit thee." "Go at once, then," returned the scholar, "and prithee, see that a good fire be kindled, that, when I get in, I may warm myself, for I am now so chilled through and through that I have scarce any feeling left." "That can scarce be," rejoined the lady, "if it be true, what thou hast so protested in thy letters, that thou art all afire for love of me: 'tis plain to me now that thou didst but mock me. I now take my leave of thee: wait and be of good cheer."

So the lady and her lover, who, to his immense delight, had heard all that passed, betook them to bed; however, little sleep had they that night, but spent the best part of it in disporting themselves and making merry over the unfortunate scholar, who, his teeth now chattering to such a tune that he seemed to have been metamorphosed into a stork, perceived that he had been befooled, and after making divers fruitless attempts to open the door and seeking means of egress to no better purpose, paced to and fro like a lion, cursing the villainous weather, the long night, his simplicity, and the perversity of the lady, against whom (the vehemence of his wrath suddenly converting the love he had so long borne her to bitter and remorseless enmity) he now plotted within himself divers and grand schemes of revenge, on which he was far more bent than ever he had been on forgathering with her.

Slowly the night wore away, and with the first streaks of dawn the maid, by her mistress's direction, came down, opened the door of the courtyard, and putting on a compassionate air, greeted Rinieri with: – "Foul fall him that came here yestereve; he has afflicted us with his presence all night long, and has kept thee a freezing out here: but harkye, take it not amiss; that which might not be to-night shall be another time: well wot I that nought could have befallen that my lady could so ill brook." For all his wrath, the scholar, witting, like the wise man he was, that menaces serve but to put the menaced on his guard, kept pent within his breast that which unbridled resentment would have uttered, and said quietly, and without betraying the least trace of anger: – "In truth 'twas the worst night I ever spent, but I understood quite well that the lady was in no wise to blame, for that she herself, being moved to pity of me, came down here to make her excuses, and to comfort me; and, as thou sayst, what has not been to-night will be another time: wherefore commend me to her, and so, adieu!" Then, well-nigh paralysed for cold, he got him, as best he might, home, where, weary and fit to die for drowsiness, he threw himself on his bed, and fell into a deep sleep, from which he awoke to find that he had all but lost the use of his arms and legs. He therefore sent for some physicians, and having told them what a chill he had gotten, caused them have a care to his health. But, though they treated him with active and most drastic remedies, it cost them some time and no little trouble to restore to the cramped muscles their wonted pliancy, and, indeed, but for his youth and the milder weather that was at hand, 'twould have gone very hard with him.

However, recover he did his health and lustihood, and nursing his enmity, feigned to be vastly more enamoured of his widow than ever before. And so it was that after a while Fortune furnished him with an opportunity of satisfying his resentment, for the gallant of whom the widow was enamoured, utterly regardless of the love she bore him, grew enamoured of another lady, and was minded no more to pleasure the widow in aught either by word or by deed; wherefore she now pined in tears and bitterness of spirit. However, her maid, who commiserated her not a little, and knew not how to dispel the dumps that the loss of her lover had caused her, espying the scholar pass along the street, as he had been wont, conceived the silly idea that the lady's lover might be induced to return to his old love by some practice of a necromantic order, wherein she doubted not that the scholar must be a thorough adept; which idea she imparted to her mistress. The lady, being none too well furnished with sense, never thinking that, if the scholar had been an adept in necromancy, he would have made use of it in his own behoof, gave heed to what her maid said, and forthwith bade her learn of the scholar whether he would place his skill at her service, and assure him that, if he so did, she, in guerdon thereof, would do his pleasure. The maid did her mistress's errand well and faithfully. The scholar no sooner heard the message, than he said to himself: – Praised be Thy name, O God, that the time is now come, when with Thy help I may be avenged upon this wicked woman of the wrong she did me in requital of the great love I bore her. Then, turning to the maid, he said: – "Tell my lady to set her mind at ease touching this matter; for that, were her lover in India, I would forthwith bring him hither to crave her pardon of that wherein he has offended her. As to the course she should take in the matter, I tarry but her pleasure to make it known to her, when and where she may think fit: tell her so, and bid her from me to be of good cheer." The maid carried his answer to her mistress, and arranged that they should meet in the church of Santa Lucia of Prato. Thither accordingly they came, the lady and the scholar, and conversed apart, and the lady, quite oblivious of the ill-usage by which she had well-nigh done him to death, opened all her mind to him, and besought him, if he had any regard to her welfare, to aid her to the attainment of her desire. "Madam," replied the scholar, "true it is that among other lore that I acquired at Paris was this of necromancy, whereof, indeed, I know all that may be known; but, as 'tis in the last degree displeasing to God, I had sworn never to practise it either for my own or for any other's behoof. 'Tis also true that the love I bear you is such that I know not how to refuse you aught that you would have me do for you; and so, were this single essay enough to consign me to hell, I would adventure it to pleasure you. But I mind me that 'tis a matter scarce so easy of performance as, perchance, you suppose, most especially when a woman would fain recover the love of a man, or a man that of a woman, for then it must be done by the postulant in proper person, and at night, and in lonely places, and unattended, so that it needs a stout heart; nor know I whether you are disposed to comply with these conditions." The lady, too enamoured to be discreet, made answer: – "So shrewdly does Love goad me, that there is nought I would not do to bring him back to me who wrongfully has deserted me; but tell me, prithee, wherein it is that I have need of this stout heart." "Madam," returned the despiteful scholar, "'twill be my part to fashion in tin an image of him you would fain lure back to you: and when I have sent you the image, 'twill be for you, when the moon is well on the wane, to dip yourself, being stark naked, and the image, seven times in a flowing stream, and this you must do quite alone about the hour of first sleep, and afterwards, still naked, you must get you upon some tree or some deserted house, and facing the North, with the image in your hand, say certain words that I shall give you in writing seven times; which, when you have done, there will come to you two damsels, the fairest you ever saw, who will greet you graciously, and ask of you what you would fain have; to whom you will disclose frankly and fully all that you crave; and see to it that you make no mistake in the name; and when you have said all, they will depart, and you may then descend and return to the spot where you left your clothes, and resume them and go home. And rest assured, that before the ensuing midnight your lover will come to you in tears, and crave your pardon and mercy, and that thenceforth he will never again desert you for any other woman."

  The lady gave entire credence to the scholar's words, and deeming her lover as good as in her arms again, recovered half her wonted spirits: wherefore: – "Make no doubt," quoth she, "that I shall do as thou biddest; and indeed I am most favoured by circumstance; for in upper Val d'Arno I have an estate adjoining the river, and 'tis now July, so that to bathe will be delightful. Ay, and now I mind me that at no great distance from the river there is a little tower, which is deserted, save that now and again the shepherds will get them up by the chestnut-wood ladder to the roof, thence to look out for their strayed sheep; 'tis a place lonely indeed, and quite out of ken; and when I have clomb it, as climb it I will, I doubt not 'twill be the best place in all the world to give effect to your instructions."

Well pleased to be certified of the lady's intention, the scholar, to whom her estate and the tower were very well known, made answer: – "I was never in those parts, Madam, and therefore know neither your estate nor the tower, but, if 'tis as you say, 'twill certainly be the best place in the world for your purpose. So, when time shall serve, I will send you the image and the orison. But I pray you, when you shall have your heart's desire, and know that I have done you good service, do not forget me, but keep your promise to me." "That will I without fail," quoth the lady; and so she bade him farewell, and went home. The scholar, gleefully anticipating the success of his enterprise, fashioned an image, and inscribed it with certain magical signs, and wrote some gibberish by way of orison, which in due time he sent to the lady, bidding her the very next night do as he had prescribed: and thereupon he hied him privily with one of his servants to the house of a friend hard by the tower, there to carry his purpose into effect. The lady, on her part, set out with her maid, and betook her to her estate, and, night being come, sent the maid to bed, as if she were minded to go to rest herself; and about the hour of first sleep stole out of the house and down to the tower, beside the Arno; and when, having carefully looked about her, she was satisfied that never a soul was to be seen or heard, she took off her clothes and hid them under a bush; then, with the image in her hand, she dipped herself seven times in the river; which done, she hied her with the image to the tower. The scholar, having at nightfall couched himself with his servant among the willows and other trees that fringed the bank, marked all that she did, and how, as she passed by him, the whiteness of her flesh dispelled the shades of night, and scanning attentively her bosom and every other part of her body, and finding them very fair, felt, as he bethought him what would shortly befall them, some pity of her; while, on the other hand, he was suddenly assailed by the solicitations of the flesh which caused that to stand which had been inert, and prompted him to sally forth of his ambush and take her by force, and have his pleasure of her. And, what with his compassion and passion, he was like to be worsted; but then as he bethought him who he was, and what a grievous wrong had been done him, and for what cause, and by whom, his wrath, thus rekindled, got the better of the other affections, so that he swerved not from his resolve, but suffered her to go her way.

The lady ascended the tower, and standing with her face to the North, began to recite the scholar's orison, while he, having stolen into the tower but a little behind her, cautiously shifted the ladder that led up to the roof on which the lady stood, and waited to observe what she would say and do. Seven times the lady said the orison, and then awaited the appearance of the two damsels; and so long had she to wait – not to mention that the night was a good deal cooler than she would have liked – that she saw day break; whereupon, disconcerted that it had not fallen out as the scholar had promised, she said to herself: – I misdoubt me he was minded to give me such a night as I gave him; but if such was his intent, he is but maladroit in his revenge, for this night is not as long by a third as his was, besides which, the cold is of another quality. And that day might not overtake her there, she began to think of descending, but, finding that the ladder was removed, she felt as if the world had come to nought beneath her feet, her senses reeled, and she fell in a swoon upon the floor of the roof. When she came to herself, she burst into tears and piteous lamentations, and witting now very well that 'twas the doing of the scholar, she began to repent her that she had first offended him, and then trusted him unduly, having such good cause to reckon upon his enmity; in which frame she abode long time. Then, searching if haply she might find some means of descent, and finding none, she fell a weeping again, and bitterly to herself she said: – Alas for thee, wretched woman! what will thy brothers, thy kinsmen, thy neighbours, nay, what will all Florence say of thee, when 'tis known that thou hast been found here naked? Thy honour, hitherto unsuspect, will be known to have been but a shew, and shouldst thou seek thy defence in lying excuses, if any such may be fashioned, the accursed scholar, who knows all thy doings, will not suffer it. Ah! poor wretch! that at one and the same time hast lost thy too dearly cherished gallant and thine own honour! And therewith she was taken with such a transport of grief, that she was like to cast herself from the tower to the ground. Then, bethinking her that if she might espy some lad making towards the tower with his sheep, she might send him for her maid, for the sun was now risen, she approached one of the parapets of the tower, and looked out, and so it befell that the scholar, awakening from a slumber, in which he had lain a while at the foot of a bush, espied her, and she him. Whereupon: – "Good-day, Madam," quoth he: – "are the damsels yet come?" The lady saw and heard him not without bursting afresh into a flood of tears, and besought him to come into the tower, that she might speak with him: a request which the scholar very courteously granted. The lady then threw herself prone on the floor of the roof; and, only her head being visible through the aperture, thus through her sobs she spoke: – "Verily, Rinieri, if I gave thee a bad night, thou art well avenged on me, for, though it be July, meseemed I was sore a cold last night, standing here with never a thread upon me, and, besides, I have so bitterly bewept both the trick I played thee and my own folly in trusting thee, that I marvel that I have still eyes in my head. Wherefore I implore thee, not for love of me, whom thou hast no cause to love, but for the respect thou hast for thyself as a gentleman, that thou let that which thou hast already done suffice thee to avenge the wrong I did thee, and bring me my clothes, that I may be able to get me down from here, and spare to take from me that which, however thou mightst hereafter wish, thou couldst not restore to me, to wit, my honour; whereas, if I deprived thee of that one night with me, 'tis in my power to give thee many another night in recompense thereof, and thou hast but to choose thine own times. Let this, then, suffice, and like a worthy gentleman be satisfied to have taken thy revenge, and to have let me know it: put not forth thy might against a woman: 'tis no glory to the eagle to have vanquished a dove; wherefore for God's and thine own honour's sake have mercy on me."

The scholar, albeit his haughty spirit still brooded on her evil entreatment of him, yet saw her not weep and supplicate without a certain compunction mingling with his exultation; but vengeance he had desired above all things, to have wreaked it was indeed sweet, and albeit his humanity prompted him to have compassion on the hapless woman, yet it availed not to subdue the fierceness of his resentment; wherefore thus he made answer: – "Madam Elena, had my prayers (albeit art I had none to mingle with them tears and honeyed words as thou dost with thine) inclined thee that night, when I stood perishing with cold amid the snow that filled thy courtyard, to accord me the very least shelter, 'twere but a light matter for me to hearken now to thine; but, if thou art now so much more careful of thy honour than thou wast wont to be, and it irks thee to tarry there naked, address thy prayers to him in whose arms it irked thee not naked to pass that night thou mindest thee of, albeit thou wist that I with hasty foot was beating time upon the snow in thy courtyard to the accompaniment of chattering teeth: 'tis he that thou shouldst call to succour thee, to fetch thy clothes, to adjust the ladder for thy descent; 'tis he in whom thou shouldst labour to inspire this tenderness thou now shewest for thy honour, that honour which for his sake thou hast not scrupled to jeopardize both now and on a thousand other occasions. Why, then, call'st thou not him to come to thy succour? To whom pertains it rather than to him? Thou art his. And of whom will he have a care, whom will he succour, if not thee? Thou askedst him that night, when thou wast wantoning with him, whether seemed to him the greater, my folly or the love thou didst bear him: call him now, foolish woman, and see if the love thou bearest him, and thy wit and his, may avail to deliver thee from my folly. 'Tis now no longer in thy power to shew me courtesy of that which I no more desire, nor yet to refuse it, did I desire it. Reserve thy nights for thy lover, if so be thou go hence alive. Be they all thine and his. One of them was more than I cared for; 'tis enough for me to have been flouted once. Ay, and by thy cunning of speech thou strivest might and main to conciliate my good-will, calling me worthy gentleman, by which insinuation thou wouldst fain induce me magnanimously to desist from further chastisement of thy baseness. But thy cajoleries shall not now cloud the eyes of my mind, as did once thy false promises. I know myself, and better now for thy one night's instruction than for all the time I spent at Paris. But, granted that I were disposed to be magnanimous, thou art not of those to whom 'tis meet to shew magnanimity. A wild beast such as thou, having merited vengeance, can claim no relief from suffering save death, though in the case of a human being 'twould suffice to temper vengeance with mercy, as thou saidst. Wherefore I, albeit no eagle, witting thee to be no dove, but a venomous serpent, mankind's most ancient enemy, am minded, bating no jot of malice or of might, to harry thee to the bitter end: natheless this which I do is not properly to be called vengeance but rather just retribution; seeing that vengeance should be in excess of the offence, and this my chastisement of thee will fall short of it; for, were I minded to be avenged on thee, considering what account thou madest of my heart and soul, 'twould not suffice me to take thy life, no, nor the lives of a hundred others such as thee; for I should but slay a vile and base and wicked woman. And what the Devil art thou more than any other pitiful baggage, that I should spare thy little store of beauty, which a few years will ruin, covering thy face with wrinkles? And yet 'twas not for want of will that thou didst fail to do to death a worthy gentleman, as thou but now didst call me, of whom in a single day of his life the world may well have more profit than of a hundred thousand like thee while the world shall last. Wherefore by this rude discipline I will teach thee what it is to flout men of spirit, and more especially what it is to flout scholars, that if thou escape with thy life thou mayst have good cause ever hereafter to shun such folly. But if thou art so fain to make the descent, why cast not thyself down, whereby, God helping, thou wouldst at once break thy neck, be quit of the torment thou endurest, and make me the happiest man alive? I have no more to say to thee. 'Twas my art and craft thus caused thee climb; be it thine to find the way down: thou hadst cunning enough, when thou wast minded to flout me."

While the scholar thus spoke, the hapless lady wept incessantly, and before he had done, to aggravate her misery, the sun was high in the heaven. However, when he was silent, thus she made answer: – "Ah! ruthless man, if that accursed night has so rankled with thee, and thou deemest my fault so grave that neither my youth and beauty, nor my bitter tears, nor yet my humble supplications may move thee to pity, let this at least move thee, and abate somewhat of thy remorseless severity, that 'twas my act alone, in that of late I trusted thee, and discovered to thee all my secret, that did open the way to compass thy end, and make me cognizant of my guilt, seeing that, had I not confided in thee, on no wise mightst thou have been avenged on me; which thou wouldst seem so ardently to have desired. Turn thee, then, turn thee, I pray thee, from thy wrath, and pardon me. So thou wilt pardon me, and get me down hence, right gladly will I give up for ever my faithless gallant, and thou shalt be my sole lover and lord, albeit thou sayst hard things of my beauty, slight and shortlived as thou wouldst have it to be, which, however it may compare with others, is, I wot, to be prized, if for no other reason, yet for this, that 'tis the admiration and solace and delight of young men, and thou art not yet old. And albeit I have been harshly treated by thee, yet believe I cannot that thou wouldst have me do myself so shamefully to death as to cast me down, like some abandoned wretch, before thine eyes, in which, unless thou wast then, as thou hast since shewn thyself, a liar, I found such favour. Ah! have pity on me for God's and mercy's sake! The sun waxes exceeding hot, and having suffered not a little by the cold of last night, I now begin to be sorely afflicted by the heat."

"Madam," rejoined the scholar, who held her in parley with no small delight, "'twas not for any love that thou didst bear me that thou trustedst me, but that thou mightst recover that which thou hadst lost, for which cause thou meritest but the greater punishment; and foolish indeed art thou if thou supposest that such was the sole means available for my revenge. I had a thousand others, and, while I feigned to love thee, I had laid a thousand gins for thy feet, into one or other of which in no long time, though this had not occurred, thou must needs have fallen, and that too to thy more grievous suffering and shame; nor was it to spare thee, but that I might be the sooner rejoiced by thy discomfiture that I took my present course. And though all other means had failed me, I had still the pen, with which I would have written of thee such matters and in such a sort, that when thou wist them, as thou shouldst have done, thou wouldst have regretted a thousand times that thou hadst ever been born. The might of the pen is greater far than they suppose, who have not proved it by experience. By God I swear, so may He, who has prospered me thus far in this my revenge, prosper me to the end! that I would have written of thee things that would have so shamed thee in thine own – not to speak of others' – sight that thou hadst put out thine eyes that thou mightst no more see thyself; wherefore chide not the sea, for that it has sent forth a tiny rivulet. For thy love, or whether thou be mine or no, nought care I. Be thou still his, whose thou hast been, if thou canst. Hate him as I once did, I now love him, by reason of his present entreatment of thee. Ye go getting you enamoured, ye women, and nought will satisfy you but young gallants, because ye mark that their flesh is ruddier, and their beards are blacker, than other folk's, and that they carry themselves well, and foot it featly in the dance, and joust; but those that are now more mature were even as they, and possess a knowledge which they have yet to acquire. And therewithal ye deem that they ride better, and cover more miles in a day, than men of riper age. Now that they dust the pelisse with more vigour I certainly allow, but their seniors, being more experienced, know better the places where the fleas lurk; and spare and dainty diet is preferable to abundance without savour: moreover hard trotting will gall and jade even the youngest, whereas an easy pace, though it bring one somewhat later to the inn, at any rate brings one thither fresh. Ye discern not, witless creatures that ye are, how much of evil this little shew of bravery serves to hide. Your young gallant is never content with one woman, but lusts after as many as he sets eyes on; nor is there any but he deems himself worthy of her: wherefore 'tis not possible that their love should be lasting, as thou hast but now proved and mayst only too truly witness. Moreover to be worshipped, to be caressed by their ladies they deem but their due; nor is there aught whereon they plume and boast them so proudly as their conquests: which impertinence has caused not a few women to surrender to the friars, who keep their own counsel. Peradventure thou wilt say that never a soul save thy maid, and I wist aught of thy loves; but, if so, thou hast been misinformed, and if thou so believest, thou dost misbelieve. Scarce aught else is talked of either in his quarter or in thine; but most often 'tis those most concerned whose ears such matters reach last. Moreover, they rob you, these young gallants, whereas the others make you presents. So, then, having made a bad choice, be thou still his to whom thou hast given thyself, and leave me, whom thou didst flout, to another, for I have found a lady of much greater charms than thine, and that has understood me better than thou didst. And that thou mayst get thee to the other world better certified of the desire of my eyes than thou wouldst seem to be here by my words, delay no more, but cast thyself down, whereby thy soul, taken forthwith, as I doubt not she will be, into the embrace of the Devil, may see whether thy headlong fall afflicts mine eyes, or no. But, for that I doubt thou meanest not thus to gladden me, I bid thee, if thou findest the sun begin to scorch thee, remember the cold thou didst cause me to endure, wherewith, by admixture, thou mayst readily temper the sun's heat."

The hapless lady, seeing that the scholar's words were ever to the same ruthless effect, burst afresh into tears, and said: – "Lo, now, since nought that pertains to me may move thee, be thou at least moved by the love thou bearest this lady of whom thou speakest, who, thou sayst, is wiser than I, and loves thee, and for love of her pardon me, and fetch me my clothes, that I may resume them, and get me down hence." Whereat the scholar fell a laughing, and seeing that 'twas not a little past tierce, made answer: – "Lo, now, I know not how to deny thee, adjuring me as thou dost by such a lady: tell me, then, where thy clothes are, and I will go fetch them, and bring thee down." The lady, believing him, was somewhat comforted, and told him where she had laid her clothes. The scholar then quitted the tower, bidding his servant on no account to stir from his post, but to keep close by, and, as best he might, bar the tower against all comers until his return: which said, he betook him to the house of his friend, where he breakfasted much at his ease, and thereafter went to sleep. Left alone upon the tower, the lady, somewhat cheered by her fond hope, but still exceeding sorrowful, drew nigh to a part of the wall where there was a little shade, and there sate down to wait. And now lost in most melancholy brooding, now dissolved in tears, now plunged in despair of ever seeing the scholar return with her clothes, but never more than a brief while in any one mood, spent with grief and the night's vigil, she by and by fell asleep. The sun was now in the zenith, and smote with extreme fervour full and unmitigated upon her tender and delicate frame, and upon her bare head, insomuch that his rays did not only scorch but bit by bit excoriate every part of her flesh that was exposed to them, and so shrewdly burn her that, albeit she was in a deep sleep, the pain awoke her. And as by reason thereof she writhed a little, she felt the scorched skin part in sunder and shed itself, as will happen when one tugs at a parchment that has been singed by the fire, while her head ached so sore that it seemed like to split, and no wonder. Nor might she find place either to lie or to stand on the floor of the roof, but ever went to and fro, weeping. Besides which there stirred not the least breath of wind, and flies and gadflies did swarm in prodigious quantity, which, settling upon her excoriate flesh, stung her so shrewdly that 'twas as if she received so many stabs with a javelin, and she was ever restlessly feeling her sores with her hands, and cursing herself, her life, her lover, and the scholar.

Thus by the exorbitant heat of the sun, by the flies and gadflies, harassed, goaded, and lacerated, tormented also by hunger, and yet more by thirst, and, thereto by a thousand distressful thoughts, she panted herself erect on her feet, and looked about her, if haply she might see or hear any one, with intent, come what might, to call to him and crave his succour. But even this hostile Fortune had disallowed her. The husbandmen were all gone from the fields by reason of the heat, and indeed there had come none to work that day in the neighbourhood of the tower, for that all were employed in threshing their corn beside their cottages: wherefore she heard but the cicalas, while Arno, tantalizing her with the sight of his waters, increased rather than diminished her thirst. Ay, and in like manner, wherever she espied a copse, or a patch of shade, or a house, 'twas a torment to her, for the longing she had for it. What more is to be said of this hapless woman? Only this: that what with the heat of the sun above and the floor beneath her, and the scarification of her flesh in every part by the flies and gadflies, that flesh, which in the night had dispelled the gloom by its whiteness, was now become red as madder, and so besprent with clots of blood, that whoso had seen her would have deemed her the most hideous object in the world.

Thus resourceless and hopeless, she passed the long hours, expecting death rather than aught else, until half none was come and gone; when, his siesta ended, the scholar bethought him of his lady, and being minded to see how she fared, hied him back to the tower, and sent his servant away to break his fast. As soon as the lady espied him, she came, spent and crushed by her sore affliction, to the aperture, and thus addressed him: – "Rinieri, the cup of thy vengeance is full to overflowing: for if I gave thee a night of freezing in my courtyard, thou hast given me upon this tower a day of scorching, nay, of burning, and therewithal of perishing of hunger and thirst: wherefore by God I entreat thee to come up hither, and as my heart fails me to take my life, take it thou, for 'tis death I desire of all things, such and so grievous is my suffering. But if this grace thou wilt not grant, at least bring me a cup of water wherewith to lave my mouth, for which my tears do not suffice, so parched and torrid is it within." Well wist the scholar by her voice how spent she was; he also saw a part of her body burned through and through by the sun; whereby, and by reason of the lowliness of her entreaties, he felt some little pity for her; but all the same he made answer: – "Nay, wicked woman, 'tis not by my hands thou shalt die; thou canst die by thine own whenever thou art so minded; and to temper thy heat thou shalt have just as much water from me as I had fire from thee to mitigate my cold. I only regret that for the cure of my chill the physicians were fain to use foul-smelling muck, whereas thy burns can be treated with fragrant rose-water; and that, whereas I was like to lose my muscles and the use of my limbs, thou, for all thy excoriation by the heat, wilt yet be fair again, like a snake that has sloughed off the old skin." "Alas! woe's me!" replied the lady, "for charms acquired at such a cost, God grant them to those that hate me. But thou, most fell of all wild beasts, how hast thou borne thus to torture me? What more had I to expect of thee or any other, had I done all thy kith and kin to death with direst torments? Verily, I know not what more cruel suffering thou couldst have inflicted on a traitor that had put a whole city to the slaughter than this which thou hast allotted to me, to be thus roasted, and devoured of the flies, and therewithal to refuse me even a cup of water, though the very murderers condemned to death by the law, as they go to execution, not seldom are allowed wine to drink, so they but ask it. Lo now, I see that thou art inexorable in thy ruthlessness, and on no wise to be moved by my suffering: wherefore with resignation I will compose me to await death, that God may have mercy on my soul. And may this that thou doest escape not the searching glance of His just eyes." Which said, she dragged herself, sore suffering, toward the middle of the floor, despairing of ever escaping from her fiery torment, besides which, not once only, but a thousand times she thought to choke for thirst, and ever she wept bitterly and bewailed her evil fate. But at length the day wore to vespers, and the scholar, being sated with his revenge, caused his servant to take her clothes and wrap them in his cloak, and hied him with the servant to the hapless lady's house, where, finding her maid sitting disconsolate and woebegone and resourceless at the door: – "Good woman," quoth he, "what has befallen thy mistress?" Whereto: – "Sir, I know not," replied the maid. "I looked to find her this morning abed, for methought she went to bed last night, but neither there nor anywhere else could I find her, nor know I what is become of her; wherefore exceeding great is my distress; but have you, Sir, nought to say of the matter?" "Only this," returned the scholar, "that I would I had had thee with her there where I have had her, that I might have requited thee of thy offence, even as I have requited her of hers. But be assured that thou shalt not escape my hands, until thou hast from me such wage of thy labour that thou shalt never flout man more, but thou shalt mind thee of me." Then, turning to his servant, he said: – "Give her these clothes, and tell her that she may go bring her mistress away, if she will." The servant did his bidding; and the maid, what with the message and her recognition of the clothes, was mightily afraid, lest they had slain the lady, and scarce suppressing a shriek, took the clothes, and, bursting into tears, set off, as soon as the scholar was gone, at a run for the tower.

Now one of the lady's husbandmen had had the misfortune to lose two of his hogs that day, and, seeking them, came to the tower not long after the scholar had gone thence, and peering about in all quarters, if haply he might have sight of his hogs, heard the woeful lamentation that the hapless lady made, and got him up into the tower, and called out as loud as he might: – "Who wails up there?" The lady recognized her husbandman's voice, and called him by name, saying: – "Prithee, go fetch my maid, and cause her come up hither to me." The husbandman, knowing her by her voice, replied: – "Alas! Madam, who set you there? Your maid has been seeking you all day long: but who would ever have supposed that you were there?" Whereupon he took the props of the ladder, and set them in position, and proceeded to secure the rounds to them with withies. Thus engaged he was found by the maid, who, as she entered the tower, beat her face and breast, and unable longer to keep silence, cried out: – "Alas, sweet my lady, where are you?" Whereto the lady made answer as loud as she might: – "O my sister, here above am I, weep not, but fetch me my clothes forthwith." Well-nigh restored to heart, to hear her mistress's voice, the maid, assisted by the husbandman, ascended the ladder, which he had now all but set in order, and gaining the roof, and seeing her lady lie there naked, spent and fordone, and liker to a half-burned stump than to a human being, she planted her nails in her face and fell a weeping over her, as if she were a corpse. However, the lady bade her for God's sake be silent, and help her to dress, and having learned from her that none knew where she had been, save those that had brought her her clothes and the husbandman that was there present, was somewhat consoled, and besought her for God's sake to say nought of the matter to any. Thus long time they conversed, and then the husbandman took the lady on his shoulders, for walk she could not, and bore her safely out of the tower. The unfortunate maid, following after with somewhat less caution, slipped, and falling from the ladder to the ground, broke her thigh, and roared for pain like any lion. So the husbandman set the lady down upon a grassy mead, while he went to see what had befallen the maid, whom, finding her thigh broken, he brought, and laid beside the lady: who, seeing her woes completed by this last misfortune, and that she of whom, most of all, she had expected succour, was lamed of a thigh, was distressed beyond measure, and wept again so piteously that not only was the husbandman powerless to comfort her, but was himself fain to weep. However, as the sun was now low, that they might not be there surprised by night, he, with the disconsolate lady's approval, hied him home, and called to his aid two of his brothers and his wife, who returned with him, bearing a plank, whereon they laid the maid, and so they carried her to the lady's house. There, by dint of cold water and words of cheer, they restored some heart to the lady, whom the husbandman then took upon his shoulders, and bore to her chamber. The husbandman's wife fed her with sops of bread, and then undressed her, and put her to bed.

They also provided the means to carry her and the maid to Florence; and so 'twas done. There the lady, who was very fertile in artifices, invented an entirely fictitious story of what had happened as well in regard of her maid as of herself, whereby she persuaded both her brothers and her sisters and every one else, that 'twas all due to the enchantments of evil spirits. The physicians lost no time, and, albeit the lady's suffering and mortification were extreme, for she left more than one skin sticking to the sheets, they cured her of a high fever, and certain attendant maladies; as also the maid of her fractured thigh. The end of all which was that the lady forgot her lover, and having learned discretion, was thenceforth careful neither to love nor to flout; and the scholar, learning that the maid had broken her thigh, deemed his vengeance complete, and was satisfied to say never a word more of the affair. Such then were the consequences of her flouts to this foolish young woman, who deemed that she might trifle with a scholar with the like impunity as with others, not duly understanding that they – I say not all, but the more part – know where the Devil keeps his tail. Wherefore, my ladies, have a care how you flout men, and more especially scholars.

Eighth Day

Novel VIII

— Two men keep with one another: the one lies with the other's wife: the other, being ware thereof, manages with the aid of his wife to have the one locked in a chest, upon which he then lies with the wife of him that is locked therein. —

GRIEVOUS AND DISTRESSFUL was it to the ladies to hear how it fared with Elena; but as they accounted the retribution in a measure righteous, they were satisfied to expend upon her but a moderate degree of compassion, albeit they censured the scholar as severe, intemperately relentless, and indeed ruthless, in his vengeance. However, Pampinea having brought the story to a close, the queen bade Fiammetta follow suit; and prompt to obey, Fiammetta thus spoke: –

Debonair my ladies, as, methinks, your feelings must have been somewhat harrowed by the severity of the resentful scholar, I deem it meet to soothe your vexed spirits with something of a more cheerful order. Wherefore I am minded to tell you a little story of a young man who bore an affront in a milder temper, and avenged himself with more moderation. Whereby you may understand that one should be satisfied if the ass and the wall are quits, nor by indulging a vindictive spirit to excess turn the requital of a wrong into an occasion of wrong-doing. You are to know, then, that at Siena, as I have heard tell, there dwelt two young men of good substance, and, for plebeians, of good family, the one Spinelloccio Tanena, the other Zeppa di Mino, by name; who, their houses being contiguous in the Camollia, kept ever together, and, by what appeared, loved each other as brothers, or even more so, and had each a very fine woman to wife. Now it so befell that Spinelloccio, being much in Zeppa's house, as well when Zeppa was not, as when he was there, grew so familiar with Zeppa's wife, that he sometimes lay with her; and on this wise they continued to forgather a great while before any one was ware of it. However, one of these days Zeppa being at home, though the lady wist it not, Spinelloccio came in quest of him; and, the lady sending word that he was not at home, he forthwith went upstairs and found the lady in the saloon, and seeing none else there, kissed her, as did she him.

Zeppa saw all that passed, but said nothing and kept close, being minded to see how the game would end, and soon saw his wife and Spinelloccio, still in one another's arms, hie them to her chamber and lock themselves in: whereat he was mightily incensed. But, witting that to make a noise, or do aught else overt, would not lessen but rather increase his dishonour, he cast about how he might be avenged on such wise that, without the affair getting wind, he might content his soul; and having, after long pondering, hit, as he thought, upon the expedient, he budged not from his retreat, until Spinelloccio had parted from the lady. Whereupon he hied him into the chamber, and there finding the lady with her head-gear, which Spinelloccio in toying with her had disarranged, scarce yet readjusted: – "Madam, what dost thou?" quoth he. Whereto: – "Why, dost not see?" returned the lady. "Troth do I," rejoined he, "and somewhat else have I seen that I would I had not." And so he questioned her of what had passed, and she, being mightily afraid, did after long parley confess that which she might not plausibly deny, to wit, her intimacy with Spinelloccio, and fell a beseeching him with tears to pardon her. "Lo, now, wife," quoth Zeppa, "thou hast done wrong, and, so thou wouldst have me pardon thee, have a care to do exactly as I shall bid thee; to wit, on this wise: thou must tell Spinelloccio, to find some occasion to part from me to-morrow morning about tierce, and come hither to thee; and while he is here I will come back, and when thou hearest me coming, thou wilt get him into this chest, and lock him in there; which when thou hast done, I will tell thee what else thou hast to do, which thou mayst do without the least misgiving, for I promise thee I will do him no harm." The lady, to content him, promised to do as he bade, and she kept her word.

The morrow came, and Zeppa and Spinelloccio being together about tierce, Spinelloccio, having promised the lady to come to see her at that hour, said to Zeppa: – "I must go breakfast with a friend, whom I had lief not keep in waiting; therefore, adieu!" "Nay, but," quoth Zeppa, "'tis not yet breakfast-time." "No matter," returned Spinelloccio, "I have business on which I must speak with him; so I must be in good time." Whereupon Spinelloccio took his leave of Zeppa, and having reached Zeppa's house by a slightly circuitous route, and finding his wife there, was taken by her into the chamber, where they had not been long together when Zeppa returned. Hearing him come, the lady, feigning no small alarm, bundled Spinelloccio into the chest, as her husband had bidden her, and having locked him in, left him there. As Zeppa came upstairs: – "Wife," quoth he, "is it breakfast time?" "Ay, husband, 'tis so," replied the lady. Whereupon: – "Spinelloccio is gone to breakfast with a friend to-day," quoth Zeppa, "leaving his wife at home: get thee to the window, and call her, and bid her come and breakfast with us." The lady, whose fear for herself made her mighty obedient, did as her husband bade her; and after much pressing Spinelloccio's wife came to breakfast with them, though she was given to understand that her husband would not be of the company. So, she being come, Zeppa received her most affectionately, and taking her familiarly by the hand, bade his wife, in an undertone, get her to the kitchen; he then led Spinelloccio's wife into the chamber, and locked the door. Hearing the key turn in the lock: – "Alas!" quoth the lady, "what means this, Zeppa? Is't for this you have brought me here? Is this the love you bear Spinelloccio? Is this your loyalty to him as your friend and comrade?" By the time she had done speaking, Zeppa, still keeping fast hold of her, was beside the chest, in which her husband was locked. Wherefore: – "Madam," quoth he, "spare me thy reproaches, until thou hast heard what I have to say to thee. I have loved, I yet love, Spinelloccio as a brother; and yesterday, though he knew it not, I discovered that the trust I reposed in him has for its guerdon that he lies with my wife, as with thee. Now, for that I love him, I purpose not to be avenged upon him save in the sort in which he offended. He has had my wife, and I intend to have thee. So thou wilt not grant me what I crave of thee, be sure I shall not fail to take it; and having no mind to let this affront pass unavenged, will make such play with him that neither thou nor he shall ever be happy again." The lady hearkening, and by dint of his repeated asseverations coming at length to believe him: – "Zeppa mine," quoth she, "as this thy vengeance is to light upon me, well content am I; so only thou let not this which we are to do embroil me with thy wife, with whom, notwithstanding the evil turn she has done me, I am minded to remain at peace." "Have no fear on that score," replied Zeppa; "nay, I will give thee into the bargain a jewel so rare and fair that thou hast not the like." Which said, he took her in his arms and fell a kissing her, and having laid her on the chest, in which her husband was safe under lock and key, did there disport himself with her to his heart's content, as she with him.

Spinelloccio in the chest heard all that Zeppa had said, and how he was answered by the lady, and the Trevisan dance that afterwards went on over his head; whereat his mortification was such that for a great while he scarce hoped to live through it; and, but for the fear he had of Zeppa, he would have given his wife a sound rating, close prisoner though he was. But, as he bethought him that 'twas he that had given the first affront, and that Zeppa had good cause for acting as he did, and that he had dealt with him considerately and as a good fellow should, he resolved that if it were agreeable to Zeppa, they should be faster friends than ever before. However, Zeppa, having had his pleasure with the lady, got down from the chest, and being reminded by the lady of his promise of the jewel, opened the door of the chamber and brought his wife in. Quoth she with a laugh: – "Madam, you have given me tit for tat," and never a word more. Whereupon: – "Open the chest," quoth Zeppa; and she obeying, he shewed the lady her Spinelloccio lying therein. 'Twould be hard to say whether of the twain was the more shame-stricken, Spinelloccio to be confronted with Zeppa, knowing that Zeppa wist what he had done, or the lady to meet her husband's eyes, knowing that he had heard what went on above his head. "Lo, here is the jewel I give thee," quoth Zeppa to her, pointing to Spinelloccio, who, as he came forth of the chest, blurted out: – "Zeppa, we are quits, and so 'twere best, as thou saidst a while ago to my wife, that we still be friends as we were wont, and as we had nought separate, save our wives, that henceforth we have them also in common." "Content," quoth Zeppa; and so in perfect peace and accord they all four breakfasted together. And thenceforth each of the ladies had two husbands, and each of the husbands two wives; nor was there ever the least dispute or contention between them on that score.

Eighth Day

Novel IX

— *Bruno and Buffalmacco prevail upon Master Simone, a physician, to betake him by night to a certain place, there to be enrolled in a company that go the course. Buffalmacco throws him into a foul ditch, and there they leave him.* —

WHEN THE LADIES had made merry a while over the partnership in wives established by the two Sienese, the queen, who now, unless she were minded to infringe Dioneo's privilege, alone remained to tell, began on this wise: –

Fairly earned indeed, loving ladies, was the flout that Spinelloccio got from Zeppa. Wherefore my judgment jumps with that which Pampinea expressed a while ago, to wit, that he is not severely to be censured who bestows a flout on one that provokes it or deserves it; and as Spinelloccio deserved it, so 'tis my purpose to tell you of one that provoked it, for I deem that those from whom he received it, were rather to be commended than condemned. The man that got it was a physician, who, albeit he was but a blockhead, returned from Bologna to Florence in mantle and hood of vair.

'Tis matter of daily experience that our citizens come back to us from Bologna, this man a judge, that a physician, and the other a notary, flaunting it in ample flowing robes, and adorned with the scarlet and the vair and other array most goodly to see; and how far their doings correspond with this fair seeming, is also matter of daily experience. Among whom 'tis not long since Master Simone da Villa, one whose patrimony was more ample than his knowledge, came back wearing the scarlet and a broad stripe on the shoulder, and a doctor, as he called himself, and took a house in the street that we now call Via del Cocomero. Now this Master Simone, being thus, as we said, come back, had this among other singular habits, that he could never see a soul pass along the street, but he must needs ask any that was by, who that man was; and he was as observant of all the doings of men, and as sedulous to store his memory with such matters, as if they were to serve him to compound the drugs that he was to give his patients. Now, of all that he saw, those that he eyed most observantly were two painters, of whom here to-day mention has twice been made, Bruno, to wit, and Buffalmacco, who were ever together, and were his neighbours. And as it struck him that they daffed the world aside and lived more lightheartedly than any others that he knew, as indeed they did, he enquired of not a few folk as to their rank. And learning on all hands that they were poor men and painters, he could not conceive it possible that they should live thus contentedly in poverty, but made his mind up that, being, as he was informed, clever fellows, they must have some secret source from which they drew immense gains; for which reason he grew all agog to get on friendly terms with them, or any rate with one of them, and did succeed in making friends with Bruno.

Bruno, who had not needed to be much with him in order to discover that this physician was but a dolt, had never such a jolly time in palming off his strange stories upon him, while the physician, on his part, was marvellously delighted with Bruno; to whom, having bidden him to breakfast, and thinking that for that reason he might talk familiarly with him, he expressed the amazement with which he regarded both him and Buffalmacco, for that, being but poor men, they lived so lightheartedly, and asked him to tell him how they managed. At which fresh proof of the doctor's simplicity and fatuity Bruno was inclined to laugh; but, bethinking him that 'twere best to answer him according to his folly, he said: – "Master, there are not many persons to whom I would disclose our manner of life, but, as you are my friend, and I know you will not let it go further, I do not mind telling you. The fact is that my comrade and I live not only as lightheartedly and jovially as you see, but much more so; and yet neither our art, nor any property that we possess, yields us enough to keep us in water: not that I would have you suppose that we go a thieving: no, 'tis that we go the course, and thereby without the least harm done to a soul we get all that we need, nay, all that we desire; and thus it is that we live so lightheartedly as you see." Which explanation the doctor believing none the less readily that he knew not what it meant, was lost in wonder, and forthwith burned with a most vehement desire to know what going the course might be, and was instant with Bruno to expound it, assuring him that he would never tell a soul. "Alas! Master," said Bruno, "what is this you ask of me? 'Tis a mighty great secret you would have me impart to you: 'twould be enough to undo me, to send me packing out of the world, nay, into the very jaws of Lucifer of San Gallo, if it came to be known. But such is the respect in which I hold your quiditative pumpionship of Legnaia, and the trust I repose in you, that I am not able to deny you aught you ask of me; and so I will tell it you, on condition that you swear by the cross at Montesone that you will keep your promise, and never repeat it to a soul."

The Master gave the required assurance. Whereupon: – "You are then to know," quoth Bruno, "sweet my Master, that 'tis not long since there was in this city a great master in necromancy, hight Michael Scott, for that he was of Scotland, and great indeed was the honour in which he was held by not a few gentlemen, most of whom are now dead; and when the time came that he must needs depart from Florence, he at their instant entreaty left behind him two pupils, adepts both, whom he bade hold themselves ever ready to pleasure those gentlemen who had done him honour. And very handsomely they did serve the said gentlemen in certain of their love affairs and other little matters; and finding the city and the manners of the citizens agreeable to them, they made up their minds to stay here always, and grew friendly and very intimate with some of the citizens, making no distinction between gentle and simple, rich or poor, so only they were such as were conformable to their ways. And to gratify these their friends they formed a company of perhaps twenty-five men, to meet together at least twice a month in a place appointed by them; where, when they are met, each utters his desire, and forthwith that same night they accomplish it. Now Buffalmacco and I, being extraordinarily great and close friends with these two adepts, were by them enrolled in this company, and are still members of it. And I assure you that, as often as we are assembled together, the adornments of the saloon in which we eat are a marvel to see, ay, and the tables laid as for kings, and the multitudes of stately and handsome servants, as well women as men, at the beck and call of every member of the company, and the basins, and the ewers, the flasks and the cups, and all else that is there for our service in eating and drinking, of nought but gold and silver, and therewithal the abundance and variety of the viands, suited to the taste of each, that are set before us, each in due course, these too be marvels. 'Twere vain for me to seek to describe to you the sweet concord that is there of innumerable instruments of music, and the tuneful songs that salute our ears; nor might I hope to tell you how much wax is burned at these banquets, or compute the quantity of the comfits that are eaten, or the value of the wines that are drunk. Nor, my pumpkin o' wit, would I have you suppose that, when we are there, we wear our common clothes, such as you now see me wear; nay, there is none there so humble but he shews as an emperor, so sumptuous are our garments, so splendid our trappings. But among all the delights of the place none may compare with the fair ladies, who, so one do but wish, are brought thither from every part of the world. Why, you might see there My Lady of the Barbanichs, the Queen of the Basques, the Consort of the Soldan, the Empress of Osbech, the Ciancianfera of Nornieca, the Semistante of Berlinzone, and the Scalpedra of Narsia. But why seek to enumerate them all? They include all the queens in the world, ay, even to the Schinchimurra of Prester John, who has the horns sprouting out of her nether end: so there's for you. Now when these ladies have done with the wine and the comfits, they tread a measure or two, each with the man at whose behest she is come, and then all go with their gallants to their chambers. And know that each of these chambers shews as a very Paradise, so fair is it, ay, and no less fragrant than the cases of aromatics in your shop when you are pounding the cumin: and therein are beds that you would find more goodly than that of the Doge of Venice, and 'tis in them we take our rest; and how busily they ply the treadle, and how lustily they tug at the frame to make the stuff close and compact, I leave you to imagine. However, among the luckiest of all I reckon Buffalmacco and myself; for that Buffalmacco for the most part fetches him the Queen of France, and I do the like with the Queen of England, who are just the finest women in the world, and we have known how to carry it with them so that we are the very eyes of their heads. So I leave it to your own judgment to determine whether we have not good cause to live and bear ourselves with a lighter heart than others, seeing that we are beloved of two such great queens, to say nothing of the thousand or two thousand florins that we have of them whenever we are so minded. Now this in the vulgar we call going the course, because, as the corsairs prey upon all the world, so do we; albeit with this difference, that, whereas they never restore their spoil, we do so as soon as we have done with it. So now, my worthy Master, you understand what we mean by going the course; but how close it behoves you to keep such a secret, you may see for yourself; so I spare you any further exhortations."

The Master, whose skill did not reach, perhaps, beyond the treatment of children for the scurf, took all that Bruno said for gospel, and burned with so vehement a desire to be admitted into this company, that he could not have longed for the summum bonum itself with more ardour. So, after telling Bruno that indeed 'twas no wonder they bore them lightheartedly, he could scarce refrain from asking him there and then to have him enrolled, albeit he deemed it more prudent to defer his suit, until by lavishing honour upon him he had gained a right to urge it with more confidence. He therefore made more and more of him, had him to breakfast and sup with him, and treated him with extraordinary respect. In short, such and so constant was their intercourse that it seemed as though the Master wist not how to live without Bruno. As it went so well with him, Bruno, to mark his sense of the honour done him by the doctor, painted in his saloon a picture symbolical of Lent, and an Agnus Dei at the entrance of his chamber, and an alembic over his front door, that those who would fain consult him might know him from other physicians, besides a battle of rats and mice in his little gallery, which the doctor thought an extremely fine piece. And from time to time, when he had not supped with the Master, he would say to him: – "Last night I was with the company, and being a little tired of the Queen of England, I fetched me the Gumedra of the great Can of Tarisi." "Gumedra," quoth the Master; "what is she? I know not the meaning of these words." "Thereat, Master," replied Bruno, "I marvel not; for I have heard tell that neither Porcograsso nor Vannacena say aught thereof." "Thou wouldst say Ippocrasso and Avicenna," returned the Master. "I'faith I know not," quoth Bruno. "I as ill know the meaning of your words as you of mine. But Gumedra in the speech of the great Can signifies the same as Empress in ours. Ah! a fine woman you would find her, and plenty of her! I warrant she would make you forget your drugs and prescriptions and plasters." And so, Bruno from time to time whetting the Master's appetite, and the Master at length thinking that by his honourable entreatment of him he had fairly made a conquest of Bruno, it befell that one evening, while he held the light for Bruno, who was at work on the battle of rats and mice, he determined to discover to him his desire; and as they were alone, thus he spoke: – "God knows, Bruno, that there lives not the man, for whom I would do as much as for thee: why, if thou wast to bid me go all the way from here to Peretola, I almost think I would do so; wherefore I trust thou wilt not deem it strange if I talk to thee as an intimate friend and in confidence. Thou knowest 'tis not long since thou didst enlarge with me on thy gay company and their doings, which has engendered in me such a desire as never was to know more thereof. Nor without reason, as thou wilt discover, should I ever become a member of the said company, for I straightway give thee leave to make game of me, should I not then fetch me the fairest maid thou hast seen this many a day, whom I saw last year at Cacavincigli, and to whom I am entirely devoted; and by the body of Christ I offered her ten Bolognese groats, that she should pleasure me, and she would not. Wherefore I do most earnestly entreat thee to instruct me what I must do to fit myself for membership in the company; and never doubt that in me you will have a true and loyal comrade, and one that will do you honour. And above all thou seest how goodly I am of my person, and how well furnished with legs, and of face as fresh as a rose; and therewithal I am a doctor of medicine, and I scarce think you have any such among you; and not a little excellent lore I have, and many a good song by heart, of which I will sing thee one;" and forthwith he fell a singing.

Bruno had such a mind to laugh, that he could scarce contain himself; but still he kept a grave countenance; and, when the Master had ended his song, and said: – "How likes it thee?" he answered: – "Verily, no lyre of straw could vie with you, so artargutically you refine your strain." "I warrant thee," returned the Master, "thou hadst never believed it, hadst thou not heard me." "Ay, indeed, sooth sayst thou," quoth Bruno. "And I have other songs to boot," said the Master; "but enough of this at present. Thou must know that I, such as thou seest me, am a gentleman's son, albeit my father lived in the contado; and on my mother's side I come of the Vallecchio family. And as thou mayst have observed I have quite the finest library and wardrobe of all the physicians in Florence. God's faith! I have a robe that cost, all told, close upon a hundred pounds in bagattines more than ten years ago. Wherefore I make most instant suit to thee that thou get me enrolled, which if thou do, God's faith! be thou never so ill, thou shalt pay me not a stiver for my tendance of thee." Whereupon Bruno, repeating to himself, as he had done many a time before, that the doctor was a very numskull: – "Master," quoth he, "shew a little more light here, and have patience until I have put the finishing touches to the tails of these rats, and then I will answer you." So he finished the tails, and then, putting on an air as if he were not a little embarrassed by the request: – "Master mine," quoth he, "I should have great things to expect from you; that I know: but yet what you ask of me, albeit to your great mind it seems but a little thing, is a weighty matter indeed for me; nor know I a soul in the world, to whom, though well able, I would grant such a request, save to you alone: and this I say not for friendship's sake alone, albeit I love you as I ought, but for that your discourse is so fraught with wisdom, that 'tis enough to make a beguine start out of her boots, much more, then, to incline me to change my purpose; and the more I have of your company, the wiser I repute you. Whereto I may add, that, if for no other cause, I should still be well disposed towards you for the love I see you bear to that fair piece of flesh of which you spoke but now. But this I must tell you: 'tis not in my power to do as you would have me in this matter; but, though I cannot myself do the needful in your behalf, if you will pledge your faith, whole and solid as may be, to keep my secret, I will shew you how to go about it for yourself, and I make no doubt that, having this fine library and the other matters you spoke of a while ago, you will compass your end." Quoth then the Master: – "Nay, but speak freely; I see thou dost yet scarce know me, and how well I can keep a secret. There were few things that Messer Guasparruolo da Saliceto did, when he was Podestà of Forlinpopoli, that he did not confide to me, so safe he knew they would be in my keeping: and wouldst thou be satisfied that I say sooth? I assure you I was the first man whom he told that he was about to marry Bergamina: so there's for thee." "Well and good," said Bruno, "if such as he confided in you, well indeed may I do the like. Know, then, that you will have to proceed on this wise: – Our company is governed by a captain and a council of two, who are changed every six months: and on the calends without fail Buffalmacco will be captain, and I councillor: 'tis so fixed: and the captain has not a little power to promote the admission and enrolment of whomsoever he will: wherefore, methinks, you would do well to make friends with Buffalmacco and honourably entreat him: he is one that, marking your great wisdom, will take a mighty liking to you forthwith; and when you have just a little dazzled him with your wisdom and these fine things of yours, you may make your request to him; and he will not know how to say no – I have already talked with him of you, and he is as well disposed to you as may be – and having so done you will leave the rest to me." Whereupon: – "Thy words are to me for an exceeding great joy," quoth the Master: "and if he be one that loves to converse with sages, he has but to exchange a word or two with me, and I will answer for it that he will be ever coming to see me; for so fraught with wisdom am I, that I could furnish a whole city therewith, and still remain a great sage."

Having thus set matters in train, Bruno related the whole affair, point by point, to Buffalmacco, to whom it seemed a thousand years till he should be able to give Master Noodle that of which he was in quest. The doctor, now all agog to go the course, lost no time, and found no difficulty, in making friends with Buffalmacco, and fell to entertaining him, and Bruno likewise, at breakfast and supper in most magnificent style; while they fooled him to the top of his bent; for, being gentlemen that appreciated excellent wines and fat capons, besides other good cheer in plenty, they were inclined to be very neighbourly, and needed no second bidding, but, always letting him understand that there was none other whose company they relished so much, kept ever with him.

However, in due time the Master asked of Buffalmacco that which he had before asked of Bruno. Whereat Buffalmacco feigned to be not a little agitated, and turning angrily to Bruno, made a great pother about his ears, saying: – "By the Most High God of Pasignano I vow I can scarce forbear to give thee that over the head that should make thy nose fall about thy heels, traitor that thou art, for 'tis thou alone that canst have discovered these secrets to the Master." Whereupon the Master interposed with no little vigour, averring with oaths that 'twas from another source that he had gotten his knowledge; and Buffalmacco at length allowed himself to be pacified by the sage's words. So turning to him: – "Master," quoth he, "'tis evident indeed that you have been at Bologna, and have come back hither with a mouth that blabs not, and that 'twas on no pippin, as many a dolt does, but on the good long pumpkin that you learned your A B C; and, if I mistake not, you were baptized on a Sunday; and though Bruno has told me that 'twas medicine you studied there, 'tis my opinion that you there studied the art of catching men, of which, what with your wisdom and your startling revelations, you are the greatest master that ever I knew." He would have said more, but the doctor, turning to Bruno, broke in with: – "Ah! what it is to consort and converse with the wise! Who but this worthy man would thus have read my mind through and through? Less quick by far to rate me at my true worth wast thou. But what said I when thou toldst me that Buffalmacco delighted to converse with sages? Confess now; have I not kept my word?" "Verily," quoth Bruno, "you have more than kept it." Then, addressing Buffalmacco: – "Ah!" cried the Master, "what hadst thou said, hadst thou seen me at Bologna, where there was none, great or small, doctor or scholar, but was devoted to me, so well wist I how to entertain them with my words of wisdom. Nay more; let me tell thee that there was never a word I spoke but set every one a laughing, so great was the pleasure it gave them. And at my departure they all deplored it most bitterly, and would have had me remain, and by way of inducement went so far as to propose that I should be sole lecturer to all the students in medicine that were there; which offer I declined, for that I was minded to return hither, having vast estates here, that have ever belonged to my family; which, accordingly, I did." Quoth then Bruno to Buffalmacco: – "How shews it, now, man? Thou didst not believe me when I told thee what he was. By the Gospels there is never a physician in this city that has the lore of ass's urine by heart as he has: verily, thou wouldst not find his like between here and the gates of Paris. Now see if thou canst help doing as he would have thee." "'Tis even as Bruno says," observed the doctor, "but I am not understood here. You Florentines are somewhat slow of wit. Would you could see me in my proper element, among a company of doctors!" Whereupon: – "Of a truth, Master," quoth Buffalmacco, "your lore far exceeds any I should ever have imputed to you; wherefore, addressing you as 'tis meet to address a man of your wisdom, I give you disjointedly to understand that without fail I will procure your enrolment in our company."

After this promise the honours lavished by the doctor upon the two men grew and multiplied; in return for which they diverted themselves by setting him a prancing upon every wildest chimera in the world; and promised, among other matters, to give him by way of mistress, the Countess of Civillari, whom they averred to be the goodliest creature to be found in all the Netherlands of the human race; and the doctor asking who this Countess might be: – "Mature my gherkin," quoth Buffalmacco, "she is indeed a very great lady, and few houses are there in the world in which she has not some jurisdiction; nay, the very Friars Minors, to say nought of other folk, pay her tribute to the sound of the kettle-drum. And I may tell you that, when she goes abroad, she makes her presence very sensibly felt, albeit for the most part she keeps herself close: however, 'tis no great while since she passed by your door one night on her way to the Arno to bathe her feet and get a breath of air; but most of her time she abides at Laterina. Serjeants has she not a few that go their rounds at short intervals, bearing, one and all, the rod and the bucket in token of her sovereignty, and barons in plenty in all parts, as Tamagnino della Porta, Don Meta, Manico di Scopa, Squacchera, and others, with whom I doubt not you are intimately acquainted, though you may not just now bear them in mind. Such, then, is the great lady, in whose soft arms we, if we delude not ourselves, will certainly place you, in which case you may well dispense with her of Cacavincigli."

The doctor, who had been born and bred at Bologna, and understood not their words, found the lady quite to his mind; and shortly afterwards the painters brought him tidings of his election into the company. Then came the day of the nocturnal gathering, and the doctor had the two men to breakfast; and when they had breakfasted, he asked them after what manner he was to join the company. Whereupon: – "Lo, now, Master," quoth Buffalmacco, "you have need of a stout heart; otherwise you may meet with some let, to our most grievous hurt; and for what cause you have need of this stout heart, you shall hear. You must contrive to be to-night about the hour of first sleep on one of the raised tombs that have been lately placed outside of Santa Maria Novella; and mind that you wear one of your best gowns, that your first appearance may impress the company with a proper sense of your dignity, and also because, as we are informed, for we were not present at the time, the Countess, by reason that you are a gentleman, is minded to make you a Knight of the Bath at her own charges. So you will wait there, until one, whom we shall send, come for you: who, that you may know exactly what you have to expect, will be a beast black and horned, of no great size; and he will go snorting and bounding amain about the piazza in front of you, with intent to terrify you; but, when he perceives that you are not afraid, he will draw nigh you quietly, and when he is close by you, then get you down from the tomb, fearing nothing; and, minding you neither of God nor of the saints, mount him, and when you are well set on his back, then fold your arms upon your breast, as in submission, and touch him no more. Then, going gently, he will bear you to us; but once mind you of God, or the saints, or give way to fear, and I warn you, he might give you a fall, or dash you against something that you would find scarce pleasant; wherefore, if your heart misgives you, you were best not to come, for you would assuredly do yourself a mischief, and us no good at all." Quoth then the doctor: – "You know me not as yet; 'tis perchance because I wear the gloves and the long robe that you misdoubt me. Ah! did you but know what feats I have done in times past at Bologna, when I used to go after the women with my comrades, you would be lost in amazement. God's faith! on one of those nights there was one of them, a poor sickly creature she was too, and stood not a cubit in height, who would not come with us; so first I treated her to many a good cuff, and then I took her up by main force, and carried her well-nigh as far as a cross-bow will send a bolt, and so caused her, willy-nilly, come with us. And on another occasion I mind me that, having none other with me but my servant, a little after the hour of Ave Maria, I passed beside the cemetery of the Friars Minors, and, though that very day a woman had been there interred, I had no fear at all. So on this score you may make your minds easy; for indeed I am a man of exceeding great courage and prowess. And to appear before you with due dignity, I will don my scarlet gown, in which I took my doctor's degree, and it remains to be seen if the company will not give me a hearty welcome, and make me captain out of hand. Let me once be there, and you will see how things will go; else how is it that this countess, that has not yet seen me, is already so enamoured of me that she is minded to make me a Knight of the Bath? And whether I shall find knighthood agreeable, or know how to support the dignity well or ill, leave that to me." Whereupon: – "Well said, excellent well said," quoth Buffalmacco: "but look to it you disappoint us not, either by not coming or by not being found, when we send for you; and this I say, because 'tis cold weather, and you medical gentlemen take great care of your health." "God forbid," replied the doctor, "I am none of your chilly folk; I fear not the cold: 'tis seldom indeed, when I leave my bed a nights, to answer the call of nature, as one must at times, that I do more than throw a pelisse over my doublet; so rest assured that I shall be there."

So they parted; and towards nightfall the Master found a pretext for leaving his wife, and privily got out his fine gown, which in due time he donned, and so hied him to the tombs, and having perched himself on one of them, huddled himself together, for 'twas mighty cold, to await the coming of the beast. Meanwhile Buffalmacco, who was a tall man and strong, provided himself with one of those dominos that were wont to be worn in certain revels which are now gone out of fashion; and enveloped in a black pelisse turned inside out, shewed like a bear, save that the domino had the face of a devil, and was furnished with horns: in which guise, Bruno following close behind to see the sport, he hied him to the piazza of Santa Maria Novella. And no sooner wist he that the Master was on the tomb, than he fell a careering in a most wild and furious manner to and fro the piazza, and snorting and bellowing and gibbering like one demented, insomuch that, as soon as the Master was ware of him, each several hair on his head stood on end, and he fell a trembling in every limb, being in sooth more timid than a woman, and wished himself safe at home: but as there he was, he strove might and main to keep his spirits up, so overmastering was his desire to see the marvels of which Bruno and Buffalmacco had told him. However, after a while Buffalmacco allowed his fury to abate, and came quietly up to the tomb on which the Master was, and stood still. The Master, still all of a tremble with fear, could not at first make up his mind, whether to get on the beast's back, or no; but at length, doubting it might be the worse for him if he did not mount the beast, he overcame the one dread by the aid of the other, got down from the tomb, saying under his breath: – "God help me!" and seated himself very comfortably on the beast's back; and then, still quaking in every limb, he folded his arms as he had been bidden.

Buffalmacco now started, going on all-fours, at a very slow pace, in the direction of Santa Maria della Scala, and so brought the Master within a short distance of the Convent of the Ladies of Ripoli. Now, in that quarter there were divers trenches, into which the husbandmen of those parts were wont to discharge the Countess of Civillari, that she might afterwards serve them to manure their land. Of one of which trenches, as he came by, Buffalmacco skirted the edge, and seizing his opportunity, raised a hand, and caught the doctor by one of his feet, and threw him off his back and headforemost right into the trench, and then, making a terrific noise and frantic gestures as before, went bounding off by Santa Maria della Scala towards the field of Ognissanti, where he found Bruno, who had betaken him thither that he might laugh at his ease; and there the two men in high glee took their stand to observe from a distance how the bemired doctor would behave. Finding himself in so loathsome a place, the Master struggled might and main to raise himself and get out; and though again and again he slipped back, and swallowed some drams of the ordure, yet, bemired from head to foot, woebegone and crestfallen, he did at last get out, leaving his hood behind him. Then, removing as much of the filth as he might with his hands, knowing not what else to do, he got him home, where, by dint of much knocking, he at last gained admittance; and scarce was the door closed behind the malodorous Master, when Bruno and Buffalmacco were at it, all agog to hear after what manner he would be received by his wife. They were rewarded by hearing her give him the soundest rating that ever bad husband got. "Ah!" quoth she, "fine doings, these! Thou hast been with some other woman, and wast minded to make a brave shew in thy scarlet gown. So I was not enough for thee! not enough for thee forsooth, I that might content a crowd! Would they had choked thee with the filth in which they have soused thee; 'twas thy fit resting-place. Now, to think that a physician of repute, and a married man, should go by night after strange women!" Thus, and with much more to the like effect, while the doctor was busy washing himself, she ceased not to torment him until midnight.

On the morrow, Bruno and Buffalmacco, having painted their bodies all over with livid patches to give them the appearance of having been thrashed, came to the doctor's house, and finding that he was already risen, went in, being saluted on all hands by a foul smell, for time had not yet served thoroughly to cleanse the house. The doctor, being informed that they were come to see him, advanced to meet them, and bade them good morning. Whereto Bruno and Buffalmacco, having prepared their answer, replied: – "No good morning shall you have from us: rather we pray God to give you bad years enough to make an end of you, seeing that there lives no more arrant and faithless traitor. 'Tis no fault of yours, if we, that did our best to honour and pleasure you, have not come by a dog's death; your faithlessness has cost us to-night as many sound blows as would more than suffice to keep an ass a trotting all the way from here to Rome; besides which, we have been in peril of expulsion from the company in which we arranged for your enrolment. If you doubt our words, look but at our bodies, what a state they are in." And so, baring their breasts they gave him a glimpse of the patches they had painted there, and forthwith covered them up again. The doctor would have made them his excuses, and recounted his misfortunes, and how he had been thrown into the trench. But Buffalmacco broke in with: – "Would he had thrown you from the bridge into the Arno! Why must you needs mind you of God and the saints? Did we not forewarn you?" "God's faith," returned the doctor, "that did I not." "How?" quoth Buffalmacco, "you did not? You do so above a little; for he that we sent for you told us that you trembled like an aspen, and knew not where you were. You have played us a sorry trick; but never another shall do so; and as for you, we will give you such requital thereof as you deserve." The doctor now began to crave their pardon, and to implore them for God's sake not to expose him to shame, and used all the eloquence at his command to make his peace with them. And if he had honourably entreated them before, he thenceforth, for fear they should publish his disgrace, did so much more abundantly, and courted them both by entertaining them at his table and in other ways. And so you have heard how wisdom is imparted to those that get it not at Bologna.

Eighth Day

Novel X

— A Sicilian woman cunningly conveys from a merchant that which he has brought to Palermo; he, making a shew of being come back thither with far greater store of goods than before, borrows money of her, and leaves her in lieu thereof water and tow. —

HOW MUCH in divers passages the queen's story moved the ladies to laughter, it boots not to ask: none was there in whose eyes the tears stood not full a dozen times for excess of merriment. However, it being ended, and Dioneo witting that 'twas now his turn, thus spake he: –

Gracious ladies, 'tis patent to all that wiles are diverting in the degree of the wiliness of him that is by them beguiled. Wherefore, albeit stories most goodly have been told by you all, I purpose to relate one which should afford you more pleasure than any that has been told, seeing that she that was beguiled was far more cunning in beguiling others than any of the beguiled of whom you have spoken.

There was, and perhaps still is, a custom in all maritime countries that have ports, that all merchants arriving there with merchandise, should, on discharging, bring all their goods into a warehouse, called in many places "dogana," and maintained by the state, or the lord of the land; where those that are assigned to that office allot to each merchant, on receipt of an invoice of all his goods and the value thereof, a room in which he stores his goods under lock and key; whereupon the said officers of the dogana enter all the merchant's goods to his credit in the book of the dogana, and afterwards make him pay duty thereon, or on such part as he withdraws from the warehouse. By which book of the dogana the brokers not seldom find out the sorts and quantities of the merchandise that is there, and also who are the owners thereof, with whom, as occasion serves, they afterwards treat of exchanges, barters, sales and other modes of disposing of the goods. Which custom obtained, as in many other places, so also at Palermo in Sicily, where in like manner there were and are not a few women, fair as fair can be, but foes to virtue, who by whoso knows them not would be reputed great and most virtuous ladies. And being given not merely to fleece but utterly to flay men, they no sooner espy a foreign merchant in the city, than they find out from the book of the dogana how much he has there and what he is good for; and then by caressing and amorous looks and gestures, and words of honeyed sweetness, they strive to entice and allure the merchant to their love, and not seldom have they succeeded, and wrested from him great part or the whole of his merchandise; and of some they have gotten goods and ship and flesh and bones, so delightsomely have they known how to ply the shears.

Now 'tis not long since one of our young Florentines, Niccolo da Cignano by name, albeit he was called Salabaetto, arrived there, being sent by his masters with all the woollen stuffs that he had not been able to dispose of at Salerno fair, which might perhaps be worth five hundred florins of gold; and having given the invoice to the officers of the dogana and stored the goods, Salabaetto was in no hurry to get them out of bond, but took a stroll or two about the city for his diversion. And as he was fresh-complexioned and fair and not a little debonair, it so befell that one of these ladies that plied the shears, and called herself Jancofiore, began to ogle him. Whereof he taking note, and deeming that she was a great lady, supposed that she was taken by his good looks, and cast about how he might manage this amour with all due discretion; wherefore, saying nought to a soul, he began to pass to and fro before her house. Which she observing, occupied herself for a few days in inflaming his passion, and then affecting to be dying of love for him, sent privily to him a woman that she had in her service, and who was an adept in the arts of the procuress. She, after not a little palaver, told him, while the tears all but stood in her eyes, that for his handsome person and winsome air her mistress was so enamoured of him, that she found no peace by day or by night; and therefore, if 'twere agreeable to him, there was nought she desired so much as to meet him privily at a bagnio: whereupon she drew a ring from her purse, and gave it him by way of token from her mistress. Overjoyed as ne'er another to hear such good news, Salabaetto took the ring, and, after drawing it across his eyes and kissing it, put it on his finger, and told the good woman that, if Madonna Jancofiore loved him, she was well requited, for that he loved her more dearly than himself, and that he was ready to meet her wherever and whenever she might see fit. With which answer the procuress hied her back to her mistress, and shortly afterwards Salabaetto was informed that he was to meet the lady at a certain bagnio at vespers of the ensuing day.

So, saying nought to a soul of the matter, he hied him punctually at the appointed hour to the bagnio, and found that it had been taken by the lady; nor had he long to wait before two female slaves made their appearance, bearing on their heads, the one a great and goodly mattress of wadding, and the other a huge and well-filled basket; and having laid the mattress on a bedstead in one of the rooms of the bagnio, they covered it with a pair of sheets of the finest fabric, bordered with silk, and a quilt of the whitest Cyprus buckram, with two daintily-embroidered pillows. The slaves then undressed and got into the bath, which they thoroughly washed and scrubbed: whither soon afterwards the lady, attended by other two female slaves, came, and made haste to greet Salabaetto with the heartiest of cheer; and when, after heaving many a mighty sigh, she had embraced and kissed him: – "I know not," quoth she, "who but thou could have brought me to this, such a fire hast thou kindled in my soul, little dog of a Tuscan!" Whereupon she was pleased that they should undress, and get into the bath, and two of the slaves with them; which, accordingly, they did; and she herself, suffering none other to lay a hand upon him, did with wondrous care wash Salabaetto from head to foot with soap perfumed with musk and cloves; after which she let the slaves wash and shampoo herself. The slaves then brought two spotless sheets of finest texture, which emitted such a scent of roses, that 'twas as if there was nought there but roses, in one of which having wrapped Salabaetto, and in the other the lady, they bore them both to bed, where, the sheets in which they were enfolded being withdrawn by the slaves as soon as they had done sweating, they remained stark naked in the others. The slaves then took from the basket cruets of silver most goodly, and full, this of rose-water, that of water of orange-blossom, a third of water of jasmine-blossom, and a fourth of nanfa water, wherewith they sprinkled them: after which, boxes of comfits and the finest wines being brought forth, they regaled them a while. To Salabaetto 'twas as if he were in Paradise; a thousand times he scanned the lady, who was indeed most beautiful; and he counted each hour as a hundred years until the slaves should get them gone, and he find himself in the lady's arms.

At length, by the lady's command, the slaves departed, leaving a lighted torch in the room, and then the lady and Salabaetto embraced, and to Salabaetto's prodigious delight, for it seemed to him that she was all but dissolved for love of him, tarried there a good while. However, the time came when the lady must needs rise: so she called the slaves, with whose help they dressed, regaled them again for a while with wine and comfits, and washed their faces and hands with the odoriferous waters. Then as they were going, quoth the lady to Salabaetto: – "If it be agreeable to thee, I should deem it a very great favour if thou wouldst come to-night to sup and sleep with me." Salabaetto, who, captivated by her beauty and her studied graciousness, never doubted but he was dear to her as her very heart, made answer: – "Madam, there is nought you can desire but is in the last degree agreeable to me; wherefore to-night and ever 'tis my purpose to do whatsoever you may be pleased to command." So home the lady hied her, and having caused a brave shew to be made in her chamber with her dresses and other paraphernalia, and a grand supper to be prepared, awaited Salabaetto; who, being come there as soon as 'twas dark, had of her a gladsome welcome, and was regaled with an excellent and well-served supper. After which, they repaired to the chamber, where he was saluted by a wondrous sweet odour of aloe-wood, and observed that the bed was profusely furnished with birds, after the fashion of Cyprus, and that not a few fine dresses were hanging upon the pegs. Which circumstances did, one and all, beget in him the belief that this must be a great and wealthy lady; and, though he had heard a hint or two to the contrary touching her life, he would by no means credit them; nor, supposing that she had perchance taken another with guile, would he believe that the same thing might befall him. So to his exceeding great solace, he lay with her that night, and ever grew more afire for her. On the morrow, as she was investing him with a fair and dainty girdle of silver, with a goodly purse attached: – "Sweet my Salabaetto," quoth she, "prithee forget me not; even as my person, so is all that I have at thy pleasure, and all that I can at thy command."

Salabaetto then embraced and kissed her, and so bade her adieu, and betook him to the place where the merchants were wont to congregate. And so it befell that he, continuing to consort with her from time to time, and being never a denier the poorer thereby, disposed of his merchandise for ready money and at no small profit; whereof not by him but by another the lady was forthwith advised. And Salabaetto being come to see her one evening, she greeted him gaily and gamesomely, and fell a kissing and hugging him, and made as if she were so afire for love of him that she was like to die thereof in his arms; and offered to give him two most goodly silver cups that she had, which Salabaetto would not accept, having already had from her (taking one time with another) fully thirty florins of gold, while he had not been able to induce her to touch so much as a groat of his money. But when by this shew of passion and generosity she had thoroughly kindled his flame, in came, as she had arranged, one of her slaves, and spoke to her; whereupon out of the room she went, and after a while came back in tears, and threw herself prone on the bed, and set up the most dolorous lamentation that ever woman made. Whereat Salabaetto wondering, took her in his arms, and mingled his tears with hers, and said: – "Alas! heart of my body! what ails thee thus of a sudden? Wherefore art thou so distressed? Ah! tell me the reason, my soul." The lady allowed him to run on in this strain for a good while, and then: – "Alas! sweet my lord," quoth she, "I know not either what to do or what to say. I have but now received a letter from Messina, in which my brother bids me sell, if need be, all that I have here, and send him without fail within eight days a thousand florins of gold: otherwise he will forfeit his head. I know not how to come by them so soon: had I but fifteen days, I would make a shift to raise them in a quarter where I might raise a much larger sum, or I would sell one of our estates; but, as this may not be, would I had been dead or e'er this bad news had reached me!" Which said, affecting to be utterly broken-hearted, she ceased not to weep.

Salabaetto, the ardour of whose passion had in great measure deprived him of the sagacity which the circumstances demanded, supposed that the tears were genuine enough, and the words even more so. Wherefore: – "Madam," quoth he, "I could not furnish you with a thousand, but if five hundred florins of gold would suffice, they are at your service, if you think you could repay them within fifteen days; and you may deem yourself in luck's way, for 'twas only yesterday that I sold my woollens, which had I not done, I could not have lent you a groat." "Alas" returned the lady, "then thou hast been in straits for money? Oh! why didst thou not apply to me? Though I have not a thousand at my command, I could have given thee quite a hundred, nay indeed two hundred florins. By what thou hast said thou hast made me hesitate to accept the service that thou proposest to render me." Which words fairly delivered Salabaetto into the lady's hands, insomuch that: – "Madam," quoth he, "I would not have you decline my help for such a scruple; for had my need been as great as yours, I should certainly have applied to you." Quoth then the lady: – "Ah! Salabaetto mine, well I wot that the love thou bearest me is a true and perfect love, seeing that, without waiting to be asked, thou dost so handsomely come to my aid with so large a sum of money. And albeit I was thine without this token of thy love, yet, assuredly, it has made me thine in an even greater degree; nor shall I ever forget that 'tis to thee I owe my brother's life. But God knows I take thy money from thee reluctantly, seeing that thou art a merchant, and 'tis by means of money that merchants conduct all their affairs; but, as necessity constrains me, and I have good hope of speedily repaying thee, I will even take it, and by way of security, if I should find no readier method, I will pawn all that I have here." Which said, she burst into tears, and fell upon Salabaetto, pressing her cheek upon his.

Salabaetto tried to comfort her; and having spent the night with her, on the morrow, being minded to shew himself her most devoted servant, brought her, without awaiting any reminder, five hundred fine florins of gold: which she, laughing at heart while the tears streamed from her eyes, took, Salabaetto trusting her mere promise of repayment. Now that the lady had gotten the money, the complexion of affairs began to alter; and whereas Salabaetto had been wont to have free access to her, whenever he was so minded, now for one reason or another he was denied admittance six times out of seven; nor did she greet him with the same smile, or shower on him the same caresses, or do him the same cheer as of yore. So a month, two months, passed beyond the time when he was to have been repaid his money; and when he demanded it, he was put off with words. Whereby Salabaetto, being now ware of the cheat which his slender wit had suffered the evil-disposed woman to put upon him, and also that, having neither writing nor witness against her, he was entirely at her mercy in regard of his claim, and being, moreover, ashamed to lodge any complaint with any one, as well because he had been forewarned of her character, as because he dreaded the ridicule to which his folly justly exposed him, was chagrined beyond measure, and inly bewailed his simplicity. And his masters having written to him, bidding him change the money and remit it to them, he, being apprehensive that, making default as he must, he should, if he remained there, be detected, resolved to depart; and having taken ship, he repaired, not, as he should have done, to Pisa, but to Naples; where at that time resided our gossip, Pietro dello Canigiano, treasurer of the Empress of Constantinople, a man of great sagacity and acuteness, and a very great friend of Salabaetto and his kinsfolk; to whom trusting in his great discretion, Salabaetto after a while discovered his distress, telling him what he had done, and the sorry plight in which by consequence he stood, and craving his aid and counsel, that he might the more readily find means of livelihood there, for that he was minded never to go back to Florence. Impatient to hear of such folly: – "'Twas ill done of thee," quoth Canigiano, "thou hast misbehaved thyself, wronged thy masters, and squandered an exorbitant sum in lewdness; however, 'tis done, and we must consider of the remedy." And indeed, like the shrewd man that he was, he had already bethought him what was best to be done; and forthwith he imparted it to Salabaetto.

Which expedient Salabaetto approving, resolved to make the adventure; and having still a little money, and being furnished with a loan by Canigiano, he provided himself with not a few bales well and closely corded, and bought some twenty oil-casks, which he filled, and having put all on shipboard, returned to Palermo. There he gave the invoice of the bales, as also of the oil-casks, to the officers of the dogana, and having them all entered to his credit, laid them up in the store-rooms, saying that he purposed to leave them there until the arrival of other merchandise that he expected.

Which Jancofiore learning, and being informed that the merchandise, that he had brought with him, was worth fully two thousand florins of gold, or even more, besides that which he expected, which was valued at more than three thousand florins of gold, bethought her that she had not aimed high enough, and that 'twere well to refund him the five hundred, if so she might make the greater part of the five thousand florins her own. Wherefore she sent for him, and Salabaetto, having learned his lesson of cunning, waited on her. Feigning to know nought of the cargo he had brought with him, she received him with marvellous cheer, and began: – "Lo, now, if thou wast angry with me because I did not repay thee thy money in due time:" but Salabaetto interrupted her, saying with a laugh: – "Madam 'tis true I was a little vexed, seeing that I would have plucked out my heart to pleasure you; but listen, and you shall learn the quality of my displeasure. Such and so great is the love I bear you, that I have sold the best part of all that I possess, whereby I have already in this port merchandise to the value of more than two thousand florins, and expect from the Levant other goods to the value of above three thousand florins, and mean to set up a warehouse in this city, and live here, to be ever near you, for that I deem myself more blessed in your love than any other lover that lives." Whereupon: – "Harkye, Salabaetto," quoth the lady, "whatever advantages thee is mighty grateful to me, seeing that I love thee more than my very life, and right glad am I that thou art come back with intent to stay, for I hope to have many a good time with thee; but something I must say to thee by way of excuse, for that, whilst thou wast thinking of taking thy departure, there were times when thou wast disappointed of seeing me, and others when thou hadst not as gladsome a welcome as thou wast wont to have, and therewithal I kept not the time promised for the repayment of thy money. Thou must know that I was then in exceeding great trouble and tribulation, and whoso is thus bested, love he another never so much, cannot greet him with as gladsome a mien, or be as attentive to him, as he had lief; and thou must further know that 'tis by no means an easy matter for a lady to come by a thousand florins of gold: why, 'tis every day a fresh lie, and never a promise kept; and so we in our turn must needs lie to others; and 'twas for this cause, and not for any fault of mine, that I did not repay thee thy money; however, I had it but a little while after thy departure, and had I known whither to send it, be sure I would have remitted it to thee; but, as that I wist not, I have kept it safe for thee." She then produced a purse, in which were the very same coins that he had brought her, and placed it in his hand, saying: – "Count and see if there are five hundred there." 'Twas the happiest moment Salabaetto had yet known, as, having told them out, and found the sum exact, he made answer: – "Madam, I know that you say sooth, and what you have done abundantly proves it; wherefore, and for the love I bear you, I warrant you there is no sum you might ask of me on any occasion of need, with which, if 'twere in my power, I would not accommodate you; whereof, when I am settled here, you will be able to assure yourself."

Having thus in words reinstated himself as her lover, he proceeded to treat her as his mistress, whereto she responded, doing all that was in her power to pleasure and honour him, and feigning to be in the last degree enamoured of him. But Salabaetto, being minded to requite her guile with his own, went to her one evening, being bidden to sup and sleep with her, with an aspect so melancholy and dolorous, that he shewed as he had lief give up the ghost. Jancofiore, as she embraced and kissed him, demanded of him the occasion of his melancholy. Whereto he, having let her be instant with him a good while, made answer: – "I am undone, for that the ship, having aboard her the goods that I expected, has been taken by the corsairs of Monaco, and held to ransom in ten thousand florins of gold, of which it falls to me to pay one thousand, and I have not a denier, for the five hundred thou repaidst me I sent forthwith to Naples to buy stuffs for this market, and were I to sell the merchandise I have here, as 'tis not now the right time to sell, I should scarce get half the value; nor am I as yet so well known here as to come by any to help me at this juncture, and so what to do or what to say I know not; but this I know that, if I send not the money without delay, my merchandise will be taken to Monaco, and I shall never touch aught of it again." Whereat the lady was mightily annoyed, being apprehensive of losing all, and bethought her how she might prevent the goods going to Monaco: wherefore: – "God knows," quoth she, "that for the love I bear thee I am not a little sorry for thee: but what boots it idly to distress oneself? Had I the money, God knows I would lend it thee forthwith, but I have it not. One, indeed, there is that accommodated me a day or two ago with five hundred florins that I stood in need of, but he requires a heavy usance, not less than thirty on the hundred, and if thou shouldst have recourse to him, good security must be forthcoming. Now for my part I am ready, so I may serve thee, to pledge all these dresses, and my person to boot, for as much as he will tend thee thereon; but how wilt thou secure the balance?"

 Salabaetto divined the motive that prompted her thus to accommodate him, and that she was to lend the money herself; which suiting his purpose well, he first of all thanked her, and then said that, being constrained by necessity, he would not stand out against exorbitant terms, adding that, as to the balance, he would secure it upon the merchandise that he had at the dogana by causing it to be entered in the name of the lender; but that he must keep the key of the storerooms, as well that he might be able to shew the goods, if requested, as to make sure that none of them should be tampered with or changed or exchanged. The lady said that this was reasonable, and that 'twas excellent security. So, betimes on the morrow, the lady sent for a broker, in whom she reposed much trust, and having talked the matter over with him, gave him a thousand florins of gold, which the broker took to Salabaetto, and thereupon had all that Salabaetto had at the dogana entered in his name; they then had the script and counterscript made out, and, the arrangement thus concluded, went about their respective affairs. Salabaetto lost no time in getting aboard a bark with his five hundred florins of gold, and being come to Naples, sent thence a remittance which fully discharged his obligation to his masters that had entrusted him with the stuffs: he also paid all that he owed to Pietro dello Canigiano and all his other creditors, and made not a little merry with Canigiano over the trick he had played the Sicilian lady. He then departed from Naples, and being minded to have done with mercantile affairs, betook him to Ferrara.

 Jancofiore, surprised at first by Salabaetto's disappearance from Palermo, waxed after a while suspicious; and, when she had waited fully two months, seeing that he did not return, she caused the broker to break open the store-rooms. And trying first of all the casks, she found them full of sea-water, save that in each there was perhaps a hog's-head of oil floating on the surface. Then undoing the bales, she found them all, save two that contained stuffs, full of tow, and in short their whole contents put together were not worth more than two hundred florins. Wherefore Jancofiore, knowing herself to have been outdone, regretted long and bitterly the five hundred florins of gold that she had refunded, and still more the thousand that she had lent, repeating many a time to herself: – Who with a Tuscan has to do, Had need of eyesight quick and true. Thus, left with the loss and the laugh against her, she discovered that there were others as knowing as she.

No sooner was Dioneo's story ended, than Lauretta, witting that therewith the end of her sovereignty was come, bestowed her meed of praise on Pietro Canigiano for his good counsel, and also on Salabaetto for the equal sagacity which he displayed in carrying it out, and then, taking off the laurel wreath, set it on the head of Emilia, saying graciously: – "I know not, Madam, how debonair a queen you may prove, but at least we shall have in you a fair one. Be it your care, then, that you exercise your authority in a manner answerable to your charms." Which said, she resumed her seat.

Not so much to receive the crown, as to be thus commended to her face and before the company for that which ladies are wont to covet the most, Emilia was a little shamefast; a tint like that of the newly-blown rose overspread her face, and a while she stood silent with downcast eyes: then, as the blush faded away, she raised them; and having given her seneschal her commands touching all matters pertaining to the company, thus she spake: – "Sweet my ladies, 'tis matter of common experience that, when the oxen have swunken a part of the day under the coercive yoke, they are relieved thereof and loosed, and suffered to go seek their pasture at their own sweet will in the woods; nor can we fail to observe that gardens luxuriant with diversity of leafage are not less, but far more fair to see, than woods wherein is nought but oaks. Wherefore I deem that, as for so many days our discourse has been confined within the bounds of certain laws, 'twill be not only meet but profitable for us, being in need of relaxation, to roam a while, and so recruit our strength to undergo the yoke once more. And therefore I am minded that to-morrow the sweet tenor of your discourse be not confined to any particular theme, but that you be at liberty to discourse on such wise as to each may seem best; for well assured am I that thus to speak of divers matters will be no less pleasurable than to limit ourselves to one topic; and by reason of this enlargement my successor in the sovereignty will find you more vigorous, and be therefore all the more forward to reimpose upon you the wonted restraint of our laws." Having so said, she dismissed all the company until supper-time.

All approved the wisdom of what the queen had said; and being risen betook them to their several diversions, the ladies to weave garlands and otherwise disport them, the young men to play and sing; and so they whiled away the hours until supper-time; which being come, they gathered about the fair fountain, and took their meal with gay and festal cheer. Supper ended, they addressed them to their wonted pastime of song and dance. At the close of which the queen, notwithstanding the songs which divers of the company had already gladly accorded them, called for another from Pamfilo, who without the least demur thus sang: –

So great, O Love, the bliss
Through thee I prove, so jocund my estate,
That in thy flame to burn I bless my fate!

Such plenitude of joy my heart doth know
Of that high joy and rare,
Wherewith thou hast me blest,
As, bounds disdaining, still doth overflow,
And by my radiant air
My blitheness manifest;
For by thee thus possessed

> With love, where meeter 'twere to venerate,
> I still consume within thy flame elate.
>
> Well wot I, Love, no song may e'er reveal,
>   Nor any sign declare
>   What in my heart is pent
> Nay, might they so, that were I best conceal,
>   Whereof were others ware,
>   'Twould serve but to torment
>   Me, whose is such content,
> That weak were words and all inadequate
> A tittle of my bliss to adumbrate.
>
> Who would have dreamed that e'er in mine embrace
>   Her I should clip and fold
>   Whom there I still do feel,
>   Or as 'gainst her face e'er to lay my face
>   Attain such grace untold,
>   And unimagined weal?
>   Wherefore my bliss I seal
> Of mine own heart within the circuit strait,
> And still in thy sweet flame luxuriate.

So ended Pamfilo his song: whereto all the company responded in full chorus; nor was there any but gave to its words an inordinate degree of attention, endeavouring by conjecture to penetrate that which he intimated that 'twas meet he should keep secret. Divers were the interpretations hazarded, but all were wide of the mark. At length, however, the queen, seeing that ladies and men alike were fain of rest, bade all betake them to bed.

— Endeth here the eighth day of the Decameron, beginneth the ninth, in which, under the rule of Emilia, discourse is had, at the discretion of each, of such matters as most commend themselves to each in turn. —

THE LUMINARY, before whose splendour the night takes wing, had already changed the eighth heaven from azure to the lighter blue, and in the meads the flowerets were beginning to lift their heads, when Emilia, being risen, roused her fair gossips, and, likewise, the young men. And so the queen leading the way at an easy pace, and the rest of the company following, they hied them to a copse at no great distance from the palace. Where, being entered, they saw the goats and stags and other wild creatures, as if witting that in this time of pestilence they had nought to fear from the hunter, stand awaiting them with no more sign of fear than if they had been tamed: and so, making now towards this, now towards the other of them as if to touch them, they diverted themselves for a while by making them skip and run. But, as soon as the sun was in the ascendant, by common consent they turned back, and whoso met them, garlanded as they were with oak-leaves, and carrying store of fragrant herbs or flowers in their hands might well have said: – "Either shall death not vanquish these, or they will meet it with a light heart." So, slowly wended they their way, now singing, now bandying quips and merry jests, to the palace, where they found all things in order meet, and their servants in blithe and merry cheer. A while they rested, nor went they to table until six ditties, each gayer than that which went before, had been sung by the young men and the ladies; which done, they washed their hands, and all by the queen's command were ranged by the seneschal at the table; and, the viands being served, they cheerily took their meal: wherefrom being risen, they trod some measures to the accompaniment of music; and then, by the queen's command, whoso would betook him to rest. However, the accustomed hour being come, they all gathered at the wonted spot for their discoursing, and the queen, bending her regard upon Filomena, bade her make a beginning of the day's story-telling, which she with a smile did on this wise: –

The DECAMERON
GIOVANNI BOCCACCIO
100 TALES of LIFE & LOVE
NINTH DAY

Ninth Day

Novel I

— Madonna Francesca, having two lovers, the one Rinuccio, the other Alessandro, by name, and loving neither of them, induces the one to simulate a corpse in a tomb, and the other to enter the tomb to fetch him out: whereby, neither satisfying her demands, she artfully rids herself of both. —

MADAM, SINCE so it pleases you, well pleased am I that in this vast, this boundless field of discourse, which you, our Lady Bountiful, have furnished us withal, 'tis mine to run the first course; wherein if I do well, I doubt not that those, who shall follow me, will do not only well but better. Such, sweet my ladies, has been the tenor of our discourse, that times not a few the might of Love, how great and singular it is, has been set forth, but yet I doubt the topic is not exhausted, nor would it be so, though we should continue to speak of nought else for the space of a full year. And as Love not only leads lovers to debate with themselves whether they were not best to die, but also draws them into the houses of the dead in quest of the dead, I am minded in this regard to tell you a story, wherein you will not only discern the power of Love, but will also learn how the ready wit of a worthy lady enabled her to disembarrass herself of two lovers, whose love was displeasing to her.

Know, then, that there dwelt aforetime in the city of Pistoia a most beauteous widow lady, of whom it so befell that two of our citizens, the one Rinuccio Palermini, the other Alessandro Chiarmontesi, by name, tarrying at Pistoia, for that they were banished from Florence, became, neither witting how it stood with the other, in the last degree enamoured. Wherefore each used all his arts to win the love of Madonna Francesca de' Lazzari – such was the lady's name – and she, being thus continually plied with ambassages and entreaties on the part of both, and having indiscreetly lent ear to them from time to time, found it no easy matter discreetly to extricate herself, when she was minded to be rid of their pestering, until it occurred to her to adopt the following expedient, to wit, to require of each a service, such as, though not impracticable, she deemed none would actually perform, to the end that, they making default, she might have a decent and colourable pretext for refusing any longer to receive their ambassages. Which expedient was on this wise. One day there died in Pistoia, and was buried in a tomb outside the church of the Friars Minors, a man, who, though his forbears had been gentlefolk, was reputed the very worst man, not in Pistoia only, but in all the world, and therewithal he was of form and feature so preternaturally hideous that whoso knew him not could scarce see him for the first time without a shudder. Now, the lady pondering her design on the day of this man's death, it occurred to her that he might in a measure subserve its accomplishment: wherefore she said to her maid: – "Thou knowest to what worry and annoyance I am daily put by the ambassages of these two Florentines, Rinuccio, and Alessandro. Now I am not disposed to gratify either of them with my love, and therefore, to shake them off, I am minded, as they make such great protestations, to put them to the proof by requiring of each something which I am sure he will not perform, and thus to rid myself of their pestering: so list what I mean to do. Thou knowest that this morning there was interred in the ground of the Friars Minors this Scannadio (such was the name of the bad man of whom we spoke but now) whose aspect, while he yet lived, appalled even the bravest among us. Thou wilt therefore go privily, to Alessandro, and say to him: – 'Madonna Francesca sends thee word by me that the time is now come when thou mayst win that which thou hast so much desired, to wit, her love and joyance thereof, if thou be so minded, on the following terms. For a reason, which thou shalt learn hereafter, one of her kinsmen is to bring home to her to-night the corpse of Scannadio, who was buried this morning; and she, standing in mortal dread of this dead man, would fain not see him; wherefore she prays thee to do her a great service, and be so good as to get thee this evening at the hour of first sleep to the tomb wherein Scannadio is buried, and go in, and having wrapped thyself in his grave-clothes, lie there, as thou wert Scannadio, himself, until one come for thee, when thou must say never a word, but let him carry thee forth, and bear thee to Madonna Francesca's house, where she will give thee welcome, and let thee stay with her, until thou art minded to depart, and, for the rest, thou wilt leave it to her.' And if he says that he will gladly do so, well and good; if not, then thou wilt tell him from me, never more to shew himself where I am, and, as he values his life, to have a care to send me no more ambassages. Which done, thou wilt go to Rinuccio Palermini, and wilt say to him: – 'Madonna Francesca lets thee know that she is ready in all respects to comply with thy wishes, so thou wilt do her a great service, which is on this wise: to-night, about midnight, thou must go to the tomb wherein was this morning interred Scannadio, and saying never a word, whatever thou mayst hear or otherwise be ware of, bear him gently forth to Madonna Francesca's house, where thou shalt learn wherefore she requires this of thee, and shalt have thy solace of her; and if thou art not minded to obey her in this, see that thou never more send her ambassage.'"

The maid did her mistress's errand, omitting nothing, to both the men, and received from each the same answer, to wit, that to pleasure the lady, he would adventure a journey to hell, to say nothing of entering a tomb. With which answer the maid returned to the lady, who waited to see if they would be such fools as to make it good. Night came, and at the hour of first sleep Alessandro Chiarmontesi, stripped to his doublet, quitted his house, and bent his steps towards Scannadio's tomb, with intent there to take the dead man's place. As he walked, there came upon him a great fear, and he fell a saying to himself: – Ah! what a fool am I! Whither go I? How know I that her kinsmen, having detected my love, and surmising that which is not, have not put her upon requiring this of me, in order that they may slay me in the tomb? In which event I alone should be the loser, for nought would ever be heard of it, so that they would escape scot-free. Or how know I but that 'tis some machination of one of my ill-wishers, whom perchance she loves, and is therefore minded to abet? And again quoth he to himself: – But allowing that 'tis neither the one nor the other, and that her kinsmen are really to carry me to her house, I scarce believe that 'tis either that they would fain embrace Scannadio's corpse themselves, or let her do so: rather it must be that they have a mind to perpetrate some outrage upon it, for that, perchance, he once did them an evil turn. She bids me say never a word, no matter what I may hear or be otherwise ware of. Suppose they were to pluck out my eyes, or my teeth, or cut off my hands, or treat me to some other horse-play of the like sort, how then? how could I keep quiet? And if I open my mouth, they will either recognize me, and perchance do me a mischief, or, if they spare me, I shall have been at pains for nought, for they will not leave me with the lady, and she will say that I disobeyed her command, and I shall never have aught of her favours.

As thus he communed with himself, he was on the point of turning back; but his overmastering love plied him with opposing arguments of such force that he kept on his way, and reached the tomb; which having opened, he entered, and after stripping Scannadio, and wrapping himself in the grave-clothes, closed it, and laid himself down in Scannadio's place. He then fell a thinking of the dead man, and his manner of life, and the things which he had heard tell of as happening by night, and in other less appalling places than the houses of the dead; whereby all the hairs of his head stood on end, and he momently expected Scannadio to rise and cut his throat. However, the ardour of his love so fortified him that he overcame these and all other timorous apprehensions, and lay as if he were dead, awaiting what should betide him.

Towards midnight Rinuccio, bent likewise upon fulfilling his lady's behest, sallied forth of his house, revolving as he went divers forebodings of possible contingencies, as that, having Scannadio's corpse upon his shoulders, he might fall into the hands of the Signory, and be condemned to the fire as a wizard, or that, should the affair get wind, it might embroil him with his kinsfolk, or the like, which gave him pause. But then with a revulsion of feeling: – Shall I, quoth he to himself, deny this lady, whom I so much have loved and love, the very first thing that she asks of me? And that too when I am thereby to win her favour? No, though 'twere as much as my life is worth, far be it from me to fail of keeping my word. So on he fared, and arrived at the tomb, which he had no difficulty in opening, and being entered, laid hold of Alessandro, who, though in mortal fear, had given no sign of life, by the feet, and dragged him forth, and having hoisted him on to his shoulders, bent his steps towards the lady's house. And as he went, being none too careful of Alessandro, he swung him from time to time against one or other of the angles of certain benches that were by the wayside; and indeed the night was so dark and murky that he could not see where he was going. And when he was all but on the threshold of the lady's house (she standing within at a window with her maid, to mark if Rinuccio would bring Alessandro, and being already provided with an excuse for sending them both away), it so befell that the patrol of the Signory, who were posted in the street in dead silence, being on the look-out for a certain bandit, hearing the tramp of Rinuccio's feet, suddenly shewed a light, the better to know what was toward, and whither to go, and advancing targes and lances, cried out: – "Who goes there?" Whereupon Rinuccio, having little leisure for deliberation, let Alessandro fall, and took to flight as fast as his legs might carry him. Alessandro, albeit encumbered by the graveclothes, which were very long, also jumped up and made off. By the light shewn by the patrol the lady had very plainly perceived Rinuccio, with Alessandro on his back, as also that Alessandro had the grave-clothes upon him; and much did she marvel at the daring of both, but, for all that, she laughed heartily to see Rinuccio drop Alessandro, and Alessandro run away. Overjoyed at the turn the affair had taken, and praising God that He had rid her of their harass, she withdrew from the window, and betook her to her chamber, averring to her maid that for certain they must both be mightily in love with her, seeing that 'twas plain they had both done her bidding.

Crestfallen and cursing his evil fortune, Rinuccio nevertheless went not home, but, as soon as the street was clear of the patrol, came back to the spot where he had dropped Alessandro, and stooped down and began feeling about, if haply he might find him, and so do his devoir to the lady; but, as he found him not, he supposed the patrol must have borne him thence, and so at last home he went; as did also Alessandro, knowing not what else to do, and deploring his mishap. On the morrow, Scannadio's tomb being found open and empty, for Alessandro had thrown the corpse into the vault below, all Pistoia debated of the matter with no small diversity of opinion, the fools believing that Scannadio had been carried off by devils. Neither of the lovers, however, forbore to make suit to the lady for her favour and love, telling her what he had done, and what had happened, and praying her to have him excused that he had not perfectly carried out her instructions. But she, feigning to believe neither of them, disposed of each with the same curt answer, to wit, that, as he had not done her bidding, she would never do aught for him.

Ninth Day
Novel II

— An abbess rises in haste and in the dark, with intent to surprise an accused nun abed with her lover: thinking to put on her veil, she puts on instead the breeches of a priest that she has with her: the nun, espying her headgear, and doing her to wit thereof, is acquitted, and thenceforth finds it easier to forgather with her lover. —

SO ENDED FILOMENA; and when all had commended the address shewn by the lady in ridding herself of the two lovers that she affected not, and contrariwise had censured the hardihood of the two lovers as not love but madness, the queen turned to Elisa, and with a charming air: – "Now, Elisa, follow," quoth she: whereupon Elisa began on this wise: –

Dearest ladies, 'twas cleverly done of Madonna Francesca, to disembarrass herself in the way we have heard: but I have to tell of a young nun, who by a happy retort, and the favour of Fortune, delivered herself from imminent peril. And as you know that there are not a few most foolish folk, who, notwithstanding their folly, take upon themselves the governance and correction of others; so you may learn from my story that Fortune at times justly puts them to shame; which befell the abbess, who was the superior of the nun of whom I am about to speak.

You are to know, then, that in a convent in Lombardy of very great repute for strict and holy living there was, among other ladies that there wore the veil, a young woman of noble family, and extraordinary beauty. Now Isabetta – for such was her name – having speech one day of one of her kinsmen at the grate, became enamoured of a fine young gallant that was with him; who, seeing her to be very fair, and reading her passion in her eyes, was kindled with a like flame for her: which mutual and unsolaced love they bore a great while not without great suffering to both. But at length, both being intent thereon, the gallant discovered a way by which he might with all secrecy visit his nun; and she approving, he paid her not one visit only, but many, to their no small mutual solace. But, while thus they continued their intercourse, it so befell that one night one of the sisters observed him take his leave of Isabetta and depart, albeit neither he nor she was ware that they had thus been discovered. The sister imparted what she had seen to several others. At first they were minded to denounce her to the abbess, one Madonna Usimbalda, who was reputed by the nuns, and indeed by all that knew her, to be a good and holy woman; but on second thoughts they deemed it expedient, that there might be no room for denial, to cause the abbess to take her and the gallant in the act. So they held their peace, and arranged between them to keep her in watch and close espial, that they might catch her unawares. Of which practice Isabetta recking, witting nought, it so befell that one night, when she had her lover to see her, the sisters that were on the watch were soon ware of it, and at what they deemed the nick of time parted into two companies of which one mounted guard at the threshold of Isabetta's cell, while the other hasted to the abbess's chamber, and knocking at the door, roused her, and as soon as they heard her voice, said: – "Up, Madam, without delay: we have discovered that Isabetta has a young man with her in her cell."

Now that night the abbess had with her a priest whom she used not seldom to have conveyed to her in a chest; and the report of the sisters making her apprehensive lest for excess of zeal and hurry they should force the door open, she rose in a trice; and huddling on her clothes as best she might in the dark, instead of the veil that they wear, which they call the psalter, she caught up the priest's breeches, and having clapped them on her head, hied her forth, and locked the door behind her, saying: – "Where is this woman accursed of God?" And so, guided by the sisters, all so agog to catch Isabetta a sinning that they perceived not what manner of headgear the abbess wore, she made her way to the cell, and with their aid broke open the door; and entering they found the two lovers abed in one another's arms; who, as it were, thunderstruck to be thus surprised, lay there, witting not what to do. The sisters took the young nun forthwith, and by command of the abbess brought her to the chapter-house. The gallant, left behind in the cell, put on his clothes and waited to see how the affair would end, being minded to make as many nuns as he might come at pay dearly for any despite that might be done his mistress, and to bring her off with him. The abbess, seated in the chapter-house with all her nuns about her, and all eyes bent upon the culprit, began giving her the severest reprimand that ever woman got, for that by her disgraceful and abominable conduct, should it get wind, she had sullied the fair fame of the convent; whereto she added menaces most dire. Shamefast and timorous, the culprit essayed no defence, and her silence begat pity of her in the rest; but, while the abbess waxed more and more voluble, it chanced that the girl raised her head and espied the abbess's headgear, and the points that hung down on this side and that. The significance whereof being by no means lost upon her, she quite plucked up heart, and: – "Madam," quoth she, "so help you God, tie up your coif, and then you may say what you will to me." Whereto the abbess, not understanding her, replied: – "What coif, lewd woman? So thou hast the effrontery to jest! Think'st thou that what thou hast done is a matter meet for jests?" Whereupon: – "Madam," quoth the girl again, "I pray you, tie up your coif, and then you may say to me whatever you please." Which occasioned not a few of the nuns to look up at the abbess's head, and the abbess herself to raise her hands thereto, and so she and they at one and the same time apprehended Isabetta's meaning. Wherefore the abbess, finding herself detected by all in the same sin, and that no disguise was possible, changed her tone, and held quite another sort of language than before, the upshot of which was that 'twas impossible to withstand the assaults of the flesh, and that, accordingly, observing due secrecy as theretofore, all might give themselves a good time, as they had opportunity. So, having dismissed Isabetta to rejoin her lover in her cell, she herself returned to lie with her priest. And many a time thereafter, in spite of the envious, Isabetta had her gallant to see her, the others, that lacked lovers, doing in secret the best they might to push their fortunes.

Ninth Day
Novel III

— *Master Simone, at the instance of Bruno and Buffalmacco and Nello, makes Calandrino believe that he is with child. Calandrino, accordingly, gives them capons and money for medicines, and is cured without being delivered.* —

WHEN ELISA had ended her story, and all had given thanks to God that He had vouchsafed the young nun a happy escape from the fangs of her envious companions, the queen bade Filostrato follow suit; and without expecting a second command, thus Filostrato began: –

Fairest my ladies, the uncouth judge from the Marches, of whom I told you yesterday, took from the tip of my tongue a story of Calandrino, which I was on the point of narrating: and as nought can be said of him without mightily enhancing our jollity, albeit not a little has already been said touching him and his comrades, I will now give you the story which I had meant yesterday to give you. Who they were, this Calandrino and the others that I am to tell of in this story, has already been sufficiently explained; wherefore, without more ado, I say that one of Calandrino's aunts having died, leaving him two hundred pounds in petty cash, Calandrino gave out that he was minded to purchase an estate, and, as if he had had ten thousand florins of gold to invest, engaged every broker in Florence to treat for him, the negotiation always falling through, as soon as the price was named. Bruno and Buffalmacco, knowing what was afoot, told him again and again that he had better give himself a jolly time with them than go about buying earth as if he must needs make pellets; but so far were they from effecting their purpose, that they could not even prevail upon him to give them a single meal. Whereat as one day they grumbled, being joined by a comrade of theirs, one Nello, also a painter, they all three took counsel how they might wet their whistle at Calandrino's expense; and, their plan being soon concerted, the next morning Calandrino was scarce gone out, when Nello met him, saying: – "Good day, Calandrino:" whereto Calandrino replied: – "God give thee a good day and a good year." Nello then drew back a little, and looked him steadily in the face, until: – "What seest thou to stare at?" quoth Calandrino. "Hadst thou no pain in the night?" returned Nello; "thou seemest not thyself to me." Which Calandrino no sooner heard, than he began to be disquieted, and: – "Alas! How sayst thou?" quoth he. "What tak'st thou to be the matter with me?" "Why, as to that I have nothing to say," returned Nello; "but thou seemest to be quite changed: perchance 'tis not what I suppose;" and with that he left him.

Calandrino, anxious, though he could not in the least have said why, went on; and soon Buffalmacco, who was not far off, and had observed him part from Nello, made up to him, and greeted him, asking him if he was not in pain. "I cannot say," replied Calandrino; "'twas but now that Nello told me that I looked quite changed: can it be that there is aught the matter with me?" "Aught?" quoth Buffalmacco, "ay, indeed, there might be a trifle the matter with thee. Thou look'st to be half dead, man." Calandrino now began to think he must have a fever. And then up came Bruno; and the first thing he said was: – "Why, Calandrino, how ill thou look'st! thy appearance is that of a corpse. How dost thou feel?" To be thus accosted by all three left no doubt in Calandrino's mind that he was ill, and so: – "What shall I do?" quoth he, in a great fright. "My advice," replied Bruno, "is that thou go home and get thee to bed and cover thee well up, and send thy water to Master Simone, who, as thou knowest, is such a friend of ours. He will tell thee at once what thou must do; and we will come to see thee, and will do aught that may be needful." And Nello then joining them, they all three went home with Calandrino, who, now quite spent, went straight to his room, and said to his wife: – "Come now, wrap me well up; I feel very ill." And so he laid himself on the bed, and sent a maid with his water to Master Simone, who had then his shop in the Mercato Vecchio, at the sign of the pumpkin. Whereupon quoth Bruno to his comrades: – "You will stay here with him, and I will go hear what the doctor has to say, and if need be, will bring him hither." "Prithee, do so, my friend," quoth Calandrino, "and bring me word how it is with me, for I feel as how I cannot say in my inside." So Bruno hied him to Master Simone, and before the maid arrived with the water, told him what was afoot. The Master, thus primed, inspected the water, and then said to the maid: – "Go tell Calandrino to keep himself very warm, and I will come at once, and let him know what is the matter with him, and what he must do." With which message the maid was scarce returned, when the Master and Bruno arrived, and the Master, having seated himself beside Calandrino, felt his pulse, and by and by, in the presence of his wife, said: – "Harkye, Calandrino, I speak to thee as a friend, and I tell thee that what is amiss with thee is just that thou art with child." Whereupon Calandrino cried out querulously: – "Woe's me! 'Tis thy doing, Tessa, for that thou must needs be uppermost: I told thee plainly what would come of it," Whereat the lady, being not a little modest, coloured from brow to neck, and with downcast eyes, withdrew from the room, saying never a word by way of answer. Calandrino ran on in the same plaintive strain: – "Alas! woe's me! What shall I do? How shall I be delivered of this child? What passage can it find? Ah! I see only too plainly that the lasciviousness of this wife of mine has been the death of me: God make her as wretched as I would fain be happy! Were I as well as I am not, I would get me up and thrash her, till I left not a whole bone in her body, albeit it does but serve me right for letting her get the upper place; but if I do win through this, she shall never have it again; verily she might pine to death for it, but she should not have it."

Which to hear, Bruno and Buffalmacco and Nello were like to burst with suppressed laughter, and Master Scimmione laughed so frantically, that all his teeth were ready to start from his jaws. However, at length, in answer to Calandrino's appeals and entreaties for counsel and succour: – "Calandrino," quoth the Master, "thou mayst dismiss thy fears, for, God be praised, we were apprised of thy state in such good time that with but little trouble, in the course of a few days, I shall set thee right; but 'twill cost a little." "Woe's me," returned Calandrino, "be it so, Master, for the love of God: I have here two hundred pounds, with which I had thoughts of buying an estate: take them all, all, if you must have all, so only I may escape being delivered, for I know not how I should manage it, seeing that women, albeit 'tis much easier for them, do make such a noise in the hour of their labour, that I misdoubt me, if I suffered so, I should die before I was delivered." "Disquiet not thyself," said the doctor: "I will have a potion distilled for thee; of rare virtue it is, and not a little palatable, and in the course of three days 'twill purge thee of all, and leave thee in better fettle than a fish; but thou wilt do well to be careful thereafter, and commit no such indiscretions again. Now to make this potion we must have three pair of good fat capons, and, for divers other ingredients, thou wilt give one of thy friends here five pounds in small change to purchase them, and thou wilt have everything sent to my shop, and so, please God, I will send thee this distilled potion to-morrow morning, and thou wilt take a good beakerful each time." Whereupon: – "Be it as you bid, Master mine," quoth Calandrino, and handing Bruno five pounds, and money enough to purchase three pair of capons, he begged him, if it were not too much trouble, to do him the service to buy these things for him. So away went the doctor, and made a little decoction by way of draught, and sent it him. Bruno bought the capons and all else that was needed to furnish forth the feast, with which he and his comrades and the doctor regaled them. Calandrino drank of the decoction for three mornings, after which he had a visit from his friends and the doctor, who felt his pulse, and then: – "Beyond a doubt, Calandrino," quoth he, "thou art cured, and so thou hast no more occasion to keep indoors, but needst have no fear to do whatever thou hast a mind to." Much relieved, Calandrino got up, and resumed his accustomed way of life, and, wherever he found any one to talk to, was loud in praise of Master Simone for the excellent manner in which he had cured him, causing him in three days without the least suffering to be quit of his pregnancy. And Bruno and Buffalmacco and Nello were not a little pleased with themselves that they had so cleverly got the better of Calandrino's niggardliness, albeit Monna Tessa, who was not deceived, murmured not a little against her husband.

Ninth Day

Novel IV

— *Cecco, son of Messer Fortarrigo, loses his all at play at Buonconvento, besides the money of Cecco, son of Messer Angiulieri; whom, running after him in his shirt and crying out that he has robbed him, he causes to be taken by peasants: he then puts on his clothes, mounts his palfrey, and leaves him to follow in his shirt.* —

ALL THE COMPANY laughed beyond measure to hear what Calandrino said touching his wife: but, when Filostrato had done, Neifile, being bidden by the queen, thus began: –

Noble ladies, were it not more difficult for men to evince their good sense and virtue than their folly and their vice, many would labour in vain to set bounds to their flow of words: whereof you have had a most conspicuous example in poor blundering Calandrino, who, for the better cure of that with which in his simplicity he supposed himself to be afflicted, had no sort of need to discover in public his wife's secret pleasures. Which affair has brought to my mind one that fell out contrariwise, inasmuch as the guile of one discomfited the good sense of another to the grievous loss and shame of the discomfited: the manner whereof I am minded to relate to you.

'Tis not many years since there were in Siena two young men, both of age, and both alike named Cecco, the one being son of Messer Angiulieri, the other of Messer Fortarrigo. Who, albeit in many other respects their dispositions accorded ill, agreed so well in one, to wit, that they both hated their fathers, that they became friends, and kept much together. Now Angiulieri, being a pretty fellow, and well-mannered, could not brook to live at Siena on the allowance made him by his father, and learning that there was come into the March of Ancona, as legate of the Pope, a cardinal, to whom he was much bounden, resolved to resort to him there, thinking thereby to improve his circumstances. So, having acquainted his father with his purpose, he prevailed upon him to give him there and then all that he would have given him during the next six months, that he might have the wherewith to furnish himself with apparel and a good mount, so as to travel in a becoming manner. And as he was looking out for some one to attend him as his servant, Fortarrigo, hearing of it, came presently to him and besought him with all earnestness to take him with him as his groom, or servant, or what he would, and he would be satisfied with his keep, without any salary whatsoever. Whereto Angiulieri made answer that he was not disposed to take him, not but that he well knew that he was competent for any service that might be required of him, but because he was given to play, and therewithal would at times get drunk. Fortarrigo assured him with many an oath that he would be on his guard to commit neither fault, and added thereto such instant entreaties, that Angiulieri was, as it were, vanquished, and consented. So one morning they took the road for Buonconvento, being minded there to breakfast. Now when Angiulieri had breakfasted, as 'twas a very hot day, he had a bed made in the inn, and having undressed with Fortarrigo's help, he composed himself to sleep, telling Fortarrigo to call him on the stroke of none. Angiulieri thus sleeping, Fortarrigo repaired to the tavern, where, having slaked his thirst, he sate down to a game with some that were there, who speedily won from him all his money, and thereafter in like manner all the clothes he had on his back: wherefore he, being anxious to retrieve his losses, went, stripped as he was to his shirt, to the room where lay Angiulieri; and seeing that he was sound asleep, he took from his purse all the money that he had, and so went back to the gaming-table, and staked it, and lost it all, as he had his own.

By and by Angiulieri awoke, and got up, and dressed, and called for Fortarrigo; and as Fortarrigo answered not, he supposed that he must have had too much to drink, and be sleeping it off somewhere, as was his wont. He accordingly determined to leave him alone; and doubting not to find a better servant at Corsignano, he let saddle his palfrey and attach the valise; but when, being about to depart, he would have paid the host, never a coin could he come by. Whereat there was no small stir, so that all the inn was in an uproar, Angiulieri averring that he had been robbed in the house, and threatening to have them all arrested and taken to Siena; when, lo, who should make his appearance but Fortarrigo in his shirt, intent now to steal the clothes, as he had stolen the moneys, of Angiulieri? And marking that Angiulieri was accoutred for the road: – "How is this, Angiulieri?" quoth he. "Are we to start so soon? Nay, but wait a little. One will be here presently that has my doublet in pawn for thirty-eight soldi; I doubt not he will return it me for thirty-five soldi, if I pay money down." And while they were yet talking, in came one that made it plain to Angiulieri that 'twas Fortarrigo that had robbed him of his money, for he told him the amount that Fortarrigo had lost. Whereat Angiulieri, in a towering passion, rated Fortarrigo right soundly, and, but that he stood more in fear of man than of God, would have suited action to word; and so, threatening to have him hanged by the neck and proclaimed an outlaw at the gallows-tree of Siena, he mounted his horse.

Fortarrigo, making as if 'twas not to him, but to another, that Angiulieri thus spoke, made answer: – "Come now, Angiulieri, we were best have done with all this idle talk, and consider the matter of substance: we can redeem for thirty-five soldi, if we pay forthwith, but if we wait till to-morrow, we shall not get off with less than thirty-eight, the full amount of the loan; and 'tis because I staked by his advice that he will make me this allowance. Now why should not we save these three soldi?" Whereat Angiulieri waxed well-nigh desperate, more particularly that he marked that the bystanders were scanning him suspiciously, as if, so far from understanding that Fortarrigo had staked and lost his, Angiulieri's money, they gave him credit for still being in funds: so he cried out: – "What have I to do with thy doublet? 'Tis high time thou wast hanged by the neck, that, not content with robbing me and gambling away my money, thou must needs also keep me in parley here and make mock of me, when I would fain be gone." Fortarrigo, however, still persisted in making believe that Angiulieri did not mean this for him, and only said: – "Nay, but why wilt not thou save me these three soldi? Think'st thou I can be of no more use to thee? Prithee, an thou lov'st me, do me this turn. Wherefore in such a hurry? We have time enough to get to Torrenieri this evening. Come now, out with thy purse. Thou knowest I might search Siena through, and not find a doublet that would suit me so well as this: and for all I let him have it for thirty-eight soldi, 'tis worth forty or more; so thou wilt wrong me twice over." Vexed beyond measure that, after robbing him, Fortarrigo should now keep him clavering about the matter, Angiulieri made no answer, but turned his horse's head, and took the road for Torrenieri. But Fortarrigo with cunning malice trotted after him in his shirt, and 'twas still his doublet, his doublet, that he would have of him: and when they had thus ridden two good miles, and Angiulieri was forcing the pace to get out of earshot of his pestering, Fortarrigo espied some husbandmen in a field beside the road a little ahead of Angiulieri, and fell a shouting to them amain: – "Take thief! take thief!" Whereupon they came up with their spades and their mattocks, and barred Angiulieri's way, supposing that he must have robbed the man that came shouting after him in his shirt, and stopped him and apprehended him; and little indeed did it avail him to tell them who he was, and how the matter stood. For up came Fortarrigo with a wrathful air, and: – "I know not," quoth he, "why I spare to kill thee on the spot, traitor, thief that thou art, thus to despoil me and give me the slip!" And then, turning to the peasants: – "You see, gentlemen," quoth he, "in what a trim he left me in the inn, after gambling away all that he had with him and on him. Well indeed may I say that under God 'tis to you I owe it that I have thus come by my own again: for which cause I shall ever be beholden to you." Angiulieri also had his say; but his words passed unheeded. Fortarrigo with the help of the peasants compelled him to dismount; and having stripped him, donned his clothes, mounted his horse, and leaving him barefoot and in his shirt, rode back to Siena, giving out on all hands that he had won the palfrey and the clothes from Angiulieri. So Angiulieri, having thought to present himself to the cardinal in the March a wealthy man, returned to Buonconvento poor and in his shirt; and being ashamed for the time to shew himself in Siena, pledged the nag that Fortarrigo had ridden for a suit of clothes, and betook him to his kinsfolk at Corsignano, where he tarried, until he received a fresh supply of money from his father. Thus, then, Fortarrigo's guile disconcerted Angiulieri's judicious purpose, albeit when time and occasion served, it was not left unrequited.

Ninth Day

Novel V

— *Calandrino being enamoured of a damsel, Bruno gives him a scroll, averring that, if he but touch her therewith, she will go with him: he is found with her by his wife who subjects him to a most severe and vexatious examination.* —

SO, AT NO great length, ended Neifile her story, which the company allowed to pass with none too much laughter or remark: whereupon the queen, turning to Fiammetta, bade her follow suit. Fiammetta, with mien most gladsome, made answer that she willingly obeyed, and thus began: –

As I doubt not, ye know, ladies most debonair, be the topic of discourse never so well worn, it will still continue to please, if the speaker knows how to make due choice of time and occasion meet. Wherefore, considering the reason for which we are here (how that 'tis to make merry and speed the time gaily, and that merely), I deem that there is nought that may afford us mirth and solace but here may find time and occasion meet, and, after serving a thousand turns of discourse, should still prove not unpleasing for another thousand. Wherefore, notwithstanding that of Calandrino and his doings not a little has from time to time been said among us, yet, considering that, as a while ago Filostrato observed, there is nought that concerns him that is not entertaining, I will make bold to add to the preceding stories another, which I might well, had I been minded to deviate from the truth, have disguised, and so recounted it to you, under other names; but as whoso in telling a story diverges from the truth does thereby in no small measure diminish the delight of his hearers, I purpose for the reason aforesaid to give you the narrative in proper form.

Niccolo Cornacchini, one of our citizens, and a man of wealth, had among other estates a fine one at Camerata, on which he had a grand house built, and engaged Bruno and Buffalmacco to paint it throughout; in which task, for that 'twas by no means light, they associated with them Nello and Calandrino, and so set to work. There were a few rooms in the house provided with beds and other furniture, and an old female servant lived there as caretaker, but otherwise the house was unoccupied, for which cause Niccolo's son, Filippo, being a young man and a bachelor, was wont sometimes to bring thither a woman for his pleasure, and after keeping her there for a few days to escort her thence again. Now on one of these occasions it befell that he brought thither one Niccolosa, whom a vile fellow, named Mangione, kept in a house at Camaldoli as a common prostitute. And a fine piece of flesh she was, and wore fine clothes, and for one of her sort, knew how to comport herself becomingly and talk agreeably.

Now one day at high noon forth tripped the damsel from her chamber in a white gown, her locks braided about her head, to wash her hands and face at a well that was in the courtyard of the house, and, while she was so engaged, it befell that Calandrino came there for water, and greeted her familiarly. Having returned his salutation, she, rather because Calandrino struck her as something out of the common, than for any other interest she felt in him, regarded him attentively. Calandrino did the like by her, and being smitten by her beauty, found reasons enough why he should not go back to his comrades with the water; but, as he knew not who she was, he made not bold to address her. She, upon whom his gaze was not lost, being minded to amuse herself at his expense, let her glance from time to time rest upon him, while she heaved a slight sigh or two. Whereby Calandrino was forthwith captivated, and tarried in the courtyard, until Filippo called her back into the chamber. Returned to his work, Calandrino sighed like a furnace: which Bruno, who was ever regardful of his doings for the diversion they afforded him, failed not to mark, and by and by: – "What the Devil is amiss with thee, comrade Calandrino?" quoth he. "Thou dost nought but puff and blow." "Comrade," replied Calandrino, "I should be in luck, had I but one to help me." "How so?" quoth Bruno. "Why," returned Calandrino, "'tis not to go farther, but there is a damsel below, fairer than a lamia, and so mightily in love with me that 'twould astonish thee. I observed it but now, when I went to fetch the water." "Nay, but, Calandrino, make sure she be not Filippo's wife," quoth Bruno. "I doubt 'tis even so," replied Calandrino, "for he called her and she joined him in the chamber; but what signifies it? I would circumvent Christ Himself in such case, not to say Filippo. Of a truth, comrade, I tell thee she pleases me I could not say how." "Comrade," returned Bruno, "I will find out for thee who she is, and if she be Filippo's wife, two words from me will make it all straight for thee, for she is much my friend. But how shall we prevent Buffalmacco knowing it? I can never have a word with her but he is with me." "As to Buffalmacco," replied Calandrino: "I care not if he do know it; but let us make sure that it come not to Nello's ears, for he is of kin to Monna Tessa, and would spoil it all." Whereto: – "Thou art in the right," returned Bruno.

Now Bruno knew what the damsel was, for he had seen her arrive, and moreover Filippo had told him. So, Calandrino having given over working for a while, and betaken him to her, Bruno acquainted Nello and Buffalmacco with the whole story; and thereupon they privily concerted how to entreat him in regard of this love affair. Wherefore, upon his return, quoth Bruno softly: – "Didst see her?" "Ay, woe's me!" replied Calandrino: "she has stricken me to the death." Quoth Bruno: – "I will go see if she be the lady I take her to be, and if I find that 'tis so, leave the rest to me." Whereupon down went Bruno, and found Filippo and the damsel, and fully apprised them what sort of fellow Calandrino was, and what he had told them, and concerted with them what each should do and say, that they might have a merry time together over Calandrino's love affair. He then rejoined Calandrino, saying: – "'Tis the very same; and therefore the affair needs very delicate handling, for, if Filippo were but ware thereof, not all Arno's waters would suffice to cleanse us. However, what should I say to her from thee, if by chance I should get speech of her?" "I'faith," replied Calandrino, "why, first, first of all, thou wilt tell her that I wish her a thousand bushels of the good seed of generation, and then that I am her servant, and if she is fain of – aught – thou tak'st me?" "Ay," quoth Bruno, "leave it to me."

Supper-time came; and, the day's work done, they went down into the courtyard, Filippo and Niccolosa being there, and there they tarried a while to advance Calandrino's suit. Calandrino's gaze was soon riveted on Niccolosa, and such and so strange and startling were the gestures that he made that they would have given sight to the blind. She on her part used all her arts to inflame his passion, primed as she had been by Bruno, and diverted beyond measure as she was by Calandrino's antics, while Filippo, Buffalmacco and the rest feigned to be occupied in converse, and to see nought of what passed. However, after a while, to Calandrino's extreme disgust, they took their leave; and as they bent their steps towards Florence: – "I warrant thee," quoth Bruno to Calandrino, "she wastes away for thee like ice in the sunlight; by the body o' God, if thou wert to bring thy rebeck, and sing her one or two of thy love-songs, she'd throw herself out of window to be with thee." Quoth Calandrino: – "Think'st thou, comrade, think'st thou, 'twere well I brought it?" "Ay, indeed," returned Bruno. Whereupon: – "Ah! comrade," quoth Calandrino, "so thou wouldst not believe me when I told thee to-day? Of a truth I perceive there's ne'er another knows so well what he would be at as I. Who but I would have known how so soon to win the love of a lady like that? Lucky indeed might they deem themselves, if they did it, those young gallants that go about, day and night, up and down, a strumming on the one-stringed viol, and would not know how to gather a handful of nuts once in a millennium. Mayst thou be by to see when I bring her the rebeck! thou wilt see fine sport. List well what I say: I am not so old as I look; and she knows it right well: ay, and anyhow I will soon let her know it, when I come to grapple her. By the very body of Christ I will have such sport with her, that she will follow me as any love-sick maid follows her swain." "Oh!" quoth Bruno, "I doubt not thou wilt make her thy prey: and I seem to see thee bite her dainty vermeil mouth and her cheeks, that shew as twin roses, with thy teeth, that are as so many lute-pegs, and afterwards devour her bodily." So encouraged, Calandrino fancied himself already in action, and went about singing and capering in such high glee that 'twas as if he would burst his skin. And so next day he brought the rebeck, and to the no small amusement of all the company sang several songs to her. And, in short, by frequently seeing her, he waxed so mad with passion that he gave over working; and a thousand times a day he would run now to the window, now to the door, and anon to the courtyard on the chance of catching sight of her; nor did she, astutely following Bruno's instructions, fail to afford him abundance of opportunity. Bruno played the go-between, bearing him her answers to all his messages, and sometimes bringing him messages from her. When she was not at home, which was most frequently the case, he would send him letters from her, in which she gave great encouragement to his hopes, at the same time giving him to understand that she was at the house of her kinsfolk, where as yet he might not visit her.

On this wise Bruno and Buffalmacco so managed the affair as to divert themselves inordinately, causing him to send her, as at her request, now an ivory comb, now a purse, now a little knife, and other such dainty trifles; in return for which they brought him, now and again, a counterfeit ring of no value, with which Calandrino was marvellously pleased. And Calandrino, to stimulate their zeal in his interest, would entertain them hospitably at table, and otherwise flatter them. Now, when they had thus kept him in play for two good months, and the affair was just where it had been, Calandrino, seeing that the work was coming to an end, and bethinking him that, if it did so before he had brought his love affair to a successful issue, he must give up all hopes of ever so doing, began to be very instant and importunate with Bruno. So, in the presence of the damsel, and by preconcert with her and Filippo, quoth Bruno to Calandrino: – "Harkye, comrade, this lady has vowed to me a thousand times that she will do as thou wouldst have her, and as, for all that, she does nought to pleasure thee, I am of opinion that she leads thee by the nose: wherefore, as she keeps not her promises, we will make her do so, willy-nilly, if thou art so minded." "Nay, but, for the love of God, so be it," replied Calandrino, "and that speedily." "Darest thou touch her, then, with a scroll that I shall give thee?" quoth Bruno. "I dare," replied Calandrino. "Fetch me, then," quoth Bruno, "a bit of the skin of an unborn lamb, a live bat, three grains of incense, and a blessed candle; and leave the rest to me." To catch the bat taxed all Calandrino's art and craft for the whole of the evening; but having at length taken him, he brought him with the other matters to Bruno: who, having withdrawn into a room by himself, wrote on the skin some cabalistic jargon, and handed it to him, saying: – "Know, Calandrino, that, if thou touch her with this scroll, she will follow thee forthwith, and do whatever thou shalt wish. Wherefore, should Filippo go abroad to-day, get thee somehow up to her, and touch her; and then go into the barn that is hereby – 'tis the best place we have, for never a soul goes there – and thou wilt see that she will come there too. When she is there, thou wottest well what to do." Calandrino, overjoyed as ne'er another, took the scroll, saying only: – "Comrade, leave that to me."

Now Nello, whom Calandrino mistrusted, entered with no less zest than the others into the affair, and was their confederate for Calandrino's discomfiture; accordingly by Bruno's direction he hied to Florence, and finding Monna Tessa: – "Thou hast scarce forgotten, Tessa," quoth he, "what a beating Calandrino gave thee, without the least cause, that day when he came home with the stones from Mugnone; for which I would have thee be avenged, and, so thou wilt not, call me no more kinsman or friend. He is fallen in love with a lady up there, who is abandoned enough to go closeting herself not seldom with him, and 'tis but a short while since they made assignation to forgather forthwith: so I would have thee go there, and surprise him in the act, and give him a sound trouncing." Which when the lady heard, she deemed it no laughing matter; but started up and broke out with: – "Alas, the arrant knave! is't thus he treats me? By the Holy Rood, never fear but I will pay him out!" And wrapping herself in her cloak, and taking a young woman with her for companion, she sped more at a run than at a walk, escorted by Nello, up to Camerata. Bruno, espying her from afar, said to Filippo: – "Lo, here comes our friend." Whereupon Filippo went to the place where Calandrino and the others were at work, and said: – "My masters, I must needs go at once to Florence; slacken not on that account." And so off he went, and hid himself where, unobserved, he might see what Calandrino would do. Calandrino waited only until he saw that Filippo was at some distance, and then he went down into the courtyard, where he found Niccolosa alone, and fell a talking with her. She, knowing well what she had to do, drew close to him, and shewed him a little more familiarity than she was wont: whereupon Calandrino touched her with the scroll, and having so done, saying never a word, bent his steps towards the barn, whither Niccolosa followed him, and being entered, shut the door, and forthwith embraced him, threw him down on the straw that lay there, and got astride of him, and holding him fast by the arms about the shoulders, suffered him not to approach his face to hers, but gazing upon him, as if he were the delight of her heart: – "O Calandrino, sweet my Calandrino," quoth she, "heart of my body, my very soul, my bliss, my consolation, ah! how long have I yearned to hold thee in my arms and have thee all my own! Thy endearing ways have utterly disarmed me; thou hast made prize of my heart with thy rebeck. Do I indeed hold thee in mine embrace?" Calandrino, scarce able to move, murmured: – "Ah! sweet my soul, suffer me to kiss thee." Whereto: – "Nay, but thou art too hasty," replied Niccolosa. "Let me first feast mine eyes on thee; let me but sate them with this sweet face of thine."

Meanwhile Bruno and Buffalmacco had joined Filippo, so that what passed was seen and heard by all three. And while Calandrino was thus intent to kiss Niccolosa, lo, up came Nello with Monna Tessa. "By God, I swear they are both there," ejaculated Nello, as they entered the doorway; but the lady, now fairly furious, laid hold of him and thrust him aside, and rushing in, espied Niccolosa astride of Calandrino. Niccolosa no sooner caught sight of the lady, than up she jumped, and in a trice was beside Filippo. Monna Tessa fell upon Calandrino, who was still on the floor, planted her nails in his face, and scratched it all over: she then seized him by the hair, and hauling him to and fro about the barn: – "Foul, pestilent cur," quoth she, "is this the way thou treatest me? Thou old fool! A murrain on the love I have borne thee! Hast thou not enough to do at home, that thou must needs go falling in love with strange women? And a fine lover thou wouldst make! Dost not know thyself, knave? Dost not know thyself, wretch? Thou, from whose whole body 'twere not possible to wring enough sap for a sauce! God's faith, 'twas not Tessa that got thee with child: God's curse on her, whoever she was: verily she must be a poor creature to be enamoured of a jewel of thy rare quality." At sight of his wife, Calandrino, suspended, as it were, between life and death, ventured no defence; but, his face torn to shreds, his hair and clothes all disordered, fumbled about for his capuche, which having found, up he got, and humbly besought his wife not to publish the matter, unless she were minded that he should be cut to pieces, for that she that was with him was the wife of the master of the house. "Then God give her a bad year," replied the lady. Whereupon Bruno and Buffalmacco, who by this time had laughed their fill with Filippo and Niccolosa, came up as if attracted by the noise; and after not a little ado pacified the lady, and counselled Calandrino to go back to Florence, and stay there, lest Filippo should get wind of the affair, and do him a mischief. So Calandrino, crestfallen and woebegone, got him back to Florence with his face torn to shreds; where, daring not to shew himself at Camerata again, he endured day and night the grievous torment of his wife's vituperation. Such was the issue, to which, after ministering not a little mirth to his comrades, as also to Niccolosa and Filippo, this ardent lover brought his amour.

Ninth Day

Novel VI

— Two young men lodge at an inn, of whom the one lies with the host's daughter, his wife by inadvertence lying with the other. He that lay with the daughter afterwards gets into her father's bed and tells him all, taking him to be his comrade. They bandy words: whereupon the good woman, apprehending the circumstances, gets her to bed with her daughter, and by divers apt words re-establishes perfect accord. —

CALANDRINO AS on former occasions, so also on this, moved the company to laughter. However, when the ladies had done talking of his doings, the queen called for a story from Pamfilo, who thus spoke: –

Worshipful ladies, this Niccolosa, that Calandrino loved, has brought to my mind a story of another Niccolosa; which I am minded to tell you, because 'twill shew you how a good woman by her quick apprehension avoided a great scandal.

In the plain of Mugnone there was not long ago a good man that furnished travellers with meat and drink for money, and, for that he was in poor circumstances, and had but a little house, gave not lodging to every comer, but only to a few that he knew, and if they were hard bested. Now the good man had to wife a very fine woman, and by her had two children, to wit, a pretty and winsome girl of some fifteen or sixteen summers, as yet unmarried, and a little boy, not yet one year old, whom the mother suckled at her own breast. The girl had found favour in the eyes of a goodly and mannerly young gentleman of our city, who was not seldom in those parts, and loved her to the point of passion. And she, being mightily flattered to be loved by such a gallant, studied how to comport herself so debonairly as to retain his regard, and while she did so, grew likewise enamoured of him; and divers times, by consent of both their love had had its fruition, but that Pinuccio – such was the gallant's name – shrank from the disgrace that 'twould bring upon the girl and himself alike. But, as his passion daily waxed apace, Pinuccio, yearning to find himself abed with her, bethought him that he were best contrive to lodge with her father, deeming, from what he knew of her father's economy, that, if he did so, he might effect his purpose, and never a soul be the wiser: which idea no sooner struck him, than he set about carrying it into effect.

So, late one evening Pinuccio and a trusty comrade, Adriano by name, to whom he had confided his love, hired two nags, and having set upon them two valises, filled with straw or such-like stuff, sallied forth of Florence, and rode by a circuitous route to the plain of Mugnone, which they reached after nightfall; and having fetched a compass, so that it might seem as if they were coming from Romagna, they rode up to the good man's house, and knocked at the door. The good man, knowing them both very well, opened to them forthwith: whereupon: – "Thou must even put us up to-night," quoth Pinuccio; "we thought to get into Florence, but, for all the speed we could make, we are but arrived here, as thou seest, at this hour." "Pinuccio," replied the host, "thou well knowest that I can but make a sorry shift to lodge gentlemen like you; but yet, as night has overtaken you here, and time serves not to betake you elsewhere, I will gladly give you such accommodation as I may." The two gallants then dismounted and entered the inn, and having first looked to their horses, brought out some supper that they had carried with them, and supped with the host.

Now the host had but one little bedroom, in which were three beds, set, as conveniently as he could contrive, two on one side of the room, and the third on the opposite side, but, for all that, there was scarce room enough to pass through. The host had the least discomfortable of the three beds made up for the two friends; and having quartered them there, some little while afterwards, both being awake, but feigning to be asleep, he caused his daughter to get into one of the other two beds, while he and his wife took their places in the third, the good woman setting the cradle, in which was her little boy, beside the bed. Such, then, being the partition made of the beds, Pinuccio, who had taken exact note thereof, waited only until he deemed all but himself to be asleep, and then got softly up and stole to the bed in which lay his beloved, and laid himself beside her; and she according him albeit a timorous yet a gladsome welcome, he stayed there, taking with her that solace of which both were most fain.

Pinuccio being thus with the girl, it chanced that certain things, being overset by a cat, fell with a noise that aroused the good woman, who, fearing that it might be a matter of more consequence, got up as best she might in the dark, and betook her to the place whence the noise seemed to proceed. At the same time Adriano, not by reason of the noise, which he heeded not, but perchance to answer the call of nature, also got up, and questing about for a convenient place, came upon the cradle beside the good woman's bed; and not being able otherwise to go by, took it up, and set it beside his own bed, and when he had accomplished his purpose, went back, and giving never a thought to the cradle got him to bed. The good woman searched until she found that the accident was no such matter as she had supposed; so without troubling to strike a light to investigate it further, she reproved the cat, and returned to the room, and groped her way straight to the bed in which her husband lay asleep; but not finding the cradle there, quoth she to herself: – Alas! blunderer that I am, what was I about? God's faith! I was going straight to the guests' bed; and proceeding a little further, she found the cradle, and laid herself down by Adriano in the bed that was beside it, taking Adriano for her husband; and Adriano, who was still awake, received her with all due benignity, and tackled her more than once to her no small delight.

Meanwhile Pinuccio fearing lest sleep should overtake him while he was yet with his mistress, and having satisfied his desire, got up and left her, to return to his bed; but when he got there, coming upon the cradle, he supposed that 'twas the host's bed; and so going a little further, he laid him down beside the host, who thereupon awoke. Supposing that he had Adriano beside him: – "I warrant thee," quoth Pinuccio to the host, "there was never so sweet a piece of flesh as Niccolosa: by the body of God, such delight have I had of her as never had man of woman; and, mark me, since I left thee, I have gotten me up to the farm some six times." Which tidings the host being none too well pleased to learn, said first of all to himself: – What the Devil does this fellow here? Then, his resentment getting the better of his prudence: – "'Tis a gross affront thou hast put upon me, Pinuccio," quoth he; "nor know I what occasion thou hast to do me such a wrong; but by the body of God I will pay thee out." Pinuccio, who was not the most discreet of gallants, albeit he was now apprised of his error, instead of doing his best to repair it, retorted: – "And how wilt thou pay me out? What canst thou do?" "Hark what high words our guests are at together!" quoth meanwhile the host's wife to Adriano, deeming that she spoke to her husband. "Let them be," replied Adriano with a laugh: – "God give them a bad year: they drank too much yestereve." The good woman had already half recognized her husband's angry tones, and now that she heard Adriano's voice, she at once knew where she was and with whom. Accordingly, being a discreet woman, she started up, and saying never a word, took her child's cradle, and, though there was not a ray of light in the room, bore it, divining rather than feeling her way, to the side of the bed in which her daughter slept; and then, as if aroused by the noise made by her husband, she called him, and asked what he and Pinuccio were bandying words about. "Hearest thou not," replied the husband, "what he says he has this very night done to Niccolosa?" "Tush! he lies in the throat," returned the good woman: "he has not lain with Niccolosa; for what time he might have done so, I laid me beside her myself, and I have been wide awake ever since; and thou art a fool to believe him. You men take so many cups before going to bed that then you dream, and walk in your sleep, and imagine wonders. 'Tis a great pity you do not break your necks. What does Pinuccio there? Why keeps he not in his own bed?"

Whereupon Adriano, in his turn, seeing how adroitly the good woman cloaked her own and her daughter's shame: – "Pinuccio," quoth he, "I have told thee a hundred times, that thou shouldst not walk about at night; for this thy bad habit of getting up in thy dreams and relating thy dreams for truth will get thee into a scrape some time or another: come back, and God send thee a bad night." Hearing Adriano thus confirm what his wife had said, the host began to think that Pinuccio must be really dreaming; so he took him by the shoulder, and fell a shaking him, and calling him by his name, saying: – "Pinuccio, wake up, and go back to thy bed." Pinuccio, taking his cue from what he had heard, began as a dreamer would be like to do, to talk wanderingly; whereat the host laughed amain. Then, feigning to be aroused by the shaking, Pinuccio uttered Adriano's name, saying: – "Is't already day, that thou callest me?" "Ay, 'tis so," quoth Adriano: "come hither." Whereupon Pinuccio, making as if he were mighty drowsy, got him up from beside the host, and back to bed with Adriano. On the morrow, when they were risen, the host fell a laughing and making merry touching Pinuccio and his dreams. And so the jest passed from mouth to mouth, while the gallants' horses were groomed and saddled, and their valises adjusted: which done, they drank with the host, mounted and rode to Florence, no less pleased with the manner than with the matter of the night's adventure. Nor, afterwards, did Pinuccio fail to find other means of meeting Niccolosa, who assured her mother that he had unquestionably dreamed. For which cause the good woman, calling to mind Adriano's embrace, accounted herself the only one that had watched.

Ninth Day
Novel VII

— *Talano di Molese dreams that a wolf tears and rends all the neck and face of his wife: he gives her warning thereof, which she heeds not, and the dream comes true.* —

WHEN PAMFILO had brought his story to a close, and all had commended the good woman's quick perception, the queen bade Pampinea tell hers; and thus Pampinea began: –

A while ago, debonair my ladies, we held discourse of the truths that dreams shew forth, which not a few of us deride; for which cause, albeit the topic has been handled before, I shall not spare to tell you that which not long ago befell a neighbour of mine, for that she disbelieved a dream that her husband had.

I wot not if you knew Talano di Molese, a man right worthy to be had in honour; who, having married a young wife – Margarita by name – fair as e'er another, but without her match for whimsical, fractious, and perverse humours, insomuch that there was nought she would do at the instance of another, either for his or her own good, found her behaviour most grievous to bear, but was fain to endure what he might not cure. Now it so befell that Talano and Margarita being together at an estate that Talano had in the contado, he, sleeping, saw in a dream a very beautiful wood that was on the estate at no great distance from the house, and his lady there walking. And as she went, there leapt forth upon her a huge and fierce wolf that griped her by the throat, and bore her down to the ground, and (she shrieking the while for succour) would have carried her off by main force; but she got quit of his jaws, albeit her neck and face shewed as quite disfigured. On the morrow, as soon as he was risen, Talano said to his wife: – "Albeit for thy perversity I have not yet known a single good day with thee, yet I should be sorry, wife, that harm should befall thee; and therefore, if thou take my advice, thou wilt not stir out of doors to-day." "Wherefore?" quoth the lady; and thereupon he recounted to her all his dream.

The lady shook her head, saying: – "Who means ill, dreams ill. Thou makest as if thou wast mighty tender of me, but thou bodest of me in thy dream that which thou wouldst fain see betide me. I warrant thee that to-day and all days I will have a care to avoid this or any other calamity that might gladden thy heart." Whereupon: – "Well wist I," replied Talano, "that thou wouldst so say, for such is ever the requital of those that comb scurfy heads; but whatever thou mayst be pleased to believe, I for my part speak to thee for thy good, and again I advise thee to keep indoors to-day, or at least not to walk in the wood." "Good," returned the lady, "I will look to it," and then she began communing with herself on this wise: – Didst mark how artfully he thinks to have scared me from going into the wood to-day? Doubtless 'tis that he has an assignation there with some light o' love, with whom he had rather I did not find him. Ah! he would sup well with the blind, and what a fool were I to believe him! But I warrant he will be disappointed, and needs must I, though I stay there all day long, see what commerce it is that he will adventure in to-day.

Having so said, she quitted the house on one side, while her husband did so on the other; and forthwith, shunning observation as best she might, she hied her to the wood, and hid her where 'twas most dense, and there waited on the alert, and glancing, now this way and now that, to see if any were coming. And while thus she stood, nor ever a thought of a wolf crossed her mind, lo, forth of a close covert hard by came a wolf of monstrous size and appalling aspect, and scarce had she time to say, God help me! before he sprang upon her and griped her by the throat so tightly that she might not utter a cry, but, passive as any lambkin, was borne off by him, and had certainly been strangled, had he not encountered some shepherds, who with shouts compelled him to let her go. The shepherds recognized the poor hapless woman, and bore her home, where the physicians by dint of long and careful treatment cured her; howbeit the whole of her throat and part of her face remained so disfigured that, fair as she had been before, she was ever thereafter most foul and hideous to look upon. Wherefore, being ashamed to shew her face, she did many a time bitterly deplore her perversity, in that, when it would have cost her nothing, she would nevertheless pay no heed to the true dream of her husband.

Ninth Day
Novel VIII

— *Biondello gulls Ciacco in the matter of a breakfast: for which prank Ciacco is cunningly avenged on Biondello, causing him to be shamefully beaten.* —

ALL THE COMPANY by common consent pronounced it no dream but a vision that Talano had had in his sleep, so exactly, no circumstance lacking, had it fallen out according as he had seen it. However, as soon as all had done speaking, the queen bade Lauretta follow suit; which Lauretta did on this wise: –

As, most discreet my ladies, those that have preceded me to-day have almost all taken their cue from somewhat that has been said before, so, prompted by the stern vengeance taken by the scholar in Pampinea's narrative of yesterday, I am minded to tell you of a vengeance that was indeed less savage, but for all that grievous enough to him on whom it was wreaked.

Wherefore I say that there was once at Florence one that all folk called Ciacco, a man second to none that ever lived for inordinate gluttony, who, lacking the means to support the expenditure which his gluttony demanded, and being, for the rest, well-mannered and well furnished with excellent and merry jests, did, without turning exactly court jester, cultivate a somewhat biting wit, and loved to frequent the houses of the rich, and such as kept good tables; whither, bidden or unbidden, he not seldom resorted for breakfast or supper. There was also in those days at Florence one that was called Biondello, a man very short of stature, and not a little debonair, more trim than any fly, with his blond locks surmounted by a coif, and never a hair out of place; and he and Ciacco were two of a trade.

Now one morning in Lent Biondello, being in the fish-market purchasing two mighty fat lampreys for Messer Vieri de' Cerchi, was observed thus engaged by Ciacco, who came up to him, and: – "What means this?" quoth he. "Why," replied Biondello, "'tis that yestereve Messer Corso Donati had three lampreys much finer than these and a sturgeon sent to his house, but as they did not suffice for a breakfast that he is to give certain gentlemen, he has commissioned me to buy him these two beside. Wilt thou not be there?" "Ay, marry, that will I," returned Ciacco. And in what he deemed due time he hied him to Messer Corso Donati's house, where he found him with some of his neighbours not yet gone to breakfast. And being asked by Messer Corso with what intent he was come, he answered: – "I am come, Sir, to breakfast with you and your company." "And welcome art thou," returned Messer Corso, "go we then to breakfast, for 'tis now the time." So to table they went, where nought was set before them but pease and the inward part of the tunny salted, and afterwards the common fish of the Arno fried. Wherefore Ciacco, not a little wroth at the trick that he perceived Biondello had played him, resolved to pay him out. And not many days after Biondello, who had meanwhile had many a laugh with his friends over Ciacco's discomfiture, met him, and after greeting him, asked him with a laugh what Messer Corso's lampreys had been like. "That question," replied Ciacco, "thou wilt be able to answer much better than I before eight days are gone by." And parting from Biondello upon the word, he went forthwith and hired a cozening rogue, and having thrust a glass bottle into his hand, brought him within sight of the Loggia de' Cavicciuli; and there, pointing to a knight, one Messer Filippo Argenti, a tall man and stout, and of a high courage, and haughty, choleric and cross-grained as ne'er another, he said to him: – "Thou wilt go, flask in hand, to Messer Filippo, and wilt say to him: – 'I am sent to you, Sir, by Biondello, who entreats you to be pleased to colour this flask for him with some of your good red wine, for that he is minded to have a good time with his catamites.' And of all things have a care that he lay not hands upon thee, for he would make thee rue the day, and would spoil my sport." "Have I aught else to say?" enquired the rogue. "Nothing more," returned Ciacco: "and now get thee gone, and when thou hast delivered the message, bring me back the flask, and I will pay thee."

So away went the rogue, and did the errand to Messer Filippo, who forthwith, being a hasty man, jumped to the conclusion that Biondello, whom he knew, was making mock of him, and while an angry flush overspread his face: – "Colour the flask, forsooth!" quoth he, "and 'Catamites!' God send thee and him a bad year!" and therewith up he started, and reached forward to lay hold of the rogue, who, being on the alert, gave him the slip and was off, and reported Messer Filippo's answer to Ciacco, who had observed what had passed. Having paid the rogue, Ciacco rested not until he had found Biondello, to whom: – "Wast thou but now," quoth he, "at the Loggia de' Cavicciuli?" "Indeed no," replied Biondello: "wherefore such a question?" "Because," returned Ciacco, "I may tell thee that thou art sought for by Messer Filippo, for what cause I know not." "Good," quoth Biondello, "I will go thither and speak with him." So away went Biondello, and Ciacco followed him to see what course the affair would take.

Now having failed to catch the rogue, Messer Filippo was still very wroth, and inly fumed and fretted, being unable to make out aught from what the rogue had said save that Biondello was set on by some one or another to flout him. And while thus he vexed his spirit, up came Biondello; whom he no sooner espied than he made for him, and dealt him a mighty blow in the face, and tore his hair and coif, and cast his capuche on the ground, and to his "Alas, Sir, what means this?" still beating him amain: – "Traitor," cried he; "I will give thee to know what it means to send me such a message. 'Colour the flask,' forsooth, and 'Catamites!' Dost take me for a stripling, to be befooled by thee?" And therewith he pummelled Biondello's face all over with a pair of fists that were liker to iron than aught else, until it was but a mass of bruises; he also tore and dishevelled all his hair, tumbled him in the mud, rent all his clothes upon his back, and that without allowing him breathing-space to ask why he thus used him, or so much as utter a word. "Colour me the flask!" and "Catamites!" rang in his ears; but what the words signified he knew not. In the end very badly beaten, and in very sorry and ragged trim, many folk having gathered around them, they, albeit not without the utmost difficulty, rescued him from Messer Filippo's hands, and told him why Messer Filippo had thus used him, censuring him for sending him such a message, and adding that thenceforth he would know Messer Filippo better, and that he was not a man to be trifled with. Biondello told them in tearful exculpation that he had never sent for wine to Messer Filippo: then, when they had put him in a little better trim, crestfallen and woebegone, he went home imputing his misadventure to Ciacco. And when, many days afterwards, the marks of his ill-usage being gone from his face, he began to go abroad again, it chanced that Ciacco met him, and with a laugh: – "Biondello," quoth he, "how didst thou relish Messer Filippo's wine?" "Why, as to that," replied Biondello, "would thou hadst relished the lampreys of Messer Corso as much!" "So!" returned Ciacco, "such meat as thou then gavest me, thou mayst henceforth give me, as often as thou art so minded; and I will give thee even such drink as I have given thee." So Biondello, witting that against Ciacco his might was not equal to his spite, prayed God for his peace, and was careful never to flout him again.

Ninth Day
Novel IX

— *Two young men ask counsel of Solomon; the one, how he is to make himself beloved, the other, how he is to reduce an unruly wife to order. The King bids the one to love, and the other to go to the Bridge of Geese.* —

NONE NOW remained to tell save the queen, unless she were minded to infringe Dioneo's privilege. Wherefore, when the ladies had laughed their fill over the misfortunes of Biondello, thus gaily the queen began: –

Observe we, lovesome ladies, the order of things with a sound mind, and we shall readily perceive that we women are one and all subjected by Nature and custom and law unto man, by him to be ruled and governed at his discretion; wherefore she, that would fain enjoy quietude and solace and comfort with the man to whom she belongs, ought not only to be chaste but lowly, patient and obedient: the which is the discreet wife's chief and most precious possession. And if the laws, which in all matters have regard unto the common weal, and use and wont or custom (call it what you will), a power very great and to be had in awe, should not suffice to school us thereto; yet abundantly clear is the witness of Nature, which has fashioned our frames delicate and sensitive, and our spirits timorous and fearful, and has decreed that our bodily strength shall be slight, our voices tunable, and our movements graceful; which qualities do all avouch that we have need of others' governance. And whoso has need of succour and governance ought in all reason to be obedient and submissive and reverent towards his governor. And whom have we to govern and succour us save men? 'Tis then our bounden duty to give men all honour and submit ourselves unto them: from which rule if any deviate, I deem her most deserving not only of grave censure but of severe chastisement. Which reflections, albeit they are not new to me, I am now led to make by what but a little while ago Pampinea told us touching the perverse wife of Talano, on whom God bestowed that chastisement which the husband had omitted; and accordingly it jumps with my judgment that all such women as deviate from the graciousness, kindliness and compliancy, which Nature and custom and law prescribe, merit, as I said, stern and severe chastisement. Wherefore, as a salutary medicine for the healing of those of us who may be afflicted with this disease, I am minded to relate to you that which was once delivered by Solomon by way of counsel in such a case. Which let none that stands not in need of such physic deem to be meant for her, albeit a proverb is current among men; to wit: –

> *Good steed, bad steed, alike need the rowel's prick,*
> *Good wife, bad wife, alike demand the stick.*

Which whoso should construe as a merry conceit would find you all ready enough to acknowledge its truth. But even in its moral significance I say that it ought to command assent. For women are all by nature apt to be swayed and to fall; and therefore, for the correction of the wrong-doing of such as transgress the bounds assigned to them, there is need of the stick punitive; and also for the maintenance of virtue in others, that they transgress not these appointed bounds, there is need of the stick auxiliary and deterrent. However, to cut short this preachment, and to come to that which I purpose to tell you, I say:

That the bruit of the incomparable renown of the prodigious wisdom of Solomon, as also of the exceeding great liberality with which he accorded proof thereof to all that craved such assurance, being gone forth over well-nigh all the earth, many from divers parts were wont to resort to him for counsel in matters of most pressing and arduous importance; among whom was a young man, Melisso by name, a very wealthy nobleman, who was, as had been his fathers before him, of Lazistan, and there dwelt. And as Melisso fared toward Jerusalem, on his departure from Antioch he fell in with another young man, Giosefo by name, who was going the same way, and with whom, after the manner of travellers, he entered into converse. Melisso, having learned from Giosefo, who and whence he was, asked him whither he went, and on what errand: whereupon Giosefo made an answer that he was going to seek counsel of Solomon, how he should deal with his wife, who had not her match among women for unruliness and perversity, insomuch that neither entreaties nor blandishments nor aught else availed him to bring her to a better frame. And thereupon he in like manner asked Melisso whence he was, and whither he was bound, and on what errand: whereto: – "Of Lazistan, I," replied Melisso, "and like thyself in evil plight; for albeit I am wealthy and spend my substance freely in hospitably entertaining and honourably entreating my fellow-citizens, yet for all that, passing strange though it be to think upon, I find never a soul to love me; and therefore I am bound to the self-same place as thou, to be advised how it may come to pass that I be beloved."

So the two men fared on together, and being arrived at Jerusalem, were, by the good offices of one of Solomon's barons, ushered into his presence, and Melisso having briefly laid his case before the King, was answered in one word: – "Love." Which said, Melisso was forthwith dismissed, and Giosefo discovered the reason of his coming. To whom Solomon made no answer but: – "Get thee to the Bridge of Geese." Whereupon Giosefo was likewise promptly ushered out of the King's presence, and finding Melisso awaiting him, told him what manner of answer he had gotten. Which utterances of the King the two men pondered, but finding therein nought that was helpful or relevant to their need, they doubted the King had but mocked them, and set forth upon their homeward journey.

Now when they had been some days on the road, they came to a river, which was spanned by a fine bridge, and a great caravan of sumpter mules and horses being about to cross, they must needs tarry, until the caravan had passed by. The more part of which had done so, when it chanced that a mule turned sulky, as we know they will not seldom do, and stood stock still; wherefore a muleteer took a stick and fell a beating the mule therewith, albeit at first with no great vigour, to urge the mule forward. The mule, however, swerving, now to this, now to the other side of the bridge, and sometimes facing about, utterly refused to go forward. Whereat the muleteer, wroth beyond measure, fell a belabouring him with the stick now on the head, now on the flanks, and anon on the croup, never so lustily, but all to no purpose. Which caused Melisso and Giosefo ofttimes to say to him: – "How now, caitiff? What is this thou doest? Wouldst kill the beast? Why not try if thou canst not manage him kindly and gently? He would start sooner so than for this cudgelling of thine." To whom: – "You know your horses," replied the muleteer, "and I know my mule: leave me to deal with him." Which said, he resumed his cudgelling of the mule, and laid about him on this side and on that to such purpose that he started him; and so the honours of the day rested with the muleteer. Now, as the two young men were leaving the bridge behind them, Giosefo asked a good man that sate at its head what the bridge was called, and was answered: – "Sir, 'tis called the Bridge of Geese." Which Giosefo no sooner heard than he called to mind Solomon's words, and turning to Melisso: – "Now, comrade, I warrant thee I may yet find Solomon's counsel sound and good, for that I knew not how to beat my wife is abundantly clear to me; and this muleteer has shewn me what I have to do."

Now some days afterwards they arrived at Antioch, where Giosefo prevailed upon Melisso to tarry with him and rest a day or two; and meeting with but a sorry welcome on the part of his wife, he told her to take her orders as to supper from Melisso, who, seeing that such was Giosefo's will, briefly gave her his instructions; which the lady, as had been her wont, not only did not obey, but contravened in almost every particular. Which Giosefo marking: – "Wast thou not told," quoth he angrily, "after what fashion thou wast to order the supper?" Whereto: – "So!" replied the lady haughtily: "what means this? If thou hast a mind to sup, why take not thy supper? No matter what I was told, 'tis thus I saw fit to order it. If it like thee, so be it: if not, 'tis thine affair." Melisso heard the lady with surprise and inward disapprobation: Giosefo retorted: – "Ay wife, thou art still as thou wast used to be; but I will make thee mend thy manners." Then, turning to Melisso: – "Friend," quoth he, "thou wilt soon prove the worth of Solomon's counsel: but, prithee, let it not irk thee to look on, and deem that what I shall do is but done in sport; and if thou shouldst be disposed to stand in my way, bear in mind how we were answered by the muleteer, when we pitied his mule." "I am in thy house," replied Melisso, "and thy pleasure is to me law."

Thereupon Giosefo took a stout cudgel cut from an oak sapling, and hied him into the room whither the lady had withdrawn from the table in high dudgeon, seized her by the hair, threw her on to the floor at his feet, and fell a beating her amain with the cudgel. The lady at first uttered a shriek or two, from which she passed to threats; but seeing that, for all that, Giosefo slackened not, by the time she was thoroughly well thrashed, she began to cry him mercy, imploring him not to kill her, and adding that henceforth his will should be to her for law. But still Giosefo gave not over, but with ever fresh fury dealt her mighty swingeing blows, now about the ribs, now on the haunches, now over the shoulders; nor had he done with the fair lady, until, in short, he had left never a bone or other part of her person whole, and he was fairly spent. Then, returning to Melisso: – "To-morrow," quoth he, "we shall see whether 'Get thee to the Bridge of Geese' will prove to have been sound advice or no." And so, having rested a while, and then washed his hands, he supped with Melisso. With great pain the poor lady got upon her feet and laid herself on her bed, and having there taken such rest as she might, rose betimes on the morrow, and craved to know of Giosefo what he was minded to have to breakfast. Giosefo, laughing with Melisso over the message, gave her his directions, and when in due time they came to breakfast, they found everything excellently ordered according as it had been commanded: for which cause the counsel, which they had at first failed to understand, now received their highest commendation.

Some few days later Melisso, having taken leave of Giosefo, went home, and told a wise man the counsel he had gotten from Solomon. Whereupon: – "And no truer or sounder advice could he have given thee," quoth the sage: "thou knowest that thou lovest never a soul, and that the honours thou payest and the services thou renderest to others are not prompted by love of them, but by love of display. Love, then, as Solomon bade thee, and thou shalt be loved." On such wise was the unruly chastised; and the young man, learning to love, was beloved.

Ninth Day

Novel X

— *Dom Gianni at the instance of his gossip Pietro uses an enchantment to transform Pietro's wife into a mare; but, when he comes to attach the tail, Gossip Pietro, by saying that he will have none of the tail, makes the enchantment of no effect.* —

THE QUEEN'S STORY evoked some murmurs from the ladies and some laughter from the young men; however, when they were silent, Dioneo thus began: –

Dainty my ladies, a black crow among a flock of white doves enhances their beauty more than would a white swan; and so, when many sages are met together, their ripe wisdom not only shews the brighter and goodlier for the presence of one that is not so wise, but may even derive pleasure and diversion therefrom. Wherefore as you, my ladies, are one and all most discreet and judicious, I, who know myself to be somewhat scant of sense, should, for that by my demerit I make your merit shew the more glorious, be more dear to you, than if by my greater merit I eclipsed yours, and by consequence should have more ample license to reveal myself to you as I am; and therefore have more patient sufferance on your part than would be due to me, were I more discreet, in the relation of the tale which I am about to tell you. 'Twill be, then, a story none too long, wherefrom you may gather with what exactitude it behoves folk to observe the injunctions of those that for any purpose use an enchantment, and how slight an error committed therein make bring to nought all the work of the enchanter.

A year or so ago there was at Barletta a priest named Dom Gianni di Barolo, who, to eke out the scanty pittance his church afforded him, set a pack-saddle upon his mare, and took to going the round of the fairs of Apulia, buying and selling merchandise. And so it befell that he clapped up a close acquaintance with one Pietro da Tresanti, who plied the same trade as he, albeit instead of a mare he had but an ass; whom in token of friendship and good-fellowship Dom Gianni after the Apulian fashion called ever Gossip Pietro, and had him to his house and there lodged and honourably entreated him as often as he came to Barletta. Gossip Pietro on his part, albeit he was very poor and had but a little cot at Tresanti, that scarce sufficed for himself, his fair, young wife, and their ass, nevertheless, whenever Dom Gianni arrived at Tresanti, made him welcome, and did him the honours of his house as best he might, in requital of the hospitality which he received at Barletta. However, as Gossip Pietro had but one little bed, in which he slept with his fair wife, 'twas not in his power to lodge Dom Gianni as comfortably as he would have liked; but the priest's mare being quartered beside the ass in a little stable, the priest himself must needs lie beside her on the straw. Many a time when the priest came, the wife, knowing how honourably he entreated her husband at Barletta, would fain have gone to sleep with a neighbour, one Zita Carapresa di Giudice Leo, that the priest might share the bed with her husband, and many a time had she told the priest so howbeit he would never agree to it, and on one occasion: – "Gossip Gemmata," quoth he, "trouble not thyself about me; I am well lodged; for, when I am so minded, I turn the mare into a fine lass and dally with her, and then, when I would, I turn her back into a mare; wherefore I could ill brook to part from her." The young woman, wondering but believing, told her husband what the priest had said, adding: – "If he is even such a friend as thou sayst, why dost thou not get him to teach thee the enchantment, so that thou mayst turn me into a mare, and have both ass and mare for thine occasions? We should then make twice as much gain as we do, and thou couldst turn me back into a woman when we came home at night."

    Gossip Pietro, whose wit was somewhat blunt, believed that 'twas as she said, approved her counsel, and began adjuring Dom Gianni, as persuasively as he might, to teach him the incantation. Dom Gianni did his best to wean him of his folly; but as all was in vain: – "Lo, now," quoth he, "as you are both bent on it, we will be up, as is our wont, before the sun to-morrow morning, and I will shew you how 'tis done. The truth is that 'tis in the attachment of the tail that the great difficulty lies, as thou wilt see." Scarce a wink of sleep had either Gossip Pietro or Gossip Gemmata that night, so great was their anxiety; and towards daybreak up they got, and called Dom Gianni; who, being risen, came in his shirt into Gossip Pietro's little bedroom, and: – "I know not," quoth he, "that there is another soul in the world for whom I would do this, save you, my gossips; however, as you will have it so, I will do it, but it behoves you to do exactly as I bid you, if you would have the enchantment work." They promised obedience, and Dom Gianni thereupon took a light, which he handed to Gossip Pietro, saying: – "Let nought that I shall do or say escape thee; and have a care, so thou wouldst not ruin all, to say never a word, whatever thou mayst see or hear; and pray God that the tail may be securely attached." So Gossip Pietro took the light, and again promised obedience; Dom Gianni caused Gossip Gemmata to strip herself stark naked, and stand on all fours like a mare, at the same time strictly charging her that, whatever might happen, she must utter no word. Then, touching her head and face: – "Be this a fine head of a mare," quoth he; in like manner touching her hair, he said: – "Be this a fine mane of a mare;" touching her arms: – "Be these fine legs and fine hooves of a mare;" then, as he touched her breast and felt its firm roundness, and there awoke and arose one that was not called: – "And be this a fine breast of a mare," quoth he; and in like manner he dealt with her back, belly, croup, thighs, and legs. Last of all, the work being complete save for the tail, he lifted his shirt and took in his hand the tool with which he was used to plant men, and forthwith thrust it into the furrow made for it, saying: – "And be this a fine tail of a mare." Whereat Gossip Pietro, who had followed everything very heedfully to that point, disapproving that last particular, exclaimed: – "No! Dom Gianni, I'll have no tail, I'll have no tail." The essential juice, by which all plants are propagated, was already discharged, when Dom Gianni withdrew the tool, saying: – "Alas! Gossip Pietro, what hast thou done? Did I not tell thee to say never a word, no matter what thou mightst see? The mare was all but made; but by speaking thou hast spoiled all; and 'tis not possible to repeat the enchantment." "Well and good," replied Gossip Pietro, "I would have none of that tail. Why saidst thou not to me: – 'Make it thou'? And besides, thou wast attaching it too low." "'Twas because," returned Dom Gianni, "thou wouldst not have known, on the first essay, how to attach it so well as I." Whereupon the young woman stood up, and in all good faith said to her husband: – "Fool that thou art, wherefore hast thou brought to nought what had been for the good of us both? When didst thou ever see mare without a tail? So help me God, poor as thou art, thou deservest to be poorer still." So, after Gossip Pietro's ill-timed speech, there being no way left of turning the young woman into a mare, downcast and melancholy she resumed her clothes; and Gossip Pietro plied his old trade with his ass, and went with Dom Gianni to the fair of Bitonto, and never asked him so to serve him again.

    What laughter this story drew from the ladies, who understood it better than Dioneo had wished, may be left to the imagination of the fair one that now laughs thereat. However, as the stories were ended, and the sun now shone with a tempered radiance, the queen, witting that the end of her sovereignty was come, stood up and took off the crown, and set it on the head of Pamfilo, whom alone it now remained thus to honour; and said with a smile: – "My lord, 'tis a great burden that falls upon thee, seeing that thou, coming last, art bound to make good my shortcomings and those of my predecessors; which God give thee grace to accomplish, even as He has given me grace to make thee king." With gladsome acknowledgment of the honour: – "I doubt not," replied Pamfilo, "that, thanks to your noble qualities and those of my other subjects, I shall win even such praise as those that have borne sway before me." Then, following the example of his predecessors, he made all meet arrangements in concert with the seneschal: after which, he turned to the expectant ladies, and thus spoke: – "Enamoured my ladies, Emilia, our queen of to-day, deeming it proper to allow you an interval of rest to recruit your powers, gave you license to discourse of such matters as should most commend themselves to each in turn; and as thereby you are now rested, I judge that 'tis meet to revert to our accustomed rule. Wherefore I ordain that for to-morrow you do each of you take thought how you may discourse of the ensuing theme: to wit, of such as in matters of love, or otherwise, have done something with liberality or magnificence. By the telling, and (still more) by the doing of such things, your spirits will assuredly be duly attuned and animated to emprise high and noble; whereby our life, which cannot but be brief, seeing that 'tis enshrined in a mortal body, fame shall perpetuate in glory; which whoso serves not the belly, as do the beasts, must not only covet, but with all zeal seek after and labour to attain."

The gay company having, one and all, approved the theme, rose at a word from their new king, and betook them to their wonted pastimes, and so, according as they severally had most lief, diverted them, until they blithely reunited for supper, which being served with all due care and despatched, they rose up to dance, as they were wont, and when they had sung, perhaps, a thousand ditties, fitter to please by their words than by any excellence of musical art, the king bade Neifile sing one on her own account. And promptly and graciously, with voice clear and blithe, thus Neifile sang: –

> *In prime of maidenhood, and fair and feat*
> *'Mid spring's fresh foison chant I merrily:*
> *Thanks be to Love and to my fancies sweet.*
>
> *As o'er the grassy mead I, glancing, fare,*
> *I mark it white and yellow and vermeil dight*
> *With flowers, the thorny rose, the lily white:*
> *And all alike to his face I compare,*
> *Who, loving, hath me ta'en, and me shall e'er*
> *Hold bounden to his will, sith I am she*
> *That in his will findeth her joy complete.*
>
> *Whereof if so it be that I do find*
> *Any that I most like to him approve,*
> *That pluck I straight and kiss with words of love,*
> *Discovering all, as, best I may, my mind;*
> *Yea, all my heart's desire; and then entwined*
> *I set it in the chaplet daintily,*
> *And with my yellow tresses bind and pleat.*
> *And as mine eyes do drink in the delight*
> *Which the flower yields them, even so my mind,*

> *Fired with his sweet love, doth such solace find,*
> *As he himself were present to the sight:*
> *But never word of mine discover might*
> *That which the flower's sweet smell awakes in me:*
> *Witness the true tale that my sighs repeat.*
>
> *For from my bosom gentle and hot they fly,*
> *Not like the gusty sighs that others heave,*
> *Whenas they languish and do sorely grieve;*
> *And to my love incontinent they hie:*
> *Whereof when he is ware, he, by and by,*
> *To meward hasting, cometh suddenly,*
> *When: – "Lest I faint," I cry, "come, I entreat."*

The king and all the ladies did not a little commend Neifile's song; after which, as the night was far spent, the king bade all go to rest until the morrow.

– Endeth here the ninth day of the Decameron, and beginneth the tenth, in which, under the rule of Pamfilo, discourse is had of such as in matters of love, or otherwise, have done something with liberality or magnificence. –

SOME CLOUDLETS in the West still shewed a vermeil flush, albeit those of the eastern sky, as the sun's rays smote them anear, were already fringed as with most lucent gold, when uprose Pamfilo, and roused the ladies and his comrades. And all the company being assembled, and choice made of the place whither they should betake them for their diversion, he, accompanied by Filomena and Fiammetta, led the way at a slow pace, followed by all the rest. So fared they no little space, beguiling the time with talk of their future way of life, whereof there was much to tell and much to answer, until, as the sun gained strength, they returned, having made quite a long round, to the palace; and being gathered about the fountain, such as were so minded drank somewhat from beakers rinsed in its pure waters; and then in the delicious shade of the garden they hied them hither and thither, taking their pleasure until breakfast-time. Their meal taken, they slept as they were wont; and then, at a spot chosen by the king, they reassembled, where Neifile, having received his command to lead the way, blithely thus began.

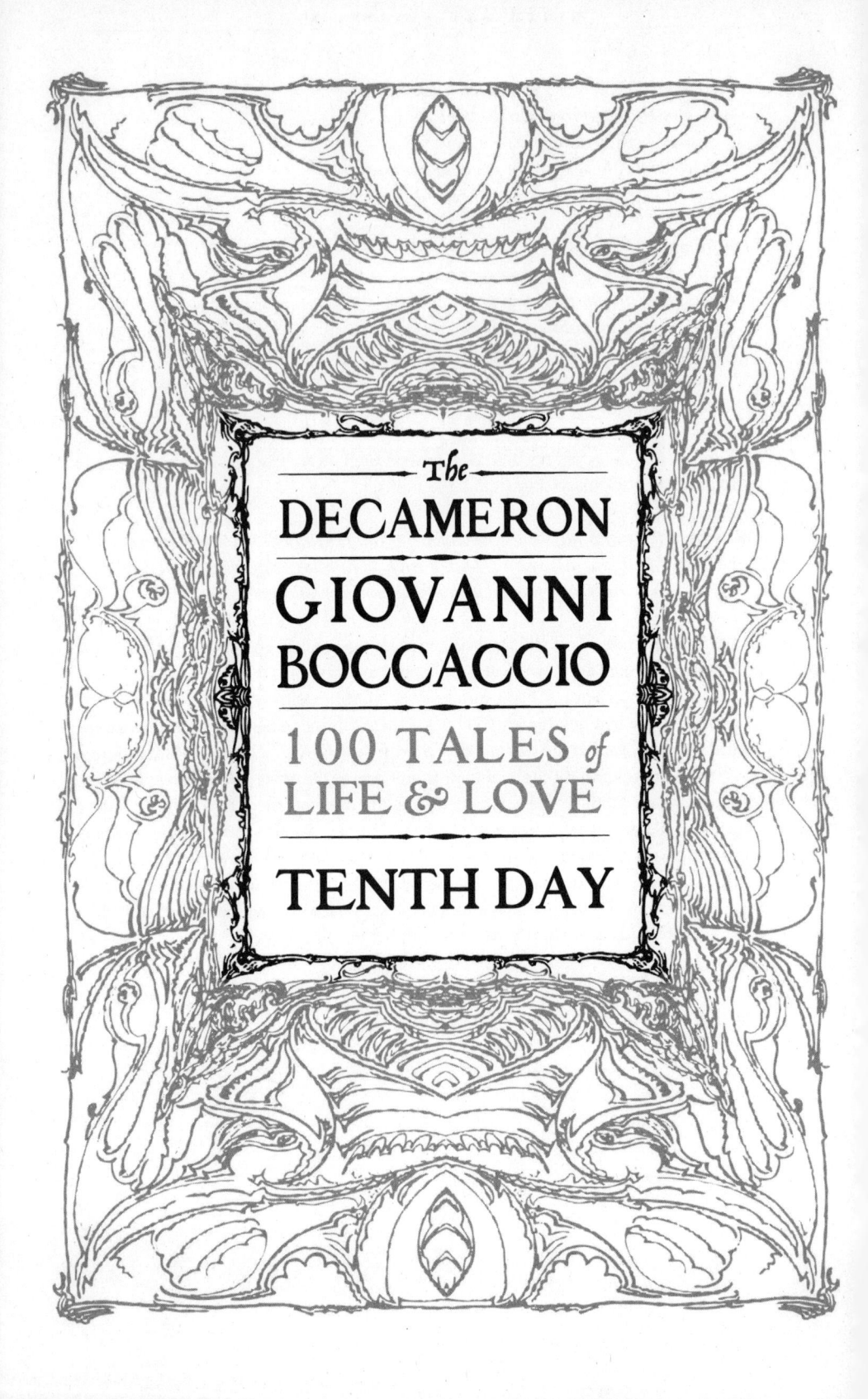

The DECAMERON
GIOVANNI BOCCACCIO
100 TALES of LIFE & LOVE
TENTH DAY

Tenth Day

Novel I

— A knight in the service of the King of Spain deems himself ill requited. Wherefore the King, by most cogent proof, shews him that the blame rests not with him, but with the knight's own evil fortune; after which, he bestows upon him a noble gift. —

HIGHLY GRACED, indeed, do I deem myself, honourable my ladies, that our king should have given to me the precedence in a matter so arduous to tell of as magnificence: for, as the sun irradiates all the heaven with his glory and beauty, even so does magnificence enhance the purity and the splendour of every other virtue. I shall therefore tell you a story, which, to my thinking, is not a little pretty; and which, assuredly, it must be profitable to call to mind.

You are to know, then, that, among other honourable knights that from days of old even until now have dwelt in our city, one, and perchance the worthiest of all, was Messer Ruggieri de' Figiovanni. Who, being wealthy and magnanimous, reflecting on the customs and manner of life of Tuscany, perceived that by tarrying there he was like to find little or no occasion of shewing his mettle, and accordingly resolved to pass some time at the court of Alfonso, King of Spain, who for the fame of his high qualities was without a peer among the potentates of his age. So, being well provided with arms and horses and retinue suitable to his rank, he hied him to Spain, where he was graciously received by the King. There tarrying accordingly, Messer Ruggieri very soon, as well by the splendid style in which he lived as by the prodigious feats of arms that he did, gave folk to know his high desert.

Now, having tarried there some while, and observed the King's ways with much care, and how he would grant castles, cities, or baronies, to this, that, or the other of his subjects, he deemed that the King shewed therein but little judgment, seeing that he would give them to men that merited them not. And for that nought was given to him, he, knowing his merit, deemed himself gravely injured in reputation; wherefore he made up his mind to depart the realm, and to that end craved license of the King; which the King granted him, and therewith gave him one of the best and finest mules that was ever ridden, a gift which Messer Ruggieri, as he had a long journey to make, did not a little appreciate. The King then bade one of his discreet domestics contrive, as best he might, to ride with Messer Ruggieri on such wise that it might not appear that he did so by the King's command, and charge his memory with whatever Messer Ruggieri might say of him, so that he might be able to repeat it; which done, he was on the very next morning to bid Ruggieri return to the King forthwith. The King's agent was on the alert, and no sooner was Ruggieri out of the city, than without any manner of difficulty he joined his company, giving out that he was going towards Italy. As thus they rode, talking of divers matters, Messer Ruggieri being mounted on the mule given him by the King: – "Methinks," quoth the other, it being then hard upon tierce, "that 'twere well to give the beasts a voidance;" and by and by, being come to a convenient place, they voided all the beasts save the mule. Then, as they continued their journey, the squire hearkening attentively to the knight's words, they came to a river, and while there they watered the beasts, the mule made a voidance in the stream. Whereat: – "Ah, foul fall thee, beast," quoth Messer Ruggieri, "that art even as thy master, that gave thee to me!" Which remark, as also many another that fell from Ruggieri as they rode together throughout the day, the squire stored in his memory; but never another word did he hear Ruggieri say touching the King, that was not laudatory to the last degree.

On the morrow, when they were gotten to horse, and had set their faces towards Tuscany, the squire apprised Ruggieri of the King's command, and thereupon Ruggieri turned back. On his arrival the King, having already heard what he had said touching the mule, gave him gladsome greeting, and asked him wherefore he had likened him to the mule, or rather the mule to him. Whereto Messer Ruggieri answered frankly: – "My lord, I likened you to the mule, for that, as you bestow your gifts where 'tis not meet, and where meet it were, bestow them not, so the mule where 'twas meet, voided not, and where 'twas not meet, voided." "Messer Ruggieri," replied the King, "'tis not because I have not discerned in you a knight most good and true, for whose desert no gift were too great, that I have not bestowed on you such gifts as I have bestowed upon many others, who in comparison of you are nothing worth: the fault is none of mine but solely of your fortune, which would not suffer me; and that this which I say is true, I will make abundantly plain to you." "My lord," returned Messer Ruggieri, "mortified am I, not that you gave me no gift, for thereof I had no desire, being too rich, but that you made no sign of recognition of my desert; however, I deem your explanation sound and honourable, and whatever you shall be pleased that I should see, that gladly will I, albeit I believe you without attestation."

The King then led him into one of the great halls, in which, by his preordinance, were two chests closed under lock and key, and, not a few others being present, said to him: – "Messer Ruggieri, one these chests contains my crown, sceptre and orb, with many a fine girdle, buckle, ring, and whatever else of jewellery I possess; the other is full of earth: choose then, and whichever you shall choose, be it yours; thereby you will discover whether 'tis due to me or to your fortune that your deserts have lacked requital." Such being the King's pleasure, Messer Ruggieri chose one of the chests, which at the King's command being opened and found to be that which contained the earth: – "Now, Messer Ruggieri," quoth the King with a laugh, "your own eyes may warrant you of the truth of what I say touching Fortune; but verily your merit demands that I take arms against her in your cause. I know that you are not minded to become a Spaniard, and therefore I shall give you neither castle nor city; but that chest, which Fortune denied you, I bestow on you in her despite, that you may take it with you to your own country, and there with your neighbours justly vaunt yourself of your deserts, attested by my gifts." Messer Ruggieri took the chest, and having thanked the King in a manner befitting such a gift, returned therewith, well pleased, to Tuscany.

Tenth Day
Novel II

— *Ghino di Tacco captures the Abbot of Cluny, cures him of a disorder of the stomach, and releases him. The abbot, on his return to the court of Rome, reconciles Ghino with Pope Boniface, and makes him prior of the Hospital.* —

WHEN AN END was made of extolling the magnificence shewn by King Alfonso towards the Florentine knight, the king, who had listened to the story with no small pleasure, bade Elisa follow suit; and forthwith Elisa began: –

Dainty my ladies, undeniable it is that for a king to be magnificent, and to entreat magnificently one that has done him service, is a great matter, and meet for commendation. What then shall we say when the tale is of a dignitary of the Church that shewed wondrous magnificence towards one whom he might well have entreated as an enemy, and not have been blamed by a soul? Assuredly nought else than that what in the king was virtue was in the prelate nothing less than a miracle, seeing that for superlative greed the clergy, one and all, outdo us women, and wage war to the knife upon every form of liberality. And albeit all men are by nature prone to avenge their wrongs, 'tis notorious that the clergy, however they may preach longsuffering, and commend of all things the forgiving of trespasses, are more quick and hot to be avenged than the rest of mankind. Now this, to wit, after what manner a prelate shewed magnificence, will be made manifest to you in my story.

Ghino di Tacco, a man redoubtable by reason of his truculence and his high-handed deeds, being banished from Siena, and at enmity with the Counts of Santa Fiore, raised Radicofani in revolt against the Church of Rome, and there abiding, harried all the surrounding country with his soldiers, plundering all wayfarers. Now Pope Boniface VIII. being at Rome, there came to court the Abbot of Cluny, who is reputed one of the wealthiest prelates in the world; and having there gotten a disorder of the stomach, he was advised by the physicians to go to the baths of Siena, where (they averred) he would certainly be cured. So, having obtained the Pope's leave, reckless of the bruit of Ghino's exploits, he took the road, being attended by a great and well-equipped train of sumpter-horses and servants. Ghino di Tacco, getting wind of his approach, spread his nets to such purpose as without the loss of so much as a boy to surround the abbot, with all his servants and effects, in a strait pass, from which there was no exit. Which done, he sent one of his men, the cunningest of them all, with a sufficient retinue to the abbot, who most lovingly on Ghino's part besought the abbot to come and visit Ghino at the castle. Whereto the abbot, very wroth, made answer that he would none of it, for that nought had he to do with Ghino; but that he purposed to continue his journey, and would fain see who would hinder him. "Sir," returned the envoy, assuming a humble tone, "you are come to a part of the country where we have no fear of aught save the might of God, and where excommunications and interdicts are one and all under the ban; wherefore you were best be pleased to shew yourself agreeable to Ghino in this particular." As they thus spoke, Ghino's soldiers shewed themselves on every side, and it being thus manifest to the abbot that he and his company were taken prisoners, he, albeit mightily incensed, suffered himself with all his train and effects to be conducted by the envoy to the castle; where the abbot, being alighted, was lodged in a small and very dark and discomfortable room, while his retinue, according to their several conditions, were provided with comfortable quarters in divers parts of the castle, the horses well stabled and all the effects secured, none being in any wise tampered with. Which done, Ghino hied him to the abbot, and: – "Sir," quoth he, "Ghino, whose guest you are, sends me to entreat you to be pleased to inform him of your destination, and the purpose of your journey." The abbot, vailing his pride like a wise man, told whither he was bound and for what purpose. Whereupon Ghino left him, casting about how he might cure him without a bath. To which end he kept a great fire ever burning in the little chamber, and had it closely guarded, and returned not to the abbot until the ensuing morning, when he brought him in a spotless napkin two slices of toast and a great beaker of vernaccia of Corniglia, being of the abbot's own vintage; and: – "Sir," quoth he to the abbot, "Ghino, as a young man, made his studies in medicine, and avers that he then learned that there is no better treatment for disorder of the stomach than that which he will afford you, whereof the matters that I bring you are the beginning; wherefore take them and be of good cheer."

    The abbot, being far too hungry to make many words about the matter, ate (albeit in high dudgeon) the toast, and drank the vernaccia; which done, he enlarged on his wrongs in a high tone, with much questioning and perpending; and above all he demanded to see Ghino. Part of what the abbot said Ghino disregarded as of no substance, to other part he replied courteously enough; and having assured him that Ghino would visit him as soon as might be, he took his leave of him; nor did he return until the morrow, when he brought him toast and vernaccia in the same quantity as before; and so he kept him several days: then, having marked that the abbot had eaten some dried beans that he had secretly brought and left there of set purpose, he asked him in Ghino's name how he felt in the stomach. "Were I but out of Ghino's hands," replied the abbot, "I should feel myself well, indeed: next to which, I desire most of all a good breakfast, so excellent a cure have his medicines wrought on me." Whereupon Ghino caused the abbot's servants to furnish a goodly chamber with the abbot's own effects, and there on the morrow make ready a grand banquet, at which all the abbot's suite and not a few of the garrison being assembled, he hied him to the abbot, and: – "Sir," quoth he, "'tis time you left the infirmary, seeing that you now feel yourself well;" and so saying, he took him by the hand, and led him into the chamber made ready for him, and having left him there with his own people, made it his chief concern that the banquet should be magnificent. The abbot's spirits revived as he found himself again among his men, with whom he talked a while, telling them how he had been entreated, wherewith they contrasted the signal honour which they, on the other hand, had, one and all, received from Ghino.

    Breakfast-time came, and with order meet the abbot and the rest were regaled with good viands and good wines, Ghino still suffering not the abbot to know who he was. But when the abbot had thus passed several days, Ghino, having first had all his effects collected in a saloon, and all his horses, to the poorest jade, in the courtyard below, hied him to the abbot and asked him how he felt, and if he deemed himself strong enough to ride. The abbot replied that he was quite strong enough, and that 'twould be well indeed with him, were he once out of Ghino's hands. Ghino then led him into the saloon in which were his effects and all his retinue, and having brought him to a window, whence he might see all his horses: – "Sir Abbot," quoth he, "you must know that 'tis not for that he has an evil heart, but because, being a gentleman, he is banished from his home, and reduced to poverty, and has not a few powerful enemies, that in defence of his life and honour, Ghino di Tacco, whom you see before you, has become a robber of highways and an enemy to the court of Rome. But such as I am, I have cured you of your malady of the stomach, and taking you to be a worthy lord, I purpose not to treat you as

I would another, from whom, were he in my hands, as you are, I should take such part of his goods as I should think fit; but I shall leave it to you, upon consideration of my need, to assign to me such portion of your goods as you yourself shall determine. Here are they before you undiminished and unimpaired, and from this window you may see your horses below in the courtyard; wherefore take the part or take the whole, as you may see fit, and be it at your option to tarry here, or go hence, from this hour forth."

The abbot marvelled to hear a highway robber speak thus liberally, and such was his gratification that his wrath and fierce resentment departed from him, nay, were transformed into kindness, insomuch that in all cordial amity he hasted to embrace Ghino, saying: – "By God I swear, that to gain the friendship of a man such I now deem thee to be, I would be content to suffer much greater wrong than that which until now, meseemed, thou hadst done me. Cursed be Fortune that constrains thee to ply so censurable a trade." Which said, he selected a very few things, and none superfluous, from his ample store, and having done likewise with the horses, ceded all else to Ghino, and hied him back to Rome; where, seeing him, the Pope, who to his great grief had heard of his capture, asked him what benefit he had gotten from the baths. Whereto the abbot made answer with a smile: – "Holy Father, I found nearer here than the baths a worthy physician who has wrought a most excellent cure on me:" he then recounted all the circumstances, whereat the Pope laughed. Afterwards, still pursuing the topic, the abbot, yielding to the promptings of magnificence, asked a favour of the Pope; who, expecting that he would ask somewhat else than he did, liberally promised to give him whatever he should demand. Whereupon: – "Holy Father," quoth the abbot, "that which I would crave of you is that you restore Ghino di Tacco, my physician, to your favour; seeing that among the good men and true and meritorious that I have known, he is by no means of the least account. And for the evil life that he leads, I impute it to Fortune rather than to him: change then his fortune, by giving him the means whereby he may live in manner befitting his rank, and I doubt not that in a little while your judgment of him will jump with mine." Whereto the Pope, being magnanimous, and an admirer of good men and true, made answer that so he would gladly do, if Ghino should prove to be such as the abbot said; and that he would have him brought under safe conduct to Rome. Thither accordingly under safe conduct came Ghino, to the abbot's great delight; nor had he been long at court before the Pope approved his worth, and restored him to his favour, granting him a great office, to wit, that of prior of the Hospital, whereof he made him knight. Which office he held for the rest of his life, being ever a friend and vassal of Holy Church and the Abbot of Cluny.

Tenth Day
Novel III

— Mitridanes, holding Nathan in despite by reason of his courtesy, journeys with intent to kill him, and falling in with him unawares, is advised by him how to compass his end. Following his advice, he finds him in a copse, and recognizing him, is shame-stricken, and becomes his friend. —

VERILY LIKE to a miracle seemed it to all to hear that a prelate had done aught with magnificence; but when the ladies had made an end of their remarks, the king bade Filostrato follow suit; and forthwith Filostrato began: –

Noble ladies, great was the magnificence of the King of Spain, and perchance a thing unheard-of the magnificence of the Abbot of Cluny; but peradventure 'twill seem not a whit less marvellous to you to hear of one who, to shew liberality towards another, did resolve artfully to yield to him his blood, nay, his very life, for which the other thirsted, and had so done, had the other chosen to take them, as I shall shew you in a little story.

Beyond all question, if we may believe the report of certain Genoese, and other folk that have been in those regions, there dwelt of yore in the parts of Cathay one Nathan, a man of noble lineage and incomparable wealth. Who, having a seat hard by a road, by which whoso would travel from the West eastward, or from the East westward, must needs pass, and being magnanimous and liberal, and zealous to approve himself such in act, did set on work cunning artificers not a few, and cause one of the finest and largest and most luxurious palaces that ever were seen, to be there builded and furnished in the goodliest manner with all things meet for the reception and honourable entertainment of gentlemen. And so, keeping a great array of excellent servants, he courteously and hospitably did the honours of his house to whoso came and went: in which laudable way of life he persevered, until not only the East, but well-nigh all the West had heard his fame; which thus, what time he was well-stricken in years, albeit not for that cause grown weary of shewing courtesy, reached the ears of one Mitridanes, a young man of a country not far distant. Who, knowing himself to be no less wealthy than Nathan, grew envious of the renown that he had of his good deeds, and resolved to obliterate, or at least to obscure it, by a yet greater liberality. So he had built for himself a palace like that of Nathan, of which he did the honours with a lavish courtesy that none had ever equalled, to whoso came or went that way; and verily in a short while he became famous enough.

Now it so befell that on a day when the young man was all alone in the courtyard of the palace, there came in by one of the gates a poor woman, who asked of him an alms, and had it; but, not content therewith, came again to him by the second gate, and asked another alms, and had it, and after the like sort did even unto the twelfth time; but, she returning for the thirteenth time: – "My good woman," quoth Mitridanes, "thou art not a little pertinacious in thy begging:" howbeit he gave her an alms. Whereupon: – "Ah! the wondrous liberality of Nathan!" quoth the beldam: – "thirty-two gates are there to his palace, by every one of which I have entered, and asking alms of him, was never – for aught he shewed – recognized, or refused, and here, though I have entered as yet by but thirteen gates, I am recognized and reprimanded." And therewith she departed, and returned no more. Mitridanes, who accounted the mention of Nathan's fame an abatement of his own, was kindled by her words with a frenzy of wrath, and began thus to commune with himself: – Alas! when shall I attain to the grandeur of Nathan's liberality, to say nought of transcending it, as I would fain, seeing that in the veriest trifles I cannot approach him? Of a surety my labour is in vain, if I rid not the earth of him: which, since old age relieves me not of him, I must forthwith do with mine own hands. And in the flush of his despite up he started, and giving none to know of his purpose, got to horse with a small company, and after three days arrived at the place where Nathan abode; and having enjoined his comrades to make as if they were none of his, and knew him not, and to go quarter themselves as best they might until they had his further orders, he, being thus alone, towards evening came upon Nathan, also alone, at no great distance from his splendid palace. Nathan was recreating himself by a walk, and was very simply clad; so that Mitridanes, knowing him not, asked him if he could shew him where Nathan dwelt. "My son," replied Nathan gladsomely, "that can none in these parts better than I; wherefore, so it please thee, I will bring thee thither." The young man replied that 'twould be mighty agreeable to him, but that, if so it might be, he had a mind to be neither known nor seen by Nathan. "And herein also," returned Nathan, "since 'tis thy pleasure, I will gratify thee." Whereupon Mitridanes dismounted, and with Nathan, who soon engaged him in delightsome discourse, walked to the goodly palace. Arrived there Nathan caused one of his servants take the young man's horse, and drawing close to him, bade him in a whisper to see to it without delay that none in the house should tell the young man that he was Nathan: and so 'twas done.

Being come into the palace, Nathan quartered Mitridanes in a most goodly chamber, where none saw him but those whom he had appointed to wait upon him; and he himself kept him company, doing him all possible honour. Of whom Mitridanes, albeit he reverenced him as a father, yet, being thus with him, forbore not to ask who he was. Whereto Nathan made answer: – "I am a petty servant of Nathan: old as I am, I have been with him since my childhood, and never has he advanced me to higher office than this wherein thou seest me: wherefore, howsoever other folk may praise him, little cause have I to do so." Which words afforded Mitridanes some hope of carrying his wicked purpose into effect with more of plan and less of risk than had otherwise been possible. By and by Nathan very courteously asked him who he was, and what business brought him thither; offering him such counsel and aid as he might be able to afford him. Mitridanes hesitated a while to reply: but at last he resolved to trust him, and when with no little circumlocution he had demanded of him fidelity, counsel and aid, he fully discovered to him who he was, and the purpose and motive of his coming thither. Now, albeit to hear Mitridanes thus unfold his horrid design caused Nathan no small inward commotion, yet 'twas not long before courageously and composedly he thus made answer: – "Noble was thy father, Mitridanes, and thou art minded to shew thyself not unworthy of him by this lofty emprise of thine, to wit, of being liberal to all comers: and for that thou art envious of Nathan's merit I greatly commend thee; for were many envious for a like cause, the world, from being a most wretched, would soon become a happy place. Doubt not that I shall keep secret the design which thou hast confided to me, for the furtherance whereof 'tis good advice rather than substantial aid that I have to offer thee. Which advice is this. Hence, perhaps half a mile off, thou mayst see a copse, in which almost every morning Nathan is wont to walk, taking his pleasure, for quite a long while: 'twill be an easy matter for thee to find him there, and deal with him as thou mayst be minded. Now, shouldst thou slay him, thou wilt get thee home with less risk of let, if thou take not the path by which thou camest hither, but that which thou seest issue from the copse on the left, for, though 'tis somewhat more rough, it leads more directly to thy house, and will be safer for thee."

Possessed of this information, Mitridanes, when Nathan had left him, privily apprised his comrades, who were likewise lodged in the palace, of the place where they were to await him on the ensuing day; which being come, Nathan, inflexibly determined to act in all respects according to the advice which he had given Mitridanes, hied him forth to the copse unattended, to meet his death. Mitridanes, being risen, took his bow and sword, for other arms he had none with him, mounted his horse, and rode to the copse, through which, while he was yet some way off, he saw Nathan passing, quite alone. And being minded, before he fell upon him, to see his face and hear the sound of his voice, as, riding at a smart pace, he came up with him, he laid hold of him by his head-gear, exclaiming: – "Greybeard, thou art a dead man." Whereto Nathan answered nought but: – "Then 'tis but my desert." But Mitridanes, hearing the voice, and scanning the face, forthwith knew him for the same man that had welcomed him heartily, consorted with him familiarly, and counselled him faithfully; whereby his wrath presently subsided, and gave place to shame. Wherefore, casting away the sword that he held drawn in act to strike, he sprang from his horse, and weeping, threw himself at Nathan's feet, saying: – "Your liberality, dearest father, I acknowledge to be beyond all question, seeing with what craft you did plot your coming hither to yield me your life, for which, by mine own avowal, you knew that I, albeit cause I had none, did thirst. But God, more regardful of my duty than I myself, has now, in this moment of supreme stress, opened the eyes of my mind, that wretched envy had fast sealed. The prompter was your compliance, the greater is the debt of penitence that I owe you for my fault; wherefore wreak even such vengeance upon me as you may deem answerable to my transgression." But Nathan raised Mitridanes to his feet, and tenderly embraced him, saying: – "My son, thy enterprise, howsoever thou mayst denote it, whether evil or otherwise, was not such that thou shouldst crave, or I give, pardon thereof; for 'twas not in malice but in that thou wouldst fain have been reputed better than I that thou ensuedst it. Doubt then no more of me; nay, rest assured that none that lives bears thee such love as I, who know the loftiness of thy spirit, bent not to heap up wealth, as do the caitiffs, but to dispense in bounty thine accumulated store. Think it no shame that to enhance thy reputation thou wouldst have slain me; nor deem that I marvel thereat. To slay not one man, as thou wast minded, but countless multitudes, to waste whole countries with fire, and to raze cities to the ground has been well-nigh the sole art, by which the mightiest emperors and the greatest kings have extended their dominions, and by consequence their fame. Wherefore, if thou, to increase thy fame, wouldst fain have slain me, 'twas nothing marvellous or strange, but wonted."

Whereto Mitridanes made answer, not to excuse his wicked design, but to commend the seemly excuse found for it by Nathan, whom at length he told how beyond measure he marvelled that Nathan had not only been consenting to the enterprise, but had aided him therein by his counsel. But Nathan answered: – "Liefer had I, Mitridanes, that thou didst not marvel either at my consent or at my counsel, for that, since I was my own master and of a mind to that emprise whereon thou art also bent, never a soul came to my house, but, so far as in me lay, I gave him all that he asked of me. Thou camest, lusting for my life; and so, when I heard thee crave it of me, I forthwith, that thou mightst not be the only guest to depart hence ill content, resolved to give it thee; and to that end I gave thee such counsel as I deemed would serve thee both to the taking of my life and the preservation of thine own. Wherefore yet again I bid thee, nay, I entreat thee, if so thou art minded, to take it for thy satisfaction: I know not how I could better bestow it. I have had the use of it now for some eighty years, and pleasure and solace thereof; and I know that, by the course of Nature and the common lot of man and all things mundane, it can continue to be mine for but a little while; and so I deem that 'twere much better to bestow it, as I have ever bestowed and dispensed my wealth, than to keep it, until, against my will, it be reft from me by Nature. 'Twere but a trifle, though 'twere a hundred years: how insignificant, then, the six or eight years that are all I have to give! Take it, then, if thou hadst lief, take it, I pray thee; for, long as I have lived here, none have I found but thee to desire it; nor know I when I may find another, if thou take it not, to demand it of me. And if, peradventure, I should find one such, yet I know that the longer I keep it, the less its worth will be; wherefore, ere it be thus cheapened, take it, I implore thee."

Sore shame-stricken, Mitridanes made answer: – "Now God forefend that I should so much as harbour, as but now I did, such a thought, not to say do such a deed, as to wrest from you a thing so precious as your life, the years whereof, so far from abridging, I would gladly supplement with mine own." "So then," rejoined Nathan promptly, "thou wouldst, if thou couldst, add thy years to mine, and cause me to serve thee as I never yet served any man, to wit, to take from thee that which is thine, I that never took aught from a soul!" "Ay, that would I," returned Mitridanes. "Then," quoth Nathan, "do as I shall bid thee. Thou art young: tarry here in my house, and call thyself Nathan; and I will get me to thy house, and ever call myself Mitridanes." Whereto Mitridanes made answer: – "Were I but able to discharge this trust, as you have been and are, scarce would I hesitate to accept your offer; but, as too sure am I that aught that I might do would but serve to lower Nathan's fame, and I am not minded to mar that in another which I cannot mend in myself, accept it I will not."

After which and the like interchange of delectable discourse, Nathan and Mitridanes, by Nathan's desire, returned to the palace; where Nathan for some days honourably entreated Mitridanes, and by his sage counsel confirmed and encouraged him in his high and noble resolve; after which, Mitridanes, being minded to return home with his company, took his leave of Nathan, fully persuaded that 'twas not possible to surpass him in liberality.

Tenth Day
Novel IV

— *Messer Gentile de' Carisendi, being come from Modena, disinters a lady that he loves, who has been buried for dead. She, being reanimated, gives birth to a male child; and Messer Gentile restores her, with her son, to Niccoluccio Caccianimico, her husband.* —

A THING MARVELLOUS seemed it to all that for liberality a man should be ready to sacrifice his own life; and herein they averred that Nathan had without doubt left the King of Spain and the Abbot of Cluny behind. However, when they had discussed the matter diversely and at large, the king, bending his regard on Lauretta, signified to her his will that she should tell; and forthwith, accordingly, Lauretta began: –

Goodly matters are they and magnificent that have been recounted to you, young ladies; nay, so much of our field of discourse is already filled by their grandeur, that for us that are yet to tell, there is, methinks, no room left, unless we seek our topic there where matter of discourse germane to every theme does most richly abound, to wit, in the affairs of love. For which cause, as also for that our time of life cannot but make us especially inclinable thereto, I am minded that my story shall be of a feat of magnificence done by a lover: which, all things considered, will, peradventure, seem to you inferior to none that have been shewn you; so it be true that to possess the beloved one, men will part with their treasures, forget their enmities, and jeopardize their own lives, their honour and their reputation, in a thousand ways.

Know, then, that at Bologna, that most famous city of Lombardy, there dwelt a knight, Messer Gentile Carisendi by name, worshipful alike for his noble lineage and his native worth: who in his youth, being enamoured of a young gentlewoman named Madonna Catalina, wife of one Niccoluccio Caccianimico, and well-nigh despairing, for that the lady gave him but a sorry requital of his love, betook him to Modena, being called thither as Podesta. Now what time he was there, Niccoluccio being also away from Bologna, and his lady gone, for that she was with child, to lie in at a house she had some three miles or so from the city, it befell that she was suddenly smitten with a sore malady of such and so virulent a quality that it left no sign of life in her, so that the very physicians pronounced her dead. And for that the women that were nearest of kin to her professed to have been told by her, that she was not so far gone in pregnancy that the child could be perfectly formed, they, without more ado, laid her in a tomb in a neighbouring church, and after long lamentation closed it upon her.

Whereof Messer Gentile being forthwith apprised by one of his friends, did, for all she had been most niggardly to him of her favour, grieve not a little, and at length fell a communing with himself on this wise: – So, Madonna Catalina, thou art dead! While thou livedst, never a glance of thine might I have; wherefore, now that thou art dead, 'tis but right that I go take a kiss from thee. 'Twas night while he thus mused; and forthwith, observing strict secrecy in his departure, he got him to horse with a single servant, and halted not until he was come to the place where the lady was interred; and having opened the tomb he cautiously entered it. Then, having lain down beside her, he set his face against hers; and again and again, weeping profusely the while, he kissed it. But as 'tis matter of common knowledge that the desires of men, and more especially of lovers, know no bounds, but crave ever an ampler satisfaction; even so Messer Gentile, albeit he had been minded to tarry there no longer, now said to himself: – Wherefore touch I not her bosom a while? I have never yet touched it, nor shall I ever touch it again. Obeying which impulse, he laid his hand on her bosom, and keeping it there some time, felt, as he thought, her heart faintly beating. Whereupon, banishing all fear, and examining the body with closer attention, he discovered that life was not extinct, though he judged it but scant and flickering: and so, aided by his servant, he bore her, as gently as he might, out of the tomb; and set her before him upon his horse, and brought her privily to his house at Bologna, where dwelt his wise and worthy mother, who, being fully apprised by him of the circumstances, took pity on the lady, and had a huge fire kindled, and a bath made ready, whereby she restored her to life. Whereof the first sign she gave was to heave a great sigh, and murmur: – "Alas! where am I?" To which the worthy lady made answer: – "Be of good cheer; thou art well lodged." By and by the lady, coming to herself, looked about her; and finding herself she knew not where, and seeing Messer Gentile before her, was filled with wonder, and besought his mother to tell her how she came to be there.

Messer Gentile thereupon told her all. Sore distressed thereat, the lady, after a while, thanked him as best she might; after which she besought him by the love that he had borne her, and of his courtesy, that she might, while she tarried in his house, be spared aught that could impair her honour and her husband's; and that at daybreak he would suffer her to return home. "Madam," replied Messer Gentile, "however I did affect you in time past, since God in His goodness has, by means of the love I bore you, restored you to me alive, I mean not now, or at any time hereafter, to entreat you either here or elsewhere, save as a dear sister; but yet the service I have to-night rendered you merits some guerdon, and therefore lief had I that you deny me not a favour which I shall ask of you." Whereto the lady graciously made answer that she would be prompt to grant it, so only it were in her power, and consonant with her honour. Said then Messer Gentile: – "Your kinsfolk, Madam, one and all, nay, all the folk in Bologna are fully persuaded that you are dead: there is therefore none to expect you at home: wherefore the favour I crave of you is this, that you will be pleased to tarry privily here with my mother, until such time – which will be speedily – as I return from Modena. And 'tis for that I purpose to make solemn and joyous donation of you to your husband in presence of the most honourable folk of this city that I ask of you this grace." Mindful of what she owed the knight, and witting that what he craved was seemly, the lady, albeit she yearned not a little to gladden her kinsfolk with the sight of her in the flesh, consented to do as Messer Gentile besought her, and thereto pledged him her faith. And scarce had she done so, when she felt that the hour of her travail was come; and so, tenderly succoured by Messer Gentile's mother, she not long after gave birth to a fine boy. Which event did mightily enhance her own and Messer Gentile's happiness. Then, having made all meet provision for her, and left word that she was to be tended as if she were his own wife, Messer Gentile, observing strict secrecy, returned to Modena.

His time of office there ended, in anticipation of his return to Bologna, he appointed for the morning of his arrival in the city a great and goodly banquet at his house, whereto were bidden not a few of the gentlemen of Bologna, and among them Niccoluccio Caccianimico. Whom, when he was returned and dismounted, he found awaiting him, as also the lady, fairer and more healthful than ever, and her little son doing well; and so with a gladness beyond compare he ranged his guests at table, and regaled them with many a course magnificently served. And towards the close of the feast, having premonished the lady of his intention, and concerted with her how she should behave, thus he spoke: – "Gentlemen, I mind me to have once heard tell of (as I deem it) a delightsome custom which they have in Persia; to wit, that, when one would do his friend especial honour, he bids him to his house, and there shews him that treasure, be it wife, or mistress, or daughter, or what not, that he holds most dear; assuring him that yet more gladly, were it possible, he would shew him his heart. Which custom I am minded to observe here in Bologna. You, of your courtesy, have honoured my feast with your presence, and I propose to do you honour in the Persian fashion, by shewing you that which in all the world I do, and must ever, hold most dear. But before I do so, tell me, I pray you, how you conceive of a nice question that I shall lay before you. Suppose that one has in his house a good and most faithful servant, who falls sick of a grievous disorder; and that the master tarries not for the death of the servant, but has him borne out into the open street, and concerns himself no more with him: that then a stranger comes by, is moved to pity of the sick man, and takes him to his house, and by careful tendance and at no small cost restores him to his wonted health. Now I would fain know whether the first master has in equity any just cause to complain of or be aggrieved with the second master, if he retain the servant in his employ, and refuse to restore him, when so required."

The gentlemen discussed the matter after divers fashions, and all agreed in one sentence, which they committed to Niccoluccio Caccianimico, for that he was an eloquent and accomplished speaker, to deliver on the part of them all. Niccoluccio began by commending the Persian custom: after which he said that he and the others were all of the same opinion, to wit, that the first master had no longer any right in his servant, since he had not only abandoned but cast him forth; and that by virtue of the second master's kind usage of him he must be deemed to have become his servant; wherefore, by keeping him, he did the first master no mischief, no violence, no wrong. Whereupon the rest that were at the table said, one and all, being worthy men, that their judgment jumped with Niccoluccio's answer. The knight, well pleased with the answer, and that 'twas Niccoluccio that gave it, affirmed that he was of the same opinion; adding: – "'Tis now time that I shew you that honour which I promised you." He then called two of his servants, and sent them to the lady, whom he had caused to be apparelled and adorned with splendour, charging them to pray her to be pleased to come and gladden the gentlemen with her presence. So she, bearing in her arms her most lovely little son, came, attended by the two servants, into the saloon, and by the knight's direction, took a seat beside a worthy gentleman: whereupon: – "Gentlemen," quoth the knight, "this is the treasure that I hold, and mean ever to hold, more dear than aught else. Behold, and judge whether I have good cause."

The gentlemen said not a little in her honour and praise, averring that the knight ought indeed to hold her dear: then, as they regarded her more attentively, there were not a few that would have pronounced her to be the very woman that she was, had they not believed that woman to be dead. But none scanned her so closely as Niccoluccio, who, the knight being withdrawn a little space, could no longer refrain his eager desire to know who she might be, but asked her whether she were of Bologna, or from other parts. The lady, hearing her husband's voice, could scarce forbear to answer; but yet, not to disconcert the knight's plan, she kept silence. Another asked her if that was her little boy; and yet another, if she were Messer Gentile's wife, or in any other wise his connection. To none of whom she vouchsafed an answer. Then, Messer Gentile coming up: – "Sir," quoth one of the guests, "this treasure of yours is goodly indeed; but she seems to be dumb: is she so?" "Gentlemen," quoth Messer Gentile, "that she has not as yet spoken is no small evidence of her virtue." "Then tell us, you, who she is," returned the other. "That," quoth the knight, "will I right gladly, so you but promise me, that, no matter what I may say, none of you will stir from his place, until I have ended my story." All gave the required promise, and when the tables had been cleared, Messer Gentile, being seated beside the lady, thus spoke: – "Gentlemen, this lady is that loyal and faithful servant, touching whom a brief while ago I propounded to you my question, whom her own folk held none too dear, but cast out into the open street as a thing vile and no longer good for aught, but I took thence, and by my careful tendance wrested from the clutch of death; whom God, regardful of my good will, has changed from the appalling aspect of a corpse to the thing of beauty that you see before you. But for your fuller understanding of this occurrence, I will briefly explain it to you." He then recounted to them in detail all that had happened from his first becoming enamoured of the lady to that very hour whereto they hearkened with no small wonder; after which: – "And so," he added, "unless you, and more especially Niccoluccio, are now of another opinion than you were a brief while ago, the lady rightly belongs to me, nor can any man lawfully reclaim her of me."

None answered, for all were intent to hear what more he would say. But, while Niccoluccio, and some others that were there, wept for sympathy, Messer Gentile stood up, and took the little boy in his arms and the lady by the hand, and approached Niccoluccio, saying: – "Rise, my gossip: I do not, indeed, restore thee thy wife, whom thy kinsfolk and hers cast forth; but I am minded to give thee this lady, my gossip, with this her little boy, whom I know well to be thy son, and whom I held at the font, and named Gentile: and I pray thee that she be not the less dear to thee for that she has tarried three months in my house; for I swear to thee by that God, who, peradventure, ordained that I should be enamoured of her, to the end that my love might be, as it has been, the occasion of her restoration to life, that never with her father, or her mother, or with thee, did she live more virtuously than with my mother in my house." Which said, he turned to the lady, saying: – "Madam, I now release you from all promises made to me, and so deliver you to Niccoluccio." Then, leaving the lady and the child in Niccoluccio's embrace, he returned to his seat.

Thus to receive his wife and son was to Niccoluccio a delight great in the measure of its remoteness from his hope. Wherefore in the most honourable terms at his command he thanked the knight, whom all the rest, weeping for sympathy, greatly commended for what he had done, as did also all that heard thereof. The lady, welcomed home with wondrous cheer, was long a portent to the Bolognese, who gazed on her as on one raised from the dead. Messer Gentile lived ever after as the friend of Niccoluccio, and his and the lady's kinsfolk.

Now what shall be your verdict, gracious ladies? A king's largess, though it was of his sceptre and crown, an abbot's reconciliation, at no cost to himself, of a malefactor with the Pope, or an old man's submission of his throat to the knife of his enemy – will you adjudge that such acts as these are comparable to the deed of Messer Gentile? Who, though young, and burning with passion, and deeming himself justly entitled to that which the heedlessness of another had discarded, and he by good fortune had recovered, not only tempered his ardour with honour, but having that which with his whole soul he had long been bent on wresting from another, did with liberality restore it. Assuredly none of the feats aforesaid seem to me like unto this.

Tenth Day

Novel V

— Madonna Dianora craves of Messer Ansaldo a garden that shall be as fair in January as in May. Messer Ansaldo binds himself to a necromancer, and thereby gives her the garden. Her husband gives her leave to do Messer Ansaldo's pleasure: he, being apprised of her husband's liberality, releases her from her promise; and the necromancer releases Messer Ansaldo from his bond, and will take nought of his. —

EACH OF THE gay company had with superlative commendation extolled Messer Gentile to the skies, when the king bade Emilia follow suit; and with a good courage, as burning to speak, thus Emilia began: –

Delicate my ladies, none can justly say that 'twas not magnificently done of Messer Gentile; but if it be alleged that 'twas the last degree of magnificence, 'twill perchance not be difficult to shew that more was possible, as is my purpose in the little story that I shall tell you.

In Friuli, a country which, though its air is shrewd, is pleasantly diversified by fine mountains and not a few rivers and clear fountains, is a city called Udine, where dwelt of yore a fair and noble lady, Madonna Dianora by name, wife of a wealthy grandee named Giliberto, a very pleasant gentleman, and debonair. Now this lady, for her high qualities, was in the last degree beloved by a great and noble baron, Messer Ansaldo Gradense by name, a man of no little consequence, and whose fame for feats of arms and courtesy was spread far and wide. But, though with all a lover's ardour he left nought undone that he might do to win her love, and to that end frequently plied her with his ambassages, 'twas all in vain. And the lady being distressed by his importunity, and that, refuse as she might all that he asked of her, he none the less continued to love her and press his suit upon her, bethought her how she might rid herself of him by requiring of him an extraordinary and, as she deemed, impossible feat. So one day, a woman that came oftentimes from him to her being with her: – "Good woman," quoth she, "thou hast many a time affirmed that Messer Ansaldo loves me above all else; and thou hast made proffer to me on his part of wondrous rich gifts which I am minded he keep to himself, for that I could never bring myself to love him or pleasure him for their sake; but, if I might be certified that he loves me as much as thou sayst, then without a doubt I should not fail to love him, and do his pleasure; wherefore, so he give me the assurance that I shall require, I shall be at his command." "What is it, Madam," returned the good woman, "that you would have him do?" "This," replied the lady; "I would have this next ensuing January, hard by this city, a garden full of green grass and flowers and flowering trees, just as if it were May; and if he cannot provide me with this garden, bid him never again send either thee or any other to me, for that, should he harass me any further, I shall no longer keep silence, as I have hitherto done, but shall make my complaint to my husband and all my kinsmen, and it shall go hard but I will be quit of him."

The gentleman being apprised of his lady's stipulation and promise, notwithstanding that he deemed it no easy matter, nay, a thing almost impossible, to satisfy her, and knew besides that 'twas but to deprive him of all hope that she made the demand, did nevertheless resolve to do his endeavour to comply with it, and causing search to be made in divers parts of the world, if any he might find to afford him counsel or aid, he lit upon one, who for a substantial reward offered to do the thing by necromancy. So Messer Ansaldo, having struck the bargain with him for an exceeding great sum of money, gleefully expected the appointed time. Which being come with extreme cold, insomuch that there was nought but snow and ice, the adept on the night before the calends of January wrought with his spells to such purpose that on the morrow, as was averred by eye-witnesses, there appeared in a meadow hard by the city one of the most beautiful gardens that was ever seen, with no lack of grass and trees and fruits of all sorts. At sight whereof Messer Ansaldo was overjoyed, and caused some of the finest fruits and flowers that it contained to be gathered, and privily presented to his lady, whom he bade come and see the garden that she had craved, that thereby she might have assurance of his love, and mind her of the promise that she had given him and confirmed with an oath, and, as a loyal lady, take thought for its performance. When she saw the flowers and fruits, the lady, who had already heard not a few folk speak of the wondrous garden, began to repent her of her promise. But for all that, being fond of strange sights, she hied her with many other ladies of the city to see the garden, and having gazed on it with wonderment, and commended it not a little, she went home the saddest woman alive, bethinking her to what it bound her: and so great was her distress that she might not well conceal it; but, being written on her face, 'twas marked by her husband, who was minded by all means to know the cause thereof.

The lady long time kept silence: but at last she yielded to his urgency, and discovered to him the whole matter from first to last. Whereat Giliberto was at first very wroth; but on second thoughts, considering the purity of the lady's purpose, he was better advised, and dismissing his anger: – "Dianora," quoth he, "'tis not the act of a discreet or virtuous lady to give ear to messages of such a sort, nor to enter into any compact touching her chastity with any man on any terms. Words that the ears convey to the heart have a potency greater than is commonly supposed, and there is scarce aught that lovers will not find possible. 'Twas then ill done of thee in the first instance to hearken, as afterwards to make the compact; but, for that I know the purity of thy soul, that thou mayst be quit of thy promise, I will grant thee that which, perchance, no other man would grant, being also swayed thereto by fear of the necromancer, whom Messer Ansaldo, shouldst thou play him false, might, peradventure, cause to do us a mischief. I am minded, then, that thou go to him, and contrive, if on any wise thou canst, to get thee quit of this promise without loss of virtue; but if otherwise it may not be, then for the nonce thou mayst yield him thy body, but not thy soul." Whereat the lady, weeping, would none of such a favour at her husband's hands. But Giliberto, for all the lady's protestations, was minded that so it should be.

Accordingly, on the morrow about dawn, apparelled none too ornately, preceded by two servants and followed by a chambermaid, the lady hied her to Messer Ansaldo's house. Apprised that his lady was come to see him, Messer Ansaldo, marvelling not a little, rose, and having called the necromancer: – "I am minded," quoth he, "that thou see what goodly gain I have gotten by thine art." And the twain having met the lady, Ansaldo gave way to no unruly appetite, but received her with a seemly obeisance; and then the three repaired to a goodly chamber, where there was a great fire, and having caused the lady to be seated, thus spoke Ansaldo: – "Madam, if the love that I have so long borne you merit any guerdon, I pray you that it be not grievous to you to discover to me the true occasion of your coming to me at this hour, and thus accompanied." Shamefast, and the tears all but standing in her eyes, the lady made answer: – "Sir 'tis neither love that I bear you, nor pledged you, that brings me hither, but the command of my husband, who, regarding rather the pains you have had of your unbridled passion than his own or my honour, has sent me hither; and for that he commands it, I, for the nonce, am entirely at your pleasure."

If Messer Ansaldo had marvelled to hear of the lady's coming, he now marvelled much more, and touched by Giliberto's liberality, and passing from passion to compassion: – "Now, God forbid, Madam," quoth he, "that, it being as you say, I should wound the honour of him that has compassion on my love; wherefore, no otherwise than as if you were my sister shall you abide here, while you are so minded, and be free to depart at your pleasure; nor crave I aught of you but that you shall convey from me to your husband such thanks as you shall deem meet for courtesy such as his has been, and entreat me ever henceforth as your brother and servant." Whereat overjoyed in the last degree: – "Nought," quoth the lady, "by what I noted of your behaviour, could ever have caused me to anticipate other sequel of my coming hither than this which I see is your will, and for which I shall ever be your debtor." She then took her leave, and, attended by a guard of honour, returned to Giliberto, and told him what had passed; between whom and Messer Ansaldo there was thenceforth a most close and loyal friendship.

Now the liberality shewn by Giliberto towards Messer Ansaldo, and by Messer Ansaldo towards the lady, having been marked by the necromancer, when Messer Ansaldo made ready to give him the promised reward: – "Now God forbid," quoth he, "that, as I have seen Giliberto liberal in regard of his honour, and you liberal in regard of your love, I be not in like manner liberal in regard of my reward, which accordingly, witting that 'tis in good hands, I am minded that you keep." The knight was abashed, and strove hard to induce him to take, if not the whole, at least a part of the money; but finding that his labour was in vain, and that the necromancer, having caused his garden to vanish after the third day, was minded to depart, he bade him adieu. And the carnal love he had borne the lady being spent, he burned for her thereafter with a flame of honourable affection. Now what shall be our verdict in this case, lovesome ladies? A lady, as it were dead, and a love grown lukewarm for utter hopelessness! Shall we set a liberality shewn in such a case above this liberality of Messer Ansaldo, loving yet as ardently, and hoping, perchance, yet more ardently than ever, and holding in his hands the prize that he had so long pursued? Folly indeed should I deem it to compare that liberality with this.

Tenth Day

Novel VI

— *King Charles the Old, being conqueror, falls in love with a young maiden, and afterward growing ashamed of his folly bestows her and her sister honourably in marriage.* —

WHO MIGHT fully recount with what diversity of argument the ladies debated which of the three, Giliberto, or Messer Ansaldo, or the necromancer, behaved with the most liberality in the affair of Madonna Dianora? Too long were it to tell. However, when the king had allowed them to dispute a while, he, with a glance at Fiammetta, bade her rescue them from their wrangling by telling her story. Fiammetta made no demur, but thus began: –

Illustrious my ladies, I have ever been of opinion that in companies like ours one should speak so explicitly that the import of what is said should never by excessive circumscription afford matter for disputation; which is much more in place among students in the schools, than among us, whose powers are scarce adequate to the management of the distaff and the spindle. Wherefore I, that had in mind a matter of, perchance, some nicety, now that I see you all at variance touching the matters last mooted, am minded to lay it aside, and tell you somewhat else, which concerns a man by no means of slight account, but a valiant king, being a chivalrous action that he did, albeit in no wise thereto actuated by his honour.

There is none of you but may not seldom have heard tell of King Charles the Old, or the First, by whose magnificent emprise, and the ensuing victory gained over King Manfred, the Ghibellines were driven forth of Florence, and the Guelfs returned thither. For which cause a knight, Messer Neri degli Uberti by name, departing Florence with his household and not a little money, resolved to fix his abode under no other sway than that of King Charles. And being fain of a lonely place in which to end his days in peace, he betook him to Castello da Mare di Stabia; and there, perchance a cross-bow-shot from the other houses of the place, amid the olives and hazels and chestnuts that abound in those parts, he bought an estate, on which he built a goodly house and commodious, with a pleasant garden beside it, in the midst of which, having no lack of running water, he set, after our Florentine fashion, a pond fair and clear, and speedily filled it with fish. And while thus he lived, daily occupying himself with nought else but how to make his garden more fair, it befell that King Charles in the hot season betook him to Castello da Mare to refresh himself a while, and hearing of the beauty of Messer Neri's garden, was desirous to view it. And having learned to whom it belonged, he bethought him that, as the knight was an adherent of the party opposed to him, he would use more familiarity towards him than he would otherwise have done; and so he sent him word that he and four comrades would sup privily with him in his garden on the ensuing evening. Messer Neri felt himself much honoured; and having made his preparations with magnificence, and arranged the order of the ceremonies with his household, did all he could and knew to make the King cordially welcome to his fair garden.

When the King had viewed the garden throughout, as also Messer Neri's house, and commended them, he washed, and seated himself at one of the tables, which were set beside the pond, and bade Count Guy de Montfort, who was one of his companions, sit on one side of him, and Messer Neri on the other, and the other three to serve, as they should be directed by Messer Neri. The dishes that were set before them were dainty, the wines excellent and rare, the order of the repast very fair and commendable, without the least noise or aught else that might distress; whereon the King bestowed no stinted praise. As thus he gaily supped, well-pleased with the lovely spot, there came into the garden two young maidens, each perhaps fifteen years old, blonde both, their golden tresses falling all in ringlets about them, and crowned with a dainty garland of periwinkle-flowers; and so delicate and fair of face were they that they shewed liker to angels than aught else, each clad in a robe of finest linen, white as snow upon their flesh, close-fitting as might be from the waist up, but below the waist ample, like a pavilion to the feet. She that was foremost bore on her shoulders a pair of nets, which she held with her left hand, carrying in her right a long pole. Her companion followed, bearing on her left shoulder a frying-pan, under her left arm a bundle of faggots, and in her left hand a tripod, while in the other hand she carried a cruse of oil and a lighted taper. At sight of whom the King marvelled, and gazed intent to learn what it might import. The two young maidens came forward with becoming modesty, and did obeisance to the King; which done they hied them to the place of ingress to the pond, and she that had the frying-pan having set it down, and afterward the other things, took the pole that the other carried, and so they both went down into the pond, being covered by its waters to their breasts. Whereupon one of Messer Neri's servants, having forthwith lit a fire, and set the tripod on the faggots and oil therein, addressed himself to wait, until some fish should be thrown to him by the girls. Who, the one searching with the pole in those parts where she knew the fish lay hid, while the other made ready the nets, did in a brief space of time, to the exceeding great delight of the King, who watched them attentively, catch fish not a few, which they tossed to the servant, who set them, before the life was well out of them, in the frying-pan. After which, the maidens, as pre-arranged, addressed them to catch some of the finest fish, and cast them on to the table before the King, and Count Guy, and their father. The fish wriggled about the table to the prodigious delight of the King, who in like manner took some of them, and courteously returned them to the girls; with which sport they diverted them, until the servant had cooked the fish that had been given him: which, by Messer Neri's command, were set before the King rather as a side-dish than as aught very rare or delicious.

When the girls saw that all the fish were cooked, and that there was no occasion for them to catch any more, they came forth of the pond, their fine white garments cleaving everywhere close to their flesh so as to hide scarce any part of their delicate persons, took up again the things that they had brought, and passing modestly before the King, returned to the house. The King, and the Count, and the other gentlemen that waited, had regarded the maidens with no little attention, and had, one and all, inly bestowed on them no little praise, as being fair and shapely, and therewithal sweet and debonair; but 'twas in the King's eyes that they especially found favour. Indeed, as they came forth of the water, the King had scanned each part of their bodies so intently that, had one then pricked him, he would not have felt it, and his thoughts afterwards dwelling upon them, though he knew not who they were, nor how they came to be there, he felt stir within his heart a most ardent desire to pleasure them, whereby he knew very well that, if he took not care, he would grow enamoured; howbeit he knew not whether of the twain pleased him the more, so like was each to the other. Having thus brooded a while, he turned to Messer Neri, and asked who the two damsels were. Whereto: – "Sire," replied Messer Neri, "they are my twin daughters, and they are called, the one, Ginevra the Fair, and the other, Isotta the Blonde." Whereupon the King was loud in praise of them, and exhorted Messer Neri to bestow them in marriage. To which Messer Neri demurred, for that he no longer had the means. And nought of the supper now remaining to serve, save the fruit, in came the two young damsels in gowns of taffeta very fine, bearing in their hands two vast silver salvers full of divers fruits, such as the season yielded, and set them on the table before the King. Which done, they withdrew a little space and fell a singing to music a ditty, of which the opening words were as follows: –

> *Love, many words would not suffice*
> *There where I am come to tell.*

And so dulcet and delightsome was the strain that to the King, his eyes and ears alike charmed, it seemed as if all the nine orders of angels were descended there to sing. The song ended, they knelt and respectfully craved the King's leave to depart; which, though sorely against his will, he gave them with a forced gaiety.

Supper ended, the King and his companions, having remounted their horses, took leave of Messer Neri, and conversing of divers matters, returned to the royal quarters; where the King, still harbouring his secret passion, nor, despite affairs of state that supervened, being able to forget the beauty and sweetness of Ginevra the Fair, for whose sake he likewise loved her twin sister, was so limed by Love that he could scarce think of aught else. So, feigning other reasons, he consorted familiarly with Messer Neri, and did much frequent his garden, that he might see Ginevra. And at length, being unable to endure his suffering any longer, and being minded, for that he could devise no other expedient, to despoil their father not only of the one but of the other damsel also, he discovered both his love and his project to Count Guy; who, being a good man and true, thus made answer: – "Sire, your tale causes me not a little astonishment, and that more especially because of your conversation from your childhood to this very day, I have, methinks, known more than any other man. And as no such passion did I ever mark in you, even in your youth, when Love should more readily have fixed you with his fangs, as now I discern, when you are already on the verge of old age, 'tis to me so strange, so surprising that you should veritably love, that I deem it little short of a miracle. And were it meet for me to reprove you, well wot I the language I should hold to you, considering that you are yet in arms in a realm but lately won, among a people as yet unknown to you, and wily and treacherous in the extreme, and that the gravest anxieties and matters of high policy engross your mind, so that you are not as yet able to sit you down, and nevertheless amid all these weighty concerns you have given harbourage to false, flattering Love. This is not the wisdom of a great king, but the folly of a feather-pated boy. And moreover, what is far worse, you say that you are resolved to despoil this poor knight of his two daughters, whom, entertaining you in his house, and honouring you to the best of his power, he brought into your presence all but naked, testifying thereby, how great is his faith in you, and how assured he is that you are a king, and not a devouring wolf. Have you so soon forgotten that 'twas Manfred's outrageous usage of his subjects that opened you the way into this realm? What treachery was he ever guilty of that better merited eternal torment, than 'twould be in you to wrest from one that honourably entreats you at once his hope and his consolation? What would be said of you if so you should do? Perchance you deem that 'twould suffice to say: – 'I did it because he is a Ghibelline.' Is it then consistent with the justice of a king that those, be they who they may, who seek his protection, as this man has sought yours, should be entreated after this sort? King, I bid you remember that exceeding great as is your glory to have vanquished Manfred, yet to conquer oneself is a still greater glory: wherefore you, to whom belongs the correction of others, see to it that you conquer yourself, and refrain this unruly passion; and let not such a blot mar the splendour of your achievements."

Sore stricken at heart by the Count's words, and the more mortified that he acknowledged their truth, the King heaved a fervent sigh or two, and then: – "Count," quoth he, "that enemy there is none, however mighty, but to the practised warrior is weak enough and easy to conquer in comparison of his own appetite, I make no doubt, but, great though the struggle will be and immeasurable the force that it demands, so shrewdly galled am I by your words, that not many days will have gone by before I shall without fail have done enough to shew you that I, that am the conqueror of others, am no less able to gain the victory over myself." And indeed but a few days thereafter, the King, on his return to Naples, being minded at once to leave himself no excuse for dishonourable conduct, and to recompense the knight for his honourable entreatment of him, did, albeit 'twas hard for him to endow another with that which he had most ardently desired for himself, none the less resolve to bestow the two damsels in marriage, and that not as Messer Neri's daughters, but as his own. Wherefore, Messer Neri consenting, he provided both with magnificent dowries, and gave Ginevra the Fair to Messer Maffeo da Palizzi, and Isotta the Blonde to Messer Guglielmo della Magna, noble knights and great barons both; which done, sad at heart beyond measure, he betook him to Apulia, and by incessant travail did so mortify his vehement appetite that he snapped and broke in pieces the fetters of Love, and for the rest of his days was no more vexed by such passion.

Perchance there will be those who say that 'tis but a trifle for a king to bestow two girls in marriage; nor shall I dispute it: but say we that a king in love bestowed in marriage her whom he loved, neither having taken nor taking, of his love, leaf or flower or fruit; then this I say was a feat great indeed, nay, as great as might be.

After such a sort then did this magnificent King, at once generously rewarding the noble knight, commendably honouring the damsels that he loved, and stoutly subduing himself.

Tenth Day
Novel VII

— *King Pedro, being apprised of the fervent love borne him by Lisa, who thereof is sick, comforts her, and forthwith gives her in marriage to a young gentleman, and having kissed her on the brow, ever after professes himself her knight.* —

WHEN FIAMMETTA was come to the end of her story, and not a little praise had been accorded to the virile magnificence of King Charles, albeit one there was of the ladies, who, being a Ghibelline, joined not therein, Pampinea, having received the king's command, thus began: –

None is there of discernment, worshipful my ladies, that would say otherwise than you have said touching good King Charles, unless for some other cause she bear him a grudge; however, for that there comes to my mind the, perchance no less honourable, entreatment of one of our Florentine girls by one of his adversaries, I am minded to recount the same to you.

What time the French were driven forth of Sicily there dwelt at Palermo one of our Florentines, that was an apothecary, Bernardo Puccini by name, a man of great wealth, that by his lady had an only and exceeding fair daughter, then of marriageable age. Now King Pedro of Arragon, being instated in the sovereignty of the island, did at Palermo make with his barons marvellous celebration thereof; during which, as he tilted after the Catalan fashion, it befell that Bernardo's daughter, Lisa by name, being with other ladies at a window, did thence espy him in the course, whereat being prodigiously delighted, she regarded him again and again, and grew fervently enamoured of him; nor yet, when the festivities were ended, and she was at home with her father, was there aught she could think of but this her exalted and aspiring love. In regard whereof that which most irked her was her sense of her low rank, which scarce permitted her any hope of a happy issue; but, for all that, give over her love for the King she would not; nor yet, for fear of worse to come, dared she discover it. The King, meanwhile, recking, witting nothing of the matter, her suffering waxed immeasurable, intolerable; and her love ever growing with ever fresh accessions of melancholy, the fair maiden, overborne at last, fell sick, and visibly day by day wasted like snow in sunlight. Distraught with grief thereat, her father and mother afforded her such succour as they might with words of good cheer, and counsel of physicians, and physic; but all to no purpose; for that she in despair of her love was resolved no more to live.

Now her father assuring her that there was no whim of hers but should be gratified, the fancy took her that, if she might find apt means, she would, before she died, make her love and her resolve known to the King: wherefore one day she besought her father to cause Minuccio d'Arezzo, to come to her; which Minuccio, was a singer and musician of those days, reputed most skilful, and well seen of King Pedro. Bernardo, deeming that Lisa desired but to hear him play and sing a while, conveyed her message to him; and he, being an agreeable fellow, came to her forthwith, and after giving her some words of loving cheer, sweetly discoursed some airs upon his viol, and then sang her some songs; whereby, while he thought to comfort her, he did but add fire and flame to her love. Presently the girl said that she would fain say a few words to him in private, and when all else were withdrawn from the chamber: – "Minuccio," quoth she, "thee have I chosen, deeming thee most trusty, to be the keeper of my secret, relying upon thee in the first place never to betray it to a soul, and next to lend me in regard thereof such aid as thou mayst be able; and so I pray thee to do. Thou must know, then, Minuccio mine, that on the day when our lord King Pedro held the great festival in celebration of his triumph, I, seeing him tilt, was so smitten with love of him that thereof was kindled within my soul the fire which has brought me, as thou seest, to this pass; and knowing how ill it beseems me to love a king, and being unable, I say not to banish it from my heart, but so much as to bring it within bounds, and finding it exceeding grievous to bear, I have made choice of death as the lesser pain; and die I shall. But should he wot not of my love before I die, sore disconsolate should I depart; and knowing not by whom more aptly than by thee I might give him to know this my frame, I am minded to entrust the communication thereof to thee; which office I entreat thee not to refuse, and having discharged it, to let me know, that dying thus consoled, I may depart this pain." Which said, she silently wept.

Marvelling at the loftiness of the girl's spirit and her desperate determination, Minuccio commiserated her not a little; and presently it occurred to him that there was a way in which he might honourably serve her: wherefore: – "Lisa," quoth he, "my faith I plight thee, wherein thou mayst place sure confidence that I shall never play thee false, and lauding thy high emprise, to wit, the setting thine affections upon so great a king, I proffer thee mine aid, whereby, so thou wilt be of good cheer, I hope, and believe, that, before thou shalt see the third day from now go by, I shall have brought thee tidings which will be to thee for an exceeding great joy; and, not to lose time, I will set to work at once." And so Lisa, assuring him that she would be of good cheer, and plying him afresh with instant obsecrations, bade him Godspeed; and Minuccio, having taken leave of her, hied him to one Mico da Siena, a very expert rhymester of those days, who at his instant request made the ensuing song: –

> Hence hie thee, Love; and hasting to my King,
> Give him to know what torment dire I bear,
> How that to death I fare,
> Still close, for fear, my passion harbouring.
>
> Lo, Love, to thee with clasped hands I turn,
> And pray thee seek him where he tarrieth,
> And tell him how I oft for him do yearn,
> So sweetly he my heart enamoureth;
> And of the fire, wherewith I throughly burn,
> I think to die, but may the hour uneath
> Say, when my grievous pain shall with my breath
> Surcease; till when, neither may fear nor shame
> The least abate the flame.
> Ah! to his ears my woeful story bring.
>
> Since of him I was first enamoured,
> Never hast thou, O Love, my fearful heart
> With any such fond hope encouraged,
> As e'er its message to him to impart,
> To him, my lord, that me so sore bested
> Holds: dying thus, 'twere grievous to depart:
> Perchance, were he to know my cruel smart,

> 'Twould not displease him; might I but make bold
> My soul to him to unfold,
> And shew him all my woeful languishing.
>
> Love, since 'twas not thy will me to accord
> Such boldness as that e'er unto my King
> I may discover my sad heart's full hoard,
> Or any word or sign thereof him bring:
> This all my prayer to thee, O sweet my Lord:
> Hie thee to him, and so him whispering
> Mind of the day I saw him tourneying
> With all his paladins environed,
> And grew enamoured
> Ev'n to my very heart's disrupturing.

Which words Minuccio forthwith set to music after a soft and plaintive fashion befitting their sense; and on the third day thereafter hied him to court, while King Pedro was yet at breakfast. And being bidden by the King to sing something to the accompaniment of his viol, he gave them this song with such sweet concord of words and music that all the folk that were in the King's hall seemed, as it were, entranced, so intent and absorbed stood they to listen, and the King rather more than the rest. And when Minuccio had done singing, the King asked whence the song came, that, as far as he knew, he had never heard it before. "Sire," replied Minuccio, "'tis not yet three days since 'twas made, words and music alike." And being asked by the King in regard of whom 'twas made: – "I dare not," quoth he, "discover such a secret save to you alone." Bent on hearing the story, the King, when the tables were cleared, took Minuccio into his privy chamber; and there Minuccio told him everything exactly as he had heard it from Lisa's lips. Whereby the King was much gratified, and lauded the maiden not a little, and said that a girl of such high spirit merited considerate treatment, and bade Minuccio be his envoy to her, and comfort her, and tell her that without fail that very day at vespers he would come to visit her. Overjoyed to bear the girl such gladsome tidings, Minuccio tarried not, but hied him back to the girl with his viol, and being closeted with her, told her all that had passed, and then sang the song to the accompaniment of his viol. Whereby the girl was so cheered and delighted that forthwith there appeared most marked and manifest signs of the amendment of her health, while with passionate longing (albeit none in the house knew or divined it) she awaited the vesper hour, when she was to see her lord.

Knowing the girl very well, and how fair she was, and pondering divers times on what Minuccio had told him, the King, being a prince of a liberal and kindly disposition, grew ever more compassionate. So, about vespers, he mounted his horse, and rode forth, as if for mere pleasure, and being come to the apothecary's house, demanded access to a very goodly garden that the apothecary had, and having dismounted, after a while enquired of Bernardo touching his daughter, and whether he had yet bestowed her in marriage. "Sire," replied Bernardo, "she is not yet married; and indeed she has been and still is very ill howbeit since none she is wonderfully amended." The significance of which amendment being forthwith apprehended by the King: – "In good faith," quoth he, "'twere a pity so fair a creature were reft from the world so early; we would go in and visit her." And presently, attended only by two of his lords and Bernardo, he betook him to her chamber, where being entered, he drew nigh the bed, whereon the girl half reclined, half sate in eager expectation of his coming; and taking her by the hand: – "Madonna," quoth he, "what means this? A maiden like you should be the comfort of others, and you suffer yourself to languish. We would entreat you that for love of us you be of good cheer, so as speedily to recover your health." To feel the touch of his hand whom she loved above all else, the girl, albeit somewhat shamefast, was so enraptured that 'twas as if she was in Paradise; and as soon as she was able: – "My lord," she said, "'twas the endeavour, weak as I am, to sustain a most grievous burden that brought this sickness upon me; but 'twill not be long ere you will see me quit thereof, thanks to your courtesy." The hidden meaning of which words was apprehended only by the King, who momently made more account of the girl, and again and again inly cursed Fortune, that had decreed that she should be the daughter of such a man. And yet a while he tarried with her, and comforted her, and so took his leave. Which gracious behaviour of the King was not a little commended, and accounted a signal honour to the apothecary and his daughter.

The girl, glad at heart as was ever lady of her lover, mended with reviving hope, and in a few days recovered her health, and therewith more than all her wonted beauty. Whereupon the King, having taken counsel with the Queen how to reward so great a love, got him one day to horse with a great company of his barons, and hied him to the apothecary's house; and being come into the garden, he sent for the apothecary and his daughter; and there, being joined by the Queen with not a few ladies, who received the girl into their company, they made such cheer as 'twas a wonder to see. And after a while the King and Queen having called Lisa to them, quoth the King: – "Honourable damsel, by the great love that you have borne us we are moved greatly to honour you; and we trust that, for love of us, the honour that we design for you will be acceptable to you. Now 'tis thus we would honour you: to wit, that, seeing that you are of marriageable age, we would have you take for husband him that we shall give you; albeit 'tis none the less our purpose ever to call ourself your knight, demanding no other tribute of all your love but one sole kiss." Scarlet from brow to neck, the girl, making the King's pleasure her own, thus with a low voice replied: – "My lord, very sure am I that, should it come to be known that I was grown enamoured of you, most folk would hold me for a fool, deeming, perchance, that I was out of my mind, and witless alike of my own rank and yours; but God, who alone reads the hearts of us mortals, knows that even then, when first I did affect you, I wist that you were the King, and I but the daughter of Bernardo the apothecary, and that to suffer my passion to soar so high did ill become me; but, as you know far better than I, none loves of set and discreet purpose, but only according to the dictates of impulse and fancy; which law my forces, albeit not seldom opposed, being powerless to withstand, I loved and still love and shall ever love you. But as no sooner knew I myself subjugated to your love, than I vowed to have ever no will but yours; therefore not only am I compliant to take right gladly him whom you shall be pleased to give me for husband, thereby conferring upon me great honour and dignity; but if you should bid me tarry in the fire, delighted were I to obey, so thereby I might pleasure you. How far it beseems me to have you, my King, for my knight, you best know; and therefore I say nought thereof; nor will the kiss which you crave as your sole tribute of my love be granted you save by leave of my Lady the Queen. Natheless, may you have of this great graciousness that you and my Lady the Queen have shewn me, and which I may not requite, abundant recompense in the blessing and favour of God;" and so she was silent.

The Queen was mightily delighted with the girl's answer, and deemed her as discreet as the King had said. The King then sent for the girl's father and mother, and being assured that his intention had their approval, summoned to his presence a young man, Perdicone by name, that was of gentle birth, but in poor circumstances, and put certain rings into his hand, and (he nowise gainsaying) wedded him to Lisa. Which done, besides jewels many and precious that he and the Queen gave the girl, he forthwith bestowed upon Perdicone two domains, right goodly and of ample revenues, to wit, Ceffalu and Calatabellotta, saying: – "We give them to thee for thy wife's dowry; what we have in store for thee thou wilt learn hereafter." Which said, he turned to the girl, and: – "Now," quoth he, "we are minded to cull that fruit which is due to us of thy love;" and so, taking her head between both his hands, he kissed her brow. Wherefore, great was the joy of Perdicone, and the father and mother of Lisa, and Lisa herself, and mighty the cheer they made, and gaily did they celebrate the nuptials. And, as many affirm, right well did the King keep his promise to the girl; for that ever, while he lived, he called himself her knight, nor went to any passage of arms bearing other device than that which he had from her.

Now 'tis by doing after this sort that sovereigns win the hearts of their subjects, give others occasion of well-doing, and gain for themselves an imperishable renown. At which mark few or none in our times have bent the bow of their understanding, the more part of the princes having become but cruel tyrants.

Tenth Day
Novel VIII

— Sophronia, albeit she deems herself wife to Gisippus, is wife to Titus Quintius Fulvus, and goes with him to Rome, where Gisippus arrives in indigence, and deeming himself scorned by Titus, to compass his own death, avers that he has slain a man. Titus recognizes him, and to save his life, alleges that 'twas he that slew the man: whereof he that did the deed being witness, he discovers himself as the murderer. Whereby it comes to pass that they are all three liberated by Octavianus; and Titus gives Gisippus his sister to wife, and shares with him all his substance. —

SO CEASED PAMPINEA; and when all the ladies, and most of all the Ghibelline, had commended King Pedro, Filomena by command of the king thus began: –

Magnificent my ladies, who wots not that there is nought so great but kings, when they have a mind, may accomplish it? As also that 'tis of them that magnificence is most especially demanded? Now whoso, being powerful, does that which it appertains to him to do, does well; but therein is no such matter of marvel, or occasion of extolling him to the skies, as in his deed, of whom, for that his power is slight, less is demanded. Wherefore, as you are so profuse of your words in exaltation of the fine deeds, as you deem them, of monarchs, I make no manner of doubt, but that the doings of our peers must seem to you yet more delectable and commendable, when they equal or surpass those of kings. Accordingly 'tis a transaction, laudable and magnificent, that passed between two citizens, who were friends, that I purpose to recount to you in my story.

I say, then, that what time Octavianus Caesar, not as yet hight Augustus, but being in the office called Triumvirate, swayed the empire of Rome, there dwelt at Rome a gentleman, Publius Quintius Fulvus by name, who, having a son, Titus Quintius Fulvus, that was a very prodigy of wit, sent him to Athens to study philosophy, and to the best of his power commended him to a nobleman of that city, Chremes by name, who was his very old friend. Chremes lodged Titus in his own house with his son Gisippus, and placed both Titus and Gisippus under a philosopher named Aristippus, to learn of him his doctrine. And the two youths, thus keeping together, found each the other's conversation so congruous with his own, that there grew up between them a friendship so close and brotherly that 'twas never broken by aught but death; nor knew either rest or solace save when he was with the other. So, gifted alike with pre-eminent subtlety of wit, they entered on their studies, and with even pace and prodigious applause scaled together the glorious heights of philosophy. In which way of life, to the exceeding great delight of Chremes, who entreated Titus as no less his son than Gisippus, they continued for full three years. At the end whereof, it befell (after the common course of things mundane) that Chremes (being now aged) departed this life. Whom with equal grief they mourned as a common father; and the friends and kinsfolk of Chremes were alike at a loss to determine whether of the twain stood in need of the more consolation upon the bereavement.

Some months afterward the friends and kinsfolk of Gisippus came to him and exhorted him, as did also Titus, to take a wife, and found him a maiden, wondrous fair, of one of the most noble houses of Athens, her name Sophronia, and her age about fifteen years. So a time was appointed for their nuptials, and one day, when 'twas near at hand, Gisippus bade Titus come see the maiden, whom as yet he had not seen; and they being come into her house, and she sitting betwixt them, Titus, as he were fain to observe with care the several charms of his friend's wife that was to be, surveyed her with the closest attention, and being delighted beyond measure with all that he saw, grew, as inly he extolled her charms to the skies, enamoured of her with a love as ardent, albeit he gave no sign of it, as ever lover bore to lady. However, after they had tarried a while with her, they took their leave, and went home, where Titus repaired to his chamber, and there gave himself over to solitary musing on the damsel's charms, and the longer he brooded, the more he burned for her. Whereon as he reflected, having heaved many a fervent sigh, thus he began to commune with himself: – Ah! woe worth thy life, Titus! Whom makest thou the mistress of thy soul, thy love, thy hope? Knowest thou not that by reason as well of thy honourable entreatment by Chremes and his kin as of the wholehearted friendship that is between thee and Gisippus, it behoves thee to have his betrothed in even such pious regard as if she were thy sister? Whither art thou suffering beguiling love, delusive hope, to hurry thee? Open the eyes of thine understanding, and see thyself, wretched man, as thou art; obey the dictates of thy reason, refrain thy carnal appetite, control thine inordinate desires, and give thy thoughts another bent; join battle with thy lust at the outset, and conquer thyself while there is yet time. This which thou wouldst have is not meet, is not seemly: this which thou art minded to ensue, thou wouldst rather, though thou wert, as thou art not, sure of its attainment, eschew, hadst thou but the respect thou shouldst have, for the claims of true friendship. So, then, Titus, what wilt thou do? What but abandon this unseemly love, if thou wouldst do as it behoves thee?

But then, as he remembered Sophronia, his thoughts took the contrary direction, and he recanted all he had said, musing on this wise: – The laws of Love are of force above all others; they abrogate not only the law of human friendship, but the law Divine itself. How many times ere now has father loved daughter, brother sister, step-mother step-son? aberrations far more notable than that a friend should love his friend's wife, which has happened a thousand times. Besides which, I am young, and youth is altogether subject to the laws of Love. Love's pleasure, then, should be mine. The seemly is for folk of riper years. 'Tis not in my power to will aught save that which Love wills. So beauteous is this damsel that there is none but should love her; and if I love her, who am young, who can justly censure me? I love her not because she is the affianced of Gisippus; no matter whose she was, I should love her all the same. Herein is Fortune to blame, that gave her to my friend, Gisippus, rather than to another. And if she is worthy of love, as for beauty she is, Gisippus, if he should come to know that I love her, ought to be less jealous than another.

Then, scorning himself that he should indulge such thoughts, he relapsed into the opposing mood, albeit not to abide there, but ever veering to and fro, he spent not only the whole of that day and the ensuing night, but many others; insomuch that, being able neither to eat nor to sleep, he grew so weak that he was fain to take to his bed. Gisippus, who had marked his moodiness for some days, and now saw that he was fairly sick, was much distressed; and with sedulous care, never quitting his side, he tended, and strove as best he might to comfort, him, not seldom and most earnestly demanding to know of him the cause of his melancholy and his sickness. Many were the subterfuges to which Titus resorted; but, as Gisippus was not to be put off with his fables, finding himself hard pressed by him, with sighs and sobs he made answer on this wise: – "Gisippus, had such been the will of the Gods, I were fain rather to die than to live, seeing that Fortune has brought me to a strait in which needs must my virtue be put to the ordeal, and, to my most grievous shame, 'tis found wanting: wherefore I confidently expect my due reward, to wit, death, which will be more welcome to me than to live, haunted ever by the memory of my baseness, which, as there is nought that from thee I either should or can conceal, I, not without burning shame, will discover to thee." And so he recounted the whole story from first to last, the occasion of his melancholy, its several moods, their conflict, and with which of them the victory rested, averring that he was dying of love for Sophronia, and that, knowing how ill such love beseemed him, he had, for penance, elected to die, and deemed the end was now not far off. Gisippus, hearing his words and seeing his tears, for a while knew not what to say, being himself smitten with the damsel's charms, albeit in a less degree than Titus; but ere long he made up his mind that Sophronia must be less dear to him than his friend's life.

And so, moved to tears by his friend's tears: – "Titus," quoth he between his sobs, "but that thou art in need of comfort, I should reproach thee, that thou hast offended against our friendship in that thou hast so long kept close from me this most distressful passion; and albeit thou didst deem it unseemly, yet unseemly things should no more than things seemly be withheld from a friend, for that, as a friend rejoices with his friend in things seemly, so he does his endeavour to wean his friend from things unseemly: but enough of this for the nonce: I pass to that which, I wot, is of greater moment. If thou ardently lovest Sophronia, my affianced, so far from marvelling thereat, I should greatly marvel were it not so, knowing how fair she is, and how noble is thy soul, and thus the apter to be swayed by passion, the more excelling is she by whom thou art charmed. And the juster the cause thou hast to love Sophronia, the greater is the injustice with which thou complainest of Fortune (albeit thou dost it not in so many words) for giving her to me, as if thy love of her had been seemly, had she belonged to any other but me; whereas, if thou art still the wise man thou wast wont to be, thou must know that to none could Fortune have assigned her, with such good cause for thee to thank her, as to me. Had any other had her, albeit thy love had been seemly, he had loved her as his own, rather than as thine; which, if thou deem me even such a friend to thee as I am, thou wilt not apprehend from me, seeing that I mind me not that, since we were friends, I had ever aught that was not as much thine as mine. And so should I entreat thee herein as in all other matters, were the affair gone so far that nought else were possible; but as it is, I can make thee sole possessor of her; and so I mean to do; for I know not what cause thou shouldst have to prize my friendship, if, where in seemly sort it might be done, I knew not how to surrender my will to thine. 'Tis true that Sophronia is my betrothed, and that I loved her much, and had great cheer in expectation of the nuptials: but as thou, being much more discerning than I, dost more fervently affect this rare prize, rest assured that she will enter my chamber not mine but thine. Wherefore, away with thy moodiness, banish thy melancholy, recover thy lost health, thy heartiness and jollity, and gladsomely, even from this very hour, anticipate the guerdon of thy love, a love worthier far than mine."

Delightful as was the prospect with which hope flattered Titus, as he heard Gisippus thus speak, no less was the shame with which right reason affected him, admonishing him that the greater was the liberality of Gisippus, the less it would become him to profit thereby. Wherefore, still weeping, he thus constrained himself to make answer: – "Gisippus, thy generous and true friendship leaves me in no doubt as to the manner in which it becomes me to act. God forefend that her, whom, as to the more worthy, He has given to thee, I should ever accept of thee for mine. Had He seen fit that she should be mine, far be it from thee or any other to suppose that He would ever have awarded her to thee. Renounce not, then, that which thy choice and wise counsel and His gift have made thine, and leave me, to whom, as unworthy, He has appointed no such happiness, to waste my life in tears; for either I shall conquer my grief, which will be grateful to thee, or it will conquer me, and so I shall be quit of my pain." Quoth then Gisippus: – "If our friendship, Titus, is of such a sort as may entitle me to enforce thee to ensue behests of mine, or as may induce thee of thine own free will to ensue the same, such is the use to which, most of all, I am minded to put it; and if thou lend not considerate ear unto my prayers, I shall by force, that force which is lawful in the interest of a friend, make Sophronia thine. I know the might of Love, how redoubtable it is, and how, not once only, but oftentimes, it has brought ill-starred lovers to a miserable death; and thee I see so hard bested that turn back thou mightst not, nor get the better of thy grief, but holding on thy course, must succumb, and perish, and without doubt I should speedily follow thee. And so, had I no other cause to love thee, thy life is precious to me in that my own is bound up with it. Sophronia, then, shall be thine; for thou wouldst not lightly find another so much to thy mind, and I shall readily find another to love, and so shall content both thee and me. In which matter, peradventure, I might not be so liberal, were wives so scarce or hard to find as are friends; wherefore, as 'tis so easy a matter for me to find another wife, I had liefer – I say not lose her, for in giving her to thee lose her I shall not, but only transfer her to one that is my alter ego, and that to her advantage – I had liefer, I say, transfer her to thee than lose thee. And so, if aught my prayers avail with thee, I entreat thee extricate thyself from this thy woeful plight, and comfort at once thyself and me, and in good hope, address thyself to pluck that boon which thy fervent love craves of her for whom thou yearnest."

Still scrupling, for shame, to consent that Sophronia should become his wife, Titus remained yet a while inexorable; but, yielding at last to the solicitations of Love, reinforced by the exhortations of Gisippus, thus he made answer: – "Lo now, Gisippus, I know not how to call it, whether 'tis more thy pleasure than mine, this which I do, seeing that 'tis as thy pleasure that thou so earnestly entreatest me to do it; but, as thy liberality is such that my shame, though becoming, may not withstand it, I will even do it. But of this rest assured, that I do so, witting well that I receive from thee, not only the lady I love, but with her my very life. And, Fate permitting, may the Gods grant me to make thee such honourable and goodly requital as may shew thee how sensible I am of the boon, which thou, more compassionate of me than I am of myself, conferrest on me." Quoth then Gisippus: – "Now, for the giving effect to our purpose, methinks, Titus, we should proceed on this wise. Thou knowest that Sophronia, by treaty at length concluded between my family and hers, is become my betrothed: were I now to say that she should not be my wife, great indeed were the scandal that would come thereof, and I should affront both her family and mine own; whereof, indeed, I should make no account, so it gave me to see her become thine; but I fear that, were I to give her up at this juncture, her family would forthwith bestow her upon another, perchance, than thee, and so we should both be losers. Wherefore methinks that, so thou approve, I were best to complete what I have begun, bring her home as my wife, and celebrate the nuptials, and thereafter we can arrange that thou lie with her, privily, as thy wife. Then, time and occasion serving, we will disclose the whole affair, and if they are satisfied, well and good; if not, 'twill be done all the same, and as it cannot be undone, they must perforce make the best of it."

Which counsel being approved by Titus, Gisippus brought the lady home as his wife, Titus being now recovered, and quite himself again; and when they had made great cheer, and night was come, the ladies, having bedded the bride, took their departure. Now the chambers of Titus and Gisippus were contiguous, and one might pass from one into the other: Gisippus, therefore, being come into his room, extinguished every ray of light, and stole into that of Titus, and bade him go get him to bed with his lady. Whereat Titus gave way to shame, and would have changed his mind, and refused to go in; but Gisippus, no less zealous at heart than in words to serve his friend, after no small contention prevailed on him to go thither. Now no sooner was Titus abed with the lady, than, taking her in his arms, he, as if jestingly, asked in a low tone whether she were minded to be his wife. She, taking him to be Gisippus, answered, yes; whereupon he set a fair and costly ring on her finger, saying: – "And I am minded to be thy husband." And having presently consummated the marriage, he long and amorously disported him with her, neither she, nor any other, being ever aware that another than Gisippus lay with her.

Now Titus and Sophronia being after this sort wedded, Publius, the father of Titus, departed this life. For which cause Titus was bidden by letter to return forthwith to Rome to see to his affairs; wherefore he took counsel with Gisippus how he might take Sophronia thither with him; which might not well be done without giving her to know how matters stood. Whereof, accordingly, one day, having called her into the chamber, they fully apprised her, Titus for her better assurance bringing to her recollection not a little of what had passed between them. Whereat she, after glancing from one to the other somewhat disdainfully, burst into a flood of tears, and reproached Gisippus that he had so deluded her; and forthwith, saying nought of the matter to any there, she hied her forth of Gisippus' house and home to her father, to whom and her mother she recounted the deceit which Gisippus had practised upon them as upon her, averring that she was the wife not of Gisippus, as they supposed, but of Titus. Whereby her father was aggrieved exceedingly, and prolonged and grave complaint was made thereof by him and his own and Gisippus' families, and there was not a little parleying, and a world of pother. Gisippus earned the hatred of both his own and Sophronia's kin, and all agreed that he merited not only censure but severe punishment. He, however, averred that he had done a thing seemly, and that Sophronia's kinsfolk owed him thanks for giving her in marriage to one better than himself.

All which Titus witnessed with great suffering, and witting that 'twas the way of the Greeks to launch forth in high words and menaces, and refrain not until they should meet with one that answered them, whereupon they were wont to grow not only humble but even abject, was at length minded that their clavers should no longer pass unanswered; and, as with his Roman temper he united Athenian subtlety, he cleverly contrived to bring the kinsfolk, as well of Gisippus as of Sophronia, together in a temple, where, being entered, attended only by Gisippus, thus (they being intent to hear) he harangued them: – "'Tis the opinion of not a few philosophers that whatsoever mortals do is ordained by the providence of the immortal Gods; for which cause some would have it that nought either is, or ever shall be, done, save of necessity, albeit others there are that restrict this necessity to that which is already done. Regard we but these opinions with some little attention, and we shall very plainly perceive that to censure that which cannot be undone is nought else but to be minded to shew oneself wiser than the Gods; by whom we must suppose that we and our affairs are swayed and governed with uniform and unerring wisdom. Whereby you may very readily understand how vain and foolish a presumption it is to pass judgment on their doings, and what manner and might of chains they need who suffer themselves to be transported to such excess of daring. Among whom, in my judgment, you must one and all be numbered, if 'tis true, what I hear, to wit, that you have complained and do continue to complain that Sophronia, albeit you gave her to Gisippus, is, nevertheless, become my wife; not considering that 'twas ordained from all eternity that she should become, not the wife of Gisippus, but mine, as the fact does now declare.

"But, for that discourse of the secret providence and purposes of the Gods seems to many a matter hard and scarce to be understood, I am willing to assume that they meddle in no wise with our concerns, and to descend to the region of human counsels; in speaking whereof I must needs do two things quite at variance with my wont, to wit, in some degree praise myself and censure or vilify another. But, as in either case I mean not to deviate from the truth, and 'tis what the occasion demands, I shall not fail so to do. With bitter upbraidings, animated rather by rage than by reason, you cease not to murmur, nay, to cry out, against Gisippus, and to harass him with your abuse, and hold him condemned, for that her, whom you saw fit to give him, he has seen fit to give me, to wife; wherein I deem him worthy of the highest commendation, and that for two reasons, first, because he has done the office of a friend, and secondly, because he has done more wisely than you did. After what sort the sacred laws of friendship prescribe that friend shall entreat friend, 'tis not to my present purpose to declare; 'twill suffice to remind you that the tie of friendship should be more binding than that of blood, or kinship; seeing that our friends are of our own choosing, whereas our kinsfolk are appointed us by Fortune; wherefore, if my life was more to Gisippus than your goodwill, since I am, as I hold myself, his friend, can any wonder thereat?

"But pass we to my second reason; in the exposition whereof I must needs with yet more cogency prove to you that he has been wiser than you, seeing that, methinks, you wot nought of the providence of the Gods, and still less of the consequences of friendship. I say then, that, as 'twas your premeditated and deliberate choice that gave Sophronia to this young philosopher Gisippus, so 'twas his that gave her to another young philosopher. 'Twas your counsel that gave her to an Athenian; 'twas his that gave her to a Roman: 'twas your counsel that gave her to a man of gentle birth; 'twas his that gave her to one of birth yet gentler: wealthy was he to whom your counsel gave her, most wealthy he to whom his counsel gave her. Not only did he to whom your counsel gave her, love her not, but he scarce knew her, whereas 'twas to one that loved her beyond all other blessings, nay, more dearly than his own life, that his counsel gave her. And to the end that it may appear more plainly that 'tis even as I say, and Gisippus' counsel more to be commended than yours, let us examine it point by point. That I, like Gisippus, am young and a philosopher, my countenance and my pursuits may, without making more words about the matter, sufficiently attest. We are also of the same age, and have ever kept pace together in our studies. Now true it is that he is an Athenian, and I am a Roman. But, as touching the comparative glory of the cities, should the matter be mooted, I say that I am of a free city, and he of a city tributary; that I am of a city that is mistress of all the world, and he of one that is subject to mine; that I am of a city that flourishes mightily in arms, in empire, and in arts; whereas he cannot boast his city as famous save in arts.

"Moreover, albeit you see me here in the guise of a most humble scholar, I am not born of the dregs of the populace of Rome. My halls and the public places of Rome are full of the antique effigies of my forefathers, and the annals of Rome abound with the records of triumphs led by the Quintii to the Roman Capitol; and so far from age having withered it, to-day, yet more abundantly than ever of yore, flourishes the glory of our name. Of my wealth I forbear, for shame, to speak, being mindful that honest poverty is the time-honoured and richest inheritance of the noble citizens of Rome; but, allowing for the nonce the opinion of the vulgar, which holds poverty in disrepute, and highly appraises wealth, I, albeit I never sought it, yet, as the favoured of Fortune, have abundant store thereof. Now well I wot that, Gisippus being of your own city, you justly prized and prize an alliance with him; but not a whit less should you prize an alliance with me at Rome, considering that there you will have in me an excellent host, and a patron apt, zealous and potent to serve you as well in matters of public interest as in your private concerns. Who, then, dismissing all bias from his mind, and judging with impartial reason, would deem your counsel more commendable than that of Gisippus? Assuredly none. Sophronia, then, being married to Titus Quintius Fulvus, a citizen of Rome, of an ancient and illustrious house, and wealthy, and a friend of Gisippus, whoso takes umbrage or offence thereat, does that which it behoves him not to do, and knows not what he does.

"Perchance some will say that their complaint is not that Sophronia is the wife of Titus, but that she became his wife after such a sort, to wit, privily, by theft, neither friend nor any of her kin witting aught thereof; but herein is no matter of marvel, no prodigy as yet unheard-of. I need not instance those who before now have taken to them husbands in defiance of their fathers' will, or have eloped with their lovers and been their mistresses before they were their wives, or of whose marriages no word has been spoken, until their pregnancy or parturition published them to the world, and necessity sanctioned the fact: nought of this has happened in the case of Sophronia; on the contrary, 'twas in proper form, and in meet and seemly sort, that Gisippus gave her to Titus. And others, peradventure, will say that 'twas by one to whom such office belonged not that she was bestowed in marriage. Nay, but this is but vain and womanish querulousness, and comes of scant consideration. Know we not, then, that Fortune varies according to circumstances her methods and her means of disposing events to their predetermined ends? What matters it to me, if it be a cobbler, rather than a philosopher, that Fortune has ordained to compass something for me, whether privily or overtly, so only the result is as it should be? I ought, indeed, to take order, if the cobbler be indiscreet, that he meddle no more in affairs of mine, but, at the same time, I ought to thank him for what he has done. If Gisippus has duly bestowed Sophronia in marriage, it is gratuitous folly to find fault with the manner and the person. If you mistrust his judgment, have a care that it be not in his power to do the like again, but thank him for this turn.

"Natheless, you are to know that I used no cunning practice or deceit to sully in any degree the fair fame of your house in the person of Sophronia; and, albeit I took her privily to wife, I came not as a ravisher to despoil her of her virginity, nor in any hostile sort was I minded to make her mine on dishonourable terms, and spurn your alliance; but, being fervently enamoured of her bewitching beauty and her noble qualities, I wist well that, should I make suit for her with those formalities which you, perchance, will say were due, then, for the great love you bear her, and for fear lest I should take her away with me to Rome, I might not hope to have her. Accordingly I made use of the secret practice which is now manifest to you, and brought Gisippus to consent in my interest to that whereto he was averse; and thereafter, ardently though I loved her, I sought not to commingle with her as a lover, but as a husband, nor closed with her, until, as she herself by her true witness may assure you, I had with apt words and with the ring made her my lawful wife, asking her if she would have me to husband, whereto she answered, yes. Wherein if she seem to have been tricked, 'tis not I that am to blame, but she, for that she asked me not who I was.

"This, then, is the great wrong, sin, crime, whereof for love and friendship's sake Gisippus and I are guilty, that Sophronia is privily become the wife of Titus Quintius: 'tis for this that you harass him with your menaces and hostile machinations. What more would you do, had he given her to a villein, to a caitiff, to a slave? Where would you find fetters, dungeons, crosses adequate to your vengeance? But enough of this at present: an event, which I did not expect, has now happened; my father is dead; and I must needs return to Rome; wherefore, being fain to take Sophronia with me, I have discovered to you that which otherwise I had, perchance, still kept close. Whereto, if you are wise, you will gladly reconcile yourselves; for that, if I had been minded to play you false, or put an affront upon you, I might have scornfully abandoned her to you; but God forefend that such baseness be ever harboured in a Roman breast. Sophronia, then, by the will of the Gods, by force of law, and by my own love-taught astuteness, is mine. The which it would seem that you, deeming yourselves, peradventure, wiser than the Gods, or the rest of mankind, do foolishly set at nought, and that in two ways alike most offensive to me; inasmuch as you both withhold from me Sophronia, in whom right, as against me, you have none, and also entreat as your enemy Gisippus, to whom you are rightfully bounden. The folly whereof I purpose not at present fully to expound to you, but in friendly sort to counsel you to abate your wrath and abandon all your schemes of vengeance, and restore Sophronia to me, that I may part from you on terms of amity and alliance, and so abide: but of this rest assured, that whether this, which is done, like you or not, if you are minded to contravene it, I shall take Gisippus hence with me, and once arrived in Rome, shall in your despite find means to recover her who is lawfully mine, and pursuing you with unremitting enmity, will apprise you by experience of the full measure and effect of a Roman's wrath."

Having so said, Titus started to his feet, his countenance distorted by anger, and took Gisippus by the hand, and with manifest contempt for all the rest, shaking his head at them and threatening them, led him out of the temple. They that remained in the temple, being partly persuaded by his arguments to accept his alliance and friendship, partly terrified by his last words, resolved by common consent that 'twas better to have the alliance of Titus, as they had lost that of Gisippus, than to add to that loss the enmity of Titus. Wherefore they followed Titus, and having come up with him, told him that they were well pleased that Sophronia should be his, and that they should prize his alliance and the friendship of dear Gisippus; and having ratified this treaty of amity and alliance with mutual cheer, they departed and sent Sophronia to Titus. Sophronia, discreetly making a virtue of necessity, transferred forthwith to Titus the love she had borne Gisippus, and being come with Titus to Rome, was there received with no small honour. Gisippus tarried in Athens, held in little account by well-nigh all the citizens, and being involved in certain of their broils, was, not long afterwards, with all his household, banished the city, poor, nay, destitute, and condemned to perpetual exile. Thus hard bested, and at length reduced to mendicancy, he made his way, so as least discomfortably he might, to Rome, being minded to see whether Titus would remember him: and there, learning that Titus lived, and was much affected by all the Romans, and having found out his house, he took his stand in front of it, and watched until Titus came by; to whom, for shame of the sorry trim that he was in, he ventured no word, but did his endeavour that he might be seen of him, hoping that Titus might recognize him, and call him by his name: but Titus passing on, Gisippus deeming that he had seen and avoided him, and calling to mind that which aforetime he had done for him, went away wroth and desperate. And fasting and penniless, and – for 'twas now night – knowing not whither he went, and yearning above all for death, he wandered by chance to a spot, which, albeit 'twas within the city, had much of the aspect of a wilderness, and espying a spacious grotto, he took shelter there for the night; and worn out at last with grief, on the bare ground, wretchedly clad as he was, he fell asleep.

Now two men that had that night gone out a thieving, having committed the theft, came towards morning to the grotto, and there quarrelled, and the stronger slew the other, and took himself off. Aroused by the noise, Gisippus witnessed the murder, and deeming that he had now the means of compassing, without suicide, the death for which he so much longed, budged not a jot, but stayed there, until the serjeants of the court, which had already got wind of the affair, came on the scene, and laid violent hands upon him, and led him away. Being examined, he confessed that he had slain the man, and had then been unable to make his escape from the grotto. Wherefore the praetor, Marcus Varro by name, sentenced him to death by crucifixion, as was then the custom. But Titus, who happened at that moment to come into the praetorium, being told the crime for which he was condemned, and scanning the poor wretch's face, presently recognized him for Gisippus, and marvelled how he should come to be there, and in such a woeful plight. And most ardently desiring to succour him, nor seeing other way to save his life except to exonerate him by accusing himself, he straightway stepped forward, and said with a loud voice: – "Marcus Varro, call back the poor man on whom thou hast passed sentence, for he is innocent. 'Tis enough that I have incurred the wrath of the Gods by one deed of violence, to wit, the murder of him whom your serjeants found dead this morning, without aggravating my offence by the death of another innocent man." Perplexed, and vexed that he should have been heard by all in the praetorium, but unable honourably to avoid compliance with that which the laws enjoined, Varro had Gisippus brought back, and in presence of Titus said to him: – "How camest thou to be so mad as, though no constraint was put upon thee, to confess a deed thou never didst, thy life being at stake? Thou saidst that 'twas thou by whom the man was slain last night, and now comes this other, and says that 'twas not thou but he that slew him." Gisippus looked, and seeing Titus, wist well that, being grateful for the service rendered by him in the past, Titus was now minded to save his life at the cost of his own: wherefore, affected to tears, he said: – "Nay but, Varro, in very sooth I slew him, and 'tis now too late, this tender solicitude of Titus for my deliverance." But on his part: – "Praetor," quoth Titus, "thou seest this man is a stranger, and was found unarmed beside the murdered man; thou canst not doubt that he was fain of death for very wretchedness: wherefore discharge him, and let punishment light on me who have merited it."

Marvelling at the importunity of both, Varro readily surmised that neither was guilty. And while he was casting about how he might acquit them, lo, in came a young man, one Publius Ambustus, a desperate character, and known to all the Romans for an arrant thief. He it was that had verily committed the murder, and witting both the men to be innocent of that of which each accused himself, so sore at heart was he by reason of their innocence, that, overborne by an exceeding great compassion, he presented himself before Varro, and: – "Praetor," quoth he, "'tis destiny draws me hither to loose the knot of these men's contention; and some God within me leaves me no peace of his whips and stings, until I discover my offence: wherefore know that neither of these men is guilty of that of which each accuses himself. 'Tis verily I that slew the man this morning about daybreak; and before I slew him, while I was sharing our plunder with him, I espied this poor fellow asleep there. Nought need I say to clear Titus: the general bruit of his illustrious renown attests that he is not a man of such a sort. Discharge him, therefore, and exact from me the penalty prescribed by the laws."

The affair had by this time come to the ears of Octavianus, who caused all three to be brought before him, and demanded to know the causes by which they had been severally moved to accuse themselves; and, each having told his story, Octavianus released the two by reason of their innocence, and the third for love of them. Titus took Gisippus home, having first chidden him not a little for his faint-heartedness and diffidence, and there, Sophronia receiving him as a brother, did him marvellous cheer; and having comforted him a while, and arrayed him in apparel befitting his worth and birth, he first shared with him all his substance, and then gave him his sister, a young damsel named Fulvia, to wife, and said to him: – "Choose now, Gisippus, whether thou wilt tarry here with me, or go back to Achaia with all that I have given thee."

Partly perforce of his banishment from his city, partly for that the sweet friendship of Titus was justly dear to him, Gisippus consented to become a Roman. And so, long and happily they lived together at Rome, Gisippus with his Fulvia, and Titus with his Sophronia, in the same house, growing, if possible, greater friends day by day.

Exceeding sacred then, is friendship, and worthy not only to be had in veneration, but to be extolled with never-ending praise, as the most dutiful mother of magnificence and seemliness, sister of gratitude and charity, and foe to enmity and avarice; ever, without waiting to be asked, ready to do as generously by another as she would be done by herself. Rarely indeed is it to-day that twain are found, in whom her most holy fruits are manifest; for which is most shamefully answerable the covetousness of mankind, which, regarding only private interest, has banished friendship beyond earth's farthest bourne, there to abide in perpetual exile. How should love, or wealth, or kinship, how should aught but friendship have so quickened the soul of Gisippus that the tears and sighs of Titus should incline his heart to cede to him the fair and gracious lady that was his betrothed and his beloved? Laws, menaces, terror! How should these, how should aught but friendship, have withheld Gisippus, in lonely places, in hidden retreats, in his own bed, from enfolding (not perchance unsolicited by her) the fair damsel within his youthful embrace? Honours, rewards, gains! Would Gisippus for these, would he for aught but friendship, have made nothing of the loss of kindred – his own and Sophronia's – have made nothing of the injurious murmurs of the populace, have made nothing of mocks and scorns, so only he might content his friend? And on the other hand, for what other cause than friendship had Titus, when he might decently have feigned not to see, have striven with the utmost zeal to compass his own death, and set himself upon the cross in Gisippus' stead? And what but friendship had left no place for suspicion in the soul of Titus, and filled it with a most fervent desire to give his sister to Gisippus, albeit he saw him to be reduced to extreme penury and destitution? But so it is that men covet hosts of acquaintance, troops of kinsfolk, offspring in plenty; and the number of their dependants increases with their wealth; and they reflect not that there is none of these, be he who he may, but will be more apprehensive of the least peril threatening himself than cumbered to avert a great peril from his lord or kinsman, whereas between friends we know 'tis quite contrariwise.

Tenth Day

Novel IX

— *Saladin, in guise of a merchant, is honourably entreated by Messer Torello. The Crusade ensuing, Messer Torello appoints a date, after which his wife may marry again: he is taken prisoner, and by training hawks comes under the Soldan's notice. The Soldan recognizes him, makes himself known to him, and entreats him with all honour. Messer Torello falls sick, and by magic arts is transported in a single night to Pavia, where his wife's second marriage is then to be solemnized, and being present thereat, is recognized by her, and returns with her to his house.* —

SO ENDED FILOMENA her story, and when all alike had commended the magnificence shewn by Titus in his gratitude, the king, reserving the last place for Dioneo, thus began: –

Lovesome my ladies, true beyond all question is what Filomena reports of friendship, and with justice did she deplore in her closing words the little account in which 'tis held to-day among mortals. And were we here for the purpose of correcting, or even of censuring, the vices of the age, I should add a copious sequel to her discourse; but as we have another end in view, it has occurred to me to set before you in a narrative, which will be of considerable length, but entertaining throughout, an instance of Saladin's magnificence, to the end that, albeit, by reason of our vices, it may not be possible for us to gain to the full the friendship of any, yet by the matters whereof you shall hear in my story we may at least be incited to take delight in doing good offices, in the hope that sooner or later we may come by our reward thereof.

I say, then, that in the time of the Emperor Frederic I., as certain writers affirm, the Christians made common emprise for the recovery of the Holy Land. Whereof that most valiant prince, Saladin, then Soldan of Babylonia, being in good time apprised, resolved to see for himself the preparations made by the Christian potentates for the said emprise, that he might put himself in better trim to meet them. So, having ordered all things to his mind in Egypt, he made as if he were bound on a pilgrimage, and attended only by two of his chiefest and sagest lords, and three servants, took the road in the guise of a merchant. And having surveyed many provinces of Christendom, as they rode through Lombardy with intent to cross the Alps, they chanced, between Milan and Pavia, to fall in with a gentleman, one Messer Torello d'Istria da Pavia, who with his servants and his dogs and falcons was betaking him to a fine estate that he had on the Ticino, there to tarry a while. Now Messer Torello no sooner espied Saladin and his lords than he guessed them to be gentlemen and foreigners; and, being zealous to do them honour, when Saladin asked one of his servants how far off Pavia might still be, and if he might win there in time to enter the town, he suffered not the servant to make answer, but: – "No, gentlemen," quoth he, "by the time you reach Pavia 'twill be too late for you to enter." "So!" replied Saladin, "then might you be pleased to direct us, as we are strangers, where we may best be lodged?" "That gladly will I," returned Messer Torello. "I was but now thinking to send one of these my men on an errand to Pavia; I will send him with you, and he will guide you to a place where you will find very comfortable quarters." Then, turning to one of his most trusty servants, he gave him his instructions, and despatched him with them: after which, he repaired to his estate, and forthwith, as best he might, caused a goodly supper to be made ready, and the tables set in his garden; which done, he stationed himself at the gate on the look-out for his guests.

The servant, conversing with the gentlemen of divers matters, brought them by devious roads to his lord's estate without their being ware of it. Whom as soon as Messer Torello espied, he came forth afoot to meet them, and said with a smile: – "A hearty welcome to you, gentlemen." Now Saladin, being very quick of apprehension, perceived that the knight had doubted, when he met them, that, were he to bid them to his house, they might not accept his hospitality; and accordingly, that it might not be in their power to decline it, had brought them to his house by a ruse. And so, returning his greeting: – "Sir," quoth he, "were it meet to find fault with those that shew courtesy, we should have a grievance against you, for that, to say nought of somewhat delaying our journey, you have in guerdon of a single greeting constrained us to accept so noble a courtesy as yours." Whereto the knight, who was of good understanding and well-spoken, made answer: – "Gentlemen, such courtesy as we shew you will, in comparison of that which, by what I gather from your aspect, were meet for you, prove but a sorry thing; but in sooth this side of Pavia you might not anywhere have been well lodged; wherefore take it not amiss that you have come somewhat out of your way to find less discomfortable quarters." And as he spoke, about them flocked the servants, who, having helped them to dismount, saw to their horses; whereupon Messer Torello conducted them to the chambers that were made ready for them, where, having caused them to be relieved of their boots, and refreshed with the coolest of wines, he held pleasant converse with them until supper-time. Saladin and his lords and servants all knew Latin, so that they both understood and made themselves understood very well, and there was none of them but adjudged this knight to be the most agreeable and debonair man, and therewithal the best talker, that he had ever seen; while to Messer Torello, on the other hand, they shewed as far greater magnificoes than he had at first supposed, whereby he was inly vexed that he had not been able that evening to do them the honours of company, and a more ceremonious banquet. For which default he resolved to make amends on the ensuing morning: wherefore, having imparted to one of his servants that which he would have done, he sent him to his most judicious and highminded lady at Pavia, which was close by, and where never a gate was locked. Which done, he brought the gentlemen into the garden, and courteously asked them who they were. "We are Cypriote merchants," replied Saladin, "and 'tis from Cyprus we come, and we are on our way to Paris on business." Quoth then Messer Torello: – "Would to God that our country bred gentlemen of such a quality as are the merchants that I see Cyprus breeds!" From which they passed to discourse of other matters, until, supper-time being come, he besought them to seat them at table; whereat, considering that the supper was but improvised, their entertainment was excellent and well-ordered.

The tables being cleared, Messer Torello, surmising that they must be weary, kept them no long time from their rest, but bestowed them in most comfortable beds, and soon after went to rest himself. Meanwhile the servant that he had sent to Pavia did his lord's errand to the lady, who, in the style rather of a queen than of a housewife, forthwith assembled not a few of Messer Torello's friends and vassals, and caused all meet preparation to be made for a magnificent banquet, and by messengers bearing torches bade not a few of the noblest of the citizens thereto; and had store of silken and other fabrics and vair brought in, and all set in order in every point as her husband had directed. Day came, and the gentlemen being risen, Messer Torello got him to horse with them, and having sent for his hawks, brought them to a ford, and shewed them how the hawks flew. By and by, Saladin requesting of him a guide to the best inn at Pavia: – "I myself will be your guide," returned Messer Torello, "for I have occasion to go thither." Which offer they, nothing doubting, did gladly accept, and so with him they set forth;

and about tierce, being come to the city, and expecting to be directed to the best inn, they were brought by Messer Torello, to his own house, where they were forthwith surrounded by full fifty of the greatest folk of the city, gathered there to give the gentlemen a welcome; and 'twas who should hold a bridle or a stirrup, while they dismounted. Whereby Saladin and his lords more than guessing the truth: – "Messer Torello," quoth they, "'twas not this that we craved of you. Honour enough had we from you last night, and far in excess of our desires; wherefore thou mightst very well have left us to go our own road." Whereto: – "Gentlemen," replied Messer Torello, "for that which was done yestereve I have to thank Fortune rather than you: seeing that Fortune surprised you on the road at an hour when you must needs repair to my little house: for that which shall be done this morning I shall be beholden to you, as will also these gentlemen that surround you, with whom, if you deem it courteous so to do, you may refuse to breakfast, if you like."

Fairly conquered, Saladin and his lords dismounted, and heartily welcomed by the gentlemen, were conducted to the chambers which had been most sumptuously adorned for their use; and having laid aside their riding dress, and taken some refreshment, repaired to the saloon, where all had been made ready with splendour. There, having washed their hands, they sat them down to table, and were regaled with a magnificent repast of many courses, served with all stately and fair ceremony, insomuch that, had the Emperor himself been there, 'twould not have been possible to do him more honour. And albeit Saladin and his lords were grandees and used to exceeding great displays of pomp and state, nevertheless this shewed to them as not a little marvellous, and one of the greatest they had ever seen, having regard to the quality of their host, whom they knew to be but a citizen, and no lord. Breakfast done, and the tables cleared, they conversed a while of high matters, and then, as 'twas very hot, all the gentlemen of Pavia – so it pleased Messer Torello – retired for their siesta, while he remained with his three guests; with whom he presently withdrew into a chamber, whither, that there might be nought that he held dear which they had not seen, he called his noble lady. And so the dame, exceeding fair and stately of person, and arrayed in rich apparel, with her two little boys, that shewed as two angels, on either hand, presented herself before them, and graciously greeted them. Whereupon they rose, and returned her salutation with reverence, and caused her to sit down among them, and made much of her two little boys. But after some interchange of gracious discourse, Messer Torello being withdrawn somewhat apart, she asked them courteously, whence they came and whither they were bound, and had of them the same answer that Messer Torello had received. "So!" quoth the lady with a joyful air, "then I see that my woman's wit will be of service to you; wherefore I pray you as a special favour neither to reject nor to despise the little gift that I am about to present to you; but reflecting that, as women have but small minds, so they make but small gifts, accept it, having regard rather to the good will of the giver than the magnitude of the gift." She then caused bring forth for each of them two pair of robes, lined the one with silk, the other with vair, no such robes as citizens or merchants, but such as lords, use to wear, and three vests of taffeta, besides linen clothes, and: – "Take them," quoth she. "The robes I give you are even such as I have arrayed my lord withal: the other things, considering that you are far from your wives, and have come a long way, and have yet a long way to go, and that merchants love to be neat and trim, may, albeit they are of no great value, be yet acceptable to you."

Wondering, the gentlemen acknowledged without reserve that there was no point of courtesy wherein Messer Torello was not minded to acquit himself towards them. And noting the lordly fashion of the robes, unsuited to the quality of merchants, they misdoubted that Messer Torello had recognized them. However, quoth one of them to the lady: – "Gifts great indeed are these, Madam, nor such as lightly to accept, were it not that thereto we are constrained by your prayers, to which we may on no account say, no." Whereupon, Messer Torello being now come back, the lady bade them adieu, and took her leave of them; and in like manner did she cause their servants to be supplied with equipment suitable to them. The gentlemen, being much importuned thereto by Messer Torello, consented to tarry the rest of the day with him; and so, having slept, they donned their robes, and rode a while with him about the city; and supper-time being come, they feasted magnificently, and with a numerous and honourable company. And so in due time they betook them to rest; and at daybreak, being risen, they found, in lieu of their jaded nags, three stout and excellent palfreys, and in like manner fresh and goodly mounts for their servants. Which Saladin marking turned to his lords, and: – "By God," quoth he, "never was gentleman more complete and courteous and considerate than this Messer Torello, and if the Christian kings are as kingly as he is knightly, there is none of them whose onset the Soldan of Babylon might well abide, to say nought of so many as we see making ready to fall upon him." However, knowing that 'twas not permissible to refuse, he very courteously thanked Messer Torello: and so they got them to horse. Messer Torello with a numerous company escorted them far beyond the gate of the city, until, loath though Saladin was to part from him, so greatly did he now affect him, yet as he must needs speed on, he besought him to turn back. Whereupon, albeit it irked him to take leave of them: – "Gentlemen," quoth Messer Torello, "since such is your pleasure, I obey; but this I must say to you. Who you are I know not, nor would I know more than you are pleased to impart; but whoever you may be, you will not make me believe that you are merchants this while; and so adieu!" To whom Saladin, having already taken leave of all his company, thus made answer: – "Peradventure, Sir, we shall one day give you to see somewhat of our merchandise, and thereby confirm your belief: and so adieu!"

Thus parted Saladin and his company from Messer Torello, Saladin burning with an exceeding great desire, if life should be continued to him, and the war, which he anticipated, should not undo him, to shew Messer Torello no less honour than he had received at his hands, and conversing not a little with his lords both of Messer Torello himself and of his lady, and all that he did and that in any wise concerned him, ever more highly commending them. However, having with much diligence spied out all the West, he put to sea, and returned with his company to Alexandria; and having now all needful information, he put himself in a posture of defence. Messer Torello, his mind full of his late guests, returned to Pavia; but, though he long pondered who they might be, he came never at or anywhere near the truth.

Then with great and general mustering of forces came the time for embarking on the emprise, and Messer Torello, heeding not the tearful entreaties of his wife, resolved to join therein. So, being fully equipped and about to take horse, he said to his lady, whom he most dearly loved: – "Wife, for honour's sake and for the weal of my soul, I go, as thou seest, on this emprise: our substance and our honour I commend to thy care. Certain I am of my departure, but, for the thousand accidents that may ensue, certitude have I none of my return: wherefore I would have thee do me this grace, that, whatever be my fate, shouldst thou lack certain intelligence that I live, thou wilt expect me a year and a month and a day from this my departure, before thou marry again." Whereto the lady, weeping bitterly, made answer: – "Messer Torello, I know not how I shall support the distress in which, thus departing, you leave me; but should my life not fail beneath it, and aught befall thee, live and die secure that I shall live and die the wife of Messer Torello, and of his memory." Whereupon: – "Wife," returned Messer Torello, "well assured I am that, so far as in thee shall lie, this promise of thine will be kept; but thou art young, and fair, and of a great family, and thy virtue is rare and generally known: wherefore I make no doubt that, should there be any suspicion of my death, thou wilt be asked of thy brothers and kinsmen by many a great gentleman: against whose attacks, though thou desire it never so, thou wilt not be able to hold out, but wilt perforce be fain to gratify one or other of them; for which cause it is that I ask thee to wait just so long and no longer." "As I have said," replied the lady, "so, in so far as I may, I shall do; and if I must needs do otherwise, rest assured that of this your behest I shall render you obedience. But I pray God that He bring neither you nor me to such a strait yet a while." Which said, the lady wept, and having embraced Messer Torello, drew from her finger a ring, and gave it to him, saying: – "Should it betide that I die before I see you again, mind you of me, when you look upon it."

Messer Torello took the ring, and got him to horse, and having bidden all adieu, fared forth on his journey; and being arrived with his company at Genoa, he embarked on a galley, and having departed thence, in no long time arrived at Acre, and joined the main Christian host; wherein there by and by broke out an exceeding great and mortal sickness; during which, whether owing to Saladin's strategy, or his good fortune, he made an easy capture of well-nigh all the remnant of the Christians that were escaped, and quartered them in divers prisons in many cities; of which captives Messer Torello being one, was brought to Alexandria and there confined. Where, not being known, and fearing to make himself known, he, under constraint of necessity, applied him to the training of hawks, whereof he was a very great master; and thereby he fell under the notice of Saladin, who took him out of the prison, and made him his falconer. The Soldan called him by no other name than "Christian," and neither recognized, nor was recognized by, him, who, his whole soul ever in Pavia, essayed many a time to escape, that he might return thither, but still without success: wherefore, certain Genoese, that were come to Alexandria as ambassadors to the Soldan for the redemption of some of their townsfolk, being about to return, he resolved to write to his lady, how that he lived, and would come back to her, as soon as he might, and that she should expect his return; and having so done, he earnestly besought one of the ambassadors, whom he knew, to see that the letter reached the hands of the Abbot of San Pietro in Ciel d'Oro, who was his uncle.

Now, such being the posture of Messer Torello's affairs, it befell one day that, while he talked with Saladin of his hawks, he smiled; whereby his mouth shaped itself in a fashion, of which Saladin had taken particular note, while he was at Pavia. And so, recalling Messer Torello to mind, he fixed his gaze upon him, and it seemed to him that 'twas indeed Messer Torello; wherefore, leaving the matter of which they were conversing: – "Tell me, Christian," quoth he, "of what country art thou in the West?" "My lord," replied Messer Torello, "I am a Lombard, of a city called Pavia, a poor man, and of humble condition." Which when he heard, Saladin, well-nigh resolved of his doubt, said joyfully to himself: – "God has provided me with occasion meet to prove to this man what store I set by his courtesy;" and without another word he brought him into a room where he kept all his wearing apparel, and said: – "Look, Christian, if among these robes there be any that thou hast ever seen before." So Messer Torello examined the robes, and espied those which his lady had given to Saladin; but, deeming they could not be the same, he replied: – "My lord, there is no robe here that I recognize, albeit 'tis true that those two robes are such as I once wore myself, in company with three merchants that came to my house." Whereupon Saladin could refrain himself no longer; but, tenderly embracing him: – "You," quoth he, "are Messer Torello d'Istria, and I am one of those three merchants to whom your lady gave these robes; and now is the time to warrant you of the quality of my merchandise, as, when I parted from you, I told you might come to pass." Which to hear, Messer Torello was at once overjoyed and abashed, overjoyed to have entertained so illustrious a guest, and abashed, for that it seemed to him that he had given him but a sorry entertainment. To whom: – "Messer Torello," quoth Saladin, "since hither has God sent you to me, deem that 'tis no more I that am lord here, but you." And so they made great cheer together; and then Saladin caused Messer

Torello to be royally arrayed; and presented him to all his greatest lords, and having extolled his merit in no stinted measure, bade all, as they hoped for grace from him, honour Messer Torello even as himself. And so from that hour did they all; but most especially the two lords that had been with Saladin at Messer Torello's house.

The glory, to which Messer Torello thus suddenly found himself raised, somewhat diverted his mind from the affairs of Lombardy, and the more so, for that he entertained no doubt that his letter had reached his uncle's hands. But for that in the camp, or rather army, of the Christians, on the day when they were taken by Saladin, there died and was buried one Messer Torello de Dignes, an obscure knight of Provence, whereas Messer Torello d'Istria was known to all the host for a right noble gentleman, whoso heard tell that Messer Torello was dead, supposed that 'twas Messer Torello d'Istria, and not Messer Torello de Dignes; nor did what happened after, to wit, the capture, avail to undeceive them; for not a few Italians had carried the report home with them; among whom there were some who made bold to say that they had seen Messer Torello d'Istria's dead body, and had been present at its interment. Which rumour coming to the ears of his lady and his kinsfolk, great indeed, nay, immeasurable was the distress that it occasioned not only to them, but to all that had known him. The mode and measure of his lady's grief, her mourning, her lamentation, 'twere tedious to describe. Enough that, after some months spent in almost unmitigated tribulation, her sorrow shewed signs of abatement; whereupon, suit being made for her hand by some of the greatest men of Lombardy, her brothers and other kinsfolk began to importune her to marry again. Times not a few, and with floods of tears, she refused; but, overborne at last, she consented to do as they would have her, upon the understanding that she was to remain unmarried until the term for which she had bound herself to Messer Torello was fulfilled.

Now the lady's affairs being in this posture at Pavia, it befell that some eight days or so before the time appointed for her marriage, Messer Torello one day espied in Alexandria one that he had observed go with the Genoese ambassadors aboard the galley that took them to Genoa; wherefore he called him, and asked him what sort of a voyage they had had, and when they had reached Genoa. "My lord," replied the other, "the galley made but a sorry voyage of it, as I learned in Crete, where I remained; for that, while she was nearing Sicily, there arose a terrible gale from the North that drove her on to the shoals of Barbary, and never a soul escaped, and among the rest my two brothers were lost." Which report believing – and 'twas indeed most true – and calling to mind that in a few days the term that he had asked of his wife would be fulfilled, and surmising that there could be no tidings of him at Pavia, Messer Torello made no question but that the lady was provided with another husband; whereby he sank into such a depth of woe that he lost all power to eat, and betook him to his bed and resigned himself to die. Which when Saladin, by whom he was most dearly beloved, learned, he came to him, and having plied him with many and most instant entreaties, learned at length the cause of his distress and sickness; and, having chidden him not a little that he had not sooner apprised him thereof, he besought him to put on a cheerful courage, assuring him, that, if so he did, he would bring it to pass that he should be in Pavia at the time appointed, and told him how. Believing Saladin's words the more readily that he had many times heard that 'twas possible, and had not seldom been done, Messer Torello recovered heart, and was instant with Saladin that he should make all haste.

Accordingly Saladin bade one of his necromancers, of whose skill he had already had proof, to devise a method whereby Messer Torello should be transported abed in a single night to Pavia: the necromancer made answer that it should be done, but that 'twere best he put Messer Torello to sleep. The matter being thus arranged, Saladin hied him back to Messer Torello, and finding him most earnestly desirous to be in Pavia at the time appointed, if so it might be, and if not, to die: – "Messer Torello," quoth he, "if you dearly love your lady, and misdoubt that she may become the bride of another, no wise, God wot, do I censure you, for that, of all the ladies that ever I saw, she, for bearing, manners, and address – to say nought of beauty, which is but the flower that perishes – seems to me the most worthy to be lauded and cherished. Much had I been gratified, since Fortune has sent you hither to me, that, while you and I yet live, we had exercised equal lordship in the governance of this my realm, and, if such was not God's will, and this must needs come upon you, that you are fain either to be at Pavia at the time appointed or to die, I had desired of all things to have been apprised thereof at such a time that I might have sent you home with such honourable circumstance and state and escort as befit your high desert; which not being vouchsafed me, and as nought will content you but to be there forthwith, I do what I can, and speed you thither on such wise as I have told you." "My lord," replied Messer Torello, "had you said nought, you have already done enough to prove your goodwill towards me, and that in so high a degree as is quite beyond my deserts, and most assured of the truth of what you say shall I live and die, and so had done, had you not said it; but, seeing that my resolve is taken, I pray you that that, which you promise to do, be done speedily, for that after to-morrow I may no longer count on being expected."

Saladin assured him that 'twas so ordered that he should not be disappointed. And on the morrow, it being his purpose to speed him on his journey that same night, he caused to be set up in one of his great halls a most goodly and sumptuous bed composed of mattresses, all, as was their wont, of velvet and cloth of gold, and had it covered with a quilt, adorned at certain intervals with enormous pearls, and most rare precious stones, insomuch that 'twas in after time accounted a priceless treasure, and furnished with two pillows to match it. Which done, he bade array Messer Torello, who was now quite recovered, in a robe after the Saracenic fashion, the richest and goodliest thing of the kind that was ever seen, and wrap about his head, according to their wont, one of their huge turbans. Then, at a late hour, Saladin, attended by certain of his lords, entered the chamber where Messer Torello was, and seating himself beside him, all but wept as thus he began: – "Messer Torello, the time is nigh at hand when you and I must part; wherefore, since I may neither give you my own, nor others' company (the journey that you are about to make not permitting it), I am come here, as 'tis fitting, in this chamber to take my leave of you. Wherefore, before I bid you adieu, I entreat you, by that friendship, that love, which is between us, that you forget me not, and that, if it be possible, when you have settled your affairs in Lombardy, you come at least once, before our days are ended, to visit me, that thereby I may both have the delight of seeing you again, and make good that omission which, by reason of your haste, I must needs now make; and that in the meanwhile it irk thee not to visit me by letter, and to ask of me whatever you shall have a mind to, and be sure that there lives not the man whom I shall content more gladly than you." Messer Torello could not refrain his tears, and so, with words few, and broken by his sobs, he answered that 'twas impossible that the Soldan's generous deeds and chivalrous character should ever be forgotten by him, and that without fail he would do as he bade him, so soon as occasion should serve him. Whereupon Saladin tenderly embraced and kissed him, and with many a tear bade him adieu, and quitted the chamber. His lords then took leave of Messer Torello, and followed Saladin into the hall, where he had had the bed made ready.

'Twas now late, and the necromancer being intent to hasten Messer Torello's transit, a physician brought him a potion, and having first shewn him what he was to give him by way of viaticum, caused him to drink it; and not long after he fell asleep. In which state he was carried by Saladin's command, and laid on the goodly bed, whereon he set a large and fair and most sumptuous crown, marking it in such sort that there could be no mistake that it was sent by

Saladin to Messer Torello's wife. He next placed on Messer Torello's finger a ring, in which was set a carbuncle of such brilliance that it shewed as a lighted torch, and of well-nigh inestimable value. After which he girded on him a sword, the appointments of which might not readily be appraised. And therewithal he adorned him in front with a pendant, wherein were pearls, the like of which had never been seen, and not a few other rare jewels. And, moreover, on either side of him he set two vast basins of gold full of pistoles; and strings of pearls not a few, and rings and girdles, and other things, which 'twere tedious to enumerate, he disposed around him. Which done, he kissed Messer Torello again, and bade the necromancer speed him on his journey. Whereupon, forthwith, the bed, with Messer Torello thereon, was borne away from before Saladin's eyes, and he and his barons remained conversing thereof.

The bed, as Messer Torello had requested, had already been deposited in the church of San Piero in Ciel d'Oro at Pavia, and Messer Torello, with all the aforesaid jewels and ornaments upon and about him, was lying thereon, and still slept, when, upon the stroke of matins, the sacristan came into the church, light in hand, and presently setting eyes on the sumptuous bed, was not only amazed, but mightily terrified, insomuch that he turned back, and took to flight. Which the abbot and monks observing with no small surprise, asked wherefore he fled and he told them. Whereupon: – "Oh," quoth the abbot, "thou art no longer a child, nor yet so new to this church, that thou shouldst so lightly be appalled: go we now, and see who it is that has given thee this childish fright." So, with a blaze of torches, the abbot, attended by his monks, entered the church, and espied this wondrous costly bed whereon the knight slept, and while, hesitant and fearful, daring not to approach the bed, they scanned the rare and splendid jewels, it befell that, the efficacy of the potion being exhausted, Messer Torello awoke and heaved a great sigh. Whereat the monks and the abbot quaking and crying out: – "Lord, help us!" one and all took to flight. Messer Torello, opening his eyes and looking about him, saw, to his no small satisfaction, that without a doubt he was in the very place where he had craved of Saladin to be; so up he sate, and taking particular note of the matters with which he was surrounded, accounted the magnificence of Saladin to exceed even the measure, great though it was, that he already knew. However, he still kept quiet, save that, perceiving the monks in flight, and surmising the reason, he began to call the abbot by name, bidding him be of good courage, for that he was his nephew, Torello. Whereat the abbot did but wax more terrified, for that he deemed Torello had been many a month dead; but, after a while, as he heard himself still called, sound judgment got the better of his fears, and making the sign of the cross, he drew nigh Torello; who said to him: – "Father, what is't you fear? By God's grace I live, and hither am come back from overseas." Whom, for all he had grown a long beard and was dressed in the Saracenic fashion, the abbot after a while recognized, and now, quite reassured, took by the hand, saying: – "Son, welcome home:" then: – "No cause hast thou to marvel at our fears," he went on, "seeing that there is never a soul in these parts but firmly believes thee to be dead, insomuch that I may tell thee that Madonna Adalieta, thy wife, overborne by the entreaties and menaces of her kinsfolk, and against her will, is provided with another husband, to whom she is this morning to go, and all is made ready for the nuptials and the attendant festivities."

Whereupon Messer Torello, being risen from the sumptuous bed, did the abbot and the monks wondrous cheer, and besought them, one and all, to tell never a soul of his return, until he had completed something that he had on hand. After which, having put the costly jewels in safe keeping, he recounted to the abbot all the story of his adventures to that very hour. The abbot, rejoicing in his good fortune, joined with him in offering thanks to God. Messer Torello then asked him who might be his wife's new husband, and the abbot told him. Quoth then Messer Torello: – "Before my return be known, I purpose to see how my wife will comport herself at the nuptials: wherefore, though 'tis not the wont of men of religion to go to such gatherings, I had lief that for love of me you arranged for us to go thither together." The abbot answered that, he would gladly do so, and as soon as 'twas day, he sent word to the bridegroom that he had thoughts of being present at his nuptials, accompanied by a friend; whereto the gentleman made answer that he was much gratified. So, at the breakfast hour Messer Torello, dressed as he was, hied him with the abbot to the bridegroom's house, as many as saw them gazing on him with wonder, but none recognizing him, and the abbot giving all to understand that he was a Saracen sent by the Soldan as ambassador to the King of France. Messer Torello was accordingly seated at a table directly opposite that of his lady, whom he eyed with exceeding great delight, the more so that he saw that in her face which shewed him that she was chagrined by the nuptials. She in like manner from time to time bent her regard on him; howbeit, what with his long beard, and his foreign garb, and her firm persuasion that he was dead, she had still no sort of recollection of him. However, Messer Torello at length deemed it time to make trial of her, whether she would remember him; wherefore he took the ring that the lady had given, him on his departure, and keeping it close in the palm of his hand, he called to him a page that waited upon her, and said to him: – "Tell the bride from me that 'tis the custom in my country, that, when a stranger, such as I, eats with a bride, like herself, at her wedding-feast, she, in token that he is welcome to her board, sends him the cup from which she herself drinks, full of wine; and when the stranger has drunk his fill, he closes the cup, and the bride drinks what is left therein."

The page carried the message to the lady, who, being of good understanding and manners, and supposing him to be some very great man, by way of shewing that she was gratified by his presence, commanded that a gilt cup, that was on the table before her, should be rinsed, and filled with wine, and borne to the gentleman. Which being done, Messer Torello, having privily conveyed her ring into his mouth, let it fall (while he drank) into the cup on such wise that none wist thereof; and leaving but a little wine at the bottom, closed the cup and returned it to the lady; who, having taken it, that she might do full honour to the custom of her guest's country, lifted the lid, and set the cup to her mouth; whereby espying the ring, she thereon mutely gazed a while, and recognizing it for that which she had given Messer Torello on his departure, she steadfastly regarded the supposed stranger, whom now she also recognized. Whereupon well-nigh distracted, oversetting the table in front of her, she exclaimed: – "'Tis my lord, 'tis verily Messer Torello;" and rushing to the table at which he sate, giving never a thought to her apparel, or aught that was on the table, she flung herself upon it; and reaching forward as far as she could, she threw her arms about him, and hugged him; nor, for aught that any said or did, could she be induced to release his neck, until Messer Torello himself bade her forbear a while, for that she would have time enough to kiss him thereafter. The lady then stood up, and for a while all was disorder, albeit the feast was yet more gladsome than before by reason of the recovery of so honourable a knight: then, at Messer Torello's entreaty, all were silent, while he recounted to them the story of his adventures from the day of his departure to that hour, concluding by saying that the gentleman who, deeming him to be dead, had taken his lady to wife, ought not to be affronted, if he, being alive, reclaimed her. The bridegroom, albeit he was somewhat crestfallen, made answer in frank and friendly sort, that 'twas for Messer Torello to do what he liked with his own. The lady resigned the ring and the crown that her new spouse had given her, and put on the ring she had taken from the cup, and likewise the crown sent her by the Soldan; and so, forth they hied them, and with full nuptial pomp wended their way to Messer Torello's house; and there for a great while they made merry with his late disconsolate friends and kinsfolk and all the citizens, who accounted his restoration as little short of a miracle.

Messer Torello, having bestowed part of his rare jewels upon him who had borne the cost of the wedding-feast, and part on the abbot, and many other folk; and having by more than one messenger sent word of his safe home-coming and prosperous estate to Saladin, acknowledging himself ever his friend and vassal, lived many years thereafter with his worthy lady, acquitting himself yet more courteously than of yore. Such, then, was the end of the troubles of Messer Torello and his dear lady, and such the reward of their cheerful and ready courtesies.

Now some there are that strive to do offices of courtesy, and have the means, but do them with so ill a grace, that, ere they are done, they have in effect sold them at a price above their worth: wherefore, if no reward ensue to them thereof, neither they nor other folk have cause to marvel.

Tenth Day

Novel X

— *The Marquis of Saluzzo, overborne by the entreaties of his vassals, consents to take a wife, but, being minded to please himself in the choice of her, takes a husbandman's daughter. He has two children by her, both of whom he makes her believe that he has put to death. Afterward, feigning to be tired of her, and to have taken another wife, he turns her out of doors in her shift, and brings his daughter into the house in guise of his bride; but, finding her patient under it all, he brings her home again, and shews her her children, now grown up, and honours her, and causes her to be honoured, as Marchioness.* —

ENDED THE KING'S long story, with which all seemed to be very well pleased, quoth Dioneo with a laugh: – "The good man that looked that night to cause the bogey's tail to droop, would scarce have contributed two pennyworth of all the praise you bestow on Messer Torello:" then, witting that it now only remained for him to tell, thus he began: –

Gentle my ladies, this day, meseems, is dedicate to Kings and Soldans and folk of the like quality; wherefore, that I stray not too far from you, I am minded to tell you somewhat of a Marquis; certes, nought magnificent, but a piece of mad folly, albeit there came good thereof to him in the end. The which I counsel none to copy, for that great pity 'twas that it turned out well with him.

There was in olden days a certain Marquis of Saluzzo, Gualtieri by name, a young man, but head of the house, who, having neither wife nor child, passed his time in nought else but in hawking and hunting, and of taking a wife and begetting children had no thought; wherein he should have been accounted very wise: but his vassals, brooking it ill, did oftentimes entreat him to take a wife, that he might not die without an heir, and they be left without a lord; offering to find him one of such a pattern, and of such parentage, that he might marry with good hope, and be well content with the sequel. To whom: – "My friends," replied Gualtieri, "you enforce me to that which I had resolved never to do, seeing how hard it is to find a wife, whose ways accord well with one's own, and how plentiful is the supply of such as run counter thereto, and how grievous a life he leads who chances upon a lady that matches ill with him. And to say that you think to know the daughters by the qualities of their fathers and mothers, and thereby – so you would argue – to provide me with a wife to my liking, is but folly; for I wot not how you may penetrate the secrets of their mothers so as to know their fathers; and granted that you do know them, daughters oftentimes resemble neither of their parents. However, as you are minded to rivet these fetters upon me, I am content that so it be; and that I may have no cause to reproach any but myself, should it turn out ill, I am resolved that my wife shall be of my own choosing; but of this rest assured, that, no matter whom I choose, if she receive not from you the honour due to a lady, you shall prove to your great cost, how sorely I resent being thus constrained by your importunity to take a wife against my will."

The worthy men replied that they were well content, so only he would marry without more ado. And Gualtieri, who had long noted with approval the mien of a poor girl that dwelt on a farm hard by his house, and found her fair enough, deemed that with her he might pass a tolerably happy life. Wherefore he sought no further, but forthwith resolved to marry her; and having sent for her father, who was a very poor man, he contracted with him to take her to wife. Which done, Gualtieri assembled all the friends he had in those parts, and: – "My friends," quoth he, "you were and are minded that I should take a wife, and rather to comply with your wishes, than for any desire that I had to marry, I have made up my mind to do so. You remember the promise you gave me, to wit, that, whomsoever I should take, you would pay her the honour due to a lady. Which promise I now require you to keep, the time being come when I am to keep mine. I have found hard by here a maiden after mine own heart, whom I purpose to take to wife, and to bring hither to my house in the course of a few days. Wherefore bethink you, how you may make the nuptial feast splendid, and welcome her with all honour; that I may confess myself satisfied with your observance of your promise, as you will be with my observance of mine." The worthy men, one and all, answered with alacrity that they were well content, and that, whoever she might be, they would entreat her as a lady, and pay her all due honour as such. After which, they all addressed them to make goodly and grand and gladsome celebration of the event, as did also Gualtieri. He arranged for a wedding most stately and fair, and bade thereto a goodly number of his friends and kinsfolk, and great gentlemen, and others, of the neighbourhood; and therewithal he caused many a fine and costly robe to be cut and fashioned to the figure of a girl who seemed to him of the like proportions as the girl that he purposed to wed; and laid in store, besides, of girdles and rings, with a costly and beautiful crown, and all the other paraphernalia of a bride.

The day that he had appointed for the wedding being come, about half tierce he got him to horse with as many as had come to do him honour, and having made all needful dispositions: – "Gentlemen," quoth he, "'tis time to go bring home the bride." And so away he rode with his company to the village; where, being come to the house of the girl's father, they found her returning from the spring with a bucket of water, making all the haste she could, that she might afterwards go with the other women to see Gualtieri's bride come by. Whom Gualtieri no sooner saw, than he called her by her name, to wit, Griselda, and asked her where her father was. To whom she modestly made answer: – "My lord, he is in the house." Whereupon Gualtieri dismounted, and having bidden the rest await him without, entered the cottage alone; and meeting her father, whose name was Giannucolo: – "I am come," quoth he, "to wed Griselda, but first of all there are some matters I would learn from her own lips in thy presence." He then asked her, whether, if he took her to wife, she would study to comply with his wishes, and be not wroth, no matter what he might say or do, and be obedient, with not a few other questions of a like sort: to all which she answered, ay. Whereupon Gualtieri took her by the hand, led her forth, and before the eyes of all his company, and as many other folk as were there, caused her to strip naked, and let bring the garments that he had had fashioned for her, and had her forthwith arrayed therein, and upon her unkempt head let set a crown; and then, while all wondered: – "Gentlemen," quoth he, "this is she whom I purpose to make my wife, so she be minded to have me for husband." Then, she standing abashed and astonied, he turned to her, saying: – "Griselda, wilt thou have me for thy husband?" To whom: – "Ay, my lord," answered she. "And I will have thee to wife," said he, and married her before them all. And having set her upon a palfrey, he brought her home with pomp.

The wedding was fair and stately, and had he married a daughter of the King of France, the feast could not have been more splendid. It seemed as if, with the change of her garb, the bride had acquired a new dignity of mind and mien. She was, as we have said, fair of form and feature; and therewithal she was now grown so engaging and gracious and debonair, that she shewed no longer as the shepherdess, and the daughter of Giannucolo, but as the daughter of some noble lord, insomuch that she caused as many as had known her before to marvel. Moreover, she was so obedient and devoted to her husband, that he deemed himself the happiest and luckiest man in the world. And likewise so gracious and kindly was she to her husband's vassals, that there was none of them but loved her more dearly than himself, and was zealous to do her honour, and prayed for her welfare and prosperity and aggrandisement, and instead of, as erstwhile, saying that Gualtieri had done foolishly to take her to wife, now averred that he had not his like in the world for wisdom and discernment, for that, save to him, her noble qualities would ever have remained hidden under her sorry apparel and the garb of the peasant girl. And in short she so comported herself as in no long time to bring it to pass that, not only in the marquisate, but far and wide besides, her virtues and her admirable conversation were matter of common talk, and, if aught had been said to the disadvantage of her husband, when he married her, the judgment was now altogether to the contrary effect.

She had not been long with Gualtieri before she conceived; and in due time she was delivered of a girl; whereat Gualtieri made great cheer. But, soon after, a strange humour took possession of him, to wit, to put her patience to the proof by prolonged and intolerable hard usage; wherefore he began by afflicting her with his gibes, putting on a vexed air, and telling her that his vassals were most sorely dissatisfied with her by reason of her base condition, and all the more so since they saw that she was a mother, and that they did nought but most ruefully murmur at the birth of a daughter. Whereto Griselda, without the least change of countenance or sign of discomposure, made answer: – "My lord, do with me as thou mayst deem best for thine own honour and comfort, for well I wot that I am of less account than they, and unworthy of this honourable estate to which of thy courtesy thou hast advanced me." By which answer Gualtieri was well pleased, witting that she was in no degree puffed up with pride by his, or any other's, honourable entreatment of her. A while afterwards, having in general terms given his wife to understand that the vassals could not endure her daughter, he sent her a message by a servant. So the servant came, and: – "Madam," quoth he with a most dolorous mien, "so I value my life, I must needs do my lord's bidding. He has bidden me take your daughter and…" He said no more, but the lady by what she heard, and read in his face, and remembered of her husband's words, understood that he was bidden to put the child to death. Whereupon she presently took the child from the cradle, and having kissed and blessed her, albeit she was very sore at heart, she changed not countenance, but placed it in the servant's arms, saying: – "See that thou leave nought undone that my lord and thine has charged thee to do, but leave her not so that the beasts and the birds devour her, unless he have so bidden thee." So the servant took the child, and told Gualtieri what the lady had said; and Gualtieri, marvelling at her constancy, sent him with the child to Bologna, to one of his kinswomen, whom he besought to rear and educate the child with all care, but never to let it be known whose child she was.

Soon after it befell that the lady again conceived, and in due time was delivered of a son, whereat Gualtieri was overjoyed. But, not content with what he had done, he now even more poignantly afflicted the lady; and one day with a ruffled mien: – "Wife," quoth he, "since thou gavest birth to this boy, I may on no wise live in peace with my vassals, so bitterly do they reproach me that a grandson of Giannucolo is to succeed me as their lord; and therefore I fear that, so I be not minded to be sent a packing hence, I must even do herein as I did before, and in the end put thee away, and take another wife." The lady heard him patiently, and answered only: – "My lord, study how thou mayst content thee and best please thyself, and waste no thought upon me, for there is nought I desire save in so far as I know that 'tis thy pleasure." Not many days after, Gualtieri, in like manner as he had sent for the daughter, sent for the son, and having made a shew of putting him to death, provided for his, as for the girl's, nurture at

Bologna. Whereat the lady shewed no more discomposure of countenance or speech than at the loss of her daughter: which Gualtieri found passing strange, and inly affirmed that there was never another woman in the world that would have so done. And but that he had marked that she was most tenderly affectionate towards her children, while 'twas well pleasing to him, he had supposed that she was tired of them, whereas he knew that 'twas of her discretion that she so did. His vassals, who believed that he had put the children to death, held him mightily to blame for his cruelty, and felt the utmost compassion for the lady. She, however, said never aught to the ladies that condoled with her on the death of her children, but that the pleasure of him that had begotten them was her pleasure likewise.

Years not a few had passed since the girl's birth, when Gualtieri at length deemed the time come to put his wife's patience to the final proof. Accordingly, in the presence of a great company of his vassals he declared that on no wise might he longer brook to have Griselda to wife, that he confessed that in taking her he had done a sorry thing and the act of a stripling, and that he therefore meant to do what he could to procure the Pope's dispensation to put Griselda away, and take another wife: for which cause being much upbraided by many worthy men, he made no other answer but only that needs must it so be. Whereof the lady being apprised, and now deeming that she must look to go back to her father's house, and perchance tend the sheep, as she had aforetime, and see him, to whom she was utterly devoted, engrossed by another woman, did inly bewail herself right sorely: but still with the same composed mien with which she had borne Fortune's former buffets, she set herself to endure this last outrage. Nor was it long before Gualtieri by counterfeit letters, which he caused to be sent to him from Rome, made his vassals believe that the Pope had thereby given him a dispensation to put Griselda away, and take another wife. Wherefore, having caused her to be brought before him, he said to her in the presence of not a few: – "Wife, by license granted me by the Pope, I am now free to put thee away, and take another wife; and, for that my forbears have always been great gentlemen and lords of these parts, whereas thine have ever been husbandmen, I purpose that thou go back to Giannucolo's house with the dowry that thou broughtest me; whereupon I shall bring home a lady that I have found, and who is meet to be my wife."

'Twas not without travail most grievous that the lady, as she heard this announcement, got the better of her woman's nature, and suppressing her tears, made answer: – "My lord, I ever knew that my low degree was on no wise congruous with your nobility, and acknowledged that the rank I had with you was of your and God's bestowal, nor did I ever make as if it were mine by gift, or so esteem it, but still accounted it as a loan. 'Tis your pleasure to recall it, and therefore it should be, and is, my pleasure to render it up to you. So, here is your ring, with which you espoused me; take it back. You bid me take with me the dowry that I brought you; which to do will require neither paymaster on your part nor purse nor packhorse on mine; for I am not unmindful that naked was I when you first had me. And if you deem it seemly that that body in which I have borne children, by you begotten, be beheld of all, naked will I depart; but yet, I pray you, be pleased, in guerdon of the virginity that I brought you and take not away, to suffer me to bear hence upon my back a single shift – I crave no more – besides my dowry." There was nought of which Gualtieri was so fain as to weep; but yet, setting his face as a flint, he made answer: – "I allow thee a shift to thy back; so get thee hence." All that stood by besought him to give her a robe, that she, who had been his wife for thirteen years and more, might not be seen to quit his house in so sorry and shameful a plight, having nought on her but a shift. But their entreaties went for nothing: the lady in her shift, and barefoot and bareheaded, having bade them adieu, departed the house, and went back to her father amid the tears and lamentations of all that saw her. Giannucolo, who had ever deemed it a thing incredible that Gualtieri should keep his daughter to wife, and had looked for this to happen every day, and had kept the clothes that she had put off on the morning that Gualtieri had wedded her, now brought them to her; and she, having resumed them, applied herself to the petty drudgery of her father's house, as she had been wont, enduring with fortitude this cruel visitation of adverse Fortune.

Now no sooner had Gualtieri dismissed Griselda, than he gave his vassals to understand that he had taken to wife a daughter of one of the Counts of Panago. He accordingly made great preparations as for the nuptials, during which he sent for Griselda. To whom, being come, quoth he: – "I am bringing hither my new bride, and in this her first home-coming I purpose to shew her honour; and thou knowest that women I have none in the house that know how to set chambers in due order, or attend to the many other matters that so joyful an event requires; wherefore do thou, that understandest these things better than another, see to all that needs be done, and bid hither such ladies as thou mayst see fit, and receive them, as if thou wert the lady of the house, and then, when the nuptials are ended, thou mayst go back to thy cottage." Albeit each of these words pierced Griselda's heart like a knife, for that, in resigning her good fortune, she had not been able to renounce the love she bore Gualtieri, nevertheless: – "My lord," she made answer, "I am ready and prompt to do your pleasure." And so, clad in her sorry garments of coarse romagnole, she entered the house, which, but a little before, she had quitted in her shift, and addressed her to sweep the chambers, and arrange arras and cushions in the halls, and make ready the kitchen, and set her hand to everything, as if she had been a paltry serving-wench: nor did she rest until she had brought all into such meet and seemly trim as the occasion demanded. This done, she invited in Gualtieri's name all the ladies of those parts to be present at his nuptials, and awaited the event. The day being come, still wearing her sorry weeds, but in heart and soul and mien the lady, she received the ladies as they came, and gave each a gladsome greeting.

Now Gualtieri, as we said, had caused his children to be carefully nurtured and brought up by a kinswoman of his at Bologna, which kinswoman was married into the family of the Counts of Panago; and, the girl being now twelve years old, and the loveliest creature that ever was seen, and the boy being about six years old, he had sent word to his kinswoman's husband at Bologna, praying him to be pleased to come with this girl and boy of his to Saluzzo, and to see that he brought a goodly and honourable company with him, and to give all to understand that he brought the girl to him to wife, and on no wise to disclose to any, who she really was. The gentleman did as the Marquis bade him, and within a few days of his setting forth arrived at Saluzzo about breakfast-time with the girl, and her brother, and a noble company, and found all the folk of those parts, and much people besides, gathered there in expectation of Gualtieri's new bride. Who, being received by the ladies, was no sooner come into the hall, where the tables were set, than Griselda advanced to meet her, saying with hearty cheer: – "Welcome, my lady." So the ladies, who had with much instance, but in vain, besought Gualtieri, either to let Griselda keep in another room, or at any rate to furnish her with one of the robes that had been hers, that she might not present herself in such a sorry guise before the strangers, sate down to table; and the service being begun, the eyes of all were set on the girl, and every one said that Gualtieri had made a good exchange, and Griselda joined with the rest in greatly commending her, and also her little brother. And now Gualtieri, sated at last with all that he had seen of his wife's patience, marking that this new and strange turn made not the least alteration in her demeanour, and being well assured that 'twas not due to apathy, for he knew her to be of excellent understanding, deemed it time to relieve her of the suffering which he judged her to dissemble under a resolute front; and so, having called her to him in presence of them all, he said with a smile: – "And what thinkst thou of our bride?" "My lord," replied Griselda, "I think mighty well of her; and if she be but as discreet as she is fair – and so I deem her – I make no doubt but you may reckon to lead with her a life of incomparable felicity; but with all earnestness I entreat you, that you spare her those tribulations which you did once inflict upon another that was yours, for I scarce think she would be able to bear them, as well because she is younger, as for that she has been delicately nurtured, whereas that other had known no respite of hardship since she was but a little child." Marking that she made no doubt but that the girl was to be his wife, and yet spoke never a whit the less sweetly, Gualtieri caused her to sit down beside him, and: – "Griselda," said he, "'tis now time that thou see the reward of thy long patience, and that those, who have deemed me cruel and unjust and insensate, should know that what I did was done of purpose aforethought, for that I was minded to give both thee and them a lesson, that thou mightst learn to be a wife, and they in like manner might learn how to take and keep a wife, and that I might beget me perpetual peace with thee for the rest of my life; whereof being in great fear, when I came to take a wife, lest I should be disappointed, I therefore, to put the matter to the proof, did, and how sorely thou knowest, harass and afflict thee. And since I never knew thee either by deed or by word to deviate from my will, I now, deeming myself to have of thee that assurance of happiness which I desired, am minded to restore to thee at once all that, step by step, I took from thee, and by extremity of joy to compensate the tribulations that I inflicted on thee. Receive, then, this girl, whom thou supposest to be my bride, and her brother, with glad heart, as thy children and mine. These are they, whom by thee and many another it has long been supposed that I did ruthlessly to death, and I am thy husband, that loves thee more dearly than aught else, deeming that other there is none that has the like good cause to be well content with his wife."

Which said, he embraced and kissed her; and then, while she wept for joy, they rose and hied them there where sate the daughter, all astonied to hear the news, whom, as also her brother, they tenderly embraced, and explained to them, and many others that stood by, the whole mystery. Whereat the ladies, transported with delight, rose from table and betook them with Griselda to a chamber, and, with better omen, divested her of her sorry garb, and arrayed her in one of her own robes of state; and so, in guise of a lady (howbeit in her rags she had shewed as no less) they led her back into the hall. Wondrous was the cheer which there they made with the children; and, all overjoyed at the event, they revelled and made merry amain, and prolonged the festivities for several days; and very discreet they pronounced Gualtieri, albeit they censured as intolerably harsh the probation to which he had subjected Griselda, and most discreet beyond all compare they accounted Griselda.

Some days after, the Count of Panago returned to Bologna, and Gualtieri took Giannucolo from his husbandry, and established him in honour as his father-in-law, wherein to his great solace he lived for the rest of his days. Gualtieri himself, having mated his daughter with a husband of high degree, lived long and happily thereafter with Griselda, to whom he ever paid all honour.

Now what shall we say in this case but that even into the cots of the poor the heavens let fall at times spirits divine, as into the palaces of kings souls that are fitter to tend hogs than to exercise lordship over men? Who but Griselda had been able, with a countenance not only tearless, but cheerful, to endure the hard and unheard-of trials to which Gualtieri subjected her? Who perhaps might have deemed himself to have made no bad investment, had he chanced upon one, who, having been turned out of his house in her shift, had found means so to dust the pelisse of another as to get herself thereby a fine robe.

So ended Dioneo's story, whereof the ladies, diversely inclining, one to censure where another found matter for commendation, had discoursed not a little, when the king, having glanced at the sky, and marked that the sun was now low, insomuch that 'twas nigh the vesper hour, still keeping his seat, thus began: – "Exquisite my ladies, as, methinks, you wot, 'tis not only in minding them of the past and apprehending the present that the wit of mortals consists; but by one means or the other to be able to foresee the future is by the sages accounted the height of wisdom. Now, to-morrow, as you know, 'twill be fifteen days since, in quest of recreation and for the conservation of our health and life, we, shunning the dismal and dolorous and afflicting spectacles that have ceased not in our city since this season of pestilence began, took our departure from Florence. Wherein, to my thinking, we have done nought that was not seemly; for, if I have duly used my powers of observation, albeit some gay stories, and of a kind to stimulate concupiscence, have here been told, and we have daily known no lack of dainty dishes and good wine, nor yet of music and song, things, one and all, apt to incite weak minds to that which is not seemly, neither on your part, nor on ours, have I marked deed or word, or aught of any kind, that called for reprehension; but, by what I have seen and heard, seemliness and the sweet intimacy of brothers and sisters have ever reigned among us. Which, assuredly, for the honour and advantage which you and I have had thereof, is most grateful to me. Wherefore, lest too long continuance in this way of life might beget some occasion of weariness, and that no man may be able to misconstrue our too long abidance here, and as we have all of us had our day's share of the honour which still remains in me, I should deem it meet, so you be of like mind, that we now go back whence we came: and that the rather that our company, the bruit whereof has already reached divers others that are in our neighbourhood, might be so increased that all our pleasure would be destroyed. And so, if my counsel meet with your approval, I will keep the crown I have received of you until our departure, which, I purpose, shall be tomorrow morning. Should you decide otherwise, I have already determined whom to crown for the ensuing day."

Much debate ensued among the ladies and young men; but in the end they approved the king's proposal as expedient and seemly; and resolved to do even as he had said. The king therefore summoned the seneschal; and having conferred with him of the order he was to observe on the morrow, he dismissed the company until supper-time. So, the king being risen, the ladies and the rest likewise rose, and betook them, as they were wont, to their several diversions. Supper-time being come, they supped with exceeding great delight. Which done, they addressed them to song and music and dancing; and, while Lauretta was leading a dance, the king bade Fiammetta give them a song; whereupon Fiammetta right debonairly sang on this wise: –

> *So came but Love, and brought no jealousy,*
>   *So blithe, I wot, as I,*
>   *Dame were there none, be she whoe'er she be.*
>
> *If youth's fresh, lusty pride*
>   *May lady of her lover well content,*
>   *Or valour's just renown,*
>   *Hardihood, prowess tried,*
>   *Wit, noble mien, discourse most excellent,*
>   *And of all grace the crown;*
>   *That she am I, who, fain for love to swoun,*
>   *There where my hope doth lie*
>   *These several virtues all conjoined do see.*

*But, for that I less wise
  Than me no whit do other dames discern,
  Trembling with sore dismay,
  I still the worst surmise,
  Deeming their hearts with the same flame to burn
  That of mine maketh prey:
  Wherefore of him that is my hope's one stay
  Disconsolate I sigh,
  Yea mightily, and daily do me dree.*

*If but my lord as true
  As worthy to be loved I might approve,
  I were not jealous then:
  But, for that charmer new
  Doth all too often gallant lure to love,
  Forsworn I hold all men,
  And sick at heart I am, of death full fain;
  Nor lady doth him eye,
  But I do quake, lest she him wrest from me.*

*'Fore God, then, let each she
  List to my prayer, nor e'er in my despite
  Such grievous wrong essay;
  For should there any be
  That by or speech or mien's allurements light
  Of him to rob me may
  Study or plot, I, witting, shall find way,
  My beauty it aby!
  To cause her sore lament such frenesie.*

As soon as Fiammetta had ended her song, Dioneo, who was beside her, said with a laugh: – "Madam, 'twould be a great courtesy on your part to do all ladies to wit, who he is, that he be not stolen from you in ignorance, seeing that you threaten such dire resentment." Several other songs followed; and it being then nigh upon midnight, all, as the king was pleased to order, betook them to rest. With the first light of the new day they rose, and, the seneschal having already conveyed thence all their chattels, they, following the lead of their discreet king, hied them back to Florence; and in Santa Maria Novella, whence they had set forth, the three young men took leave of the seven ladies, and departed to find other diversions elsewhere, while the ladies in due time repaired to their homes.

The Author's Epilogue

MOST NOBLE DAMSELS, for whose solace I addressed me to this long and toilsome task, meseems that, aided by the Divine grace, the bestowal whereof I impute to the efficacy of your pious prayers, and in no wise to merits of mine, I have now brought this work to the full and perfect consummation which in the outset thereof I promised you. Wherefore, it but remains for me to render, first to God, and then to you, my thanks, and so to give a rest to my pen and weary hand. But this I purpose not to allow them, until, briefly, as to questions tacitly mooted – for well assured I am that these stories have no especial privilege above any others, nay, I forget not that at the beginning of the Fourth Day I have made the same plain – I shall have answered certain trifling objections that one of you, maybe, or some other, might advance. Peradventure, then, some of you will be found to say that I have used excessive license in the writing of these stories, in that I have caused ladies at times to tell, and oftentimes to list, matters that, whether to tell or to list, do not well beseem virtuous women. The which I deny, for that there is none of these stories so unseemly, but that it may without offence be told by any one, if but seemly words be used; which rule, methinks, has here been very well observed. But assume we that 'tis even so (for with you I am not minded to engage in argument, witting that you would vanquish me), then, I say that for answer why I have so done, reasons many come very readily to hand. In the first place, if aught of the kind in any of these stories there be, 'twas but such as was demanded by the character of the stories, which let but any person of sound judgment scan with the eye of reason, and 'twill be abundantly manifest that, unless I had been minded to deform them, they could not have been otherwise recounted. And if, perchance, they do, after all, contain here and there a trifling indiscretion of speech, such as might ill sort with one of your precious prudes, who weigh words rather than deeds, and are more concerned to appear, than to be, good, I say that so to write was as permissible to me, as 'tis to men and women at large in their converse to make use of such terms as hole, and pin, and mortar, and pestle, and sausage, and polony, and plenty more besides of a like sort. And therewithal privilege no less should be allowed to my pen than to the pencil of the painter, who without incurring any, or at least any just, censure, not only will depict St. Michael smiting the serpent, or St. George the dragon, with sword or lance at his discretion; but male he paints us Christ, and female Eve, and His feet that for the salvation of our race willed to die upon the cross he fastens thereto, now with one, now with two nails.

Moreover, 'tis patent to all that 'twas not in the Church, of matters whereto pertaining 'tis meet we speak with all purity of heart and seemliness of phrase, albeit among her histories there are to be found not a few that will ill compare with my writings; nor yet in the schools of the philosophers, where, as much as anywhere, seemliness is demanded, nor in any place where clergy or philosophers congregate, but in gardens, in pleasaunces, and among folk, young indeed, but not so young as to be seducible by stories, and at a time when, if so one might save one's life, the most sedate might without disgrace walk abroad with his breeches for headgear, that these stories were told. Which stories, such as they are, may, like all things else, be baneful or profitable according to the quality of the hearer. Who knows not that wine is, as Cinciglione and Scolaio and many another aver, an excellent thing for the living creature, and yet noxious to the fevered patient? Are we, for the mischief it does to the fever-stricken, to say that 'tis a bad thing? Who knows not that fire is most serviceable, nay, necessary, to mortals? Are we to say that, because it burns houses and villages and cities, it is a bad thing? Arms, in like manner, are the safeguard of those that desire to live in peace, and also by them are men not seldom maliciously slain, albeit the malice is not in them, but in those that use them for a malicious purpose. Corrupt mind did never yet understand any word in a wholesome sense; and as such a mind has no profit of seemly words, so such as are scarce seemly may as little avail to contaminate a healthy mind as mud the radiance of the sun, or the deformities of earth the splendours of the heavens. What books, what words, what letters, are more sacred, more excellent, more venerable, than those of Holy Writ? And yet there have been not a few that, perversely construing them, have brought themselves and others to perdition. Everything is in itself good for somewhat, and being put to a bad purpose, may work manifold mischief. And so, I say, it is with my stories. If any man shall be minded to draw from them matters of evil tendency or consequence, they will not gainsay him, if, perchance, such matters there be in them, nor will such matters fail to be found in them, if they be wrested and distorted. Nor, if any shall seek profit and reward in them, will they deny him the same; and censured or accounted as less than profitable and seemly they can never be, if the times or the persons when and by whom they are read be such as when they were recounted. If any lady must needs say paternosters or make cakes or tarts for her holy father, let her leave them alone; there is none after whom they will run a begging to be read: howbeit, there are little matters that even the beguines tell, ay, and do, now and again.

In like manner there will be some who will say that there are stories here which 'twere better far had been omitted. Granted; but 'twas neither in my power, nor did it behove me, to write any but such stories as were narrated; wherefore, 'twas for those by whom they were told to have a care that they were proper; in which case they would have been no less so as I wrote them. But, assuming that I not only wrote but invented the stories, as I did not, I say that I should take no shame to myself that they were not all proper; seeing that artist there is none to be found, save God, that does all things well and perfectly. And Charlemagne, albeit he created the Paladins, wist not how to make them in such numbers as to form an army of them alone. It must needs be that in the multitude of things there be found diversities of quality. No field was ever so well tilled but that here and there nettle, or thistle, or brier would be found in it amid the goodlier growths. Whereto I may add that, having to address me to young and unlearned ladies, as you for the most part are, I should have done foolishly, had I gone about searching and swinking to find matters very exquisite, and been sedulous to speak with great precision. However, whoso goes a reading among these stories, let him pass over those that vex him, and read those that please him. That none may be misled, each bears on its brow the epitome of that which it hides within its bosom.

Again, I doubt not there will be such as will say that some of the stories are too long. To whom, once more, I answer, that whoso has aught else to do would be foolish to read them, albeit they were short. And though, now that I approach the end of my labours, 'tis long since I began to write, I am not, therefore, oblivious that 'twas to none but leisured ladies that I made proffer of my pains; nor can aught be long to him that reads but to pass the time, so only he thereby accomplish his purpose. Succinctness were rather to be desired by students, who are at pains not merely to pass, but usefully to employ, their time, than by you, who have as much time at your disposal as you spend not in amorous delights. Besides which, as none of you goes either to Athens, or to Bologna, or to Paris to study, 'tis meet that what is meant for you should be more diffuse than what is to be read by those whose minds have been refined by scholarly pursuits.

Nor make I any doubt but there are yet others who will say that the said stories are too full of jests and merry conceits, and that it ill beseems a man of weight and gravity to have written on such wise. To these I am bound to render, and do render, my thanks, for that, prompted by well-meant zeal, they have so tender a regard to my reputation. But to that, which they urge against me, I reply after this sort: – That I am of weight I acknowledge, having been often weighed in my time; wherefore, in answer to the fair that have not weighed me, I affirm that I am not of gravity; on the contrary I am so light that I float on the surface of the water; and considering that the sermons which the friars make, when they would chide folk for their sins, are to-day, for the most part, full of jests and merry conceits, and drolleries, I deemed that the like stuff would not ill beseem my stories, written, as they were, to banish women's dumps. However, if thereby they should laugh too much, they may be readily cured thereof by the Lament of Jeremiah, the Passion of the Saviour, or the Complaint of the Magdalen.

And who shall question but that yet others there are who will say that I have an evil tongue and venomous, because here and there I tell the truth about the friars? Now for them that so say there is forgiveness, for that 'tis not to be believed but that they have just cause; seeing that the friars are good folk, and eschew hardship for the love of God, and grind intermittently, and never blab; and, were they not all a trifle malodorous, intercourse with them would be much more agreeable. Nevertheless, I acknowledge that the things of this world have no stability, but are ever undergoing change; and this may have befallen my tongue, albeit, no great while ago, one of my fair neighbours – for in what pertains to myself I trust not my own judgment, but forgo it to the best of my power – told me 'twas the goodliest and sweetest tongue in the world; and in sooth, when this occurred, few of the said stories were yet to write; nor, for that those who so tax me do it despitefully, am I minded to vouchsafe them any further answer.

So, then, be every lady at liberty to say and believe whatever she may think fit: but 'tis now time for me to bring these remarks to a close, with humble thanks to Him, by whose help and guidance I, after so long travail, have been brought to the desired goal. And may you, sweet my ladies, rest ever in His grace and peace; and be not unmindful of me, if, peradventure, any of you may, in any measure, have been profited by reading these stories.

— *Endeth here the tenth and last day of the book called Decameron, otherwise Prince Galeotto.* —

THE END

Biographies

Giovanni Boccaccio
(*The Decameron*)
Giovanni Boccaccio (1313–1375) was one of the most significant authors in Western literature, his most notable work being *The Decameron*. Boccaccio's originality and his experimentation with literary trends and genres of the time broke the traditionally formulaic approach to fiction that once dominated. Based in Florence, Italy, Boccaccio's influence on the Renaissance literary scene spread far beyond national borders to position him as a key figure of the humanist movement in Europe. His work influenced such authors as Geoffrey Chaucer, Miguel de Cervantes, and countless others over the centuries.

J.M. Rigg
(Translator of *The Decameron*)
J.M. Rigg (1855–1926) was an English translator and historian. His translation of Giovanni Boccaccio's *The Decameron* is his best-known work, and it is considered by many to be the definitive English translation from the original Italian. Also a prolific biographer, Rigg contributed numerous articles to the *Dictionary of National Biography* between 1885 and 1900. In addition, he worked as a barrister-at-law at the Honourable Society of Lincoln's Inn.

Dr Susanna Barsella
(Foreword to this new edition of *The Decameron*)
Dr Susanna Barsella graduated from The Johns Hopkins University and is Professor of Italian for the Modern Languages and Literatures Department and the Center for Medieval Studies at Fordham University, NYC. Dr Barsella's main area of research is in Italian Medieval literature with a specific interest in the literature of Early Humanism. She has published on Dante, Petrarch, Boccaccio, Michelangelo and the idea of work from antiquity to the Middle Ages. Dr Barsella's interests also embrace twentieth-century literature with publications on Pirandello, Gadda and twentieth-century poetry. Her books include *In the Light of the Angels: Angelology and Cosmology in Dante's Divina Commedia* (Olschki, 2010); *Niccolò Acciaiuoli, Boccaccio e la Certosa del Galluzzo: Politica, religione ed economia nell'Italia del Trecento* (as co-editor, Viella, 2020); and *The Decameron Ninth Day in Perspective* (co-edited with Simone Marchesi, University of Toronto Press, 2022). She has served as a member of the Council of the Dante Society of America and as Treasurer and Vice-President of the American Boccaccio Association. She is currently a co-organizer of the ABA-ENGB (American Boccaccio Association – Ente Nazionale Giovanni Boccaccio) Summer School in Latin Paleography.

Sources

The Decameron, translated by J.M. Rigg Originally published in two volumes by A.H. Bullen, London, 1903.

FLAME TREE PUBLISHING
Epic, Dark, Thrilling & Gothic

New & Classic Writing

Flame Tree's Gothic Fantasy books offer a carefully curated series of new titles, each with combinations of original and classic writing:

*Chilling Horror • Chilling Ghost • Asian Ghost • Science Fiction • Murder Mayhem
Crime & Mystery • Swords & Steam • Dystopia Utopia • Supernatural Horror
Lost Worlds • Time Travel • Heroic Fantasy • Pirates & Ghosts • Agents & Spies
Endless Apocalypse • Alien Invasion • Robots & AI • Lost Souls • Haunted House
Cosy Crime • American Gothic • Urban Crime • Epic Fantasy • Detective Mysteries
Detective Thrillers • A Dying Planet • Footsteps in the Dark
Bodies in the Library • Strange Lands • Weird Horror
Lovecraft Mythos • Terrifying Ghosts • Black Sci-Fi • Chilling Crime
Compelling Science Fiction • Christmas Gothic • First Peoples Shared Stories
Alternate History • Hidden Realms • Immigrant Sci-Fi*

Also, new companion titles offer rich collections of
classic fiction, myths and tales in the gothic fantasy tradition:

*Charles Dickens Supernatural • George Orwell Visions of Dystopia • H.G. Wells
Sherlock Holmes • Edgar Allan Poe • Bram Stoker Horror • Mary Shelley Horror
Lovecraft • M.R. James Ghost Stories • The Divine Comedy • The Age of Queen Victoria
Brothers Grimm Fairy Tales • Hans Christian Andersen Fairy Tales • Moby Dick
Alice's Adventures in Wonderland • King Arthur & The Knights of the Round Table
The Wonderful Wizard of Oz • Ramayana • The Odyssey and the Iliad • The Aeneid
Paradise Lost • The Decameron • One Thousand and One Arabian Nights
Persian Myths & Tales • African Myths & Tales • Celtic Myths & Tales
Greek Myths & Tales • Norse Myths & Tales • Chinese Myths & Tales
Japanese Myths & Tales • Native American Myths & Tales • Irish Fairy Tales
Heroes & Heroines Myths & Tales • Gods & Monsters Myths & Tales
Beasts & Creatures Myths & Tales • Witches, Wizards, Seers & Healers Myths & Tales*

Available from all good bookstores, worldwide, and online at
flametreepublishing.com

See our new fiction imprint
FLAME TREE PRESS | FICTION WITHOUT FRONTIERS
New and original writing in Horror, Crime, SF and Fantasy

And join our monthly newsletter with offers and more stories:
FLAME TREE FICTION NEWSLETTER
flametreepress.com

GOTHIC FANTASY

For our books, calendars, blog
and latest special offers please see:
flametreepublishing.com